THE VALKYRIE CHRONICLES

PAUL HEINGARTEN

Published by Decatur Media
New Orleans, Louisiana
www.decaturmedia.com

ISBN: # 978-0-9972626-5-0

Cover design by Y. Nikolova at Ammonia Book Covers

Ana Crucinal character artwork © Wenjuinn Png

ACKNOWLEDGMENTS

First and foremost, thank you to my wife Andrea, thank you for loving me and for your endless support, I couldn't do this without you.

To my family, for endless love, support, and encouragement.

To my editor Kit, who never ceases to amaze me with the depth of her work in pulling out the best version of my stories possible.

To Lisa Herrington, thank you once again for your friendship and continual encouragement.

To my PA Jenny Bodle, for your efforts in helping me get the word out about my books, and for being a great sounding board as I navigate the Indie Author seas.

To Carissa Andrews, for your help, pep talks, inspiration, and for being an awesome author in your own right.

To the Bayou Writers Club. Thank you for hours of discussions about writing, the camaraderie, and for your support.

The term "Hell Hawk" used in this series is derived from the nickname given to several military units during WWII, including the 365th Fighter Group of the Air Force and Marine Fighting Squadron 213.

Special thanks to my street team, the "Krewe of Paul" for helping me become the best writer I can. Find out how you can join the Krewe of Paul and get free books at my site www.paulheingarten.com

For Andrea, with all my love

MENACE ASCENDING

STORIES OF THE VALKYRIE

PAUL HEINGARTEN

ONE

ANA CRUCINAL STARED AT THE graduation credential in her hands. Legs crossed, she sat on her bed and pawed over the translucent document. She was finished with her training in Lebabolis as a Worker Product, and the next thing for her was a series of assignments. All classes of Products: Worker, Warrior, and Intellectual, waited after completing their training for the word, the small announcement that dictated for each of them the course of their life from that moment forward.

A luminous, black video screen faced her bed. The Lebabolis national crest shimmered on the digital monitor. It looked back at Ana like a watchful parent. The MODOSNet updates ran daily, but it wasn't time yet. Even when it was, Ana knew anything that came in the system report wasn't going to be about her work obligation. All she knew was that, as a Worker Product, she'd be sent somewhere like a plant for making parts for other machines or processing Valentium, a rock-like substance discovered by Intellectual Products as a source of fuel.

Like the notice about their job placement, there was another designation to be given, the Pairing, where she'd be sent to live with another Worker Product, the idea being that together they'd produce offspring under that same Product registration, per the laws of Lebabolis.

The roar of a Hell Hawk engine boomed outside. The sleek airships were used for their maneuverability and ran regular patrols through the Sectors of Lebabolis, where they searched for Deviants, those who couldn't or wouldn't follow along with the policies and laws of the nation. Some had problems with the food allotments. Others took issue with the work or pairing assignments. As for the rest, their resistance was a mystery. Or at least it was to the nation's leaders. Lebabolis did what it could to weed out nonconformists.

In its second century of existence, Lebabolis stood as a beacon for many, as hope that the planet Earth could somehow arise from the ashes from its last great war and those who survived built a new world again. One of safety, security, and purpose.

The lights flickered in Ana's room. She glanced up at them until they returned to full brightness. The Valentium cores were switched out every so often and sometimes it involved a power dip for a few moments. Deposits of Valentium were found in a lot of places around Lebabolis as well as the Outlands, which made regular runs to the Outlands important.

The only problem with venturing out into the Outlands was the risk of running into one of the random groups of Scavengers moving about. The origins of the Scavengers were a mystery. Some were believed to be outcasts from Lebabolis, but others could have been from elsewhere. Regardless of the Scavengers' origins, a contingent of Warrior Products from Lebabolis accompanied all Lebabolis excursions into the Outlands—for Valentium harvesting and any other trips considered necessary by the nation's ruling group, the Coursons.

A rumble of quick footsteps grew louder outside Ana's door. She shook her head as a huge smile formed on her face while she counted, "3 . . . 2 . . . 1 . . ."

Varrick, Ana's little brother, burst into the room and leaped onto her lap. Ana let out a fake groan and giggled.

"Well, hello to you, too. How's my little man?" She ran her fingers through his hair as he smiled and eyed her with wonder.

Varrick blew a puff of air that moved the locks of his hair from his face, and then he nuzzled Ana's midsection. As usual, Ana found any concerns about what was ahead for her weren't even a thought when her brother was nearby.

"Play with me."

Ana snaked her arms around him and touched her forehead to his. "Now? It's almost mealtime."

Varrick responded by shifting his weight with some small whimpers. Ana had only been back at home for a week since completing her training, and it wasn't enough time for Varrick; he hadn't gotten his fill of playtime with his big sister.

Ana gently shook her brother. "What you wanna play? Warrior Stand? I can show you some moves."

"Yeah. Show me what Treg does."

Ana paused for a second. She couldn't have kept her secret sessions with Treg from Varrick, he knew when she was out after mealtime and before curfew and why. Treg was a fellow resident, but a Warrior Product. He and Ana grew up together, and toward the end of their Product training he had started showing her, in their free time after instruction sessions, a few things he'd learned. It was something Ana wished was more hidden than it had managed to be, with her family knowing about it. They knew it was illegal for a Product to demonstrate any training they'd received during their instruction phase to someone of a different Product registration.

Ana moved onto her knees and wrestled with Varrick. She did a submission move and tipped Varrick, but held him so he was suspended for a few seconds before she let him fall gently to the soft mattress.

"I wanna be a Warrior Product." Varrick got to his feet, his arms flexed like a fighter.

"Little man, you can't, remember? We're Workers, and that's what we do. One day soon I'll be sent to a plant and work there."

"Can I go with you?"

Ana chuckled. "I wish. But you've gotta stay with Mom and Dad for now. You'll start your own training one day, too, ya know."

"Are you leaving soon?" Varrick's lip twitched.

"I am, honey. I have to go when they tell me."

"Why?"

They'd had this conversation before, and every time Ana repeated the rule of the Pairing to him, it got harder for her to explain it without a voice of doubt in her head that wondered, like Varrick did, just why it had to be.

The logical side of Ana knew it was just the law. Violation meant classification as a Deviant and scheduling for discipline, up to Realignment, a cruel chemical alteration that removed all thought processes and left a person a compliant but mindless creature, a Drone Product.

The video screen blared the shrill MODOSNet update tone, which made them both jump. Varrick huddled back on Ana's bed with her as they watched.

Charista Mantisword, the military leader of Lebabolis, appeared on the screen. She wasn't the most senior member of the Coursons, but she was the face of the military and the Sentries who enforced the laws of Lebabolis, and the person most Products were familiar with. Her face looked pretty hard, as if it were carved out of a single piece of tree trunk. Steely gray eyes darted about, and she faced the screen as she gave her regular address to the nation. Reports from Charista were mostly about the condition of the border and reports of any attempts at crossing it, either way.

This particular update was more about the Deviants, a listing of counts, by the Sector, of escapees caught, and also showing the disciplinary results for each. It was meant to deter others from considering doing the same thing and trying to break the laws or escape, but for Ana it just made her wonder what was making more people break free? They had a structured life, but there was also food. Weren't the

Outlands much harder? She couldn't imagine living on her own out there, not knowing when or even what her next meal would be.

Varrick snuggled closer to Ana. "They should help them."

"Who?"

"The Deviants. Maybe they just want help."

Ana marveled, despite Varrick's young age, just how much he thought of others. "Yeah, that would be nice. I guess Charista wants to keep them from hurting other people. Besides, you don't want to be sent for Realignment for trying to help Deviants, huh?"

Varrick squirmed at the mention of Realignment. "What's it like?"

Ana paused. She knew exactly what it was like, but she wasn't ready for Varrick to hear it. It was a subject in their school, and just the idea of what they did to a human freaked her out. She rocked back and forth with Varrick as her mind worked out a version that wasn't as brutal for a child's ears. "Well, I heard they inject you with something and it freezes your mind. When it's over, you can still walk and talk, move around and carry things, but you can't speak and you don't even know who you are."

Varrick lay still against Ana. "I wouldn't know you?"

"No. It's real bad."

"I don't want that."

Ana nuzzled Varrick until his soft hair tickled her nose. "Me either, little man. But we have to do our work and build a stable world for Lebabolis. It's not fun, but it's important. And you know what, one thing we can keep doing is dreaming. They haven't been able to stop that, except for the Link." The Links were new, but spread quickly throughout Lebabolis. No longer satisfied with the information sent to citizens through the video screens, the next version of MODOSNet relied on implanted chips within the brains of Lebabolis's fair Products. Ana received hers toward the end of her training, but she was told it wouldn't be activated until she began her work assignment.

Charista's face became animated more when she talked about the tech advancements. Varrick pointed to the screen. "She's mean."

Ana kissed Varrick's head as she rocked back and forth while they studied one of their fiercest leaders. "Mmm, yeah. I wonder how old she is."

"She's grown up. She's like 80."

Ana let loose with a cackle. "Eighty? Come on, you're just being silly."

"No, she is."

Ana pulled Varrick into a bear hug, enough that she saw the mirthful grin on his face. In response, her fingers poked Varrick's midsection a bit. He squirmed and giggled. "I was just thinking, I may not have a whole lot more chances for this, so I better get to it while I can." With that, Ana tickled Varrick roughly. His giggles burst into squeals of laughter and delight as he flung himself about on Ana's lap, but her grip held firm.

"Try all you want, there's no escape!" Ana added a menacing enough fake growl to her playful antics. The only thing that stopped them was their mother's voice.

"Now why couldn't I have recorded this?" Emily stood in the doorway, her hands on her hips and a huge smile on her face. Ana lifted Varrick up and as Emily reached for him, she stopped short. "Oooh, you feel a little warm, baby."

"We were just playing." Ana shrugged.

Emily's eyes were shrouded with worry as they met Ana's. "Uh huh, but what about the other two times last week?" She set Varrick down and they made their way to the dining room.

Mealtime consisted of a selection of rations from Lebabolis. The provisions were small, but enough so they weren't hungry. Emily watched Varrick to make sure he ate, and then she asked Ana, "Have you heard about your assignment?"

"No, but it's supposed to be anytime now." She sighed.

Ana's father Jordan leaned back in his chair. His body had been sculpted by years of hard labor in a fabrication plant. He folded his hands behind his head, and his wiry arms looked like they were about to thrust his own head down onto the table. He and Ana said nothing for a moment, just traded glances. His eyes showed a lot of concern for Ana, and Ana figured this was just part of the letting-go process for a parent. She wondered how she'd be when it was her time to send her own kids away.

Ana studied the package of rations in front of her. Sector 3 produced the food that all of Lebabolis ate. Ana wondered just how that one Sector managed to get all that food for them and the rest of Lebabolis day after day, with no interruption. Like clockwork, shipments were distributed through the Central Depot in each Sector to all Products.

Ana eyed Jordan. "Is it normal to feel odd about this?"

Jordan shrugged. "Of course. Don't worry, it's an adjustment, just like you not being here will be for us."

"I still get these feelings, sometimes. Not sure about this whole idea."

Emily shrugged. "Change isn't easy. But remember, you've got to go along with what they've set up. The Product system exists for a reason. You don't want to be labeled as a Deviant, do you?"

"At least we have this one to keep us company for a while longer." Jordan squeezed Varrick's arm before he turned back to the monitor. "Speaking of Deviants, the other day at Central Depot I heard talk about a raid at one of the Sectors."

"What kind of talk?" Ana asked.

Jordan's eyes widened a bit, as if he'd forgotten for a moment that it wasn't just Emily in the room with him. He eyed Ana. "Oh, mostly just rumors. I was on a run for the rations and heard some talk at one of the loading platforms."

Emily threw Jordan a worried look. "Dear, you know there's plenty that gets said around there that's not the least bit true."

"I know." Jordan shrugged.

Ana looked at both of her parents, they said nothing for a bit after that and the subject festered in the room like a buzzing insect. "Come on, Dad, what happened?"

Jordan shut his eyes. "I'd heard it had something to do with Baudricort." The name hung in the air like the scent of burned bread. Baudricort was a leading system architect, who had designed a great number of systems for Lebabolis, including MODOSNet, the nation-wide tool that allowed all citizens to be tracked and served regularly. He wasn't ever seen on the video updates, but he was certainly the power behind the throne, of sorts. And Products in Lebabolis knew his name, although it wasn't often spoken.

It was more of a topic of late because for the past several months Baudricort had been among the missing. Even stranger was that he never showed up in a border search, while Charista made a regular point of announcing them on the updates. Everyone knew he was either dead, escaped to the Outlands, or was for the moment hidden very successfully somewhere in Lebabolis.

Emily shook her head. "If he isn't dead, he will be as soon as he shows his face."

"Or maybe he got with the Action. Did you hear anything about that?" Ana asked.

"Now that's a subject we definitely shouldn't discuss." Emily leveled a glare both at Ana and Jordan. The Action was the underground resistance to Lebabolis. Ana had only heard whispers and rumors about them, but even those had a way of propagating, like forgotten weeds that grew between the cracks of a stone. Enough people knew about the Lebabolis Resistance to make it some unknown specter that waited and watched from the shadows for the right time to appear. Ana had heard about it back in her training. Updates claimed it was contained. Ana wondered.

"If there is an Action, there won't be for long," Jordan said as he chewed on a slice of meat.

Ana thought about it, and how her parents both seemed uneasy at all this. She felt that if Products knew about these rumors, the Coursons would've known more. And wouldn't it have been better if they just talked about the rumors in the open so everyone knew what was really happening? "Why don't they ever share that information on the updates, Dad?" Ana asked.

Jordan stared at the monitor on the wall near them. His eyes darted back to Ana, but he didn't respond. Instead, he returned to his meal and tapped the table so Varrick stopped playing with his food.

Emily eyed Jordan and waited for him to respond to his daughter. When he held silent, she shrugged and eyed Ana. "Maybe they don't want to give those people strength by acknowledging them. You're going to have to learn—I thought it would've come up in your school —but sometimes giving your enemies notice is just what they want to get stronger."

"It just makes me wonder why he left. You think maybe he found the Valkyrie?" asked Ana, but Jordan responded with a stern gaze. Ana regretted the mention of that name, but her curiosity was too great. The problem was the only thing more forbidden to be mentioned than Baudricort was the Valkyrie. It was a distant memory for some, a more familiar one for older Products. The stories about how the Valkyrie kept Lebabolis safe went from recent history to folk-lore to contraband in a matter of generations.

"Ana, you know that's a sensitive subject." Jordan's lips drew into a line.

"I'm just wondering, after all she did back then to protect us, why aren't they trying to locate her or bring her back?" Ana shrugged.

"It's because she committed treason, you know this, sweetheart." Jordan's face looked a little shiny from sweat. He forced a smile back onto his face. "Come on. We don't have too many more evenings with you here, we should focus on happier things for now."

Ana's muscles had locked up, even after her parents returned to acting pleasant again. Even though her parents looked to have settled back into normal everyday conversation, she felt something was off. Mealtime was always a time for them when as a family they talked about things. The Action had been a rumor for some time, but it hadn't been a taboo before then. "Is everything all right?"

Jordan and Emily's eyes met. "Of course, dear. Come on, let's eat before it gets cold." Emily patted the table near Varrick and they resumed their meal. Varrick gave Ana a small grin.

Ana managed a smile in kind, and tried to remember, for just a moment, a time when she was Varrick's age and things were too easy to forget. She returned to her food.

After a few more bites of his dinner, Varrick winced a bit and clutched his arm. Emily's face got more contorted with worry and she grasped his arm to check it. She then checked his forehead with the back of her hand. "You feeling okay, sweetie?"

Varrick shrugged and mumbled a bit in response.

"What was that?"

"It hurts."

"Where?"

Varrick frowned and pointed to his midsection. Emily's face melted to a frown. "Can you eat any more?"

Varrick responded with a quick shake of his head. His face twisted in pain.

"Okay, let's see if we can get that under control with a med pack."

Ana worried about her brother. But she knew she had something else to be ready for. As Emily was busy with Varrick and Jordan watched them both, Ana rose slowly from her seat. "Mom, I'm gonna go out for a bit before lights out, okay?"

Emily called out to Ana from the table and their eyes met. "Be careful. You know I'm still responsible for you until you're paired off."

Ana sighed. "Mom, it's fine. There's nothing to worry about."

As Ana passed Jordan on her way out, he caught her arm. "Don't let anyone see you, okay?"

TWO

"EASY. THIS TAKES TIME."

Ana laughed at Treg's words. If she were anywhere else other than on her back, looking up at the treetops, she may have thought Treg's comment was genuine. But she and Treg had done this for a few years already, in the wilderness on the outskirts of Sector 5. As useless as these outings were for Ana's future career and life, she found it beyond easy to make time for them. She wondered if these sessions were just more of a comfort to Treg or herself, some piece of their childhood they wanted or needed preserved.

The air was filled with the scent of leaves in the early decay of fall. The wind whistled through the foliage overhead, and Ana wished the gusts of air would take with them some of the worry she had about her future. If it wasn't for the soreness in her belly and her thoughts about her future right then, the scenery would've been pretty peaceful.

Treg stood over Ana, his hand outstretched. Their practice area was a large group of trees in the wilderness area at the outskirts of Sector 5. Back on her feet, Ana glanced around and attempted to see which direction the border was. It seemed so easy in the Sector, but the woods were thick enough that it was anyone's guess where the border really was. Treg cleared his throat and Ana looked back toward him and eyed their weapons. "Glad we can still do this. Can't tell you how dull Worker Training was. Soon, I'll be working in some plant and making babies 'til I'm dead."

"We'll both be working and raising families." Treg smirked and shook his head as if their talk about parental lifestyles came from someone else nearby, not either of them. He looked off in thought. "You think we'll still see each other?"

"Of course, dummy. We'll still be in the same Sector. It'll be kinda hard to miss you for long."

"That's not what I meant," Treg muttered.

Ana swallowed the lump in her throat.

Their eyes met again. Ana shrugged. "I don't know. I hope so." It was happening so fast, and for them, things were set. Their lives of work and family waited for them in the close distance, delivered to them like a serving of food. But what about those in Lebabolis like the Deviants, who weren't taken care of the same way? Varrick's comment about helping the Deviants had Ana thinking about what made some people unworthy and others treated like family members.

Didn't everyone deserve help? Wasn't there a better way, where people weren't just parts that were remolded if they didn't fit?

Maybe the word about the Outlands wasn't the truth? Could it be that it wasn't so much about Products being kept out of the Outlands as it was them being kept in Lebabolis? As bad as it was for some in Lebabolis, was the unknown really better?

Ana folded her arms. "You're going to the Outlands someday, aren't you?"

"Oh yeah, at least part of the time. You might be too, you know."

"Yeah, maybe. You nervous?"

"About what?"

"Everything, you know. Your future, the work assignments, the pairing?" Ana folded her arms and sighed.

Treg steeled his gaze. "Warriors don't get nervous."

"Oh don't give me that."

Treg's eyes narrowed a bit, and Ana followed suit. If it were anyone else, Treg would've quickly responded next with a sharp verbal response for cutting the person down to size. But Ana's lips curled up in a playful smirk and that was all it took for Treg to bust out with a chuckle. "You know I can't keep this up around you."

Ana took a few playful steps toward Treg. "That's 'cause I've known you from when you were little." She laughed and patted his arm. "Hey, it's okay. You remind me of when I didn't worry about anything."

"Same here. And yeah, I don't know exactly what I'll be doing, but there's a good chance it's gonna involve escorts to the Outlands, at some point."

"How about Nycole?"

"What, you suddenly got blind and deaf on me, Crucinal?"

Nycole, another Warrior Product from Ana and Treg's age group, had been announced as earning a top slot in Charista's upper tier security. It was common for the top placing Products in each group and class to get a mention on the MODOSNet updates.

"Oh yeah, I heard something. That she's better than you." Ana fought the smile that clutched her face but it was useless.

Treg twirled his staff around, his lips upturned at one side. "Just because she made the top slot in the Warrior Product at school doesn't mean she's better."

Ana's brow raised. "Sure sounds like it."

Treg twirled his staff around over his head and swung it in a wide arc back down until one end smashed into the ground in a loud thud. "Ratings are based on each round of training, and you know that. People can have a bad day anytime."

Ana looked into Treg's eyes as their smiles faded. "I'm kidding. Besides, I wouldn't have anyone else doing this training stuff with me."

Treg looked away. "Training. Is that all this is?" Their eyes locked again, but this time his look was far deeper than the gaze of a concerned trainer. This gaze had a lot of years of feelings behind it, and unspoken words that flew across the few feet of air between them. He leaned on his staff, his own brow raised a bit. Ana felt something stir in her with their shared glance. A feeling settled on her like morning dew, images of a life not under the confines of Lebabolis. Her life with someone who very well could've been Treg. Scenes of children, a house, and much more freedom. Dreams were thankfully still possible in Lebabolis, as long as they remained dreams. She stayed in the thought for a moment longer, but then shook herself out of it.

Ana's voice was a little broken when she replied, "You know we can't do that."

Treg sighed and glanced at his boots. "Yeah, I know. Another time, another place. Come on, there's still time left before curfew." Just like that, the wistfulness in Treg's eyes was gone, in its place was the slightly weary but still focused Warrior stare Ana had gotten used to from him.

They dropped their staves and went to empty hand fighting. They moved in a circle, and Treg tossed jabs, while Ana responded with her own punches and a few kicks. His moves were fluid. Hers were slower, but compared to when she started, much better. Instead of her awkward jabs and thrusts earlier, she'd gotten smoother.

"You're looking like some of the Warrior Products in the final days of training," Treg said.

Ana's eyes stung with sweat. "Doing what I can." She huffed as she kept her pace brisk to match Treg's.

"You've always been a fast learner."

Ana dove to the ground and rolled over before she sprang back up. "What can I say, just kinda feels natural. So what's with all this training they gave you?"

"What do you mean?"

"Well, since we've been doing this you've shown me shooting weapons, fighting, grappling, self-defense. But everywhere I've been in Lebabolis is pretty peaceful. I mean, there's the Deviants and I see

Lebabolis Sentries taking care of 'em. But the military and Charista, don't you ever wonder why they're so formed up?"

"Eh, I guess. But you know we've got the Outlands. The Sentries keep order in country, but there's always someone outside to watch out for, and it isn't always who's in front of you."

With that, Treg landed a soft blow on Ana's face. She countered with a jab to Treg's chin. "And now we're getting philosophical," Ana said and chuckled.

"Laugh all you want, but you know it's true."

"Maybe so, Warrior Product. Show me that power move you just did again."

As they reset, Ana said, "My dad said he heard something about Baudricort at Central Depot."

That stopped Treg cold. His eyes showed a glimmer of wonder for a moment, but a wave of dread washed back over them at the thought of the name Ana dared to speak. "You better not mention that too loud."

Ana froze and blinked.

"I'm serious, Ana. You know his name's banned, and even mentioning it isn't something you should ever do."

"Treg, come on. It's really bothering me, and my parents got really quiet about it at dinner, like they'd let a secret slip or something. I had to tell someone, and you're the only one I completely trust."

"What did they say?"

"Some people spotted him."

Treg froze.

"Where?"

"Inside the border, near this Sector."

Treg looked off and processed the idea that the most wanted fugitive to Lebabolis could be in their very neighborhood. "Any talk about Baudricort is just rumors at this point."

"You've been a Warrior Product graduate for all of about a week, what makes you so sure?"

"I think we'd have seen a pretty sizable unit here to catch him if it were true, don't you? It's just talk. People like to tell stories and so far they haven't gotten us all on the Link, so spoken information isn't tracked."

"Right, of course. Look, I know he's a mystery, and people like to chatter. It doesn't mean it's all false though. What do you think about Baudricort, Treg?"

The name again stung Treg like a blow to his gut. He mulled his response for a bit while he grabbed his staff and swung it around his head. "I dunno. He seems like a crazy old man. Maybe with all that access to the data it got too much for him? Seeing that much information about people's gotta mess with your mind after a while. You know everything. It's gotta be almost like being a god or something. Maybe he just couldn't handle it."

Ana's mind wasn't able to grasp any reason for Baudricort's disappearance that made sense. Maybe he was taken by the Action, if that was for real? "You'd think Charista would've suspected something. It would be tough for him to just disappear. I bet Charista and the Coursons knew when it happened pretty quick."

Treg stomped his boot into the ground in a loud thud that sent a flurry of leaves and twigs up into the air. "Yeah, maybe. But then he could've just taken off, too. Maybe he knew what they were planning and left without it."

"You think that's true about the Action?"

Treg sent a steely look toward Ana. He shook his head and scoffed in response. He swiveled his battering stick about, and watched the twirling motion, lost in thought. Still focused on his moves, he opted instead for another subject. "How's Varrick doing?"

Ana watched Treg's stance. She noticed that she'd mimicked his moves with her own body, without even realizing it. "Well, he's been getting these fevers lately. Just had another one this evening. Mom's treating him, but they still keep happening."

Treg stopped his swivel move and stood up straight, facing Ana. "Fevers, huh? One of the Warrior Products I trained with, a guy named Sendi, came down with something they're calling the Pox. It was pretty nasty, they had to treat him in some kind of quarantine facility."

Ana kept an eye on Treg's midsection and saw the slight shift in his weight. When she thrust her arm up and caught Treg's arm in a block, she squinted as a barrage of images that popped into her head. Sights of Varrick ill and being pulled around in a hospital bed scared her. She wasn't going to let that be his life, or hers. She silently pleaded that her mother and father could figure out a way to get him better.

"I hope it's not that. Besides, kids get sick all the time. Didn't you have some hives when you were younger?" Ana nudged Treg in the gut. He laughed and swung his hand down to gently push Ana away.

"All right, now. Yeah, I got sick." Treg flung his arms around. The thick muscles of his biceps and forearms jumped about, and he narrowed his gaze again. Illness was treated quickly in Lebabolis, but there was no speed to this cure for Varrick.

"The big, bad Warrior got something wrong?"

Treg laughed. "All right, now you're asking for it."

Ana's smile changed to a defiant smirk. After a few moments it was back on. Her face tightened up as Treg's did. He thrust the stick up and Ana blocked it with her right arm. Ana winced at the sharp soreness where Treg's stick made contact.

"You have to be able to fight someone who's overpowering you," Treg commented. He swiveled the stick more. Ana ducked and weaved. Treg grunted with his attack on Ana, not letting up on her. "Out there, there's no mercy. In the real fight it's live or die, not just win or lose."

"I'm gonna miss these moments, ya know." Ana stopped, her eyes tinted with sadness.

Treg nodded as well. "Yeah. Me, too."

A few times, Treg came close to contact with her head. He held back from dealing any serious blows. Any marks on Ana would be suspicious, especially for a Worker Product. It wasn't typical for assaults to happen without Lebabolis Sentries being involved. And Ana, a Worker Product one week out of training, wouldn't be in any kind of scuffle at all, except if she were less than eager to leave the only home she'd known to that point.

"Treg, you ever think about just running from this life?" Ana clutched Treg's arms. He eyed her hand on his bicep, then looked deep into her eyes.

"Sure, would be nice not having to do something I didn't want to."

"I'd want Varrick well and with me, though, and you, too."

Treg glanced on her with warmth. "As if there's any doubt."

"How about the others, you hear from Otto and Kado?"

"The Intellectuals of the group? Nah, they've been on advanced studies. They'll be designing systems and replace Baudricort in a few years. The Circle is gonna run this country, one day."

That was the name they had for their friends, Ana, Treg, Norg, Kado, Zengus, and Otto: the Circle. Six friends who grew up in Sector 5 together, and were within a few years of each other. In their early years, they played together, as all Lebabolis children did, regardless of Product. Then, they went their own ways in the division of Lebabolis, Ana with the Workers, Treg, Zengus, and Norg with the Warriors, and Otto and Kado with the Intellectuals. But there remained that connection they had.

Treg glanced back toward the housing units. The light from the sun had turned a deep amber, the dark shadows on the housing unit building had grown long. "Hey, let's wrap this up before the night security sweep comes."

THREE

ANA RETURNED TO HER HOUSING UNIT, 517. She glanced at the Digisign that stood two hundred feet from her residence. The black and steel squared-off pillar rose up twenty feet, and its always-running video screen made it seem like a lighthouse in the early evening. The screen alternated between the Lebabolis national crest and updates about productivity in sectors, and, of course, ration delivery, so Products knew when to head to Central Depot.

Ana heard a familiar voice to her side as she got to the main entrance to her housing complex.

"Out a little late, aren't we?"

Vega Nyx, Ana's instructor from Lebabolis Product school, leaned against the wall near the entrance. Vega's face was framed by her warm smile and a short crop of hair. It was pretty normal for Workers to keep their hair at a shorter length, mostly for safety purposes.

"I was visiting a friend." Ana looked off to the side for a moment. She didn't want to look into Vega's eyes in the hope her omission about her visit with Treg wasn't obvious.

"It's okay, I just wanted to see how one of my favorite students was doing."

"Oh, just fine, I guess. Waiting to hear about my assignment."

"Yes, of course. I understand a new Valentium plant is coming online. If it were my bet, I'd say that's where you'll be."

"That should work, I guess. I was more thinking about my pairing."

A slight bit of color came to Vega's face. She smiled and stroked Ana's arm. "Of course. It's not as scary as it seems. Remember, they're in the same position you are, it's something new and you'll get used to it. It's just a simple adjustment."

The sound of Vega's voice, her soft tone and the warmth in her eyes always put Ana at ease, and Ana was glad that still held true. It was no mystery to Ana why Vega was her favorite teacher, and in a sense still was. Ana's fears about the change ahead seemed unnecessary, hearing Vega's explanation of it with the ease of a class lecture about machinery assembly.

Ana took a relaxed breath and smiled. "How are things with you? New crop of students coming in soon, right?"

"Indeed. But there are enough familiar faces that I'm not starting from scratch completely."

They shared a laugh. Students attended school in Lebabolis from an early age, but started focusing on their specific product training from the age of ten. That gave them a thirteen-year run of training with their future work assignments.

Vega's mouth drew into a line, her eyes filled with compassion. "You'll be fine. Don't you worry about anything. Things work out; they always do."

"Thanks. It's good seeing you again."

Vega clasped Ana's shoulders. "You can always ask me for help. Just because you're not my student anymore doesn't mean you can't, all right?"

Ana dipped her head. "That's one thing I always had trouble

remembering, the asking for help part. Okay, I need to get in before curfew."

"Of course. Me, too. Good night!"

FOUR

T HE DAYS CONTINUED ON. Ana focused on what she knew was happening at the moment, time with her parents and Varrick, and some training with Treg. This return to a regular routine after a few days almost made her concern about her future a distant memory. Until one day, on her walk home, when she got close to the Digisign by her complex, a klaxon alarm and series of red lights in the distance by the pathways startled Ana and stopped her short.

Ana crouched down, and felt her sides seize up with fear. She wondered how Warrior Products handled fear, or if they ever even felt it. The way Treg went on, it sounded like Warrior Products had fear removed in some kind of medical procedure.

In the early evening light, it was tough to make out anything, but Ana was determined to see something. After what she'd heard from her parents, Treg, and others around the housing sector, she wanted to know what the problem was, and why Charista's updates never seemed to focus on this in particular.

Ana heard a quick set of footsteps off to her left. Evening was a time for slowing down, and it was unusual for anyone to be near the housing units in a hurry for anything.

She decided to check out whoever it was and headed in that direction. She hadn't seen anything and was soon near the trash receptacles. A hand slammed firmly onto her shoulder in a tight grip. She let out a short shriek and felt herself freeze, as she was dragged behind the large refuse bin into the growing shadows of twilight. Ana felt a grimy hand slide over her mouth.

"Careful," the voice whispered in her ear. It was scratchy and sounded feminine. "I'm not supposed to be here. You gonna turn me in?"

The hand over Ana's mouth went free. Ana stammered. "What? I —don't even know what you look like."

The person pushed Ana to the ground. Ana got a glimpse of them in the dimming light. It was a girl. A mane of dirty, blonde hair covered her face, and she swiped at it with an arm that had more than its share of tattoos.

Tattoo girl eyed Ana, one of her eyebrows arched. After a few seconds, it was obvious to Ana this girl wasn't in any kind of sharing mood, other than wanting Ana for something, probably leverage with the Sentries.

"Sorry about that. You were in my way, and I couldn't risk you calling me out to anyone. You're not gonna, are you?"

Ana was surprised by her words, spoken as if a threat from someone who wasn't in the vulnerable position they were right then. Tattoo girl's brow creased, her arms flexed a bit as she braced for Ana's response.

Ana's fear gave a little, shifting to mild annoyance about being pulled into whatever this girl was about. Ana figured she was probably a Deviant. Ana had never come face to face with one before, and age-wise she was easily within a year or two of Ana. "Guess I have no reason to. Besides, I don't even know your name."

Tattoo girl's mouth curved upward at one side. "Marlene."

"How come I haven't seen you around here before?"

"'Cause I'm from Sector 3. I'm making my way to the next pickup point for the Action."

"So, Marlene, why are you leaving, anyway?"

Marlene flashed her left wrist to Ana. Even in the dim light the skin brand of a Deviant was distinct. Their eyes met and Marlene nodded. "Yeah, I was a few hours away from Realignment. They had me paired, and I lasted about a year, but then my dad got sick. When I found out, I wasn't keeping away from blood. Screw the Pairing law. I also wasn't gonna let him be treated by the Lebabolis medical wing."

"Wait." Ana's eyes widened. "Why not?"

Marlene's mouth twitched and a bead of moisture trickled from her eye. "All I know is anyone they take in to 'heal' isn't heard from again. So, I raided the Central Depot for extra food and whatever med packs I could swipe. All of this happened because I wanted to take care of my father. I'm sick of it all." She swiped a tear from her eye as she glanced downward.

"So you're abandoning him." Ana scoffed.

"No, I'm making a play. The Action's getting people out, in case you haven't heard. But it's not a free ride. You get out, you help others do the same. They'll get my dad, soon enough. That's how they've worked it, and so far it's gone all right."

Marlene's eyes darted about every few seconds at the noises in the evening. "All right" wasn't even in the deck of cards Ana wanted to play on care for Varrick. It amazed her, how much Marlene must've been pushed to consider an escape attempt. Ana felt for her, and she had to admit the extra rations Marlene asked for seemed perfectly reasonable. To be punished so hard for something like that, what would Ana or her parents be in for if they pushed the issue with Varrick?

Ana clasped Marlene's arm. Marlene flinched at Ana's touch, her eyes scanned the area once more, then met Ana's again.

Ana took a measured breath, and checked around them for anyone sneaking up close. "I get what you're doing, really I do. But, going to the Outlands with the Action . . . ? How long will you last?

Lebabolis is hunting you down. What if they can't get back to pull your dad out?"

"The way I figure, my dad and I have a lot better chance there than here. The sooner you realize this ain't some place for you either, the better."

Ana stifled a laugh. It was so easy for these people, she mused. There had to be a better way than the Realignment Marlene faced if caught. Ana felt resolve course through her veins. She couldn't have argued she was in paradise, but she had needs to be met. "We're being fed, and my brother needs help."

"Oh does he? Let me guess, the Pox?"

Ana bolted upright at Marlene's tone and the way she made the terrible sickness Varrick faced sound like a sorry excuse. Ana quickly found herself edged up onto her haunches. "He's got a disease. How about some compassion?"

Marlene leaned back a bit her hands outstretched. "Easy. Hear me out before you do something stupid."

"Why the hell should I listen to anything else you say?"

Marlene's lips trembled. "Because the second I show my face to any Lebabolis Sentry, I'm dead. I've got a lot to lose. Sounds like you've got plenty, too. Look, I've screwed things up for me and probably my dad, too. I won't argue that. At least let me help you before it's over for me."

Marlene's eyes pleaded with Ana in the darkness. Ana's annoyance dissolved into pity for her. Ana held her ground while Marlene spilled her information. That Lebabolis Products were being weeded for something other than the Pairing and Product system that had been as much a part of their lives as daily sunlight. She talked about Baudricort, not as some distant fugitive, but as a nearby organizer and leader who could just as well have been on the other side of their current hiding position, much less hidden in the far corners of Lebabolis.

The thought of the Action being an option for Ana bludgeoned its way into her mind. She was annoyed it made it into her thoughts like it did, but she also wasn't able to push it out easily. Ana thought if she were crazy enough to try the Outlands, the last place she wanted to be was with a group of known fugitives who were Lebabolis's number one priority to find. "Okay, suppose I believe you. What then?"

"Gimme a few of your rations? You can split food with your family for a few days, huh? I don't know how soon we'll be able to eat and I need something."

Marlene's eyes peered up like an animal that waited for the hunter to vacate the scene. She eyed Ana up and down. "You wanna come with? You're practically aiding a Deviant right now, anyway. If they catch you, that won't go too well for ya . . . what are you anyway? Let me guess. I've seen bigger arms on some people, but you got dirty hands for sure. You got Worker Product all over you, honey. No freaking contest."

Ana felt her face flush hot in the cool evening air. "So what if I am? Besides, what you're trying isn't the way. I gotta stick by my brother. If he has the Pox, here's our best shot."

Marlene winced, her eyes dimmed with despair in response. "Well. maybe they'll find it in their black hearts to help. You wanna roll the dice on that, it's your call. Me, I'm done waiting for something to happen." She shook her head.

Ana chuckled a bit at the realization that the rumors she'd heard about the resistance weren't just fantasies of the desperate. "So the Action is real."

"Damn right they are. They got a cache of gear, too. Even some Hell Hawks they managed to swipe. They make runs across the border when they can. Supposed to be around once a month."

"Not for long. Charista said the borders were being shut down."

A hoarse chuckle rolled off Marlene's lips. "Oh, you really are one of them, aren't you? Honey, they tell you that to keep you feeling nice and cozy over here in your life so you'll keep producing and popping out other babies—excuse me—*Products* so Lebabolis keeps churning along, bleeding us all dry."

Ana opened her mouth to answer, but never got the chance.

A chorus of mechanical buzzes and whirrs filled the air around them. Marlene bolted up, a pulse pistol in her hands. Her weapon made an angry whine as it activated. Ana gasped at the sight of a Radomet, the mechanized soldiers that worked with the Sentries in policing the Deviants of Lebabolis. The smooth steel of the Radomet's body gave a few reflections of the distant lights around the housing unit. A sharp reddish glow came from the face of the android. Ana's pulse throbbed in her throat at the sight of a Radomet closer than she'd ever been to one.

Ana watched the Radomet as it cast a measured gaze around them. Ana noticed there were no eyes visible behind the metal and visor. She'd heard these soldiers were once humans, but what looked at her just seemed to be a mechanism.

When it saw Marlene and her drawn weapon, the Radomet responded with its own pulse gun, a red dot appeared at the center of Marlene's chest. "Freeze, Deviant. Relinquish your weapon," its robotic voice directed.

Marlene checked out her pursuers and thought for a moment. She glanced at Ana, but their eyes met, and an unspoken conversation happened. Marlene's eyes teetered between the Radomet and Ana, until she gave Ana a slight smile. Ana hoped Marlene thought enough about her and Varrick and didn't try using Ana as a hostage.

Ana held a breath as things seemed slowed down at that point. Marlene's head twisted until her eyes locked with Ana again and Marlene muttered barely above a whisper, "Get out before it's too late, and tell Vega I'm sorry."

Ana felt a chill at the mention of her instructor. *What did Vega know about this?*

In the next instant, things sped back up, and Marlene fired a few pulse bolts at the Radomet. The shots glanced off the armor, as Marlene made a beeline for the forested area. The Radomet swung its arm around and shot an electrotase pulse of bluish energy bolts that wrapped around Marlene like a cocoon. Her screams were soon muffled by the electronic buzzing sound of the containment energy current.

A group of Lebabolis Sentries collected her and carried her to a large transport vehicle that arrived near the front of the complex.

After Marlene's unconscious body was loaded, one of the Lebabolis guards approached Ana. "Are you injured? Did she tell you anything?"

Ana felt her pulse quicken and her throat started to close. "No, she wanted me as a—hostage." Her gaze darted about, and saw the name Wayland on the Sentry's uniform.

Wayland's eyes narrowed, his lips in a line. "We'll need to run a scan on you before you can go. Standard protocol." Ana felt her throat tighten as Wayland led her over to the transport vehicle and hooked a series of wires up to her arm. Her vision got cloudy with a series of static before images of her and Marlene played back. Sounds of their conversation were heard on speakers.

Ana noticed Wayland watched the monitor screen with her as the talk between Ana and Marlene played back.

Wayland nodded. "She gave a pretty standard story for an escaping Deviant. We're running into this more and more. It's best you tell no one about this."

"Of course."

"We're unable to wipe your memory of this out with the Link for now, so I'll need to put you on a watch for a few weeks. The Action is a terrorist organization. Their aim is to disrupt, and destroy our way of life, and the sooner they are eradicated, the better. That's all you need to know." Wayland's voice was even and measured, and Ana noticed how much it sounded like it was rehearsed. Or maybe even programmed?

"Sounds like you tried talking her out of it, which makes me glad. Just be careful."

Ana felt her body relax, but then Wayland said, "There is something else. At other times, we've seen you heading to the outer portions of the Sector. That's a great way to arouse suspicion."

Wayland disconnected the device and eyed Ana for a few moments. "Care to tell me what you were doing out there?"

Ana's gut tensed and she felt her face heat up. He knew about her and Treg. How did he?

Then she realized.

The Link. They've already activated mine.

How much had they seen?

If they knew about me and Treg. Why hadn't they approached me before now?

Had they talked with Treg? He didn't say anything about it. Wouldn't he have told me something if they did?

Ana took a slow breath, but still her pulse rattled in her throat. "Nothing at all, trying to get some fresh air."

"Sorry, gonna need more of an answer than that. Try again." Wayland regarded Ana for several moments, a glare deepened into his face.

What was he doing? Should I run now? Does he already know about me training with Warrior stuff? She tried slowing her breaths, but the longer they stood there, the worse it got.

I'm surrounded. Marlene even had a weapon and it didn't help at all. Ana felt her pulse throb in her neck and her breaths came fast and short. She began to brace and wondered if there was another electrotase coming, this time for her.

Thankfully, Jordan interrupted their conversation. "There you are, I've been worried about you!" He turned toward the Sentry. "What's the meaning of this?"

"She was seen in the company of a Deviant and I just asked about her trips to the wooded area. It's not typical for a Worker Product to be concerned with things like that."

Jordan gave Ana a concerned look that all but spoke the words to Ana, "I told you so." He then turned to Wayland. "What exactly did you see?"

Wayland looked at them both, then gave Ana a pointed stare. "Well, the Links aren't active one hundred percent but we saw her approach the tree line area several times. There's no reason for a Worker Product to be taking that many trips that way."

Jordan eyed Ana with a smile. "She's always been an active girl, she just wanted to get some exercise. I don't think anyone would mind a Worker Product in better shape for their job, right?"

Wayland studied the monitor once again, on it was a map of their sector and the wooded area. He finally looked back at Jordan. "She'll be on monitor for a time. We can't be too careful."

"Of course not. Can she go now?"

Wayland eyed Jordan, his glare traded between Jordan and Ana for a few moments. He glanced back at the monitor screen then jabbed his head toward their housing unit. "Inside and stay there, curfew is in effect."

FIVE

"**I**'M WORRIED ABOUT VARRICK."

Emily's words hung in the room like the still air before an approaching storm. No one had a response, at least not one that included a cure.

Varrick lay still on the bed. Emily sat at his bedside and rubbed a cold damp cloth over his head. His brow was creased, and Ana felt the pain in his eyes in her gut. "The medics said they don't know what else it could be. I'm just waiting for this fever to break." Emily said.

Ana and Jordan stood near the back of the room and watched Emily and Varrick. "So, what happened with that Deviant?" Jordan asked.

"She jumped me while she was trying to escape. Tried to get me to come along."

"What did they tell you?"

Ana froze at the question. Whenever Deviants or the Action came up in conversation before, Jordan talked about not giving either of them any thought, but now he wanted information about them. Also, Ana noticed a strange glint to his eyes. Ana wondered why he was all of a sudden interested in someone who'd spoken about the Action, a subject that was supposed to be so forbidden. "She talked about the Action and that they were making runs across the border."

Ana glanced back to the bed and caught the pained look in Emily's eyes. Ana felt her throat tense up. She wanted to say so much at that moment, but none of it had anything to do with a cure for Varrick.

Jordan wrapped his arm around Ana and pulled her outside of the room.

"He can't die, Dad. There's got to be a way, somehow." Ana swallowed a lump in her throat.

Jordan gazed into her eyes, and softly clasped her shoulders. He nodded in silent agreement with her, but Ana noticed something else brewing behind his eyes. "Ana, please listen to me. Things will get worse before they get better. I wish I could—just stay safe, please. I can't have anything happen to you. I think you need to stop with Treg for now. It won't be long, you'll be getting your assignments soon. Just please, I can't have something happen to you and Varrick, too."

"Dad, you've gotta do something."

"Don't worry, we will."

SIX

VARRICK'S CONDITION LINGERED ON. His fever lowered a little, but he remained weak and spent most of the days in bed. Emily kept her watch over him, and Ana and Jordan chipped in as best they could.

Ana's pairing assignment arrived with no fanfare or notice. She was surprised at how simply it came. A basic announcement that dictated just how she was to live the rest of her life came with the pomp and spectacle of chewing a bite of food. Her task assignment was Valentium Plant 915, the new one Vega had mentioned. And with it came her Pairing Assignment and Photo. Ana ran a finger over the picture of the man who'd be with her for the rest of her life. A thick mane of dirty blonde hair swept low, stopping just above his eyes. A heavy jawline and deep bluish eyes framed the rest of his face. *Well, at least he won't be bad to look at,* she mused.

Once she had her assignment, and her life presented to her, Ana felt a calmness drift over her. It wasn't her choice, but at least it was no longer a mystery. The certainty of it settled over her and she felt herself breathe a little easier. She was at least relieved that wondering wasn't her big hobby anymore. *Mom and dad were able to do it, why*

35

shouldn't I, too? She supposed her days ahead were going to be filled with more regular work and discussions like her parents were having with her soon-to-be new family.

Ana sat down, her back to the base of the Digisign in front of housing unit 517 and looked toward the sunset one evening before curfew. Things were quiet outside the housing complex. An eerie stillness hovered over the area. Ana remembered something Treg had said about a calm before a fight, like an ambush.

The sudden feel of a hand on her arm sent a wave of panic through her. She stifled a scream, but quickly a hand was over her mouth and she was face to face with Vega. Her face was scraggly, her eyes wild. Vega glanced around for any signs of other people. Her eyes were steeped with fear. "Shhh, listen, there's no time. I'm sorry I couldn't tell you this or do more, but I've been monitored for a long time. I'm making a break for the Outlands with the Action soon and you should think about it."

Vega's words confused Ana. So strange, hearing about these scary things like the Outlands and the Action as if they were safe places to run to for a change. She had always been told to avoid both of these and now it was the opposite. What was going on?

"What about Varrick? He's getting sicker. They think it's the Pox."

Vega winced. "Listen, don't let them take him in. That's not a cure, you understand me?"

"Well, what then?"

"I know it's a risk for you, going with the Action, but it's the safest bet any of us have right now. Besides, I want to know what she told you."

"Who?"

"You know who, Marlene."

The memory of Marlene, cocooned in a mesh of electricity, popped into Ana's head. She had been so desperate to escape.

Ana's eyes met Vega again, and Vega nodded in understanding.

"She was supposed to meet for pickup but Lebabolis upped their patrols and she was spotted."

Ana took a shuddered breath. "She said to tell you she's sorry."

Vega shut her eyes tight. "She was a Warrior Product from Sector 3. We connected on the underground network the Action set up. She came here for something, but then she was spotted, and I couldn't risk anything. Better one of us go down than these slip out."

Vega palmed Ana's hand and she felt a cold metal disc against her flesh. "This is what Marlene came for. It's is a credential for the Action for getting onto one of the convoys. I want you to use it. You've got to move though, time is short. We can't be too careful anymore. I'm afraid if I don't go now it won't be safe for me, maybe not even you."

"Me? I haven't done anything!"

Vega's mouth bent into a sad smile. "Even if you haven't, you're associated with me. When they investigate Deviants, they first review anyone that person had contact with, anyone they could've reached and tried to turn—"

"Like one of their students?" Ana's eyes widened.

"Now you're getting it. I'm sorry, Ana. I didn't want this for you, but you'd better stop worrying about your safety here and start thinking about how to survive this. You'll be much better off in the end. I've seen you with Treg. Would he leave with you?"

"Maybe. I don't know."

"Well, you better be sure, but I suggest you look for another pick up and get yourself out of here fast. Use that credential, it's the only thing that gets you on one of the Action pick-ups."

"You're making a break for it?"

Vega's mouth formed into a line. "I've got to. Get out while you can. This will only get worse for you the longer you stay. Trust me, it's the only way."

Ana's pulse quickened. Fear sent a deep ache into her chest and she felt rooted in place. She held the credential out to Vega. "I can't.

Not with my brother being sick. Now look, you're saying Lebabolis can't cure him and Marlene said something similar, but they're treating people anyway, aren't they? So exactly what happens to them?"

Vega looked at the credential and gave Ana another concerned look. She slowly gripped Ana's arms, and bowed her head in thought. "I was on an excursion one day, doing a plant review, standard stuff. One of the operators wasn't as secretive and they showed me what they do to people with the Pox."

"What do they do?"

Vega's eyes were rimmed with tears. She opened her mouth but paused. Her eyes flashed dread and Ana had an eerie feeling Vega was holding back just like Ana herself had with Varrick when he had asked about Realignment. The thought of whatever it was that Vega knew but seemed almost physically unable to repeat sent a sharp chill up Ana's spine. "Come on, Vega, tell me."

Vega's voice shuddered when she spoke again. "Ana, best I can say they've been experimenting with a cure. It didn't look too promising what I saw though. I don't think you'd want your brother connected up like a piece of equipment."

Ana's arms got sore under Vega's grip. She remembered Treg's friend, who was at the top of his skills as a warrior and never returned after he became ill.

Vega took a shaky breath. "I've been hiding, but they've found me. More and more are being marked and I can't promise you'll be safe here for long."

Ana felt torn to leave, but her brother held her in place. "How do I do this?"

"There's a transport coming tomorrow evening. You'd be best to be ready for it and don't wait a moment longer. Get Treg, get your brother, and get out of here. Remember, use that credential."

SEVEN

ANA RAN INTO TREG THE NEXT DAY in the common area between the housing complexes and the wilderness, and she told him about the meeting with Vega. Ana paced, her head clasped between her hands. "The Action's been brewing. This isn't a few renegades anymore, it's a movement. Charista's turning up the heat on them, and will stop 'em."

Treg gazed off, his eyes wide, a glimmer of hope bursting in them. "So, it's all true then. Ana, you should go." Treg's words hovered over Ana for a second, and she at first thought she'd imagined them.

Leave Lebabolis?

Leave Varrick and my family, while Varrick is this sick?

For what?

A chance to live off of dirt and maybe get killed after a week of running? That's if I don't manage to get myself caught and sent for Realignment. Charista's going to step up the penalties for people who leave, that's obvious. She's gonna want to make as strong an example for the rest of Lebabolis Products as she can.

"Sounds like they're taking the sick too, from what Vega said," Treg said.

"Maybe. Marlene thought otherwise."

"It's worth a shot, Ana. You and Varrick should go. Besides, who'd turn away a sick child?"

"What about you?"

Treg's jawline twitched. "If you go, I'll do whatever I can to protect you."

"Yeah, but will you go?"

Treg looked back toward the housing unit, and a tinge of guilt crept over his face. They both knew at most Varrick would be with them for sure, anyone else of their family and friends were on their own. "Yeah. I can't be a part of what they're doing here anymore."

Their eyes met and they both smiled. "The Circle."

"Always."

Ana sighed. "Do I really want to move him, Treg? What if something bad happens and I can't take care of him?"

"Ana, something bad is already happening. At least for now you can do something about it."

EIGHT

KLAXON ALARMS BLARED IN THE SECTOR, with a broadcast warning:

"Deviants have been spotted in the area. All Products must proceed at once to Central Depot for Safekeeping until further notice."

Ana's comm unit rang and she at first figured it was another form of the warning, but the readout on her device had a different message.

Unit 517 Distress—Emily to Ana.

The message was simple, and in regular times it could've been just a check in or an alert about a Valentium core rupture at a plant, a concerned note from her mom about checking on her family. But these weren't regular times, and a very uneasy feeling crept over Ana, her old worries about the future swept back over her and she'd gotten a terrible idea about her family, and what made them send that message.

This time, it wasn't about a work assignment or a pairing.

This time, it was survival.

Treg reached for Ana. "Hey, you all right? What is it?"

But Ana said nothing. Instead, she bolted for the housing unit, with Treg's voice screaming behind her to stop. Ana kept running until she was at unit 517.

A large crowd of Products had already begun exiting the housing complexes in the sector, including Ana's. She watched as the horde of people were directed by the Sentries into lines that snaked down the pathways toward the Central Depot. The Products moved in a regular pace, and Ana noticed that their faces weren't full of anything like panic. It was more resignation, response to another order.

They aren't even questioning this, she thought.

She squirmed her way past the oncoming traffic and weaved through the hallways until she got to the door of her family's unit. It had been pried open.

Ana called out for her parents and Varrick, but only silence greeted her. She pressed a hand against the door and swung it further. The furniture was thrown about and the video screen, displaying a deviant alert warning, hung over on its side.

Emily and Jordan were nowhere to be found.

Ana sank to the floor and looked at the table, its chairs over-turned, where her family had eaten.

Maybe they heard the warning and left early?

If so, that doesn't explain the mess someone made here. Ana clutched her head and raced back over the past few minutes, and her run in with Vega.

What's going on, she wondered.

Were my parents the Deviants the alert was about?

And, where was Varrick?

Ana's comm rang and her heart about stopped. It was a message from Emily. Ana had never heard this tone in her mother's voice before. Her pulse quickened the more she listened to her mother's frazzled tone.

"Ana, I hope this gets to you. There's not much time, but you must listen. Don't follow the evacuation to the Depot, whatever you do. Your father and I are heading off to help the Action and we want you to join us. I've hidden Varrick in the woods near where you and

Treg meet. Find him and get to the border. Another run is coming soon and you need to be on it. We wanted to tell you more, but we've been monitored for a while now and there was no way we could've risked it without calling the Sentries down on us much sooner. Protect Varrick. Stick with Treg and you get Varrick to the convoys for the Action. Jordan and I are going to help the Action make their pick-ups across the border. Find Baudricort, he'll explain everything. I love you, and I'm sorry."

Ana was stunned. Her thoughts went to Varrick, and how he was left alone like that. As sick as he was, how could she have abandoned him?

A hurricane of emotions surged through Ana. She wondered if she'd ever feel settled again.

Ana's thoughts went immediately to Varrick. She raced to his room but like the rest it was in shambles with him nowhere near. And he was due for his latest round of meds. A wave of panic hit Ana.

Did the people know about his illness, did they even care?

How could they have left him alone like that?

They always told me to look out for him and now they and he are gone. What am I doing?

Ana's personal comm rang, it was Treg.

"Ana, are you all right?"

"I don't know."

Ana froze, her throat closed as if an invisible hand squeezed it tight. The room around her began to dim and she felt her heart race. A few seconds later, she gasped for air.

"Ana, talk to me."

The concern in Treg's voice snapped Ana back and she took a labored breath. "Treg, they're gone. They're all gone." Ana's voice shook with a sob. Her vision blurred with tears as she stood at the table, the one thing left undisturbed, a grim reminder of the only life she'd known, that was now and for always gone. She slammed her fist to the floor. The pain welled up and throbbed at her wrist. She paused and felt the soreness as it pulsated through her hand up to her wrist. She let the pain happen: it was the one thing right then she had definite control over.

Treg broke into her thoughts. "Hey, listen. They can't be far. I haven't seen any patrols around for Deviants, yet. Maybe they just got scared and headed to Central Depot for safety. Come by and we'll look for them."

"They didn't go to Central, Treg. They're with the Action, if they even made it that far." She bit her lip as she scanned the ransacked room around her. "Treg, somebody trashed this place. If they left, why would anyone do that, unless they were looking for someone, or something? What about your folks?"

"They're headed to Central Depot and joining the Warriors. Said it was better to go in than try anything right now. Too many armed soldiers around."

"Don't you have to report with the Warriors?"

"I don't care about that right now. Let me help you. We need to find Varrick, make sure he's okay."

"Sure. Meet me back at our spot in the woods in ten minutes."

"On my way."

Ana let a few more sobs out, and soon felt a rage build inside her. The thought of her family possibly destroyed was too much for her. It was bad enough she was soon for leaving them under normal conditions, but the idea of that base not being there wasn't anything she was ready, or even willing, to accept without a major brawl.

I'll kill someone if he's hurt. You bastards want a fight, you want a war? Test me on this, I dare you.

Ana spied one of Varrick's jackets on the floor. She grabbed it on her way out. *He's still my family, no matter what. I'm not leaving him while I don't know if he's okay.* She stopped at the door for one more look at the place she'd known, the life she'd known. The family she knew, her present, and even her future were all now steeped in chaos, and she just wanted something to settle so her feet could find steady ground again.

Ana grabbed a spare med pack for Varrick and fled outside. She started to bolt for the wilderness when she was stopped short by a hand on her collar. She turned into the agitated face of a Sentry. He clutched a rifle with one hand and gripped the back of Ana's shirt tight.

"Where do you think you're going?"

Ana's pulse rattled in her throat and she glanced around. "T-to find my brother. He wasn't at home when the evacuation was ordered. I need to find him, I think he went to the woods."

The Sentry said nothing for a few moments, his measured breath his only response. His eyes darted to the evacuation line and back to Ana. "You've got ten minutes. If you aren't back by then, we're coming after you, weapons hot."

Treg and Ana scoured the area of the woods and yelled for Varrick, but nothing. The light was dimming. Ana sighed. "I'm not leaving without him. I'd rather die first. 'Protect Varrick.' That's what mom said."

Ana dropped to the ground. "It's all going too fast. Treg, I don't know anything anymore. All I know is I have to find Varrick. He needs me and I need . . ." Ana's voice broke off in a whimper as she took off through the woods. She neared clumps of trees and bushes and ducked her head into gaping stumps and what looked like holes in the ground. "I won't go anywhere he isn't. If he gets sent for Realignment, I'll be on the gurney next to him."

Treg folded his arms. "Okay, I know. We'll find him. Look there's no way of knowing where he is, or if he's still here at all." His voice shook as the reality of what he was saying settled on them like a leaf drifting to the ground.

Ana was on her feet quickly. Her reddened eyes shot a gaze that bored into Treg's. "I will act as if he's alive until I have proof otherwise. If I have to stay out here until my limbs fall off so he knows I'm here, that's what I'll do, understand?"

Treg's mouth formed a line. He gently patted Ana's arms. "Of course."

They kept up their search until they heard faint whimpers.

Varrick sat low in a clump of bushes. His skin was clammy and his jaw twitched. His face brightened at the sight of Ana. "Mom said wait here, and you'd come for me."

Ana's vision blurred and she let out a whimpered gasp at the sight of her brother. Once she was able to speak at all, her voice came out in choked sobs. She pulled Varrick into her arms as she trembled. "Of course I will, little man. Always. Shh, we're getting out of here." They embraced and wept together. For a few minutes, Ana welcomed and basked in the relief of at least knowing Varrick was safe. Even with all the doubt around them, the comfort of knowing Varrick was with them gave her new energy to press onward.

In spite of their situation, Treg was moved at the sight of brother and sister reunited and he felt compelled to let them breathe for a minute. He returned to a vigilant gaze around the area.

Varrick held up a small shiny device with a digital readout to Ana. "Mom said give you this."

Ana grabbed it and eyed Treg. "Ever see one of these?"

"Yeah, that's a beacon." Treg took it from Ana's hand and worked the buttons on it. "See here? It's giving coordinates, they look like they're close to the border."

"Little man, did mom say anything else about it?"

"She said that's where the Action will be next."

Treg smiled. "Well then, guess we got our ticket out together after all. Let's move."

As they walked they heard shouting ahead and some weapons fire. They all crouched, and Treg edged up onto his knees for a look. "They've got some people up ahead. Maybe Deviants. Sentries are drawn on them. They . . . oh."

Ana's gut seized up. "What, Treg, what?"

He gave Ana a pained glance. "It's your parents."

Ana was upright as fast as a startled cat. Treg grabbed her arm but she shook him loose and moved up behind a tree for a closer look. About twenty yards ahead, a Sentry vehicle was parked with several Sentries on foot in front. Their weapons were drawn and Ana saw

Emily and Jordan facing them with a group of four others. They shouted at each other and then Radomet came into the area with their weapons drawn.

"We've gotta help 'em." Ana hissed.

"With what? A beacon and our clothes? No way. We go there, we'll be just as bad off as they are. We gotta get free from this."

"Treg, we have to—"

Emily glanced for a moment in their direction and her expression softened a bit. Her eyes switched back between Ana and the Sentries before she gave Ana another glance. Emily's mouth curled in a pout. A lone tear snaked its way down her cheek as she mouthed, "Go".

NINE

THE THREE OF THEM MADE IT to the convoy. They weren't as lucky as some escapees but Ana showed her worth in spades. After a tense ride in a transport and a run-in with a patrol at the border, Ana came face to face with Baudricort. His hair was tousled, his face with several days' growth of facial hair. He gazed at her with curious eyes and gave her a once over.

"Hi, we haven't met. I run the Action, and I'd like you to stick close to me for now."

"As long as my brother is with me, I don't mind. I'm not going anywhere without him."

"Family is important. I believe in that, too." He smiled and offered Ana a seat. "Sorry about your parents."

Ana's eyes stung with new tears. "What happened to 'em, do you know?"

"They were captured holding off Sentries to let a group get to a convoy. They didn't make it."

"Oh." Ana bowed her head as tears streamed down her face. She huddled over while her body was racked with sobs for several minutes. "They figured Varrick had a better shot with me, I guess." She swiped her eyes quickly.

Baudricort sat next to her and wrapped his arm around her, hugging gently. "I know they loved you. And they wanted you and your brother to be safe, which you are now."

Ana glanced around, the walls of the room were covered with video screens, and packs of gear were strewn about—a sign of a hurried escape.

Ana's voice trembled when she was able to reply. "This is all nice, but would you just mind dropping us off?"

"Drop you off?"

"Yeah. I'm not a soldier and Varrick is sick."

"How do you expect to care for him out here, alone?"

"Like I always do, figure something out."

"We're in the Outlands now. You have any idea what's out here?"

"Am I supposed to?"

Baudricort's eyes narrowed, and a smile crept over his lips. "There are random groups of people, who've only survived because they can fight and take what they want from whoever else is out there. We're barreling through that and we don't always have the best luck with them, and we're a group with Warrior Products in the mix. What exactly are a Worker Product and a child going to do?"

"I can take care of myself." Ana narrowed her eyes as she sniffled.

"Okay, well what about meds? We've got Pox treatments here. They hold the disease at bay."

Ana watched him, her voice still shook. "Oh yeah, what's that, poison? I heard the cure for Pox was a joke."

"No, it's not a joke. It's not a cure yet, but it's a start. We've been helping others with Pox get by." Baudricort watched her for a second. "Look, I know a bit about you. Treg filled me in on what you did during the convoy trip here. Why don't you just give it a little while, huh? We're heading west, as far as we can go. There's this mountain range we're headed to for safety. It's rocky, and it should be easy to defend once we get there. We have enough supplies with us to last until we get established. What have you got to lose?"

Baudricort's talk about supplies made Ana think of Marlene and how she wanted food even in the middle of avoiding capture. Ana's burning stomach chimed in, too, and gave her even more to think about.

"Treg's with Varrick as he's getting settled into the medical unit. I promise you we'll take care of your brother. Let us take care of you, too, for now."

Ana gazed back at Baudricort. "Okay."

Ana chewed her food slowly and watched Baudricort as he met with others in uniforms about maps and movements. This was her new life. She had no idea where she was going, but she definitely knew she was never going back to where she'd been.

CATACLYSM EPOCH

THE VALKYRIE CHRONICLES

BOOK 1

PAUL HEINGARTEN

"The most beautiful people we have known are those who have known defeat, known suffering, known struggle, known loss, and have found their way out of the depths. These persons have an appreciation, a sensitivity, and an understanding of life that fills them with compassion, gentleness, and a deep loving concern. Beautiful people do not just happen."

DR. ELISABETH KÜBLER-ROSS (DEATH: THE FINAL STAGE OF GROWTH, 1975)

ONE

(ANA)

THAT ROOF WAS GONE if it had one more direct hit.

Everyone else in the room focused on it each time a blast rumbled or when the building creaked from the attack outside. For a mobile facility, this place was pretty stable unless of course someone tried to have it bombed to hell.

For the last month or so, I'd traveled with these people, The Action. My rescuers from my former life. Yeah, well, it wasn't really my life.

The lights flickered as another explosion rumbled. Soldiers scurried about with pulse rifles, several headed outside. This was the third attack since I'd been here, but it was anybody's guess. At least for me everything kinda ran together, days and nights. I was one of many rescued in the Exodus, the great escape from Lebabolis. And now we were on the run from raids like this one.

They called this place Encampment 2, one of the many separate Encampments of people in the Action. Baudricort explained since they were spread out over the Outlands it made it that much harder for Lebabolis to shut the Action down all at once. Lebabolis kept their

55

search up though, and every now and then they found one of these places.

I gazed at the faces that swarmed around me. Tired faces. Some looked beaten. But clear eyes, all of 'em. Not that haze they had when they were Lebabolis Products. Some of them worked at the Encampment facilities when they were used for mining for Valentium, the ore that was all over the Outlands. Others, like me, were just ready to get the hell away from what we left behind.

The air was stuffed with voices. I had no idea how these people managed when things got like this. If I screamed, no one would've noticed. My stomach churned with a nagging soreness, so I checked the crates strewn about the room and grabbed rations for Varrick and me. Baudricort met me on my way out of the room.

"More love letters from Charista?" I nodded toward the sounds outside. Charista was head of Lebabolis military, and she made bringing us back her primary mission.

The room tipped a bit with another blast. Baudricort steadied himself for a moment and checked the others in the room. "Mmmhm. Knew this wouldn't be easy."

He eyed my rations and smiled. "How's he doing, Ana?"

"About the same."

"I'm glad you both made the Exodus. You know we can keep him safe." He grabbed my chin and added, "You too." His eyes widened a bit. He had looked after Varrick and me ever since they got us out. I figured he felt bad about how my parents disappeared before we fled.

I managed a small smirk. "Thank you. And I owe you for that, I do." I sighed and added, "But we both know, Varrick won't get better here."

"I know you're in a hard spot."

Varrick had what they called The Pox. He came down with it a month or so before we fled. I decided his best shot was for me to get us far north out of anyone's way here so I could look for some people I'd heard about who could help treat him.

If I had any inkling Varrick could've been treated back there in

Lebabolis, I'd have stayed behind even as bad as I had it. But I knew better. And Baudricort knew damn well what else we wanted to get away from.

A soldier ran up to Baudricort and updated him on the situation outside as I looked around for water. Baudricort led The Action so he was always pulled in a million directions, sometimes between different Encampments.

The hallways in this place were just big enough for two people to pass each other. Of course with all the scrambling going on, stumbling about was a regular thing.

As I made my way down the hallway, I felt the pang of guilt searing my midsection.

Even with Varrick sick, I thought about what these people had done for us. Baudricort called it the Exodus: they crept through Lebabolis after dark and took people, sometimes one or two at a time, anyone who wanted out. It was always a risk, and there was never a guarantee you'd even survive the escape part. But it was a chance at a better life, or a life at all.

So far, the Action had given me more than I ever had where I was. Back in Lebabolis I was just a piece of equipment that made things and future generations of slaves. We all were.

Even with whatever gear I grabbed, I'd never been on my own before or even defended myself in a tough spot. Treg showed me a little, but training and a real situation weren't the same.

Someone knocked me into the wall. The stinging coolness of the steel on my cheek made me jump a bit, but it felt kinda good too. I felt a dull ache on my side and heard a voice I wished I hadn't.

"You hoarding?"

Remy stood there and flashed his lopsided grin. His hands gripped a rifle like an infant might have held a chair for the first time. Not a surprise; as an Intellectual Product he little to no time with weapons. And with his attitude, I doubted anyone helped him much with training or anything.

"You know damn well who it's for." I straightened myself out.

"Well, better not take over your ration or Varrick's."

"Mmmhm, got it. Shouldn't you be, I dunno, pointing and shooting that thing?"

We exchanged glares for a moment before he turned and sped off. I was sick of him not long after I got here. He was one of the earlier escapees and acted like the whole damn Action was his idea. Baudricort had that honor though. He and the other leaders they called the Cadre were scattered around at other Encampments, where they did whatever they could so they and the people around them survived another day.

I glanced down to my side. The soreness went away quickly, but I knew what caused it.

The dagger.

I straightened myself and the sheath at my side. It was made of faded canvas and stood out from anything I'd seen for gear. It was very old, which I'm sure was why no one else bothered with it.

Baudricort made me carry it. He never said why, but weapons weren't in huge supply here, so I never asked.

Baudricort barked more orders as I headed for Varrick.

I GOT to the stairs that led to the medical facility when I heard another familiar voice.

"Ms. Crucinal, I presume."

Treg was in full gear, helmet too. A pulse rifle was slung over one shoulder. I took him in. That halfway smile. Those eyes that had already seen way too much.

We embraced. "Hey, you."

"Keeping yourself entertained?"

I shrugged. "I'm a guest. No rec time with those assholes around, right?"

He nodded. "Or the moves. Sure would love to see whatever map Baudricort's using for this Exodus."

"Right? Would love to figure out why we keep running into these patrols."

We both laughed a bit. The word from anyone I asked was we headed west, aside from the twists and turns which avoided the Lebabolis raids for the most part. Baudricort told me he wanted to get to some mountain group called the Range because it had enough shelter for the Action, or whatever they considered themselves, which meant a chance for a new start.

As crazy as it was, the frequent moves, the rationed food, the occasional raids, it started to feel more like I was part of something. People looked out for each other here, instead of everyone's heads held down in fear of being noticed otherwise. I'd even seen a smile from people on occasion here.

"You came in for something?" I asked Treg.

He shrugged. "Just got back from the Valentium run. Your brother's asking for ya."

"I'm headed that way."

"All secure that way. I better join the, uh, fun outside." He glanced down the hallway with a grim smile. Valentium was our fuel. There were deposits of it scattered around outside of Lebabolis borders in the Outlands.

I studied his expression. "How'd it go?"

He bit his lip and pondered a second. "OK, I suppose. No one got zapped this time."

I sighed. "Am I crazy, trying to leave?"

He swung his rifle behind his neck. He always seemed more natural with a weapon than not. "You're protecting your brother, trying to get him well. Nothing crazy about that."

"And getting us both away from Cataclysm." I sighed. Cataclysm had already happened, but a lot of people were sure another one was coming. All I'd heard about the first one was stories; it had happened before I was born. But it tore up Lebabolis pretty bad, enough that people were terrified of the idea that another one was coming.

Treg rubbed a boot against the other leg. "Could just be a myth."

"I'm not taking any chances." I smiled.

Treg and I had grown up in the same sector. Neighbors, but different "Products", as they called it. I was a Worker Product. We handled things like assembly of mechanical items, food distribution, and a whole lot more. Treg was a Warrior Product. They handled security inside and outside the borders. The Product system just mattered in Lebabolis, but people still referred to it out of habit.

I tapped the handle of the dagger in thought and gazed off for a moment. Treg said, "See you got Baudricort's present still." He nodded toward the knife.

"Yeah, made me keep it. Dunno why, with all those rifles around."

We both chuckled. A knife was the last thing anyone wanted with pulse weapon fire, bombs and who the hell knew what else on top of us. I figured every weapon was spoken for, with how broad the Action reached into the Outlands. Baudricort gave it to me right after I arrived. It had a basic handle but with a strange emblem on it. I guessed it was from an old unit or a relic. Whatever it was, it wasn't important enough to pass to their soldiers.

Treg's smile faded as he asked, "Still thinking of heading north?"

I scanned the floor around my boots. "Mmmhm. Try and ditch these raids, get more help."

"If there are people up that way."

"It's rumors for now, but the way it is here-" I waved my hands around and shook my head. "Almost anywhere else would be better."

Treg gazed at me. No matter where we were or what went on, whenever I saw his glance it gave me this feeling that, I dunno, things were OK. They were ever since they sent him for me when I broke free from Lebabolis, aside from the scraps we ended up in like this one.

Soldiers passed between us, headed toward the exit. Treg started after 'em, his rifle clutched firm. He caught himself and met my eyes. "Take care of yourself, OK?"

"Don't I always?"

He smiled big. "Oh yeah."

I watched him head outside. At least there were enough Warrior Products here for protection. Not every Encampment was as lucky. The Action was a grab bag, and everyone pulled their weight, no matter what the job was.

I turned toward the stairs and grabbed for the railing but missed as a very loud bang rocked the building and sent me to the floor.

TWO

(ANA)

T FIRST, I THOUGHT THE WIND had knocked down a commo tower. Or a thunderstorm had kicked up. But then the shouting started.

The lights blinked once, then shut off. A wave of heat rushed over me, and my pulse throttled in my throat.

I got back on my feet when I heard footsteps and the rattle of gear behind me. I groaned as I was knocked against a wall. The breath from my nose brushed against the metal in the darkness. The chirp of activated pulse rifles filled my ears, and the light their displays put off cast a faint glow in the hall.

Somewhere in all of this Baudricort yelled, "Ambush! They hit the infirmary!"

No, Varrick!

I grabbed for the railing. The rations slipped away when I surged up the stairs, weaved and scooted around people or whatever was in my way in the dark. The entrance to the infirmary was a shattered mess. There was just enough light to see dim outlines and the gaping hole in the roof.

Several Action soldiers were about the room, firing up into the night air. The wind howled and right above the hole was a Hell Hawk hovercraft. It floated above us, like a hungry predator that pondered its next meal. Beams of light from the front of the ship sliced the room like brilliant tentacles. Dust blew everywhere, along with the rotten smell of engine exhaust.

"Take cover!" yelled one soldier. A pulse shot skewered a soldier near me. His body fell backward with the impact, and his screams joined the chorus of the whining turbines above and general shouting. Something warm splashed my arm; I saw it was blood.

I crouched behind supply crates as the entire medical facility was showered with pulse fire. More Action soldiers poured in and joined the fight. I saw very little in the dim light and smoke from the pulse shots that tore into everything, steel, fabric, people.

Chaos erupted among soldiers in the room like an agitated volcano. The soldiers I watched scurried about with not much direction. They fired at the ship above us, though it did little good. With the sea of shouting mixed with screams and weaponry at play, I heard nothing that resembled any kind of command.

Baudricort crouched behind a counter area and fired back on the Hell Hawk. I strained my eyes in the fray, but things were too crazy.

I crawled over to Baudricort. "What happened?" I yelled.

"What's it look like?"

The roof looked like it was cut pretty clean off, like someone had taken a big knife and sliced it off.

Baudricort grunted. "That roof wasn't blasted from the outside."

He flinched as a shower of dust rained on us. He growled and slapped his weapon as it malfunctioned.

I scanned the edges of the hole in the structure. "Was it charges? Booby trap?"

He glanced at me. His eyes went wild as he pondered who may have done it. In the Action, sabotage was not so much of an if but a when and a who. "Stay down and keep close."

At last I saw the sick bed area through the haze. Several Action soldiers crouched low and returned pulse fire as best they could.

Most of the fights I'd seen between the Action and Lebabolis had been very one sided. Lebabolis sent large groups on raids and the Action often couldn't provide enough troops for a raid. It was better to spread and take a few losses than to risk greater casualties, they said.

Even with the mixed groups in the Action, Intellectuals like Baudricort even handled weapons. They kept up a pretty good fight against the Lebabolis army a lot of the time.

A ramp lowered on the Hell Hawk, and several dark forms dropped out. Metallic soldiers. They looked human, but when I saw the deep red glowing lights in their chests, I knew what they were.

Radomet.

The result of Lebabolis experiments, their own super soldier force. Select Warrior Products who went through a series of modifications. The Radomet weren't human, but then again anyone who accepted that assignment wasn't ever human at all.

At least ten Radomet advanced toward the patient area. The pulse fire sprayed the room like a sideward electric monsoon. The voices on the Radomet crackled over the air. They sounded like electronic growls, speaking a strange mechanical code to each other.

The story I heard was that Radomet voices produced a pitch that paralyzed people with fear if their minds weren't strong enough. It was one way they cornered the runaways back in Lebabolis.

Most of the Action pulse fire glanced off Radomet armor with no sign of damage. Several more Action soldiers fell; their screams filled the silences between weapon fire.

"We gotta get over there!" I said to Baudricort. I inched toward the patient area, but he grabbed my arm. "No, Ana, wait!"

I fought his grip. "Let go! You want 'em to get our people?"

The room shook with another blast, and I was knocked down again. A new burst of dust and smoke wafted over us. My vision clouded even more as I struggled back onto my knees.

Then, in the mayhem, one soldier confirmed my worst fear.

"They're taking our people!"

Loud metallic shrieking rang as the Radomet surged past, each carrying pods with people in 'em. They all charged back to their ship.

"Varrick!" I screamed. I lunged with my hands outstretched as if I could've pulled him back from where I was.

My gut erupted with a deep ache, and tears filled my vision. I was so fixed on the sight of Varrick carried away in a pod, helpless, I hadn't heard the metallic motorized whine of the Radomet to my side, and before I knew what happened I felt a blow to my head and dropped to the ground. My vision blacked out, and my eyes stung. A deep ache throbbed from my head at the point I was struck. I blinked and rubbed my eyes, but it was pointless.

As I rolled on the ground, a few pulse shots from our people rang out. Baudricort bellowed, "Stop! You might hit one of ours!"

A deep aching dread burst in my gut as I watched Varrick loaded onto the Hell Hawk. I lurched up on my knees. "Shoot the cockpit!" I yelled. "We can disable it!"

"No!" Baudricort yelled back and signaled the others to stop. He shook his head. "Too risky."

My face flushed as I gazed at the ship. *No. Not him. He's all I have left.*

The Hell Hawk engines fired up and blasted the room with warm air. A shower of debris swirled around in the warm tempest of heat and engine exhaust.

I failed him. I told him I'd get us away from here, and I failed him.

I saw him in front of me, the little boy before he was sick. How he played with me, how I held him. How I protected him, or was supposed to.

Now... gone.

I yelled at Baudricort, "Do something!"

He winced and eyed the rest of the troops and the Hell Hawk. "We're overpowered. They won this one; there'll be others."

I grabbed Baudricort by the front of his shirt and shook him. "That's my brother!"

"I know! I know Ana, I-- I'm sorry." His lips twitched, and he was speechless. I'd seen him most days. He directed so many people around and spoke to the entire Action in person and over the comm network announcements. Silence wasn't normal for him.

His eyes burned, and I wished I knew what went through his mind at that point. He said nothing, but I still wondered. My gaze slid to the aircraft. "Why aren't they finishing us off?"

Baudricort had no answer.

The engines on the Hell Hawk revved up and sent more waves of hot putrid wind down into the busted room. I squinted as bits of dust scraped my face.

I released my grip on Baudricort. He watched me a little while longer and stroked my arm. Part of me wanted him to say something, anything. The other part wanted to take a swing at him for letting our people go.

Then, almost like a vehicle switching gears, he spun on his heel and barked orders to everyone around. Whatever it was that had him frozen was gone, and he was back into command mode.

Everyone started the clean up and tended to the wounded. I joined in; it was better than simmering in a pool of pity. While I helped out, I picked up bits of conversation from people around me about the next move. A raid like this meant Relocation came soon after. They moved around every few weeks, as the raids happened all over the Outlands.

I made my way around the mobile facility and spotted Baudricort inside one of the comm rooms. The door wasn't all the way closed, so I peered in enough and saw Baudricort with Otto. They watched a monitor with Charista on screen. Her dark eyes always gave me a chill. She read a message to the Action. After a few seconds, Baudricort flicked his head to the side and stopped the video.

"What do you think you're doing?"

I opened the door further. "The door wasn't secure."

He turned around. His face melded into a scowl, and he reached for the door. "You need to help with the Relo prep and mind your own business."

"I'm leaving to get him."

He stopped with his hand on the door. "You're what?"

"I'm going. I'm rescuing him-"

"Hold it, just hold it." He swung the door back, his brow furrowed. That look had gotten familiar pretty quick. I sensed one of his offers was coming. He sure had a way with people. After all, he had started the move from Lebabolis. A few weeks ago I wouldn't have questioned him, but now that Varrick was taken...

Before he got started, I had my own piece. "I dunno why you didn't make your case to her. If it was so damn important we took off with their gear and people, couldn't you reason with the General of the Lebabolis Army and save us the trouble?"

He smiled and shook his head. "Don't you think I would've considered that?"

"Well, what was that I just saw? Charista reaching out to you?"

Baudricort eyed Otto. "She's trying to force a truce. Same thing she always does."

I narrowed my eyes at him, and he added, "You saw what they did. This'll get worse, believe me. I know you want your brother. I want everyone they took back." He patted my shoulder as he added, "I have a plan."

I knew it.

Otto watched me from over Baudricort's shoulders. He was Baudricort's number one tech person, at least that's how Baudricort described him. Otto's gaze was a great indicator of the truth, unlike other people's. Otto fixed his glasses and nodded, his eyes wide and with a sincere grin.

I looked back toward Baudricort. "What?"

He narrowed his eyes, as if he searched for the answer I wanted to hear. "I think it's best you do go. But not for Varrick, not yet."

"Why not?"

"It's too dangerous, and I can't help you." He grimaced. "We're already down several soldiers. I can't just grab a few and send them with you to rescue Varrick."

My lip trembled. He tried his best to soothe me. "Hey, I hate this, I do. And they took more than him, remember? Thing is, they found us. And once that happens, they get even better at zeroing us in."

Once again, I was on my own. "So you don't want me to go for Varrick and you don't want me to stay here. What the hell does that leave?"

"I'm sending a small team on a special mission. It's a group of three and one Landcrawler. I want you with them."

I wrinkled my nose. "How's that safer?"

"We're in the Outlands. Nowhere's safe. Please trust me." He wiped a small piece of debris from my cheek with his finger. "This is better for now. We'll figure out a rescue soon enough."

My eyes darted to the side. "Keep talking."

"I'm working on hacks to MODOSNet with Otto." Baudricort nodded toward Otto, whose fingers jabbed the keyboard in front of him and produced a constant rattle of clicks and taps. "It's not done, but maybe by the time you come back."

Baudricort always attempted hacks into MODOSNet. They were used for a lot of things, from locating food shipments that we raided to breaches of the security system. Hacks were how he got so many of us out in Exodus, but of course they had made the system more impenetrable ever since.

"So I ride along, for safety?"

"For now. Getting you to another Encampment is too difficult, and then you got the same problem as here. A small group is easier to hide and move. Stay out of the way of the Warrior Products; they'll handle the rest. Come to the briefing room, you should meet each other."

THREE

(ANA)

THE MEETING ROOM, like most things with the Action, was haphazard. Exo-suits lined much of the walls, along with equipment for harvesting Valentium. They made runs for fuel whenever it was safe or whenever supply ran low. It was always a risk, but so was being stranded in the Outlands.

Baudricort stood next to a screen against one wall, which displayed maps of the area as I and the other three watched from a table close by.

"I know you've heard talk about plans, strategies, heading west to the Range, this and that. I'm saying we're keeping our move up and trying to make it as far west as possible. It takes awhile to move this many people and keep them safe, or at least try to."

I winced at that part about 'keeping people safe', at least he had the sense to qualify that.

He glanced over his shoulder. "We're also trying to get as many to escape Lebabolis." His eyes slid to me when he added, "And everyone they took back from us."

My mind still puzzled about why the Radomet had stolen our sick. No one I asked knew. Maybe it was for human collateral, so we were lured into the open? Or was it for more of their experiments. My mind shuddered at the thought. It was bad enough that every Lebabolis citizen slept connected to the Link each night.

"What about Cataclysm?" I asked.

Baudricort's eyes widened. Even if I derailed what he was about to say, it felt good. I bet these guys and everyone else wondered the same thing. "I've seen nothing that indicates Cataclysm has begun again, and we are keeping an eye on that. So far, that threat is minimal, and that's also part of why I'm moving us to the Range. And of course, getting out the way of these raids. Now if you'll wait a second, I'll tell you why you're here."

He leaned against the wall next to the screen and folded his arms. Whenever he did that I remembered the last time I saw him with my parents. They had a long talk, and he had his arms folded the entire time. Soon after that, I never saw my folks again.

"What I'm about to say doesn't leave this room."

The others at the table shared glances.

Baudricort tapped more controls and a picture appeared over the maps: a man in his late twenties. Smoky brown hair and deep hazel eyes. He looked pensive.

"Who knows about Xander?"

We all raised our hands.

Baudricort smirked, and faced the screen again. "So you paid attention in Lebabolis instruction. Yep, Xander. The prophet of Lebabolis. The man who wrote the book that Lebabolis believes is our future." He paused then corrected himself. "Their future."

Of course we knew Xander. Every Product in Lebabolis was sent to Instruction from the age of five, and one of the first things they hammered into our brains was about Xander, who years ago had written about this great society that saved humanity from destruction.

Then there were the Prophecy Centers that people attended and praised Xander. I went to services, like everyone was required to. Some people looked forward to them, I just felt empty before and afterward.

Remy said, "I've heard the regular messages through the Link. Is there anything special we haven't been told yet?"

Baudricort replied, "I'm not interested in what Lebabolis says about Xander." He studied the picture for a moment, and swiveled back to us quick.

"I'm sending one of you to meet him."

I swallowed hard.

Meet Xander? But that meant the Verge.

The Verge wasn't new but it was new to me. What I knew about it was a mixture of hearsay, speculation, and a little impossibility too. The story I had heard was the areas with high concentrations of Valentium around opened up these pockets in time.

The first few were found by accident. Several people slipped through while they harvested Valentium. A few less came back. A little while later, Intellectual Products figured how to control the access and return.

"Are we delivering a message, sir?" asked Remy.

Baudricort shook his head. "We need to bring him here."

Remy looked around the table, his eyes glowered through blonde tousled bangs. Something about him struck me, like I'd seen him somewhere years back, but it hadn't registered from where yet. He shot me a look every now and then, as if I was an insect he needed squished. Whatever it was about, I was glad I was a pain in his ass for whichever reason his thin brain decided.

Yag, on my left, scratched his chin. His broad shoulders moved as he took a thoughtful breath. "All this time I thought he was a myth."

Baudricort paused. "No, he's very much real."

"Sir, with respect, what are we hoping to accomplish?" Remy asked.

Baudricort frowned. "Lebabolis wants us all back. They're facing this enemy, the Omegans, and they need every able-bodied Product. They seem to think that Xander will give them more leverage. They want to fan the flames around that whole belief system and stop those leaving through Exodus. It's their best play, so I want to get him first so no one else uses Xander to communicate on the Link to everyone in Lebabolis. This way, we get to set the message."

The Link was what every Lebabolis citizen wore on their head when they slept. It fed us information like work assignments, but it also gave us information about the state of Lebabolis and how good everything was. Whatever they wanted came through the Link. And to most people, it was rock solid truth.

"Haven't the hacks to the Link been working?" Remy asked.

"Some," Baudricort replied. "Our moles are getting more people to stop using it, but it's taking too long. We need to step it up before they end us."

Remy motioned to me. "Why is she here?"

I eyed Remy, and Baudricort responded, "What's that?"

Remy's eyes darted between Baudricort and me. "Well, I understand you've got the Warrior Products for security. So what's she got to offer?"

Baudricort drew his lips in a straight line and took a deep nasal breath. His jaw clenched in thought, and thrust his chest toward Remy. "You forget who's running things, boy? Well, let me clear it up for you. I'm in charge. I'm the one who's getting us to safety, so you better listen to what Otto and I have to say; it might come in handy for you very soon," he snapped.

Remy shook his head and snorted.

Oh.

That snort reminded me of who Remy was. He busted that aggravating nasal sound out back in Instruction when he was this mealy little Intellectual Product. He always ratted on other kids for misbehavior so he looked better in front of the teachers, and he was put first in every good thing possible. I narrowed my eyes at him. *Lemme just show you what I can do, little boy.*

"So Xander, how do we get him to come here?" Wick asked.

Baudricort produced a book. As he rifled through it, a little dust launched into the room. "You're too young to remember books, I'm sure, unless you've seen the caches." He nodded at me, and I smiled at the mention of caches. I stumbled upon one of 'em with Treg. Ancient containers of artifacts from centuries ago. I always wondered who put 'em there, and why.

Baudricort said, "This book is what Xander's prophecies in Lebabolis Deism are based on." He handed it to Yag, and we passed it around. While it was very faded, I made out the title, *Cataclysm Epoch*, and a name on the cover: "Xander Lee". I had seen a few books in the cache, but none like this. It had an awful rotten smell to it. I ran my fingers over the coarse pages that felt dust covered. There they were, words that people spoke about Xander and what Lebabolis was for us and the world.

"You'll need to explain to Xander, best you can, that we need his help. We're sending one of you through the Verge to get him." Baudricort added, "Once you convince him to come back, place the tether bracelet for the Verge on his wrist and return. Remember, like you he can't travel through the Verge without wearing a tether or he'll be lost in time forever. Locate beacons and rendezvous at Encampment 13, medical will be ready."

"Bringing someone forward in a Verge from their base time, has that ever even happened?" Wick asked. The thick muscles on his arms flexed on the table as he spoke, and it almost looked like his arms were the only thing that kept the table on the floor.

"No. And under normal circumstances, I wouldn't even consider it. But we all saw what happened. Lebabolis is stepping up their patrols on every Encampment. We'll keep moving west, but we've still got a long way to go, and that means more Valentium and supply runs. Sooner or later, we'll run out of luck again."

Baudricort showed the Verge location for our mission on the map. It was in a large group of trees on a hill. If it was guarded from a distance, we'd have known easily, he explained. While Lebabolis sent their patrols where the larger groups would be like the Encampments, Valentium sites were always important.

He turned to us. "Remy, you're the Verge jumper. Otto's gonna brief you on details of the period and as much as we know about

Xander, which isn't a whole lot." His lips drew in a grim smile. "Yag, Wick, your job is to get Remy to the Verge. No matter what. Got me?"

"Affirmative," they replied.

"So if things go, let's say... crappy. What's our move?" I asked.

Everyone looked at me for a few seconds, and Baudricort half smiled. "Locate the nearest Encampment beacon and head straight for it. Don't engage any troops, you'd probably be outnumbered and outgunned. Alright, I'll have Otto meet you outside. Take a Landcrawler and head to Encampment 12 for tech and locale briefing."

WHEN THE MEETING BROKE UP, I headed outside toward the rear of the main mobile building and waited for the others. The cool air kissed my face and I was glad for it, but even happier I was away from Remy for a little bit.

Of all the people Baudricort could've stuck me with. I hoped that Verge jump happened quick. The sooner I was away from him the better.

The late afternoon sky was smeared with a few clouds. Charred trees littered the area, victims of the fight. I watched the details as they buried the lost soldiers. They never had time for more than a mass grave, but it wasn't even a question. Everyone in the Action got at least that respect. I rubbed the sores on my head from where I'd worn the Link up until a few months ago.

It was dangerous for someone living in Lebabolis if they hadn't worn the Link. Anyone caught was labeled Deviant and sent for punishment like Realignment, kind of a mind erase. At that point you weren't anything other than a Drone Product. Totally obedient and mindless. More or less a Radomet without the mechanical enhancements. But somehow, Lebabolis placed a higher value on Drones. They loved it when someone was under their control. Having access through MODOSNet wasn't enough for them.

My thoughts returned to escape. Treg could've helped me. I doubted anyone else would've noticed, and Remy wished I would vanish. What a sniveler. He even ratted me out to our Sector Proctor about how Treg had taught me weapons and unarmed fighting in rec time.

I slowed my thoughts down as I thought about everything in steps. If Remy came through, and Baudricort did his bit, I was home free. This had to work.

But if it didn't, I knew in my gut there was another way, even if it meant I had to make one myself. Heaven help the idiot who got in my way.

FOUR

(NELSON)

T HE LIGHT NEXT TO MY HEAD flickered a bit.

I looked at it from my seat on the couch. Probably the neighbor's microwave again. Damn prehistoric wiring. If everyone in this place fired up their microwaves at once the whole building would've exploded.

I swiped at the back of my neck to wipe away some of the moisture. Aside from the kooky wiring, this place wasn't bad for an apartment in the Marigny, tucked away in the recesses of New Orleans far enough that vomit from the Bourbon Street touristy parts missed it. It was modest for an IT consultant's salary like mine. The exposed bricks and old time fixtures gave it just enough of an air of that funky vibe that I liked.

The place was quiet for the most part at night, even as close to the Quarter as it was. Still, the occasional loud drunks who stumbled by or distant gunshots kept me alert.

I wished my landlord was more educated on the wonders of modern pesticides and sprayed the place.

A jolt shot through my entire body at the sound of my phone's ringtone. My stomach knotted up as usual, since these days, at this time of night, any phone call may have been the one I feared most.

I stomped on a skittering cockroach and answered to Dad's shaky voice on the other end.

"Hey, can you come over?"

"Sure. How is she?"

Dad paused. "Not responding much. Come over, huh? Quick."

Under normal circumstances, I dreaded calls from Dad since they could mean a number of bad things. But his voice this time was more erratic than usual. I stammered a bit and finally replied, "Need anything? Need me to call someone?"

"No, just get here."

I swallowed hard. "Be right there."

Mom had struggled through multiple rounds of radiation and chemotherapy that all but destroyed her body. She fought so hard the whole way. But after months of this, she barely stayed awake at all anymore. Dad and I did our best, though neither of us had a clue about anything besides what the doctors told us. It was a lost cause no matter what. Her body was about done. We had set up hospice last week, and she had been bed ridden ever since.

The glow of my laptop screen caught my attention. On the screen was the title page for my manuscript, Cataclysm Epoch. I stood back as if it dared me to have worked it more. I had toyed around with it earlier that night. I hammered on it here and at the library when I needed a change of pace. Yeah, I kinda saw myself as a novelist in disguise. I even figured out the perfect pen name: Xander Lee. Hey, if I made it in writing, that would've solved my clock punching problem forever.

Then again, I could've also won the Powerball.

In honesty, writing wasn't easy, in particular these days. I had a hard enough time with nagging voices: "You're not good enough to write", "You should take better care of your parents", "You think you're a good worker? What a joke."

I yawned deep and powered my laptop down. After I ran my

hands through my hair a few times, I grabbed my keys. The stays over by Mom and Dad's varied in length. I came over during off hours from work, and I'd burned a few sick hours from work so Dad got a break.

On the drive over, my right hand was fidgety, so I treated myself to a concert via my MP3 player random mode. Aside from my writing aspirations, I had a decent job but with a royal dick of a boss. He jumped on every little thing I did, and waited or hoped to find that I messed something up, like it was a damn game. The fact he'd been so gracious about me taking time off for Mom was less about his generosity and more like HR cutting me a break.

My phone buzzed with a text while I was at a light. A lump in my throat formed. One of my biggest fears was being away when it happened. Even if it meant I held her hand and comforted myself that I comforted her.

I held up the phone in the dim lights from the street.

_____

From: Tina
To: Nelson
Hey babe

______

I tossed the phone on the seat next to me. I'd met Tina one night in the Quarter a few weeks ago. I needed a night away from things and, Well, we hit it off - enough for a few booty calls. She was fun and the perfect distraction for me. Alright, she was a good lay. She was cute but a little on the needy side. After a few times I got the idea she hid from something or someone while she was with me. She knew about Mom. Guess she figured I needed more distractions at the moment.

Not now.

The only place that felt right was with Mom and Dad. Besides, another world competed for my thoughts too. My story. Mom's fight the past several months had inspired this tale. The fire, and absolute determination in the face of horrible odds.

Maybe I made you too real? I wish you were here right now. You'd hug me and tell me to keep going, wouldn't you? You'd never let me feel sorry for myself or anything.

Damn. Obsessed over a fictional character. Maybe I was crazy after all.

———

I RUBBED MY EYES, but everything was still blurry. I massaged my temples in hopes it would ease the painful throbbing. Of course, the pungent smell of hospital sanitizers wasn't a help at all. The clock's luminous numbers stared back at me: 2:00AM. I'd been at my parents' house for a few days and kept watch over Mom. I'd hoped for any response from her, but she gave nothing.

I heard Dad's footsteps toward the back of the house. He and I had this odd kind of shift thing for watching over Mom, like some weird one person hospital, or bed and breakfast for the terminal.

My hand stretched to the hospital bed next to me, and I held her frail, withering hand. She felt cold. She lay still without much indication she was alive.

Her cancer was pretty nasty, and even after the operation she never really recovered. The doctors zapped her with radiation and chemo, but they had no idea how much damage the actual therapy may have added on top of everything else.

Hospice had been by earlier, just one part of the horrific waiting game the three of us played.

I gazed about the room, then back to her. This house had been so full of good times. I hated it had to be the setting for this. There was nothing good and nothing to do except to take it. I looked for a hint of life behind those half closed eyes. Nothing. Only the hum of the oxygen pump, the faint rise and fall of her chest and her labored breathing were remnants of this woman, once so full of life. The woman who had raised me and made me what I was.

"Anything new?" Dad stood behind me.

"No, been pretty peaceful for at least two hours now."

"Oh, well they said it wouldn't last much longer."

"Had a good nap?"

"So-so. Still used to being up at weird hours on account of her."

Dad's weary gaze extended to his entire body. His schedule had been turned upside down from Mom's situation. I pitched in as much as I could, but a full time job and the novel took up most of my time.

I glanced back at Mom and sighed before I turned back to Dad. "I should be going. Gotta check in with work tomorrow afternoon."

"Want some food? I heated up that meatloaf."

"Naah. Too late. I'll catch a snack." I clenched my jaw so I wouldn't bawl. Even so, my voice was shaky enough that anything would've caused it. But somehow, I held it in check. Whenever I saw Mom's vacant face or Dad's beaten look, it shook me inside.

I stayed strong for them.

I had to.

Mom's quiet breaths became louder and more strained. Her body twisted and turned, her hands kneaded the bed sheets firmly. I stroked the sides of her face. I hid my true emotions from my voice as much as I could. "It's alright, Mom. Dad and I are here. You're safe."

Dad added, "Love you, baby. Try and relax."

Dad reached for the morphine bottle on the table next to the bed. He drew a small amount into the dropper as I ran my palm softly over Mom's hair and face. "Stay with us, Mom." I whispered to Dad, "How long are we going to keep doing this?"

"Long as we have to. I don't want her in any pain."

"Me either, but Dad-"

"I'm not ready yet."

Mom let out a huge gasp and went completely silent for a few seconds. She took another slow breath and held it for several moments. This continued for a little while. Her hands went from the bed sheets to up in the air, as if she caressed a face seen only to her.

Dad's voice lifted a little with nervous energy. "Honey, baby, we're here. You're alright."

She ignored Dad's reassurance. One more slow gasp of air and her hands limply fell to her side. She exhaled slowly.

The room froze. Everything was still. My stomach sank as her presence left us at that moment. There were so many things I had left unsaid to her, so many things I should have told her. I took advantage of her and Dad in my younger years. I put them through shit they never needed nor deserved.

Had I made amends?

I hoped so.

This was wrong. Unnatural. Not fair. Why her? Why now? It was too quiet. She passed away, and I hadn't even heard the sound of breathing in the room. My throat tightened up and my vision blurred with tears that meandered down my cheeks unchecked. A deep soreness flared in my stomach, and I wanted it to. I wanted the hurt. It was a reminder of losing Mom, whether or not I needed it.

I grasped her hand and kissed it gently as my tears fell freely. "I love you, Mom."

The shock hit Dad a few moments later. "No, dammit, no! Not like this. Please don't leave me!" He collapsed into sobs over her body. I put my hand on his shoulder. Speech failed me at that moment. The grief washed over me and my sobs picked up, echoed by Dad's whimpers.

We sat like that for what seemed hours. At last I said, "Dad, we need to call somebody."

"Hospice, number's on the fridge."

Dad remained frozen, his head bowed. He still clung to the rail of Mom's bed. I sprang up. I felt like the more I moved, the less time I dwelled on how my world was ripped in half.

"Hospice said they're sending someone right now. Ten, fifteen minutes."

I returned to the bed, stood over Dad and gazed on Mom. He stroked her hand; perhaps he hoped she wasn't gone yet. Maybe this was apnea?

The hospice nurse arrived and confirmed Mom was gone. Dad

leaned over her and kissed her one last time. I sunk down into a chair. The woman who had driven me to every little league game, who cheered for me from the crowd at the band concerts, who always had a hug and a kiss for me whenever I came to visit, no matter how badly I'd screwed up in the world, was gone.

I went to Dad and placed my hands on his shoulders. "She's at peace, Dad. That's all we could ask."

"I know. Can't imagine how I'll go on now." His shoulders slumped as the thought of what he said sunk in.

"Me either. But we have each other."

"I have a card for a funeral home. Blazier Funeral Home, I think."

"I'll call," the nurse said. I saw this ache in her eyes, a reflection of what we'd been through and were going through.

Dad weakly gestured to the kitchen table. I sifted through the mound of papers and envelopes stacked on it for a few minutes. I got a chill when I saw the vast number of unopened window envelopes. At least a few of those were bills. It all looked like a window into their lives, now on pause and forever changed. I found the card and handed it to the nurse.

About an hour later, the funeral home undertakers arrived. Two men in suits. The hospice nurse had left Dad and me with the two men. With great care they handled Mom's body, transferred her to a gurney and wrapped her snugly in several heavy blankets. I stood by Dad, my arm draped around him, and clutched his hand. None of it seemed real, her lifeless body escorted out like this.

The men stood next to Mom once they finished with her. One of them asked, "Would you like one last look before we go?"

Dad shook his head. I said, "Give me a moment with her." The man nodded and stood back as I approached her.

I leaned over and kissed her forehead again. I spoke softly, "Goodbye, Mom. I'm going to make you proud of me. I'm gonna finish what I said I'd do, somehow. I love you."

My tears streamed when I moved back from her. I nodded to the two men, and they somberly wheeled her out of the house, then returned and shook our hands with offers of condolences before they departed.

The house looked different. Like a room had been removed. Dad stared into blank space. "We should try and sleep."

I looked at the clock and it was a quarter to four. *Sleep? What sleep?* I felt my phone vibrate with a text. I read it once, rubbed my eyes, and checked it a second time and saw I hadn't dreamed it. I read it again and swallowed the lump in my throat that still refused to leave.

From: UNKNOWN
Xander, we need you. Will be in touch.

(ANA)

OTTO SAT IN THE REAR for the trip to our briefing for the Verge jump. The Landcrawler rumbled through the brush on a twisting and winding path. Branches tapped out a random cadence against the doors and windows. Sometimes, the path took us on straighter, clearer roads.

I'd seen every kind of ground in the Outlands, from overgrown forests to jagged patches of old paths from years gone by, now overgrown and almost impassable. Then there were the occasional smooth clearings and of course the Valentium sites, which were their own things altogether.

The vehicle dipped, and I braced myself. The Landcrawler we rode in was about average. They were never made for comfort, just to get you from one spot to another. They handled the road, but of course you felt every damn bump along the way.

Yag drove with Wick on shotgun. They chatted it up with Remy and ignored us in the back, which was fine for what I cared.

There wasn't much that I missed in Lebabolis, but the roads there sure were easier to handle than this.

Otto was fixated on the P-LAD on his lap. He never said a word until I held my hand over his screen.

"Quit that."

"So you can still talk. Come on, I'm bored. Tell me anything." Otto was interested in just about everything, for as long as I had known him. I remembered him when we were kids, he even studied the trees around our housing area. Some people weren't sure about him and that crazy look he sometimes got in his eyes. But I always figured his mind was just too busy. He never minded my questions even when they became endless.

After a few moments, he said, "I may have descrambled the checkpoint algorithm for checkpoints inside the border."

Beyond the move to the west and all the Relos, Baudricort's next greatest love were the hacks they tried into MODOSNet, the network system for Lebabolis. I wished they were as concerned about Cataclysm as they were about their hacks.

I smiled at Otto. "Not quite what I was hoping for but it sounds important?"

"Yes, would help a lot for when we rescue the others."

The sharp pang in my gut flared again. Very important. If only Baudricort was interested in our people the way Otto was. " I know you talk a lot about tech. Heard anything else?"

He set the P-LAD down and cracked his knuckles. While Baudricort hid information pretty well, Otto wasn't as opaque. He looked out the window, then back to me. "Nothing really."

I smiled a bit as my brow furrowed. "Otto, one thing I love about you is you're the worst liar I know. Come on, what is it? You can tell me." I patted his arm.

Otto flashed me a quick grin, and eyed the others at the front in case they caught any of our conversation. "You remember the odd symbols that showed up around Lebabolis when we were young?"

I thought about it for a minute until it came back to me. Odd symbols painted onto buildings in the sectors. Not all at once, and not in the same places. They were always covered up quick with paint with no explanation from Lebabolis Security.

"I always thought they were Deviant code."

"Not at all." His eyes lightened up as he sat up in his seat. I really loved how he was this bona fide tech genius in one second and in the next he was still the kid who had grown up near me in the sector, a bright and inquisitive Intellectual Product.

Otto said, "I found data on them. It looks like it's from a military unit."

"Like the Omegans?"

His eyes left mine and darted back to the P-LAD. "Nobody knows for sure."

"Then, Lebabolis security?"

"I don't know, honest!" He looked back at me, his eyes wide.

"Does Baudricort know about this?"

"I showed him, but he said nothing about it."

Another group out there. I stared off in thought, until an idea came to me. It seemed farfetched, but what the hell? "What if it's the Valkyrie returning?"

"Naah. They were sent for Realignment, and the leader was executed."

According to what we were told in instruction, the Valkyrie led a special unit in the earlier days of Lebabolis. They faced off the Omegans, an invading army that almost tore the nation up. They would've succeeded if it wasn't for Cataclysm hitting and crippling their forces.

The Valkyrie and their group defended Lebabolis from the remaining Omegans back then, but when the leader refused to stand down and follow the Coursons, things ended badly for 'em.

When we were young, kids like Otto and me, and even Remy, played Valkyrie with sticks and whatever else we found lying around the woods near housing. However it went, we always did their salute: your arms crossed in an X over your head, like the symbol of the

Valkyrie. We conquered the world until one or more parents had had enough and ended the fun.

So far, the only people who gave us trouble here were Lebabolis. But if the Omegans had come back for revenge, it sure was a good time I left for awhile.

Toward the front, Remy snickered. I figured it was a crude and demeaning joke. Yag and Wick laughed too. I glared at the three of 'em. Was me being here a fancy idea of punishment for me by Baudricort?

At least I knew about Wick, he and Treg were pretty close. And if Treg vouched for someone, that was enough for me. I slapped my legs in thought. "Ugh, that guy." I glanced at Otto and asked him, "Could he be more annoying?"

Otto shrugged. "I find ignoring him helps."

"Oh? I thought you Intellectuals stuck together."

Otto half chuckled and frowned in response. "We're in the Outlands; anything goes. Besides, it's One or None, right?"

One or None was Baudricort's brainchild. It was how he reminded everyone in the Action that we were together, even as spread apart as we were. It was a rally cry; a few people said it every day. Whenever Exodus dragged on and the raids came, Baudricort aimed everyone's attention on how our goal was to the west, and together was the only way there.

I smiled and patted Otto's leg and looked away before the worry got to my face. They believed in it so much. It grew on me too, after awhile. But since Varrick was gone, thoughts of him washed over any growing sense of belonging I had.

I remembered one day before he came down with the Pox, we had played in the woods close by our living area. I told him what I knew about the Product assignments as he listened, his eyes rapt with attention.

"Can I stay with you after I finish instruction?"

I chuckled. "No, dear. You'll be assigned a breeding partner and you'll go with 'em, just like me with mine."

"Won't we see each other again?" His eyes sank a bit.

I ran my fingers through his hair. "Oh, of course we will. There is still rec time, but you'll have your own place. You'll see."

That was when I first thought of escape. The caches cemented it. Treg and I found one near our housing area. The container was made of some strange metal, and when we opened it the hinges made a whine like a suffocated person who fought for breath.

Inside were books like the one Baudricort gave Remy. The people in those pictures from the caches looked so different than me and everyone else I knew. The stories I had read about growing food off the land; I had no idea how but I figured it was something I would learn. They traveled in strange vehicles. Some of them moved through the air, but they were way different than Hell Hawks looked.

As happy as I was away from Lebabolis, I still had doubts about the Action. Baudricort was OK, and I knew he wouldn't have sent me anywhere more dangerous than where I already was.

My mind raced as images of Varrick poured through it. Baudricort better get his plans figured out fast. I was beyond tired of this.

"One or None," I said to Otto and sighed.

SIX

(NELSON)

DAD AND I SAT in the Arrangement Room of Blazier Funeral Home Tuesday afternoon. The whole place felt uncomfortable, like a pair of pants that squeezed you to the point of pain. The room itself looked fake even. The vase with flowers in the center of the table was a bit much. I guess they had done some study on how flowers soothed people who had just had their hearts ripped out. A few shelves in the corner and a picture of butterflies on the wall opposite us rounded things out.

I rubbed my arms while we waited for the funeral director, and checked the time on my phone for the sixth time in the past five minutes. My hands kneaded the leather covered armrests of my chair.

Dad said, "We didn't have any prearranged plan or anything."

"I'm sure they'll help us figure it out."

A man in a dark suit entered the room. He flashed a compassionate smile as he sat down at the opposite side of the table and placed a binder to his side. After he shook our hands, he said, "Hello, my name is James Bruel. First of all, my deepest condolences on your loss. I assure you we're here for you and will do our best to make this go as smooth as possible."

"Thank you very much," Dad replied. "We, uh, don't have a lot of money."

Bruel watched Dad, but his gaze slid to me every so often. His compassionate expression was framed by his neat trimmed black hair. This guy would've been right at home in a bank, I mused, where he could've hawked the latest CDs or other top rate investment opportunities.

Bruel grabbed the binder and flipped through several pages. "Alright. Let's see what's reasonable." He stopped and glanced at me. "So you're the only son?"

"Yes."

He winced, his mouth in a tight line. "I'm so sorry, this must be difficult."

"Very. Least I was with her at the end." With that, the ache in my stomach returned. Even the mention of her death felt like it skipped me back to that very moment again, when the pain was so fresh and new.

"Well, that's a comfort, I'm sure." He smiled again, and I wondered if these were lines he recited for all of his customers.

He stopped at one page in the binder and turned it toward us. "Here are some modest arrangements we can offer, if you're on a budget."

I gazed at the pages and froze. There they were, like on the pages of a damn furniture catalog: coffins and urns. On the following pages, floral arrangements. It was all so odd. Everything with a price tag, a catalog of death. It was very creepy, but what should I have expected? My face flushed. "What do you think, Dad?"

He flipped through a few pages, stopped and pointed. "How about this?"

On the page was a package that included the basic items, a cremation and internment in a mausoleum for $6500.

I looked at it for a few minutes. Dad ran his finger over the pictures, as if he felt the actual flowers through the glossed page. I turned to him. "That what you want?"

He said nothing at first, then cleared his throat. "Yeah, I think that'll be nice."

I looked up and saw Mr. Bruel's gaze on me. "Mr. Bruel, can you excuse us for a moment?"

Nodding, he stood up and left.

"Dad, tell me what you need."

He sighed. "I can't cover all of this, but if you can give me say, $4,000 that should do it."

My face got real hot.

"D-dad. I don't have that kind of money."

He watched me, his glum eyes studied me while he processed my response in depth. His nod sent a tear down his cheek. My pulse quickened, and I glared at the catalog. How could we have failed Mom this bad? My mind decided to add extra torture to my woes and conjured up a tally of various life debts I owed her that left me on the short end of everything. Mom deserved the best. There had to be a way for this to happen.

I shook my head and cleared my thought train. "We'll figure it out," I said as Bruel reentered and sat back down.

"Figure what?" he asked.

I looked at Dad but he remained silent. My voice scratched as I began. "Mr. Bruel, I'm afraid we can't afford to pay you if you need up front money. Is there anything we can-" My words and rope ran out at the same time.

Bruel slid the binder to the side. His brow creased in thought, and his expression faded from warmth to one a bit more stoic. "I see. Well, we do have financing options available, if you can make an upfront deposit, say 20%?"

$1300 was a whole lot better than $6500. Dad nodded his agreement. "Yes, we can work that out," I said. I breathed a little deeper with relief. Dad relaxed a bit in his chair. He was the only one who wanted this finished more than I did.

I slid my card over to Bruel for the initial payment. "We'll take the $6500 package," I said and pointed to the binder. "Page 15."

He grabbed the binder, nodded in agreement and turned the book back towards himself. "Very well. I need basic information from you about the deceased and we'll handle payment next." He pulled a form from the binder. "Name of the deceased?"

"Marie Forrester."

He stopped for a moment and stared at the name he had written. "Wow, that's interesting."

"What?" I asked.

"Oh, that name: Forrester. I, er, my family had a close tie with a Forrester family growing up. Where are you from?"

"New Orleans," Dad responded.

"Oh I see. Well, I hail from Austin, Texas. Perhaps they're distant relatives."

Dad eyed me and shrugged.

Bruel smiled before he went back to the form. "And your names?"

"I'm Nelson Forrester, and my father is Jerry."

Bruel stopped again, his grip on the pen tightened a bit.

"Something wrong?" Dad asked.

Bruel stared at his handwriting on the page for a few seconds, then looked at us. "It's nothing. I'm sorry. I had a rough morning. Work troubles, you know how it is." He added a hasty chuckle.

Dad said, "Always a challenge, but that's why they call it work."

We all laughed at that.

After several more minutes, Bruel finished the form, and we looked it over. Everything was addressed, Mom's cremation, the flowers and a modest mausoleum for her.

"Looks about right," I said. Dad nodded in agreement.

"OK, I'll need your contact information and method of payment so we can get this started."

We gave Bruel our address and phone numbers, and he left the room again. Dad slumped back in his chair like a weightlifter at the end of an all-day workout. "So glad we're almost done."

"I know, Dad. It's gonna be alright." I wondered if I said that more for Dad or for me.

Dad managed a slight smile, and patted my shoulder. "Want to eat out tonight?"

The mention of food was welcomed into my brain like the guest of honor at a surprise party. "Yeah, sure. My treat."

"Alright, my boy."

Bruel returned into the office and handed our cards back. "OK, we're set, except for scheduling."

I turned to Dad. He scratched his chin in thought. "Can we have this done very soon, like tomorrow?"

"That's a bit close, but I can still check. Are you waiting on any family to be notified?"

"No, just a few other friends I can tell today. Not much family."

"OK, well how about I call you this afternoon and let you know?"

"Alright. And if you can't tomorrow?"

"Perhaps we pick one other day to be safe." I suggested.

Dad thought a bit. "This Thursday?"

"Two days from now on Thursday. I think we can arrange that. Morning or afternoon?"

"Morning."

"Morning, right. I'll call and let you know when." We stood up from the table. Bruel shook our hands and wished us well.

(ANA)

WE GATHERED AROUND the tech storehouse in Encampment 12 for a run through of the mission. Gear was piled up high against the walls, and it looked like at any moment it may have fallen on us. I leaned against the table and watched Otto while he wrote directions for Remy.

"The Verge will take you to a remote part of the city. We don't have an exact location on Xander, so you'll need to be resourceful," Otto said.

"Any risks of talking with the ancients?" Remy asked.

Otto shook his head. "Not any more than the usual. Keep interactions at a minimum, but yeah, you'll need to ask around a bit. Be careful you don't let anyone get your tech." With that, Otto laid a P-LAD in front of Remy. Remy flipped it around and powered it up. His greedy hands pawed all over it. He disgusted me. All that showing off, and the extra care he took when he watched the supply stores even though it was never his assigned task. And then, he had proof of how much he was needed.

It was too much for me, and silence escaped me yet again. "You may have to ask for directions."

Simple as that remark was, it turned his knuckles white, and he met my eyes with a stern gaze. "Don't you have anything better to do?"

I enjoyed his reaction way more than I should've. "No, doesn't look that way."

"Ahh, right. Your protector gave you a free pass." Remy scoffed and looked around the table for support. "Instead of packing and moving an Encampment and doing real work, you tag along with us."

"Remy." Otto reached toward him, but Remy waved him off and instead faced everyone. "I wonder if the rest of you know who's really sitting with us."

My gut flexed, and I felt my face flush. I wasn't sure what his deal was, and the empty looks from the others told me at least here Remy was alone.

His arms folded, Remy said, "See, I know a lot about you, Ana. And your parents, your REAL parents." He smirked, and I imagined how it would've felt with my hands around his throat. My fist burned from how much I squeezed my fingers together. Otto furrowed his brow.

"See, Ana's parents were known pretty well by Charista. They made a name for themselves by looking for any Deviants they could find, and especially anyone who was with the Action. They'd rat them out and get them hauled away for Realignment." Remy shook his head. "Happened to someone in my housing section."

The heat beneath my shirt started an itch up and down my spine. The others looked at me. I bit my lip so hard I was sure it bled.

Otto said, "Remy, you know Deviants were always hunted by Lebabolis, and they had their own forces looking for people, I've never heard about anyone working from the inside."

"Of course not," Remy snickered. "They didn't want it recorded, so it was done off the record, not through MODOSNet."

I thought back to what I remembered about my parents, and how they disappeared. I remembered a few strange people by our housing unit, but... no, ridiculous. He just always had it in for me.

"How convenient." I sighed. "You've got 'em branded, me too, with no evidence besides a wild story."

Remy pointed a shaky fist at me. "You're only here because of orders. Stay outta my way until this is over, or so help me."

"I'm not leaving this room. Why don't you pay attention, little helper, I think you've got bigger problems right now." At that point I flashed him a look of daggers.

Otto coughed. His eyes flipped between Remy and me. "We don't have maps of the area, but with that P-LAD you'll be able to take a sig of a vehicle for tracking purposes. It's crude, but this and plain old eyesight should get you around."

"What kind of transportation do they have?"

"There are vehicles, but be cautious. Again, the more you interact, the more suspicion you draw. It's best to move around at night as much as possible. No killing unless it's life or death for you. Try not to be seen by too many people. And for God's sake, don't get arrested or anything."

Otto talked about who else was looking for Xander. Lebabolis had a special group that handled security and discipline. They were a group within the Security Force, under Charista's watch, but with their own commander. They included the best Warrior Products and were known for things like Realignment. As much as Remy irked me, I still shuddered at the thought of him up against 'em, alone. Even one on one with 'em was a scary thought.

"What about Omegans in the Verge?" Remy asked.

"We've never had any proof they've been through them, but stay sharp and act quick. We don't know if Lebabolis isn't just out to terminate Xander."

Otto handed two tethers to Remy. "These are for the Verge. One for you, the other for Xander. Once you acquire him, make the Verge jump and you should return to the Outlands, near Encampment 13. Bring him in for evaluation." He turned to Yag and Wick. "Baudricort said he filled you guys in already. Get Remy to the Verge and return to Encampment 12 with Ana. Don't stand too close when

Remy makes the jump, or the aftershock might pull you in too. And Remy, watch this Xander guy when you get him back here. This big a jump, we can't be sure how his body will take it, even with a bracelet."

I PULLED Remy aside as we left the meeting. "I dunno where you get your delusions, but we both know Baudricort wouldn't sabotage his own mission."

Remy shrugged.

I clenched his shirt around his chest. "And don't spout whatever that was about my parents. For all you know, that's a rumor."

He broke my grip and leaned close. "Just because you're here doesn't mean I have to like it or even talk with you." He squinted at me, and I saw a brief flash of doubt in his eyes. At last, it sunk in how dangerous this Verge jump was for him. He was needed and had his ass on the line at the same time, and the most ever in his life. And he was alone on this. Without another word, he brushed past me, headed outside.

I had never heard for sure what happened to Mom and Dad, and the fact I even entertained the possibility that what he said was true bothered me. Sure, Realignment was a thing, and they targeted Deviants for it. But were the plants by Lebabolis true, so the Action would be squashed before it ever started? Was that why Baudricort kept everyone spread out and always moving?

While the rest of the group checked the gear for the trip, I found Otto back in the Encampment lab.

"You'd tell me if you knew something, right?" I asked.

He stopped. "Of course. You're my friend... Hey, Remy's nuts. I was in advanced training with the guy, remember? I don't know where that came from, honest." He managed a small smile.

Otto's word was enough for now. But when I got back, Baudricort owed me answers.

———

THE RIDE to the Verge site took twenty minutes. I was even happier than before for the seating arrangements. Remy pretended I no longer existed, which was fine with me.

I stared out the window into the wilderness. It wasn't all the way dark outside, but it was pretty close. I braced myself against the vehicle's jostling and thought back for any sliver of a memory about my parents. I'd never heard they disappeared because of Realignment, those were posted on the MODOSNet update anyway. They wanted everyone to know who broke the rules and also that we saw how far and how small their mercy went. No one I asked in my housing unit knew either. Treg thought they were held for interrogation, but nothing was ever known.

My com unit buzzed to life, and I saw Treg's face on the screen.

"Hey, nice to see you." I smiled.

"Everything decent?"

I glanced toward the front of the vehicle. "Your guy's OK. But, Remy. Of everyone they could've stuck me with. Yeesh."

Treg squinted. "Oh yeah, he's a prick. Least you won't be around him for long. They scout the Verge location?"

"Otto gave us the rundown."

"Good. Ya know, I saw one of those symbols again."

I sat up. "Yeah? Like the ones from the buildings?"

He nodded. "In a clearing not far from the new Encampment spot. I was scouting the area."

"Yeah, Otto mentioned finding out more about those symbols. He said it might be the Omegans."

"Whatever it is, we're on high alert. No sense taking chances."

"Exactly. Well, I'm gonna get wherever I can when this is over and will let you know."

"Please do. I'll let you know what I can about Baudricort."

I touched his face on the screen. "Thanks. See you soon, I hope."

EIGHT

(ANA)

W E PULLED UP A HUNDRED FEET or so from the time rip location. At least five Lebabolis troops stood guard around it, and who knew how many more waited in the woods? A concrete bunker stood about fifty feet from the Verge point. I winced at the structure, a relic from when people attempted installation of power generation facilities around Valentium deposits. I looked at the concrete castle and wondered how many lives that little experiment cost.

Yag and Wick kept low, their rifles pointed toward the Verge. Their optical scopes checked the visible soldiers, their weapon stores, and body armor types. Remy watched for anyone behind or to the side of us.

I shivered and ran my hands under my armpits in the gentle breeze.

"So much for slipping past unnoticed," Remy said.

Yag wiped his brow. "We can double back later, look for an alternate spot."

Remy shook his head. "No, there are none that close. Remember, the longer we wait, the more time they have to kill Xander."

Remy peered at the Verge with a bit of awe mixed with that scared look he flashed me back at the Encampment. I watched the center of the Verge. An amber colored ball that was the size of an average person lit the immediate area.

Remy wiped his brow. "Anyone near that will be a major target."

Wick motioned toward the Landcrawler, and we met back there. I shoved a few branches back to squat down, and I was rewarded with scratches on my hands. Wick held up a few disk shaped objects. They weren't guns or anything Treg had shown me before. "We're not letting anyone stop this party. I've got mines; if we get them close enough each of these can take out at least two people."

"If they're close enough," Yag said.

Remy eyed the mines. "Think it'll work?"

"As far as surprise, it's as good as we got. Once that happens, we'll lay down fire. You haul ass to that Verge point," Wick said.

Remy nodded. "And where should we be when you do this?"

Yag looked toward the Verge point. "Close by where we were a minute ago. We'll fan out in an arc. Stand in between Wick and me. We'll throw them. Soon as they pop, haul your skinny ass into that light."

"What about me?" I asked.

"Stay close to me, and keep low," Wick replied.

We crept back up toward the Verge, and got into position. As Wick checked the mines, I looked over to Yag and Remy, crouched low and ready.

"Treg said a lot of good things about you, Wick."

He smiled as he set the mine controls. "Did he now? He's a good fella."

"Yeah, too bad he couldn't have taken Remy's place."

"Ahhh, don't worry about that guy. He's more pissed he don't have a better job yet. Like we're all in the Action to be the honcho."

Wick caught Yag's attention, and with several hand signals, they got ready. They almost activated the mine sequences when the sound of thunder rolled across the sky above us. A Hell Hawk descended fast, and came to a shuddering halt a little above tree top level. The gust of hot wind tossed leaves, twigs and other debris around us along with that familiar rotten smell of hot rotten death engine exhaust. We crouched next to the tree, and kept still. Wick signaled Yag "stand down", and we all eyed the hovercraft.

OK, either they had a trace on this area and found a few extra heat signatures, or this was just some kinda social call.

The Hell Hawk descended a bit further, into the clearing around the Verge, and a man leapt out. Whoever it was, he was easily the tallest one. He wore a backpack and addressed the nearby soldiers, who got in line pretty quick. Whoever it was, they were important.

Their clothes were strange, nothing I'd ever seen anyone here wear.

Well, I'd seen it, but somewhere else.

I swallowed hard when I realized why I recognized the garb. When you saw pictures of clothing from a centuries old cache, you remembered a thing or two.

"He's going back. To the time Remy is," I said.

"What?" Wick whispered. "How do you even know?"

"A hunch." I sighed. "He's dressed for it. Bet he's going for Xander."

"So where'd he get those ancient clothes?" Wick asked.

I wished I knew. We watched as the man stood near the time rip zone and waved the Hell Hawk clear.

"Wick, the aftershock," I whispered, and he nodded. He signaled Yag to be ready. Each held their mines up.

I watched the soldiers as they moved back as well. Two of 'em took shelter in the bunker.

The man stepped into the time rip. A loud thump shook the ground, and I wobbled a bit. The swarm of electrical tentacles lashed out and came close to a few soldiers to the right of us.

The leaves and branches about us rustled loudly as everything shimmered about us. A hum followed, so loud it was all I heard for several moments.

As the aftershock faded, Wick and Yag tapped the releases on their mines and tossed 'em. Wick's flew fifteen feet, bounced a bit and landed on the ground about ten feet from the Verge. Yag's landed twenty feet from the Verge.

I ducked low and waited for the blasts. Nothing.

"Damnit!" Wick said.

Lights stabbed the darkness, and the air around us lit with pulse fire. I fell to the ground as Wick and Yag returned fire. I looked up enough to see Remy as he half crawled, half scrambled to his feet toward the Verge.

Wick charged the bunker, and before anyone shot at him, he blasted the two soldiers inside and rendered 'em smoldered corpses. I crawled close and kept as low as possible. From further back, another group of soldiers opened fire on Wick.

"Get over here, Ana!" he bellowed. I dashed over and joined him inside the bunker. I fell inside and closed the door. Wick fired at various points in the distance.

"You good?" he yelled between shots.

"Yeah, I think so." I got to my knees and dusted myself off as best I could.

The air around us sizzled with heat from the pulse fire as branches and leaves showered the bunker. The flashes of light from the pulse fire lit things enough that I caught sight of Yag pinned down, clasping one leg with a bloodied hand.

"Yag's hit!" I screamed.

"Damn it! Where the hell's Remy?" Wick shouted.

We heard the Lebabolis soldiers' shouts as they moved around to the front of the bunker. "If they get a pulse grenade in here, we're done for!" Wick said.

A shape appeared to my right. I jumped back, my fist cocked until I saw Remy's face. Blood trailed down his mouth.

"Help," he said with a raspy voice.

I pulled him inside the bunker, and he crumpled to the floor. In the dim light I saw that he was bleeding from his chest, and the look on his face told me how bad it was. He clutched the Verge tethers in one blood soaked hand.

"What now?" I asked. Remy shuddered and wheezed, a blob of blood oozing over his lips. His coughs became convulsions when he sat up.

"Yag!" Wick yelled. "He's not moving! How's Remy?"

Remy said nothing. He slumped onto his back, his eyes fell to me. He looked off in thought for a second, then back to me when he pushed the tethers into my hand.

"What, am I supposed to?" I asked, but he only motioned to his P-LAD. Wick continued his barrage of fire on the Lebabolis troops. He growled as shots hit the bunker and sent more debris raining inside.

Time was short. Escape was the only option.

But how? And to where?

I might have made it, if they were still occupied with Wick.

You're not going anywhere.

I flinched at the voice.

I glanced at Remy. His eyes watched me as he writhed on the floor. While I felt an odd pity at the sight of him like this, I recalled his words about me, *"Why is she here?"*

Was this Baudricort's plan all along?

Was I Remy's backup?

"Can't hold them much longer!" Wick screamed. A shot tore through his arm. "Shit!" The bunker lit up again with a flash and a wave of heat.

Move it, soldier!

I lunged out of the bunker as I heard Wick's moans. Shots came my way but zoomed past with a quick wave of heat in their wake. Only a few more feet left. I snapped a tether on my wrist, like Otto had shown Remy. It sent a tingling warm surge through my arm.

Out the corner of my eye, a Lebabolis soldier raced toward me, his gun sprayed the air all around me. Ten more feet.

One met me head on. My right foot planted into the ground, and

I leapt into 'em as they raised their rifle, which sent us both to the ground.

My feet dug in one more time, I jumped right into the Verge point, and my world was undone.

———

THE BACK of my head felt like I had been struck with a steel pipe. A dull ache bored from the base of my neck all the way up and into my forehead as I found myself in a glow of light. Things floated past in an endless stream: images, people, places, events. A few things I recognized, a lot more I didn't.

A vibrating hum warbled my hearing to the point of deafness. A large group of people rushed past me. Soldiers. One waved a resistance flag. I couldn't make out any of their faces though. Another soldier walked right in front of me. Fierce eyes, she ordered the Action troops about. She looked at me, and I felt her gaze like it came out the back of my head. She yelled at me, "Move out!" but I soon realized it wasn't directed at me. She wore battle armor, and the troops rallied around her. I saw explosions off to either side, and the mysterious woman charged toward 'em, the troops behind her.

Next, a man rushed toward me. I shuddered when I recognized him from the Verge. I was never quite sure if what I saw on these time rips was fellow travelers or phantoms from my imagination, but according to Otto, no one could do anything to anyone seen in a time rip. The only thing that really existed here was your mind. Anything you felt as far as pain, or fear, was a projection of your mind.

The strange man fired a pulse weapon. One of his eyes looked like it was made out of metal. He was a Lebabolis Sentry.

The images jumbled as the Verge accelerated. The strange man melted away, and I sped through a tunnel of bright colors. I felt a burning sensation in my chest and on the wrist with the tether. I looked at it and forced my mind away from thoughts of the worst.

Otto said this was the furthest back they'd sent someone with a monitor bracelet. There were no guarantees from 'em.

Or for me.

I shook those thoughts from my head and focused on Varrick.

The burning in my chest became like fire, and I screamed. My arms were thrust to my sides. It felt like my body was pulled apart, stretched from limb to limb and my skin being ripped off my face one strip at a time.

My vision blurred as I kept my thoughts on the goal that was now mine and not the fear that something had gone wrong. But the more time passed, and the more I felt like I had dissolved into nothing, the more the fear persisted.

Anxiety gripped my throat like a pair of hands, and my breaths almost stopped.

I won't make it.

I can't keep this up.

My heart felt like it was ripped from my chest. Another loud thud and huge flash of light, and I felt weightless. My arms slid back by my side, and I drifted downward.

Then, everything went black.

NINE

(NELSON)

I T STARTED LIKE AN EARTHQUAKE.

The ground rocked so intense that no one could stay on their feet. Trees were uprooted, buildings fell. Then the earth opened up and shot geysers of lava hundreds of feet into the air. The wind howled like a thousand angry spirits, it ripped through and around people and objects, until everything whipped into a massive tornado. The lava was spread about, and everyone who wasn't incinerated scrambled for whatever foothold and shelter they could possibly find.

It felt a little strange when I wrote about Cataclysm in my book. All the stress over mom and what would happen with my job had to come out somewhere, and drinking hadn't really helped settle me that much. Tina was a help but that was only very recent. As horrific as it was, I felt good I could shove my anger and fear into one safe place like that.

I WOKE up Wednesday morning with a dull headache. Probably should've skipped that fourth glass of wine, but oh well. It wasn't every day that I handled my mother's funeral arrangements.

My vacation from work had been good up until next week. My mind raced with thoughts of sadness and anger. I felt like doing everything and nothing at the same time. I even moved in slow motion, like I had a bad fever and the assorted aches and pains of a flu.

My brain needed a diversion before I went crazy.

I figured my best bet was the novel. After my initial burst about Cataclysm and general word vomit, I stopped and stared at my laptop for several minutes. I hoped that somehow I could just will the words onto the page. Oh, if it were that simple.

The phone jolted me out of my semi daze. It was Bruel.

"Mr. Nelson Forrester?"

"Speaking."

"Hi, sorry to bother you. I tried calling your father but there was no answer."

"What's going on?"

"We neglected to go over the obituary for your mother."

A stabbing headache sliced my head right between the eyes. Every time I thought things were done with Mom, I was pulled right back in for something else. "Oh, what do you need?"

"Several words about her, her life, surviving family. Things like that. You can email it to me."

"Do they have a word limit?"

"No, but remember you're budgeted for $300 so keep it to 250 words or less."

"Sure. I'll work on it."

I opened up a new file on the laptop and typed away. Alright, Mom's obituary counted as writing, I supposed. It ended up being easier than I thought. My only challenge was length. 250 words was insufficient to do her justice. But I guessed that's what a life came down to in the end, the allotted space for a newspaper and website.

After a few minutes, I had it done. It was simple. I stared at the screen, and her life contained in those few words. It mentioned her charity work and how she loved gardening. I felt like it did her proud.

I called Dad up on his cell phone. After several rings he answered, "Hello?"

"Hey, Dad, Mr. Bruel from the funeral home called. We didn't do an obituary for Mom."

"Oh boy."

"I typed one up. Want me to read it?"

"No, I trust you. I can't do it right now."

"I know. I'll send it. Anything else you need?"

"No, think I'm gonna watch TV."

"Alright. Talk soon."

I stared at the screen a little more. As I glanced over the words, my mind flashed back to Bruel. He seemed a little shaky in the meeting. His job must've really sucked... a funeral director? Meetings with sad people about their dead loved ones all day? I bet he wanted the distraction of a phone call, even if it was about yet another deceased person.

I stared more at the screen but felt nothing. Writer's block was still in effect. Fuck this.

A conversation with someone was the answer. Dad wasn't really in shape for a chat, so I called my buddy Harvey at his office.

"Harvey Preston."

"Hey, man."

"Yo, how are you?"

"Pretty bad. Got a minute?"

"Uh, yeah. Hang on a second."

He spoke to someone else, then he returned. "OK, what's going on? How's your mom?"

I took a shuddered breath. "She's gone, man."

"No! I'm so sorry, man. That's awful."

"Thanks, yeah, she at least went peaceful at home." Even as I repeated the words about what had happened, it still felt like fiction.

"Well, that's good."

"Dad and I were with her, and she isn't suffering anymore."

"Right. Well, if there is anything I can do, please let me know."

I leaned back and scratched my leg. "Just talking is great." I was amazed how calmer I felt after just a few minutes on the phone with Harvey.

"I can sure do that. So, made the funeral plans yet?"

"Yeah, it's tomorrow, Thursday at the latest."

"Oh, wow. I'll try getting over for a few minutes. Let me know when you have the definite time."

"I will. Hey, how about a drink soon?"

"Sure! Say when and where."

"Thanks, dude."

"Hey, what are ex college roommates for?"

We both laughed. Harvey and I met in school, where I wound up with him as my roommate by sheer luck of the draw. He was there for me in good times, bad times, and shitty times too. My folks always liked him. He loved when they had him over and Mom made her lasagna.

I hung up with Harvey and stared at my laptop. The manuscript stared back, as if it mocked me. Unlike the screen of warmth and kindness about mom's life, these words sneered back at me with a taunt. "Where the hell are you?" I glared at the screen. "Come together, damn it!"

My phone buzzed to life again with a voicemail message. That was weird; usually I heard the call waiting first. I opened the voicemail system. The automated date/time stamp announcement played. A chill ran through me as I heard the message. The voice sounded mechanical, and at times was garbled:

Nelson Forrester, listen carefully. I've been assigned to protect you from people trying to kill you. It's imperative you contact me at once. Don't disregard this message; your family is also in danger.

I played the message again.

Someone wanted me dead? Why?

I scrambled to think of what could have brought that kind of threat on. Alright, I'd been with several women, a few were already attached, but this wasn't a jealous boyfriend.

So how was it they knew my name and number?

TEN

(ANA)

A STEADY THROB PULSED in my head, like it could have exploded as I lay on the ground.

There was a loud hum somewhere.

Or it was just my headache.

I sat up and looked around. I licked my lips and tasted the salty sweat that had beaded up there. I blinked for a few seconds until I realized it was mostly dark wherever I was. A few lights cast a faint glow in the distance. After a minute or so my eyes adjusted and revealed more shapes to me. A large building to my right. Several small walls to my left.

A dog barked in the distance. I soon saw what made the humming sound. It stood right across from me. A large metal tower and a lot of cables. It soared into the sky so high, I wondered if it was a transit system.

I scratched my head and ran back through the events that had led me here. At least three people I knew were dead. Would I have done the same if the positions were switched and one of them had a clear shot at the Verge?

111

I was safer than I was back there, sure. But I had less than half the chance Remy had. He was trained for this; I wasn't.

"You've got more of a chance than you know."

I spun around and saw nobody. *Please tell me I'm not going crazy,* I thought. *Really don't have the time, like ever.*

"Relax, you can do this. You know the goal, you have your target. Find him."

The voice was a woman, but none I recognized. And from the look of it, whoever it was wasn't with me in person, either.

The monitor on my wrist showed May 2014. I wiped a bead of sweat from my forehead and slipped off my jacket. I noticed I was on a stone platform. Off about fifty yards away, sets of lights passed down a path.

Transportation. I needed some.

As I neared the path with the lights a man's warbled voice from the ground mumbled, "Hey, did ya see that?"

I looked for the source of the voice and saw a clump of blankets on the ground with a head and feet stuck out from either side. What I made out of his face looked ragged, more so than a lot of the Encampment people I'd seen, who moved from place to place, some-times at a moment's notice. I stooped down, put my hand on his shoulder and gazed upon the face of a dirty and bewildered man. "See what?" I asked, hoping he hadn't meant the crazy girl who'd talked to herself.

He pointed towards my arrival point. With a scratchy voice that sounded like he had just rinsed his mouth with a bag of rocks, he replied, "Back there, ssss-some kinda light or somethin'. Loud bang too."

I humored him and looked in that direction. "Dunno. Nothing now."

He said nothing for a second. His eyes wandered, almost like he had forgotten about me. Then he returned to our conversation. "Well, see t'morrow in daylight."

"What's your name?" I asked.

He moved about a little and scratched himself. "Louie. I'm Louie."

"Hi, Louie. I'm Ana. You're gonna be OK." I smiled and patted his shoulder. He murmured something that sounded along the lines of "Sugah." He slid back down and drifted off to sleep. He seemed harmless enough. If he was the only one who had seen anything, I was fine.

I left Louie and made my way up to the path. A few other people were scattered around, but Louie was the only one who talked to me. I kept my eyes low. I'd already spoken with more people than Otto had suggested.

I ran back over the meeting at Encampment 12 in my mind, what Otto had told Remy about. No interactions with people unless absolutely necessary. Well, that had gone out the door once Remy took a shot in the gut and died on us.

Hopefully, Otto had the right location and I wasn't too far away from Xander.

As I checked for vehicles, I noticed something black on the ground in front of me.

It reminded me of pictures from the cache. They called these things hats.

The fabric was smooth under my hands. The edges were a little stiff, and it looked like it had been stepped on or a vehicle had rolled over it a few times. But I wasn't picky.

I mused how useless it was, if someone from Lebabolis had a bead on me. But, Otto suggested anything that blended in. This was a start.

The sides felt cool on my head. It slipped low over my eyes until I tilted it back a little.

I came across a vehicle parked along the street. It was smaller than a Landcrawler. I pointed the P-LAD toward it and activated the electropulse. Its lights came on and after a few seconds of click sounds from the front of the vehicle, whatever motor it had came to life. I smiled at Otto and his magical toys.

It took me a few minutes with the controls before the vehicle moved at all. Soon after, it shuddered. I cursed it a bit, as if that prevented any problems. I needed a way around this place before I convinced someone I had never met that I was from the future and made sure they followed me back my way.

That wasn't so hard, right? Whomever that woman's voice I heard thought so. That was good enough for now, I guessed. I clutched the monitor bracelet in my hand. At least MODOSNet had no trace on my whereabouts.

I fought with the controls until the vehicle lurched ahead. At least the paths here were open and clear. After a few minutes, I pulled the vehicle over and checked Remy's P-LAD for whatever details it had.

Not only was every Lebabolis citizen registered in MODOSNet, their locations were tracked at all times. Any changes for things like health conditions required your Product status be updated. Each sector proctor reviewed those who hadn't properly updated their information, and if you violated this enough they had you "convinced" about compliance.

It wasn't sudden, all that control. They worked it in slow. Basic services, food, shelter, medical, were tied to MODOSNet. No registration meant you received no food. A few tried their luck and lived off the land instead, but the areas for that were kind of sparse, and you may have been devoured by the wild animals around, so there was that.

I had to watch myself. I wasn't the only dog in this hunt.

ELEVEN

(NELSON)

I RETURNED TO THE OFFICE the following Monday. I worked for a consulting firm called QuickSolve. We handled software for law enforcement agencies. As far as jobs went, we did fine a few years back. Work was the fuel for my writing time, anyway. I reminded myself of that when things got bad, which was often as of late.

My recent time off was a bit of a challenge with these people. At least the owner allowed me time with Mom as needed. My immediate boss Travis, however, used it to his advantage after awhile.

I checked voicemail while my computer started up. Fifteen messages from last week. Typical. I needed coffee before I started in on them.

My cubicle sat in the middle of a sea of them, like some corporate based coral colony. People were in and around, tapping away on keyboards, some on their headsets on support calls. I'd forgotten the dull roar of this place when the busy morning hit. Once I'd settled back in for a bit, that old familiar caffeine pang reared its ugly head, and I knew what my next move was.

Of course, the coffee pot had a half inch of sludge that might've passed for coffee on the bottom if chewable semi-burnt coffee was a thing. On my way to the kitchen, I heard the voice I had hoped I could've avoided for the moment.

"Well, look who's back."

I turned and saw Travis, a file folder clutched in his hand as if it were a poisonous snake. Travis looked like those guys who were always like two seconds away from stories about his yacht club or a lame trip where he looked at waterfalls. The neatly trimmed hair, the Ed Hardy shirts; he must've taught guys lessons on douche bag behavior in his off hours.

"Hey, Travis."

He folded his arms and trapped the folder beneath them. His aqua marine polo and frosted hair were pretentious enough on their own without his help.

"How's it going; you getting situated?" He threw in a pretend sympathetic smile.

"Trying to, yes."

"Well, don't let me keep you from coffee duties. Come see me in a bit." He glanced at the pot and snorted before he walked off.

Travis was already my boss for a few months too long. We never gelled. And I had a great supervisor right before him too. Of course, they left for a better job, and I had been stuck with Travis ever since. Travis made a big splash with some interagency web application that coordinated drug enforcement agencies and made sure their undercover work never overlapped. Alright yeah, it was brilliant. But a lot of people actually did the work that he took credit for. Travis was good like that.

After I had cured my coffee deficiency and waded through support calls and email updates from network admins about server issues, I strode over to Travis' office. I knocked on his door, and he yelled from inside, "Yeah?"

I entered, and he waved me over to a seat, which happened to be a few inches lower than his desk and chair. Being in his office always felt like court. In honesty though, I'd have much preferred it be court. At least there I had a halfway decent shot at explaining myself to an impartial judge.

Travis folded his hands, his forearms draped across the desk almost as if he were praying. Ah yes, the silent game- one of his favorites. He waited for people to say anything that gave him a target for pouncing.

My eyes squinted a bit. I had forgotten how bright he kept it. He claimed it was because of an eye issue. Sure.

His smirk faded a little. "So, first off, sorry about your mom."

"Thanks."

"How're you handling it?"

"Oh, as good as I can, I guess. Good days and bad days, you know?"

He eyed me for a second. "Mmmhm," he offered. He made a few keystrokes and spun the monitor on his desk toward me and I saw an oh so familiar site: the Service Call Tracker.

"So, on to business. Your support call stats are bad, and have been for awhile now, way before you took off." He grabbed the keyboard at his desk and typed away for a few minutes. Several graphs appeared on the screen from the support tracker software the company used for efficiency measurements.

He pointed at the screen and said, "As you know, we shoot for minor issues to be resolved in one to three days max. Major issues we allow up to two weeks for resolution. I checked your times over the past two months, and you're taking too long." He turned back to me. "So what's going on?"

My stomach tightened, and my breaths came a little quicker. "Um, I don't know, lotta users don't respond when I check on their status."

"Yeah, a few like that." He glanced back at the screen, ran his hands through his hair and faced me again. "Look, I know these cops get pulled away a lot. But this is happening all over the place, man."

"Alright. I'll work on it."

He studied me for a few seconds and offered what I thought was a half smile. "You realize if these agencies aren't happy with us, they stop paying our fees. And you know what that means, right?"

"Yeah, yeah. I gotcha."

"Fix it, Nelson. All I'm saying." He waved his hand to the door, then turned back to the screen and became engrossed with it. His typing built into a moderate rattle of fingers on keys and served as my cue that my presence was no longer even on his radar. What a jackass. And he had thrown that thing in about Mom first so he appeared sympathetic.

I always felt like I needed a shower to wash the smarminess off after dealing with Travis. The calls he rode me so hard about were for our jail management software. It was in use all day and night and yeah, any down time for those customers whatsoever was bad. The others in my group and I rotated on support at night and on the weekends.

I never had much leeway from Travis, not even with a dying mother. I wondered how my unavailability over the past two weeks had further affected my standings. And I hated the fact it was even a source of worry for me.

Beyond the new voicemails that came during my thrill ride of fun with Travis, another was from a telemarketer. Heh - easy delete.

I sipped my coffee and played the next message:

Nelson Forrester, you don't know me, but I know you. Be careful. I need to see you as soon as possible. Don't disregard this, there is too much at stake. Sorry I can't say any more right now, but I'll be in touch.

I sat back for a moment. After another sip of coffee, I listened to it a few more times.

Careful?

I was a support analyst at a modest IT company. The list of my worries pretty much consisted of carpal tunnel and eye strain.

I deleted the message and shook my head. Another message - this was either a horrendous wrong number case, or my imagination had gotten the best of me at last.

Now, the world I wrote about was full of danger. As bad as my prick supervisor was, at least my existence here was pretty mundane.

TWELVE

(ANA)

I FLOATED IN A MURKEY DARK FOG.

Dim shapes floated by, and a young child whimpered some-where close. Then, the fog cleared and I drifted around a room. Two dark figures huddled over a bed as I watched from a corner. The rest of the room looked plain, bare other than a table near the bed with several pumps on it and tubes connected to the child on the bed. It reminded me of a medical station from an Encampment hospital.

The child's sobs echoed in my head. One of the dark figures spoke with a gruff male voice. The child cried out, and a chill grabbed me as I recognized the voice.

Varrick.

My heart raced, and my breath quickened.

The child cried out, "Sister!"

He reached up, but the dark figures steadied him. Their faces were still too dark to see. Varrick's eyes were full of fright, and he focused on one of the dark figures.

Sweat rolled down Varrick's forehead, and mingled with his tears. He breathed faster, and looked at the figures. His eyes pleaded for relief.

Please no.

I moved closer to the bed, almost as if pushed by something or someone. They made sure I saw everything. I reached toward Varrick. I wanted him soothed, anything where I was a help. But it was useless.

Varrick's pleas were audible as I neared the bed. I looked around, but the walls of the room faded into blackness.

I heard more discussions between the two dark figures. The larger of the two held the child against the bed while the other figure grabbed a needle and injected it into Varrick's arm.

They waited. Varrick's breaths hadn't changed. He glanced about for a few moments.

Then he screamed.

His scream echoed over and over in the room and ripped through me. It felt like my soul was burned from inside my body. The agony shot through him, and his body shook on the bed as he was still braced by one of the figures.

His eyes shut.

Whatever I was in this place crumbled inside. Tears clouded my vision. I swung at the dark figures, but nothing happened.

Varrick shook once more then was still. A thin trail of blood oozed from his nose. The figures stood, still faced away from me.

The larger figure spoke clearly, a man's voice. "Well done. I know that wasn't easy."

The other responded with a raspy, "He had the Pox, it was a death sentence anyway."

The large figure turned and grabbed the other's shoulder. "We need to take care of the rest like this. I wanted you to understand – we can't save them, but we can decide how to help them."

"Of course."

"Now you're truly ready to lead, Ana."

What?

The other figure turned, and I saw my face. But the eyes weren't mine. They were icy and soulless. My entire being clenched so tight a gasp escaped my lips, and grew into a scream.

"No!"

I was back in 2014, and near where I first arrived. Drenched in sweat, my heart pounded in my throat. I looked around. Several of the people stared at me, including Louie.

"Rough dream?" he asked.

I nodded and shook my head.

"Sure you're fine, sugah? Got some food from the Mission if you want." Louie held up a tray toward me. I was just too bewildered for any kind of rations.

"Thanks, I'm OK." I slid back and eased my thoughts as best I could and tried for peaceful sleep. Dawn came soon. I had a job to do and needed focus.

ALL OF MY attempts at the data sources with the P-LAD failed. Their technology was too ancient. I figured Xander must've had friends somewhere. I just hoped whoever I asked wasn't from Lebabolis in disguise.

The day after my arrival, I wandered roads in the dark hours. I watched vehicles and people passing while I stuck to the side of the large paths. Better I avoided vehicles for now, since that would've made me more noticeable pretty quick.

After a few twists and turns down quieter paths I came up to a large one. A large gap divided the two rows of buildings, with trees in the middle. Several signs lined up in front of the buildings I walked next to. Up ahead, a few people entered and exited this one location. The glowing signs in front of the building read "Checkpoint Charlie's". As I headed toward the door, I pondered if it was a waypoint system. Checkpoints?

The blare of conversations and music greeted me when I entered the checkpoint. A few people were inside, some at tables, others in a row along one side. It looked a little like our food halls. A large man stood against the wall and eyed me as I approached. "Drink?" He huffed.

I looked at the others as I took a seat. I lowered my shoulders to the bar and leaned toward him. "So, are you Charlie?"

He wrinkled his brow. "Huh? No, I'm Jimmy. Getcha drink?"

"No, thanks. I was wondering if you could help me though."

Jimmy scratched his bald head, his brow furrowed. Then he broke into a smile, but I didn't think I wanted to know the thought behind it. "Maybe."

My hands kneaded a bit. "I'm looking for somebody."

Someone yelled at the other end. Jimmy craned his head over for a second, then back to me. "Boyfriend?"

"No."

He studied me for another moment. "Girlfriend?"

"No, no." I checked to see if anyone else was listening before I leaned in. "You know a Xander Lee?"

He narrowed his eyes in response and shook his head. "Naah, never heard'a no Xander." He grabbed a rag and wiped the counter. After a few seconds he added, "Sure you don't want no drink?"

"Yeah. Look, I really need to find 'em. Any suggestions?"

He folded the rag back and shrugged. "Google?"

"What's Google?"

He stared at me. "Ya never heard of Google? Where you from?" He shook his head and slipped away to the other end of the counter with a snort. His belly smashed up against the ledge as he tended to other people alongside it. He laughed at something someone said. He peered back in my direction and chuckled.

Maybe if I canvassed the city, however long that took. Or if I locked in on a beacon from the Lebabolis group, if they were stupid enough and left theirs on.

Maybe, but even that was a long shot.

I could've tried another Verge location. But how long would it be before I found one, with no gear for location.

If I checked whatever enforcement agency existed around here, the heat on me would be raised. No way I needed that kind of attention.

Or maybe Louie knew another way.

"Hey, honey."

I jumped in my seat to see Jimmy right in front of me again. He watched me with a half smile. "Why dontcha try the library? They can help with dat."

(ANA)

AFTER I ASKED a few more questions and gave into Jimmy's insistence that I have a drink of water, I got what I hoped were directions to this library place. I rode my vehicle there the next day. A musky smell greeted me when I entered the building. My nose twitched at the pungent air, and I coughed a little. The place reminded me of the Encampments at first. A large desk stood in the center with rows of shelves that lined the walls. Several tables were scattered around. People's murmurs floated by from different points in the room. They were all about, a few at tables, others walking along the large shelves and gazing at the books.

I'd never seen so many books in one place except the few from the caches. I wondered who had made them, and if it had been the same person or not.

One worker led me through the library to a room and handed me a large book, much bigger than the Xander book. As I sat at a table with it, the worker hovered nearby.

My fingers slid across the coarse paper. So this was how they searched for things. The pages crinkled as I turned 'em, and more of the musty smell greeted me as I flipped through the tome. The book was a directory of names and locations, housing quarters, I guessed. As I got to the "L" section, my stomach tightened.

I leaned in close while my finger scanned the lines of names. Nothing. I tried again; zip. I checked the pages before and after, no luck still. My heart sank a bit.

"Is this the complete city directory?" I asked the worker and patted the pages.

"Well, it's a few years old, but it's the newest we've got." She shrugged and eyed it, then me.

I gazed at the book and turned a few pages. "He's not here."

"Who?"

I whispered, "Xander Lee."

She cocked her head, but nothing in her eyes gave any hint of recognition. "I'm sorry, never heard of them." She flipped the pages back to the beginning. "Could you have the wrong name?"

I gritted my teeth. *How much should I say?* I was in this far already.

"No." I thought back to Jimmy's suggestion. "Do you have a Google?"

She replied with a nervous giggle but caught herself and straightened up. "I'm sorry, you mean, you want to try Google?"

"Yes, would Google know?"

"Uh, y-yes. Probably so. You can sign up for a computer; I'll need your card for that."

I stared at her. "My what?"

"Your card, you know, library card?" She smiled.

"Oh, I don't seem to have one."

"Ahh, well we need some other identification. Driver's license?"

"Afraid I don't have any." My fists clenched in my pockets.

"Oh," she said as she closed the book. "Forgot it?"

"Yeah, well. Something like that."

She nodded. "Well, come back when you do, and I'll set you up." She smiled and took the book in her arms. My gut tightened into a ball of soreness, and I felt my heartbeat leap into my throat. *I've got to get to him.*

As she turned, I grasped her shoulder. Either she was that jittery or my hold was a little too hard, but the book slipped out her arm and made a loud echoey thud against the floor.

She looked from the book back to me, her eyes wider. "Y-yes?"

Two people at a nearby table now looked our way. I smiled at the worker, my voice still low. "I'm sorry, I really need to find this person. Is there anything else you can do?"

"Um, ma'am? I'm sorry, but without proper ID I can't grant you computer access. You're welcome to stay and browse, but we have rules. Now if you'll excuse me." She brushed past me and darted off. She passed by a man at another table. He also looked my way. His eyes squinted a bit at me, then he returned to his work. My gut tightened when I recognized those deep brown eyes. They were the same ones that stared back at me from the screen in that meeting room with Baudricort.

As I approached him, a rattling sound came from the table. He grabbed a small device and held it to his ear and talked for a few seconds, then picked up the items spread out on the table, packed 'em up and left the building.

I followed him with my eyes as he hurried out.

Found you, Xander Lee.

(ANA)

I WATCHED XANDER as he left the building and got into his vehicle. I took a sig of the car with the P-LAD and thought more about what would've convinced him when I got the chance. I yanked his book out, flipped through a few pages.

What if I mention Varrick to him? I bet he has kids of his own. Saving a sick child would convince him, right?

Back on my P-LAD, I thought more about his reactions and how I would've handled 'em. *He wouldn't believe it's real. I shouldn't blame him. I dunno; I'd feel different in his place.*

A few others left the library building and stood outside near me, so I slid the P-LAD out of view. Vehicles passed by in the darkness, their lights casting quick flashes of brightness on the area.

I was about to get up when a booming voice wafted out to my side. "Never a cab when you need one."

Out the corner of my eye I noticed a figure leaned over the back of the bench to my right. A man in a dark suit. Our eyes met, and he offered a smile.

"Mind if I join you?"

I could've easily ignored him and left. My quota for speaking with people was way over any reasonable limit. Something stopped me, though. It was better I stayed put right then. If I ran, that would've drawn more attention, or he could've chased me. If I jumped back into my vehicle and he was anybody I needed to worry about, it would've made tracking me even easier.

Much of his face blended into the evening light. I offered a "Guess so" and made room on the bench for him to sit.

I pulled my hat down lower and peeked at him and watched the vehicles more.

He ruffled his shirt a bit and sighed. "The heat in this city is insane. Even at night, it's like a stew around here."

I shook my top a bit and enjoyed the brief coolness from that. While I agreed, I remained silent. I hoped he was just an oddball out at night, lonely for a friend, like Jimmy at the checkpoint place. I did my best to become invisible to him.

"My name's Jesse. What's yours?" he asked.

I shook his hand. An agitated sigh escaped me.

"Joan."

"Hi, Joan, what do you do?" His body turned toward me, his arm snaked along the back of the seat in my direction.

"Sightseeing."

He glanced behind us. "In the library?"

"Oh, I was... I'm waiting for a friend."

"Oh, is that right?" His eyes peered into me, a little too deep.

I swallowed, but the lump that formed in my throat was still there. "Yeah." I looked back toward the road. A few vehicles passed us. This conversation went on too long already.

He stretched a bit. "Too bad you weren't a little earlier, could've seen Jazz Fest a few weeks back."

I nodded. "Yeah, well, I should be going. We were supposed to meet but something must have happened."

I stood up and felt his gaze on me as I walked to the sidewalk. He said, "Well, you know, I can help you reach your friend or at least stay with you while you wait."

He approached me and added, "It's not safe to be alone at night."

The little crowd from a few minutes ago had thinned out. It felt more and more like I was being sized up. I balled my left hand into a fist. He was bigger than me but if I dropped him to his knees long enough, I could get the hell away.

He eyed my tensed arm and quickly showed his hands, a conciliatory smile on his face. "Oh no, please don't misunderstand. I know what this must look like, but I'm harmless, believe me."

Yeah, sure.

He pulled out a card and waved it at me. "I'm sorry, I know we just met. I'm in the hospitality business, and it's my nature. Here, look at my card. Would I give you this if I was trying to pull something?"

When I reached for the card, I noticed it on his wrist.

No one else would have thought twice about it. It would've been another piece of jewelry to 'em.

But I knew better.

It was a Verge tether.

***

"SUPPOSE I SHOULD WALK IT," I said as I turned up the street.

He grabbed my arm tight and pulled me back so we were face to face. A deep soreness flared in my arm and I felt throbbing where he held me. His eyes had darkened with a sinister recognition. My gut tightened and my mind raced. *What to do, next move, Ana? Come on, think.*

"Not so fast, Deviant." He got up, my arm still firmly in his grasp.

I started to shake. "W-who?"

He cocked his head with contempt. "Give it up, it's over."

I wriggled under his grasp, but it was pointless. No one was around us anymore, and whoever rode past on the road must have thought we were two lovers in a fight. Or, they were too busy to have noticed anything?

"Who are you?" I asked as I struggled under his grip.

He scowled a bit. "Shut up." He grinned at my efforts under his grasp. "Not that it really matters to you at this point, but you can call me Azrael."

I wasn't familiar with him, but according to Baudricort, he suspected Lebabolis had sent Brenn Havens. He was one of the, excuse me, goons who worked under Charista and the Security Police. These guys lived for moments like this – Deviants like me in their custody who they had their way with. Whatever they did when they caught Deviants lasted awhile, so I had heard. Sometimes it was Realignment, but I'd always heard there were other types of torture too. Guess they felt the quick and clean kills were too boring.

"How'd you find me?" I asked.

He laughed. "You steal our tech and bastardize it, and think we can't find you? How naive." He glanced around for any onlookers, then led me down along the vehicle path.

"Your tech sucks," I said. "Otherwise, you'd have Xander by now."

He stopped short and glared. "How do you know we don't already?" His glare faded to a grin.

"Because you'd have killed me already. Guess you don't have all the answers, you and Miss Queen Charista."

His voice raised to a grow. "Shut up." He pulled me down into an alley. The air got thick with a heavy stench, so much I almost gagged. Azrael grunted while he dragged me further. He shoved me against a metal container with one hand and grabbed a comm unit from his jacket pocket. "Deviant apprehended, proceed with neutralization?"

The reply came a few moments later. "Affirmative. Contact again when complete and meet at rendezvous point. Out."

The alley was empty. A vehicle passed by several hundred yards away. We were next to another path for vehicles; too bad none used it at that moment. I craved for any distraction possible.

My eyes scanned the ground for anything useful. Twisted pieces of something that cast a slight shimmer in the dim light. Some other kind of trash; I had no idea what it was. "So what're you going to do, kill me and Xander?"

"You'd like to know that, wouldn't you?" He sneered back.

My feet skidded across the ground through piles of trash. "You don't want to kill him. Not with the Omegans and Cataclysm, you need all the help you can get, don't be stu-"

"We're well aware of all that. Charista just wants to clear the field first."

He grabbed both my elbows and spun me around. My dagger sailed a few feet away, and made a loud clanging noise on the street. "Mmmhm, believe I do. Nice try, by the way. Think that would work on a security police?"

"It had crossed my mind."

He lifted me up a bit. My feet dangled, my gut tightened.

Focus, Ana.

Remember what you learned.

What Treg taught you.

Find a way. Keep him talking, off centered. Don't let the bastard direct the situation.

I stared at the dagger, only visible in the minimal light because I had seen where it landed. It was still too far.

He grabbed both arms now. "You never learned your place. None of you did. You're a Worker Product, and a mediocre one at that. How you tricked anyone into thinking you were any kind of warrior, I'll never know. Your little insurrection will soon be over."

My breath hitched a bit from the pain. "Well, there is a big difference between me and you."

"Oh, of that I'm certain." He chuckled.

"No, you don't understand. You fight because you're required. And, it's how you earn respect. The only way you earn respect. I fight for myself, my family, and people who refuse to be slaves. People who'll smash Lebabolis into dust one day."

His eyes widened with a crazed look. "You have no idea who

you're up against. Besides, I could rip your arms out right now and watch you bleed out for the enjoyment."

His grip tightened. My biceps flared with a deep ache, and my heart thumped into my throat with a rapid throb. My mind raced over what options I had in this situation, but more and more the pain took precedence.

A loud squawk blared and shook us both out of our focus. It echoed over and over in the alley, followed by lights. A vehicle moved fast toward us. If it wasn't for the lights and screech of the alarm, I wouldn't have heard the engine at all; Landcrawlers were never that silent.

The vehicle shone white lights with blue and red flashing ones, they washed over the buildings like brilliant temporary paint. Azrael glanced in their direction, and I drove my knees into his midsection.

Lucky for me, he was without a Lebabolis body suit or I'd have only smashed my knees. But no, I connected, and it knocked him back a bit, his grip on me broke and I landed in a crouch on the ground. As he staggered and wheezed, I dove toward the knife.

As I heard the familiar sound of an activated pulse weapon, the knife handle was flush against my palm. I launched the knife deep into his forehead. His eyes opened and glazed over. His arms went limp, and he dropped his pulse rifle as the large vehicle neared. It slowed, and I saw two people inside. They stared with their mouths wide open, and looked at Azrael's limp body and me. One grabbed some kind of device and spoke into it. The vehicle drove past down the alley, the alarm squawked more as it turned the corner. I saw the name 'Ambulance' emblazoned on the back. Whoever it was, I was in for it now. Spotted as I had killed someone.

Time for high gear.

FIFTEEN

(NELSON)

I HADN'T BEEN BACK on the job a week when Travis fired me. He waited long enough that I was back after Mom's funeral before he laid this on me. Of course, he softened it with "Contracts are not coming in as much, we need to tighten up for now, call you when things change," blah blah.

Well, at least I had all the writing time I needed.

I DROVE NOWHERE and everywhere for an hour or so. I still wasn't ready for anything productive. My mind reeled. What was the point of anything anymore? I was kidding myself, my usefulness was imaginary. Mom was dead, and now I was now unemployed.

I needed a release.

As fate or my muscle memory would have it, I ended up next to a bar. I leaned on my car for a minute, my feet slid along the gravel in the parking lot. The early afternoon sun cast a judgmental glow on me while I headed into the small watering hole. The place was pretty quiet. One long bar held up the far wall, a few tables and a

134

pool table welcomed me like I was a long lost relative at a family reunion.

Just fine.

Three stools each held up a person at the bar, along with several more empty ones. The bartender looked like he was a few seconds away from a nap.

"Gimme a whiskey sour," I said as I approached.

He tossed a coaster on the bar and busied himself as I took a seat. A TV over the bar ran a slew of commercials, Dial-A-Sue Attorneys and the reality show du jour promos. Reality was furthest from my mind. It was all about fantasy for me right then.

My phone blared my ringtone "Pick up the Pieces", and I felt a lusty smile on my face when I saw Tina's number on the caller ID. *Speaking of fantasy...*

"Hey, what's up?" I asked.

"You tell me, baby. How you doing?"

I heard the rattle of ice cubes and saw my drink ready for me. I ran my finger around the moisture on my glass. "Eh, been better. What's going on?"

"Well, I thought you needed a little to get your mind off things."

A burst of heat rippled through me at the thought. *You have no idea, honey.*

She added, "I don't work until morning. Wanna come over?"

I swiveled on the stool and eyed the others at the bar. All of a sudden a drink wasn't the first thing on my mind anymore. And with the swirl of crap on me, getting laid made everything else less crucial for now. "So tell me, what you wearing?"

"T shirt and panties, baby. Come over; you know you wanna," she laughed.

I licked my lips. "You're on."

I grabbed a plastic cup for my drink and cashed out. I cast another look at my fellow patrons, fellow members of the "Life is shitty so I'm drinking all day" club. Two guys in identical work shirts sat together. Off to the far side was this girl. Our eyes met. She gazed deep into mine, enough that I felt weird about looking away and even stranger that I couldn't break my gaze either.

Who was she?

I swished my drink and listened to the clink of ice cubes while I ran through a litany of people she could've been. Maybe she was a movie star? Stranger things have happened in this town.

I've had my share of one night stands, but she wasn't that kind of familiar. I'd never seen eyes like that ever.

The bartender returned with my receipt, and it snapped me back. I had a hornier place to be than here. "Here ya go, buddy."

I grabbed the pen, and I heard this female voice. "Hello?"

There she was, right next to me. Dressed rough, but not in a homeless kinda way. She seemed pleasant, but who knew? Sure wasn't shy about things.

"Yeah?"

She took a few steps closer. "Have we met?"

"Mmmhm, I get that a lot." I tossed the pen and receipt on the bar. "You move pretty fast, you know? My mom always warned me about women like you."

"I need to talk with you."

I caught her eyes again, and I froze. They were so intense they almost glowed in the dim light. "Yeah? What's with the outfit, you going to a comic con?" I grinned and stood up.

"Xander?"

I stopped short and spun on my heel at the name. "Whadya say?"

She stepped closer. Her gaze deepened, and I lost interest in leaving the bar for the moment.

"Xander. You're him, aren't you?" She pulled out a very old and tattered book. A paperback novel. But damn, this may have been an early printing of the Bible from all appearances.

She showed me the front cover. In the dim light I made out the words on it. *Cataclysm Epoch*.

"What is that?"

She eyed it and ran her hand over the cover. "It's written by

Xander Lee." Her eyes tracked back to me. "It's about a war on Earth that could destroy the planet."

Another flash of warm rushed over me, this time fear instead of lust. I took a swig and swirled the tart alcohol around my tongue for a second before I swallowed. This sounded like my synopsis. The synopsis that I had showed no one. Oh, and the pen name Xander, which I mentioned to no one. And the tiny miniscule fact I hadn't even finished the damn thing yet, but there it was, like it was dropped off by the Amazon Weird Shit drone.

"How the - where the hell did you—"

"So you're Xander Lee? You sure look like him." She turned the book around to the back cover. Still faded but I saw a photo on it. Me.

"When did you get this?"

"It was in a cache."

"What's a cache?"

She grinned. "I think your people call 'em time capsules?"

"A time capsule? Really? Who the fuck are you? What are you doing? Did someone put you up to this?" I reached for the book. It was my manuscript alright. Part of it, anyway. The last half, I'd never seen before. But it had my characters in it. I felt a soreness in my gut, like I'd been punched in it.

"Xander-"

"Alright, first off, my name's not Xander. It's Nelson."

She squinted at me, and looked back at the book. "Then why Xander?"

"What do you care? I could be William S. Burroughs for all you know." She glanced at me with blank eyes. "Never mind." I shook my head. My brain ached with thoughts of how this elaborate ruse was put together. Or was it even a ruse? Was everything getting to me at last?

"Xan- Nelson, what I'm about to say is gonna be difficult for you to believe. But you have to trust me."

Maybe this is a dream. "I'm not in the mood for any shit right now. I lost my job, my mom died, and I can't write a novel for shit.

Well, at least I can't write all of one." I stabbed a finger toward the book.

She grabbed my arm. "Nelson, please hear me out. I'm sorry for your troubles. I have to tell you a few things."

My thoughts swayed between sex with Tina and my troubles forgotten for a few moments, and how this girl I'd never met had a published copy of a book I never even finished yet.

For some strange reason, whenever I focused on her eyes, it stopped me, like a stick shift car stuck between two gears. Any thoughts of leaving, even for Tina, were gone from my head once I locked eyes with this girl.

I motioned back to the bar. "Might as well sit; it looks like you're gonna tell me you're having my baby."

"What?"

"Forget it."

She put the book on the bar and sat down. "No, not even close."

"Want anything to drink?"

She winced at the sight of the beer taps. "Water."

I signaled the bartender and studied her a bit more. I had another look at her clothes – I noticed a pattern to them, almost like fatigues. But nothing I'd ever seen.

"Alright, you have my attention. You've got some crazy finished copy of a book that I'm still writing, you look like you came from a war, what else?"

"I have come from a war."

"Where are you from?"

"Nelson, I'm from Earth. But the future."

She talked about where she lived, the time, the threats. The more she said, the more I dreaded where she headed with it all. Details mixed together and painted a picture that was way too familiar.

"So you mean to tell me this world that I've created for a fictional novel is real?"

She nodded.

"And it happens, on Earth, several hundred years from now?"

"Yes."

"What is your name?"

She smiled a little. "Don't you know?"

I studied her face: her piercing eyes were bordered with a full head of downward swept dark hair. She smiled a little as she waited for my epiphany.

"No clue."

She blinked and reached for my hand. "I'm Ana Crucinal."

I sipped my drink and crunched an ice cube. "Sorry, never heard of ya." I snorted.

Her eyes narrowed.

"Offended?"

She pondered a moment. "A little. Can't blame you for being skeptical though." She turned away and sighed. "Not sure I believe it either."

I set my glass down. "I never wrote of or even heard of you before. Yeah, I wrote a novel that you somehow have."

Her gaze softened. She grabbed the book and pet it like it was a puppy. "I need your help."

"But I never finished it. I think you need 'future me' or something."

"Please."

"What if I say no?" I slammed the glass down.

Her eyes sharpened up quick when the glass thumped the bar. "You could. But no matter what, other people from my time are coming for you, and if you don't accept my help, you're gonna end up dead or worse."

That comment brought me over my limit, which I had reached earlier that day, thanks to Travis. I knew I had two choices: either I let this day spun more and more out of control, or I took control of one of the few things I still could.

Amazing enough, even my lusty link up faded away from my thoughts. I wouldn't have been good for Tina like this, I wasn't sure I was even good for myself.

I pulled out a ten-dollar bill for the extra drinks and set it on the bar. I wiped my mouth and gazed at her. "Well, Ana, very nice meeting you, but I'm gonna take this as a sign to cut myself off on the booze. Have a nice afternoon and evening."

Her eyes widened as I spoke, and as I darted for the door I heard her behind me. "Wait, Nelson! You gotta listen!"

I was in my car in seconds and on the road. Soon as I got home, I locked the door behind me. This couldn't have been real. I sunk onto the sofa as I dozed off to sleep, my head full of wishes the world kept a safe distance from me.

SIXTEEN

(ANA)

NELSON'S CAR ROCKETED away and disappeared around a corner. I thought about what I had said. What he had said. How I could've convinced him further.

I didn't know. It was a pretty tall order to start. Remy wouldn't have done much better. But that wasn't consolation either.

At least Nelson wasn't compromised.

Not yet.

If he had, they'd have been all over me the second I showed up.

My vehicle, like most I'd seen, was nothing like the Landcrawlers. The seats inside were soft, with a fabric covering, unlike the cold hard insides of our vehicles back home. It would've been a lot nicer riding in one of these in the Outlands.

A small marker with a word "Ford" on it was what I saw for any indication of it. I parked down the road from the location where I had landed. Several people lay on the ground, and a few were in makeshift tents in a large open area by several large buildings. It reminded me a little of the Encampments back home.

Since we moved around so much, there wasn't much time for anything more than a few fighting positions, tents and if you were lucky enough, the mobile housing units. A few always stayed outside though, in a wide perimeter as a watch for any Lebabolis patrols.

I drew a crude map on the P-LAD of the areas I'd seen Nelson in for my next move. I brushed my hands on my pants to dry them off a bit from the night air.

"There she is," a gravel rough voice said. My friend Louie from the other day. He and another man stood over me. I quickly slid the device into my jacket pocket but not quick enough. Louie's friend stooped down. "Whatcha got?" His eyebrows were so large they formed one straight line above his eyes.

"Oh, something I found."

Eyebrows regarded me for a second, sizing me up. "Lemme see it."

"Mike, leave her 'lone. She didn't do nuthin."

Mike ignored him, his eyes locked on mine like an animal studying its prey. My arms flexed a bit, and I imagined his look if I sprung for him.

Instead, I tried the verbal approach. "I saw it first."

Mike grunted. I bet he wasn't used to rejection, or he just made sure everyone was scared of him. Big mistake on his part. I had complied with others way too long. This moron was close to a painful lesson from me.

I got on one knee, hunched my shoulders. "Mike, I'm looking at it. That's all."

Mike grunted again, and Louie grabbed his shoulder. "C'mon, Mike. Stevie got food from the Mission. Let's go eat."

One mention of food and Mike's attention was diverted. He glanced past my shoulder for a moment. He smacked his lips and looked at Louie. "Shit, I could eat. Let's go." As they walked off, he gave me the eye.

I returned his icy gaze and waited until he looked away before I pulled the P-LAD back out.

SEVENTEEN

(NELSON)

I ALMOST EXPLODED.

I had never had it this intense before.

I slid my hands over Tina's ample thighs as she lay atop me. I felt the curves and tone of her frame and gasped as she took me inside of her ever so slowly.

She gazed darkly at me and cooed, "Give it to me, baby. I want it."

The glow of the street lights peeked into the room with a few slivers of light, enough so I saw her tattooed body and her sultry gaze as I felt her tighten around me.

The sensation and the sight of her over me was too much; couldn't hold out long at all. I released loudly as she shuddered. After a few seconds, I unfroze and rolled to her side while I caught my breath. She gently nuzzled me in the dark.

"You needed that, didn't you?" she whispered, panting.

"Um, yeah. Way more than I can say." I chuckled as she laughed as well.

She brushed a strand of hair from my face. "You're lucky I had you back after you stood me up." She patted my cheek.

"Sorry about that, baby. Had car trouble, and it ran awhile."

"Mmmhm. Well, ain't no call like the booty call, huh?"

"Yeah. Thanks, been a rough few days. We should do this again soon."

"Call me, baby. You know the number."

She slid away as I tossed the condom and got dressed.

My phone growled to life on the bed behind me. I grabbed it as Tina slinked under the covers more.

There was a new text:

From: UNKNOWN

Xander - Seize Your Destiny. Meet me on the Moonwalk near Jax Brewery tomorrow.

FIRST THE WEIRD texts and voicemails and now the weird girl at the bar. Why was my crazy quota upped? I felt like I was falling for a second and thrust my hands out. Tina eyed me, her eyebrow arched. "You doing OK?"

I managed a nod in response. Once the feeling stopped, I almost threw the phone against the wall. No, not the right time nor place. I leaned over, kissed Tina, and headed out.

I focused on what I knew. Dad needed me. Maybe my imagination was running crazy with everything that had happened. This wasn't real, right? First things first. I needed a new job before I got Dad situated.

Writing was on the back burner again. How my book world became real was none of my business. And whatever crazy stalker bitch gunned for me, a little tasing would've settled her down a bit.

I WALKED into the Kerry Irish Pub right after five. The place felt as comfortable as a warm blanket on a cold night. It had that French Quarter feel that those remote Metairie bars just never touched. The bar was already filled with a few regulars. I meandered around the tables in front of the bar until I slid onto a stool at the far end from the door.

The air was filled with loud discussions and the occasional laughter, people glad they weren't at work for at least a few hours. The loud clicking of glasses and bottles punctuated the conversations around me.

After I ordered a pint of Guinness, I texted Harvey. I needed a dose of lucid common sense and a fresh perspective on things. If nothing else, a change of subject was enough.

May 3, 2014
5:13PM
Dude, you busy? I need to talk. @ Kerry. Call/Text or come by.

I scoped out the others nearby. A few familiar faces, but no one I trusted with this kind of story. Alright, it was pretty freaky how close she'd gotten on things. But the part I hadn't written yet? Someone had played me in a freaky way, that was all.

But how? And who?

Was Travis that vindictive? What else was there that he wanted, my head on the wall next to his vacation picture at "Yo-See-Me" Park? He already got me axed from the company. Maybe he caught my writing on the printer at work, but he had no reason for pranks now that I was gone, right?

The first pint of Guinness stood no chance with me. I ordered an Irish Car Bomb as Harvey walked up. "Hey man, you in a hurry?"

"Dude, I'm unemployed and job hunting. I don't need the stress, alright?"

"Well, damn, that sucks. Sorry to hear that." He grabbed a stool and patted my back in support. "What's on your mind?"

"You'd better get a drink first, might help you absorb it better."

"More than your mom dying and you being fired?"

"Much."

He flagged the bartender. Once he got a sip of beer, he nodded to me. "Go."

"You know that novel I'm writing?"

"Um, yeah. That sci-fi thing, right?"

"Yep. Few days ago, right after I got canned, I was out and met this girl."

"Yeah?" he raised his glass and winked.

"No, we didn't, hook up or anything. We talked. And I swear this is the freakiest shit ever. Got a strong feeling this is a joke. But it's too wild for a set up."

"What happened? Tell me." His lips curled with intrigue.

"Alright. She knows about my book."

"What do you mean? You told her?"

"No, man. She told me about it. With details. Specific details. I never told anyone about it, except you and my folks."

He shook his head. "I haven't said anything."

"That's not all, either." I leaned to Harvey's ear and lowered my voice. "She wants me to come to the future with her."

Harvey leaned back in his seat and gave me a hard and not the most supportive gaze. "What?"

"Yeah."

He arched an eyebrow, which was his typical look when he detected a line of BS. "You copacetic, man?" He grabbed my shoulder, and looked at me like a doctor about to give a patient some awful test results.

"I'm fine. Look, I'm telling you, it happened. I was in a bar with other people around. She was standing right in front of me, talking like we are now."

"That's insane."

"I know, right? I mean, yeah, a few people know about the book." I paused. "You're not fucking with me are you?"

He set his drink on the bar, eyed my almost empty glass, then clutched my arm. "Look, I know you're in a tough spot, but try and get a handle on things, man. I think you should lay off on the drinking for a little while."

"You didn't deny it."

"Nelson, it's not me. It's not anyone. Damn, I don't know what to tell you, buddy. You've been pretty stressed these days, it's getting to you."

I squeezed the bar as if I could've splintered that mahogany under my hands. Would've been nice if I could've. Maybe Harvey was right, it sounded too wild for reality. Had my writing brain concocted this?

"I should get more sleep."

"Couldn't hurt, buddy. Give it a break. Take a few days. How about some exercise? I can get you to my gym on a treadmill. That'd be good for you."

The gym? If sex hadn't gotten my head straight... "Thanks for coming out, and sorry to lay this on you, man. How're you doing?"

"No worries. I'm good, working as usual. Real estate biz kind of slow at the moment, but it always picks up sooner or later."

"I see. Well, I'm sure you'll figure that out. You usually have some kind of plan."

"Hope so. How's your dad?"

"He's adjusting. Slow though. Guess it'll be awhile."

"Gotta be rough. How many years were they together?"

"Forty."

"Oh damn. Yeah, so rough. I feel for him."

"Yeah, it's hard."

"And you, how're you handling things?"

"Don't know. Mom and I were real close. Tough not having her around to call or anything."

"Sorry, man. Wish I knew what to say."

"It's alright. You're listening, and that's a lot right there."

My smart phone rang. I checked the number, but it wasn't familiar. It was too soon for a call back about the jobs I'd sent resumes out for. Whatever it was would be handled later.

I ordered another Guinness. I held it before myself and gazed at the glass of dark brew and its thick whitish head for a moment. "So, real estate is kicking your ass right now as opposed to the opposite?"

"Yeah, the condo market is fucking fierce, dude. I'm scrapping for whatever I can get."

As soon as anything real estate entered the conversation, Harvey took on a whole new energy. Even though real estate was the last thing I'd ever have considered for a career, Harvey's flailing arms and bright expressions as he discussed it made it as compelling as it could've been to me.

Then again, I already knew the IT rat race. I hated the idea of having to learn another line of work. "So, I shouldn't try and jump careers into yours, from what you're telling me."

"Are you nuts? Stay where you are, dude. IT is great. Something's bound to come along. And now you have time off you can work more on that book, right?"

"Yeah, if I can get myself into writing it."

"Well, you should look for that girl again and see if she can 'inspire' you."

We both laughed at that. My head cleared a bit and I chuckled a little more, both at Harvey's off putting jokes and at how my imagination would be considered a dangerous weapon in every state, in particular, my state of mind.

EIGHTEEN

(NELSON)

AFTER A FEW WEEKS of scouring job websites, Craigslist and anywhere else I thought might hire me, I landed an interview with a consulting firm in town. The pay was a step down, but I wasn't very picky at the time.

The interview went well, with a "We'll be in touch" at the end. Yeah, I had heard that one before. Long as I kept up the search, I figured something was coming my way. I sounded like Dad.

I left their office building and walked down Poydras. The hot and burned rubber smell of bus exhaust greeted me on the street. I weaved around people and was almost back to my car when I heard a familiar voice behind me.

"Nelson!"

Oh, not her again.

She was about ten feet back, a faint smile on her lips. People walked past her as if she were a smooth stone in a rushing stream. Her eyes stayed locked on me; I don't think she even blinked. She approached me slow.

I squinted at her. "What are you doing?"

"I have to talk with you."

Even in the daylight, her eyes gleamed, and I was fixated on her that quick again. But this time, I shook the thoughts from my mind and glared at her. "No, you don't. And I don't appreciate the weird messages and crap, alright?"

"Messages?"

"Yeah, I'm assuming that's you telling me to meet at the Moonwalk and everything?"

Her eyes narrowed. "What's a moonwalk?"

"Forget it. I'm gone, you stay away." I turned back toward my car. About two steps later I felt a hand on my shoulder.

"Stop."

Either her hand or her tone sent a chill straight through me.

"You know, some people would consider this stalking." I looked over my shoulder at her. Her eyes pleaded with me and, I don't know what happened, but I gave at that moment. I felt like whatever it was, whatever she needed, I at least should listen after all she'd done to get in front of me more than once.

"I really need to give you the details. Gimme five minutes."

"Alright, Ana. I've got an idea, let's go down to the Moonwalk, should be decent this time of day for a brief conversation."

Her eyes darted about when I said "Moonwalk" again. "Wait, that's not good."

"Oh? Few seconds ago you were dying to talk and now you aren't so social?"

She sighed and glanced downward. She looked like she was a second away from taking off down the street. "Remember I told you I wasn't the only one looking for you?"

"Mmmhm."

"Well, that person, whoever left you that message, Nelson, don't you realize? If they know you're Xander-"

"-Well, you can both have a nice reunion and fly away on the Millennium Falcon on whatever the hell you rode to get here."

Her jawbone moved back and forth, and her eyes burned into me. "You refuse to make this easy, don't you?"

"Honey, if you knew half of what I'd been through lately. Excuse me if I'm not completely sold on this story about me predicting the damn future over a thousand years from now."

I tried to leave again, but she gripped my shirt and pulled me closer. The top locks of her hair slid down a bit over her eyes, but they still showed up, almost too well. "Yag."

"Huh?"

"Wick, Remy."

"What are you talking about?" I asked.

Her eyes widened a bit. "They're people who tried to get to you. And now they're dead."

"Friends of yours?"

She nodded, slowly. "It wasn't even supposed to be me who came, but that's what it is."

My mind ached in calculations over these names I'd never heard of, and I thought more about what I wrote about.

"Cataclysm. Did it happen?"

Her gaze softened a little. She shook her head. "A small one, but the world's not gone, not yet anyway. Look, I know you're hurting. You're not the only one in pain."

My chest tightened at the idea, and I saw in her eyes the same look that nurse gave me back at the house after Mom died. I saw the hurt that I'd felt but hadn't been able to explain to anyone, waved in front of my face like a ninety foot billboard.

Her voice hitched. "My little brother. He's not dead, but he doesn't have long."

"I'm sorry."

Her lip twitched, and she glanced downward. "Me too. If there was anything I could do to prove this to you, believe me, I would."

Her grip on my shirt relaxed, but her breaths remained agitated.

I grabbed for her hands. My throat quavered and my voice began to break. "My mom died, not three weeks ago, alright? I try to not think about it, I... it's tough. I'm so damned angry. I don't know what good I am for anything right now."

She looked away, her eyes faded shut.

"I don't know what you think I can do, but you got my attention with that book. I can at least hear you out. Let's get somewhere less visible first."

I took her over to PJ's in the Quarter. Besides the barista, the place was empty. No surprise for that time of day. I grabbed a table in the far corner with a view of the street.

I sipped a café au lait as she laid everything out. The classification system, the punishments, the torture, done in the name of a better world.

"Is it my fault?" I asked.

"People in power make choices that affect the rest. They didn't pull this trigger because they were told to. At some point people have to take responsibility. Anyone can wage war, doesn't mean they have to."

"I imagined a major disaster that would just about destroy the planet. But people would somehow survive."

"We are open to suggestions." She flashed a quick half smile.

"I can't believe I wrote this." I set the cup down and drummed my fingers on the table. "Sounds like it's set in stone. Can we really make a difference now?"

"Baudricort thinks so."

"Who's that?"

"He's in charge of the Action. It's what they call the resistance."

"And what about you; what are you in this for?"

She shrugged and studied her water bottle. "I want my brother back so I can get us away from it all."

"Yeah, but you said the raids and patrols happen all over the Outlands. Think you'll ever be away from that?"

"If I can get away from the Action, and the Valentium, which is what Lebabolis wants, I won't be around anything valuable anymore."

"And the Omegans?"

"Best I can tell, they just want to be superior, with no one to challenge them. If I'm out of their view, and don't pose a threat, can't see why they'd waste their time."

She spoke pretty plain in spite of everything she said. I was never one who roughed it, and I couldn't have imagined me on my own in the wilderness, much less with someone I took care of.

"Ya got balls, have to say. Still don't know what I make of this. And suppose I start rewriting this book. I can change it or even destroy it. Maybe that's the best option."

She watched me as I spoke. "Well, someone else had that same idea. You already said you didn't finish it, remember?"

"Yeah. Well, we're back to me not being able to help you, I suppose."

She slapped her hand on the table. "I'm bringing you back, and that's all there-"

Her voice trailed when her eyes slid toward the counter at someone else who'd entered, a tall man in a dark outfit. His face was hidden behind the counter displays, but when he backed up a bit I recognized him. Ana crouched lower on the table, her head almost lying down on it.

"What's Bruel doing here?" I asked.

Ana dropped her voice to a hissing whisper, her face twisted in agitation. "Who's Bruel? That's him, the guy I told you about!"

"What guy?"

"You know, the man sent to kill you."

I looked back at her on the table. "Alright, you've gotta chill, dear. I know this guy. Look, I'll get him to join us, you'll see." I walked over to the counter and caught Bruel's attention.

"Why, hello. Mr. Forrester, right?" Bruel smiled warmly.

"Yeah, didn't think I'd run into you here." I chuckled.

"Well, who doesn't enjoy coffee?"

I nodded and glanced back toward my table.

Ana was gone.

NINETEEN

(ANA)

I RAN EVEN THOUGH my sides ached. I sucked down gulps of air until my lungs scorched and I worked my way to the side of the road.

I leaned against a building and glanced back toward where I had left Nelson with the one person who knew who I was and would've killed me without a passing thought.

My pulse thumped in my throat. Did Azrael get a message to Brenn before I killed him? Had Brenn followed me?

OK.

Focus. I hunched down by the road, pressed my arms close, and thought about next moves, theirs and mine. Nelson's family relations were also a target, in case he wasn't grabbed. If I convinced them about everything and they reached out to Nelson...

No more games. I pulled out the bloody piece of paper from Azrael and read the location: 3117 Fleur De Lis Drive.

I PARKED my vehicle under a large concrete structure, an elevated vehicle road. I squirmed over the soreness in my back and pressed myself into the soft cushion of the seat, but that didn't help the pain any. One of these days I was gonna sleep for a month and let everything heal for a change.

Once my eyes focused, I glanced at the screen of my P-LAD in the darkness until my mind drifted back to Treg. How he wanted me around him in the Action.

"Would rather have someone I can trust with me," he had said. "So many Encampments, we'll be making regular supply and Valentium runs, and you know how those can go. We need people who can deal with problems like that, like you can."

"I know. We could still make a break for it."

Treg. My mentor. My best friend. I wished he were with me. He knew how Warrior Products thought. I was blind here, and anything would've helped.

A loud noise startled me, and I realized I'd dozed off. A blue light pierced and enveloped the inside of the vehicle. My eyes ached from the intrusive glare. I squinted and saw another vehicle alongside mine. A loud squawk sound like I had heard in the alley with Azrael rang out into the night.

I silenced my device and laid it on the seat next to me.

Whatever it was looked like some kind of security force. The loud squawk changed to a man's voice. "Driver, exit the vehicle and place your hands on the hood."

I swallowed hard and shoved the P-LAD under the seat as I got out. Once I was in place, they exited their vehicle, approached me and stood to my side.

"Whatcha think you're doin'?" he asked gruffly.

"I was just-"

"-License and registration."

I nodded slowly. "I... what?"

"You think I'm playin around? Let's go." He tapped the metal on my vehicle. I shook my head in response.

He eyed me for another moment, spun around and spoke into some device on his chest.

Great. Time to improvise.

I had gotten a better look at his vehicle as I exited mine. NOPD emblazoned on the side, and the blue lights atop it blinked rapidly. The squawk sounds still came from inside like it was some kind of comm unit.

He nodded toward my vehicle. "I won't find drugs in there, will I?"

"Drugs? I don't know what-"

"Cut the bullshit, you ain't in this part of town right now if you aren't dealing, honey." I felt his glare on me. "This car was reported stolen. You don't have any ID on you?"

"That's right."

"Well, you need somethin', or I gotta take you in." I lurched forward when he kicked my feet further apart. He clutched the back of my jacket and added, "Spread your hands, dammit!"

His hands ran up my legs and around my midsection. My whole body tensed up like a rope yanked tight. Otto's words to Remy echoed in my head.

No killing unless it's life or death for you. Try not to be seen by too many people. And for God's sake don't get arrested or anything.

So much for that.

I recalled when Treg and Nycole held an exhibition for us while we were in instruction. Each Product demonstrated some of their skills to the entire school. One time, Treg and Nycole showed unarmed fighting techniques like escape from various holds. Nycole braced against a wall, and Treg stood behind her. In a few short moves, she flipped Treg around and slammed his body to the ground like a rag doll. Had there not been a padded mat he'd have been in bad shape. He still had the wind knocked out of him.

My mind raced as I thought back on what I saw her do. When he grabbed one wrist, I spun around, and speared a hand at his throat. He gasped and took a few steps back, then thrust a small can in my face. "Get the fuck on the ground now!" he yelled, his face crumpled in anger.

Instead, I lunged for him and connected with his head in a round-house kick as he sprayed me with the contents of the can. Scorching liquid hit my eyes. I shut them but the pain was as bad either way. I heard his groans and the sound of his body as it hit the ground. My eyes burned and it hurt like hell, but I kept 'em open, enough for blurry vision. I dove into my vehicle and groped until I clasped the P-LAD, and took off down the street. As I fled, I heard him in the distance as he yelled into his comm unit.

I leaped into a large clump of bushes near a building, and hoped whatever was in my eyes wore off soon. Damn, this crap stung! We could've used some of whatever this was back in 3192.

Next stop for me was that Fleur De Lis location. I only hoped I still had time.

TWENTY

(NELSON)

I T WAS THE DAY AFTER Ana vanished from PJ's, and I hadn't heard anymore from her or got any further messages. Maybe she had had her fill. That suited me fine. I made more interview rounds and was more than ready for a few drinks. I strolled down Decatur near the Jax Brewery early afternoon when a text from Harvey buzzed on my phone.

What's the name of that chick you hooked up with?

Alright, he asked me for the name of a booty call? Maybe he needed some drinks himself, or a nice long weekend on the gulf coast at Beau Rivage.

Tina, why?

No response came for a few minutes. I almost texted him back when he replied again.

Check the local news on TV

I ducked into the lobby of Bienville House hotel. The bright creamy yellow interior and posters of Jazz Fests gone by made me feel a little like I was out of town, but here for a visit.

A couple inside lounged on two lobby chairs and thumbed through brochures, in a debate over which tourist trap was the most suitable for their next jaunt.

The TV was on at the end of the narrow lobby. I breezed past the engrossed tourists and flipped to a newscast.

When I saw it, I felt the room sway and spin. Or that was just my head. I blinked several times, but the image on screen stayed the same.

There were pictures of Tina, and her apartment complex. The graphic on the screen read, "Local girl found dead in apartment."

I leaned on a chair back and watched the news for a few minutes. The couple with the brochures glanced up at me for a second before they returned to their tourist shopping.

According to the reporter, there wasn't a suspect yet, but a few people in the complex were around when Tina's body was found. I watched the story almost like it was a movie. But, I knew the victim. Worse yet, I had been with her a few hours earlier.

When they showed a police sketch of the victim, my gut about burst. Wouldn't be tough to have convinced someone the sketch looked a lot like me. I felt sick. I shielded my face and called Harvey as I walked back outside.

"Hey man, you see it?"

A car horn blared on the street next to me and I almost dropped my phone. "Yeah," I groaned. "Unreal."

My head throbbed. I strolled down Decatur and made contact with no one, and Harvey did his best with me. "She ever give any hints about being in trouble?"

"Naah, none. Course, we weren't exactly having deep life conver sations either."

"Could be a pimp thing?"

A motorcycle thundered past and I jumped a foot off the ground. "Um, I think I'd know by now if she was a hooker."

Harvey said nothing for a bit. "Nelson, what really happened with you and her?"

"Dude, we had sex. That's it, alright? I left, and she was fine. That's everything I know."

"Alright, alright, I believe you." He paused again, then added, "You still watching TV?"

"Naah, I ditched. They still talking about it?"

"No, but they did the usual. Crimestoppers reward for info and all that. Didn't name a suspect yet. So whatcha gonna do?"

"Working on it," I said. I brushed past a large person who came the other way. I glanced back and said, "Sorry," and caught their irritated look. *Keep walking, Nelson, they're some random person. Focus. One reality sandwich, hold the paranoia, please.* "I should go in, talk with them, right? I don't have anything to hide, I didn't do it."

"Call them up, cooperate. Good."

"Yeah, but from home. I mean if they want me to come down, fingerprints or something, I'll do it. But why should they, right?"

"Don't know what they'll do, man, but you're cooperating, that's gotta look better for you."

I HOPPED BACK in my car and sped home before anything else happened. Still shook me to the core to think I may actually be considered as a murder suspect. First things first, that had to be cleared up.

I slumped on the couch with the phone. It took a few rings before NOPD answered. I heard a bit of commotion on the other end, then a raspy voice stabbed through the din.

"Sixth Precinct, Sergeant Daughtry."

"Hi, I'm, calling about the, uh, girl on the news?"

"You mean Tina Guirard?"

"Yeah, that's right."

"What about her?"

I swallowed hard. "I was with her the night before she died."

They paused. "What's your name?"

"Nelson Forrester."

"Where you located?"

"The Marigny, Esplanade Avenue."

"You wish to make a statement in this matter?"

"Yeah, I wanted to tell someone there-"

"-hold please."

The background chatter and the voice cut out while I was transferred. A few more seconds and another voice, a smoother one, came on the line. "Homicide, Detective Costello speaking."

"Hi, I'm Nelson Forrester, and I was with Tina Guirard the night before she was murdered."

I heard what sounded like papers shuffled around a bit. "OK, let's get a little information from you first. We're doing our investigation and may call you to come in if necessary." He coughed a bit and cleared his throat. "Alright, how did you know the victim?"

I shifted a bit in my seat. "It was more or less a physical thing."

"Physical?"

"Yeah, you know, hooking up?"

"Mmmhm," he replied. "How long were you acquainted?"

My mind spun out of control for the answer to that. And how much had we known each other, from drinks together and some hook ups after just over a month?

Then there was the way he asked it. I felt more like I had become their suspect and not someone who wanted the air cleared. I leaned back on the couch. "Little more than a month?"

The questions went on from there. The more he talked, the less relieved I felt. I really doubted this did any good for me. We ended the call, and I flipped on my iPod deck for a few minutes when the phone rang again. I figured Harvey wanted an update on how it went with the cops. "Hey man, I called the cops."

A surprised voice, which wasn't Harvey, replied, "Um, Mr. Forrester?"

"Oh, yeah? I'm sorry, who's this?"

"It's James Bruel from Blazier Funeral home."

I sighed deep and sat up. "Wow, hi. You're the last person I expected to hear from right now."

Bruel chuckled a bit. "I bet. It's funny, I should've mentioned this when I saw you in PJ's the other day, but it was so unexpected. We need you to stop by our office, I'm afraid."

I sat up. "I see."

"Yes, there's been a billing mix-up for your mother's funeral and your family is owed a slight refund of overpayment."

TWENTY-ONE

(NELSON)

BRUEL GREETED ME INSIDE the front entrance to Blazier Funeral Home. The building was empty except for us. Maybe I still reeled about Tina's death, or it was Bruel's manner in general, but all of a sudden I felt like this was the last place I should've been. I never thought of a funeral home as a comedy fest, but something didn't set right with me.

Most of the inside was dark. The only lights on were a few at the front and in the hallway. Also, Bruel was almost too glad I was there, someone he owed a refund to on a funeral plan. What if he friended me on Facebook next or showed me pictures of his coffin collection?

"Mr. Forrester, thank you so much for coming. Sorry about the inconvenience."

I nodded hello and glanced past him into the hallway. "Staff on strike?"

He managed a modest chuckle. "Oh, we had a training session today, finished up a bit early."

I motioned down the hall. "Let's finish this."

"Of course." When we got to his office, he pointed me to a chair in front of his desk. Once we both sat, he stared at me for a bit.

"What?" I asked. "I need to sign something or what?"

He regarded me for another moment. "Mr. Forrester, may I call you Nelson?"

"Yeah, sure."

"Nelson, I'm going to level with you. I'm not just a funeral director. You might say I have a part time job on the side."

"Uh, alright?"

He looked deep into my eyes a little too deep, like a detective at an interrogation. About what, I hadn't the slightest idea.

"Just what are you getting at?"

"See, I knew you'd wonder. I mean, who wouldn't, right? Besides, anyone with your talent for writing would suspect anyone coming at them from a mile away."

A sharp pang hit my gut, and I shifted in my seat. "How do you know I write?"

"Ahh Nelson, I know a lot about you." With that, he placed what looked like two bracelets on the desk. "Tell me, in the past week or so, has anything odd happened to you?"

"Odd in what way?"

Bruel pondered his answer. "Have you met anyone that came off a bit strange to you?"

I saw her face as he asked the question. I almost said her name. But I stopped, and instead, I answered, "It's New Orleans; there's odd people all over."

He responded with a laugh that couldn't have been more fake if he were a morning TV news personality. He smiled, but that quickly faded to a frown. He studied me for what seemed like ten minutes. Finally, he said, "What if I told you I know what happened to Tina?"

My gut tightened.

"Who?"

His frown deepened. "Mr. Forrester, I think we'd both do each other a great service if we don't beat around the bush. The girl, Tina, of your acquaintance. I know what happened to her."

My throat tensed. "Did you kill her?"

"Of course not. But," he leaned back in his chair, "I don't think I need to tell you who did."

I thought about how much she pleaded with me. She was so desperate. No, she couldn't have - or...

Bruel's lips curled in a triumphant smirk. "What did she tell you?"

"About my book. The future. Me in a lot of danger."

"You're lucky you got away from her alive." His eyebrows arched.

"She wanted me to travel with her, in time."

He twirled one bracelet around a finger. "I don't know how you managed to get away from the likes of her but I'm here to tell you, she's dangerous."

"So those messages on my phone were you?"

He blinked. "Guilty. It wasn't my intent to alarm you. Warning someone in these circumstances takes a little finesse. I'm sorry if I went overboard." He offered that TV news smile again, which made me cringe all the more.

I was two seconds from making a break for it. I stood up, and he said, "And I apologize for the charade in having you come here, but I'm afraid you're going with me."

"What, why?"

"You're in danger, but the truth is it's from Ana. Nelson, I know this is very difficult, but what you've heard about the future, I'm afraid it's correct."

My face felt like it burst into flames. "So you've seen my - copies of my-"

"-*Cataclysm Epoch*. Yes, and I'm familiar with Xander."

My heart pounded in my chest. The dizziness I felt when I was with Tina returned, and it was ten times worse this time. I clutched my head and sucked for air. I felt like the target of a massive manhunt for something I was wrongly accused of. *What is even happening? Have I lost it? Does anything even matter anymore? I wrote a damn book. That was it. Fiction. How was any of this real? Wake up, Nelson, wake up!*

I thrust my hands up. "What can I possibly do? I have no control over any of this!"

Bruel eased himself closer. "You're wrong. Please, come with me. Let me show you what you - who you really are."

"Ana said you wanted to kill me."

He winced, his eyes oozing sympathy. "Nelson, I was sent to protect you and bring you to the future where you can be safe."

I glanced to the door. "What if I take off, leave town or something?"

"Won't do any good, they'll track you. You'll be found. There's also a good chance she'll get your father."

"What?"

"Look how I found you; think she isn't that resourceful too?"

"Seems more of a risk, going with you."

"You're smart, and I understand your reservations." He still smiled, but now his hand kneaded my shoulder a bit, the pressure making my shoulder ache. I leaned away from him but he held me in place.

First the messages, then Ana, now this? "I'm sorry, no. Please leave me alone."

He glanced downward and sighed. "Nelson, this is your purpose." He shook me, as if the idea would've sunk in better that way. His grip was taut, a slow and steady throb built in my arms.

My eyes returned to the door. I'd have been through it by now if he hadn't clutched me like this. I whipped my arm around and broke his grasp. I strode to the door and said, "I don't know what's happening, or who you think you are, but I'm never leaving-"

A dull thud on the back of my head knocked me down, and the room went dark.

TWENTY-TWO

(NELSON)

A SHARP THROBBING in my head woke me up. I blinked, but everything was blurry. I lay on something that felt like a mattress. I tried a stretch, but my hands were held fast.

Shackles?

When I called out, my throat seared with a burn so strong I coughed out of control for a few seconds. It felt like I'd drank a gallon of Drano.

After a few minutes, I managed a very raspy "Hello?"

Nothing.

"Anyone hear me?"

The room came a bit more into focus. A cabinet with lots of drawers in one corner. A light overhead that was shut off. It looked like some kind of doctor's office. Who knew where?

Or when

Bruel entered and stood before me. The room exploded in light that made my eyes burn almost as bad as my throat. He glanced behind me and tapped on a panel on the wall, which responded with a series of beeps. He checked me over as he said, "Nelson, I'm sorry, but you weren't listening to reason."

I tugged my hands against the restraints. "Was this really necessary?"

He nodded. "Afraid so. We were in a hurry and I wanted to be safe."

"Yeah, alright." I groaned. My eyes still hadn't focused yet. "Thanks for knocking me out. Really, helped a lot. I was hoping I'd have a splitting headache today, so great job."

He grabbed my shoulders while I struggled on the bed. "Soon, I hope you'll realize I'm trying to protect you."

"Shackling me is protecting me?"

He studied me for a little while, held the bindings on my wrists and took a small gray device out. A few seconds later, the bindings snapped open. "Again, sorry. The Verge can be messy and I didn't want you hurting yourself."

I held my wrists. "Too late." I reached for him, but he grasped my arms. "Nelson, don't make me knock you out again. You've come all this way-"

"-to where?"

His brow creased, and his mouth drew in a thin line. "3192."

The ache in my head deepened. "Just when I thought it was a bad dream." I noticed something else on my wrist. It was probably there for awhile, I noticed it as the room became more or less in focus. One of the bracelets from his desk was now on my wrist, and my skin around it felt warm.

"What's this?"

"Your tether. It links to your actual time so you won't suffer displacement sickness."

It was smooth and metallic, and I saw no seams in it at all. The underside had a readout that displayed the years 2014 and 3192, along with some other numbers.

Bruel tapped the device. "This is your lifeline. Whatever you do, don't remove it."

"Why?"

His smile faded. "You'll die."

I straightened up a bit. "Why am I here?"

Bruel stepped back and leaned against the wall behind him. "Now Xander, as much as I'm sure you've heard about that by now, what we want is simple. We want you to discredit Ana Crucinal and the Action to our people."

"And just why would I do that for you, now that you've kidnapped me?"

Bruel folded his arms. He glimpsed over me like he had forgotten to check for wounds. Then he asked, "Didn't you ever ask yourself how I came to know so much about you or wonder how I happened to be working for the very same funeral parlor you and your father visited when you were making arrangements? My dear Nelson, I've been watching you for some time now. Putting in hours of useless effort at a job that ended up letting you go, never finding that purpose you wanted in life. And then, your novel – the little book that you told almost no one except for close family and a friend. The little book that happened to be the future in print centuries later. If that's not proof of your purpose and why we need you here, I don't know what to say."

I had no response for that. I had made my mark on the world, just not the way I hoped. I'd have been glad with a sports car or two, living comfortable and all. But the feeling of this place and me, somehow tied together, was a lot to take. Maybe I had found what I was supposed to be doing after all this time.

Bruel sat down at the foot of my bed. "Once you give us some time, you'll go back home."

"How much time?"

He shrugged. "You'll see. Charista is very interested to meet you and show you what we've been working on."

I massaged my forehead a bit. "Why don't you read that damn book. I don't know anything else."

He smiled again. "I'd rather not overwhelm you yet." He looked away in thought, then added, "Traveling through a Verge can be pretty stressful for even the most experienced person, and since this is your first time, why don't I show you around?"

I sat up on the bed. "OK, sure. Let's go."

Bruel pulled a roll from his pocket and opened it to a digital screen. He ran a finger along the surface and said, "First, I need to introduce myself properly." He extended his hand. "My name is Brenn Havens. I work with Lebabolis Security."

I shook his hand, and he said, "I'm taking you to Harkson, our leader."

"What about Charista?" I rubbed my neck.

"She's there too. They'll explain what's happening and how we're going to protect you." Brenn checked the display on his digital pad.

HAVENS INTRODUCED ME TO NYCOLE, another soldier from Lebabolis Security. She looked like she spent a lot of time in the gym. Her arms were rippled with muscles that about burst out of her short sleeved shirt. The outfit looked like fatigues, with an insignia over the left chest. They weren't far off from what I saw on Ana, for that matter.

Nycole greeted me with a nod, her outstretched arm angled toward a vehicle. Her steely eyes studied me close, and her taut lips never gave away any sense of surprise at me, a man from over a thousand years ago.

Of course, I supposed time trips or whatever were old hat to these people.

The hot and humid air outside greeted me like a long-lost friend, and I stifled a chuckle. *At least the weather's familiar.*

The vehicle we rode around in looked like someone had squished a Hummer flat into a car shape. I rode in front with Havens. Nicole sat right behind me. Whatever area we were in looked like hell.

Rotted shells of buildings lined both sides of what I gathered was a street at one point in time.

I leaned back and craned my neck to look out the back and the metal frame of the seat dug into my shoulder blades.

The road we were on was made of some kind of strange material I'd never seen before. It was dark colored, with a few lines and arrows.

"Where are we?" I asked.

Havens replied, "Sector 5. Built over remains of a city long ago destroyed."

"And this road?"

Havens glanced my way with a smile. "We had to get around somehow. What was here before was mostly underwater."

I looked around at the desolation and looked back at Nycole for a moment. She too watched the scenery. Our eyes met for a moment, and hers narrowed a bit.

I marveled as we passed a rusted hulk of a building that oozed fire and belched smoke. I caught Nycole's steely but curious expression in the rear view mirror. She watched me like an irritated parent. "She here to beat me if I misbehave?"

Havens chuckled. "For your protection, Nelson, nothing more."

I looked at the surrounding decay, but none of it seemed real. Was this what I had created? And why this story? Why not anything nicer that came true?

Our vehicle stopped near a collection of large buildings. Havens patted my leg, his brow creased. "Nelson, what I'm about to show you might be tough for you to see. I just wanted to warn you."

I shifted a bit in my seat. "Alright, is this someplace I would know?"

Havens looked back at Nycole a moment, then to me. "Nelson, where we are, now, is what you know of as New Orleans."

I guffawed from sheer reflex. "It's 3192 and this place isn't underwater yet?" I took another look around. Sure enough, the buildings were extremely worn down, but a few looked a slight bit familiar.

Kind of like when you see really old photos of your great great great grandwhatever from eighty years ago.

"Unreal," I said. "I figured this would all be at the bottom of the gulf by now."

"The gulf?" Brenn asked.

I glanced at him. "Yeah, large body of water, connects to an ocean?"

He chuckled softly. "Ahh yes, water. Well, you're going to find pretty quick that water is in short supply, among other things."

I gazed at the sad looking building that looked almost like it begged for demolition and an end to its misery. "My city... no more."

"Not completely; we were able to salvage a bit of it."

"Why bother?"

"You'll see."

I watched the surrounding ruins of buildings, their bottoms partially submerged in a murky stew. I thought of all the things I knew, loved, and cared for in this city, gone. No one around. The desolation and emptiness, I'd seen before. It was like Katrina times a million.

Everyone I ever knew, loved, hated, never met but existed when I did, gone.

I realized at that moment that even if Travis was around I would've felt better. Loneliness gripped me as the full weight of what I saw pressed on me. My eyes welled up.

Had I caused this?

We drove on past the huge collection of buildings and a large open field with a sizable hill on it. It was unidentifiable, from centuries before, like a stone almost polished smooth after being in a running stream too long. Even though I knew where I was, I had little idea in what part of town we were. There was no way I'd have known this place in a million years, or even a little over a thousand.

I jumped a little as Nycole spoke. "Sector 5 handles a lot of manufacturing. Tech equipment. You'll be seeing our facilities pretty soon, they're right past the next few buildings."

She talked about a meteor for a few seconds, but Havens stopped her short.

We drove past the open field, which held a few trees, their sparse branches reached high into the air as if they pleaded for rain from the sky that wasn't common from the look of it. Then, amid the sea of decay and dying city, a gleam attracted my eye. Several buildings jut out of the rubble ahead. They stood out almost too well. It was like they were dropped by some giant.

"Sector 5 Admin. We're almost there," Havens said as he weaved our vehicle around some rubble. As we neared the buildings, the rubble and destroyed road gave way to smoother, neater streets.

"We've managed to put in a few roads over time in the sectors, enough for transport. The rest of the rubble is here to stay, I'm afraid," Havens said.

Some people walked around in front of the buildings ahead. It looked fake at first, an almost pristine building stuck out from the rest of the construction carnage like an artist sketch of a new building.

But it was real alright. A few other vehicles like the one we were in crossed the path up ahead close to the building. The console of our vehicle came to life with beeps, and a hologram display appeared. An intercom voice spoke. "Landcrawler 109, state name and purpose for security clearance."

Havens tapped a few controls. "Havens, ID Zero niner, Windshore, ID Echo four. Escorting prisoner."

Prisoner? "And I thought I was special."

The console light dimmed, and we continued on the path. "I'm keeping up appearances. Not many people know you're here," Havens explained.

A huge blast in the front of the vehicle jolted us to a stop. Smoke billowed up from the floor, and soon it was all I saw. An alarm sounded close by outside. Behind me, I heard a loud whine and the shuffling of boots on the ground. Nycole slipped outside the vehicle.

Havens grabbed my arm. He leaned toward me, his face twisted in pain. "Stay close, Nelson, this some-"

Another pop stopped him short. What looked like a beam of light pierced the window and rocketed through his chest. His body rocked with the blow and blood spattered the console. He gritted his teeth and held up a pistol, but it was too late.

I heard more shouts and pops like the one that got Havens. There were at least two voices and yells from others outside the vehicle.

My door flung open and Ana stood outside, her hand outstretched. "Are you alright? Are you hurt?"

"N-No, I'm fine."

Another explosion hit near the vehicle. Ana waved the cloud of debris away. "Look, you wanna live, get your ass outta there and follow me!"

ANA and I ran back the way I'd come with Havens and Nycole. More blasts hit, and more dust and particles rained about us. We jumped off the main path, and made our way to the second floor of an abandoned building. The windows were busted and random furniture was piled up everywhere.

We leaned up against an overturned desk, out of view of the windows and I told Ana about me and Havens in the Funeral Home.

"He had a job there?" she said as she adjusted her rifle. "How'd he get you over here?"

"He knocked me out," I said. I grasped my head on the sore spot.

She looked at me and winced. "I shoulda tried that," she snickered.

"He wanted me to discredit you and something called the Action. Still don't know what to make of this," I said, my legs stretched out.

Her lips formed into a line. "We'll figure all that out later. Right now, my number one is keeping yours and my asses alive." Her eyes darted out the window, and she kept silent for a minute. She acted like an animal that surveyed for other predators. "Look, I'm not here to hurt you, OK? I'm supposed to bring you to Baudricort, and that's it."

I stared at her. "They told me you're trying to kill me."

Her eyes warmed, and a faint smile slid over her lips. "They told you a lot, huh? Look, I'm sorry, but I've never lied to you."

"They were about to bring me to someone named Harkson, said they'd help me get home when you killed them."

She shook her head. "They said that before or after they put you in restraints and knocked you out?" She pointed back the way we came. "That place they were taking you, the nice looking building? That's their facility for Realignment."

A chill went through me when I heard the term from my book. This was real.

Her lips formed a grim smile as she caught my recognition. "That's right. Chemical lobotomy. Makes you one nice, happy, drooler, ready to die for their self-righteous bullshit."

I rested my head in my hands. "Lemme wake up, God."

She clutched my hand in hers. "Look, I'll be honest. It wasn't even my idea to bring you here. But now that you are, I'm getting you to somebody who can help. Once that's done, you go home."

She sounded like Havens, or rather Bruel. "Why should I trust you?"

She shrugged. "You could go it alone, but you think you can find a Verge site?"

"No."

"OK. Stick with me, I'll get you home."

A loud rattling tone blared out. It bounced off the buildings. Ana motioned for quiet as she peered around the desk. I heard a hum. It started low but then it loudened. Wind whistled through the air right outside.

"Hell Hawks. Hovercrafts. Sweeping the area for us." She checked outside again. The loud hum faded a bit. "We're getting the hell away from here. I can get us to the Outlands, but that's a day's walk. From there we can get a ride to the nearest Encampment."

(NELSON)

WE WALKED ALONG broken roads and around chunks of debris. I looked around at faint reminders of the city I once knew, with way more decay and atrophy than I could've ever dreamed. Patches of stone and broken concrete littered our way.

The stone we walked over was full of jagged fractures, like the whole place was pounded with a giant hammer. Overgrowth and decay hid a lot of details, but a few things registered.

I stumbled over a thin sheet of metal and gawked when I realized what it was... a street sign for Decatur Street. It was rusted for the most part but the words were still the slightest bit legible. The sight of it made me gasp, but that gasp faded into a light chuckle. My mind went to Harvey, how we got together and talked about how crazy Ana probably was and how her story was ridiculous.

Ha. Right.

I trudged behind Ana. She stepped slow and deliberate over the broken ground and rubble, her rifle poised. She craned her head about; this time her gaze stared through me when she looked my way. She looked like a lioness on a hunt. Her gaze covered the area about her and behind us. Her eyes returned to me again after a few minutes. "You OK?"

"Oh, great. Never better. Nothing like knowing everyone I ever knew is dead and my hometown is rubble along with the rest of the world." I kicked a rock.

She stopped short and faced me. "Not all of it." Her lips drew taut. "I'm sure you're thinking a lot right now. And you don't even know what to ask or even how to feel about this."

Her eyes softened, but she held her weapon up as a guardian over us. Over me. Even if I had never believed what she said before, she hadn't fed me any other stories or faked who she was like Bruel did. She also never cuffed me or knocked me out. Knocked me for a loop maybe, but I'd worry about that later.

"I'm gonna trust you," I said.

She nodded and smiled for a moment. Then, in an instant, her gaze hardened and darted behind me. A scowl popped onto her face and she murmured, "Behind me, now."

I staggered back as I heard a mechanical whine that came from her weapon. She aimed it in the dark. Her face fixed in a scowl, like a hunter focused on her kill for the day. Her legs spread into a stance and she lowered herself, the rifle rock steady and poised in her grasp.

"Who's there?" she barked.

A weak voice in the darkness replied, "Deviant."

Ana took a step forward. Her weapon made a beep sound and cast a cone of bluish light in front of us for about twenty feet. "Step out slowly."

Ana was fixed in place; her weapon never wavered or even shook. A frail looking man shuffled into the light. His tattered clothes barely clung to his body. He wheezed, and his hand partly covered a wound that oozed on his head.

"How'd you escape?"

His voice shook as he replied, "Jumped off a transport heading to Realignment."

"And your wound?"

"T-torture, Realignment camp."

Ana studied him a bit more. Then she said, "You know what I need to hear."

The man wheezed a bit, puzzled for a moment at her statement. He stood up straight, and said, "One-"

"-or None," Ana finished the phrase. She lowered her weapon, and the light disappeared. She walked to the man, her hand extended. "Ana."

He smiled as he took her hand. "Deke."

Ana nodded. "This is Nelson."

"Hello," I said. He nodded in reply.

We continued walking, Ana in the lead. She eyed Deke and asked, "So where about were you when you escaped?"

Deke coughed a bit. His eyes went back and forth between glassy and alert several times. After a little of this, he said, "Sector 4."

"Ahh," Ana replied. "Lotta tech out that way."

"Mmmhm."

"Why'd they mark you, stealing equipment?" As Ana asked the question, she glanced toward me with a perplexed look. I guessed she hadn't vetted him to her preference yet.

"Theft, yeah. Food, extra clothing."

Ana shook her head. She looked forward again while continued our trek. "See, Nelson. This happens a lot. Everyone gets a food ration depending on your age and the size of your family. Sounds fair, right?"

"I guess so," I replied.

"Only the rations are also tied to production of your Sector. And I don't mean what you do as a person. I mean the total output. They expect so much every period or you lose rations and privileges until things pick up."

"What output? What are you supposed to be making?"

"Depends on the Sector. Four and Five handle a lot of technology. Scanners, tether bracelets like the one you're wearing."

I looked at Deke as we walked. "You have family back there?"

He nodded, his eyes cast downward.

"How many?"

"Wife, two kids," he said.

"How long since you saw 'em?" Ana asked.

"Few weeks."

Deke's words about his family jolted me. What about my family? I had a dad left back home. And now I'm here in this world I created. Were these people my family too? A dull ache spread over my head when I thought about all of this, the responsibility. This is crazy, this isn't real. It just isn't.

Ana's cough snapped me back into their conversation. "They probably prepped him for Realignment until whatever batch they brought together was ready. You heard any other talk in your group? About Deviants, the Action?"

"Little bit. Been hearing about Xander, too. Some kinda way he's coming here."

Ana stopped and looked at me. "That's the rumor alright." She turned to Deke. "So no one else got out with you?"

He shook his head.

Ana looked back the way we came. The moon peeked out and cast a little light, but not too much. Her skin glowed like porcelain. Her brow furrowed. She checked her rifle again and looked at Deke. "OK. Well, the Action's sending people out to help the escapees. Glad you ran into us." She grabbed a small digital pad and tapped a few times on it. "We're far enough from any kind of monitor grid. I'll let the Action know our location; we'll be catching a ride pretty soon."

TWENTY-FOUR

(ANA)

AFTER A FEW MORE HOURS on foot, we caught a ride on one of the Hell Hawks the Action had stolen and flew over to Encampment 7. I watched out the side of the cockpit at the wings, swept up high in graceful arches. I braced myself against the seat while the ship rocked through the air. I wasn't crazy about riding in these things, but it beat another day or so walking through the Outlands with two people and only one gun.

As the medics and nurses tended to Nelson, I waited outside the operating room with Treg, our eyes on the door and the techs who worked feverishly on Nelson.

"What the hell happened at the Verge site?" he asked.

"OK, Baudricort and Otto picked a great spot. So great that Lebabolis had the same idea. They sent a jumper through while we were there."

Treg folded his arms. "So what about the others?"

I shrugged and looked away. "Remy bought it for sure. Gave me his P-LAD and tethers. Not sure about Yag and Wick."

"So you improvised." Treg nudged me. "It was a tough situation, but you handled it. I knew ya could."

My eyes found his. "Wasn't clean though. I had to sneak over to Sector 5 before I caught him."

"You were in Lebabolis territory alone?"

"Hey. I found a way. Besides, what would you've done?"

"You're lucky they didn't zap ya both." His eyebrows raised.

"You know I can handle myself."

"Yep. Remember though, you're up against people bred for this, and you weren't."

"I'll blame my teacher." I laughed.

A loud noise from the operating room startled me. A few minutes later, a medic joined us in the hall. "He's stable. Had a jolt for a little while, probably the usual Verge effects. But he's calm."

"What about his tether?" Treg asked.

"Well, it's risky to leave it on, with the tracker and everything. Of course, removing it at this point is even worse," the medic replied.

"I bet Otto can fix it," I said. "When can I see him?"

"Give him a little longer to stabilize," the medic said. "I don't want him seizing up or anything."

The medic returned inside the operating room.

"Baudricort's gonna want to see him," Treg said.

"Only when he's ready." I peered toward the door.

"Glad ya made it back safe," Treg said.

I nodded. "Thanks, me too. Well, we got 'em. Time for Baudricort's part of the deal."

Treg laid his hands on my shoulders. "This is gonna work out, soon as this guy cooperates."

I grasped Treg's hands and leaned against the wall. "I need your help with him." I glanced into the operating room. "Otto warned about the effects of the Verge. Treg, I don't like the way he looked back there. He had this weird glint in his eyes."

Treg frowned. "Maybe we should keep him sedated."

"Let's wait on that. He knows I'm not going to kill him, but getting him to do this thing for Baudricort-"

"Don't tell him too much, not right away," Treg cautioned.

I ran my fingers through my hair in thought. Another maneuver. My new goal: keep Nelson on our side without him becoming overwhelmed. My side of the bargain with Baudricort had gotten more and more complex.

TWENTY-FIVE

(NELSON)

THEY STUCK ME on another bed like the one I was chained to by Havens and gave me a good once over. This time, the room was much smaller, or it was just all the people hovering over me. It was pretty much like a hospital visit, but with a lot more gadgets than I'd ever seen, and a lot less bedside manner than I expected. Of course, they were real curious about the bracelet.

Not enough to have removed it, thank God. I hadn't bought all of this as reality 100% by then, but I wasn't the gambling type either.

One of their machines made a rattling buzz sound that I swore sounded like my alarm clock back home. But no, I wasn't that lucky to have this all be a dream.

Once they were satisfied with what they saw, Ana came and brought me to a room with a table in the middle. Chairs surrounded the table, and several screens on the walls displayed maps. The maps changed after a few minutes, each display showing a bunch of markers on it. It reminded me a little of that application Travis had claimed back at Quicksolve. And for another brief moment, I realized I kinda missed even that asshole.

After I sat, Ana left and returned with a man dressed in fatigues similar to hers. He had a slender build and was a few inches taller than her. He carried some kind of assault rifle in his wiry arms. He regarded me with an icy expression, and looked on me like a cop at a DWI checkpoint. I only wished that was all I was into.

I extended my hand. "You're one of the badasses, I guess?"

He smiled and offered me his hand. "I might be. Treg. Treg Firebreed. Nice to meet you, Nelson."

Treg placed his gun on the table, and he and Ana both sat down. He warmed up a little once he sat down. He and Ana traded a few comfortable glances.

Treg ran a hand over his neatly trimmed hair. "So, we've got plenty of questions. But before that, anything you want to ask us?"

"Got a beer?"

They looked at each other for a moment. Treg asked, "What's a beer?"

I chuckled. "It's fine. I could use water, and a side order of 'why the hell am I here'."

He handed me a canteen. "Don't drink it all, we're a bit low."

I popped the top open and sipped the lukewarm fluid. It tasted metallic, with a hint of sulfur in it. But since convenience stores weren't around anymore, I had no room for complaining.

I kept sizing people up like I'd done with Ana, Brenn, and Deke. If this turned out to be a dream, I was gonna exploit every little bit of it. And if the crazier idea of me predicting all of this was the slightest bit true, these people had better give me some space while I got adjusted.

As the odd wateresque liquid trickled down my gullet, Treg and Ana explained the situation. How we were in one of the Encampments for the Action, each of which held from a few hundred up to a thousand people. How Lebabolis spread news and rumors about how evil the Action was to their citizens through their network MODOSNet.

"They had enough problems with the Omegans before. When we

left we took a lot of their gear, enough to be a problem for them. Lebabolis wants more than anything to bring us back into their fold. They run scans of the area, looking for us."

"How'd you even get away in the first place?" I asked.

"Slow, here and there. Baudricort started the Action five years ago," Treg explained. "It was a small group of people. They call us Deviants."

"Why?"

Treg shrugged. "Misfits, unable or unwilling to follow Lebabolis law."

You mean my law.

Ana pulled out a metallic curved object. "This is the Link. It's what Lebabolis citizens... the obedient ones, wear at night. It connects to MODOSNet and feeds 'em instructions about their work." She eyed the device, then looked at me. "It's also how they keep most citizens under their control."

Treg added, "Baudricort, once he learned what they were planning, got as many as he could out. It was small groups at first, but soon, more and more people escaped."

"And now they search for you. How do you avoid them, with so many people?" I asked.

Ana set the Link down. "We move. Use beacons so the rest of the Action knows where the Encampments are."

"Does that always work?"

Treg shrugged. "Most of the time. Sometimes no. The Outlands are huge, and they can't be everywhere at once. Still, sometimes, we get zeroed."

"And then what?" I asked.

Their only response to that was a grim stare.

"So what's your plan?"

Ana shrugged. "We raid their convoys for supplies, hit their Valentium stores, try and get as many people out as we can. Help any that escape, like Deke."

I sipped more water. "So beyond that, best plan is to keep moving and hope they never find you?"

"Of course not," Treg said. "Baudricort has us heading far west. Claims there are mountains we can take shelter in while we regroup, build our numbers, and wait out Cataclysm."

He leaned back in his chair, eyed his rifle, and Ana. "We're in survival mode til we get more protection like the mountains. Lebabolis wants us intact. Much as they try to locate us, they don't want to kill us unless it's absolutely necessary."

"These Encampments started as mining units for Valentium, the power source. We're their labor." She looked at Treg. "A lot of us were."

"So can you, either of you, or anyone, help me get back home?" I asked as I slid Treg's canteen back to him.

They both nodded. "But, ya know, there are risks. You even having that tether from Havens on your wrist is a risk. We're gonna get Otto or Kado to look at it, to make sure there isn't a tracker mechanism," Treg said.

"Risks with the Verge too?"

"Yes," said Ana. "For one, the Verge locations are well known. I wouldn't be surprised if they're staking out those areas from now on. They're praying you'll be dumb enough to turn up at one. Because if you do..." She pointed at my head as if her hand was a gun. "You're dead."

I slid up in my seat. "Well, y'all seem real nice and thanks for not knocking my ass out and all, but I really don't want to stay around here the rest of my life."

Ana chuckled. "No offense." Her smile faded as she added, "We're working on it, OK?"

"If we agree to help ya, and we are," Treg said, "are ya willing to do something for us?"

I folded my hands on the table and eyed the Link. "What would that be?"

"I'm guessing Ana told you about your status here? The Prophet Xander and all that?"

I looked over at Ana. "She told me a little."

Treg said, "A lot's going out on MODOSNet about Xander and prophecies. A lot that might kill the Action if we don't stop it."

"So many got away at once, we never knew for sure if any of 'em were plants, sent over by Lebabolis, still connected to the Link, getting their little instructions," Ana added.

"And what can I do about that?" I asked.

Treg replied, "You can get a different message out on MODOS-Net, through the Link."

"Isn't that locked down?"

Treg scratched his neck. "Baudricort has hacks; he already got a few messages out. But anything sent through the Link is easy to track back to the sender. People can tell it's Baudricort. But a message from you, a prophet who predicted this, well-"

"You could get the truth out, Nelson," Ana added.

I rubbed my eyes. "So what, I get on a camera and make a video?"

They looked at each other. Ana replied, "No, it's more like telepathy." She held up the Link.

I squinted at her. Just when I thought it was already odd enough. "Excuse me?"

"Baudricort can explain it a lot better." She cringed through her smile.

Neither of them said anything further. "Alright, let's go see Baudricort." I shrugged.

"Give it- give us a few days. Things are still a little hot right now. Ya just broke out of a sector, remember? I promise they're on the hunt for you now." Treg said.

I fidgeted with my hands a bit. The idea of me as a prophet had my brain jumbled. But if they wanted my help on this and it got me out of here that much quicker...

If I had yet to have written some of this, I figured having a few days to find out more wasn't a bad idea. "Alright. I'll help, and you get me home."

Treg nodded. "We'll do our best."

TWENTY-SIX

(ANA)

ADULL BOOM came from outside. The lights flickered.

"What was that?" asked Nelson.

Treg activated his rifle and darted out of the room.

I took my weapon in one arm and steadied Nelson. "Like Treg said, sometimes, they find us."

Rumbling shook the room. Nelson planted his hands flat on the table. "So we're dead?"

His eyes got that strange look again, but when I swung my rifle to the front, it snapped him to. "You're not allowed to die. Not if I can help it. Stay close."

Two Hell Hawks hovered near the Encampment as several Action soldiers fired back on 'em. I hurried Nelson over to the Encampment bunkers. These facilities were used for locating Valentium in the past, but some were converted to radar facilities by Baudricort and other Intellectuals like Otto. No surprise, we found Otto in the bunker where he tooled with some tech.

"I thought those scramblers would keep the nasties away," I chided.

Otto shrugged. "Hey, it pretty much worked; took them two weeks to find us."

"'Pretty much' is a start, but how about we do 'always'?" I scratched his back. "Otto, this is Nelson. You know him better as Xander."

A bit surprised, Otto grabbed Nelson's hand and bowed. Nelson's brow wrinkled and he eyed me, then nodded to Otto.

"OK, OK, send that tech to sleep, Otto, or you'll be facing the business end of a pulse rifle in about two minutes."

The roar of Hell Hawks punctuated my warning. Treg headed for a forward position with Zengus, our heavy weapons guy. Further into the bunker with us was Llewyn with a few Action soldiers, all of them engrossed in digital maps and the Beacon settings.

Llewyn was the deputy commander of the Action, second to Baudricort. It would've been great if he was less of a prick, but at least I knew surrender wasn't in his vocabulary.

"What's the plan, colonel?" I asked him.

His eyes were fixed at the video maps. His broad shoulders and chest were all that moved on him as he took several slow breaths in thought. He slid a glare my way, but once I held his gaze for a second I saw a flicker in his eyes. It was a strange little game he and I played. He folded his arms. "Squadron of Hell Hawks mobilized for backup. Should be here within ten minutes."

"Ten minutes. What if this thing is over in two?"

His jawbone twitched. "You throwing in, Crucinal?"

"No, sir."

"Good. We're holding the line and setting new beacons. Relo ASAP after this is over."

With that, he turned back to the maps. He never was much for pleasantries.

I walked toward the exit and stopped by Nelson. "You'll be fine. Much as they want to scare us, they'd rather take us alive. That goes extra for you." The Hell Hawk engines punched the air with blasts of rumbling thunder. "I'm gonna check our guys outside. Be back when it's over."

He nodded and looked around at the screens. "Be careful, I'll be fine."

After a quick jog over, I jumped in with the left forward group. Norg's surly face greeted me as I slid down into position.

"Nice seeing you too, Norg."

"When did ya get back?"

"Few hours ago. Why, you missed me?"

He grunted in response. Norg was the kinda person who was happiest when he was miserable. Before he joined the Action, he was at a factory in Lebabolis that robbed him of any charm and humor, but also cultivated in him a strong physique and excessive dislike of everything that was Lebabolis.

I was one of the few he not only tolerated, but watched out for. It helped that we had grown up near each other. I also think what I did right after I joined the Exodus impressed him, but he never let on.

"Heard about Yag and those guys," Norg said.

We traded glances.

"Yeah, well. Kinda knew going in how hot it could be."

Norg sighed and clutched his weapon. "Someday this shit's gotta end."

I watched him for a second before I replied, "Damn right."

More Hell Hawks joined the others over us. It looked like four or five of 'em. They swooped down low and zoomed over the Encampment. The dust and debris clouded up around us and blocked our view of everything.

"Is this another scare?" I pondered between coughs.

"Let them come close," Norg snarled, his grip on the rifle tightened.

The rear position in the Encampment got off a few shots as the Hell Hawks passed over 'em. They arced up again in the sky. On their next run, they showered the Encampment with pulse fire. The two main barracks buildings took most of the hits. Small trenches surrounded the barracks, each filled with soldiers that returned fire. The air was a mixture of blasts, debris that fell and the screams of the wounded.

"We gotta do something!" Norg yelled over the chaos.

"Reinforcements on the way!" I shouted back.

His doubtful gaze was his only response. He flailed his hands around his feet in the darkness. "Yer soundin' like Llewyn now. Should get his ass out here, see how good he feels about reinforcements coming when they're raining fire on us."

I pointed to his pack. "Got any goodies in there?"

He pulled out a pulse missile and smiled. "Don't I always?"

I shook my head. "Glad you're on our side."

Once we got a bead on the Hell Hawks, Norg and the others stood and fired their missiles. They soared on a snaking path and left a trail of glowing dust behind them. Two found their mark. The pulse made a loud boom, and the Hell Hawks that were hit sputtered and zoomed off, then crashed a few seconds later.

My comm unit crackled a bit, and I heard Treg. "Nice shooting. Need cover from you guys when they come back. Got a little treat for them too."

Before I or anyone else replied, the whine of a rocket invaded camp and hit the bunker where I had left Nelson. The explosion sent sparks from the building, and smoke billowed. My heart sank. I activated my comm unit. "Fall back, perimeter around the admin bunker!"

"No, Ana!" Treg hollered in reply. "They're trying to draw you out-"

I ignored Treg and hauled up out of the position. Someone grabbed for my leg, but it was pointless. I ran amid the fire and smoke, dodged piles of debris, spun around obstructions and hurled myself toward the bunker.

My legs wobbled when the ground under my feet shook from a nearby explosion. I was almost there when a few people stumbled out the destroyed building in the darkness and meandered back toward the rear guard position. I screamed for Nelson, but heard nothing back.

The roaring thunderclaps started again.

Another pass.

I half ran and half jumped ahead toward the rear guard position, and I saw Llewyn. He bled from a wound on his head and bellowed into his comm unit for Zengus and the air cover.

Nelson wasn't around.

A loud thump caught me for a second. I looked toward the front of the Encampment and saw it. A large flash of light shot out arms of electrical sparks that pierced the remaining Hell Hawks. The Hell Hawks soon exploded in a brilliant cacophony, and I looked away as the light got way too bright.

"Treg, you OK?" I asked over the comm.

"We're good up here. Gonna need help with the rest though, plenty wounded around."

I looked back to Llewyn, who shook his head. "Damn lucky. We must have gotten a small patrol this time."

"What about Nelson?" I asked.

Another voice to my side answered, "Who me?" Nelson's eyebrows arched as he dusted himself off. "Nice group of friends y'all have."

LLEWYN, Nelson, and I stopped over at the barracks on our way back to the front. One of the barracks was badly damaged; even in the darkness we saw the black smoke it coughed into the air. The other looked like it took a few shots, but nothing too serious.

"I need an update on the wounded." Llewyn nodded to me.

"Talked to Baudricort yet?" I asked.

"He's at Encampment 5, yeah, I contacted him after this was over."

"What'd he say?"

"Relo at once."

"I'm glad we have him to tell us this." I shook my head. Llewyn eyed me for a second then darted off.

As medics tended to the wounded, Llewyn saw about the facility repairs. Treg and Norg found Nelson and me. Treg yanked his helmet off. His scowl bored into me. "What the hell was that?"

I pulled my helmet off and ran my hand through my hair. "You mean me trying to protect our asset?"

"How about the part where ya ran through a sea of pulse fire?" He narrowed his eyes and shook his head. "You'll get your ass chewed up and spit out if you keep pulling crazy shit like that."

"I had it under control, OK?"

Norg regarded Treg as he spoke. Treg replied, "Think smart, Ana. People look to you, whether you think they do or not. Don't go getting yourself killed."

Treg and Norg walked over and unloaded their heavy gear.

"So I'm an asset, now?" Nelson asked.

"I'm sorry, Nelson. It's not like that."

"But you said it."

"I know, I'm - things have been crazy for me."

Nelson squatted down and surveyed the cleanup work. "Crazy, huh? Like being-zapped-a-few-centuries-into-the-future-to-a-world-I-wrote-about-crazy?"

I joined him on the ground. "Yeah, I keep forgetting you've been through a lot yourself. Keep the faith, we'll both get what we want yet." I smiled and patted his leg. I looked around and made sure Llewyn wasn't in earshot before I added, "Nelson, truthfully, I could care less about you being Xander. This Xander business is really Baudricort's idea."

"What about Treg? He seemed pretty into it too."

Treg and Norg had joined up with Llewyn. The three of 'em were into an active discussion. Probably a recount of their exploits from the raid earlier. Heh.

"Treg's along for the ride. For how long, I dunno." I looked at

Nelson. "You'll need all the help you can get getting to one of those Verge zones, though." I sighed and added, "I can't do it alone."

"Yeah, those other people you lost. Does that happen a lot?"

I shrugged. "For me, that was the only time I ever did that. But yeah, I've heard it happens a lot."

"So what do you do next?"

"First, we move this Encampment and get supplies. Then Baudricort."

Hissing noises followed by a low growling hum came from every building around us. "Better stand up," I said as I grabbed for Nelson. "These things make a little ruckus when they start up."

I watched as the Encampment facilities, except for the second barracks unit, rose a few feet off the ground, revealing that they were large hover units. A team of people moved and directed 'em into a single line.

"What in the world?" Nelson gasped.

I watched his eyes. They sparkled with wonder a little like Varrick's when he was impressed. I beamed. "Welcome to the Action, Nelson. Always ready, always mobile."

TWENTY-SEVEN

(NELSON)

I RUBBED MY EYES, but it didn't help the burning sensation from the smoke around me. Ana and the rest joined in with the clean up; they looked a little too familiar with all of this.

I chuckled to myself when I thought about what had happened over the last two days. Had it just been two days? It felt like a year had passed in that time. And my rescuer, Ana, seemed to have brought me into more chaos and misery. So much for a shining knight.

The Action pulled several vehicles nearby as they loaded supplies and got people ready to move. I saw a few vehicles that looked like the car I rode in with Brenn and Nycole, and a thought landed on me like a piece of falling timber. *This is your world, Nelson. Who the hell are any of them to tell you where to go or what to do? You want answers, you go find them yourself.*

Ana strode up. "About ten more minutes and we're out of here. You OK?"

My eyes surveyed the scene again. When I caught her glance, I saw the concern in her eyes. I grasped her shoulder. "Yeah, I'm alright. Just taking things in."

She nodded and jogged off toward a group loading some heavy gear into one of their vehicles. I saw at least three of those small cars near the outer ring of transports. It was now or never; a few more minutes and I'll be in tow once again.

I walked slow at first. People still milled about; I bet most of them didn't know my name. *Did I know their names? I created this story. How could I not know people here?*

A few soldiers carrying a collection of rifles brushed past me. They were more concerned with their weaponry than who the hell I was. *They both want something from me. Well, what the hell about what I want? I never asked for this. Let me get back home. I'll delete the damn novel and let the future be something else, something that has nothing to do with me.*

I glanced back and saw Llewyn instructing a small group. He held up a digital screen that displayed some maps of the area for their next destination. *They'll* see. *It's time I take things into my own hands. Let them come begging to me for whatever they need.*

The vehicles weren't attended. I fumbled with the door for a few seconds before it slid open. The console inside looked like the one I rode in earlier. There wasn't a steering wheel, though. I thought back to what I saw Brenn doing when he drove me through Sector 5.

I tapped and slid my fingers across the console, but there was no response. I looked up, and people still milled about. I then caught sight of Ana. She'd stopped helping and peered around.

The console came to life with a series of beeps and flashing lights. An electronic voice sounded: "Destination please."

"Uh, Sector... 5?"

The engine started into a rhythmic clunking noise. The seat shuddered, and a steering wheel appeared from out of the console in front of me. The voice responded: "Warning, Sector 5 is Lebabolis territory."

I moved my feet about and found pedals below. It was close enough to a car that I could handle it. If I just knew where the hell to go.

"Nelson?" Ana called out, and I saw her walking briskly toward the car.

"Start now, get me out of here!" I yelled to the console.

"Incalculable destination," came the response.

Ana ran toward the vehicle. "What are you doing?"

"Move!" I yelled.

"Incalculable destination."

I pushed the pedals at my feet, but they only revved the engine. I was stuck. Ana was close; another twenty feet and she'd have her hand on my door.

My breaths huffed in short bursts. There had to be something, some kind of-

"-Xander! Take me to Xander!"

The console reverted to a map display. "Do you wish to locate a Prophecy Center?"

Anything that wasn't here right now. "Yes, sir, affirmative, for fuck's sake!"

The vehicle lurched back and careened into a swift 180 before it zoomed off. I clutched the wheel and prayed that the auto control would last until my head felt like it wasn't about to explode.

MY HANDS WERE sore from their grip on the wheel, but I couldn't have let go if I wanted to. My pulse raced in my throat. The freedom and the curiosity of this place had me almost trembling.

The console map updated, showing indicators of where my vehicle was and wherever the destination, a Prophecy Center was. Nice they still had GPS these days. If only they had an airport.

After about ten minutes, I ended up on a rough patch of road. I moved the wheel and guided the car around several large holes and cracks. The road looked like it was once a main thoroughfare of a city, but time had rendered it a loose patchwork of pavement and rubble.

The radio in the car hissed to life with a familiar voice.

"Nelson, come in. Pick up the handset. Talk to me."

"What, Ana?"

"What are you doing?"

"Getting away. I want to see this place for myself."

"What?"

"You heard me. It's my story, it's my world. You're just living in it."

"You're putting yourself in a lot of danger, Nelson. Why don't you stay put? I'm heading your way."

"You're not even real. Why should I listen to you?"

"Dammit, you're hysterical. I told you before, I won't let anything happen to you. Why can't you believe me?"

My gut ached a bit, and my voice hitched. "I'm going to this Prophecy Center. See what I can find out. Why don't you meet me there?"

"Will you at least wait until I can get to you?"

"Where are you?"

"Looking at your sig, I'm two miles behind you."

I checked the pedals and sure enough one slowed the vehicle to a stop. "You've got fifteen minutes." I shut the radio off.

I tapped the console until it switched displays. More maps and diagrams of buildings. It looked like some official Lebabolis documentation. Energy towers, chemical production facilities. Even staffing rosters.

A pack lay on the seat next to me. It had food rations, a light, and a small book, like a notebook. "Suspects" was written on the cover, and a few names written inside. No one I'd heard of. I put everything else back in the pack.

Ana pulled up with another soldier in a truck. Getting out, she walked up to my car. "What was that about?"

"I'm getting away from the war. In the past two days with you people here, I've been shot at, inoculated, handcuffed, and almost blown to kingdom come. Excuse me if I'm a little wary of how much your protection is worth."

She folded her arms. "Oh, is that right?"

The soldier with her stood nearby, eyeing her and me.

"Yep, and I'm sorry but no one, including you, has convinced me that this even isn't some damn dream yet. In fact, why don't I get myself killed, and we'll all see if I wake up or not?"

Ana's eyes narrowed. She stepped toward me. "Tell you what. I'll take you to the Prophecy Center, we'll do that. I'll show you what they've said about Xander, and what they are saying. And I'll also show you the Pox and what it's done to people. If you still don't believe all of this, I won't stop you; you can leave and go wherever you want."

I took a deep breath and let it out very slowly. "Thank you."

"Follow us; do not get separated. When we get there, let us check out the area, and then you can have a look."

"Got it."

<hr>

THE PROPHECY CENTER stood like some kind of ancient temple. Large columns supported a roof and gave it a look like some ancient Greek structure. The place showed some wear from weather. Black scorch marks also dotted the surface. The surrounding area was rubble with a few paths picked through.

I pulled my car in front of a statue and froze. The figure was in a dramatic pose. One arm held a book and the other was outstretched as if it cast a blessing. The face was unmistakable. It was me, Xander.

"Recognize that guy?" Ana asked.

The inside of the center was basic: more stone, fixtures along the walls. Also some computer terminals that complimented the book-shelves around the place. A doorway at the far end of the room lead into a chapel.

Ana pointed to the door and said something to the Resistance soldier before he stepped outside. She then approached me. "OK, we don't have long. Let's check the terminal."

Ana pressed several buttons on the terminal and it displayed a MODOSNet main menu. She tapped her fingers over the screen and sent the display into a quick strobe of screen changes. "Lebabolis has patrols all over the area, so we don't have time for the grand tour."

As she manipulated the controls, the displays showered pictures and updates of Xander, and pages of Cataclysm Epoch cascaded over the screen. "These people know everything about you, Nelson. They're afraid of Cataclysm and figure the only way they'll be safe is if they listen to every word you write in your book."

"You should've gotten me later on, when I was closer to finishing it," I replied. "I don't know what to make of any of this."

"But you will. It's in your mind somewhere. And Brenn wanted to pull it out." Ana winced. "No one deserves that."

"Well, what does Baudricort want?"

"He thinks you can figure out how to shut down MODOSNet. If we can do that, it's the start of ending their control. We still need to take out Charista and the leaders, but first we have to cripple them. MODOSNet is the leash they have everyone else on, keeping people quiet, and dying."

She nodded to the screen, which then displayed a video of several people lying in beds. Their bodies were full of sores and looked horrible.

"This is what Pox looks like when it's not treated, when people are close to the end," Ana muttered.

The sight was painful. It reminded me a little of Mom, on a bed and clinging to life. There were dozens on this one video.

"Is there anything that can be done?" I asked.

"Treatment, but very rare, and unavailable to us in the Action unless we swear to live by their rules."

A loud boom from outside shook the floor. Ana's gaze shot to the entrance. "Trouble. See, told you this was risky!"

The Action soldier approached the front entrance. Ana grabbed her rifle and headed out with him. "Stay behind us!"

Another vehicle joined ours outside. Two Lebabolis soldiers stood beside it, their weapons drawn on us.

"What do you think you're doing?" barked one soldier.

"Catching up on our worship." Ana scoffed.

"Forget it, Deviant. You and your kind need to learn your place. All of you, get over here. You're all under arrest."

Ana looked back to me. "You'd dare place this man, the Prophet Xander - under arrest?"

Ana stepped aside. The soldiers craned for a better look at me. "Impostor," one remarked. "Why should we believe a Deviant who claims someone is Xander?"

"No way," the other soldier added. "We're here to shut this center down anyway. So, Deviants, get your asses over here." A low hum filled the air when they activated their rifles.

Everything paused for a moment. I took a breath but it seemed to get caught in my throat. The Action soldier and Ana looked at each other. She pointed at him with two fingers and he nodded in under-standing. She turned to me and mouthed "Here we go."

Ana faced the Lebabolis soldiers and extended her hands as if for surrender. She took a few steps toward the soldiers, then reached one hand back and grasped something near the back of her neck. She flung her hand forward and launched a small knife, which lodged in the throat of one Lebabolis soldier. He fell to the ground with gasps and spurts of blood from his neck, firing his pulse rifle off in random directions.

The other soldier quickly swung his rifle straight at me. Ana yelled, "Down, Nelson!" But my legs locked into place. Ana dove straight toward me when the soldier fired. Ana collided with me, and we both tumbled to the ground.

The Action soldier fired on the Lebabolis soldier. Pieces of stone from the facility splintered off and sent clouds of dust down on us.

Ana lay on top of me. She watched me with frantic eyes. "Are you OK?"

"Y-yeah, think so."

"Stay down!" She rolled off of me. The Action soldier took a shot to his midsection and yelped in pain as he collapsed back against the Prophecy Center.

Ana's rifle had slid down the steps and was too far away. She lunged for the Action soldier's weapon and delivered a barrage that enveloped the Lebabolis solider in a spray of brilliant light.

She proceeded slow toward the Lebabolis vehicle, her rifle held up and checked the area. Once it all looked clear, she made her way back and checked on the Action soldier.

"It's OK," Ana cooed. "You're alright. You're a soldier. Remember, one or none."

The soldier's breathing slowed, and then he was still. Ana gently laid the soldier flat on the ground. She paused over him for a few minutes.

I walked near her. "You saved me. You could've let me die, but you didn't."

She kept her gaze on the fallen soldier. "You aren't here because you wanted to be. I made a promise I'd protect you until Baudricort's done with you."

She lunged toward me, hand to my throat, her voice in a tremble. "And that includes keeping you from dying, which, if you haven't figured out by now, is real. You think I would've done that if it wasn't?"

Her barrage jolted me a bit. I gazed into her eyes as she slowly lowered her hand from my throat. "Alright. This is all just too confusing."

"I know. I just wanted to get away with my brother. But that won't happen until my deal is done. Same goes for you getting home."

"I understand."

Ana took another look at the vehicle. "Encampment 7 is in full Relo. Let's loot that rig for whatever they were dumb enough to leave behind and hightail it to Encampment 3. It's closer to where we are anyway. Besides, it's time you meet Baudricort before you drag my ass the other half of the way over the Outlands."

TWENTY-EIGHT

(NELSON)

ANA AND I SAT with Baudricort in the bunker at Encampment 3. He had the disheveled look of an eccentric college professor. He gazed at me through a mop of tussled hair. "So you're Nelson Forrester," he said, his fingers steepled.

"Last I heard," I said.

His expression didn't change. It appeared humor hadn't survived into the future either. I should have written that part in.

"I understand you're ready to help us."

I eyed Ana. "You could say that. Ana gave me a look at MODOS-Net. She said you want to shut it down."

Baudricort sent Ana a quick glare, then tapped a few controls on a terminal at his desk before he looked back to me. "MODOSNet drives Lebabolis. If we can cripple or shut it off, it's a start to ending their control. It's their census, how they track people, and most important, the primary way their citizens get information."

"Information?"

"News, production statuses. It's part of keeping them quiet, giving them little pieces of information about how things are going."

He gestured with his hands as he spoke. "Keep their minds on their work and how lovely it is to be a citizen. When people have something to do and their minds are occupied with whatever distraction possible, they can be controlled."

Ana rolled her eyes at Baudricort's sprawling description.

"Where you come in," he said, "is that you're the face of what people have believed for over a century now. All this production, creation, work, has been under the idea that this system, this country, this Lebabolis, was preordained. It's the grand nation mentioned in your book. And the nation that wins the war you described."

"Does that include Cataclysm?" I asked.

He managed a small chortle. "You mustn't listen to every fairy tale you hear out there."

I crossed my arms. "But if everything I've written ends up coming true, and this great nation is Lebabolis and it so far has happened like I wrote, why are you even bothering? Why not run for the hills?"

His eyes darkened. "That won't matter. If they finish what they started, there won't be any of us they can't get to."

"How do you know this?"

He sat back, his brow furrowed. "Because I'm the architect of MODOSNet. It was supposed to be about restoring the food supply, and a sense of order too. Like their Product system, allow the natural abilities of people to develop and improve over generations while the world rebuilt itself."

"But they changed along the way?"

He nodded. "MODOSNet was only supposed to be a temporary solution to the problem, but it soon became the backbone to everything. And now, if they can perfect these Link implants—"

I stopped him. "Link implants?"

"Yeah. Like the Link devices, only they are wired directly to the brain. The Radomet were an early version of this experiment. If it worked, citizens would be fed suggestions all day and night. They'd have complete control of everyone and could order them to do whatever at anytime, anywhere."

"Did they set it up?"

"No, not yet. When I left I took everything I had been working on and data on what they were planning for real. It's kept safe, and only I and one other person know where it is."

"What are they planning?"

He looked at Ana for a moment. "That Product System of theirs? Total lie. Well, it isn't for the order they claim. They're building an army. Using Worker Products to assemble gear and supplies for them. It's about the Warrior Products. The others, once they serve their purpose, will be destroyed. Only a few Intellectual Products and the Coursons will remain, with the Warrior Products as their force."

"And this army is for the Omegans?"

Baudricort eyed Ana again, then folded his arms back behind his head. "That's right. The last time they attacked, Lebabolis almost fell." His voice stumbled when he added, "If it weren't for the small Cataclysm, they would've overrun everything."

"And the Radomet is part of that army?" I asked.

"They see anyone who can't use a weapon as a liability. They're afraid they won't be able to stop the Omegans again this time, so they're filling the ranks until more Warrior Products are old enough to replace them. Once that's complete, the Warrior and Intellectual Products will cut the rest off and move out."

"Cut the rest off?"

"Yeah, as in eliminate. Worker Products. They have this belief in the upper echelon of Lebabolis that only the strong deserve to go on. But they're riding the backs of the weak to get there. As soon as they can, they harvest what Valentium they can and set out to destroy the Omegans."

His gaze was a mix of dread and regret. I felt sorry for him, with that trapped look on his face.

"But how can I stop this? What can one person do?"

"One prophet," he corrected. "I want you to make messages for the Link. You're very recognizable as the Prophet Xander. Identify the true nation you mentioned as the Action. Then you ask people to join us. I want to get all the Workers we can to come with us, and anyone else who can be convinced. The more we get to safety, the better."

"Will that work?"

"You'd be recognized as the true Xander. That name came from your mind, no one can fake that, not even me. Lebabolis will do what they can - do their utmost to stop this. But if we keep trying, I think we can sway people. And soon, a few becomes many."

Ana clasped her hands. "And then we cut the head off the snake. Destroy MODOSNet. Right?"

Baudricort flinched a bit at Ana's remark and shot her a look. "Of course."

The room was silent for a moment. I asked, "So once I do this, I'm going home?"

He checked a few screens on his desk and said, "We'll do our best. You're their prime target now so getting you there safe won't be easy."

"Leave that to me," Ana said.

TWENTY-NINE

(ANA)

I STROLLED OUT of the meeting room and took a walk around the perimeter of Encampment 3. I thought about Baudricort's reaction to destroying MODOSNet and smirked. As bad as it was and how much it controlled, it was still his baby.

I traded waves with the sentries. The only sound in the distance was the wind as it rustled trees and kicked up a little dust.

My comm unit beeped to life with Treg's ID.

"Hey, how goes it?" I asked.

"Eventful. We scored more Valentium."

"How much?"

"Enough for one or two Encampments. It's something."

"Yeah. About time for another supply raid too."

"Right, gonna head your way. Should by be there morning. So what's doing with the honcho?"

I slid down next to a Landcrawler and leaned against one of the tires. I spied the admin building and scanned around the rest of the area. "He's gonna work on those Xander Link messages with Nelson."

"Still don't think this'll work?"

I watched the few people who walked about. A few had weapons, others made adjustments to vehicles. "I don't know. It'll take more than a few messages to save those people."

"It's a start. Have faith."

"Yeah, well. Sooner we get going the better."

He said nothing for a minute.

"You OK, Treg?"

"Yeah, yeah, fine."

"Any of our group with ya?"

"Just Norg right now. Kado is running another convoy raid in one of the sectors."

I swiped at my face as a gust of wind blew dirt over me. "Yeah, Otto is around. Once they get those messages done, we'll make a run for the Verge again."

"Oh wow."

"Yeah, well. I can't blame this guy for wanting to get home." I dug my heels into the ground and watched the little divots my boots carved. "I'm still ready whenever, you know."

"I know. Hope I'm there when ya go for him."

I traced my finger over the screen. "That'd be good."

Nelson stepped outside and looked around.

"Lemme go, Treg. Looks like they're ready for showtime."

"Check. Stay safe. Out."

Nelson caught my eye as I approached.

"So?" I asked.

"He wants me to make three messages, should be ready to go in a day." He nodded with a slight smile.

"Then you get to leave this joy behind, right?"

"Hope so, no offense."

I smirked. "Hey, it's OK. I've wanted to get away from these assholes for awhile myself."

He closed in a bit and whispered, "He also told me about the spots to try for the Verge."

"Just 'told you'? What about maps and coordinates?"

"He's loading them up for us."

A few soldiers came near us and adjusted the beacon antenna.

"This'll get pretty hairy, you know. Wherever it is. And I hope you know, we might have to try more than once."

He watched me with the same expression he had back in the library. "I know."

"Tell you what. Since you've got a little time, and you're already curious about this place, how about you join me and Treg on a supply raid tomorrow? We can have you back by the time Baudricort's ready."

"Yeah, why not?"

THIRTY

(NELSON)

T HE NEXT MORNING we boarded one of their Hell
Hawks and flew close to the border of Lebabolis. I sat in
the rear with Ana and the others while Treg piloted the
ship. The craft lurched and swayed at times, while the whine of
turbine engines revved up during the flight.

Ana chatted with the others on the trip. Their bond was obvious,
a smaller group within the larger Action.

Once we landed, we trekked through overgrown bush and some
broken trails for another half hour until we ended up on a hill that
overlooked a winding road. According to Treg, the Action made
supply raids like this every so often.

I wanted a visual clue of the sun, but all I got was an overcast sky.
Somehow I felt like if I saw the sun, things would've been more
normal.

Ana gazed toward the road through a pair of binoculars. The air
was a bit hazy, almost like a fog that tried to keep from being burned
off. Off a few feet from me, Norg, Zengus and Treg checked their
weapons.

Ana turned to me. "This road is one of the few anymore that lead

210

around the area. Lebabolis uses it to run supplies to their Sectors. We're near the border between Sectors 3 and 4."

"They don't secure it?" I asked.

Ana smiled. "It's too damn big. They can't be everywhere."

"But they'll be packing heat when they do come." Norg grunted.

I looked over at Norg while he worked at his weapon. I turned back to Ana. "When's their next run?"

"We know it happens on the first Saturday of the month, which is today, and usually around this time of day."

"So you take what you need?" I asked.

"Correct."

Ana talked like this was home landscaping, not a raid of a supply convoy guarded by armed soldiers.

They all held out their weapons and checked them over. All that firepower made me feel a little naked being unarmed. I watched Ana with her weapon. "So you've done this before, right? Anything ever go wrong?" I asked.

She shrugged. "Sometimes. Baudricort helped us pinpoint better areas to stake out. Still, we sometimes get cornered and lose a few. But there's no time for growing food when you're always on the run, so it's worth the risk to not have more people starving than already are."

"So how do we do this?"

"Let's get everyone together. Hey Treg, over here!"

After we gathered in a circle, Treg began the run down. "Zengus, set up low near the road. No matter what, you disable the first truck. Don't blow its wheels off like last time, just make sure it can't run anymore."

Zengus said, "Well, now you tell me."

Treg eyed us for a second. "Ana, you and Norg with me. Weapons at the ready, fan out and zap anyone who comes out shooting. Head and chest shots, nobody walks away."

Ana turned to me. "You better wait here, Nelson. These can get rough. Sit quiet until I call you."

"That's fine," I said.

I crouched behind a tree and watched as they made their way down to the road. Zengus ran out in a line straight in front of me, towards the bottom of the hill. Once he stopped, he blended in like a chameleon. Had I not known where he was headed, I would've missed him altogether.

Ana, Treg and Norg spread out toward my left, a little higher up on the hill. Everything was silent except for the occasional rustle of branches. Not even birds. I scanned the road for any sign of a vehicle. Nothing.

Then a low hum started, and two trucks appeared on the road soon afterward. Treg gestured to the group by the road and directed them all, as described.

I saw Zengus a little better now. He held up a long slender gun to his shoulder and pointed it down the road towards the direction of the trucks.

The trucks reached the bend to the straightaway near us. As they finished the turn, Zengus fired a rocket. Its roar echoed on the wind, and it slammed into the first truck with a loud bang. The truck shook with the impact, and smoke poured out the front. Treg yelled, and the rest charged down the hill and fired short bursts at the convoy.

Two men fell out of the cab of the first truck. One looked rather dazed by the explosion and struggled to his feet, a weapon clutched in his hands. The other was more able and crouched behind the bumper, where he returned fire on Treg's group.

More people exited the rear truck. Ana ducked between the two vehicles and fired at the soldiers to the rear. Treg advanced towards the group in the rear, while Zengus pulled up another weapon and blasted at the two in the front.

In a little while, Zengus took out the two at the front. He ran to the back, where Treg and the others stood. Before long there was one left, on his knees as Treg watched him with a rifle.

Ana called out, "Nelson! You can come down now."

I met Ana as she looked through the back of the first truck. It was full of crates. Many were marked with different types of food. A few had "Transmissible" stamped on them.

"This is good," Ana said. "Enough for several weeks, even a month or two on rations. The other Encampments can also use this stuff."

"What's the transmissible stuff?" I asked.

Her eyes flitted between the cases and me. "We can't stay too long, never know if Radomet will do a sector scan."

We climbed off the truck and met Norg and Zengus. "Good job team." Ana smiled. "How's the other vehicle looking?"

"Food and tech," Norg answered.

"Nice. Still drivable?"

"We didn't touch it, should be fine," Zengus replied.

"Where's Treg?"

"He has someone from the other truck still alive."

"Really? I thought we weren't taking prisoners."

Zengus shrugged.

I followed Ana as she crept to the back of the rear truck. When we got closer, I saw Treg, his rifle pointed at the chest of a man on the ground. Treg's body tensed. The man's body shook with each breath, a wild look in his eyes.

"Treg, you OK?" Ana asked.

"Ana, ya gotta see this."

Treg handed her a square shaped object, almost like a computer tablet, only the items on the display floated above it, like holographs.

She studied it for a few minutes and looked back at Treg a few times, as if she hadn't believed what she saw. "How did they get this?"

"No clue. Baudricort's super tight lipped about stuff, and I thought we'd gotten the moles already."

"Guess not."

Ana clenched the tablet. Her jawbone slid back and forth as her gaze narrowed. She tossed the tablet down, swung her rifle around, and pointed it at the strange man's neck. "What's all this about Cataclysm? What do you know about it?"

The man's haggard breaths gave way to a defiant hoarse chuckle. "Stupid Deviants. You can't hide much longer."

"Tell me now. This is your last chance." Ana nudged the gun into his neck.

The man sneered, and his chuckles degraded to coughs as he added, "No chance. Just like your sweet little brother."

The taunt in his words lingered over the air like smoke from a long extinguished fire. Ana's scowl deepened, and her knuckles whitened. Treg let out a gasp at the barb, and before he could stop her, she fired three shots into the man's neck and head. His body jerked and slumped down while blood spurted out. My stomach tensed, and a gasp escaped my lips.

Ana swiveled to me, her eyes wide. "Nelson, back by the truck!"

I met Zengus and Norg as they unloaded crates from the front truck. Ana and Treg came up a few moments later. Treg glanced at me for a moment and said, "OK, let's get everything we can loaded from this truck to the rear one. And make it quick, don't want Radomet putting our asses in a sling."

Ana waved me over to the crates in the front truck. I wondered what the Transmissible ones were. She had looked at me a little odd when I asked. We loaded most of the food that fit onto the rear truck. I reached for one of the Transmissible ones and Ana waved me back. "Better let us take that."

Once Ana and Treg loaded the Transmissible boxes on the back of the rear truck, we climbed in. Treg took the wheel, Ana sat on the passenger side, and I was in the middle. Zengus and Norg rode in the back. Treg drove for awhile until the hills flattened back to level ground. A dirt trail soon appeared and forked off from the road to the right. Treg took it, and soon we arrived at Encampment 9.

THE MOMENT we arrived at the Encampment, people gathered around the vehicle. Ana and company unloaded supplies like they were Christmas presents for the destitute. The crowd elbowed each other to grasp for any tidbit they could until all was gone.

"We need to talk." I grabbed Ana's arm while the others continued the charity spree.

"This isn't a good time."

"Doesn't matter."

Her eyes narrowed at me, then she nodded and we grabbed chairs in a storage area. "OK, what?"

"What? Let's start with what Treg and you were so damned worried about you had to kill an unarmed man for it."

Ana grit her teeth. Her eyes searched my face for a minute. I drew a total blank on this, and I figured she was waiting for any epiphany from me before she explained.

"Nelson, that man you saw me with back there had some information on Cataclysm. I'd hoped you knew something about it, but I guess we nabbed you before you got to that part."

She handed me the page. It was a listing of numbers and mathematical equations.

"I've been trying to figure out what or where or even when Cataclysm is going to happen. At first it was just for Varrick and me to have time for an escape. Now I want to know just how much time left I have to rescue him before it happens."

"Tell me more about Varrick. What did that comment about him having no chance mean?"

She tensed at the sound of his name. "They call it the Pox. Lots of people started getting it over the past several years. They think the new power grid is causing it."

"The Valentium?"

She nodded quickly.

"Are we in danger?"

She flopped her hand back in her lap, and sighed. "Well, if we are, you've got the least to worry. You've been here for what, a week? Me and the rest have been near this our whole lives."

"Are they going to... will Lebabolis-"

"-take care of him?" Ana said. "Baudricort thinks so."

"But you don't?"

She shrugged. "They want us back. And to be honest, he's got the best chance over there right now."

"How so?"

"They've got a scanner that removes every trace of Pox from someone. It's available in the capital to those willing to pay the price."

"The price?"

"Takes a lot of power to run it. That's why they never made it available to everyone. They figured the average Product's life wasn't worth the cost. Only upper strata get a privilege." She shook her head in disgust.

"Well, what then?"

Tears rolled down Ana's cheek. Her face wrinkled in sorrow and her voice broke. "I'm beyond sick of Baudricort and his waiting game."

Her arms writhed like a boxer, her hands balled into fists. She looked off, her face pained. Then she lowered her head.

"They won't let Varrick die, right?" Even as I heard myself say that, I clenched my gut at how naïve it sounded. Who the hell could stop anyone from dying? Could I have kept Mom alive?

"I like to hope not." She glanced back at me. "But I don't trust 'em. They'd just as soon keep me thinking he's ill and the rest of our people are sick to keep drawing us out."

I reached for Ana. Memories of Mom flushed over me. I remembered how I felt when I helplessly watched her die. What I would have done for even five more minutes with her. Thoughts of everything still flung about me, and I wanted more than anything for my feet to be on the ground, but it just wasn't there. At least I had a way to get things back on track now. They wanted something from me, and it meant I would get to go home if I cooperated.

"Get me back to Baudricort, Ana. I'll do those Link messages."

(NELSON)

T HE ROOM SPUN AROUND ME even though I was in a chair. It felt like I was on one of those spinning rides at a local fair operated by a carny dying to make it go until I retched everywhere.

The cool metal band around my head hugged my temples as a firm reminder it was still on. Every now and then I felt a slight pinch around the back of my head.

I squirmed and clutched my head. "People actually sleep with these things on?"

Baudricort adjusted my device. "All the time. Remember, this is your first experience. Most folks do this their whole lives."

Ana surveyed the whole situation from behind Baudricort. "How's it feel?"

"Like somebody's reaching into my head and pressing my eyes from the inside out," I said through clenched teeth.

Baudricort made a few more tweaks. The dizziness faded a little, but the pinching sensation didn't. "How long do I need to wear this?"

He handed me several pages of text. "Long enough to read that."

He crouched beside me. "I need you to do several of these, so we'll space them out a bit to give you a break."

I rifled through the papers.

"Citizens of Lebabolis, I bring you peace and good tidings from the Prophet Xander. The time has come for you to rise up against the silent oppression of Lebabolis. I say again, rise up! You are being held in captivity against your very nature. Your captors hide in plain sight as those who claim to shelter, clothe and feed you as Products of Lebabolis. You are being used as tools for the sole purpose of Lebabolis to conquer the world and subjugate its resources and people to the will of a few. Do not be fooled by the security and prosperity the great liar Harkson Baronage offers. Together with his mad dog Charista Mantisword, he will drain the world of all hope for true freedom and reason.

"Be strong, fear not, good people of Lebabolis. The Prophet Xander loves you and is showing you the way to true freedom."

I sat back in my chair. "So what happens after this runs?"

Baudricort handled the pages. "We give it time to get out. I can hack MODOSNet, but they're good at shutting down infiltration. I'm thinking it'll take at least a few tries before it gets heard by enough people."

Baudricort played the Link message back on speakers in the room. An odd chill ran through me as I heard a voice, my voice, that read the script as if I spoke it. According to them, this was exactly how it sounded when sent through the Link.

"You almost sound like you believe what you read," Ana said.

"It's a means to an end, Ana. You don't have to subscribe to it." Baudricort stared off and beamed like I'd given him the cure for every disease ever known.

Ana nodded at me. "Nice work, Xander."

Baudricort offered a small smile as well. "This is going well. Sit tight; there's one more thing we need to run."

He tapped a few controls, and I felt a sharp sting on the back of my neck. My body flinched by reflex. "W-what the hell?"

Ana's eyes widened. A roaring kind of static started in my ears. Baudricort's lips still moved, and I just made out his voice over the din in my head. "Nelson, just relax. I want to see if we can figure out about Cataclysm."

"What the hell is this?" Ana stepped toward Baudricort.

My body tensed and shook as the pain in my neck increased. Ana grabbed Baudricort and argued with him, but I couldn't hear a thing at that point.

The roar in my ears sounded like a rushing stream of water, and then flashes of light filled my vision. I closed my eyes, but that didn't stop them.

A tingling sensation ran down my spine, through my arms and legs. I strained against the chair, but I was held fast.

A voice penetrated the rushing noise in my ears. It was Baudricort's voice, and he asked, "Where is Cataclysm?"

His voice echoed in my head; it felt like it bounced off my skull. I gnashed my teeth and shook from the loudened roar in my ears and the tingling everywhere else.

The flashing lights in my vision flickered and I saw images float past. Places I'd been to, people I'd seen; they swirled about me in random order. There was Tina and me at a bar having a drink. Then, Travis and me at my job interview. Quick scenes that just swarmed past like a video played on high speed.

"Where is Cataclysm?" The question came again with more echoes. I moved my jaw up and down; every time my teeth clicked it sounded like a bell.

I attempted to speak. I wanted to tell him to cut this shit out, whatever the hell it was. How dumb was I? None of these people wanted to help me out. They were just out for whatever they thought I had to offer.

"Where is Cataclysm?"

My jaw clenched again, but I managed to mutter, "Ffffffuck yyyyyou."

Another series of jolts soared through me, and my eyes flew open.

I saw Ana. She held Baudricort's head back, her face twisted in anger. She gestured toward me, but I still had no idea what she was saying.

Again the voice came, "Where is Cataclysm?"

My jaw bobbed a few times. I reared up for another retort, but this time I spoke something I never planned on. I couldn't have even made this up, wouldn't have even thought of this.

"Western Range, 41.2835°N 120.2007°W." My body shook after I said that, and my eyes squeezed shut again. The roaring came to a stop, and the pain in my neck was gone. I heard shouting. My eyes peered open and I saw Ana; she was holding a knife poised at Baudricort.

"What the hell did you do to him?" They both looked at me, Ana with mild fright and Baudricort with interest through his dazed eyes.

Ana shoved Baudricort and rushed up to me.

"What the hell do you know, old man? Why are you talking about finding Cataclysm? It's an event, it happened. Right?"

Baudricort stared at her. His eyes jumped to me, then back to Ana. "I had to find out if he knew about it."

"Cataclysm, OK, you found it, you bastard. Don't you ever think about someone else before what you want? How about letting other people in on things for a change?"

She yanked my restraints off. I gasped a bit for air and she helped me upright. Baudricort's brow furrowed. "I'm sorry, Nelson. I didn't think you'd have allowed me to do that if you knew."

"Good guess." I moaned. Ana pulled me upright.

She ran her hand through my hair a few times. "I'm taking you out of here before he gets any other bright ideas. Just got a message from Encampment 7 anyway. They've taken a hit. Lots of casualties."

"They should've traded places with me." I groaned.

Ana helped me up. Baudricort tended to some data but looked up when she thrust her dagger toward his chest. "We're heading to 7. You so much as touch him like that again, I'll cut your stomach out and feed it to you."

(NELSON)

THE BOUNCING ON THE TRIP to Encampment 7 did nothing good for my headache, but being away from the torture chamber from the ninth level of hell was relief enough right then.

"I'm sorry, Nelson. I really had no idea." Ana clenched the wheel tight. "He said next to nothing about Cataclysm and now that you're around, he tries this."

She pounded the console. "I never knew." A sparkle of moisture appeared under one of her eyes.

"What was the point of that Xander message he had me do? Just a smoke and mirror thing, get me off guard for the third degree times a million?"

"I know the messages are real; we've had those for a long time. He keeps a lot to himself though. Now there's that location you blurted out. I don't get it, is that where Cataclysm starts?" She tapped a few controls on the console and pulled up a map. "That's close to our destination in the Range. Is he trying to kill us?"

The question floated in the air between us for a few minutes. She gave a sigh. "Someday I'm gonna sit his ass down and make him come clean about everything."

I wiped the sweat off my brow. I was back to square one over here. Ana had rescued me from people who were about to torture me and brought me to people who did just that. But her story about her brother and her reaction had me wondering. And she pulled me away each time. As upside down as it all was, she somehow stood apart from it. Whenever I stuck with her so far, I ended up better off.

BY THE TIME we got to Encampment 7, the efforts were already underway. This was salvage at the very best. Groups of soldiers looked at burned out buildings and checked for anyone still alive. Ana surveyed it all, the grimness of it reflected on her face.

The air was heavy with a smoky odor of burning fuel and flesh. I gagged when I saw twisted corpses, like pieces of black wood half burned to dust.

Ana shook her head. "Animals. They did this."

"This happen a lot?" I asked.

"Too much," she replied as she looked at the carnage around her. "They'd rather us dead than not with them."

A few people shouted for Ana. About fifty yards away, a group of soldiers crowded around something on the ground. As we stepped over rubble, Ana focused on that direction. Then, she said, "Oh God," and took off in a sprint.

My less nimble feet weren't as fast as hers. When I got to the circle of soldiers, Ana knelt in the center next to a wounded child who writhed on the ground.

Ana asked the group, "Anyone know her?"

Someone thought the kid was a rescued orphan. No one else knew anything. She looked around seven years old. Nasty burns smeared her face and body. Her black hair was quite stringy, and her gaze wandered. She focused on a few of us in the circle over her.

Her eyes widened when she saw Ana. Ana collected the girl into her arms as she whimpered. Ana cradled her and rocked gently. "Shh, it's OK." The girl's eyes were wild and glanced around as if she were waiting for another attack like whatever did this.

Ana calmly brushed the girl's hair from her face. "See that look, Nelson? That's how we live. Waiting for things to be better, but terrified that they'll only get worse."

Ana leaned in closer and spoke in a whisper. "What's your name, sweetheart?"

In a raspy voice, she half whispered, "Clara."

Ana's voice hitched as she replied, "Aww, how pretty. Thirsty?"

Clara nodded several times. Ana grabbed her canteen and held for her. "We'll take care of you, OK darling? You rest."

Ana kissed Clara softly on the forehead and handed her to one of the others. She surveyed the rest of the charred area as I followed her.

"I can't do this," she said after a few minutes.

"Do what?"

"Leave. Even if I could get Varrick, I can't leave 'em. Not when this keeps happening."

Her eyes filled with angry tears and her brow furrowed. "I'm an idiot."

"Why?"

Her head shook slow, her eyes scoured the scene again. "I thought I'd be safe one day if I left. But where's safety, where Baudricort's leading us? To the north? The Omegans won't be done even if they stop Lebabolis. They'll keep on and one day I'll have to deal with them anyway."

She brushed her arm past her eyes and glanced at me. "That little girl may as well be Varrick. And everyone else's kid. And their mother, or father. Someone's gotta stop this."

We sat on a pile of rubble. "What you said back there with Baudricort, about destroying MODOSNet. Do you think it's even possible?"

She chuckled for a bit and looked toward the burning structures.

"Crazy, and a long shot. We'd only do that if we got to the capital, and that's locked up rather tight, so I dunno." She picked up a twisted piece of metal and hurled it. "But it's the head. You wanna kill a snake..." She sliced the air with her hand.

The more I was around these people the more I felt for them. In part for what I did, however it happened, that created this world. The image of Clara was seared into my head too now, and I wanted it gone. No one deserved a life like these people had.

"I should stay," I said.

Her eyebrows shot up. She looked at me for awhile. Her lips bent upward a little, but she said nothing still.

We sat and watched the soldiers with the cleanup again. Then she got up and turned to me. "Nelson, this isn't your fight. You don't need this. You've got your own family, and you deserve to be with them. I'll make that happen, at least."

THIRTY-THREE

(ANA)

WHILE WE WAITED for the cleanup at 7 I got the coordinates for the Verge from Baudricort. It was the least his ass could've done.

The Verge location ended was about sixty miles away from Encampment 3, so we hitched a ride with a Hell Hawk most of the way.

This particular Verge was in thick woods. A grove of trees and brush extended from where we were around to the right, where it expanded into the woods. The air was thick with the musky smell of damp, rotted leaves. The trees formed a ring around the Verge, with a clearing of fifty yards all around the Verge location.

With the clearing, the Verge was impossible to miss. An egg shaped aura of red-purple light lit the surrounding brush up like a jewel stuck on a vine. When we got close to the Verge, our group kept low in a field of dense brush and surveyed the area.

Off to the right, the ground rose up into cliffs at the far end. A stream made a natural boundary to our right. With all the trees around, it made great cover for us – but also for anyone who wanted a shot at us.

The sun shone bright and cast thousands of shadows everywhere in the woods. It was thick, but not enough that the light wasn't all over.

We stood at the edge of the woods before the stream. Otto was off to my left. He tried a scan of all heat sigs in the area, and any other possible intruders.

"You hear that?" I asked.

Nelson turned to me. "Huh? No."

"Exactly. That's the wrong kinda quiet."

"Mmmhm." Norg alternated between a manual weapon check of his rifle and a clenched brow while he looked at whatever the hell Otto was doing. I pointed to the woods and whispered to Norg, "Think we'll find anyone in there?"

He scanned the tree line for a moment. "That's where I'd be."

Nelson admired the Verge location, a glowing aura of reddish purple light.

"Pretty, isn't it?" I asked him.

He shook his head. "I'm beyond words."

I gathered the rest around closer. We all agreed we were too few for anything other than a straight run at the Verge.

"On my go," I said, "we sweep along the shoreline of the stream, and when we're one hundred feet from the Verge, start angling toward it. Circle around Nelson. Anyone or anything starts shooting at us, repel fire from wherever, got it?"

Everyone nodded. Nelson asked, "What do I do at the Verge, how does it work?"

"Your tether is set to the correct time. You step inside and that's it."

We eased along the shoreline, a ring of humans. My view shot to the trees, and darted around the rest of the area. It was quiet, except for a few birds. The air was crisp, like another few degrees cooler and I'd have shivered. It reminded me how it felt when I made my Verge jump. The memory made my gut clench. Unlike that time, there was no bunker, just fifty yards of open ground for us to run through.

"Easy does it," I whispered. "Good going, group. Keep it up."

I glanced back at the woods across from us. We were almost past 'em and ready for the beeline to the Verge.

A loud mechanized shriek froze us in position. My bones vibrated. I held my ears and glanced at the others in the group. It wasn't a Radomet call. I hadn't heard this one before, ever. Otto mouthed something to me, but I couldn't make it out. Nelson winced like he was slugged in the belly and Norg was, well, his usual chipper self.

The shrieks continued. The Verge remained unchanged, but some clouds moved in and darkened the area. I turned back to the group and waved 'em toward it, but then I noticed it.

Whatever it was wasn't ours or from Lebabolis. I'd never seen whatever this was before: a strange black craft with silver markings. The wings were decorated with odd shapes, a language maybe. Guns protruded from the front and sides, and they aimed in our direction.

Otto's lips were taut. He held his P-LAD up, his eyes widened. On screen was the message: Signature Unknown, Foreign Entity

The shrieking was replaced by a loudspeaker with a voice that spoke some weird language. The others shook their heads.

We stepped deeper into the woods, but the ship and its guns moved a little with us. Norg was already drawn on it; I bet his glare alone would've torn a hole into it.

Otto marveled at the craft. "Omegans."

"You sure?" I asked.

"Oh yes."

"What if I just made a break for it?" asked Nelson as he lurched a bit toward the Verge.

"Don't be stupid, prophet man." Norg spat and leaned toward Nelson. "One of those guns would turn you into chopped meat."

I grasped Nelson's shoulder. "Easy. We dunno they've seen us yet, but that's not your send off party."

The loudspeaker piped up again. This time, the message was clear.

"Halt, you are under arrest. Drop your weapons and prepare to be placed into custody."

I took a slow breath and held it. My hand gripped my rifle so tight I felt a burn course through my grip. My shoulders tightened. Then, I heard the response from our group: our pulse rifles activated. A smile found my lips. I glanced around for the best ground cover.

"The hell with this," Nelson said, and he bolted toward the Verge.

"No, dammit!" I yelled after him, but it was too late.

The Omegan craft opened fire. Its glowing pulse cannon shots perforated the ground around us and sent a shower of dirt, branches and leaves onto us. I crouched to the ground.

Nelson wobbled on his feet as the ground shook under the weapons fire, but he kept upright and on a twisting path toward the Verge.

My feet wanted to take off after him, but instead I froze in place. "Stop, Nelson, lie down, they're gonna -"

A large pop and a cloud of smoke billowed about where he was. My throat tightened. "Nelson!"

Norg and the others returned fire back at the ship. "I see him!" shouted Otto. "He's on the ground!"

We made it into the grove of trees. The others formed a line and gave the strange ship enough trouble so nothing else was fired toward Nelson.

I only hoped that was why they hadn't shot anymore in that direction.

I craned my neck and checked where everyone else was. "Otto!"

"Here!" he said off to my right.

"Let Norg and the rest handle this bird. You and I need to get Nelson and bring him back before that ship gets to him."

Otto fired a few shots, then responded, "Check. After you."

We took off and added to the barrage of cover fire our group provided. After a short sprint we got to Nelson. He lay face down on the charred ground.

I turned him over. His eyes were closed, and there was no visible sign of life from him. I grabbed his arm. "Grab the other side, Otto! Let's move!"

The ground shook all about us with the weapons fire and blasts that pummeled the ground and trees. My knees were so sore they almost buckled. But I tightened my grip and surged ahead back behind Norg and Treg, who still served a healthy barrage of return fire at the strange aircraft. We were almost back to the woods when a thump and a quick burst of heat hit us. I heard Otto's groan, and Nelson's body got heavier in my grip all of a sudden. We were still about twenty feet from the brush. Someone else helped with Nelson, and I pulled Otto behind a downed tree.

"Think of something fast!" Norg bellowed. "Not gonna last long here!"

The craft pivoted back and moved straight over the Verge. Several claws dropped from it toward the Verge center, and it stopped its barrage.

"They're harvesting it. I've got an idea. Everybody, on the ground!" I yelled.

I pointed my weapon at the center of the Verge. I fired several shots, and the sky burst into a brilliant display of light. The blast sent a wave of hot air over us. The ship exploded with a loud echoing blast that sent the remnants of it off in the distance, a trail of smoke behind it.

The trees about us shook, their leaves made a frantic and angry rustle. The glowing center of the Verge flickered and faded to nothing.

THIRTY-FOUR

(NELSON)

MY EYELIDS SPLIT THE DARKNESS into a smoky haze. I felt cool bristles of grass beneath me as I shifted around. My hearing was muffled, but I heard shouting voices.

The last thing I remembered was when I ran toward the Verge location, I heard this one loud pop. I felt a solid blow to my chest, like a punch, and I was knocked down to the ground. A few dark shapes entered my view, and after I focused on them a little I saw they were people. One knelt close and Ana's face came into a slight focus. Her lips moved but everything still sounded like I was underwater.

Finally, my hearing returned enough and I heard her ask, "Are you alright?"

My voice warbled in my ears. "Can't hear much. What the hell was that?"

She frowned in reply while she and someone else pulled me to a seated position in the woods. "Otto always said the Verges are nothing more than trapped energy. I figured this ol' pulse rifle could release a little of it."

The rest checked their gear. Treg held up an electronic device with antennas like a radio. Someone wheezed nearby. I craned my head and saw Otto as he clutched his side. A bit of blood oozed over his hand. Ana said, "Easy, Otto, keep pressure on that."

"The fuck we still doing here?" Norg bellowed from behind me. "Won't be long before another patrol comes by to take us down. Lebabolis, Omegans, don't matter. We're dead meat if we take on any kinda unit in our shape now." He circled around and met my eyes. "And you, prophet man, I thought I said don't be stupid. You got Otto shot up with that little stunt of yours."

"Norg, that's enough." Ana and Norg stared at each other like two dogs in a territorial dispute. He threw me another pointed glare before he lurched off.

I got on my knees for a second but was too sore for that. "I thought I could make it."

We watched Norg as he surveyed the Verge location. "He's always had a short fuse on him." She jabbed a finger in my face. "It doesn't excuse what you did. You better just hope Otto makes it, because Norg looks about as pissed as I've ever seen, and I can't promise I can stop him if he goes for you."

I looked past Ana to the Verge location. The spot that once glowed with such a brilliant light was gone. In its place was a tremendous black spot of charred ground. Thin trails of smoke billowed from the ground, and any foliage close enough to have survived smoldered with lingering flames. My eyes flickered and my nose wrinkled against the burnt air.

"Guess we need to find a new spot," I said.

Ana nodded. "My number one is we get as far the hell away from here as possible." Her eyes fell to Otto. "And watch him; I don't like that wound."

<hr>

TREG APPROACHED US. "Took me a minute to figure this thing out. This is more Intellectual Product stuff. I located the nearest

Encampment beacon but there's too much interference from the Valentium residue for any comm contact. We'll need to hump outta here for a bit so we can link up with whoever's closest."

Ana nodded. "Can you walk, Nelson? Otto needs more attention right now."

I got on my feet, but the ground still felt a little wobbly. Ana steadied me and I held onto her for a few seconds. After a few breaths I replied, "Yeah, t-think so. I'll be alright." I saw Norg from the corner of my eye, his stare spoke enough about his disgust of the situation, most of all me.

As I got a better footing I looked away from the Verge, and back toward where we came from. I hoped whatever location they had in mind wasn't too far away.

Zengus broke my train of thought. "Otto! No, no don't... We're losing him!"

Ana and Treg scurried over as Zengus laid Otto gently on his back. His eyes smashed shut in agony, his wheezing deepened and his legs twitched. Zengus worked fast while Ana and the others kept watch for what seemed like an hour. Ana stroked his forehead and his eyes opened for a moment. I heard nothing she said as she leaned in and comforted him as best she could.

Otto nodded toward one side and grasped for something. Ana pulled out a flat screen device and looked at it for awhile. "You want me to have this?" She held it up to his face.

He huffed and nodded. A few seconds later his eyes shut again.

"Otto, talk to me," Zengus commanded. "You're gonna make it."

Otto said nothing, he just lay still for awhile longer, with only his moving chest as any indication of his state. Soon that stopped too.

Zengus glanced at Ana and Treg and shook his head. Everyone froze for a few moments. It seemed like even the wind had stopped. Not even the birds I'd seen about made any noise. I felt pulled back to the house next to Mom's bed as she breathed her last. My gut tightened and I blinked the moisture that was no longer caused by the burning landscape.

Treg kicked the ground and ambled away, his arms folded. Ana cradled Otto's head in her hands. Then, after she eased him back to the ground, she punched the ground nearby. Her scream filled the air, its echoes jarred more tears from my eyes.

———

"THIS IS YOUR FAULT."

Norg broke the silence. My stomach tightened and I swallowed hard at his engorged eyes.

He clutched his rifle tight and paced. "What's so special about him? So he wrote a damned book, and he's hot shit around here. Well, I'm pretty damn sick of losing people I care about, and if that's what helping him's gonna mean, I'm out."

Ana still knelt over Otto, she was fixated on the device Otto had handed her.

Treg stepped toward him. "Norg. Ya know we had orders for this. This was part of our deal -"

"Screw that. Call me a deserter if you want. I'm getting as far away from him as I can."

"And go where?" Ana neared my side and she slid Otto's device in her pocket. "You think I'd stay any longer than I needed to? This changes things. That ship, whoever they are, changes things. Maybe we don't know who's out there, but I sure as hell know who's right here."

She stepped around us in a circle. "We grew up together, Norg. You, me, Treg, Otto. What was it we used to say?"

Norg said, "Gonna grab the world—"

"-And make it ours," Ana completed. "We were young. Proud Products in that system. Gonna go and make a difference. And yeah, it was the wrong system. And Baudricort tried to set it right. I'm not saying he didn't make his own mistakes too, but I believe he's the one that's gonna get us there one day. We have to follow through. Everyone deserves to go home."

"Like Otto?" Norg said. "Is he worth less than Nelson?"

Ana's gaze lingered on Norg, then fell to Otto's body. She approached Norg until they were eye to eye. "Of course not. Look, I wasn't for Baudricort's game of cut, run and send Link messages. Otto believed, like Baudricort did, like all of you do, about giving us a fresh start. But oh, there's Cataclysm too. Well, Otto's just given me something on that."

"What do you mean?" Treg asked.

"It's schematics on that P-LAD. I think it's some kind of weapon."

"It's a weapon?" Norg asked.

"Looks that way. And all over these files are notes about Cataclysm."

Treg stopped his calculations and looked at me, along with the rest of them.

"Baudricort put Nelson on the Link and did a pull. He got him to give some coordinates when he asked where Cataclsym was."

I shifted on the ground. It was all I could do right then. Ana watched over me before she looked at the rest of the group. "You all know I'd do anything for you guys, and I know you'd do the same. Tell me right here and now, do any of you know about Cataclysm?"

Treg and the rest said no.

Ana's eyes narrowed. "I don't know what he's thinking, or why he and even Otto kept this quiet like this. But if it's that secret, if Baudricort's been that tight about it, I've gotta think it's worth a whole lot, maybe even to Charista."

"She could try a pull on us if she thought any of us knew, like the honcho did on Nelson." Treg commented.

I clasped my hands. "I saw her communicating with Baudricort at an Encampment. I'm getting in Baudricort's face as soon as I can and we're finding this thing. That could be what we need to get Lebabolis to let our people go, maybe even more."

"Look, we gotta leave now," Treg said. "Longer we stay, the less luck we'll have here." He swallowed and eyed us. "Someone carry Otto."

"Me," Norg replied as he ambled toward Otto's body.

We left the wooded area in a single line that snaked over the open ground. Treg walked in front with Ana. Norg walked behind me. No one talked for a long time. Whatever device Treg used earlier made beeping noises. He stopped and examined it.

"OK, better access point," he said. While he tapped the controls Ana walked over to me.

"How're you holding up?"

"Alright I guess. Look, about Otto. I'm sorry."

She eyed me. "Even without your stunt there were slim odds of everyone making it. But remember what I said."

"Of course."

Ana looked over to Treg. "These beacon sweeps can take a few minutes, better relax while we can." We grabbed a seat on the ground. While the trees were set back a bit from us, the ground still had a bit of grass that sprouted from between the rocks and gravel.

Ana swept her legs up underneath her and leaned on her rifle in thought. Her hair slid over her eyes. Her jawbone twitched.

"So did you know that girl with Brenn when you grabbed me?"

Her gaze was somewhere else but she answered, "Nycole. Yep."

"Guess she's somebody important to be escorting a prisoner like me."

She glanced to me, then back to her rifle. "Mmmhm. Treg knew her better than me, being a Warrior Product." She sighed. "Nycole was one of the best Warrior Products in school. Wouldn't be surprised if they made her an officer in the Security Force by now."

"So, why are you still helping me, after all this, and now with what happened to Otto?"

She pondered for a few moments. "Because he'd want me to."

"Baudricort?"

"Varrick." She smiled a bit. "When he was a little younger, but able to move around and talk, I used to tell him about taking care of family, and people who needed help. He'd ask 'how do I know who needs help?' and I'd say you'd know when you saw 'em."

"You keep saving me. How am I ever going to pay you back?"

She managed a half smile then glanced away. The little girl and now Otto joined my growing dread over leaving these people. And those coordinates I'd come out with, like I recited my home address, I had no idea where that came from. But they had to make it, and for whatever reason for all of this, I was the one they needed to get there.

My thoughts wandered to Mom, and I wondered about her take on this situation. She always taught me if I made a mess, I cleaned it up. But this wasn't dirty dishes in the sink. If I helped them in this mission and we failed, was that it for me?

I squinted a bit as the sun peeked from behind a cloud over us. A sharp ache hit me on the side of my head and a throbbing built between my temples. I glanced away from the sun, maybe I'd watched it too close.

The pain remained though, and the throbbing intensified. My lip quavered.

Ana's voice echoed in my head. "Nelson?" And everything went black.

THIRTY-FIVE

(ANA)

I KNELT OVER NELSON and checked his signs. "Zengus, anything in your med pack for reviving someone?"

Zengus brought his kit over. "Few things; lemme see."

I felt a slight pulse in his neck, but his skin was fiery to the touch. Zengus slipped a pill between Nelson's lips. "Displacement sickness?"

"I guess. Otto said no one's ever gone that far from base time before."

Treg walked over. "What happened?"

"Nelson passed out."

Treg cringed. "Got a fix on the nearest Encampment. Gonna be at least three hours walk. More if we're hauling these two."

Norg stood back at a distance and watched Zengus work on Nelson. I motioned Treg off to the side. "Ya know, Otto passed something to me before he died."

"Oh?"

I pulled the device out. "Yeah. You gotta see this." I activated the device. It was similar to P-LADs, but it didn't have any individual ID data.

Treg eyed the displays. "What are these schematics for?"

"I dunno. Treg, Baudricort tried to pull something out of Nelson the last time we were with him."

"Yeah? Like what?"

"He asked him about Cataclysm, where it was. I've never heard him say much about it, but all of a sudden he's curious about where it is. Does that make any sense to you?"

"Not really. But we gotta know he's onto more than he's talking about. Maybe he found out how Cataclysm starts, or at least how it moves."

It pissed me off that I had to dig around like this for something Baudricort could damn well just 'fess up. He played us sometimes almost as much as he played Charista and Lebabolis.

Treg clutched my arm. "Look, we gotta move. Let's bring this to the honcho. He's got explaining to do."

I looked at Otto's body and over to Norg as he stood and watched the area, his rifle at the ready. "We have to bury Otto first."

"Norg won't like that."

My voice hitched and a tear stung my eye. "You think I do? This is what the Action does and I'm damned if I let one of us... us... not get that respect. We owe him, Treg, and you know that."

Treg and I explained things to Norg as Zengus tended to Nelson. I'd seen burials in the Action before, but this was the first time it was someone so close to me, and someone from this group. One of our circle was gone.

I looked around for several minutes until I found a good spot. Otto deserved to be in a place where some wild animal wouldn't root through to find his body. I settled on a patch of rocks under a few trees for Otto. Treg and Norg dug the grave and buried him. Afterwards, we stood around for a few minutes. No one spoke. Part of me hoped we were wrong, that he wasn't really dead, and while they laid him in the ground his eyes would've opened. But he gave us nothing but complete stillness.

Once I'd accepted his absence, the words found me. "He believed in the Action, and in us. He loved us, and we loved him too."

Norg's jaw clenched. "Rest easy, bro. You're with us always."

I grasped Norg's shoulder. He flinched at my touch, but he nodded even though his gaze never left Otto's grave. "One or none."

A PAINFUL SUN beat several hours later while we trudged into Encampment 2. After we delivered Nelson to the medics, we found a bit of rest ourselves for a few hours. The raging soreness in my back eased a little once my body surrendered to a nap.

After I woke up, I contacted Baudricort on the comm and filled him in on our failed mission.

"Damn, glad you made it out of there."

"We were lucky. Except for Otto."

"What happened to him?"

I sucked in a breath and held it. Even though I'd seen it, I had trouble getting the words out. "He's gone."

Baudricort just stared back at me. His eyes widened and his head shook. "No, no, this can't be happening."

"Afraid so."

He dropped his head down. When he looked back up, his eyes darted about the way he did when he worked on an emergency Encampment Relo, but he was quiet.

"We lost a Verge point too."

He squinted. "How's that?"

"I blasted it."

His eyes shot open. "You did what?"

"It's a pocket of energy. We had a massive ship baring down on us. What the hell else was I supposed to-"

He nodded and shook his head fast. "No, no, you're right. I just never realized you knew about that."

"Otto told me once." The name hurt when I said it. But it felt good that he got the credit here. Even if this one had cost him his life.

"Ana, I'm sorry about Nelson. I wanted to find Cataclysm, and I thought not telling you about it would protect you." He sighed. "I never can tell how much they've got us under the Link even during the day. I thought playing this one close would be safer."

His brow wrinkled and he glanced away.

"I'm gonna be there whenever you talk with him again. Sorry, I just don't trust you alone with him after that. I think you can understand."

He watched me with sad eyes. "I'm coming there. I know some more Verge points you can try, and there's some other gear you can use."

"How soon can you make it here?"

"I can be there in a few hours. Will get you in the Admin room when I do."

"OK, see you then. Out."

***

I FOUND KADO, another of the Intellectual Products. He'd observed Nelson since we arrived.

"Ana, I don't know what's going on with him!"

"It's the Verge, right? The big gap between his base time and now?" I asked, exasperated.

"We're giving him several medications. He's stable, but I don't know why he passed out like that. It all points to the Tether. Best I can tell, the chip in his device may be malfunctioning. That's the best theory we have, but right now it's just that. Whatever happens, we can't let his Tether break, or-"

His gaze drifted off and the worry on his face spread to me. "Will he die?"

Kado gazed at me and searched for his reply. He wouldn't have soft sold anything to me. "You know I'll do whatever I can to stop that, right?"

He winced and gave a polite smile.

"I've got a P-LAD from Otto with some things on it. Maybe you can find out some other options for treating him."

"I don't think there's anything else I-"

I waved him quiet. "Find something, Kado. I'm not losing him. OK?"

THIRTY-SIX

(ANA)

WHILE THEY TENDED TO NELSON, I pulled out Otto's P-LAD and scoured it with Treg. All the maps I ever saw, all the plotting I watched Baudricort, Llewyn and the others doing, nothing ever showed up like this.

The maps showed the Range that Baudricort mentioned, with some paths marked. The notes on it were scribbled, and a lot of things were scratched out. And then there was the device. That's what we called it, since it wasn't clear what the hell it was. A series of tubes and control modules, the diagram was not very clear, but one word on it was: Cataclysm.

Treg scratched his head. "What do you make of those schematics?"

"Could be some kind of shelter – or maybe an escape vehicle. They put 'Cataclysm' on it, maybe it's some kind of counter device, something to negate the effects? I turned to Treg. "I couldn't understand much of what Otto said near the end, but he kept repeating 'Find it', and pointed to this thing."

"It's in the Range somewhere. But that thing's got to be over a thousand miles wide. If it's even in there somewhere, we'll be looking a long time unless we have some kind of clue."

Baudricort brushed everyone off who asked about Cataclysm. Had he known about these records? Otto was his number one with Tech. Wouldn't they have discussed this? And if it was something for Cataclysm, why wouldn't he have mentioned it to the Action as a group?

"Hey, how about this?" Treg tapped the screen, which revealed an archive on screen. It was a bunch of notes:

I don't have long, but I need to pass this on to someone. I hope whoever finds this knows what kind of terrible weapon is here, and that it must be destroyed. I wanted to destroy it, I should have. It was my responsibility. The Valkyrie protects, and the existence of the Cataclysm device puts the world in danger.

The person who created Cataclysm as well as myself know what people will do to get it. I'm including specific instructions for shutting down this device, but it can only be shut down in a certain way. My troops and I are overrun, and I don't have much more time. I've initiated a safety sequence, the instructions for operating it are contained in these files.

For my failure at this, my calling, the creator of Cataclysm who is so much more to me than that, and for the one other thing I've lost that hurts me the most, I have no adequate explanation other than when faced with the deepest, darkest tyranny, I did all that was left in my power to keep this weapon, and the world, safe.

To whoever finds this, if you feel any inkling of light in your soul, find whatever courage and strength you need to complete destroying this Cataclysm device. If you have other ideas, may this device burn you from the inside out.

The Valkyrie

I READ the words over and over, tried to take them in and hoped that I wasn't imagined things. Cataclysm was a device? Baudricort was always pretty clear that he knew it existed, but he had never said anything about finding it, or that it was something anyone needed to find anyway. Was he trying to keep it a secret and hope no one found out about it?

"Did Otto tell you about this?" I asked Treg.

He shook his head. "I knew about weapons, but this is way beyond anything that they'd give to a Warrior Product." He pointed to the screen. "Says here it causes massive destruction, upends the gravitational field, even reverses polarity."

"Is this what they used back then? Total catastrophic damage," I muttered. "Under someone's control. Wonder how the Valkyrie got it?"

"We can ask the old man, but as little as he's said about it so far, don't know what he'd give up now."

AFTER AN HOUR of tests and some medication, Nelson was better. I sat with him in his room while Treg contacted Baudricort on the comm. Treg and I figured that we needed to corner Baudricort on Cataclysm, and from what we had seen in Otto's P-LAD, the sooner the better.

Nelson reclined on the bed. He winced whenever he moved. "We gotta stop meeting like this."

"How are you feeling?" I patted his leg.

"Eh, alright I suppose. I just kind of dropped out, it felt like I was some kind of kitchen appliance plugged in and running and someone just yanks the power cord out and I keel over."

"I talked to the medic. They gave you some medication that should slow that down. They think it's related to your tether and just the general time sickness."

"Oh great, was afraid you'd say something like that. I gotta keep this doohickey on but it's gonna make me pass out every now and then."

"It is what it is, for now," I said. "Look, I know having a look at anything to do with Cataclysm or something Baudricort might be interested in is about the last thing on your mind at this point, but I've got some maps about that Cataclysm Treg and I were trying to make sense of. Wanna have a look?"

He squirmed a bit. "Well, seeing as how he's not around to give me the anal probe or something, why not. Whatcha got?"

I laid the P-LAD on his lap and stood over his shoulder. I flipped it through the screens slow, taking a few minutes to give him time to take it all in. The schematics, I flipped past them. The mountain ranges came up next. I cycled through the maps and ranges for a few seconds, and then he grabbed the P-LAD firm in his hands. His whole body tensed like a statue, and for a second I thought he was having a seizure.

"You OK?"

He chewed on his lip. "You ever see something and feel like you've seen it before somewhere?"

"Maybe."

His eyes locked on this image, and his hands held the P-LAD so tight I wondered if it would crack. "It's right there. I don't know why I do, but I've got this feeling and I'm telling you, save this and we'll use it to find that thing, I'm sure of it."

<hr>

TREG CAME in after a few minutes and grabbed a seat. "The honcho's headed here. Should be another hour or so. What's doing with the maps; Nelson get anything out of them?"

"Oh yeah, he did." I nudged Nelson. He smiled for the first time since he had collapsed in the field. "We should move on this soon, gotta figure out a way. If we can grab Cataclysm, we'd get all these jokers lined up to deal with us. We wouldn't need Charista, or Baudricort, or even the Omegans."

"Yeah, but what do we have to do to get there?" Treg shrugged.

"We're looking at several hundred miles easy, over open ground, and with whatever firepower we can muster up. Baudricort's not gonna give us whatever we need; I'd be surprised if he does. There's too much to protect and he's got too many other people out in the open still. No, Ana."

"He was damn near about to cut this guy's head open to find Cataclysm if I hadn't offered to rearrange his face with my blade."

"Right, but also remember how secret he kept it all. What makes you think he wants us to be anywhere near it?"

I watched the monitors that tracked Nelson's signs and thought about the rest of the Action. I wondered if I still had that reputation with people out there. "Maybe we don't need Baudricort."

"How so?"

"I can talk to people. They have to be tired, at least some of them, tired of always running. Betcha most don't even know why they're still on Exodus anymore. Maybe if I tell them what we're running to, give them something they can latch onto. All people need is something they can see. A goal, an idea."

"But what idea? Cataclysm is dangerous. You saw what the Valkyrie said about it. And she hid it pretty well."

I grabbed the P-LAD and studied the map Nelson was so excited about. It was a long way, sure. And I didn't know what kind of group we'd get on this. I figured Treg, Norg, Zengus were locks. But we needed more. A vehicle or two, some air cover even. We were just too thin to make a run.

"I'll talk with Baudricort. He and I have an – understanding."

THIRTY-SEVEN

(ANA)

ONCE BAUDRICORT ARRIVED at Nelson's room at the Encampment, the three of us laid it all on him: the P-LAD, the messages from the Valkyrie, Nelson's gut response to the pictures of the Range.

Baudricort eyed the screen with the Valkyrie's note. He ran his finger over the letters, his eyes damp. "It was so long ago," he half muttered to himself.

"You OK?" I asked.

After a few more moments, he said, "Yeah, I'm good." He leaned back, his arms folded. "Suppose I can't keep this secret any longer."

We all stared at him.

He stood and paced, his hands kneaded together like he was trying to escape from invisible handcuffs. "Cataclysm was a project began by Charista years ago. She, like many of the Coursons, thought if they could somehow harness the destructive power of what Cataclysm was supposed to be in Xander's book, we'd have the ultimate defense."

"Or weapon," I muttered.

Baudricort held his hand up to me. "It was intended as defense.

And the Valkyrie saw to it that was the only reason for it. But then things changed. The Omegan armies invaded. Charista had a choice: she could let the Lebabolis Army, led by the Valkyrie, turn back the Omegans, or they could try using Cataclysm.

"It was risky, either way. Letting the Lebabolis ground and air forces fight it out was sure to cost many lives, and may have not ended well at all. But Cataclysm was untested. There was no way of knowing it wouldn't backfire and cause even worse damage on Lebabolis.

"The Valkyrie argued against Cataclysm. She and Charaista were close, but on this they parted ways.

"Cataclysm was fired. It turned back the Omegans, but it also damaged some settlements in the Outlands. People who'd lived independent of Lebabolis for many years were killed. Charista dismissed it as collateral damage and loss of those less worthy than the Products of Lebabolis.

"The Valkyrie attempted to take out Charista, but the attempt failed. Then, in a late night raid, she stole Cataclysm away and hid it. No one except the Valkyrie's most loyal troops knew where it was. She returned and was pressed to find out where it was hidden. But the Valkyrie held fast. There was no breaking her. Charista knew as I and the Coursons did that breaking the Valkyrie's mind was impossible. Still, she tried. She then ordered the Valkyrie and her troops sent for Realignment."

"So that's what happened to her." I shook my head.

"No, not quite. I helped her. I forged the system records that made it look like she and the rest received Realignment. I also helped her unit escape north, made that look like they overpowered the security. They were part of the Regiment so it wasn't a big stretch. But the Valkyrie was locked up, and I never saw her again."

Nelson propped himself up on his elbows. "Who built Cataclysm, Baudricort?"

The question hung in the air like early morning fog. Baudricort's brow creased, and a few beads of sweat formed. He looked at Nelson, then the rest of us. But he still said nothing. He didn't have to, I knew the answer.

"You did." I stood up, my arms folded. His eyes tracked to me. I stepped toward him. "All this time, it was you. You were running from all your mistakes. MODOSNet... Realignment... and Cataclysm."

"Ana." Treg stood up.

Baudricort folded his arms. He heaved a bit and bit his lip.

I stood right next to Baudricort. "Why didn't you say anything? Tell anyone?" A million thoughts flooded my brain. On one hand, I wanted to pummel him for what he had put Nelson through, and what we all went through, before and after Exodus.

But his beaten look, his wild eyes like those of a starved animal, made me freeze in place. I looked on him with a mixture of helplessness and mild anger.

When he spoke again, his voice shook. "The Link ties you all into Lebabolis. Not just when you're asleep. They can pull information from you as well as send. That's what I tried with Nelson." He glanced to the bed. "I'm sorry for that. I'm in a horrible spin, and I'm trying to do what I can to fix it."

He stood up and faced me. "They used me. My ideas, my plans. I only wanted to rebuild. They wanted to restrict, refine, in their image. I learned later, there was no stopping Charista. The Valkyrie did too. We wanted the same thing, but we figured on different ways of getting it done. She wanted to cut the head off, but I wanted to eat away at the system over time. With messages, with cracks. Enough breaks in a wall and it will tumble."

"But you both lost." I paced about. I grabbed for the P-LAD. "But here, we've got something. At least we know where Cataclysm is."

"You'll get Charista's interest with that, but she'll never let you live if she knows you know where it is. Remember that. She needs that way more than you." Baudricort leaned against the wall.

"So what's the move here?" Treg asked.

Nelson cleared his throat. "We've got another leg up on her. I know where Cataclysm is, to the exact spot. I feel it when I see the map of the area. But I'm not connected to your Link system. So that makes me collateral, or at the very least, valuable."

"We need to get to the site, but with the Omegans and Lebabolis hunting for us and each other, it's a crapshoot heading straight there. They'd pick off a convoy like ducks. We have to throw in with one of them, at least for the time being." Ana crossed her arms.

"An uneasy alliance. You're going to have to disable it though. If Charista or the others get ahold of this and it isn't shut down, one flick of the switch and they'll upend the world," Baudricort said. "Let me see the rest of the P-LAD information from Otto.

He manipulated the screens on the device for a few minutes. "Otto and I worked on the codes here. The Valkyrie included the shut down sequence. She didn't even tell me in case they tried to pull it through on a Link. So, she coded it. I'll need a little time to work on that."

Baudricort took off for the tech lab with the P-LAD to decipher what he could out of the Valkyrie's message while Treg and I stayed with Nelson. His strength came back more and he even stood up a little bit, walking and talking with us.

We discussed Charista and what we imagined her response would be. If she would even make a deal with us after she had an idea of what we knew.

"She's gonna need proof," Treg said. "No way in hell she'll buy anything from us without that. And how do we prove something in Nelson's head?"

"What if she hooks me up to a Link and pulls it out?" Nelson asked.

"Well, maybe. But I'm not leaving you alone with her. As bad as Baudricort got with you, Miss Queen Baddie will make that look like baby steps."

"We'll need to get her attention too. She won't just come up for anyone trying to raid the border of Lebabolis," Treg said.

"All we need to do is flash that schematic. I bet if any of this means anything to her, that will. That's our plan, OK?"

They looked at the device and me, and nodded.

Nelson got to his feet and managed some wobbled steps around the room. He still winced, but his strength returned a little bit at a time. "Think I'm getting it here."

"Looks that way. You better not overdo it; if you're gonna be traveling with us to the Border, you'll need some strength." I glanced at Treg. He eyed me for a second, and he blinked his eyes as if in receipt of the wordless message I had just sent.

Treg stood up. "I'm finding you a weapon, Nelson. If we're going to be a small group, everybody needs some heat."

Treg headed to the supply closet. I guided Nelson back to the bed. He watched me as I picked his feet up off the floor. "Think this'll work?"

"The Border, the deal with Charsista? Can't say I don't have my doubts, but if I know anything about her, she's in it for the power and glory, and that's what Cataclysm is for her."

A loud blast echoed in the hall outside the room, and the lights dimmed.

"Raid?" Nelson asked.

Yelling came from the other side, people coughing and struggling about. I got to the floor and crawled over to the door, eased it open to a billow of dust. I winced and looked back into the room, coughing a bit. Then I was able to see more into the hallway. I took off to find out what happened.

Action soldiers flit about the area, some bumped into me as they moved past in one direction or another. After a few minutes of this, I spotted Treg near the end of a hallway. There was a pile of rubble near him, and he worked with some Action soldiers to clear it out.

"I didn't hear any Hell Hawks. They're getting sneakier."

"That's because there were none." Treg stopped and looked at me, his eyes wild. "This was an inside job."

My gut ached at the idea. We had heard about plants and saboteurs in the Action, but this was as close as they'd ever gotten to one of us. I looked at the rubble pile and recognized the markings on the walls. When I did, my heart sunk more.

Treg watched me and reached for me. "Ana, it's the Tech lab-"

He didn't need to say anything more. I threw myself into the effort, helping to pull pieces back. "Baudricort!" I screamed. "Can you hear us?"

Treg tried to pull me from the pile of debris, but I refused. In a few minutes there was hole big enough to get into the room. Black scorches covered the walls, and the smell of smoke from the hallway was way more intense. Baudricort lay on his back, the P-LAD from Otto damaged and resting in his hands.

"No!" I screamed, and dropped to the floor. I scampered over to his side. Seeing me near him, he smiled. His face was burned pretty bad. His teeth stood out sharp against his deep red charred flesh.

He took a breath, but he heaved and broke into coughs.

"They're calling medical; they'll be here soon." I laid a hand on his head.

He shook his head and looked at me. His eyes filled with tears, and his lips drew into a line. "I'm sorry it happened like this."

I turned back toward the hole I had entered and yelled, "Can we get some medical in here now! Baudricort is hurt. Bad!"

A medic slipped into the room and rushed to Baudricort's other side, where he started an IV and worked on whatever he could to make him more comfortable. He gave me a grim look, but I just pointed back toward Baudricort. "You keep going; he's still with us."

"That's my—girl." Baudricort rasped amid several coughs.

"What are you talking about? I'm one of those you rescued, that's all."

He shook his head. "There was never time for telling you everything. Your mother and I weren't the same Product, I didn't want you in any danger. So I forged the records in MODOSNet and had you brought to another family. People sympathetic to the Action."

A tear rolled down his face. My throat clenched, and I felt a queasiness set in. My vision blurred. I felt like I'd lived in a house for so many years, and now it had crumbled with just one statement, just a collection of words strung together made walls smashed, doors splintered, windows disintegrated. Made me undone.

I looked back to Baudricort and realized it was tears in my eyes. "Y-you're my father."

He nodded. "I wanted you out, but if anyone ever found out you were mine, you wouldn't have a chance. You'd be captured and used as ransom. You never asked for any of this; I did what I thought would protect you."

My throat was still tightened, and I felt my voice break. "I saw my parents taken away. My brother, my— Do I even have a brother? Who am I?"

"You absolutely do have a brother. You love him and he loves you. Nothing ever changes that." He gasped for air before he continued. "Ana, you've got to take this." He slid a datapod into my hand. "It's got what we talked about on it. Keep it safe."

I slipped the device into my shirt pocket and clutched his hand. My trembling increased, and the ache of what I'd just learned poured through every inch of me. "You can't leave me."

He shut his eyes tight in response and grit his teeth. The medic continued his efforts, but I wondered if the only thing keeping him going was my denial of what was really happening.

"Hey, stay with me." I watched this man I'd seen for so long, like it was the first time I'd gazed at him. How could this be my father? How could this be, how could any of this be?

Baudricort's eyes shut. The medic thrust his hands onto his chest and manipulated his cavity for several minutes. But the denial I felt wasn't strong enough. Neither was Baudricort. I slumped backward on a piece of broken wall and let the sobs flow out of me. My father was dead.

THIRTY-EIGHT

(ANA)

"GET AWAY FROM ME, TREG."

He met me after I left the room. He reached for me, but I held my arms close.

"Ana, what?"

I shook my head, a few tears flung from my face. "Treg, I need a few."

He looked over my shoulder to the room, then back to me. "I don't under-"

I brushed past him; my voice almost broke into sobs. "Later, Treg. Tell you later."

I found a quiet spot in the Encampment in a storage room and slumped against a wall. The pain overtook me for a few minutes. Thoughts rushed past me like a stream. I felt like I was about to drown any second.

Baudricort, my father, was gone.

Just the fact I knew that now felt weird. Everything I'd known up until then was wrong. Why had he hidden it from me, to protect me or just himself?

I never thanked him for what he did for me and Varrick. My brother. Was he still my brother?

Everything was unraveled. Had Baudricort known how grateful I was for what he did? Maybe, or maybe not, since we never had time to say thank you in the Action.

We had ammo with Cataclysm, but everyone was scattered by distance, and now even more without our leader. Baudricort was the glue of the Action. It was up to Llewyn now. Did he know what Baudricort did about Cataclysm?

Whether he did or not, Llewyn was in charge. If people rallied around him, maybe this wasn't for nothing.

I thought again about what Remy had said about my real parents. Had he known this, too? That little sniveler.

I pulled my knees in and wrapped my arms around my legs. I wanted away from this more than ever at that moment. I had a bad feeling Varrick was dead anyway. In my sea of worry, one thought appeared like the jagged rocks of a cliff: Varrick was and always would be my brother. Blood or not, nothing ever changed that for me.

My thoughts drifted to the girl I was during Exodus, and what I did and why so many people look at me different. No one said anything about it to my face, but I saw it in their eyes, the way they looked at me. Sometimes I imagined what they thought. *How did she do that? She's a Worker Product, there is no way. You can't be serious.* My Exodus had started like most of the others did. A team of Action soldiers came by my housing unit and got Varrick and me out overnight. We went into this transport vehicle that made it look like a routine maintenance haul. Thirteen others joined Varrick and me. Treg and Brent, two Warrior Products, handled the security. Until I saw Treg, I was afraid we'd just be picked off. Somehow, the sight of his face made me feel safer.

Our ride through the Sector was pretty quiet for a half hour or so. I watched the empty roads from out the rear of the truck. The streets were empty, of course. Curfew in Lebabolis wasn't something people tested. Anything to not be marked as a Deviant.

I shuddered when a cold blast of air stabbed through me. Everyone else in the back was quiet, which suited me fine. I figured they were as nervous as I was, and I preferred to pretend they were invisible instead. All I had for company were the low hum of the truck and the creaking of the seats and sides of the vehicle when we hit a bump in the road.

The whine alarms of Lebabolis Security broke my calm and sent my gut into a tight knot. The truck shuddered to a halt, and we heard a voice on loudspeaker: "Halt and exit the vehicle for work order inspection!"

There was no other sound for a few seconds, but then the doors opened and blasts of pulse fire echoed in the darkness. Within seconds, the security patrol rained fire on us. The flashes of pulse weapons lit the night, and small bands of hot air whipped by outside with the volleys. A few passed through the roof area of the truck. Varrick crouched low, his arms wrapped around my waist. There were no weapons in the back. The trip was supposed to be a quick pass over the border and then we were home free.

A loud pop came from near the front of our vehicle, and someone yelled in agony. My throat squeezed and my ears rang while I wondered who it was. The rest in the back of the truck braced low. These people, like me, were all Worker Products. We were never taught anything about combat, except for what we saw demonstrated by the warriors in school.

Of course, I had a little after school learning of my own.

The fear I felt everywhere began a turn. I stroked Varrick's hair and kissed him, then popped to my feet. My pulse thumped in my throat. The commotion outside hadn't stopped, and the shots that pierced the truck got more frequent. I looked at the rest in the back, my fellow Products, cowered down like beaten dogs. Distress flowed into disgust. Anxiety into anger. By the time I leapt from the truck my temper raged.

I thought back to one of Treg's many lessons: "Anger's good in a fight, but don't let it overtake you. Stay focused, stay driven. Protect yourself and yours, then attack with abandon."

I kept low and crawled up toward the front of the vehicle on the driver side. Smoke billowed from that side, and someone lay back on the windshield, a pulse rifle clutched in their hand. When I got close I made out Brent's profile, the side that wasn't a charred mess of burned flesh. Treg stood up on the other side. He fired at the patrol and kept them busy.

The Lebabolis patrol stood near their vehicle, at least three regular soldiers and one Radomet. They were so busy with Treg, they hadn't noticed when I yanked the pulse rifle from Brent's grip to my side. I dropped back low to the ground and crawled near the front tire. The Radomet lurched forward and activated its flamethrower when I sprung to my feet and answered with my own barrage.

Everyone was taken off guard, even Treg. He took out the two regular Lebabolis security troops, but the Radomet shifted to me. An electronic snarl vibrated from it, and its face locked in on me. Its red eyes bored into me. I'd heard Radomets could paralyze someone just by long enough eye contact. But at that point, I couldn't care less. Part of me almost wanted it to strike me. The rage sweltered in me as I stepped toward it and fired at it with everything that weapon had.

Shots glanced off its armor without damage, but it was still knocked a bit off balance by the impact. I walked toward it and fired more. Treg yelled behind me, "Stand clear, I'm gonna ram it!"

I aimed right for the Radomet's head and released one more barrage. It tried a swipe at my head, but it was uncentered enough that it stumbled. I jumped aside, and Treg floored it. The truck rammed the Radomet and knocked it to the ground. I scrambled over to the driver's side, and he hoisted me up before he sped us away.

"You good?" Treg asked.

I laid the rifle down and adjusted in the passenger seat. I took a few deep breaths, my inner inferno calmed to a low simmer again. "Yeah, I'm OK."

"I'd ask where you learned how to do that, but I think I know already."

A smile found my face. "You should."

"The honcho's gonna love this, Ana. You should think about helping more once we're in the Outlands."

I watched his eager expression when he talked about the Action, something I hadn't ever shared. "Thanks, but I'm making a break as soon as I can."

Was that girl still here?

———

AFTER LLEWYN SENT word to the entire cadre about Baudricort, everyone met at Encampment 8 for a discussion of our next move. Of course, no one knew who planted the bomb or whatever had killed Baudricort. All anyone had were ideas and theories so far.

Of course, there was also what I saw on Otto's P-LAD. No one else said a thing about it. I was more than done with secrecy, and I had a good verbal salvo ready for them.

The meeting room at Encampment 8 was larger than the rest, and no gear on the walls crowded our group in. The cadre, the group of leaders right under Baudricort, were there. Most of 'em were in charge of individual Encampments as well. Kaitlinn, chief of Encampment 13, sat next to Llewyn. She studied something on the table in front of her as Llewyn spoke. "We've got to continue with Baudricort's plan and get to the Range before Cataclysm hits."

Other suggestions flew about in the discussion. Destroying Valentium deposits, staking out locations for Valentium, guarding 'em better, poisoning the water system, and on.

Several squabbled about Baudricort. Others said they wanted out of the Action altogether, that even attendance at the meeting was dangerous if their leader was killed that easily.

I looked around the room. These were the uppers of the Action.

Most were in it from the start. They were many of the best and brightest of Lebabolis. All were in heated discussions and arguments, the room filled with their rumbles. Llewyn tried for order, but it was useless.

Nelson shook his head at it all.

"What do you know about Cataclysm?" I blurted out.

The room chatter died down. Llewyn eyed me. "The same thing you and everyone else does?"

With that I strode to the console on the desk. I pulled out my datapod and held it up to Llewyn. His brow creased, but he said nothing.

I placed the datapod into the port and opened the schematic on the main screen. "We're running from Cataclysm, and all this time I figured it was some natural disaster that would hit at any point." I looked to Llewyn. "It's not, is it?"

"Where did you get this?" Llewyn's eyes were wide. The room looked to him.

"Baudricort. He and Otto were working on this."

Voices and chatter in the room built again. People craned to look at the schematic, and the discussions ignited.

The discussions started up again and built to a low roar. Llewyn's voice met the rising clamor. "Let's have order in here." He swung his head back to me. "You know we've been avoiding a war, right? All the raids, and the Omegans around. Baudricort had to manage a lot of people and facilities to get Exodus to happen, and we're still not done."

After the room settled again, he said, "I know Baudricort developed this weapon at Charista's request, and it was tested, but then lost because of the Valkyrie."

"Lost? Try hidden." I slammed my fingers on the controls and pulled up the Range maps. Nelson groaned off to my right, his eyes twitched at the sight.

"Nelson over here, better known as Xander, has located where the Cataclysm device is. It's in the Range we're headed toward. But out of a few thousand miles, he's pinned it down to one particular spot."

Llewyn's glare lay on me as the room billowed in surprised conversation. "Just what are you suggesting then, Crucinal?"

I shut off the display and strode about the room. I caught a few glances of people, focused, maybe a little intrigued even. Kaitlinn, one of the Encampment commanders, sneered at me.

"Charista knows this exists, and I think it's obvious that's at least one reason she's raided us. She knows her guy developed it and thinks he still has it."

I circled the room and arrived back at my seat. "They've been chasing us halfway across the Outlands, they won't stop. The Omegans, are out too. We ran into them at a Verge and it cost one of our brightest people."

Nelson nodded.

"If we go it as we've been, it's not going to take her too much longer to separate us, and finish us off. Remember Encampment 7?"

Llewyn folded his arms. He glanced off in thought for a few moments. "You're not going to suggest we try and make peace with the people we've been escaping, are you?"

"No way." I planted my hands on the table. "I suggest we bargain. They want this thing, we know where it is."

The room gasped. I stood back up. "This war you're talking about is here. We're in it, and yes, I think the people from Encampment 7 knew that too. But if we don't get to this thing first, and Charista does, we're all doomed. She'll turn it on to destroy the Omegans and who the hell knows who else in the process. Or if we deal with her, we can control how we face her. She toked our moves all long. It's time we take control."

"You're setting yourself and anyone with you up for a slaughter."

"More than we already are? How can we keep Exodus up when we can just barely make supply runs to keep us from all out starving?"

Llewyn chuckled a bit. "So then, you want to turn the biggest weapon we've ever known to the biggest enemy we've ever had?"

"It can be disabled. We've got instructions for doing that and I'll take care of that. The Valkyrie was supposed to, but she ran out of time. I will finish the job."

"Yeah? You and what army?"

"Don't need an army. I've got a Xander."

"So you make your way to the capital and offer a deal. What's stopping them from blasting you into vapor?"

"She's craved power and control, this will give her that more than she could ever dream. She'll listen."

"But then, we bring them to this spot, and if you turn it off, you'll no longer be any use to her. What do you think, she'll just let you go then?"

"Change doesn't happen without sacrifice."

"You impressed a lot of people during Exodus, especially for a Worker Product. And you've inspired people, but this..." Llewyn's voice trailed.

I glanced about to everyone at the table, and I saw it in their eyes. A fire.

They weren't done, even now that their leader was gone.

But fires without someone who kindled them died.

"You're in this room because the Action - because Baudricort saw something in you. You wouldn't even be here if you didn't see anything in him."

"But you're talking about a suicide mission."

"It's the only way I know of to get rid of Cataclysm, and make this world safe again."

"And what about the Omegans?"

"If we've got Lebabolis with us, even if it's just a truce, we've got a shot. Who knows, maybe they'll just kill each other off before we get too dinged up."

Llewyn looked at the group. "Before we go any further, do we agree on this plan? Making a deal?"

The cadre members nodded in agreement. Llewyn steepled his hands and scanned the cadre in the room. "We're not sending two people in alone. We'll need at least a detail. I don't want anything to go wrong here."

"I'll get Treg and Zengus. Norg too."

"Do it!" Llewyn commanded. To the others at the table, he said, "We need to prep for a coordinated move, each Encampment. I want statuses and updates from each commander within the hour."

As the discussion finished, Nelson leaned over to me. "That was great."

I shrugged. "About time we finished what Baudricort started."

After the meeting, Treg and I strolled around outside the Encampment.

"Nice work," he said with a chuckle.

"They needed to know the truth; looks like more than a few had no idea."

"This is gonna work, Ana."

"I hope so. I wouldn't be doing this if I didn't have the circle with me."

"We got your back."

THIRTY-NINE

(NELSON)

THE DISCUSSIONS AND PLANS BY LLEWYN and the Cadre came down to one Landcrawler with me and Ana along with Zengus, Treg and Norg. Our goal was to get noticed at the border without drawing as much attention to bring big numbers of either Omegans or Lebabolis out. Llewyn gave the order for us to go pretty quick, though. It felt like he was just anxious for us to be out of his way for awhile, or maybe for good.

Zengus drove with Norg at shotgun while Ana, Treg, and I rode in the back. The rough and overgrown roads cleared and the path to the border stretched over smoother ground, with just a few moderate hills in our way.

We stopped near the Lebabolis border at the top of a rise, where a single winding road led downward to the actual border. A bunker beside the road was the only visible sign of any control over this entry.

Ana stared at the bunker for awhile. "If this thing turns sour, we'll be in for it. Anyone want to back out now, speak up."

Norg leaned up from the back seat. "If yer lookin' for my vote, I say what the hell are we waitin' for?"

"I'm with him," Treg said. "Let's do this."

We proceeded further down the road. A few figures appeared around the bunker ahead. No one fired, though. Either they were unprepared or - something.

An explosion behind us shoved the Landcrawler sidewards a few feet.

"What the hell was that?" Ana barked.

"Nothing from the Lebabolis side," I offered.

Ana punched the console.

Treg craned his neck around. "Behind and to the left, small squadron of craft."

"Lebabolis patrol?" Ana asked.

"Negative, unknown markings," Treg replied.

Ana looked back. "Oh no."

"What?" I turned and saw them. Black colored craft, with what looked like the same symbols from the ones that attacked us at the Verge. My pulse pounded in my throat.

Ana yelled, "Floor it, Zengus, right for the border!"

FORTY

(ANA)

FIVE OMEGAN SHIPS SWIRLED ABOUT us in a cascading arc. I grabbed my pulse rifle and directed Zengus toward the front. I fired a few shots at the black ships as we weaved toward the Lebabolis border.

"Nelson!" I called out. "Get on the comm. Anything like channels W91 through Z13. Try and raise Lebabolis. We need help. Got it?"

"Alright!"

I felt a chuckle come over me when I realized I'd just put a call in for assistance. While Nelson grabbed the headset, I surveyed the area. The shrieking of the ships above echoed across the sky. I never saw Hell Hawks move like these ships were, almost too fast for my eyes to keep up with them.

"Ana!" Nelson yelled.

"What? You get somebody?"

"Huh? Oh, no. Llewyn's on the comm; he wants an update."

A blast glanced off the hood of our Landcrawler. The super bright blue light blinded me for a second, and my head knocked the back of my seat. If that wasn't already enough to piss me off, I had

'Colonel Rear Guard' calling for a sitrep from his safe room. "Tell him we're being shot to shit, that's what!"

The black ships swept back up into the air but left one that fired upon us. Through the smoke, I saw Treg and the others lay down heavy fire on the black ship fixed on us.

The ground erupted in a fountain of rubble and people from another blast.

"We need to pull back," Nelson said.

Even as the ships swarmed around us and kept us pinned down, a word appeared at the back of my head: No!

It repeated in my mind, louder and louder until it got to my voice. "No, no we can't!" I squinted over the smoke and fired at the craft, which had its way with us.

They're just playing with us. We're sitting ducks. *We shouldn't have come. This was my idea,* and *look where it's got us.*

The air above filled with the whine of engines as ships soared about and sent plumes of flame and heat about with their weapons fire. Every so often the punch of a shot that found its mark slammed my chest as if it were a fist.

I fired shot after shot at the engines of the black ship nearest us. Norg joined me and blistered the air with his weapon fire.

"Ana, we need to ditch!" Nelson yelled over the rising rumble.

"No, a little further!" I yelled. "Keep on that comm!"

Another shot hit the hood of our Landcrawler. It sent more dazzling light out, and for a moment I saw nothing else. I closed my eyes, my rifle still aimed forward.

"Do not stop!"

More shots hit the front of our Landcrawler as we neared the front. A loud blast and huge cloud of smoke came from the front of our vehicle, and it skidded to an abrupt halt.

"Engine hit; we're stuck!" yelled Zengus.

If we don't stop 'em now, we're as good as dead.

"Aim for the engines!" I yelled. I trained my rifle on the back of the ship and opened fire. A large pop sounded, followed by smoke and an explosion as the engines of the black ship burst, and it wobbled in the air.

I clambered onto the roof of the Hell Hawk. I pointed toward the ship. "Norg, Treg, pulse grenades, hit the cockpit!"

Soon, the ship was engulfed in smoke and turned for an escape. Treg launched a pulse grenade at it, and the ship burst into an orange ball of flames.

The cheers from our group were brief as the other crafts peppered us with pulse fire.

"Take cover!" I yelled.

We dispersed back to the bush and kept up our fire at the ships overhead.

"Can we get help from Llewyn? Some kind of back up?" Nelson asked.

Blasts hit the trees above, and branches were strewn down on us. I grabbed Nelson, and we rolled away from the incendiary foliage.

"Back up?" I yelled. "We're it, baby."

A sudden roar of missiles proved me wrong, though.

The black ship that neared us was the first hit. It burst in a brilliant explosion, and showered debris over the trees. Other rockets came soon after. The remaining black crafts fell, one by one.

"Those shots came from inside Lebabolis!" Nelson said.

I looked through the smoke and flames, back to the road, but saw nothing. "You sure?" I grabbed my rifle and called to the others around me, "Keep low till we figure out what's going on!"

I tapped Nelson and waved Treg over. We crept up toward where the shots came from, inside the Lebabolis border. We made our way back toward the bunker.

Whoever it was hadn't heard Nelson's distress call. They were already there. I eyed the road ahead. "Stay sharp, everybody. Not liking this too much right now."

More figures appeared by the bunker than before, and I made out a missile launch system. But what caught my eye the most was a flag one soldier waved. Even through the haze from the smoke and flame, it looked so familiar.

It wasn't a Lebabolis flag.

As we walked, I directed the group, "Weapons ready, but don't engage unless threatened."

We passed the last burning Landcrawler, and the haze cleared. The symbol on the flag sharpened up, and I still shook my head at it. I turned to Treg. "You seeing that too?"

He shook his head and looked at me. "Yeah."

We walked slowly toward the group of Lebabolis soldiers, one of which waved the flag of the Valkyrie.

FORTY-ONE

(ANA)

WE STOOD A FEW FEET from the soldiers. Their eyes mirrored our own tense readiness. They held their pulse rifles tight. The Radomet fixed their gaze on us, their visored helmets kept a mindless watch over us for even the slightest threatening move.

I was surprised they hadn't made a move by that point. There we were, with the man they'd made a Verge to get, along with some of their least desirable Deviants. But they were all still.

I broke the silence first. "Take us to Charista."

A few of 'em traded looks, but none budged even then.

"Did I fucking stutter? Take us there now, or we might as well get this over with." I pulled my rifle up.

Still, they did nothing. I closed in on the soldier with the flag. He held it on the ground and leaned on it.

"Where'd you get that?"

"One of your Encampments."

"Oh?" I moved closer. "Would that be one you destroyed?" I asked, my fist raised.

He slid the flag between us. "Something like that."

"Easy, Ana," Nelson said.

The Radomets moved towards me as I approached the soldier, the mechanical whine of their limbs made a creepy underscore to our conversation.

I thrust my finger at 'em. "Get this: we've got Xander with us. If you don't want to be sent for Realignment, I suggest you bring us to Charista yesterday." As I eyed 'em all, I heard Treg's rifle powered up.

I almost grabbed the flag soldier's neck when a female voice stopped me.

"Cool it, hot shot."

Nycole appeared from out of the group of soldiers and approached us. "Always flying off the handle. Who do you think you are, the Valkyrie?"

I smirked at the sight of her. "Hiding behind your troops, Nycole? That's not much like a Warrior Product. What would Charista think?"

She sneered and stood next to the flag soldier. "How about a thank you for saving your collective asses."

I narrowed my eyes at her. "Oh please, we were headed for cover."

"Yeah uh huh."

"So how many times do I have to ask you to bring us to Charista? I don't have time for games."

"Whoa, hold it." Her dirty blonde hair flopped about when she swiveled back to me. "Why would I want to bring some Deviants who may well have a bomb to our leader?" She waved to Nelson. "We meet again."

"Looks that way." Nelson cradled his weapon and nodded slowly.

Her lips drew into a line. "You should've stuck with us."

"Somehow, I doubt that."

She shrugged. She and Treg exchanged nods. "Hi."

"Hi, yourself," Treg said.

"Still babysitting the would-be warriors?"

"Negative." Treg smiled at me. "More like leading."

Nycole glanced back to me, her lips curled. "I'm still waiting for you to tell me why I should be even talking with you anyway."

I eyed her for a moment. "I've got Cataclysm."

"Liar."

"Nope, it's real. I've got the specs and I even know where its located."

I brought the datapod over to the Bunker and pulled up the information for Nycole. She watched the diagrams on screen, her eyes wide. "Why do we need you, then? I can copy this and build another one."

"Not without the descrambled code. And in the meanwhile, there's already one built, just waiting to be found. You want power, you want to be able to destroy the Omegans, get that peace Charista's so hot for? You'll need a bigger stick. This is the biggest stick there is."

"But still, what do we need you for?"

"Xander here knows where it is. He can find it. And since he's not been implanted, you won't be able to retrieve it from him."

"We'll see about that."

"Or," I said, grasping my gun, "we can just bring you back to square one." I pointed my gun at Nelson's throat. "What's it worth, Nycole? You want to fumble through plans for weeks while the Omegans get further and further up your face?"

Nycole grit her teeth. "Much as I'd like to yank that rifle out of your puny hands and snap your ungrateful Deviant neck, I've got to let Charista weigh in on this."

"Now, was that so hard?" I grinned.

Nycole held her glare on me. "I'll bring you to Charista. I suggest you don't try anything, I've got no problem wasting everyone else in your crew if I have to."

FORTY-TWO

(NELSON)

OUR CONVOY FOLLOWED Charista's group into Lebabolis. We snaked through the main roads of the Sectors, which were empty. The occasional small patrol appeared, but nothing stopped our advance.

A light haze settled over us as we went. The further into Lebabolis we traveled, the thicker it got, almost like late morning fog. Through the dimmed visibility, I saw a collection of buildings. It was an odd set of pairs; for every one or two buildings that were in shambles, there was at least another one that looked like it was built more recently.

Ana glanced at the navigation console. She tapped a few controls, which changed the display a bit. Several icons appeared, scattered around near the bright green lines.

"Not sure where they're taking us, but I'll adjust our beacon to Llewyn, in case." She opened the comm. "All weapons on standby until I talk with Charista."

The roads were pretty quiet. Too quiet, to be honest. We disrupted their warning system, but I figured at least a few people would be about, a few vehicles like that convoy they had raided. But yet, nothing.

"Curious where their Hell Hawks are," I said. "Even regular vehicles. It's like they're hunkered down."

Our convoy slowed as we neared a large building. Ana and I exchanged glances. A row of heavy duty looking vehicles formed a perimeter around the building, their dark reddish armor reflecting a mean glare from the sun overhead. Ten or more Hell Hawks hovered in formation above us, poised and ready. On the ground were over two thousand foot soldiers, all armed.

There in front was a smaller crowd of people. By the look on Ana's face though, these weren't average citizens. They looked haggard, almost like they were patients under medical care. One of them wasn't dressed the same though. She was in battle armor, but more regal looking.

Ana swallowed hard. She glanced to me and nodded toward the woman. "Charista."

FORTY-THREE

(ANA)

EVER SINCE I LEFT Lebabolis, I'd thought about this moment for a long time: Me and her face to face again.

My mind was a jumble of questions and things I wanted to say to her. I wondered if she ever knew what it was like: having your family taken from you and later finding out they weren't your real family to begin with. Oh, and finding out who your father is as he died in your arms.

Charista was the reason I and so many others were on the run. When I had played this meeting out in my mind so many times in the past, it was always the two of us. She attempted an explanation of why everything happened like it did. I shut her down, and the two of us fought to the death.

I never pictured it like this.

We sat in the Landcrawler. My gut tightened as I deliberated over what the move was. Her troops stood behind her, weapons down but they all looked braced for a quick assault. *If they go for us, Zengus can floor this thing and we can at least nail a few before booking outta here.*

Baudricort still influenced my strategic mind from the beyond.

Charista's voice crackled over our comm unit. "I know you can hear me, Ana. We need to talk."

I tapped a reply. "Before or after you wipe us out?"

She scoffed. "We could've done that any time we wanted, and you know that."

I narrowed my eyes at her through our windshield. "Alright, I'm listening. You wanna threaten us or are you gonna make a point anytime soon?"

She whispered to one of the others next to her, and they took off. "I am. I want to know what you have about Cataclysm."

I eyed Nelson for a second. "We found it. Well, should say Baudricort did."

"Did he now? How is he?"

"He's dead."

Her face changed. "Baudricort is... dead?"

I nodded.

She took a slow breath. Her eyes cast downward, and I thought I saw a hint of moisture there. If I were stupid I'd think she actually cared for Baudricort from this little show. "He believed in his work and gave us so much." Her eyes found mine. "But he was a crusader. He refused to believe we needed a shield, not just more tools."

"Cataclysm doesn't sound like a shield to me."

She shrugged. "Sometimes, dear Ana, you'll find that the only way to settle aggression is with the right amount of deterrent. That is, if you ever want to be responsible for more than yourself."

My voice quavered. "Like my brother? Look, we all know how you handle people. I'm here for a truce, if you're willing to listen."

"Continue."

"We know where Cataclysm is hidden. I can show you. We're trying to get to the Range, as I'm sure you know. If you free our people, and provide us all safe passage, I'll lead you right to Cataclysm, and you can do what you want with it then."

She grinned. "I'm sure you'll do me the courtesy of giving me proof."

"I can and I will."

"Well, that is a very interesting proposition. We do have a more pressing matter right now, however."

"Like what?"

"Before we set out for Cataclysm, we need to take care of the Omegans bearing down on us. They want revenge, and we can't send anyone on a retrieval mission just yet."

"How many Omegans are we talking about?"

"We've seen scout groups, small units around, like the one you ran into at our border a little while ago. But we're also tracking a much larger force, headed for our Realignment facilities."

"We're a little short on numbers now. Can't you deal with them?"

"We're putting the Capital in a lock down mode; I need some troops for the Garrison there. But if you can help me out with support, I'm sure you can spare a few Hell Hawks you've stolen from us over the years."

I squinted at her. "Why, don't you have enough of your own?"

"Ana, I'd rather know you're as invested in this agreement as possible. Human collateral always works better than promises."

We traded glances for a bit. "I'll get with Llewyn on that. But after all this, and after you get your Cataclysm, I need to know you'll leave us be for good."

"Of course," she replied. "As soon as the threat from the Omegans is neutralized, you'll no longer be a target of interest, none of you."

I rubbed my temples and glared at her. "One more thing. Cure 'em."

"I'm sorry?"

"The Pox. Treat 'em all, or no deal. I know you can, and so do you."

She thought on it for a moment, then shook her head rapidly. "No. No, it's too costly. We don't have enough re-"

"-figure it out. You can do it. You better, or no deal."

She frowned a bit, turning to talk to a few people nearby her.

Advisors, I guessed. She looked back at me as a smile formed. "Sure, Ana. You've got a deal."

"Excellent. We should shake on this."

"Of course. Come out, and I'll have Nycole tell you everything else we know."

FORTY-FOUR

(NELSON)

AFTER A LOT OF DISCUSSION, Ana and Charista came to an agreement. From our Landcrawler, we watched the Lebabolis troops, which separated into two smaller units, one of them lined up with us.

Ana stared at the troops as they reorganized. "Am I doing right?"

"What?"

"Trusting these people? Trusting her?"

I watched Charista as she oversaw things with her troops. "If they wanted to crush us, we'd be dead already."

My eyes met Ana's. Her brow crinkled in thought, she asked, "Is that your prophecy, Xander?"

I grimaced. "Stop calling me that. And no, I don't know. Anything I can think of now is nothing more than hunches and instinct." I drummed the seat back in front of me. Even if this was my story, I hadn't written it yet.

"Guess we'll play along. I agree, though, can't see how they'd lure us in and not capture us or shoot at us if there wasn't more going on."

We moved down Lebabolis roads toward Sector 5 and the Realignment Facility. We passed through more collections of buildings with no people around. Speakers scattered about all blared an emergency announcement for evacuation toward the Lebabolis Capital.

After a few hours' drive, I found myself on a familiar path as each rubble filled street we walked turned and gave way to that familiar site where Ana had first rescued me. As we passed Jackson Square, I noticed Nycole beside Ana and me.

"We meet again," I said.

She looked at me for a moment and smiled faintly. "Oh, Mr. Forrester. Hello."

"Thanks for not abducting me this time."

Her eyes went back to the road, but she managed a "Sure."

We headed into the Realignment facility, a large three story building near the Mississippi River. Well, whatever sorry excuse for a river it was. All those centuries had not been kind. I shook my head at the river of thick grime with a rainbow of dark hues that swirled past me. And they thought pollution was bad back then.

The inside of the facility looked like a hospital. Very white and well lit. A few small windows provided the only natural light in the place. The main area was fairly large and quickly swallowed up our group.

As everyone filed in, we went into a large room for a briefing. Ana and Nycole stood at the front with a large screen behind them.

Ana said, "The Action and Lebabolis are in a pact. In return for our assistance in fighting off the Omegan assault, we're granted freedom from Lebabolis and the right to set up our own nation."

The large screen displayed the strange symbol from those crafts we had seen back at the Verge.

Nycole said, "This is our enemy. The Omegans. The last time we faced them years ago, we had luck on our side with Cataclysm. But today, we don't. We'll need to be strong on our own and turn them back. We're all that stands in their way. They want our Valentium and they want us and everyone else like us dead. If we don't stop them here, they'll march on to the Capital."

The video screen flashed pictures of their troops and aircraft like the one we had seen at the Verge.

A murmur rippled through the crowd with shouts of defiance. Ana glanced at Nycole, and they both smiled.

"That's why we're here," Nycole said.

"We're a team, and we fight together," Ana added.

"We're going to canvas the building. Seal every entrance, put units on the roof," Nycole said. "We've got air support, but not unlimited. Not sure what they'll be bringing our way, so we need to hold this ground. At all costs."

"We will!" Ana cried out, her arms outstretched.

"We will!" came the crowd's response.

(ANA)

AFTER THE ROOF AND ENTRANCES were fortified, we went outside again and set up a perimeter. The rubble provided a few spots for observation. We surrounded the building with a large circle of positions.

I watched the Radomet and Lebabolis troops side by side with us and shook my head. How had we gone so far to wind up back with them like this? What would Baudricort have said or thought? I hated that we were in with these people, and worse, that our options were so limited.

I still had no sign or idea of what or from where the attack was expected, but everything we planned was almost ready. Nycole went with a few troops up several floors in nearby building for extra eyes up top and long range shooters.

I leaned against a pile of rubble and watched the others while they finished setting up their gear. I spotted Nelson as he trotted toward me.

"Must be extra weird for you, being right back here," I said.

He marveled at the sight and almost chuckled, but it came out as light coughs. "Ain't quite the Big Easy anymore, but least I'm trying to defend it."

I patted his back. "Gonna be OK. We'll take care of these bastards and get everyone away from here soon." I reached for one of the rifles in the position and handed it to him. "Here, in case you need it. Remember, the sight's in the middle if they're more than twenty feet away."

He checked the rifle over. Either he had picked up this soldiering thing, or he faked it really well.

Several birds announced their presence with random squawks overhead. A large group of 'em soared almost right over us, headed off towards the way we came in.

"That can't be good," Nelson said.

I activated my rifle and grabbed my comm unit. "See anything, eyes in the sky?"

Nycole replied, "Negative. Bunch of birds coming through, that's it."

"Well, keep watching."

I stretched with the rifle for balance. The daylight faded a bit as the sun sank lower in the sky. After a few minutes, I jumped up and made a pass around the positions. Everyone looked ready for action. Treg held the northernmost spot, Norg had the southernmost. Llewyn woulda freaked if he saw me in the line of everything instead of in the rear, but that wasn't me. I wasn't one who led people from behind.

I returned to my position and crouched down next to Nelson.

"So the deal is," I told him, "if they attack from one side, we keep close contact and support 'em if needed. We don't run toward the fight, though, since they may try a flank."

"And if they attack from more than one side?"

"Anything that shoots at you, blow it the hell away. We got heavy artillery on the roof too, but they gotta pick their shots so we don't get wasted."

Nycole's frantic voice burst through the comm unit speaker. "Enemy spotted, enemy spotted!"

I heard the faint sound of engines, but saw nothing around. I craned my neck over, but saw nothing. "Position?" I replied.

"Overhead!"

———

TREG'S GROUP fired on the ships first. I aimed my rifle, but I froze as I counted 'em: at least fifteen ships.

They swirled in a circular pattern. Everyone fired at will. The ships responded with a pummeling barrage of fire. Loud thuds shook the ground every time one of their cannon fired. My chest pounded with each blast.

"Aim for their engines!" I bellowed to those nearby.

A blast knocked me down. I dusted myself off and saw Nelson, down low as he fired his rifle.

"You OK?"

He glanced at me, then looked back to the fight without a word, except he managed a thumbs up. *Alright, Nelson. May make you a soldier yet.*

Several large objects separated from the ships above with loud clanging noises. The smaller objects lowered to the ground around fifty feet outside our perimeter.

"Blast those things!" I yelled over the comm. "Nycole, fry 'em!"

We fired on 'em but the shots glanced off, and whatever they were, they landed. The ships above stopped their barrage for the moment. We kept up our volleys at 'em and sent a few shots toward whatever was on the ground with us now. The smoke from shots and fires around the area clouded my vision, but it looked like the objects on the ground had changed shape.

"Treg!" I called on the comm. "You seeing those things over there?"

"Check," he responded. "Whatever they are, they're heavy-"

One of the objects opened fire on Treg's spot, and it burst into a brilliant white glow.

"Treg!" I yelled and lunged toward him, but someone held me back. I turned and saw Nelson, his hand on my shoulder.

"Get down! They'll incinerate you!" he yelled.

My heart pounded when I saw what was left of Treg's position. The objects on the ground spread out and fired more shots at us randomly. They looked like heavily armored tanks.

The air filled with the burnt smell of engine exhaust. I nodded at Nelson. "We gotta get out of this hole, or we're done." The other positions around our group still returned fire, but another one of 'em burst into flames as I watched.

One tank headed in our direction. I turned to everyone in our position. "Move out, now! Follow me!"

I sprinted towards the Realignment facility. Several transport trucks lined up near the front as part of the barricade. I turned and fired a bit as I ran and saw Nelson and the others close behind me.

"Nycole," I gasped into the comm, "any pulse tech up high? Give us a hand!"

A few moments later, a barrage of greenish balls sprayed from Nycole's spot. When they landed on the ground, I motioned our group down to the ground. The bulbs ignited with a quick burst of light, and the tanks were motionless.

"Nice work," Nelson said.

"Not for long. We've got about three minutes before that wears off," I said. "Come on inside; they're attacking from the roof!"

WE MADE it to the roof in minutes. Several Omegans were there already, in a skirmish with Lebabolis troops. The figures were the same color of their ships and looked like they had exo-armor. Or it was just their bodies.

Our group crouched behind ventilation ports. We were almost

between the two groups. I signaled to Nelson and the others, and as one we jumped up from our secluded spot.

"Fire!" I yelled, and we unleashed a barrage from the flank that caught the Omegans by surprise. A few of 'em fell, but more of 'em trained their fire on us. I spotted a heavy cannon on the roof, along with what was left of the soldier who fired it. His body was badly burned and almost melted to the weapon.

We kept our barrage on the Omegans, and together with the other group on the roof we pushed 'em back a bit. I pointed Nelson toward the big gun. As he scrambled over, I felt a white hot spear as it slammed into me. The pain ripped through my shoulder. Sensations like thousands of needles jammed into that spot as well as a searing burn. I landed on my back but still screamed, "Keep going!" to those around who checked on me.

A Lebabolis soldier helped me up. I touched the spot, and almost passed out from the pain. My hand came up from the wound bloody too. I gathered what strength I had left and moved as swift as possible to Nelson. He and another soldier manned the cannon. I pointed to the ships overhead. They swiveled the big gun up and fired on 'em.

At this, the Omegans pushed up from their spot. I switched my rifle to my good arm and pointed at the Omegans on the corner of the roof.

"Push 'em off!" I yelled and charged, my voice shredded in a wild shriek.

The Omegans shot down a few of our group, but enough of us made it. I turned my rifle and shoved myself forward into the first few Omegans, so they were knocked into the others. They stopped firing and grappled with us as we pushed 'em back.

Their replies came as a series of hisses and semi mechanical noises. Whatever they were wasn't human.

We neared the edge of the roof, and the first few slipped off to the ground below. "Keep pushing!" I hollered as our group mustered up more strength and knocked the rest of 'em off the roof.

A blaring horn sounded above us as the last of the Omegans

slipped off the roof. I fell to my back, rifle pointed at the sky. One ship blasted a message:

"This is Commander Chun of the Omegan Empire. This facility is now under our control. You must evacuate immediately or face elimination." The ship trained its guns on the facility roof and us. "You have thirty seconds to comply."

I glanced to the others. The Lebabolis soldiers nodded to me, their weapons at the ready. The Radomet kept their wordless stances, their weapons also held fast. I saw the Action soldiers, their eyes burning with belief in the cause and now in me.

Nelson looked on me with resigned determination. He was ready.

I nodded back to all of 'em. All at once, we fired on the large ship. Nelson launched several more barrages from the cannon. The ship swerved away from our shots, but not before it took several hits on its wings, hull, and engines.

We walked over to the side and got a better view of the ground scene. Some tanks remained and still blasted indiscriminately at our troops. A few pockets of our people and Nycole fired off several shots while they avoided return fire.

One of the Lebabolis troops put a dressing on my shoulder as I watched the scene below. The Hell Hawks gave chase to the ships for the time being, but they were still outnumbered as well. I tried Charista or Llewyn on the comm, but no response.

"Ashton?"

"Yes, Ana?"

"What's it take to detonate the Valentium?"

He froze with a look of mild fright.

"Come on, we knew this was the deal. If we can't stop these guys, we have to keep the Valentium away from 'em, right?"

He nodded a bit. "Y-yes, of course. There is a control module below ground where we can activate the sequence."

After we secured the roof, we made our way downstairs when Ashton stopped.

"What?" I asked.

He looked at me a moment. "You know what will happen if we do this, right?"

I narrowed my eyes and nodded my head toward the commotion outside. "You know what happens if we don't stop 'em at all?"

His eyes shut as he nodded again. "They might detect the energy buildup though, blast in here-"

"This is fail-safe. Our last resort."

We continued down. Nelson panted a bit. "Thought we were gonna get outta this one."

I watched him. His brow furrowed, beads of sweat and tears dripped off his face.

"I'm sorry." I clutched his arm.

We made it to ground level. The explosions from outside sounded louder than before. The tanks were at the truck barricade, mere feet away from us.

Ashton activated the entrance to the below ground control center. He led the way in, and I was waving the rest in when I heard a new sound.

It sounded like a clap of thunder. It was soon echoed with many more.

WE BURST through the barricades around the door and got to the street. A fleet of Hell Hawks were firing on the Omegan ships, sending 'em into jumbles of debris and fire.

I activated my comm earpiece. "Action calling Hell Hawk fleet, acknowledge."

A few moments went by with no reply. I checked around and saw several groups of Lebabolis soldiers still fought with Omegan units. We headed to the defensive positions for cover. Several in our group joined back in the fight.

The area was a littered mess of burned hulks of machinery,

bodies, rubble, and random small fires. Looked like the Facility was still intact though.

My comm unit crackled to life. "Wing H5 calling Action."

"Action here, nice to see you guys. A bit unexpected, but most welcome." I waved at one passing ship.

"Roger that. Llewyn made the call and redirected us from Encampment security and transport."

I breathed a slight sigh of relief. At least we had this wave of the fight in hand. I felt certain more were on the way from Omegans though, if Charista's assessment was accurate. We needed more of a plan for 'em, but that part was up to her.

Amid the sporadic fighting, I heard shouts and cheers from the far end of the facility. Nelson and I exchanged glances. "Let's check it out," he said. We jogged over to soldiers crowded around the wrecked remains of an Omegan ship. An Omegan lay in the center on his back. Several Lebabolis soldiers had weapons pointed at 'em.

I worked my way over to Norg in the crowd. "He say anything?"

"Mostly curses and yelling." He grinned. "Looks like they're shot pretty bad, so I don't know how much more time he's got." He spat.

I broke through to the center of the crowd. The Omegan's eyes fell to me. The head looked somewhat human, except for slightly larger eyes. Cuts and dried blood framed up his face, which had a look of anger mixed with agony.

I hushed the crowd a bit. "Let me guess, Commander Chun?"

He nodded, and the murmur of the crowd grew a bit.

I gestured around myself. "Sorry to break up your little party, but looks like you're fresh out of troops."

"Swine," he blurted out, along with a small spurt of blood. "Enjoy your minor victory. It won't last." He heaved and managed a snarling smile.

The cheering subsided as more listened to him as he made promises of revenge. They sounded like veiled threats from a dying creature.

Or were they?

I swung my rifle at his head. "You're the only one here who won't last."

"It's easy to kill a dying being. Wait until you're facing our hordes!" He lurched up, twitched and coughed more from the effort. "Our army."

"Oh, you have an army?" I asked, my voice raised. I stepped onto his chest, my rifle in his mouth. "You'll need more than that."

I fired, and his head exploded into a misshapen gob of blood and tissue.

FORTY-SIX

(ANA)

THE VALENTIUM WAS SECURED on board Hell Hawks for our trip. After discussions with Charista, Llewyn and our group, we decided that we needed to pull back further to a place more easily defended. Sector 5 had too much damage and too many wide open paths.

I was watching the crews as they loaded a Hell Hawk when I heard Nelson behind me.

"Found something for you."

When I glanced at him over my shoulder, he smiled and brandished some kind of stick.

"You brought me a stick."

"No, no, no." He chuckled. "It looks like a bat, a baseball bat."

"What's baseball?"

"A game from my time. Not as important right now but this," he smacked his free hand with the stick, "can come in quite handy if you ever find yourself without a weapon."

"Oh, is that right?" I asked, my eyebrow arched. "You becoming a weapons expert?"

"Well, not like you guys. But I figure, one can never be too prepared for what's ahead."

Nodding, I stood. "Can't deny that."

He handed me the bat. It was lighter than it looked, but I bet it did damage if used in the right way. I swung the stick at a rock on the round, and it careened off into the distance. "Not bad, long as the other person doesn't have a pulse rifle." I gave it back to him with a wink as he shrugged.

An announcement sounded on the loudspeaker that Charista had a nationwide announcement for broadcast. We headed into the meeting room of the facility for perhaps the last time.

The lights dimmed. The Lebabolis insignia appeared, along with the Coursons and Charista.

"Citizens of Lebabolis, I bring you great news and hope. Our military force has met the Omegans at Sector 5 and soundly defeated them! The Omegans were intent on harvesting the Valentium we have stored, but we were able to crush their strike with minimal losses."

I turned to Nelson. *Minimal losses? Our military? She forget who helped her, or who led the damn force?*

"Furthermore, we are making plans for your continued protection. Effective immediately, our facilities and borders are under secure lockdown protocol. Please do not be alarmed, as I have no reason to believe we will have further risk of threats from the Omegans. This is merely a precautionary measure to secure the people and resources of Lebabolis and ensure our mission continues on without fail."

The screen switched to the Lebabolis insignia again, and faded to black. The room was silent. I rose up and made my way to the front of the screen.

"We won today. This fight. There'll be more though. Remember, I'm with you. We're gonna face whatever they bring next. It'll get much worse before it's over."

People's eyes veered from the screen to me.

"If we're together, nothing will stop us. Just remember this day and how we stood together. It's the only way we'll beat 'em... together."

Toward the front, Norg stood and held his arms up, crossed in the Valkyrie salute. Everyone watched him for a few moments, then Treg and Nelson joined in. Soon, even some of the Lebabolis troops stood, their arms held high in an 'X'. The Radomet kept a reserved watch on the room.

The fire in us roared as one.

SETTLING
DARKNESS
THE VALKYRIE CHRONICLES
BOOK 2
PAUL HEINGARTEN

"The night is darkest just before the dawn. And I promise you, the dawn is coming."

(THE DARK KNIGHT, 2008)

PROLOGUE

T**he story so far…**

ANA CRUCINAL, a twenty-three year old citizen of Lebabolis, has fled her home with members of the Action, the Lebabolis Resistance. The Action has worked to get as many willing citizens as possible to escape from Lebabolis and their cruel structure of forced labor in exchange for a semblance of security and purpose.

Baudricort, leader of the Action, and a former high ranking member of Lebabolis who designed many of its systems, wants to make amends for the destruction his work has done and what it has caused Lebabolis to become.

Ana's brother Varrick, who had joined Ana on the Exodus with the Action, has been kidnapped by Lebabolis, along with a number of the Action who have fallen ill to a disease known as the Pox. Ana made a deal with Baudricort to help him in exchange for a promise to get Varrick and the sick of the Action back.

When a mission to cross time to modern day New Orleans is put in jeopardy, Ana takes matters on herself and flings herself across centuries to find a man they know as Xander Lee.

Xander Lee happens to be the pen name of a man named Nelson Forrester, who lives in early 2010s New Orleans and works on a book about a nation at war known as Lebabolis. After much convincing and some bloodshed, Nelson is forcibly taken to the year 3192 and learns that what he thought was a simple literary project is actually prophecy.

Together, Ana and Nelson navigate the choppy seas of their predicament. They also learn that while they are under the gun, their enemies are closer than they think, and sometimes the best course of action involves joining with the enemy of their enemies.

A deal was struck between Ana and Charista, military leader of Lebabolis, to have the Action join Lebabolis to fight the Omegans, a strange alien race who has marauded the Earth for centuries and has set their sights on the technology Lebabolis has managed to acquire for themselves.

ONE

(ANA)

MY SKIN BURNED at the feel of the sun. The horizon bent upward over us, the walls of the crater we were in swept up like a giant hill. It was a low spot, but it was where the Omegans were headed. Which also made it the one place we had to be.

More of these craters turned up once we got further into the Outlands. Each of them had a giant ball of Valentium at their center and the Omegans were on top of a lot of them, so we had our work cut out for us keeping them away from as much of it as possible.

Three hundred of us filled up this crater. Spread out in a line that snaked up around toward the top of the crater, we stood and watched the Omegans. They'd followed us and fought us wherever they could. It was as much about payback for them as it was their Valentium. The unit we fought in Sector Five turned out to just be a scout. They waited in the wings with three regiments and once they learned what happened it was open season on us, Lebabolis, and anyone else who stood in their way. Kaitlinn and Jason commanded the two legions of troops from Lebabolis and the Action, and I ran this other unit. The

299

plan was to join back up with Kaitlinn and then I'd break off with Nelson and a few others for a run at Cataclysm like we'd agreed.

That being said, we had still been on the run a month since the attack at Sector Five. Charista promised sending help whenever she could in her updates.

Some help.

At least the Action knew more about foraging for whatever we could get our hands on to stay alive and safe. We were the Coalition now, the combination of Action and Lebabolis dedicated to turning back the Omegans. I went back and forth on how I felt about working with Lebabolis, like most of us in the Action did. Charista made a strong play when she used Varrick and our other sick people as hostages so we were convinced. I had every intention that she'd pay for that one day.

People in the Action still considered us separate from the Coalition. We were a band apart, and that was just the way it was. Once we learned about the Omegans and saw what they did in Sector Five, almost leveling the place, we knew that as bad as Lebabolis had been, taking care of the Omegans had to be our number one. So, until the Omegans weren't a problem anymore, we kept in this fight, on Charista's side. I knew though, there'd be a time we'd have to make our move, get our people back who Charista had taken from us and make our own place in this world.

Until then, our agreement was fight to destroy the Omegans, and in return Lebabolis gave the Action its own peaceful existence. But I really wondered if we'd ever go back to anything that resembled peace after this. Charista had us as her army, and I didn't see any scenario that didn't involve her keeping her claws firmly stuck into each and every one of us.

And then there was our deal about delivering Cataclysm to Charista. Nelson and I had that job, and we'd have been well on our way if it weren't for the Omegans jumping our groups every chance they got. They were more after us than Lebabolis ever was.

The Valentium rested at the bottom of the crater. We formed a perimeter around it far enough to be safe but close enough that any Omegan who tried a move was gonna get a little taste of pulse rifle in their face.

The comm was a chatter of people in the crater, also with some updates from Llewyn. Even though he was far away from here, he still kept an eye on us. His main job though was the move to the Range. His reasoning was it was Baudricort's goal to get everyone there to safety and he was determined to honor his memory, or at least let his idea live until the move succeeded. I had to admit I was happy about it too. Even though he was cryptic with answers to my questions, or just withdrawn sometimes, Baudricort and his presence held it together, held the Action together. The Action he believed in, anyway. A pang hit me whenever he came across my mind, which was pretty regular since he'd died.

I stood next to Treg while we watched the Omegan crafts hovering in the distance. "I don't like this," I said.

"Hey, what kinda talk is that? You're in the Coalition now, remember?"

"We're in a barrel here. Could there be a worse position? They just gotta rain down whatever fire they got and we're toast. So enough of that Coalition talk. It's the Action, and you know it. We're not partners, we're their escorts." I grabbed for a Digiview. "At least we know they won't blow the Valentium up."

"What makes you so sure?"

"Because they'd have done it already?" Even with a superior force about to run hell up our collective asses, a smile found my face. Guess that's what kept me from going full out crazy.

Some others in our group held positions toward the upper edges of the crater for a wider spread of fire. My gaze of our unit, sparse but geared up and ready for a fight, was distracted by the dim glint of gray bands on the arms of the Lebabolis soldiers. Even in this united group, they held onto that one piece of their identity separate from the Coalition, from us as one unit.

Our boots sank several inches into the sand with every step we took, so most people stayed put once they had their spot. We were ready.

Treg exhaled a worried breath. "Think the Hell Hawks can break through up there if we take fire from the Omegans?"

"Whadya mean if? Jacobs is up there. He'll figure out something."

"Oh, him? I just hope whatever he does won't blow us up too," Treg said.

I never thought of Jacobs as the best pilot in either Lebabolis or the Action as much as he did himself. No matter what, there was never any question that he was the craziest. Rumor had it that on one of his Exodus runs he ran out of ammo and improvised by ramming his Hell Hawk through a detachment of Lebabolis troops. I was glad he was on our side, and I hoped he stayed on the side of the living.

"Jacobs will be busy enough up there." I gazed through the Digiview at the crafts above us. "We got our own party down here too. Whoa, 2000 Omegan troop count? Great."

We'd have been well on our way to Cataclysm by now, but this was another part of our deal with Charista: the Valentium had to be secured and out of the Omegans hands so Lebabolis didn't run short on their fuel supply. We had reserves, but she wanted all the rest kept from the Omegans as much as possible. We wanted them as starved for everything as we were. Only problem with that was it kept us just as stretched out and I worried this all was gonna come down to who had more troops to lose out here. It was Charista's plan, but I wondered just how we'd pull this off.

Side doors on the overhead craft opened and waves of troops dropped from them. Their forms dotted the sky like black rain. They landed on the edge of the crater a hundred yards over and made their way toward us in a slow march.

A gruff voice shattered my already shaky train of thought. "How's it look?"

I eyed Dawn next to me, then returned to the Digiview. I wriggled my shoulder like I had an insect on it, which would've been a lot nicer than her. "Ain't good, but you knew that already."

Dawn had been sent by Charista as my own personal shadow for the trip to get Cataclysm. It was how Charista made sure we, especially me, followed every bit of our agreement. Dawn's one job I could figure was being on my ass every living moment. I was over it and her after the first ten minutes.

She sighed and scratched her arm. "I'm in contact with Charista. She'll send more troops to help."

"When, next month?"

"In time; there's a lot to handle. Jason and Kaitlinn both sent teams to secure some Valentium. Lot better than I can say for our efforts."

I wanted to slam her head with my comm piece but instead turned it on for an update. "Weapons activated and ready; they aren't here to say hey. Stand by with pulse grenades on my go."

This was our routine since Sector Five: run, fight and run some more. For me, it was more than just saving Varrick and the others who Lebabolis had taken from us. I had a promise to keep to Baudricort and to several others among the living.

After just a few months here, I shouldn't have expected the weird feelings to be gone. In very little time, I went from being this brave runaway girl to someone important, at least in a few people's eyes. It all went so fast, I hadn't time to even think about how I wanted this, or even what I wanted here. I'd seen soldiers as a child and young girl; they always seemed so sure of everything. And now I was in charge of this group of soldiers and I gave orders to people, most of them older than me. Their reactions were anything from quiet nods to sidewards glances as they waited for a royal screw up from me. I spoke quick and direct, and hoped the queasy feeling that simmered in my gut each and every day never made it to my eyes.

At least I had one thing protected. Nelson was close in the air with Jacobs. I wanted him out of the way; there wasn't room for anyone who couldn't handle the heavier weapons here. He wasn't much safer with Jacobs, but at least Jacobs could bug out quick if things got terminal.

I felt a sizzling burn on the side of my face closest to the Valentium, which glowed a deep amber. This spot wasn't in any danger of being a Verge site; there was too much Valentium in this one area. But it was a prime target for anyone who needed extra fuel or wanted to disrupt another's supply. Since Sector Five the Omegans showed over and over again that Valentium was their number one. The collateral damage they managed a few times was just a bonus.

I watched the advancing soldiers and thought about our next move. The strategy played in my head a lot. There were so many pieces: the Omegans, the Action/Coalition, Charista, the Valentium, Nelson. It had started right after Baudricort died. Each attack, every move, was like a giant board with pieces everywhere, and I had to figure it out: who to attack first, and where, and how we'd make our way out of our current shit pile. Should have known I was his daughter.

Charista's strategy at least was simple: secure the Valentium and don't let the Omegans get any of it. We needed it for fuel anyway. Supplies were thin, and runs were impossible with the Omegans around every turn. I wished to hell Charista was down here for once. She needed to see how damned tough this battle has gotten. I couldn't let anyone see how I felt, but some days it seemed like a rifle pointed into my mouth would be less dangerous. Lately, we had had to bug out and let them grab more Valentium to save our own asses. We had squadrons of Hell Hawks in the Outlands, but they couldn't be everywhere. We have secured some Valentium already, but this looked like it was gonna be another loss for us.

Our outer positions fired on the advancing Omegans. Several Radomet sprung to action; their mechanical shrieks rang and echoed in the edge of the crater. My fists still tightened at that sound and the memory of when Radomets took Varrick and the rest of our sick.

The positions were a blur of smoke and weapons fire. It was tough to tell which side did better in this fight. Whatever happened, it was up to me to keep as many of our people alive. I dropped down low, my comm pressed close to my lips.

"Central to Wing 7, copy? We need air support, like last week, over?"

A loud thump in front of me shook the ground, and I lurched onto my back. The ships above fired on us as well. "They're crazy; they'll be gone too if any of their shots hit that rock. Don't they know that?"

Treg helped me up. "I wanna know where the hell our air support is." Treg took several aimed shots at the craft. "Remind me to punch Jacobs in the mouth if we make it out of this."

The sky above was peppered with bursts of ship to ship pulse fire. I grabbed for a pulse grenade and armed it when I heard the comm crackle again. "Jacobs, on approach."

"Book it, or there won't be anyone left to rescue!" I yelled.

"They're engaging us up here. I'm circling to the southern side of the crater. Watch for red smoke, then head over."

"Wait, did we check for Darkness yet?" Treg eyed me.

We called it Darkness because there wasn't a better name for it at the time. The Omegans had a device that deactivated our weapons. Vehicles, guns, even lights were shut down by this tech. We'd heard stories about it in the Outlands, but I hadn't seen anything like it yet. It turned up in fights once the Omegan regiments made contact, but so far we hadn't seen 'em where we were.

"I got no clue. Gotta figure they'd have tried it before they sent their troops in for target practice though." A whiff of sand flew up in my face. I swatted my hand and spit the gritty particles out.

More blasts punctured the loose soil and sent it up through the air. I signaled our unit commanders and gave word on the comm to wait for my signal to bolt.

The Omegan soldiers made quick work of the outer positions nearest the crater ridge. The Radomet held up for the most part, but even they had trouble with the larger group that moved through.

Soon we were pushed back within inches of the danger point

with the Valentium. The heat on my back intensified and it felt like blisters formed there.

A dull boom rang out in the crater, and a wisp of red smoke billowed from one spot. I almost called out the order to fall back there when several gigantic pops and explosions rang in the sky. The Omegan crafts were jostled but soon steadied out and returned fire on the squadron of Hell Hawks that appeared.

I motioned everyone to the red smoke, and we took off in a run. Our steps slowed right away, as each time I planted a foot, my boots sank an extra several inches in the sand. When I pulled up, it felt like invisible hands clutched my feet and barely let go. I strained and pushed ahead, my hips sore from the extra work. The pulse fire slammed the ground about us, and we turned and fired at random toward the advancing troops. Five Hell Hawks met us at the end.

I joined the rest of the Coalition troops who returned fire on the Omegans. Once I spun back around and fired on them, I noticed that a group of their troops stopped their attack and focused on the Valentium. I hoped what we did at least gave them something to think about. The Radomet and several other troops showered the Omegans as close as possible without hitting the Valentium store in the middle.

One of the Hell Hawks ascended and shot out of the crater. A group of Omegans broke free and made their way closer to us.

Treg ended up near me. "What's the plan here?"

"Besides not getting our asses blown away? We aren't keeping this one. I'd as soon take off and blow this place from the air than stay here any longer. They'd never let us alone that long anyway. We gotta regroup with a better position. We know where they want to hit; we just have to be smarter about where and when to strike back."

Dawn trudged up beside us. "We can't just give them the Valentium, don't you remember?"

"I remember—"I spun to her—"our number one is keeping our people alive. I'd rather live to fight again. Besides, don't you think it's time we go for the real prize?"

Her lips curled, and she held a glare on me for a long moment.

She then lifted her rifle toward the oncoming Omegans. I wasn't sure who I hated more, her or Charista. The fact Dawn was in strangling distance gave her an advantage at that point.

Treg and I were headed for the nearest Hell Hawk when the ground shook under us and sent us sprawling back down, along with a few others. The Omegans made a weird guttural moan and went into some sort of charge. I looked in time and saw a group of them as they pressed forward on us quick. The Coalition troops shifted; some stumbled in the sand, scurried back and crouched for returning more fire.

Just then, another loud rumble raged above and behind us, the unmistakable sound of hundreds of thunderclaps with an angry turbine wailing through them. I glanced and saw Hell Hawk 42, Jacobs at the helm. Together with the nine other Hell Hawks, they showered the area in front of us. Their barrage tore through several Omegans; the rest pulled back further toward the Valentium.

While three Hell Hawks dropped to a fast landing, the rest stood watch in the air and served up barrages that kept the Omegans from getting closer.

"Everybody, onto the Hell Hawks now!" I bellowed. I twisted myself over and to my feet. Just when I and the others near me made it to the crafts and took off, more explosions slammed the ground. I grasped for the rails and pulled myself into a seat in the rear personnel hold along with the others.

As soon as I was inside, I looked for Nelson but saw no sign of him. I figured he was up with Jacobs with the map displays he checked like he did with the Cataclysm location.

I watched out the narrow windows and saw the rest of the Hell Hawks as they loaded troops and gear and kept as much cover as they could, but the Omegans soon moved up again.

The on board comm crackled to life and I heard that twang voice of Jacobs. "Ev'rybody settle in now. Gonna be a bumpy ride; we're booking out."

The craft lurched about. My gut tightened when I felt us leave the ground, and the wobbling made me nauseous. The angry whine of the turbines built to a shrieking chorus, and I was pulled down into my seat as we rocketed into the air. I grasped the rails near my seat and took a few deep breaths. The nausea that built in my gut was pretty serious. Most of the time I'd flown in these Hell Hawks was for simple transports or quick shots across the border or to another Encampment. Combat flying wasn't something I had much to do with, and I damned well wished I never did.

My eyes focused, and I felt a little better when I saw Treg across from me.

"They'll let anybody on these things," I muttered.

He smirked a bit. "About time Jacobs got his ass here."

"You seen Nelson? I had him on this one with Jacobs."

Treg eyed the others seated around us. "I saw him loading gear on Hell Hawk 91 when we were scrambling out. Poor guy just had to help somehow."

Nelson had settled down from when he first got here, and he wasn't much for taking off and running wild like before. But the less I knew where he was and who he was with—well, it didn't go so great for Varrick when I had let my guard down earlier.

"So we head to another Regiment?" Treg eyed me.

"It's either Kaitlinn or Jason, and she's a lot closer. The sooner we get back to friendlies, the better."

"Better ditch the Omegans first, or we'll be in even worse shape."

I stuck my rifle between my knees and squeezed the barrel in the hope it made me forget the sharp soreness in my hips. "Yeah, well. And since Charista's running the show, no telling where we'll end up."

"Or how far off track. This is such a cluster. If you and Nelson would've just left earlier, you could've nabbed Cataclysm by now."

"I won't leave troops under attack. I was taught better."

"Glad you paid attention."

"Mmmhmm. It's time we show Charista who's in charge. Not her, not the gray bands."

"Damn right."

"We're the ones who survived on our own, mobile, fighting off their raids on us."

There was never time for plans, with us always being scattered about like this. Only quick discussions, seeds of thought that got scattered to the wind. Our unit and the Regiments of Kaitlinn and Jason were supposed to be the decoys, the interference that drew fire while Llewyn kept the Encampments fixed on Baudricort's plan of moving west while the other two regiments handled defense for Lebabolis. Nelson, Dawn, and I were supposed to make our break for Cataclysm and let the bigger units keep them occupied. But Charista changed her plans from the field, and Valentium became the bigger issue quicker than I thought it would. The hope was we held the Omegans away from Valentium and kept them from getting their filthy hands on the rest of the deposits around. But so far it wasn't working. We were too strung out, and the help they gave was next to nothing.

The ship steadied out a bit and things calmed down. I hoped the queasy feeling in my gut went away soon too. "There won't be a rendezvous if the Omegans zero us in."

A loud explosion pounded the outside of the craft. The lights blinked off, and I felt the craft wobble awkwardly. The soldier to my left jutted his legs out for support.

Treg bellowed. "Ya had to say something!"

"Yeah, well if I knew it was request hour, I'd have asked for food."

The lights went off and flickered back on. The comm came to life again. "Brace for impact, we're hit and going down!"

The craft buffeted and rocked harder, and the lights blinked off again. I crouched down and clutched my legs. I tried to slow my breaths, but it was pointless. The others around me shifted in their seats, and I heard their fast and loud gasps while we tightened our bodies for the crash.

We slammed into the ground with a deep thud. I was jolted out of my seat when the craft came to a stop. The lights flickered off, then back on, followed by billows of smoke in the cabin. "Everybody out before she blows!"

Everyone pulled what they could carry and left the Hell Hawk as it burst into flame. A few grabbed several packs, and we scampered away from it into the woods nearby.

While the others gathered gear into piles, Dawn strode about like she was the commanding officer and expected a detailed report from an imaginary subordinate. She eyed the damaged craft like a mechanic about to enlighten us on how she would've fixed it. She turned to Jacobs. "What the hell was that up there?"

"Excuse me?"

"You heard me, just what do you call that?"

Jacobs narrowed his eyes. "Aerial maneuvers."

"Oh, really? And that includes sending us crashing to the ground?" Dawn closed in on Jacobs, but he just jutted his chest out more the nearer she got. I'd never seen Jacobs strike a woman, but he sure hadn't backed down one inch either.

"Honey, see these people here? I just landed that Hell Hawk safe and kept them from being torched in a burning wreck. All I'm expectin' outta you at present is a thank you while we figure things out."

Dawn's jawbone twitched, and she held her gaze on Jacobs. He returned her icy glare for a moment, then brushed her off and walked around to look at the crowd of survivors as everyone gathered gear from the Hell Hawk. "We walk from here," he said.

"Where to?" I asked out of reflex, but I knew. Jacobs lived for the fight. As much as Treg hated our situation with the Coalition, Jacobs was disgusted we were forced into being escorts for Lebabolis instead of turning our guns on the greater threat.

"We gotta get to a Storehouse." Jacobs face was taut. Lebabolis set up these Storehouses, places for weaponry and gear for any troops of theirs or the Coalition to load up in case of being overrun. They weren't part of the system, so any hacks into MODOSNet wouldn't reveal them. But Warrior Products knew where they were in their sectors; it just meant we had to slip over there to get them.

It wasn't any less risky to head for the Storehouses, but the fact that it meant we would have more weapons made it worth the risk.

While Jacobs checked his P-LAD, Dawn's eyes slid to me. "We have to get to the Capital."

"Are you nuts? Omegans are everywhere. The Capital's gotta be slammed by now. How're we gonna handle Omegans with no ship and just some pulse rifles?"

Her eyes bored into me. "I don't think I need to remind you about our little arrangement, Ana." She studied a few soldiers who cleared out wreckage and made piles of weapons and stuff they could save.

"Yeah, I know. But that arrangement includes getting our people to safety, and abandoning 'em like this is unacceptable."

Jacobs returned and stood near us. "We're near Sector Three. Figure we can search for it."

"Anybody here from that Sector?"

"No, but it's worth a hunt. I can get this bird up again for a quick hop. The targeting systems could zero it in if they're adjusted right."

I held my gaze on Dawn. "And the Capital?"

Jacobs looked at me a second, then returned to the device. "Uh, at least double that. Day or two, I'm guessin'. Why you looking for the Capital; we gotta get back to our people, right?"

Dawn grasped his shoulder. "Your people will be fine. When we make it to the Capital, you'll have everything you need to help your friends. We better move; time's wasting."

Jacobs eyes slid to Dawn's hand on his shoulder, then he looked at me with a gaze that told me he was anything but the touchy feely type and another collision was coming in seconds.

TWO

(NELSON)

ANA'S WARNINGS HAD GOTTEN easy for me to ignore again. She'd proven to me that this was all real, but that wasn't enough for me to avoid the fights like she wanted me to. But the sight of them flailing through the sand, desperate to avoid the Omegans that pounced down on them like a hungry pack of wolves, just jolted me into action. I leapt out of the craft, pulled people and gear, whatever I could reach, and helped haul things out of there.

The move sped up fast and I got so flipped around while I helped with loading several different Hell Hawks that I forgot which one I rode here on with Jacobs. I felt better when I spied Norg. He and I jumped into the closest Hell Hawk and before everyone was in a seat, we were in the air. I counted thirty total with me before the door shut us into that tight space. The air inside was putrid, like a sweaty gym locker room. No big surprise; as much as we'd been on the run, there wasn't time for things like housekeeping or even baths. I'd have luxuriated in a gas station bathroom right about then and felt like the most pampered metrosexual in this millennium.

Of course, the smell could've just as well been explained by where I was, the personnel hold. We sat fifteen each on two rows of narrow benches held fast against the walls of the ship by seat restraints. I'd been on a few of these so far, and each one reminded me of a cramped city bus, only with minimal windows. One thing I'd learned in a short time was to not stand up too fast or even for too long. These babies were pretty light and those quick dips meant a whirlwind on the digestive tract if you weren't sitting, and sometimes even if you were.

The reduced outside visibility was a blessing anyway. As much as I felt the ship jolt around, if I had the added sight of the spiraling horizon, I would've redecorated the cabin and made the already putrid odor even worse.

I only made out Norg's face next to me on my left. The rest of them were mere shapes with assorted groans and grimaces when the Hell Hawk twisted violently. The craft rocked and rolled like a ride at a fair run by a carny unconcerned with safety. Once I settled into the rhythm of the flight my thoughts went to why the Omegans were there, and I got this really sinking idea that this raid from the Omegans may have been as much about me as the Valentium, even more so. I mean, they had given chase even after we ditched the crater.

I braced myself to stay in my seat while we twisted through the air. The screech of the engines peaked and waned, like the calls of an agitated bird. Outside, random thuds and pops slammed about the walls, roof and floor. My stomach knotted up over the thought at any moment our pursuers could ram a shot right through this thing and kill us in a second.

Seconds later, Zengus' voice came over the system. "Three Omegan birds on our ass; I gotta outmaneuver them. Everybody brace, gonna get rough!"

"What's he mean, get rough?" Norg added his own private concert of groans to his retort and the increased movements of the ride. "Shit, I hate this damn flying junk."

"I thought you prepared for this."

He shot me a perturbed glance. "I was trained to fight on land. Most flights I been on ain't been so damned wild."

My sides ached from holding myself steady for so long. I jammed my eyes shut in the hope my dizziness settled down.

Ana insisted I ride in a ship instead of wait out the ground attack. Said I was too valuable to be killed.

Then I realized that the last thing I'd seen before the doors closed was her, still firing on the troops.

"Norg, did I get on the wrong craft?"

"Long as you wanted 91 you didn't."

A beam of light swung through one of the windows and lit up the sign across from me: tail number 91. "Damn. It was 42. I was supposed to be with her on 42."

"It's fine. You're alive; you made the right choice."

Aside from the pain in my midsection, there was the feeling I'd named the Pull. That was the best word for it, since that's how it felt. Ever since Baudricort hooked me to the Link, I felt this draw to get to Cataclysm. Whatever he did, it awoke something in me, and now I had this constant restless feeling. It was like if I slowed down I got uneasy in an instant, like that top of the roller coaster feeling. The more I headed in a particular direction, the better I felt. I thought for the longest it was just nerves and the rest of the catastrophes I'd been through up to then, but the location on the map, the sight of it just filled me with this urge that whatever I did and however rough it was, I had to get there.

I hauled myself up and peered out the window at Hell Hawk 42 and saw some shots careen into its side with an awful noise. I froze and felt a chill on my neck as I watched, helpless. The whine of 42's turbine engines sputtered as if it had pneumonia. The craft spun wildly and dipped lower, and a thick cloud of black smoke trailed behind it.

I glanced at Norg. He just shook his head at the floundering ship. "It's Jacobs; he's got it. He ain't our best pilot by accident." I watched the faltering plane until my vision became cloudy and I zoned out for a second. The rhythmic weaving and bobs of the flight stopped at once and I felt still and calm. I wasn't next to Norg or anyone else, and I wasn't on Hell Hawk 91 anymore either.

A splash of panic hit me. Were we blasted and killed instantaneously? No, this was different. I wasn't in the afterlife.

I was somewhere else.

I saw as clear as I'd looked in the personnel hold seconds earlier a group of people standing in the woods. Ana was there, and she was face to face with Dawn, the woman from Lebabolis who clung to Ana as part of our arrangement with Charista. I felt an odd sensation around her, but in that case it was more like the feeling of a substitute teacher who eyed me during class.

I saw Ana and Dawn in an argument. I reached out, but I couldn't touch them. Their words were muffled, but I saw their faces, Ana's twisted in anger and the other woman just glaring in response.

Another explosion clanged the outside of the ship. The woods blurred and faded as quickly as they'd appeared, and I was back in the Hell Hawk. The hum and the periodic thunder crash as the engines shifted our position, were overshadowed by a few loud whoosh sounds. Added to the mix I now had the worst pulsing headache I could remember.

"Missiles," a voice muttered. "Won't be missing us much more at this rate of fire."

Norg snorted. "They want payback. You alright, Nelson?"

"Yeah, think so; I just felt woozy."

"Well, you're in good company. Don't worry, Zengus got a few tricks yet, just hope I get to see when they blast those Omegans outta the sky." Norg snarled in contentment. He had taken personal joy in the sight of Ana with Commander Chun of the Omegans when she blasted him into bits back in Sector Five. It rallied everyone in the Action and Lebabolis, but it had brought a hell storm of fire on us for several months now.

The Omegans were strange anyway. The pulls I felt or feelings I got about things like Cataclysm and the Range, and even some people in the Action, didn't happen with the Omegans. They were odd, and the sight of them made me nauseous, but I hadn't figured out why just yet. I'd seen bits and pieces but none of them involved the Omegans.

More rumbles came from outside. I craned my neck for a glimpse through the narrow window. The three ships that careened toward us showed no sign of slowing down. I thought back to how they handled us at Sector Five. They were so clinical about it. They descended on our group like a cheetah toward a wounded gazelle. So ready to accept the surrender that we never gave them. I wondered how much they really knew about Lebabolis, or what would've made them so easily wait for a surrender. I knew I'd been through enough where giving up wasn't an option, and I was damned proud we still had enough who agreed, Coalition or no. It was crazy how that all went down. Instead of blowing us up at first sight, they waited. They didn't fire until we did.

Charista hadn't given us much information since, for someone who seemed like she had a lot of intel on the Omegan threat. The race was on, they were on a spree to harvest as much Valentium as they could find, so Llewyn was also tasked with making quick hits to get the rest of the Valentium available and Storehouse it.

Our options were limited if the Coalition didn't get most of the Valentium first. We had enough for fuel, but moving around more than we ever were, there was no way of guaranteeing this would last.

Zengus' voice burst through again on the speaker. "Norg! Get up here; I need help now!"

Norg released his seat restraint and lunged for the large cabling overhead while he muttered, "Better come too, Prophet Man, in case we need your noodle for gettin outta this."

He stopped after a few steps and looked over his shoulder. "You comin', or you gonna sit there til you puke?"

I followed Norg through several twisted corridors. A blast of hot steam hit me in the face at one point, and I swiped the moisture away. Faded yellow lights near the floor and ceiling lit our way. Now and then I swung into one side of the hull or the other and felt the ship lurch and shake. After more turns, we made it to the cockpit. Out the front of the ship, I saw the horizon twisting about while Zengus pulled and jerked the controls. The console in front of him displayed a map with three red glowing markers. My nausea welled up, so I locked my vision on them instead of the flipping scenery outside.

The muscles on Zengus' arms twitched and bulged as he grappled with the controls. The panel was covered in a wild display of blinking lights and sensors. A lone spark shot out from the center of the console every few seconds. Zengus never even turned his head. "What, ya stop to take a leak? Norg, nav and weapons console. We gotta hit these assholes with whatever this bird's got left. Nelson, to the left behind me, comm center. Raise somebody, anybody friendly. Fast!"

The comm controls lit up and after first glance, I tapped them and opened a channel. "Any idea who's closest right now?"

"Just send a distress call; anyone nearby gets it.

The craft steadied down a bit, but the vibrations from the floor that traveled up my seat through my back, and the high whine of the turbines, gave me an idea of how fast we were going. Zengus swung the controls of the ship about, and we twisted and bucked around.

I shrugged off the chills and turned back to the comm. "Anyone hear me, this is Hell Hawk 91, under fire from Omegans. Need ground to air cover, ballistics, anything, in deep shit, over!" I heard the words spoken in my voice with no hesitation, like a character I watched on screen in a movie.

The ship plunged, and my gut flung up into my throat for a second. Zengus roared and yanked the stick back hard, and we climbed again.

Beads of sweat poured off the back of Zengus' neck. "Can't keep this up. We're gonna be toast. Norg, set a course for us to ditch; least we can take cover in the bush."

The comm console flickered and switched to a map. I felt the familiar tightness in my stomach and thought it was another Pull.

But it stopped.

I tapped random controls on the comm and clung to the hope that someone friendly was nearby. It was possible, but just barely. A few other squadrons of Hell Hawks were in the Outlands, but the Omegans had been around a lot, so they were never in the same area for long.

The comm crackled and a deep voice pierced the white noise. "Stay on course, HH91, salvo loaded and ready."

"Who's there, over?" I tapped the controls, but no other response. "We got company, another unit close by."

Norg looked back. "Who is it? You get an ID?"

"No. They didn't give one."

"What? That's impossible, they ain't gotta give, its tagged on their comm. You sayin' you got a comm with a blank code?"

A few flashes of light and booms pierced the air around us. The ship shook violently and Zengus got to his feet and fought to maintain control. He heaved and wrangled the yoke as if he were a bull rider. His grunts accented the alert beeps from the control panel. His muscles rippled through his shirt and settled once the craft righted itself again. The console in front of him updated, and one of the three red markers disappeared from the screen. The remaining two changed course and headed away from us.

"Alright, 'bout time we get some help," said Norg.

"Yeah but from who? And where?" Zengus answered.

"Ain't gonna be picky over who saves our ass."

"Check the landing sequence, Norg. We gotta land somewhere fast, and it better be close to friendlies."

"No idea," I said. I looked back at the comm, but the screen was blank.

Norg popped up from his seat and leaned across me at the comm. He tapped a few controls. "Now that's strange. Don't see nothin on the register."

"Told you," I said.

Norg climbed back to where I was and pushed me aside. He

punched some controls and glared at the screen. "Nah, you don't get it. Anytime someone pops on a comm a tag shows their ID. It's how we know who's sending the info. Lebabolis and the Action tried fakin' that stuff plenty, but no matter what, there's always been some kind of marker. But there's nothing on this one."

"But you heard it, right? Both of you?" Norg furrowed his brow and shook his head as he slid past me back to his seat. I hated that I asked the question, but ever since I was hooked up to that Link, and what I went through when I saw the maps of the Range, I felt more and more tied to this world somehow. I always was, since I'm the one who wrote about it. But now, it was like I was joined with it, like physically. It made me wonder just what other people knew, saw and heard, and what was just in my head. And the vision of Ana and the rest, with no idea of when or even where that took place, made me more worried.

"There are groups in the Outlands, but they've never been loyal to anyone. They're scavengers and stay out of the way."

"You think it was one of them?"

"Yeah, or a Valentium blast. Could be the Verges; they've been unstable since the Omegans started using Darkness."

"No, someone called; that was help from somewhere."

Norg's jaw tightened. "Easy, Prophet Man, you ain't crazy on this one."

Zengus settled back in his seat. "Let's focus. That counterattack could just be a trick to pull us in closer. I'm dropping this bird low and getting cover soon. After we land we locate the nearest Regiment for med treatment and supplies soon or we won't be up for anything else."

Norg tapped the console until several maps appeared. "Kaitlinn's two clicks away; she's got air support capability. Gimme a few minutes to locate their beacon."

While Norg located Kaitlinn's group I thought back about the Pull and the Link. It changed quickly since we teamed up with Charista and the problem went from reigning in the Action to the

Omegans. They weren't sending messages anymore. Even the Xander ones weren't a thought anymore. In very little time, they weren't important at all, just a distant thought. I wondered about them and what they would've done to help things out. I guess she wasn't as concerned with the tailored messages once her people and her front yard were part of the war zone. Baudricort's great plan became barely an afterthought, except for his Exodus to the Range. And now here we were, scattered, on the run and under attack. Our only hope was that Llewyn wasn't in a similar spot. At least the groups in the field had the ability and the weapons for fighting back.

These people needed a leader to get them united; that was the only thing that went further than agreeable thoughts and distant shelter at the Range.

The Valkyrie seemed a good bet to me, based on what I'd heard so far. It sure made sense in my book that people rallied around a single person to win their fight. It was more about the Valkyrie than the Link. That work Baudricort had me do seemed like a terrific waste of time once the fighting started for real. He was more concerned about freeing his people; what was he not sharing with us? Why wasn't he more worried about the Omegans? Seemed they were the biggest problem by far. Of course, my Pull hadn't started until he hooked me in, so I wondered if that was his plan after all.

Everything I had heard since I got here told me the Valkyrie was the right choice for Lebabolis to rally behind. But I recalled my hero broke free from captivity. Ana wasn't trapped. She was on the run, sure. No one else had stepped forward, but it was obvious that as much as she was against it, she was the obvious choice.

Ana held true to what she'd said from the start. She wanted no glory or expectations from anyone about who or what she was supposed to be. She led from among the troops and didn't want any grand oath or anything. But once she had Varrick back, she was gone. She had no plans for a monarchy.

The Valkyrie brought a nation together. But what nation? Was it those people with Llewyn, scrambling into the Range to hide like cockroaches? Was it Lebabolis proper, in their ivory and metal tower, hunkered down from the rest of us less than worthy types? Was it the Omegans, who wanted to destroy the Coalition? Why? Were we the evil ones after all?

Being with the Valkyrie also meant swearing allegiance to Lebabolis, and Ana wanted no part of that. I hoped she was OK. She would've sent a comm from her ship by now though. It had to have been her ship that was shot down. Even with Jacobs with them, they were in a world of trouble. They would be flying blind and on foot with the Omegans swirling around like smoke about a campfire.

As far as we knew, Ana was missing, and that didn't set right with me. I had to know she was all right and that crash wasn't the end of her.

As Zengus eased the ship to a dense area of woods, I leaned forward. "Listen, guys, I gotta tell you, we need to watch out for Llewyn."

Norg eyed me. "The hell you talkin' bout now?"

"Look, I know it doesn't make sense. Believe me, I'm not sure why either, but I just got this really bad vibe about him."

Zengus chuckled a bit. "You do realize you're talking about the leader of the Action and the man Baudricort trusted with getting us to the Range."

I shook my head as they shrugged off my statement. I wasn't even sure myself at first about them, but just like I did with the Range and the location of Cataclysm, I felt other pulls about people. It was different with Llewyn. It was a push.

Whatever these new sensations were, there was only one person in the Coalition besides Ana Crucinal I trusted for answers, and I had to get to him as soon as possible.

(ANA)

DAWN EYED US as if she took some kind of census. Jacobs broke her concentration when he jerked his shoulder and freed her hand from his arm. "I'm helping our people." Jacobs stepped back, the P-LAD pressed flat against his chest.

"We are helping our people." She walked toward him, her eyes narrowed into a stare that danced with Jacob's in a sizzling gaze.

"Our people? Lemme tell ya something, lady." Jacobs thrust a finger in Dawn's face. "Yeah, I know what you're thinking, about Cataclysm. Well, since we got a minute to yap, I figure it's a good time to let you know I think that's BS. Far as I can see, y'all got a piece of meat on a hook for us to grab; what that is, I ain't exactly sure. But a whole lotta us gonna bite it following you before we get there."

I crouched down and traced my finger through leaves and pebbles on the ground. "Why the hell don't we just run and gun for it now? We're thirty strong; we can slip through the other mess in the Outlands."

"You'd die of exhaustion first. You agreed to this deal, you agreed to make this trip; don't get second thoughts now."

"Second thoughts; hell, the whole situation's changed. The Action's been cutting and running on Lebabolis for a good while now. We ain't never needed any help from you before. We gotta take care of our own, because no one else ever did. And that don't include some crazy ole chase into the mountains for your damned secret weapon neither."

The crowd swarmed around Jacobs and broke out in whoops and shouts. Some people yelled out "One or None!" I felt the Action pride burst out in me, but I remembered there was another side to this now.

Dawn's eyes narrowed. I wondered if she even knew how to crack a smile. "You know, the whole purpose of this Coalition was to help each side out. Your people get to stop running like the frightened mice you are, and we get to fight the real enemy without worrying you'll meddle with things and screw them up." Dawn dug her boot into the ground and sent up a brief fountain of leaves.

"I ain't never signed on for ditching my group. Neither did Ana. No way are we leaving anyone behind; the Action's as important as Cataclysm, if not more. One or None, right?"

His eyes found mine, and I saw the fire behind his, raging more than many. He lived that phrase, that rallying cry; so many of them did. There were no gray banders in this group. But for the first time, that battle cry made me ache. It had meant so much for so long, it kept us strong and got us to move and unite. Now with things this backwards, it hurt thinking about it. It was an uncomfortable memory. Did it still mean what it did after what we'd done, and who we'd sided with?

I had no love for Charista, and even less feelings for Dawn, but the deal we made stuck me. They promised protection in exchange for help from Nelson and me. And I just knew, as bad as the Omegans were and as wild as it was in the Outlands, us going it alone was suicide. This decision felt like a blade edged past my ribs into an artery; if I moved or tried to get rid of it, I'd bleed to death.

Jacobs' eyes pleaded with me and held my gaze. His glance said more than his words ever could. It was the same look I'd seen from people in the Action, and a big part of what kept me with them all this time. Even Norg, Kado, Treg and all of my friends from so long ago. They needed me here. They'd have done the same for me, and it was a safe bet the rest of our group from the Crater were looking for us right then. And Varrick, could I walk away from him being cured? If only we had left sooner. Was I really a leader, when I hadn't been able to even decide what was best for me and my own brother? Now we were ditching the Coalition, including our people, when they needed us most. Why didn't they deserve the same respect? Besides, at that point, "anyone in the Coalition" included Nelson, who I wasn't leaving behind to be stranded or hurt by a damned sight. Crazy as he was, Jacobs would've died before he let anyone else in the Action get hurt. And that went over and beyond the damned Coalition.

Jacobs was spot on about our situation: with no ship and minimal guns, we were an easy target no matter where we went. Hell, the Omegans may not even have to fire a shot if one of these roving bands in the Outlands got to us first.

I had this awful idea that Nelson was dead, but only for a few seconds. They hit us so hard in that escape, I had to think that others out of the ten took fire too. As images of Nelson among the wounded came into focus in my mind, I shook myself to get that thought away. *No, you'll crumble if you start thinking like that. Keep it together. People are watching you.*

Pulling my shoulders back, I clutched a rifle behind my shoulders and enjoyed the cool metal against my neck. I chuckled to myself when I recalled how Treg held his rifle the same way. My mind wandered to the options. Thanks to Jacobs and Dawn's quite clever yammering and insults, they were clear cut. I wondered if that was how I sounded during those fights I'd had with Baudricort, over questioning Encampment moves and arguments for more rations, or later on with ideas on securing the Action from raids. I gathered a slow breath in my lungs and imagined Baudricort. When things got rough since he died, it helped when I pictured him, like he wasn't dead just yet; he was still here, my father.

When I did that and spoke, the words came through me, and I felt my father's presence. "Jacobs is right. Making our way to the Capital over open ground with no protection is very dangerous. Not even Dawn can deny that."

Dawn shook her head. "It's not a question of denying. You made a deal and you have to honor—"

"If we get to a Storehouse, we have a chance." Jacobs interrupted.

"Hell, we could even split up, send a smaller group back to the Capital and send another group back to the fight," I added. Jacobs nodded, a smile creeping on his lips.

Dawn seethed. "That's not what we agreed to."

I swung the rifle to my side. Dawn tensed up when the muzzle moved past a straight line toward her chest. "Neither was getting shot down. What's your background, anyway? You a Warrior Product over there, 'cause it looks like they laxed requirements letting your flabby arm twitchy ass in."

She straightened herself and looked three inches taller. "I'm an Intellectual. And you're what, a Worker?"

"Had me some after school learning. You had it cushy with the Lebabolis elite. Out here, things happen and we deal with 'em. We make hard choices and handle the fallout. We don't always like it, but we go with what we're dealt. And we take care of our own. That's what the Action's about."

"There is no Action." Dawn returned a triumphant smile.

"Bullshit," said Jacobs.

"Where there's two or more of us, there's always an Action." I glared at Dawn.

"Our people are in danger, and we have to make sure they're OK. There were ten Hell Hawks in that crater. We don't know what happened to the others." Jacobs steeled his gaze for a moment. "And there's also the Guard. Maybe we can reach them."

The Guard was the elite unit of the Valkyrie. I hadn't heard anyone mention them out loud, but plenty wondered about the roving bands in the Outlands and the chance some of them were linked to the Guard. Nothing was ever known for sure; it was just a lot of interesting stories so far.

I held back a chuckle when Jacobs mentioned them. It was better having Jacobs on your side in a fight, but still sometimes he talked crazy even by his standards.

Dawn scoffed at Jacobs. "The Guard? You don't put faith in that decrepit band of warriors, do you? Calling them warriors is a stretch. You realize how long it's been since they've been any kind of formidable unit?"

"Don't matter, they're around."

"And just how do you know?"

"I've heard things."

"Oh, things. Like rumors? Fairy tales?"

I wondered what Jacobs knew. There was the Valkyrie emblem, but I was always told even talking about the Guard was forbidden. The unit only lived in memories of some older Products and random whispers around the Sectors.

"I ain't seen any proof they're gone for good, and the way they gave y'all hell back then tells me they're tough, and toughness means survival. You ask me, they're just what we need now."

Dawn shook her head. "We're low on time. As much time as we just spent talking about long lost warriors, we could've made good progress to the Capital."

"Well, just what are we getting there? Can't you clue us in so we know why this trip is so damned important?" I asked Dawn.

"Because no other way will get us there. We'll never make it on our own, not even if that Hell Hawk is flying and piloted by Captain Ego over there. You don't understand; you're trying to win a battle, I'm trying to win the war," Dawn said.

"By gettin' Cataclysm. Now who's believin' in fairy tales?" Jacobs rolled his eyes.

Dawn's gaze flopped back between Jacobs and me. "It's not like that."

I waved Jacobs off for a second. "So far it's more like a hunch, but y'all kinda got me and the Action where you want us. So again, what is so damned special at the Capital that's more important than Cataclysm now?"

Dawn eyed us and those who stood close. She hesitated, but then after she weighed out the risk of telling it, she took a deep breath. "Charista's promised us transport ships. Very sleek, very fast. They have a good chance at outrunning the Omegans. They won't outgun them, but with their speed, the Omegans won't have time to get a fix on us. But they're only in the Capital. We can't get to them anywhere else, especially not via a Storehouse."

"What if the Omegans hit it with their Darkness? They've already downed Hell Hawks with it."

"I grant you there's no guarantee with the transports either, but they've got a lot better chance than Hell Hawks; they're much faster. If we want a fighting chance at this objective—"

Jacobs had been leaning against a tree, his arms folded tight while Dawn made her case. But when she brought the transports up, he lit up like a case of explosives. He shoved off from the tree, his face twisted in a sour look, and he waved his hands about as if he were fanning the reek of Dawn's putrid idea. "Just hold it, now she's yapping about transports. Multiple, right? We been scratching and crawling like dogs to get to the Range in those land clunker facilities. Why the hell she been saving them til now? We're getting picked off—"

"We don't have enough ships for the Coalition. They're advanced prototypes, and right now Charista wants them used only for the Cataclysm run. This is just a backup plan." Dawn's lips drew in a line.

I knew the burning in my gut was there to stay until we at least knew about the rest of our people. I thought Nelson would've been safer away from me. After Baudricort was killed I thought whoever did that might come after me, especially if anyone else knew he was my father. I was glad Nelson wasn't there with me then. Just maybe he had a better chance than us.

Jacobs made his way around to the others, talking to them two, three or more at a time. Their eyes warmed to his words, and I saw their nods and curious glances my way.

I adjusted my comm for the ship Nelson was on but got no response. I dropped slowly to the ground and watched the comm as the sounds of Jacobs and Dawn arguing faded into the background.

I went to a nearby hill with Treg as he still maneuvered the P-LAD for a signal to locate the Storehouses. Even if we split up, it was up to Jacobs to give coordinates to the Capital for Dawn and whoever else attended there.

Dawn's voice surged to a shout. "Each of you is in debt to Lebabolis! You don't know what happens if you just go renegade."

"I'll entertain your crazy ass theories another day, lady," Jacobs muttered. He planted his feet, a defiant sneer on his lips.

Dawn's eyes widened, and she looked ready to unload a verbal salvo at Jacobs, but she never got to. Hell Hawk 42, already damaged from our narrow escape from the Omegans, exploded. The blast knocked several others and me down and sent the trees into a spastic, angry dance. The rattle of leaves hung in the air along with a steady column of smoke from the wreckage.

A loud ringing clouded my hearing for a few minutes, and I gagged on the odor of burning fuel and mechanical ship guts. People staggered to their feet in a daze, and if I had been alone I would have seriously doubted I'd just seen this. But it was real.

Shouts came into focus, and a few people rushed over to some who stood close enough to get hit with the flames.

Others scrambled to their feet. The moans and grumbles gave way to shouts toward the ship.

There it was, left in a smoking smoldering mass of black twisted metal. Any hopes we had of getting it flying again were gone. A mangled number 42 was most of what was left of her tail. There it lay, like a dead animal. What had kept us from being vaporized a little while ago was quickly burning down to embers and jagged pieces of metal.

I jumped up and hauled whoever I could grab away in case of a secondary blast. We settled back and collapsed again to the ground fifty yards away from the burning wreckage. I scanned the group until I saw Jacobs. His eyes had widened, but a clear spike of rage blossomed. He swung his rifle up and took a few steps toward the simmering wreckage, then turned to Dawn, his lips pursed. "What did you do?"

"Excuse me?"

"You heard me." He approached her; his rifle came to a bead on the center of her chest. "You tryin' to do us in over here; what the hell you pulling trying to blow us up?"

"Hold on; what even makes you think I'd do that? I was on that ship just like the rest of you. You really think I'd kill myself?"

"No, but you'd keep us from taking care of our own. You weren't getting takers on your Cataclysm mission, and we need a ship for gettin' back to our people. Not having one's the best reason to go 'long with you to the Capital."

"Might've been a fuel leak; did you think of that while showboating and playing hero?"

"I call it savin' your Intellectual Product ass, honey." His face twisted. "I got an idea." He powered up his pulse rifle. The whine of his weapon as it came on to firing mode froze everything in place. My breaths stopped. I felt Treg's hand on my arm, but my entire body was stuck in place. He ran over to Jacobs and Dawn.

While I watched the scene between the three of them, a weight pressed on my chest. I let out a sharp gasp, but no one noticed. Then, I heard a voice that sounded hollow with a slight echo.

+Ana.+

I glanced around. My fists clenched at the sound of my name. For a second I thought it was the Comm, but no, that was still dead.

Then I remembered.

It was the voice I'd heard before, at the Verge site and when I made my trip back to 2014. I hadn't heard it since, but it was impossible to forget. And it wasn't the Link either, like I'd thought it was once. It echoed in my head, and my thoughts became a voice in response.

Hello?

+I need your help.+

You're the one who called out to me when I went through the Verge?

+I am.+

The memory of the voice made my throat tighten, but I wasn't speaking out loud.

Who are you?

+It's not important. But you must get to the Lebabolis capital as soon as possible.+

Why? What about our people?

+They are fine.+

Nelson?

+Yes, of course. They found help and are safe for now.+

I can't; there are Omegans everywhere.

+What's at the Capital will help you defeat them. Please, you must go there.+

We're alone, with hardly any weapons. We'll be picked off.

+Do what you always do... find a way.+

We have to arm up first.

+Be quick. Someone there needs you. Someone you care about.+

Then, along in the background, I heard another voice, a young boy pleading in wails of pain.

"Varrick?" I blurted the name out in a quick sob. Dawn swiveled toward me.

+Yes. Make your way to the Capital; it's urgent. Take a small group. No more than four people. Scans might not pick you up. They look for larger units.+

The weight released off me, and my hearing cleared again. There was Jacobs, his rifle poised now at Dawn's head. Beads of sweat squirmed across and down his forehead.

Treg hollered, but Jacobs stood fast. The muscles on his arms bulged, and I realized why Treg hadn't grabbed the rifle. It was set to fire, and if he missed when he reached, Jacobs might've set it off, even just as a nervous flinch. In spite of this, Dawn wasn't fazed; at least she didn't show it. Her eyes were as cold as a Radomet visor. For once I had to admit I had just a sliver of admiration for her.

I marched up past Treg and stood between Jacobs and Dawn so the rifle was pointed at my chest.

Jacobs' face flashed in confusion. "What the hell you doing, Crucinal?"

Treg reached for my arm. "Ana, get out of—"

"No!" I swung away from Treg. "Go ahead, Jacobs. You wanna kill somebody? Shoot me."

The sweat came quicker down his forehead. I heard Dawn behind me say, "It's a wonder you people survived this long on your own."

I swiveled my head over my shoulder. "Dawn, shut the immediate hell up." Looking back to him, I said, "Jacobs, don't waste time on her. You want to get to our people, rejoin the fight and keep the Action safe. It's what Baudricort wanted, what he still wants. His dying wish was for our safety. You know we made this other deal with Lebabolis to keep that going. So I'm going with Dawn to the Capital to finish our part of it."

"Oh, are ya now?"

Jacobs stared at me in disbelief. I stared at the three orbs, the angry glow of Jacobs's rifle and his eyes that struggled to make sense of what I meant.

"It's what separates us from them. We finish what we started. We promised Lebabolis we'd go for Cataclysm, and that's what we need to do."

He lowered his rifle. "You realize you're going with the person who just tried to kill us?"

My stomach knotted when I realized I had no good counter to that. "Yeah, well, she needs me as much as she thinks we need her, Jacobs. She knows her big boss wants me alive and I've got a deal with 'em, so if anything happens to me it won't be pretty for her." I turned to her. "Isn't that right, twitchy?"

Dawn nodded.

"And I'm looking out for who we left back there too." My gut tensed when I thought about Nelson and what they may have ended up with. Maybe they weren't even as lucky to have landed as we were. They could've been captured.

He shot a glare toward Dawn, and to me a concerned look. "They'll use you and spit you out when they don't need you no more."

"I'm a soldier, and I'm completing my mission. You take care of our own and get our people safe."

Jacobs' eyes pleaded with me more, and I felt my throat hitch. "If you see Nelson, tell him I'll see him soon." The words came out half as a request, half as a sob.

"Tell you what," Dawn said. "Jacobs, you want to leave, go right ahead. That goes for the rest of you too. From what I've seen on the tracker, it won't be long before you get snatched up by an Omegan patrol or worse, and so help me I won't feel bad in the slightest."

"Back at ya, sweetheart. I'm bee lining for the Storehouses and getting back in this game." He glanced at the rest who'd gathered around us. "Anyone who wants to save our people, come with me."

That was it. Our Coalition group may as well have reverted to Action at that point. The crowd made their way around Jacobs until Dawn, Treg and I were the only ones standing apart.

"We should stay in a small group." I grabbed my rifle and

powered it down. "We'll move quicker. Jacobs needs a lot of muscle if he's gonna scrounge for a Storehouse."

Dawn checked her P-LAD then nodded. "Fine. Ana and I will do it."

"And me," Treg said as he walked closer. He winked at me and hoisted his rifle.

I looked into his eyes. A trace of the fierce calmness remained, but a glint of worry pushed through.

"I've had your back until now; not stopping anytime soon."

I offered him a smile in return. While the group with Jacobs passed around weapons, he approached me and nudged a pulse pistol into my hand. "In case."

"Thanks."

"Your old man was pretty hard headed too. Guess I shouldn't be too surprised."

"Yeah, well. Take care of yourself."

"Damn straight. And you, don't turn your back on her, you or Treg. You're out there walking through the woods, got to take a rest, even for just a second, she may get one on you. I mean it. Don't think she can't call out a squad with that P-LAD of hers neither."

Treg nodded. "Jacobs, link back up with Kaitlinn when you can, give her our update. We'll reconnect as soon as possible."

FOUR

THE REST OF THE HELL HAWKS that made it out flew off to the rendezvous point. We arrived in time to see the sun sinking below the horizon. It cast a deep amber hue on the sky, but we had no time for scenic pictures, much less the gear to take any. Six out of the original ten ships made it back. We stood around and checked for who was safe or not. The ships wheezed black smoke as their engines purred to a low hum as they were powered down.

Kaitlinn's regiment still had a decent number of troops, over a thousand at that point. The landing strip was a carved out section in the wilderness. Trees formed a jagged border that gave little protection other than an indication of where the rendezvous area ended. Toward the center of the clearing, next to the landing area was a familiar sight, the temporary buildings used for troops and storage. What Llewyn's group hadn't used in their trek to the Range was left behind to help the Coalition troops in fighting the Omegans and keeping their eyes off the main group headed for safety.

"Checked troop counts on the console before we landed and we got 1800 total here. Not bad. Just hope the rest of our wing didn't get zapped like 42."

"How about the others, like Jason?" I asked.

"He's railing it up north. Giving the Omegans some shit alright, but we hadn't heard much from him so far. Gotta think, hard ass crazy dude like that, he'll be alright. He's wild but he ain't stupid."

The whines of the Hell Hawk engines reverberated against the tree line like squawks from an agitated pack of birds. Waves of heat and engine exhaust splashed my face, and I coughed at the noxious fumes while I watched Zengus and Norg with the others. The soldiers checked on the wounded while some made adjustments to the Hell Hawks.

A group of thirteen Radomets kept a silent watch over the scene along with a collection of Coalition gray band troops. They strode the outer perimeter, the Radomets' mechanical gait almost humanlike, but with enough awkward jerks that reminded anyone they weren't human. Radomets were around and provided security here, and where they could. They just weren't able to handle the unstable terrain like the crater. Too bad; we could've really used them there.

This was a temporary fall back, according to Norg. Kaitlinn wanted time to regroup, as little time as they could grab. Even I knew we had to hit them with an even bigger force than we had here. Kaitlinn's regiment had a good punch, but without word from Jason she wasn't about to get into anything too deep in case we had to fall back to Lebabolis for a final stand.

Or head to the Range.

I wondered how it would go down if it meant protecting the Range or Mother Lebabolis, and then I realized it was obvious. We were as much on our own as we ever were if this came down to survival.

If Jacobs somehow made it up with Jason, and Ana was there, they'd be fine. I hoped she'd be alright wherever she was, but I wasn't too sure. The Pull was the only thing I'd been 100 percent on of late.

Once they saw who made it back from the Crater attack, the next step was getting back in the fight. The longer they stayed here, the more time the Omegans had to find Llewyn's group and pick them off for good.

Coalition troops hurried around the place. Some tended to the mobile facilities while others counted and checked weapons and the rest took care of the injuries in a makeshift field hospital. Wounded were directed to a med station for treatment. The whole scene felt like a busy airport or better yet, a disaster scene. Soldiers reached for equipment and shouted updates to others. Medics raced about the wounded.

I grabbed Norg. "You tried raising Jason on the comm?"

"Comms are spotty as hell. Can't even get advisories from Lebabolis right now, and that's a real bite. We're bloody and blind out here. Best we can do is hope we get word from a scout unit before another company of Omegans rolls over our asses."

"What about those guys who called our ship?"

"No idea. Let's see if Kado can figure that out. If he's even here."

Norg and Zengus joined in with the work on the Hell Hawks. The bold ships had a continuing purpose: provide whatever air support they could and keep the Omegans focused on them and not the ground troops. We had a small edge on them in the air, not with guns, but with maneuvers. And some help from other Coalition soldiers on the ground.

I left the group of soldiers that tended to Hell Hawk 91 and headed toward the med station when I heard a gruff voice over to my side. "Hey, gimme a hand over here!"

After a second I found the source. Two Coalition soldiers knelt over a third, who looked about the size of the other two combined. The soldier who called to me had a bleeding gash under one eye.

When I got closer, I saw the man on the ground they surrounded. He writhed in pain, and I felt my legs tense at the gaping wound in his midsection. A strong wave of nausea hit.

"I- I'm not a medic, fellas."

"Don't matter, let's move him to a table. Medics are too busy; help us out, huh?"

Eye Gash directed me to one side of the man while the other soldier, a taller thin man with glasses, cradled one of the man's arms. With some effort, we heaved and got the heavy guy onto a table. Heavy Guy groaned loudly and some blood splashed on my arm. I felt woozy, as much from the blood as the heavy lifting.

Eye Gash looked the man over, his mouth crinkled and his eyes stained with worry. "Hell of a damned war, ain't it?"

"Oh yeah. I'm Nelson, by the way."

"Lon. This one over here's Tayl and the wounded fella down here's Mack."

"Nice meeting y'all, aside from the circumstances. Don't suppose you know where I could find Kado?"

Tayl's voice was gruff with a slight gurgle of someone with a lung ailment. "Haven't seen him since we got here yesterday."

"If he's here, check the med station. He's gonna be pretty damned busy if he's around though, unless you been shot or worse."

"Thanks."

The med station was in total chaos when I got there. Two tables staffed by three people tended to twenty soldiers. Scattered around were bodies of those with serious wounds in various states of consciousness and life. I noticed two of them marked with the symbol that indicated they had Pox. It reminded me of Ana's brother Varrick, and made me wonder how he was, in the involuntary custody of the Lebabolis government. I thought about Charista's pledge to Ana, part of what started this whole Coalition thing, and wondered if she really could have cured the Pox in them.

Bandages were flung about like Mardi Gras parade throws while the medics worked at a frantic pace. One girl medic got close to me on her way through the crowd, where she did quick assessments of the soldiers, so I grabbed her shoulder. She jerked her head up and spun around, a scowl on her face.

"Don't touch me like that, or you'll get a hypodermic in the eye."

"Sorry. Is Kado here?"

She huffed and returned to her P-LAD, her head nodding. She shot me another nasty look before she bothered with a response. "Negative. He's doing a job for Llewyn."

"Where?"

Her eyes tipped upward to me, and her scowl deepened a bit. "Can't you see we're busy? Ask Kaitlinn."

She continued her work without another word in my direction. Even if some of them had an idea about what happened to me with the visions, there was no way any of them checked me before the wounded. What I had was filed under "Crazy". They had enough cases of "Dying" for a good while.

I trudged back toward the mobile buildings and caught sight of Kaitlinn. She held a P-LAD tight beneath her folded arms. Her broad shoulders were a random but distinct reminder of how small mine were in comparison and how I needed to find whatever gym these people used around here. I made a personal note if I ever got back home, I was gonna start a dystopian warrior workout as my surefire crazy rich retirement plan number 793.

Kaitlinn alternated between gestures to soldiers. She directed them like a seasoned symphonic conductor and gave a stoic survey of the scene of casualties between batches of orders to her subordinates. Just the sight of Kaitlinn gave me a feeling of calm. I couldn't imagine what her inner dialog was, but on the outside she looked like a battle tested general. She reminded me a little of that General Honore guy I'd seen as a kid in New Orleans after Katrina. She grasped her ear comm and rattled off lines of crisp clear orders then returned to the scene before her.

"How goes the war?"

She spun to me. From the first time I'd seen her, Kaitlinn had this ever annoyed look on her face. I figured if she ever cracked a smile, that was the moment I would drop dead from surprise. Her battle armor covered most of her body, and jagged scratches and some char-ring canvassed a good bit of the armor. She was the leader of the field troops. She came from the Lebabolis side of course, and while the Action didn't think as much of her for it, they weren't saying too much about it either. Of course, the sideward glances I noticed from the Action troops made me realize just how little they really thought of her. Like her or not though, she was in charge of the field, she and Jason anyway.

Every time she looked at me, her eyes got this weird glint as if her brain conducted some elaborate analysis of my exact purpose on this planet, with results that were so far inconclusive. Her green eyes pierced mine like a bird of prey. They reminded me of Ana's, but instead of how Ana's glance made me speechless, Kaitlinn's visage made me feel like I was under inspection from a superior officer, or even an interrogation.

"Ah. Mr. Forrester. Glad you made it out." Her tone was as flat as an empty balloon. At least with Baudricort, I gathered he was kinda interested in what I had to offer, or at least that I was around. With her, it felt like she waited for an opportunity to hand me over for ransom. She was the last person I ever wanted to play any kind of card game with. Some of her looks I swore I'd gotten from an irate Bourbon Street bouncer or two.

"What happened in the Crater?"

"We were overrun and outnumbered."

"What do these Action people think they can do?"

"If we hadn't gotten out when we did, we'd be dead. We got off some shots at them; Ana had us there."

"Ana Crucinal; yes, I know her. The darling of the Action, an untested, illegally trained Deviant. As if I didn't have enough problems on my hands, I have to deal with somebody's messiah complex."

"She's not about that."

"I'm not so sure. Anyway, poor planning and execution. If we weren't so stretched out, I'd have sent a group there myself. That's the problem letting ragtags run the show."

Kaitlinn had gotten a lot of attention earlier in the war, after the attack at Sector Five, by leading early maneuvers and turning back a division of Omegans from the Capital. It got harder and harder to keep the Capital safe, though. The Omegans had more numbers, and they forced the Coalition of Lebabolis and the Action into a regroup. The hope was this group with all Lebabolis' strength and all the Action's resourcefulness had what it took to finally stop the Omegans. Until we got Cataclysm, anyway.

Kaitlinn glanced back at her P-LAD and spoke into her comm again. She watched the Hell Hawk crews and the rest of the troops. Her feet planted as if they were two tree trunks, she stood firm and resumed her meditative stare from a few minutes earlier, the kind of trance I pictured reserved for the likes of Napoleon Bonaparte or Catherine the Great. I imagined she had a lot on her mind, and since Baudricort's murder was still a mystery, I assumed she was wary about the same thing happening to her.

No one ever discussed what had happened to Baudricort in recent months, or if anyone had ideas, they hadn't shared anything with the group. It really bothered me how they never told me here. It wasn't like I knew a whole lot about what they had planned, but still... being this much in the dark had me pretty worried. With nothing they could use for information in their fight, I was that much easier for them to take out, so they had one less thing to worry about if I wasn't around.

"Should've gotten more Valentium," she blurted out loud to no one. "We've got to be better about that. These vehicles don't power themselves, and the raids are getting more dangerous by the day. The Omegans are sealing off the Valentium one site at a time; we can't keep letting them take it."

I hated the way she brushed off what we were up against. "It's been a rough fight. Has anyone else been able to get some Valentium?"

"Of course we did. Our Warrior Products were trained more for engagements than Ana's group."

"They hit us pretty hard back there. Their force was ten times what Ana had there, easy. But we had other help once we left the crater."

She raised an eyebrow. I nodded and continued, "Somebody shot down a few of those Omegan crafts chasing us. Was that you or someone else from the Coalition?"

"No, I'd have heard if it was. Could be Jason's Regiment, but more likely it was one of the renegades. I wouldn't be too thankful. They could've easily shot you down instead."

"I assume you heard about Jacobs' group."

"Mmm. That's going to hurt. Jacobs is a good man, even if his loyalties are skewed." Kaitlinn served the praise up with the ease of someone who had a gun pointed at their head. "I understand Ana was on that flight too."

"Yeah. Heard anything from them?"

"Their beacon showed a safe landing; that's what we know. The signal went dead not long after."

"Oh?"

"It could be their attempt to avoid tracking. We're trying to raise them on the comm, but that's tricky." Her eyes darted past me and without another word, she walked toward a group of Hell Hawk pilots and briefed them.

Just past where Kaitlinn and the pilots stood, a large procession of troops formed and loaded wounded personnel and gear onto the mobile facilities. I may not have been around here long, but I was familiar with this sight: another Relo.

Kaitlinn's discussion continued with the small group, but the mechanical gasps, whirrs and other sounds that came from close by muffled most of it. The troops in her presence, however, stiffened up and regarded her with complete attention and silence. I smirked at the sight of the gray bands on most of her rapt audience. No wonder she won them over so well. She was one of Charista's best senior officers, and the more I saw her with her troops and how she and they got along, the more I saw, not just felt, what had been happening. Ana had been worried how much these two groups had really meshed, and I didn't blame her at all. I wished I knew where she was; the longer I stayed with Kaitlinn, the more I felt like a prisoner than an ally.

I knew I wasn't the only one who felt that; Ana was never that sure of Kaitlinn either. I wondered if my whole separation from Ana in the crater was part of some attempt to get me away from Ana and even more vulnerable.

I missed Ana.

The hurricane I'd entered when I got here hadn't stopped, and the damage it did hadn't happened all the way yet. The people on my team were few. Ana had my back, but her being gone made me rethink what I needed for my best shot at survival and one day getting out of this. I had the Pull, and if I could just figure out how to control or at least get back to following it, maybe I had something. I knew, just from the look in Kaitlinn's eyes when she watched me, it wasn't a good idea to share too much about the Pull too fast. I mean, I had trusted Baudricort much more and he damn near cooked my brain on that Link machine. They had the Link, they had their weapons, but information was mine and I had to watch how I used it. Without Ana nearby, my back wasn't covered, so I watched my mouth instead.

The word from several people back in the Crater was Llewyn needed another two weeks if they didn't run into any other problems or attacks. And that was one of our main goals: give the Omegans a target to shoot at. Maybe we took a few of them down in the process. I thought about my primary mission, getting Cataclysm, and how Ana and I were not on track for that.

I caught up again with Kaitlinn and her gray band cult as they were planning the Relo and their next move after that. When she noticed me in the crowd, she frowned and began using code that I didn't understand. But I definitely got the message that she wanted me gone, someway somehow, even if it came down to shooting me in the head.

I'd never missed home more. Little stupid things that I'd had, food, friends, even a cashier at the supermarket, any one of them right then and there would've made me relax if just for an inkling.

And of course, I wanted to know about Dad.

The road home was further and further away; it seemed like the grainy distance on a highway road, flickered in the distance just out of my reach. The Verge, the break in time that got me here, was thrown out of whack according to what had Kado told me back in Sector Five. As much as he knew about a lot of things, he hadn't come up with any solution to that, which worried me the most.

My gut ached at the thought of how long it had been since I left 2014 and what he must have gone through ever since. As my mind played back more memories, a stiff pain shot through my neck. I grasped for the small control device. Kado had developed it as a way to slow the effects of the Verge on me. It worked alright, except for feeling like I was being strangled every now and then. I was about to ask Kaitlinn where Kado was when I noticed her staring at me.

"Something wrong?" I asked.

She said nothing but watched me for a little while longer. I felt a lump form in my throat and swallowed to relieve the tension. It didn't help, so I tried my other option. "I'd like to see Kado. Any chance you can point me to where he's at right now?"

She arched an eyebrow. "Kado? Why do you want to see him?"

"I'm having problems with the device he gave me, I'd like him to look at it."

Her brow creased and she gave a quick sigh. "Our wounded get treated before we move out again. I can't let this large a group sit too long. I'd have moved much sooner if we didn't have this many injured. Besides, Kado's not here now anyway."

"Can you get me to him?"

"No way."

"Why?"

She faced me. "Because for reasons I'm sure I don't know fully, Charista considers you valuable. And with Omegans running wild over most of the Outlands and inside Lebabolis borders, I won't risk an asset because of minor discomfort. You read me?"

Dread settled on me like a spring rainstorm.

An asset?

My throat clenched, but then the irritation spiked. I narrowed my eyes toward her.

She responded with a glare of her own, as if she'd read what I was about to say. "I know your worth, Nelson, trust me. I'm capable of reading briefings."

"Alright, so then how the hell do you know how bad this problem I'm having is or if it won't get worse?"

"People are dying here, Nelson. We're still getting Pox outbreaks. We tend to the most pressing issues first. You'll hang on with this device, and we'll get you to Kado when we can."

Her eyes burned back against my stare. A soldier ran up to her with an update, and she took off with him. Yeah, my second class citizen status has been reconfirmed in spades.

I watched the loading in progress for a few more minutes, and Norg approached. "There's scout patrols around; we're waiting on their latest reports from the Omegan movements. We're rotating out in a day or so."

"Where to? Anywhere near a beach?"

Norg laughed. "Not quite. But I'm thinkin' I need to see Kado. Heard he's working on new weapons powered by Valentium. More powerful than we've ever had before, and we'll need 'more powerful' if we're gonna get an edge on those Omegans."

"You going? Kaitlinn told me no."

"Why?"

"Said it's too risky."

"She's not wrong, but that never stopped the Action before." Norg smirked, and a twinkle appeared in his eyes when he said Action.

"I'm all in. This thing on my neck is bugging me."

"I'll make it happen."

"Kaitlinn won't like that," I said.

"Duh. Ana can't have all the fun, right?"

I laughed. "What about Zengus?"

"Nothing doing; he's been reassigned to a flight squad. But me, I'm not gonna sit on my ass and wait. I'm a Warrior Product. We don't wait for an opportunity, we make one."

The ships were scattered about on the pad, an uneven display of firepower. While most Hell Hawks were worse for wear, the soldiers worked on them and loaded them up before the temporary encampment was broken down for their next move.

Most of them did nothing that made me feel like I was at home, but after a few surly looks and snarling rebukes from Norg I realized that he'd given me as close to a welcome as anyone. Even after what happened when we lost Otto, Ana, Norg and their Circle never held it against me, no matter that I'd taken off running and put them in a bad spot earlier. I guess they realized that just like them, I wanted to win this fight.

Kaitlinn marched about the temporary facilities while they were closed up, and I mused that she looked for a place I could fit, some kind of compartment so this 'asset' would be kept tidy and clean, like a crate of water.

She'd always kept me on the outside of her group, and at every turn I knew I was being tested. But with Ana it was more about her helping me and vice versa. I was useful. Kaitlinn made it clear to me that I wasn't.

About time I made her rethink that.

FIVE

(ANA)

THE REST OF THE TROOPS walked off with Jacobs. I watched 'em head back, ready for another fight, and wondered if Dawn was right, that they'd just be picked off. They had a fighting chance if they got to a Storehouse. But there were also the roving bands. I half wondered if Jacobs was into more than he let on, if he had information about the Guard he didn't want shared with Dawn and the non-Action side of the Coalition.

Jacobs stopped and gave me a look as the others walked about him down the path toward the Storehouse. The serious glint in his eyes faded and his lips turned up a little. He arched his arms up in the Valkyrie salute, and I returned it. We watched each other for a moment, two ragged warriors more than ready to take a break from this endless trip around the outlands but unwilling for any surrender that wasn't part of our total victory. Much as guys like him could be pricks, I knew if things really got hot, he'd have taken a shot to the chest for me. I'd have done the same for him too.

We shared this thought without a word spoken between us. He turned around again and was gone.

Dawn led the way toward the Capital at first. I was a little

346

amazed until I realized she was staring at her P-LAD for directions. I couldn't help but wonder if her intellect was limited to her technology access.

There we were, a Warrior, a Worker, and an Intellectual Product, a cross section of what Lebabolis represented in its essence. Three of us working together, but not how they had planned.

After Jacobs' outburst, Dawn claimed we had even less time than before. With Treg and me close behind, she hurried over the leaf coated ground. Her trail sent flurries of leaves around, and the branches in her way snapped back as if in surprise. I watched her relentless pace and chuckled to myself as I waited for a stumble from her. The warm air brushed past us with each step we took. The air was dank with the smell of leaves both growing and rotted.

Finally, she stumbled over an exposed root, but that only slowed her down for a second. It was like she was in a trance with just every so often making an adjustment. A slight turn here, a little jag there, but her pace was as steady as a Radomet. We pawed our way past the branches that flung back angrily in the path of Dawn's wake.

"Watch it!" Treg called out. "You may know the way, but we need to be careful."

"It's fine," she said. "I scanned this area; there are no traps." Her arms swung wide, with not even a glance back our way.

I wondered if my comment to Jacobs that she was on the up and up was gonna bite me on the ass. Treg shrugged and rolled his eyes at me as if he'd heard my worries out loud.

"Hear that, Treg? The Intellectual says there are no traps. Maybe she can get on her little play pretty there and fetch us a ride, save her precious little feet from all this abuse."

Dawn stopped short and darted back to us. As fast as she'd moved ahead, she rushed back within an arm's length from Treg and me. Her precious P-LAD was clutched tight to her side, and her deep blue eyes pierced into ours. She held her gaze on us; her only other motion was the excited heaves of her chest. Beads of sweat formed on her crinkled brow. She switched her glare between Treg and me. In her eyes was a blend of aggravation with some fear too. By sheer reflex, I felt my scowl deepen.

"You think I wanted this? You think I wanted to be out here with any of you people? I was perfectly happy where I was, in a lab doing research for Charista, when she pulled me out for this. I'm sorry that I don't see any reason to be here any longer than possible."

"We were happier when you weren't an appendage to us, too," I said speaking for both Treg and me.

"You made the deal, you live with it. Just like me."

I gave serious thought to ripping the device out of her hand and popping her with it. The tightness in my gut spread to the rest of my body and I could feel my teeth clench. I'm not sure how I managed to speak instead of whack her, but I did. "So you want to get back to your little death facility, I get that. Until then, you're not under the cozy umbrella of the Capital out here. We're a team, get it? So you best listen up to the people who've covered combat areas on foot more than you."

"How about you show me some courtesy as well?"

"How about you give me more than two feet of space," I said, raising my weapon up to my chest, and in a flat tone I whispered, "How about it?"

That's when Treg stepped in between us. She shook her head and glanced at her P-LAD until he grabbed her shoulder. "See, we don't get to play with just our own Product here. It's all about one in the Action—excuse me—the Coalition. And that means what's best for every... one. Get it?"

It was my turn to pull him back as Dawn blurted out, "You weren't so successful you didn't need to make a deal with Lebabolis, now, were you?"

For someone who was supposed to be smart, she didn't have an ounce of self-preservation.

What she did have was luck because Treg and I both felt like she wasn't worth the trouble of killing.

Treg shouldered his rifle. "Call out directions from the rear, and let us with the guns do what we do."

Dawn tapped her P-LAD in thought. "I guess you have a point." She averted her eyes and pointed in the way she'd been headed when we'd stopped. I felt a tinge of relief at what was the most progress we'd made yet on this hike.

"I'll cover the rear." When Dawn eyed me, her eyebrow arched. I added, "Don't worry, honey, I'll have his back, and I just might cover yours too."

Treg flashed me a wink and activated his rifle as he stepped out ahead. Dawn followed in the middle, and I held the rear up. We were as prepared for action as anyone could've been in our situation. My hand found the handle of my dagger. I'd be able to toss it at somebody if needed. It sure came in handy on the Verge back to 2014.

I smirked to myself thinking back to when Jacobs had his gun at her chest. He'd have blasted her wide open, and then we'd be off somewhere else. But I couldn't do that. I had a deal and I had to focus. If nothing else, for Varrick. What would become of him if I didn't?

Dawn's eyes slid to Treg then back to me every so often. She wasn't sure she could trust us, but she finally realized she didn't have a choice. Our pace was slower this time as she pointed out dips and breaks in the ground ahead.

My gut eased a tad when it looked like we had made a breakthrough with her. However, the searing hunger pains I'd felt back in the crater were creeping in much worse by now. While the thought of food was appealing, the idea of what we had to go through to get it wasn't. I took a few deep breaths and focused on ignoring the nag of my belly. I looked through the woods every chance I got but saw nothing even close to being food.

The outskirts of Lebabolis, where we were, were barren. Any worthwhile food was harvested from this place a long time ago. A person could find food if they had some know-how and some time, but we were short on both.

"Can't you find a Verge on that P-LAD of yours and get us through this quicker?"

"Not since the Omegans started using Darkness and made the Verges unstable."

We walked on in silence for an hour. The forest provided just enough sound that covered up the noise of our breaths. The periodic chirp of a bird and the smooth rustling of leaves were the only noise for a while, until my curiosity got the better of me. I thought of how wide the Coalition was, and the fact they had stuck me with Dawn, of all people. An Intellectual Product. Ok, she could've helped when it came time to work with Cataclysm, but why now? We were in a bad way out here, and another Warrior Product would've been far better.

My boredom had gotten as bad as my hunger. "So laboratory, huh. What were you making in there, more Radomets?"

Dawn glanced over her shoulder but kept walking before she said, "Not quite."

"Well, what then?"

"Chemical experiments." Her answer was squeezed out as easy as someone who'd been tortured for it.

"So then, Radomet research."

"No, not that. We were studying the effect of a new virus on humans."

That stopped me short.

A jolt of disgust hit me like a fist to the midsection. Visions of Varrick and the others with Pox flooded my head, and along with my progressing hunger it made me dizzy.

A new virus?

I knew they'd already experimented on augmentation like with Radomet, but this was the first I'd heard about there being biological weapons in their programs. "You're telling me you developed biological weapons for use on people?"

"For defense purposes."

"Defense from what?"

"Oh come on, Ana. You know about the groups out in the Outlands. You don't remember, or perhaps you were too young, but we had raids in the city. Why else do you think we made such a well-trained army?"

"OK, got me there. What kind of virus?"

"Is this really important right now?" She flashed a worried look.

"Maybe, maybe not. Ya know, you can call 'em experiments when they're in a lab, not when they are used on real people. And Dawn, when you toss me that scared look, it makes me wonder what else you're up to and why you're really here."

"What do you mean?"

"I bet you heard by now a lot of our people came down with this thing we call Pox. It's lethal, and so far no one's been able to treat it. My little brother has it, and Charista promised she'd cure him and our people. Seems a little strange to me if she'd make that claim and not have some kind of person like yourself to back that up."

"That would be strange alright."

The heat of the woods I'd been sweating off just coursed through me, but this time it was anger. It could've been the shakiness in her voice, or the weeks and months of running ragged with little to no sleep or food, or just the damn stupid smirk on her face right then, but a switch flipped in my head. Everything at that moment had to wait for me to set her straight. The Capital, the Valentium; even Cataclysm and Varrick had to wait for me to take care of this.

I grabbed her shoulder and spun her back until our eyes were directly across from each other.

Treg approached us. "What's going on?"

"A little girl talk, Treg."

My face seared, but the warm air had nothing to do with it. My gaze dug into her eyes like a needle. Dawn panted, her eyes wide. "W-what are you—"

"I'm not too happy about this either, but since you never bothered to ask Treg or me how we felt about being stuck with some low-life Lebabolis scum, I'll just say it. It sounds like you're avoiding telling me something, and I'm not too good with secrets. So I'll ask you one question, nice and easy, and you better tell me straight or you'll regret it, I promise."

"O-OK."

"Did you develop Pox?"

Multiple beads of sweat formed and trickled off her forehead. Her eyes looked in several directions before they returned to me. "What do you mean?"

"It's not a complicated question. An Intellectual Product can handle it. Did you develop Pox?"

"Does it make any difference now? Your brother, your people have—"

And she was avoiding again. Time for more persuasion. In a breath, the dagger was in my hand and at her face. She squealed at the cool blade pressed into her flesh. A tear joined the sweat that now poured off her face.

Treg gripped my arm, but I flung my shoulder and broke his grip.

"Ana, what are you—"

I held my hand up and waited for Dawn's response.

Her eyes were wide and focused on the blade an inch away from her right one. "OK, yes, yes, yes I did. But I was part of a team. I wasn't alone."

"Same difference. Doesn't make you any less guilty. Like when you blew our craft up."

"That wasn't me!"

Her eyes still hadn't convinced me. "I'm watching you, twitchy. I get any, and I do mean any, funny feelings about you, I'm knocking your ass out and dragging you to the Capital. I've been wound up for a while, and I think the exercise would do me some good."

At that moment I prayed there was a Verge nearby that I could've jumped back through so I could've eliminated every person who had developed that illness, including Dawn. But there was nothing I could do. We were stuck, and so was she. The emptiness of my options made me even angrier, and I was back to thoughts of what I'd do to Dawn to relieve some of this.

Treg squeezed my arm that held the blade. "There's no time, and you know we need her. Let's go."

I gave her another moment to wonder how far I'd take this, then pulled back and walked on with Treg. Dawn followed behind us at a safe distance.

"The hell's with you?" Treg asked.

I shrugged. "She's bugged me. For a while now."

"She's up your ass by assignment. Of course she'd bug you. Can't you just deal with it?"

"It's kinda tough when she's one of those who made my brother and the rest of our people sick. You know, people in the Action? Dammit Treg, they poisoned us. Why don't you care?"

Treg crouched under a low branch. "Hey, you know I do. But we made this play with them. We got a deal, and you heard Charista. She'll cure them if we finish it."

"If she can."

"Now we know for sure they developed Pox, so they can also stop it."

I glanced back at Dawn, several steps back. Her eyes widened when they met mine. I took a little satisfaction from her apprehensive stare as I turned back around slowly to continue our trek.

We walked in silence for another hour. The path got rougher, and each time I lifted my feet over a fallen branch or stump my hips rewarded me with shooting pains. My stomach ache had progressed into a mild burning sensation by then. I strained to think of when my last actual food was. A week? Could it have been that long?

"Treg, how bout a break, huh? This walking is killing me."

"Can't keep up with the Warriors, Worker Product?"

I tossed a branch at him. "You know better. Come on, let's rest for a few."

Dawn was surprisingly agreeable about stopping. Amazing how a blade to a person's face can change their whole disposition. We pulled up against a cluster of trees and lay back on the grass. The light from the sun dotted the leaves and ground around us and made jagged shadows on the ground of our surrounding foliage. Dawn leaned on a tree off to one side of the clearing on the far end away from us. I drank the rest of my water, which amounted to two gulps. It wasn't even enough to soothe the itchy dryness that stretched down my throat.

Treg sat across from me, his legs crossed and rifle leaned over his shoulders. His eyes scoured the land around us, but like I'd seen, there was nothing.

"Treg, we need rations. Anything. What Sector are we closest to?"

He sighed. "No clue. Better ask Dawn; she's got the nav data."

"Do I have to?"

"Wherever we are is the outskirts of Lebabolis. They trained us in spots like these, but I wasn't in this exact one."

Dawn alternated between gazes at her P-LAD, cautious looks our way and around the woods as if she could find some food and prove us both wrong. She'd be the hero Intellectual Product who got one over on the Warrior Product and warrior type who couldn't fend for themselves in the wilderness.

"Think it's a good idea we talk, based on our last conversation?" The thought made me chuckle.

Treg watched Dawn for a second, then replied, "Just be less you, and that'll be a start."

I kicked a patch of leaves into Treg's lap in response and approached Dawn. She held her water bottle up, so the scant drops in it fell into her mouth as I neared her.

"Hey."

She pulled the bottle back and jerked her head in my direction.

"We need food and water soon."

She resumed her gaze around the woods. "How about we find a stream?" Dawn looked at her P-LAD and checked the maps.

"I got another idea. Let's try a housing unit in the nearest Sector."

"That wouldn't be smart," Dawn said, avoiding my stare.

"Try necessary. Where are we; what Sector's close?"

"You realize the Omegans were spotted in groups in most Sectors?"

"I'm not saying we mount a damned offensive. We peg the housing units, we pop in, grab some rations, pop back out. We need a recharge. It's at least another half day to the Capital, right?"

"We should keep going; we've had enough delays."

"But we might have to detour again, and the Capital isn't expecting us. What if it takes a while to get through to 'em? And what if the Omegans are there too? We may have to hide and wait longer than we think or draw down on a bigger force. In either case, we should be ready to wait longer than we think."

She looked down toward the P-LAD in thought. I looked at the screen for any hint of a tracker or a link to Charista. I was waiting, hoping to see anything that would've justified what Jacobs thought and given me a green light to tear into her. But nothing except her eyes locked on mine. "You're not going without me."

"As if I didn't know that." I smirked. "Get the coordinates and we'll make it happen."

Dawn's P-LAD screen flashed into nav mode and scrolled several maps as well as our location before it displayed a jagged red line between two sites. "We're near the border between Sector Two and One. We could arrive at a housing unit, maybe 15 or 20 minutes from here."

"That sounds good." I motioned Treg over and pointed toward Dawn's P-LAD. "So according to Dawn there's several housing units nearby. We gotta be light and quick about it; you know the Omegans are in a lot of places, and the ones who aren't trying to get to the Capital are busy scouring the rest of Lebabolis for anyone who didn't make it to the Capital for Lockdown."

"If we come up against more than five of them at once, it's not gonna be pretty... for us."

"I know. There's foraging around here, but I haven't seen

anything edible since we started. Besides, there could be snares set out here. I'm sorry, but I'm not trusting what's in her little P-LAD scan here. We rely too much on that tech, and it's gonna get us killed one day. Besides, the Omegans are just as interested in pilfering the housing units as we are, so they won't rig 'em."

Charista started the Lockdown not long after the fight in Sector Five as a precaution. According to what Charista said, all Products were brought to the Capital with little to no notice. It was a little like how I left in Exodus, but this time in broad daylight. People took whatever they could get together in that short of time. My gut screamed at me that there had to be some supplies left behind. Then again maybe my gut just yammered for a meal. In any case, it was our best chance for getting food and any info besides the secret alerts Dawn chose to share with us. I was hopeful for some weapons, but the reality was we may just score a bit of food someone had no time to carry.

"Why don't we make this detour even more worthwhile and look for a Storehouse too?" Treg asked. "Would be nice having more fire-power for the rest of this trip."

"Can we locate 'em?"

"Warriors were shown the ones for their sectors, but that's about it. And this isn't where I grew up." He fluttered his lips and looked at me with a downtrodden gaze.

Treg set his rifle down and folded his arms behind his back. "Before we jump on this, what about the Valentium? They'll be around for that too, and I don't want to hit on any pockets of that stuff they just happen to have a unit guarding or anything. It'll be bad enough if we hit a roving patrol, but they'll be jacked up at the Valentium sites; they'd waste us in a blink."

"No deposits in the immediate area," Dawn said as she looked back at her P-LAD. "There's always potential they exist but don't show up on this device. I think it's worth this already risky idea."

Treg nodded me over to the side. We walked several feet away, out of earshot from Dawn.

"You think we can trust her? A minute ago you were about to fillet her throat and now we're trusting her to find us food?"

"I hate to be going off my gut right now so much, but it's all I got. I figure she's out here like us. And I gotta think, if she's that concerned with not leaving my side, she wouldn't put us or herself in a situation that would jeopardize it."

"She's gotta be hungry, like us?"

"Yeah, but she also wants to get back to her people, like us to ours. So we help her, and ourselves. It sucks, but it's the Coalition."

"Helluva motto." He nudged me.

Dawn had returned to her P-LAD. I wondered if she just had maps on it still, our nav path, or if she'd relayed some update back to Charista, our coordinates for something else. I looked forward to the time when we'd be free of her and no longer need to be under this deal that felt like anything but one.

SIX

(NELSON)

THREE LOUD BLASTS thumped me in the chest, and I gasped for air.

People around me looked at each other and me as if to ask if everyone else had felt the same thing just then. I checked the skies for any incoming craft around, but there were none. Kaitlinn passed a glance over the scene, her arched eyebrows melded into a scowl that pierced the area in a sweeping arc like a lighthouse beam until her eyes fixed on one spot. She muttered, "Damn."

The temporary facilities belched black smoke into the air. Soldiers rushed in and around the vehicles. Some checked what had happened, others rushed to help people injured in the blasts. The explosion hadn't affected the Hell Hawks for the moment, but crews near the ships stopped their repairs and fired up their engines, and sent the ships further away from the spreading flames.

Some spots burst into flames that lapped at people nearest them. Kaitlinn swung the P-LAD about, and she looked like she wanted to fling it toward the facilities in frustration.

"We've got a problem," Kaitlinn said it to no one in particular, and without any hint she caught the irony of us having a single problem amid a sea of nine million other catastrophes. I felt right then like I was a director of some weird documentary about a military commander with virtually no knowledge of their situation who made their best attempt at control out of chaos.

Kaitlinn tapped madly on her P-LAD. Diagrams flashed back and forth, and readout flickered like a strobe light. She scratched her head at some schematics which flashed over the screen very quickly.

Kaitlinn let out a deep sigh. "Kado worked on this problem ever since the Coalition was even formed. I thought we had more time before this happened."

"Before what happened?"

"These units were meant for Valentium exploration and mining, and nowhere near the level of abuse they've been getting. We're pressing them too hard."

"So what then?"

She fixed her eyes back on her P-LAD, with no acknowledgment I was even there. "Baudricort was smart, using them in his Exodus. They're the only way to move so many people out very fast. But even he'd admit this trip to the Range is a long shot. We'll get them moving somehow. There's too many people to handle otherwise."

She nodded in agreement with her own idea. I wondered just how many would've gone along with the likelihood of that. She scanned the area again until her eyes met mine and a name popped into my head. It was in part wishful thinking, but now more than ever it looked like she needed him too.

"Can Kado help us out?"

She gazed down at her P-LAD, as if the answer was already there. Maybe it was. Just then I was hit with an odd regret for the times I'd spent with my eyes glued to a smartphone or other device screen while in conversation with someone. Weird how that little nugget of perspective popped up at me right then.

"Our priority is security and defense; we can't have one without the other. It's too risky, shuttling him back and forth. No, he's safer where he is. I've got a unit guarding him. Both of you are important, too important to chance being out in the open, unprotected."

"Me continuing to, you know, breathe is pretty important to me."

She took a slow breath, her eyes pierced into me. "No, it's too dangerous. If need be, we can relay information to him on a comm."

"How about a deal?" I asked.

"Mr. Forrester, I thought I made it clear, I won't risk you out in the open like that. There's a place for you, and right now that's within my sight. If you want to be of use, keep people away from the flames."

My eyes fell to her P-LAD as she continued her argument. I saw a map of the area, and just then, a tight ball of tension built in my stomach, but I realized it was another Pull. This one was a little like the feeling I had when I saw the map with Baudricort and Ana, and located Cataclysm. Only this time, the display jumped more, and it had nothing to do with her hand.

There on the map, an overlay of icons appeared, like some kind of strange computer program. And I just knew the icons were us, the Coalition. One icon slid across the map and then several more markings of a different shape appeared. Above this the text "Omegan attack in 12 hours" in bold red letters framed the image up.

And then the air around me went into a haze and I saw more explosions. Like before, when I saw Ana in the woods, but this time I was in an open field during a battle. I felt the hot wind from ships that swooshed by above, the thundering ground from troops rushing about, Coalition and Omegans. Then there was the hot singe of pulse fire that rocketed past almost too close to avoid.

I saw Kaitlinn as she fell to the ground, and blood trickled from her mouth. Ana flashed into view too; she had a knife poised at her throat. My fear had me frozen. It was all I could do just to keep my eyes open. An Omegan attack? Was this the future? Trouble about to happen?

I heard warbled speaking and then a click. The visions faded back to the burning facilities and where I had been a moment earlier.

I looked back at Kaitlinn, who held her gaze on me. "Well, what do you have to say about that?"

"I'm sorry?"

"I asked, if you're supposed to be this prophet Xander, what should we do here?"

I chewed my lip and watched her, then looked back to the map. Just like that, this field commander of the Coalition, a decorated soldier of Lebabolis, asked for my strategic assessment. I felt like I'd just been given four kings in a hand of poker and it was time to call.

"What if I told you I knew where and when the next Omegan attack is happening?"

Her eyebrow arched. "I'd say tell me where."

"Nah uh. You know what I want."

"Oh?"

"Get me Kado, either here or there."

"Did you forget the part where I explained how dangerous that would be?"

"You need help, as do I."

"So you're holding out on me?"

"I'm bargaining. There's something wrong with this device he put on me. If you do that, or get him here, I'll tell you what I know. And you better do it before whatever this is I'm having gets worse."

Her jaw twitched. "Suppose I just yank it out of you?"

"Yeah, but you don't know that wouldn't kill me, huh? You willing to risk that?"

"I'm beginning to think it's worth a chance."

"I bet Ana would have a lot to say about that, not to mention Charista."

She inched closer to me until her breath tickled my nose. "So that's how it is?"

"Looks that way."

Her eyes reddened. They widened, and her scowl tore into me. I took several deep and noisy breaths, then swallowed the lump in my throat, but I felt my feet rock stead beneath me. She thrust the P-

LAD to her side. Her eyes narrowed and her lips drew in a line. "Norg will bring him here. You'll stay with me. Is that clear?"

"Fair enough."

"No, answer the question. Is that clear?"

"Crystal."

"While we're tending to that, I'm giving Llewyn an update. He needs to know, in case his facilities start breaking down like ours. He needs to be ready if the Omegans slip past us and the rest before we can get mobile again. We're making good on our deal to protect the Action, like you are on Cataclysm."

"Alright."

"And you'll be there when I contact them so we'll both know what's going on in that brain of yours."

"Why not? Lots of people want inside my noodle these days. At least I know you want me for my mind."

KAITLINN TOOK me into a darkened room. Three chairs stood around a table with a comm in the center, a small disk shaped object. When Kaitlinn activated the comm, Llewyn materialized above the device, a disembodied head that wafted in midair in front of us with a bluish glow. She started the conversation and rattled a lot of details off from their facilities and much of it went over my head. She spoke words that melded into gobbledygook about system problems. At best I recognized every fifth word she said. But even being back home, a mechanical conversation would've glassed me over more than listening to a golf game on TV.

All I was good for in maintenance was driving my car in to Firestone when the little red light told me so. I had a great imagination for creating this world, but imagination is where it ended. I refocused on her assessment when she got back to regular English.

"It's pretty bad. The units are having multiple issues. Ultrahydraulics, drive systems, general maintenance problems. These units aren't holding up to all this traveling. We both knew this would happen at some point, I just hoped it would've been closer to the Range."

Llewyn squinted in thought. "So what then? How do we fix this so we can keep going?"

"It'll take a lot more than elbow grease and wrenches." Kaitlinn sighed.

I leaned toward the comm as she spoke. "Look, while we're discussing options, why don't we just make a grab for Cataclysm? It's out there, and Charista's hell bent on finding it any way she can."

Kaitlinn eyed me. "Ana and Dawn are part of the deal."

I gazed into Kaitlinn's eyes in the hope that maybe I'd gotten a breakthrough from her and she'd for once listen to one of my suggestions. Instead, I got a face I'd have expected from my old high school disciplinarian. Kaitlinn's brow was creased, and her face was littered with sweat, some grime and an expression sour even by her standards. "You don't realize what you're dealing with there. Charista is adamant Dawn is to be part of the retrieval. I can't allow you to go on your own."

I figured on another approach and decided I'd flex my snark muscle. "Kaitlinn, are you afraid of not doing something Charista tells you?"

"That's none of your damned business. I'm more concerned with our people. Cataclysm is Ana's job."

"Right, but who's to say where Ana even is right now? We're not sure she's still alive." My throat tightened when I said that last part. Thinking that idea for a second, her not being around anymore, scared the hell out of me. As much as I'd been through in all of this, she was the one constant that kept me going. And my thoughts of getting home took on new life once I saw what she went through and was still going through for me. She taught me that the darkness out there was nothing I couldn't overcome and break through like the sun piercing a thick cloud front. She never flinched, coming centuries back for me, even it if meant leaving her brother behind to an illness.

Thinking of her tireless trip and continued surge filled me with energy and a sense of why I was here after all. If she made it across all those centuries to me, what was a trip of several hundred miles in comparison?

"What are you suggesting here?" Llewyn asked.

"I've got the P-LAD from the Valkyrie. It's got coordinates on it and some other text. It was encoded, and no one's been able to break that, not even Kado with his gear. But there's something he doesn't know, that none of you do either.

Kaitlinn and Llewyn's eyes were glued to me.

"I can read them."

They both cackled in response. Kaitlinn shook her head. "Ridiculous. Now I'm wondering if the time displacement sickness hasn't induced delusion in you. Perhaps you really do need an examination from Kado."

I then reached for her P-LAD, which she slid just out of my grasp. "Show me the maps for the Range."

She pulled up the diagram, and with the Link open to Llewyn I sat back and breathed deep. I was getting better at controlling the Pull when I wanted to. It was happening on demand, even deeper than I'd felt before. A tremor rippled through me at first. My throat seized for a few seconds, then I felt a trail of heat spread from my mouth down into my stomach. I took several quick breaths before I rattled off a litany of words, many of which I had no idea about. They sounded like coordinates and the Greek language. Did I know Greek? I took a class, but that was ten years ago. Back then I only knew things like how to describe my dog after he had a drink of water. What I was babbling could've been words similar to what Kaitlinn had rattled off a few minutes before. For me, it wasn't a matter of comprehension, but more like regurgitation. It was as if I had an MP3 player in my brain and someone had just pressed play on the most bizarre playlist ever. Kaitlinn's gaze faded from a cynical grin to mild amusement to downright shock.

I rattled off names and locations of not just the Range, but of other areas near it. I spoke names I'd never heard, in pronunciations I had no clue I'd known. My mind and mouth became like a water pump that spurted information out. Had I not seen the look on Kaitlinn's face, her mouth wide open in amazement, I would've happily accepted a strait jacket and an all-expense paid trip with accommodations in a padded cell.

I handed her P-LAD back and swiped my hand through my hair. "I never said anything when I first found out. Baudricort tried to jam me up to the Link and pull it out of me, and I was afraid what he might have done if I told him about this. But yeah, I can read it. The words just form into where I can read them, like magic."

"So we've got the source of this code, but not the means to get to the Range any faster. The Omegans are around, and sooner or later we'll be in the thick of this again no matter where we go."

"Can we get anyone there, Kaitlinn? It's worth a hit to your numbers if we can get Cataclysm."

"All I need is a transport and one other person." I smirked when I thought of just who I wanted. I knew if there was anyone I had a fighting chance of staying alive with, it was him.

"Give me Norg and I'll go. I'll find it."

Kaitlinn shook her head. "We must reposition first. We've got an edge if we know where Cataclysm is, but right here we're far too vulnerable, this many troops and vehicles in one spot. Besides, I won't chance us getting to Cataclysm first with two people only to have you captured or killed by the nearest Omegan group that happens along. Once this regiment is better dispersed, I'll spare a detachment for you. In the meantime, we'll get word via comm from Kado on a temporary solution to this problem so we can get going again. Once we handle the facility issue, you and a detachment take off ASAP, head straight for the Range and that location. Meanwhile, keep your comms open and report back on the first thing you see or if there's trouble, you got that?"

I released an anxious sigh. "Yeah."

(ANA)

THANKS TO DAWN'S P-LAD coordinates, we threaded ourselves through very thick brush and made it into the cleared outskirts of Sector Two. The gentle stillness of the woods was fast replaced with vacuum silence, the stale sound of nothing. It was like someone paused the sector in its tracks. The emptiness in the air made me queasy. The woods were a sea of noise compared to this.

Even knowing about the Lock Down protocol, the empty streets and buildings that greeted us felt very weird. Everything was vacant. Vehicle paths were littered with shards of clothing and rations containers, signs of a mad scramble. Tire treads from where trucks pulled people and drove them away from here snaked along the pathways headed out of the sector. The signs that normally displayed work assignments were smashed, and instead spat sparks out in a regular tempo like an electric fountain. The functional boards displayed the standard Lockdown message.

Rule one in a Lockdown was you made it to the Destination any way you could. The regular transports weren't there, of course. The whole place looked like a fake construction site, a decoy Sector. The only noise I heard was the low whine of the evac alarms while we walked around.

My gut drew taut when I felt my boot crunch over a busted P-LAD on the ground. The droning alert was the only sound around us. This weird feeling settled on me like a moth. My arms tightened, and my mind went to that place it did when there was trouble. I learned this from Treg—if you lose your bearings for too long, you become a target.

Focus. Center yourself on the immediate area.

The problem was the immediate area bugged me more than anything.

I looked around at the housing units, ten alone on the path we walked. Any decent sniper set up on top one of those buildings could've gotten a shot off at all three of us. I watched Dawn and hated to admit it, but for at least this part of the trip she was right. We had let our hunger call this move. I had a bad feeling it was gonna bite us back hard. If the Omegans or anyone else wanted to, we would've been easy pickings for even their worst soldiers.

I peered around while Treg stepped ahead of us, his rifle aimed forward. I wondered about the people who lived in these units and what had happened to 'em. Did they make it? Not too long ago I was one of 'em. In a dangerous event, we'd be ushered to a safe place. We had practiced for things like Valentium Core reactor meltdowns, but I had never seen a real evacuation by Lebabolis.

It impressed me how everyone looked to be gone; I hoped all of 'em made it to the Capital for lockdown. Of course, all Lebabolis had to do was dangle the promise of food and they'd be off. Those were the reins: food, work, purpose, ingrained through the Link. For those who accepted it anyway, acceptance meant more like absorption. They kept every product working and humming along like a well-tuned machine. Aside from the Deviants in Custody, the rest of their Products got on well with the program. The Deviants were eventually turned into Drone Products, or Radomet if they had enough physical potential.

Most Products were so lulled and guided by the direction of having work to do—the same work day in and day out—they didn't need much to have to pull up and get to the Capital any way possible. Most of 'em would've crawled there if they had to.

That's why the Exodus was still the best idea for a lot of people, even with Baudricort's absence. There wasn't time to organize it better. They just had to get as many to safety and let the sorting work itself out later, once we decided just what and who we'd be. In this system I was more warrior, but maybe there'd be another choice— farming, or even leader? What if those choices included a family of my own? A chill ran up my back at the idea I could be someone other than who I was right then.

I'd never been through a real lockdown, but the complete empti- ness of everything around us just felt strange, even wrong. I noticed scarring on some buildings and wondered if the Omegans picked off some stragglers during the move for Lockdown. But even so, if they did, where were the bodies? They wouldn't have bothered with clearing the dead away.

Or would they?

After a few minutes, my breaths slowed, and with the slight relaxing went the knotty soreness in my body. I was glad for once, being away from the fight, even if it was here. I walked further and glanced around at the peacefulness of this place. Trees were scattered around between the facilities, and small patches of grass showed some jagged darkened lines that looked like hurried steps of people in flight. The area almost looked lonely, like an abandoned animal that waited in sad silence for its owner's return.

I had time to breathe and adjust to what was going on for a change, and adjusting to people's plans weren't easy, especially Charista's. All of her moves since the Coalition were tough to figure, but so far I hadn't felt like she wanted to kill me. The Omegans were still enough of a threat, and her people, like Dawn, were here with us. I had enough value in Cataclysm alone. Problem was, what happened after I delivered it? Nelson and I had worth until then, but she wanted me to go after Cataclysm more than any of her people. There was some kind of weird trust between us, I guess.

I realized I hadn't heard that voice I'd heard at the crash site. I wondered if it knew about Baudricort and my mother. I still had so many questions, and I only felt more deep in this fog than ever. I wondered about how that bomb had killed Baudricort just moments after we'd seen him. I thought about maybe that was meant for Nelson or even me. My mind flipped through scores of faces and names, a sea of suspicion, but that's the sick and twisted game I played in my head. Like my father before me, I'd never stopped planning and working out my options. I figured as long as I kept at that, I had a chance at finding my way outta this mess and even getting Nelson back to his home.

A sharp ray of sunlight bounced off one of the windows and into my face. I winced and blinked to clear my sight of the glowing remnants in my vision. We had a play with Cataclysm, as long as we got to it first. With the mix of people in the Coalition, I was even less sure about who Nelson was left with. So help me, if I found out he was dead, whoever was responsible was gonna deal with me. I let that thought of his death linger a second, but just like earlier, I pushed it aside. I had to keep all the energy I had directed toward our next goal as much as possible.

Dawn observed her P-LAD, and I noticed some updates from Kaitlinn from over her shoulder. If Nelson was safe, he'd be with her. It was the smartest place, other than with me. Kaitlinn was Charista's top officer, and as much as Charista considered Nelson valuable, he'd be held under Kaitlinn's boot at all costs. Kaitlinn was a warrior though, and warriors aren't babysitters.

I wondered how Nelson dealt with being under constant watch from someone other than me. I mused if he'd handled it any better than I'd been with Dawn. Maybe Kaitlinn would've been easier; at least busier so she couldn't have been as close by as Dawn had been with me.

I hoped Nelson hadn't taken off on another rogue trip; there was no way I'd have known when or where to look out for him if he did.

My biggest problem was even if we delivered Cataclysm to Charista, there had to be a way out for us. We needed some kind of assurance before we delivered that kind of power to anyone. Once she used it on the Omegans, then what? Was she serious on her promise to let us go in peace? I missed Baudricort a lot more at times like this, when my brain churned in overdrive with so many scenarios and options. I strained my mind to consider what he'd do in this situation.

And then there was the "Valkyrie" business.

It started not long after we repelled the attack at Sector Five and I faced down Commander Chun. Charista made her grand show, where she announced the victory to citizens on MODOSNet and took her credit for it. But people who were there and put out the fires and buried the dead and brushed the blood, dirt, and guts off their hands by my side knew differently.

They saluted me.

It felt weird, but by reflex I returned it, my hands crossed above my head, and mirrored them. I felt pain from not knowing what to tell these people. I wasn't sure where this Coalition was going, beyond the Range anyway. Wasn't that something a leader was supposed to know? All I knew was if I pressed ahead, I wouldn't be stuck. I had people's attention, but I also had no clue on this, and felt nothing like how I figured a leader felt. A leader handles their people, makes the tough calls and leads their group to win wars. Attacking a position, leading a charge, that was more me. I'd been shown that. But this path wasn't clear cut. I dealt with people who wanted more power and to keep theirs. The straight forward fight was my zone.

I was proud of the Action and that I stood with 'em, but that Valkyrie name bugged me. When I heard it from people in the Action or the Coalition, I felt like it was meant for someone behind me. There were looks too: the beaming eyes, the gazes of respect. They made me uncomfortable, but they continued. I brushed the hopeful glances of awe off best I could. Someone could refer to me as Valkyrie, but I'd never have called myself that. People said it to me like it was for a dignitary, but for me, it felt like a criminal sentence. Besides, the Valkyrie was always declared by the Coursons, the governing body of Lebabolis. They determined the strongest, bravest of their Warrior Products.

As far as I was concerned, that was ancient history, like they were talking about someone in an ancient book from one of those caches. I didn't like being told I was anything. I was somebody who had enough, that's it. Enough of being a part of a machine that only cared I was well enough to work for them. That didn't deserve a title. If it did, then how about Clara, the little girl who survived an attack on her whole Encampment by herself? The title, directed to me, felt odd, like a bulky costume I couldn't wait to take off.

Dawn's P-LAD chimed with an alert. A swirl of holograms appeared above it and there was Kaitlinn, reading a report. Kaitlinn reported she'd secured a Valentium point for fueling. That meant they had a group of people, and I bet some from the Circle were there. Most likely Norg and Zengus, but this time helped by Lebabolis and Radomet too. Her update continued on about mechanical problems the mobile facilities had. Buildings were stalling, breaking down, even blowing up. My heart sunk when I thought about our people, out in the open on their way to the Range, and the thought of them stranded in the open with little to no protection. A pang of guilt hit me at the idea the ones we fought for to make it to the Range were stuck like that. If Jacobs made it back to 'em, he'd be able to help. We became more and more like lost animals who had to be rounded up. I hoped Jacobs and his group would get back. As long as they weren't spotted and overtaken, they'd be mixing it up in no time.

Nothing appeared about Nelson on these updates, which made me wonder even more how he was. I didn't have a comm to contact him.

The area around the housing units was empty and quiet, like the vehicle paths. Crates and other boxes were scattered around as if some windstorm had flung packages and scrambled them around the streets. The green area with grass was a complete mess, jagged patches ripped out by too many feet in a dash across to be evacuated. Treg pointed to the green areas and commented on the tracks and the type of panic that must've happened. The place was full of stories, panicked people, and judging by the black char marks on some buildings, Omegan pursuit.

I pointed the blackened areas on the buildings out to Treg. "You think the Omegans hit 'em during the evac?"

He only gave a concerned look in response.

We watched the scene, like it was a set of giant still images that we walked through.

Treg leaned close, his voice in a whisper. "I'm gettin bad vibes. Let's get some supplies and head back to the woods quick."

Dawn and I nodded our agreement. With Treg in the lead, we slipped inside the nearest Housing Unit, HS17. The main area of the building was in shambles. Chairs overturned, the monitors on walls flickered on the Lebabolis logo with a message about evacuation and the lock down protocol. Over in a corner stood four familiar metal containers for ration storage. We shared hopeful grins with each other, and I made my way over to them while Dawn and Treg canvassed the rest of the area for any other kind of information or weapons.

I looked in the food stores in the units one at a time. The first two were empty, but the third one had a few left over rations. I grabbed 'em and checked the fourth, but it was also empty. Dawn scampered about and tapped into the console to search records. Treg headed upstairs.

Dawn scanned her P-LAD for any updates regarding HS17. "The Lock Down alert came too quickly and if there was an ambush, that explains why they never cut power."

"Guess the Omegans didn't learn the rule they're supposed to allow a head start on running like hell," I muttered.

After several minutes we met back in the lobby. Treg found a few containers of water and more rations, but nothing else. We eyed each other's haul for a moment and he said, "Look at us, rooting for scraps."

"Some things never change." I shrugged and smirked.

Dawn shook her head and skirted around us for another check inside storage cases.

I shoved some ration packs into my bag and watched Dawn for a second. "We better get—"

The low hum made my gut seize. It was the first sound we'd heard other than those alarms, and it was pretty clear a vehicle was approaching. There, up the road, a dark shape in the distance caught my eye, and when I focused that way I saw a group of transports headed our way. I motioned to Treg and he watched it too. "Crap. Omegan Patrol."

"We shouldn't have come." Dawn hissed.

I ignored her glare and crouched low behind a desk unit by the front windows. I lifted my head enough for a glance toward the approaching convoy. "Maybe they're just passing through; let's hide and see."

Much as it would've been nice to throw down on 'em, we were way light on weapons and even lighter on people we'd need based on the size of the truck, unless our surprise was for our own suicide. We raced to the second floor of the housing unit and grabbed spots low near a bedroom window.

"Better pray they aren't scanning this place, or we're toast." Treg cradled his rifle close and propped himself up against the bedroom wall.

I checked my pulse pistol. It registered half charge, and that confused me. Jacobs had given me this one before we split up. I hadn't fired it yet, so why was it half charged? These guns were kept on the ship.

The hum of the vehicle got louder until it sounded like they were on the street next to us. The vehicle stopped and the engine died.

Then a low murmur built as several Omegans got out. Some of 'em worked with a large case. A few mechanical whirs later and we heard two of 'em talking. The tall and lanky one spoke with a gruff voice. "Assur is crazy; this won't work."

The other was a lot shorter and stocky. He answered, "That's not up to us. We're supposed to test the device here, so no one around sees what it will do."

The warm air in the room was more noticeable the longer we were in there, and soon we pulled at our body armor pieces, shirts, anything to release some of the heat that was building up from everywhere. Maybe they didn't kill the power, or they just killed some, like for the comfort generators.

Six others pulled a large dolly, covered with a dirty cloth. It had a dome shape and even with the six of them they struggled hauling it around. The tall and short ones directed the crew until the dolly was set how they wanted.

The short one waved to the troops to uncover the item. "Let's get this over with quick."

A few drops of sweat rolled into my eyes. I blinked back the burning and lifted up on my knees toward the window for a better look. The vehicle they rode in was parked fifty feet away from the housing unit. Two Omegans stood in a clearing another twenty feet away. A group of twenty other soldiers with weapons fanned out in an arc around them. The tall Omegan in the middle set up a mechanism on a tripod.

"What the damn hell?" Treg muttered.

They backed away from the mechanism. It was three small spheres joined together on a vertical rod. The other Omegan with the device tapped a red colored control panel and the spheres started rotating. A deep magenta glow appeared and got brighter the faster the globes spun. A loud hum built from this, and soon our window shook.

I looked back to the two Omegans. One of them swiped the air with his hand, like it was some kind of signal. The other pointed a device at the tripod. A loud roar burst from the spinning sphere, and a ripple of magenta colored light shot out from all sides. Everything shook and we were knocked backward onto the floor.

Treg's and my rifles powered down. He flipped his around for a few seconds. "It's totally dead. That thing's gotta be Darkness."

Dawn peered at the device for a few seconds, her lips drawn into a grim line. "Disruptor."

There it was. The first one I'd seen, and the very thing that had been giving us the most problems yet. Treg never explained that kind of weapon to me in our sessions; there never was enough time. I figured he knew about it from Warrior Product training.

"So that's where Darkness comes from."

Dawn eyed us with a tired glance. "You got it. If you've got any bright ideas on how to stop one of them once they've been turned on, you'd get a lot of people like Harkson, Charista, Kaitlinn, and Jason wanting to talk with you."

"There must be something we can do."

"Blowing it the hell up before they turn it on is a great start, but that won't happen. You're too late and hurling rocks is all you have left now."

I eyed Dawn with mild disbelief. Seemed a little foreign to me to not engage.

Dawn gestured out the window. "That's an Omegan platoon, thirty troops easy, most if not all armed. Think you're busting down there with two non-working guns and a lot of dirty looks?"

"Have to admit, Ana, she's got a point here. We made a dumb move 'cause we were hungry. Let's not graduate to stupid while we're at it." Treg shrugged.

My hands clenched the grip of my useless rifle. "Well, we can ID it and describe it to the others to look for it. That's better than—"

The front door to the unit opened and shut, and we heard footsteps downstairs. I yanked Dawn into the closet and snapped my fingers to Treg. My voice dropped to a hoarse whisper. "They're checking after effects, see what else it hit."

"Or they scanned for sigs after all," Dawn muttered.

"Either way, we'll get a jump on 'em if they don't see us coming."

"Right, so we can piss them off even more before they kill us."

Treg clutched both of us and gave a 'Quiet' sign.

The closet was a little cooler than the room, but just by a few degrees. By the time my pulse had sped up enough though, it made the place even warmer than the room.

My heartbeat thumped in my throat as I planted my hands against the wall behind me. I had to admit, I didn't give it much thought when I slipped in here with 'em. But what the hell else was there? If we hadn't been hungry as all get out, I wouldn't have even suggested this detour.

One of them entered the room. Their footsteps plodded slowly around the room and stopped short. They reached down, and after a short pause they grasped Treg's rifle and held it up. My breath hitched and I eyed Treg in the dim light. Treg's eyes burned and his mouth twitched. But he kept quiet, beads of sweat on his forehead his only other response.

My heart rattled in my chest when our visitor bumped against the closet door. They worked on disassembling the weapon when their comm unit burst to life.

"Eben, report."

Eben fumbled for a few seconds, then the rifle clanged loudly on the floor. "Here. Found some tech that is now disabled. The test looks to be successful. Should we check for stragglers, see if this weapon has an owner nearby?"

The reply came quick. "Wonderful. No time for anything else; Assur needs us back at base for a report on the weapon test. Let's go."

My heart thumped in my throat. I imagined Eben punching a hole through the door or even a wall and yanking us out. Treg and I could've fought him off, but what about the firing squad of a unit outside?

EIGHT

(NELSON)

NORG WASN'T TOO FAR AWAY, thank God, and made good on my idea to just go for Kado. I hadn't trusted Kaitlinn even before the call to Llewyn. I was done waiting for them to get a hold of things.

Norg and I hopped into a Landcrawler and hightailed it out of there. It felt good being on the road again, more in control of things, and unlike the last time I had protection the whole way. We drove for a few hours until we got to Kado at the test facility.

After our sudden breakout, the comm exploded with messages from Kaitlinn. Seems I was even more important to her than ever after that. She even broke off and followed us with a unit herself. I laughed at the thought of how much it pissed her off that we just went and did something not on her pre-appointed schedule. Of course, it didn't help our chances of staying hidden since she knew right where we were headed. We had a head start though, and that had to be good enough for the moment.

Kado was in a lab with Ashton, the Lebabolis regular who was there for the fight at Sector Five. Kado's hair was more messed up than usual, which really said a lot. He had the same frazzled look most in the Coalition had, but not many of us had his kind of mileage, with everything he kept running.

The lab was in disarray, and it amazed me that in spite of all the facility moves Kado still worked through plans for a new weapon. A pungent smell of burned circuits hung in the air.

Kado cradled a translucent circuit board like a father with a newborn baby. "We were lucky in Sector Five. The Omegans kept their big guns in the wings, and now it's our only hope that we somehow keep them from blowing us up."

"You mind telling me why Kaitlinn's so concerned with guns right now when these units are breaking?"

"They'll need them eventually; they'll have to stand and fight the Omegans at some point."

"I don't suppose in all your hopping around you heard anything about Ana?"

His head sank, a deep sigh escaped him. "No, and it's bugging me."

"I've got this feeling she's alright. I can't explain how—"

"That's not atypical for her. Look, she's a survivor. That much I know, and so do you. I'm one who looks for hard facts before any declaration, but I'm comfortable in that assessment for now. However, I'm more concerned about Cataclysm. Where does that mission stand?"

"Where? It's dead in the water, unless she got some miracle break that includes surviving a Hell Hawk crash."

"If Ana's around, she'll go for it. Dawn won't let her stop. I know Dawn. She's Charista's head of Tech and Research. I was surprised Charista let her out of the lab for anything."

"Can we trust Dawn?"

"No more than Charista. Cataclysm's worth the hunt, but you don't want it in anyone's hands who might abuse it."

Ashton adjusted controls on a console while Kado grabbed a device. It looked like a gun, but it was more slender than the pulse weapons I'd seen.

"We got the idea from the attack in Sector Five," Ashton explained. "I noticed the way their beams sliced into buildings and even our armor, and it gave me ideas on new approaches. I also used some of Baudricort's older notes, and here we go."

They traded places, Aston worked on the device with some tools while Kado talked to Norg and me. "It's our heaviest gun yet, power wise. It worked a lot better on the Omegan armor in tests; it'll give us more of an advantage against them."

"Fantastic," Norg remarked. "When do we field test?"

Ashton and Kado spoke a few quiet words with each other. Kado then mulled whatever they discussed and turned back to Norg. "We can test whenever."

Norg and I exchanged glances. He looked back to Kado. "How many of these ya got?"

"I've got 100 cloned up."

"That's it? Kaitlinn said we had enough for a regiment at least."

Kado clutched his head like a disparaged parent and winced as if Norg had just punched him. Which he had, only with words instead of fists. "Kaitlinn says a lot of things. Norg, in case you hadn't noticed, we're on the run right now."

"You don't know the half of it, Kado," I muttered.

"What?"

"She's coming here, or at least some of her people are."

"Now?"

"Yep. They aren't too far behind us. We aren't exactly here by her plans either."

"Yeah, well, we still need as many as we can get. In case you haven't heard, things ain't going too good for us right now." Norg slapped Kado's back.

Kado looked to me. "We'll do our best. So Nelson, what's the last you heard from Ana since the Crater?"

"Not a peep. We saw her ship crash. Kaitlinn tried raising the comms on her and that whole group with Jacobs, but nothing."

"Oh. Well, I'm sure they'll make contact as soon as they can." His eyes darted about. "She was with Jacobs? If anybody could've saved a ship, it's him. Trust me."

Kado gave Ashton and Norg a quick look before he said quietly to me, "I need to talk with you; stick around once this is over."

Kado handed the weapon to Norg, who clutched it like a boy handed his favorite toy on Christmas morning. "'Scuse me while we get acquainted."

As he headed out I blurted out, "Don't shoot your eye out, or you know, blow up the world."

While Ashton followed Norg outside, Kado motioned to the seat next to him.

"OK, first thing, you gotta check this device, man."

He glanced around my shoulder. "What's wrong?"

"I've been having these blackouts."

"Blackouts?"

"Yeah, I see people and places. I can't be sure, but they feel like they're from the future."

"You have the closest link to the timeline as anyone I've ever known, Nelson."

"Well, then there are the Pulls."

"What are those?"

"It feels like I'm being physically drawn toward Cataclysm."

"Does Kaitlinn know?"

"No."

"Good, better keep that quiet. I wouldn't even tell Norg or Ana." With that he sat me down and pawed at the device on my neck from the back. I felt nothing at first, just heard a few clicks and snaps. But then it hit me: a surge of pins and needles all over my body.

"Whoa, what the hell?"

"Sorry, Nelson. I should've warned you. This device releases a regular sedative dosage into your system. I just adjusted it to increase a little. Should stave the effects you've been describing."

"Stave, as in temporary?"

"Best I can do for now, I'm afraid. The key we're going for is so your mind doesn't lose its place on the timeline."

"So, like a bookmark?"

Kado slid back to my front. "Huh? Oh, those ancient paper tiles? Yes, I suppose. Now, I've got a few things to talk with you about before our visitor arrives." He pulled up his P-LAD and activated the holograph. A series of images floated by in a glowing blur.

"I was curious for the longest time why Charista was so interested in you and Xander. She put so much effort into those Link messages, and even Baudricort went along in his own way, trying to have you send those messages, and then to have it come to nothing. I asked whoever I could. Otto didn't know anything and Baudricort was as evasive as he usually was."

On the screen appeared a huge crossed knife and bolt, the Valkyrie symbol. Kado stared at it before he turned to me. "Besides working on new weapons and coming up with fixes to the temporary facilities, doing what I can about the wounded and sick, I've done some digging of my own."

"Yeah? Anything good?"

"Plenty. Not sure if it meets your qualifications of 'good', but it's a start."

"Alright then."

"Yeah, I suppose. Kaitlinn and Charista are desperate for some kind of edge. It really concerns me that they don't have anything in their plans beyond finding Cataclysm though, and whatever tech we can conjure up here in the meanwhile. Anyway, in my digging, what I found really was inevitable, I suppose. In every project, enhancement, weapons research I went through, I came across some transmissions from Lebabolis."

"Transmissions?"

"That's correct. Some Link message artifacts, regular comms, random traffic. Reception's been spotty though. Lebabolis is sending information where they can via MODOSNet."

"Kaitlinn said it's broken."

"Damaged but not destroyed. If you know the system, you can find a way in. I did, but I also grabbed something else I didn't expect. I've monitored channels wide open, because we never know which ones will be used or tracked, and neither does Lebabolis. And one night there was something."

"You found something you weren't expecting?"

"Absolutely not." With that he tapped in a code and a group of documents appeared in the hologram. They had a lot of text on them, but my eyes went to the picture of Baudricort.

"I've been in Baudricort's upper group with Otto for a good while. He was a good commander, but I always had this feeling he wasn't letting everything out to us. Otto and I talked about it. And right around when he started to share more details, and the maps to Cataclysm turned up, Baudricort ends up dead."

"Baudricort wanted the action to exist on its own, free from Lebabolis. We had people; we needed infrastructure. It was a long shot. But he figured the Range was our best play. At least basic shelter wasn't a concern there. This traipsing around in those portable buildings was never more than a temporary measure. Charista shrugged it off. But when the Omegans entered the picture again, she was suddenly interested in the Action."

"But why send Llewyn and those few to the Range? If there was that big a threat, why not all of Lebabolis?"

"That ivory fortress they have won't hold off the Omegans. She needs this weapon and us. She's not one to surrender either, but she'd consider a deal if it meant keeping her power."

"Lebabolis had us under their thumb. And so we broke free, Baudricort created the Action and we went with him because it was a chance for us. But instead, we ended up on the run from Charista, and as much as we fought her back and kept our move up, they still nipped at us until they once again had us—our sick were kidnapped. Ana wasn't the only one who was hit hard by those raids against our wounded."

"And now this." He grasped for the images in the air. They

billowed around by his touch, as if it was a pool of water and he just jabbed his hand into it. He yanked his hand back and there with it was: a communication from Charista.

Agreement between Harkson Baronage, Chancellor of Lebabolis, and his eminence Zakmar of the Omegan Empire. Delivery of package in return for cease fire and immediate withdrawal of Omegan troops from Lebabolis soil. Arrangements for sharing Valentium to be determined at a later date.

Deal brokered by Charista Mantisword.

I froze on the words as if they were a hypnotic image and held me in a trance. I read them over again to make sure I hadn't imagined it. Nope, still the same.

"A cease fire? No, this isn't right. This isn't playing out like the story I wrote."

"Time's fluid, Nelson, remember. We make choices, we make mistakes, we triumph, we fall. All of it qualifies as adjustments. What we do today affects centuries down the line. Just you being here is unexpected."

"Well, we do have one thing in our advantage. I know where Cataclysm is."

"Yeah?"

"Close enough, anyway. When I looked at the Range maps, it came over me, like some kind of pull. I told Kaitlinn I'd help them find the next attacks by the Omegans."

"Does that really matter anymore? The attacks aren't going to matter a whole lot if she's got this deal and is part of it with Charista. I thought they were our escorts. They're more like a delivery service for the Omegans."

"Does Llewyn know about this?"

"He said no."

"You believe him?"

"I'm inclined to, given what this came from. The communications are garbled, Nelson. There's no way of knowing this wasn't some kind of false transmission to throw off anyone who could be trying to hack into our system, like the Omegans."

"Might be an attempt to draw us out, thinking there's a cease fire."

"They'd have been all over this on the comm by now if that was real, I have to think."

"Well, what is it then, some random transmission? And what's the package they mentioned?"

Kado's brow furrowed.

I scratched my head and thought about all the pieces at work. "It could be the Valentium. Norg told me when we left the crater how the Omegans switched from attacking us to harvesting all the Valentium they could carry. They pulled back from their attack for it even."

"So she's never really meant to cooperate with us, has she? She was just playing us and the Omegans until she got the deal she wanted? And now Llewyn's heading straight for a trap!"

"I'm more surprised that the Omegans were so willing to make a compromise. After all they've done, as strong as they've come on in fighting us and pushing us around, to just agree to a simple cease fire?"

"It doesn't make sense. We've got proof Omegans are in Lebabolis sectors, looting and roaming. That's not how two groups in a truce act toward each other."

Kado flipped through more records that detailed the terms of the cease fire. And the group to be exchanged was none other than the Coalition, headed right for the Range, where I was sure they were just going to be waiting for us.

"What about Kaitlinn; you think she knows?"

"If she does, Nelson, she's said nothing. I keep my head down because telling her anything is as good as telling Charista; you remember that. If she doesn't know, I'd just as soon cut my own throat than tell her. She's Lebabolis through and through. Hell, I bet she'll get some kind of citation and promotion for helping keep the rest of us in the dark."

"Could the deal be Cataclysm? Do the Omegans even know about it?"

"Can't say for sure. But they've got other tech at their disposal like a Disruptor, so they won't need a whole lot of firepower to get the better of us if our weapons are inert. It and the Valkyrie are what stopped them before, and I'm sure they won't forget that anytime soon. But I don't think they'd have any idea of where we've located."

"Could the Disruptor stop Cataclysm?"

"There's no way of knowing that before one's used against the other. It's never been tried; can't really say. I do know it's pretty damned volatile."

"Cataclysm?"

Kado's eyes bugged out, and for a second I thought he might grab me. "Of course, Cataclysm! Think about it, you've got Valentium, this already highly unstable substance. So much that it's bent the time continuum and allowed us to travel into the past and back. Now there's this weapon that at its core channels Valentium energy and can be directed to a focused location. It gave us a hell of a lot of power, but there was no guarantee that power wouldn't be contained. That's what the Valkyrie was referring to when she had it turned off and dismantled. Charista continually rejects the idea that what she's after could end up destroying us all."

"Disruptors weren't used when Cataclysm was last in play. All I know is one thing these Disruptors have done already is affect the Verge. And the Disruptors haven't been around that long to know what they are."

I felt a shudder and lurched back in my seat. The lights in the room dimmed, and I made out Kado's voice in the distance, as if I were underwater. "Nelson, you still with me?"

Lights flashed about me and the room spun. The twisting sped up until the walls liquefied and vanished. When it stopped the walls had faded into a forest. Several figures stood in the center and after a second my eyes locked on Ana, her knife poised at someone's neck. I couldn't see who it was, though I gazed directly into Ana's eyes. They were stark and wide, fixed with rage. Treg stood beside her and held Ana back slicing into the other person.

A rumbling sound broke that vision and then I was transported to the Range in a cave with Kado, Norg, and a group of soldiers. A device was off to our side, and I knew in my soul what it was.

Cataclysm.

We were on a rise, a jetty that extended out of a mountain. From a distance I saw a huge battalion of Omegan ships and troops. They converged on us with the ease and coordination of a python that slithered for an easy kill. Norg stood nearby and fired his rifle at the Omegans along with the rest of the troops. Then, I was whisked away over to one side of the field and saw another group. All of them had long mangy hair, and they wore torn outfits, or in some cases no shirts at all. They looked coarse, but their faces and eyes were as attuned as a panther perched to strike its prey. And at the front of this group, more disheveled than I'd seen her before but with eyes as animated as I'd ever seen and her face twisted in a battle cry, was Ana. With her in the lead, they barreled toward the Omegan forces. Just when they were about to collide, the sound of a thunderbolt popped me back, and there was Kado, his hand firm on my shoulder and a concerned look on his face.

"What happened to you?"

Beads of sweat cascaded about my face, and I huffed to catch my breath, but it was no use. Kado offered me a canteen, and more of the metallic sour water, but at that point it tasted like a mountain stream. I jammed my eyes shut and took a few slow gulps.

"Kado, it just happened again. I don't know why. Either it's got to do with me being here in the first place, or this device, or something else. But I'm seeing things, more than just the Pull to Cataclysm."

"What kind of things?"

"Places, people. Things I hadn't seen, and it makes me wonder if they're the future."

"What people are you seeing?"

"Usually they involve Ana. I see her with Treg, and just now saw her in the woods with someone, about to cut their throat."

"The device I gave you is a stabilizer. You are the only person who's been this far from his base time for this long. Your body was not meant to be displaced for this length of time. We found this out after we started making these Verge jumps and a few people came down with it. We called it time sickness. It went away not long after the person returned to their base time. But we've never had someone away for more than a week or two. You've been here more than a month now, right?"

"Yeah, that's right. I'm not telling Kaitlinn this, I'm still not sure about her either. But that deal over there is scary."

"I've seen some bad cases of time displacement sickness, Nelson."

"How bad is mine?"

He paused and checked notes. "Pretty damned bad. Look, we can't wait for Kaitlinn to be ready for strategy. She's got her own battles to fight. We also can't wait for Ana; she may not even be able to make a run. We need to take care of this."

"I can't go with you, Nelson."

"What, why? Come on, we may still have a chance to leave now. They aren't here yet."

"You don't understand. She's got a tracker on me. If I leave an assigned area, she'll know. I'll only be a liability for you."

"I don't think we should wait any longer for them to arrange the trip to the Range," I said.

"I wouldn't disagree. But Kaitlinn won't provide support. If you and I break for Cataclysm on this, we're on our own, and she won't let you slip away that easily."

"I wouldn't think she would. But if we had some extra help, like Norg, we could make a better run for it. Think you could get some kind of comm up to Ana in the meanwhile? She should know about this deal."

"It's dicey at best."

"She's alive, I'm sure of it. I can feel it."

Kado smiled. "Much as she's been through, I'm sure you're right on that. Even if Treg got zapped along the way, I feel bad for the person tries to take her down."

"But your tracker, maybe we can disable it?"

"She hooked it to the Link. New tech."

"I thought that was shut down."

"The old one was, but this is tech that came online outside of that. Bloodborne microtransmitters. Removing them would involve some massive hemorrhaging, so no."

"Damn. Well, we're gonna go."

"I've got notes. I'm giving you everything I've seen written and stolen about Cataclysm. You'll need it, and I'm hoping it will make some kind of sense to you."

"Judging from the way I've seen foreign words and things appear as familiar, there's a chance."

"Alright, enough stalling and waiting. I'm going to grab whatever I can from here and load up. Kaitlinn will be contacting Charista for a report and status, so that should give us enough time to make a break for it. We get Norg and Ashton and whoever else from the Action and make a run for it."

"I'll get a Landcrawler. It'll get us going, but I won't have time to disable the security algorithm. If they tap it, we'll be on foot."

"It's better than waiting on foot." I shrugged.

The Pull came back stronger. It stung like an electrical shock, but as soon as I stepped in that direction, every little bit I progressed that way, the better I felt. I just hoped that what I'd seen of Ana was in fact the future and not just some wishful daydream. She had to be alright, she just had to.

Kado closed up his P-LAD and put it in his bag. I took another drink of water before I gathered everything I could. The sight of Ana, alive and fighting, spurred me. The feeling I'd had of falling to earth was replaced with the sensation of my feet planted firm and me ready for another fight, like Ana would've been.

If we could just get to the Range and Cataclysm, it stood there, just urging me to get to it. My bargaining chip, their leverage. My ticket home.

"Kado, I'm not waiting anymore, I'm going for Cataclysm now."

"Yeah?"

I nodded. "Kaitlinn agreed to send me with a unit after I showed her how much I know about that area and where Cataclysm is, but she still wants to wait until her regiment is situated before we make a move. I can't shake the feeling I won't come back if she sends me with her people anyway. We need to get an upper hand here while there's one to get."

"Who's going with you?"

"So far, Norg. Would be great if we could get some help from you as well."

"Well, I'd feel better about getting these units moving, but if we can nab Cataclysm, so much the better."

I told Kado the rest of the plan, about the Valentium bait and going for Cataclysm.

"They want this Delivery, let's get it to them. They're glorified scavengers. They haven't been interested in killing us as much as they want their Valentium, so we're gonna deliver it to them," I said.

"Well, if that works, and we get Cataclysm in our hands, we'll really be sitting pretty. We won't be answering to anyone anymore." Kado grinned widely.

"Just better watch our end too," Kado said. "We've been through enough already, we need to be smart about this. There are enemies on all sides, even our own."

NINE

(ANA)

THE FOOTSTEPS HEADED OUT of the room when the same voice burst over Eben's comm, this time doused in fear:

"Eben, get here now! Raiders!"

We looked at each other and wondered what that meant. Had Jacobs changed his mind and back tracked to us? Were we close to the Storehouse after all?

Our room guest's steps picked up downstairs and then there were loud pops from outside. After the noise, a roar built. Treg slid the door to the closet open and we crept back to the window for another look.

A large group of people appeared from the direction of the woods and moved toward the Omegans. Whoever they were, they weren't Jacobs' group. These soldiers looked ragged, with tattered clothing, most with faces twisted in anger. A few wore breathing masks. The roars and shouts came from them at random. A few carried pulse rifles, but most of 'em just had simple sticks or clubs.

"The hell kinda weapons are those?" Treg asked.

As we watched the makeshift weapons they carried, Dawn explained, "I told you, these groups are all over the Outlands. They do, take, and make whatever they need to survive, and that includes weapons."

Whatever rifles they had couldn't have been any better than the tech the Omegans tested. They descended on the Omegans like a pack of wild wolves, with no regard for the fact they were outgunned in every possible way.

The ones with pulse rifles aimed them at the Omegans, but they fired nothing. They must've been hit by that Darkness too. The Omegans laid down heavy fire on the ragged group, but that never fazed them. They chucked rocks and whatever they could at them, and charged right into the hail of pulse fire.

It was unreal.

One of the stones connected with the Disruptor, smashed it and sent it to the ground in several pieces. The barrage of Omegan fire hammered the ragged group and threw a few of 'em off balance. Some fell, but each one who could got back up charged more, even the wounded ones.

Were they even human?

One of them shouted, and the whole group took off in a sprint toward the Omegans, their voices raised in a collective war cry. Whoever they were, they had nothing that ID'ed them as Action or Coalition or even Lebabolis troops. I figured this was it; they'd be wasted in a quick heartbeat for that kinda behavior. But no, they kept up their fast pace, a loud chorus of yells and whoops. With no vehicles or heavy weapons on them, they ran blindly toward the Omegans.

If someone had described what I was looking at then, I'd have laughed in their face.

Yet there it was.

They ran forward, not walked, not headed for cover; they ran. The only thing they had going for them was more numbers. Even with their filthy appearance, their stance, the way they moved as if they were almost mechanical. Their motions looked like Radomet, but instead they were real flesh and blood.

How had we missed that big a group, just the three of us alone in the woods? And also, how had they missed us, and how would we be seen? Another enemy to be destroyed?

The ragged troops collided with the Omegans, and the brawl that erupted kicked up a cloud of dust like a low lying fog. Soon the scene was just a mixture of dirt, swung arms, shouts, loud smashes of stick, rock, fist and heads making contact. A few pulse shots from the Omegans rang out, but then came the cracking sound of pulse rifles snapped in two. The ragged troops broke rifles, theirs and the Omegans, with their bare hands.

Finally, a small group of Omegans, including the tall and short ones who'd checked on the Disruptor, peeled away from the melee and found their vehicle and hauled ass in reverse, but not before they fired a few shots back toward the wild ones.

The Omegans who weren't as fast got pummeled even more by the ragged soldiers, who laid them out on the ground. The rest of the Omegans piled into their vehicles and beat a hasty retreat.

"Who the hell are they?" I asked.

Dawn squinted toward the strange troops. "Nobody important. A random tribe of scavengers from the Outlands like we talked about."

Treg shook his head at the pile of mangled Omegan corpses. "Those aren't scavengers. I've fought scavengers. More to the point, I've chased away scavengers. They're human vermin, and they run at the first sight of trouble. This group didn't have a working pulse rifle, but they overran a unit that could've wasted them all. Not only that, they crushed a few—see those bodies, Dawn? Those skulls are crushed. That's brawn, muscle, sheer force. Those Omegan troops had explosives, enough to blast a square mile around us into vapor, but they were frightened. Whoever the wild ones are, they've been trained."

"I agree. That kinda crazy takes learning."

The ragged troops joined into a large crowd near the remains of the Disrupter and shouted; some of it was cheers, other parts a bit of a song. Then, in the middle of the crowd, a thin soldier swung a pole around in an arc with a tattered and faded flag attached to it. The flag was twisted at first, but it opened up as it waved.

It was the flag of the Valkyrie.

I pointed to the flag and eyed Dawn. "They're nobody, but they just happen to have a Valkyrie flag?"

"I'm telling you both, they're scavengers. Treg, maybe you never happened upon some of the more violent ones before, but that's what we're looking at here. Yes, Ana, that's a Valkyrie flag. Don't you realize, scavengers steal whatever they can? Why do you think we protected Lebabolis all those years? To keep people like them out. They're barbarians."

"Or they're the ones Lebabolis expelled because they couldn't be controlled."

"You're not going to believe that's the Guard, are you?" Dawn laughed for a second, until she saw Treg and I hadn't joined in. Her smile faded. "Any scavenger or deviant could've found that flag out here. Think about it. How much did the Action steal from Lebabolis over the years?"

Dawn's eyes pleaded with me. I watched the celebration. "I'm interested in 'em. They annihilated a disruptor and made short work of a better armed unit with a few rocks, sticks, and their bare hands. At least we hate the same people." I shrugged.

"You realize they might not even know what Lebabolis or the Omegans are? How do you know they aren't here for what we are, food?"

"They were all over the fight. That was just brute force; maybe they were scavenging for food but they aren't right now."

"Fine, I'll suppose for a minute that they are the Guard. Look at them. They look crazy. What makes you so sure they won't attack us too? It would take no time for them to knock off three more people."

"She has a point, Ana. Besides, if they're really the Guard,

Lebabolis threw them out. Why would they help us? To them, we're more of the same. They have no idea what the Action is, much less the Coalition. We'd look like Lebabolis military to them."

"I got you both. But they could just as well come up here and start rooting around like the Omegans were. We've made our play, and now we're here, dumb as it was. I say we face 'em. We're bound to come across the Omegans again. Wouldn't it be better having more numbers when we do?"

"You're reaching here, Ana. Letting them leave is prudent."

"Nah."

Dawn folded her arms. "So tell us how you expect to convince an angry mob you're a friendly."

"With this." I flung the knife up between Dawn and myself, then flipped it and caught the blade in my hand. I held the Valkyrie emblem to her face. "See, we got a matching set."

"You can't resist throwing yourself in it, can you?" Dawn asked.

"Honey, I've been in it. I want a way out. Hiding in some damned closet and cowering is what I did back in Lebabolis, and look where it's got me."

I blew past Dawn's extra warnings and curses and headed outside. My throat clenched up a bit. Sure, there wasn't any telling what they'd do once they saw me. They charged soldiers that out gunned them without any hesitation. What would they do to a single soldier? But something in me just said *go*.

The soldiers stood in a tight group and shouted when I approached. A few caught sight of me and their cheers melded into a distinctive growl. I held my arms up and walked up a few steps. I felt their eyes on me. Soon I was in the middle of them, a sea of vicious faces with smoky colored eyes that glared out at me like a sea of angry crystals.

The air was a nasty mix of body odor, blood, and from the look at their mouths, whatever these people ate for food. The pack of faces around me tightened in on me like wild animals ready for their next feast. I swallowed the tightness in my throat, took a breath, and heaved some words out over the roar of their bellows. "I come in peace—I'm against the soldiers you just smashed." They answered me with more grunts and groans like a pack of mad dogs.

Several of 'em glanced over my shoulder, and the voices picked up volume. I looked over to Treg and Dawn by the outside of the circle.

After a few minutes, a tall soldier made his way from around the others until he stood a foot from me. His gaze knifed into me. I swallowed hard but held steady.

The tall one eyed me up and down. His face was a collection of scars and cuts. His pulse rifle was slung across his back, not unlike how Treg carried his. He nudged a finger into the Coalition insignia on my chest plate. His voice was as ragged and gravel sounding as he looked. "What's that?"

"The Coalition."

"The what?"

"It's a truce between Lebabolis and the Action."

"The Action? Never heard of it. But we know about Lebabolis. You some kinda patrol?"

"No, Lebabolis is under Lock Down because of the Omegans." I gestured to the bodies on the ground.

"Oh them. Yeah, we come up on them sometimes and get the bastards running. They get off some shots and we take a few hits but not enough to stop us none." He let out a raspy laugh. "So Lebabolis... You're one of theirs, huh?" He laughed more and then swung his rifle down underneath my chin. "I hate Lebabolis. They threw us aside."

The cold steel of the barrel dug into the flesh of my neck. I felt the rattle of my pulse in my throat.

His nostrils flared. "We been scrapping for whatever and screwing up what we feel like just to make them regret the day they lost us. Fighting troops on the ground and shootin' their Hell Hawks outta the sky keeps us sharp, I 'spose. More so to be a knife in Charista's ass."

His eyes darkened as he pushed the barrel into my chin. The cool metal dug further into my flesh, and I felt my jaw press harder against the roof of my mouth. Around me, the growls increased. Through it I heard Treg's yells for them to back off, but it was useless. What the hell was I thinking?

Scarface's eyes widened in curiosity, and the barrel of the rifle pressed harder. Treg scuffled nearby and shouted, "We're fighting Omegans too; we want to destroy them!"

"Easy, boy," the tall soldier muttered. "How good a job you been doin' when they're still around?"

"We've got two Regiments of Lebabolis Warrior Products in maneuvers against them."

Scarface laughed more. "You're dreaming, all of you. You ain't stopping that lot."

"You did more just now than I'd seen in a good while." I gazed deep into his eyes.

Scarface returned my look with a stern glare. "We got lucky. Ain't always that way. Number and tech like Radomet won't stop them much either."

Treg said, "We're fighting them one at a time; it's all we can do."

"They're a disease. They'll keep going til we're wiped out. Only way of ending them is extermination. They'll never stop coming. They don't want anything but to wipe you out, don't you get that?" Scarface shook his head and looked around at his group. Some nodded in reply, the rest stood in place. A few shot me curious looks before they focused again on their leader. I hadn't won 'em over. Not yet, anyway.

"We won't stop 'em if we run. Besides, we got a deal with Lebabolis."

Scarface leaned in closer to me. My eyes watered under his rotten breath. "You mean you're their slaves. You served Lebabolis and you're still serving them as their army."

"Maybe, but it's how we stopped 'em from attacking us."

"It's the easy way."

"You got a better idea?" My eyes darted to the soldier with the flag. He held the pole up straight, the flag danced lazily in the slight breeze. "Why are you waving the Valkyrie flag?"

"What do you care?" Scarface held his rifle firmly. Beads of sweat tickled and itched my forehead as they snaked downward toward my neck.

"Because of this."

I twisted my hand back and grabbed the dagger and slowly unsheathed it. At the sound of the blade's ring of being set free, the tall soldier activated his rifle again. "One more move and I'm gonna fry the inside of your skull."

I gripped the knife and managed a small grin. One of the other ragged soldiers to my right gasped. "Where'd she get that?" Another one said. The murmurs spread until the tall soldier glanced down and saw the knife. His eyes widened, and he pulled his rifle back.

"Baudricort of the Action gave it to me for protection."

Scarface shouldered his rifle. They watched the knife like a sacred relic. He held a hand up and quieted his troops then turned back to me. "That knife belonged to the Valkyrie. Our leader. My name's Duncan. I'm commander of this—"

"The Guard?"

Duncan shrugged. "What's left of it. Banished by Lebabolis because we refused to follow anyone but the Valkyrie, the true Valkyrie. We been in the Outlands for over twenty years now, living off the land and taking what we needed to survive. Lebabolis wouldn't have us, but they knew better than to toy with us."

"You were their army, correct?"

"We served with the Valkyrie, and the Valkyrie served Lebabolis. We were the protectors of Lebabolis, and we gave the Omegans plenty to think about. There was no stopping us. We faced them down with the Valkyrie and turned their forces back."

"Well, you and Cataclysm," I said.

"We beat them down enough. You think you're tough, sneaking

in and around here, gettin' into a scrap now and then, getting some shots off? You aren't hard. You gotta eat, breathe, and sleep soldierin'. Omegans don't take any rest. They stab you, you shoot them. They shoot you, you blast them and send them straight into hell. Period. Cataclysm finished what we started, but you best listen, foolin' with that is meddling with powers that shouldn't be tested."

"Yeah, well, how did you lose Cataclysm?"

Duncan thrust a finger toward me as if it was a blade. "We didn't lose it! The Valkyrie knew it meant trouble. That kind of power shouldn't be in anyone's hands. Besides, we had things in hand and we sent them Omegans to hell right good."

"As you saw, not forever," I said. "They're back for Valentium and payback."

"So I see, but it ain't our concern. I won't fight for a country that abandoned us; neither will they."

I looked at their group and realized how much we were alike, two groups of people who were cast out by the same country. "What about the Action then? We aren't Lebabolis. We're like you, sick of lives we're forced into. We broke free from Lebabolis and we've been struggling. The Action wants freedom too, from a system that treats people like parts. We're trying to get to the Western Range and stop the Omegans."

Duncan's eyes softened, and I saw even a trace of humanity under them. He looked on me with warmth. "What's your name, fiery girl?"

"Ana Crucinal."

"You got spirit, Ana Crucinal. But this fight is yours, not ours. We done our bit for country, and paid a price we didn't deserve. Now we just want to survive in peace."

"You weren't peaceful a few seconds ago. Hell, you almost did me in." I scoffed.

"We show force and take what we need, but no more. We're not marauders, rapists or ravagers. We scavenge to survive. We hunt and use our will to survive to determine our course. Nothing more."

"I told you." Dawn shrugged.

Duncan's friendly gaze went furious in an instant as he looked toward Dawn. "You shut your mouth, gray band. You're a pawn and you know it. I got a good mind to shove this here stick down your throat, see how it tastes to ya."

I waved my hands. "If you think you'll survive with the Omegans around, you're kidding yourself. You said the words, they're brutal and they won't stop. They want Valentium, and revenge, but I've seen them up close. How can you walk from a fight like this? If the Omegans win, they'll bleed this land dry, and anyone they come across is dead meat. "

"And Lebabolis won't do the same?" Duncan asked.

I swallowed hard on that truth. "We'll figure that out when the time comes. I know we can take control if you help us. You were the elite once. You stood up to Omegans even though they were tougher, and you held them off. You became what was needed when it mattered. I'm just asking you to do it again.

"For what?" Duncan asked.

I thrust the knife into the air. "A chance to say you didn't lie down when it was most important. One last chance to make the Guard name mean something again. Omegans won't be satisfied when Lebabolis and the Action are no more; they'll keep going until the world is under their rule. Think your peaceful existence of just taking what you need will keep you out of their way? They'll come for you. Not now, not this month, but there will come a time. They'll be on you and it'll be too late. I've been on the run most of my life. I wanted for a long time more than anything to just leave this behind. But they took my brother and other sick people. They made me fight. I hate 'em for it, but I hate the Omegans even more. And there'll be a time to pay back Lebabolis too, I guarantee you."

I felt their eyes on me and thought I'd made a breakthrough with 'em, but Duncan set things straight again. "Lebabolis can crumble into the sea for all we care."

"They aren't going anywhere soon, especially once they get Cataclysm," I said.

"What do you mean, get Cataclysm?" Duncan's brow creased.

"That's what I said."

Duncan asked, "They found it?"

"Baudricort showed me, showed us."

"Impossible. It was hidden long ago, before you were born, and we've had no idea where."

"It's not only possible, but we know where it is, and we're gonna deliver it to 'em." I grimaced at the idea but reminded myself it wasn't the final plan.

I heard a ripple of chuckles through the nearby Guard soldiers. Duncan shook his head. "Are you mad?"

"No, I'm trading for something else."

"What, exactly?" Duncan's held his hands in the air.

"I don't know."

"You don't know? What the hell are you thinking then; you just want to start trouble? You might be better off with us instead of followin' some fool leader gonna toss you away soon as you give them what they need. You're high on hope, fiery girl."

"I'm against a wall; hope's all I got."

Duncan paced back and forth. He scratched his head and looked at me for a few moments in silence. "The Omegans aren't to be taken light. They're pretty fierce, and we seen that weapon of theirs. It's ruined more than a few of what we got left of our people, so I know exactly what you're saying, believe me."

Aggravation settled in on me, and I fought with myself to keep in this talk. If I flew off and left here, I'd have lost the one ally I needed most. I braced myself and focused my mind on what Baudricort would've said to them. "We get Cataclysm; even if we have to give it to 'em, we're in control."

"No, you're giving up control. You don't understand, that kind of power don't belong in one person's hands, no matter who they are."

"If we don't get this, and someone else like her does, there's no telling what'll happen. Someone's gotta try," I said.

"And you're crazy enough to. So you got a plan, and you're crazy enough to think it'll work?"

"It might, if we get some help."

"From who, us?"

I scanned the group again. "Yeah. Look, I've seen and read a lot about you. The Guard were the toughest fighters Lebabolis has ever known. When I was a kid I heard the stories, how it took three Radomet to stop a Guard member any day of the week. Yeah, times have changed, you're older and slower, but think about what you did. And what did you do to get there? It wasn't just your training, or your physical strength, even your belief in the Valkyrie. It was your hearts. They're pure and full of devotion. You don't just fight to kill. You fight to survive, to protect. Because you care, you've got loved ones. And you'd die before you let anyone get over on you. Fighting for something is more powerful than fighting against it. You became the fiercest warriors through training and service and belief in the Valkyrie. You can do it again, if you want to. And I think you do. I don't think this life you've got, scavenging around for scraps, taking pot shots at crafts that aren't even aware or can fight back to any degree is what you want. You want more. And that's what we want. We're finishing what was started by the Valkyrie. And we could really use the help. How about it?"

Duncan gazed at me for a long time. His troops had eyes fixed on me too. Their scowls melted into more thoughtful expressions. "Sorry, fiery girl. The Valkyrie is dead."

I thought about the voice and what it told me, but would they have even believed it? Maybe it was just a ghost from years back and I was lucky enough to be the haunted one. If I told people, they would've just dismissed me as this crazy girl with big plans and, as a bonus, who, oh yeah, heard voices. Who the hell would follow someone like that?

I shrugged that off though and kept on. "It's up to you. I can't make you. But you faced down an enemy that could've easily laid waste to you with no fear. We need your force."

Duncan sighed, and his head dipped a little. "We're scattered halfway across the Outlands. Even the Guard isn't one group anymore. We do what we need to survive."

"You won't survive much longer like this. Somebody's gonna fire Cataclysm. If not me, then her, and you remember what Cataclysm does, right?" I said.

"Yeah." Duncan sighed.

"Charista's turning it on the Omegans first chance she gets, and you and I know she won't stop there. She wants the whole world to fall under this umbrella of Lebabolis."

Duncan folded his arms. "Worlds fall all the time, fiery girl. We fought our fight. It's someone else's turn now." He laughed. "We're headed home; our round of foraging is done for now. I don't expect you'll see us again."

My eyes pled with them, but it was useless. Duncan gave a shrill whistle and his troops joined up together. As one, they swiveled back in the direction of the woods and marched off. A loud chorus of "One or None" followed them, and a wave of sadness hit me. Was it that hard, convincing them? Had I just failed again? Who would've thought I was any kinda leader if they'd seen me here right now? Was the Action really that much different than the Guard? Was I looking at our future, my future... a member of a bunch of scavengers who prowled the world like a starving pack of dogs just in for whatever the next scrap of meat to be stolen? How could they have used the same cry, the same call that was ingrained in the Action? Would I be a ragged, worn out leader of a troop of renegades just scraping by for whatever we could get to sustain ourselves?

"Satisfied?" Dawn asked.

"Better we ask than never know," I replied. "I thought they could've been up to the task."

"Wrong again. Let's go."

I nodded, my eyes still on the soldiers. I hated that they wouldn't or couldn't stay, and I wondered about what I'd seen behind Duncan's eyes. They said a lot more than his words, but that was just a mystery, maybe forever unsolved. His gaze was clouded with something else, like smokiness inside an otherwise clear crystal.

TEN

(NELSON)

"NELSON, WE STILL have time, there's one more thing I need to show you." Kado ushered me over to his terminal and pulled up the MODOSNet screen. He studied me with the sincere gaze of a therapist. "First, tell me again what Baudricort told you about Ana."

I thought back to those last moments with him on the floor in his busted out quarters. The smoke that wafted around from the blast itched my nose and the ringing in my ears from being so close to the explosion made it tough to make anything out. He was a mixture of emotions: fear of dying without knowing if what he had done made any difference. He was all worry and uncertainty. But I leaned in close enough for his last few words about Ana. "He just said to watch out for her."

Kado eyed me, expressionless. "Ana's a mystery to a lot of people. I know Treg trained her. But her skill, her strength, that's ingrained in Warrior Products from birth, and before. That's the whole idea of the Product system: traits survive, even if free choice doesn't. Me, I never bought she was a Worker Product. She was too strong. It takes more than training to get as capable as she is."

404

I nodded. "Treg once told me she took on a Radomet by herself."

"That's what I mean. Once the Action started, Baudricort corrupted records to keep as many people safe so they never knew the system had been compromised for people like Ana."

He then went back to his terminal. "I'm not sure why this was hidden, but our friend Ana's got a lot more going on than any of us could've guessed."

"What do you mean?"

"Baudricort never said anything to me about what I'm about to show you."

He leaned back from the screen, and I had a look. There was the MODOSNet file on Ana on the screen. Her parent entries were blank. "This happened for a lot of the Action members; Baudricort saw to it when he was wreaking havoc in the system during Exodus."

"So what, Kado? I don't understand; she's got these skills, but is she really any different from the rest who escaped? Baudricort just gave her a head start, like the others."

"Ahh, maybe. And sure, that's a safe guess. See, Lebabolis would do whatever they could to hunt down people, even if it meant tracking down their parents. But I didn't show you this so you could see what was removed." He tapped a few more controls. "I want you to see what was never in that record."

With that, he activated a video, and I found myself staring once again into the eyes of Baudricort.

"Ana, my daughter. I'm a coward. I held things from you. I thought I was protecting you, but I was really protecting myself. But now, I want to be clear. If what I think has happened, you need to be ready because you've got work to do.

"I wish I had time to tell you everything you've wanted to know about your life and where you came from. But there was never enough time. I'm marked, and I don't know how much time I have left. Your mother—"his voice wavered and he suppressed a sob—"is probably dead by now, so I must pass this onto you. I couldn't risk telling you sooner, and give Charista the chance to do a Link pull on you. But you must know her name is—"

The video crackled and the image popped blank for several seconds.

"You've gotta be kidding me." Kado adjusted and tweaked controls, but it was useless.

"I don't know what happened. Was he making this right before he died? Maybe it was a Valentium spike."

"Can't say for sure. Wait—here it comes again."

The video resumed but nothing further about Ana's mother.

"I've made so many mistakes. But maybe, if you're still alive and seeing this, there's still a chance we'll stop the bigger catastrophe. My only hope is Charista hasn't found out who you are yet. I'm even taking a risk saying this to you now, but it's time you know. I'm sorry it's too late for me to tell you in person. Cataclysm is the deadliest weapon and I was ordered... forced to create it by Charista. I used data she'd gotten from the Omegans, it... was always supposed to be secret, but I don't see the point of keeping that hidden anymore.

"Charista's the one you need to watch out for. She'll say whatever she needs; don't believe her. She'll tell you she's the Valkyrie. Watch yourself; she's also gotten into the Action with her spies somewhere, I'm sure of it. It feels like there's someone in this group who's not one of us. I just hope I figure out who before it's too late.

"I've left information with Kado on the Cataclysm device and a security system I've enacted with the Valkyrie. Cataclysm will not fire without the Failsafe enacted. I don't want to say exactly how it works here in case this is being monitored. You must get to Cataclysm and use the Failsafe system before anyone else can, or the destruction that happened before will happen again on a much bigger scale. And if Charista is in control of it, there'll be no end. She'll destroy whoever's against her: the Action, the Omegans, anyone else who doesn't fit her plan. It's vital you follow the details in the fail-safe method I've outlined."

The tears rolled free down his face and his voice got strained into a plaintive whine. "I wish I could've given you the life you wanted or deserved. You needed love from your birth parents, but you had none. You needed a family, but it was taken from you. You needed security, but you only had hiding and deception. I wish it could've been different, that I could adjust things, make things better, I do. But even with the Verges, some things still can't be done over."

"Just know, Ana—it's in your blood. You're stronger than I, your mother or anyone else. The fate of Cataclysm rests with you. It's in your blood to survive, to manage, to do whatever needs to be done to outlast the rest.

"Your mother was in danger as I was. We were two different products and weren't allowed to breed. But we loved each other. We wanted no part of a system that made such demands on people. But we knew also that we weren't able to get away just then. So we did the next best thing. We hid, we gathered resources, we bided our time. One by one, the Action grew until we were strong enough to leave. But Lebabolis wasn't oblivious. It didn't take long before their spies and scouts infiltrated us, and your mother was one of the casualties.

"I'm so sorry for everything. I only wanted to get you out, and when we did I thought just maybe I hadn't failed you both. I hoped you'd one day do what we never could and turn the evil of Lebabolis on them. You are my heart, soul and my message to Charista. I know you'll make things right.

"You'll have to fight harder and survive more and go further than we've been able to. But in the end, I know you'll be the one standing over the rest. Just remember, no matter what happens, you'll always be my daughter and I love you with all I am."

The screen flickered and faded to black. A lump formed in my throat as the words hung in the air. "I love you with all I am."

I stared at the blank screen and wondered what Ana knew about this. I felt memories of Mom push through with Baudricort's message. I wanted to hug Ana right then. How much must it have hurt her all those years, never knowing, that missing piece of her like a window missing a pane of glass? I realized how lucky I'd been, at least to have known my mom while she was alive.

"She never mentioned her mother at all," I said.

"When we left, our lives were uprooted, connections severed. Some families were even split among loyalties to Lebabolis and the Action. Even though we've rejoined, breaches like that aren't repaired as easily."

"We've got to get to her. If she's alive, she's headed to the Lebabolis capital and if she's there now, who knows what Charista is telling her?"

"It's not quite that simple." He smiled in a pained wince and drooped brow. He activated some more screens, and several items flashed up on the screen. Words in a faded green stared back at me, and Kado maneuvered his hands for awhile until there on screen was a message between Charista and the Omegans.

"Those coordinates are familiar," I muttered, my eyes agape.

"Yeah? How so?"

"That's where Llewyn and the Action are heading. Why is Charista sharing this information with the Omegans?"

"And look, there she's mentioning something about delivery of a package. What is she talking about?"

"It couldn't be Cataclysm, could it?"

"No, there's no way. She wants that all to herself."

"Maybe it's the Coalition. She's been sending us up all this time. She doesn't want a truce or even to let the Action exist outside; she's not stupid. She'll just set us up to be her enemy again someday. No, this package is us; she's delivering the Coalition to the hands of the Omegans."

"But for what? Would they go for that? They just want to destroy us anyway."

"There must be some reward in it for them as well. No one does something of that magnitude without the idea of getting something in return."

"So we're collateral? She's going to get Cataclysm and use it on the Omegans and us now?"

"Maybe she found a way to invert the mechanism."

Norg and Ashton returned. A trail of bluish smoke snaked from the end of the weapon.

"Well?" Kado asked.

Norg looked at the weapon for a second, then back to us with a mixture of a glare and a grin. "Uniquely badass. Ya done good."

"That's a relief! Nelson and I've been doing our own bit of research here."

"Yeah, how so?" Ashton asked.

"According to what Nelson's telling me, Cataclysm is in a grouping away from the Range, so we've got a shot of getting it if we can sneak over there undetected."

Norg said, "Well, what are we waiting for? You tell him Kaitlinn's on her way?"

I nodded. "Yeah, so I'm thinking we take a small group, me, Norg, Kado, a few others, and load Cataclysm onto a Hell Hawk and make our way to a safe point."

Kado's head hung. His body shook with exhaustion.

"How many hours she's had you working at all this?" I asked.

His eyes were a mix of watery and twitchy. He didn't answer me; his eyes did enough talking anyway.

"Too much for too long. I wish I had more answers or knew what to suggest to you. I-I'm sorry."

"No, no." I went to his side. "None of this is your fault. We're all being used here; that's why it's more important than ever we try this."

"There's a lot of open ground between here and there." Kado sighed. "What if we get attacked? Even with these new weapons, the Omegans won't need a lot to overpower us."

"It's risky, but what have we done that isn't?"

Norg patted Kado's arm. "He's right, man. We gotta book it on this one. Longer we stay around jabberin' and debating plans, the sooner they could happen on it. Don't think they don't have their own kinda scans running neither."

When Norg mentioned scams, Kado's face brightened a bit. "There's something else you need to know. Word from Kaitlinn is they're setting up a decoy for the Omegans. A lure. They're hoping they'll bite for the Valentium; we're putting a lot out. They'll move their deposits of Valentium to a location a good thirty miles from the Cataclysm point."

Norg shook his head. "What else aren't they telling us? I'm sick of waiting; let's go!"

Kado glanced off a bit. "Are they even sure the Omegans will go for this Valentium decoy?"

I shrugged. "Valentium hauls have been their MO of late. You weren't there for the crater attack. They had us boxed in and they let us out of there. We're giving them a nice bit of Valentium just served right up to them. It's gonna work."

Kado looked at the weapon, then back to me. His brow crinkled and he took a slow breath. "It's a risk no matter what we do. But if we nab Cataclysm, I'll figure out that Failsafe and get it to work."

Norg grinned. "If anybody can, it's you, brain child.

"Let me see that." I reached for the notes from Kado. The words on the page were gibberish alright. They were in some other language. But I just stared at the page like I did for the map, and it happened.

The letters flickered and then they rearranged themselves to me as English. I read notes from Baudricort that he had entered about the Failsafe. It was set up and tied to the Valkyrie. They prevented the operation of the Cataclysm device unless the Failsafe was triggered by transmitters located in her blood.

I said, "Kado, it's tied to her blood, the Valkyrie. The weapon's useless without it."

"What?" Kado grabbed the notes and eyed them. "We don't even know the Valkyrie is still alive. She'll work on a hack of course. We don't even know if she's aware of this Failsafe."

Norg grunted. "So let's move out then. I'm tired of waiting around for something to happen to us."

The screen rifled through a lot of different displays. Pictures, faces, details rushed past me like water over a waterfall. Then, when I got dizzy, the display jerked to a halt and there were two faces: Ana and another woman I'd never seen before.

"Baudricort was keeping the Action safe," Kado explained. "Part of that was hiding the true identities of as many people in the Action as he could, even if it meant wiping their records. This was especially for anyone Lebabolis would consider important."

Kado jabbed a finger toward the strange woman's picture. "This is Petra. I know she doesn't mean anything to you"—he glanced at me—"but she means a lot to us. She led the group that turned back the Omegans all those years ago."

I sat up. "The Valkyrie?"

Kado nodded. "And no one really knows whatever happened to her. Some say she was murdered, others say she was delivered to the Omegans as a bribe."

I said, "If I can't be with her, I figure I'm as safe as I'd be, being with you guys. You're part of the Circle, and that's good enough for me."

"So let's do this." Norg motioned to the door.

I grabbed Kado's arm. "We need to move on this now. The Omegans don't have to wait for anything. They are pressing on, and the more we wait the more time they have to get a foothold. We'll try and reach Llewyn and fill him in; he'll be at the Range soon and we need to get moving now!"

"Get moving where?" Her gruff voice entered the room before she did. The door swung open and there was Kaitlinn. Kado swallowed hard and managed a nod in her direction. The air in the room seemed to freeze. Kaitlinn tossed me a dirty look as she meandered toward us. "Some day you'll learn your safety is one of my biggest concerns." She glanced toward the weapons and then to Kado. "I trust you've tested them out thoroughly?"

"Yes, ma'am. Been through all I could put them through, given the short time frame."

"We need these passed out to the rest of the crews. I'm sending a few people out on this. For now I want you back on the facilities issue, alright? We need to get them running so we can keep our group moving."

"Affirmative." Kado nodded.

Kaitlinn looked at me. "You're coming with me, Nelson. We're going to check with Llewyn on his location. He's run into problems, and we need further assistance with the terrain and your knowledge of that area before we start for Cataclysm."

"ENOUGH DISTRACTIONS." Dawn shoved branches out of her way and walked deeper into the woods. "We could've been killed back there. You've no idea how unpredictable those people are."

"Those people?"

"The Guard, alright?"

"So you do know them."

"Yes, Ana, I do. You keeping score? Any more foolish detours you've got to suggest?"

"We needed food. Seemed a reasonable risk."

Dawn's annoyed gaze pierced into me and made me wonder just what kind of plans she had for us at the Capital. Her eyes flickered for a second, and I wondered, once I mentioned the Guard, why she brushed it off so fast.

"You knew they were still out here, didn't you? Your talk about random bands was you trying to scare us off looking for anyone. All this time, you knew. Did you contact 'em, get 'em to join you? Oh, I bet that went well. You send a messenger and what, they broke their arms?

Her eyes darted about, then they gazed back in the direction we came. She looked back at her P-LAD, but I yanked her hand, and we were face to face again. "Well?"

"We always suspected. The Action was our bigger concern. We gave the Guard up for lost. Our recon groups, when they came across any of them, it looked like what you saw back there. Can you blame us, I mean, you did see how they were right? That's how they've been. They sustained themselves and kept out of our way for the most part. Charista figured they'd eventually waste away."

"Unlike the Action? Why'd you even bother with the Action when you had them?"

"We didn't need another group of Renegades, and you were still close enough to the fold. You weren't wiped out."

"Neither are they. They're hanging tough, even away from Lebabolis this long."

"Seems so. But trust me, you don't want to be involved with them. There's no guarantee when the fight comes down to it that they'll step up, and they just might turn on you."

"How do you know?"

"Because we tried it with the Guard. We went to them years ago when they scrounged like rats and made the offer: give us another go, all will be forgotten. We offered them a chance to utilize their potential. The Omegans hadn't returned by then, but security was always a priority for Charista. The Guard took off shortly after. Living like they do, it changes you. They aren't what they were; I hope for once you'll believe me here."

Her gruff dismissal of this group surprised me. Everything I had heard about the Guard was they were extremely fierce and had been the thing that stood between Lebabolis and the Omegans for all those years. I wondered what about the Action other than our general age made us a better choice. What happened to this group that turned them into what I'd seen? Is that what we would become if things didn't end well for us in this war?

Dawn darted back out ahead as our walk continued. I fell back near Treg. "Some afternoon, huh?"

"Yeah, for sure. You good?" His brow wrinkled, a concerned look on his face.

"Pretty much. Never came up against the Guard before."

"Me either. You did great, seeing as you had a rifle at your throat."

"He wasn't gonna use it. He was testing me."

"You think?"

"Yeah, I do."

"Come on. You saw what they did to the Omegans. I can still hear the sound of one of those arms popping. He'd have mangled you if you hadn't shown that knife."

"Treg, no way."

"Why are you so sure?"

"They've been used to scavenging and they respond when there's danger, like an animal would. They survive and fight only when they have to. Yeah, they sized me up. But once they saw who we were, and that we weren't scared, and I had the knife—"

"Which could've been taken off a dead body. Hell, that's what they've been doing for years."

"The Guard was the absolute in everything. Strength, loyalty, bravery. He tested me. It was in his eyes."

"Or, you just lucked up."

"Wish they would've taken me up on joining us."

"You're thinking about who they were. You gotta see what they have become, a bunch of wasted out renegades. They've been away in the woods too long. I don't think Duncan's all there in the head, if he ever was."

"No food, Treg."

"Huh?"

"The food. The rations, what we went there for. They never took anything off us. That didn't seem odd to you?"

"They could've found theirs somewhere else. Speaking of, let's grub while we walk."

I slid a ration bar over my lips. The sweet and salty flavor melted on my tongue. The flavor mixed with my saliva as it drizzled down my throat until my stomach warmed at the first food it had had in days. I took a few quick bites until I gagged and slowed down to a moderate nibble. In mere minutes I felt eons better. We munched as we walked. Dawn went behind us and followed in silence. After a mile into the woods, I waited until she neared me. She looked at me and eyed the ration bar I offered her.

"Come on, it's why we stopped."

Her glance darted between me and the food for a second. Soon, her mouth quivered, and a bit of saliva formed on her lips. Her tongue slipped from between her lips as if she were a snake ready for its next meal. She then grasped the protein and hungrily devoured it.

I couldn't hide the smirk on my face and didn't want to either. "Looks like Treg and I weren't the only ones starving."

She spoke between bites. "Can't risk that again." She chewed a bit more and flashed a quick eye to me. "Thank you."

I pulled her chin until her eyes returned to mine. "I'm believing your story about being stuck with us against your will. I still don't like you on that thing so much, like it's a beacon to Charista you're not telling us about. But I also figure the sooner we get there, the sooner you and I don't have to see each other again."

We made it back to the deep woods just as night fell. The moonlight was scattered among the branches and leaves above us. We made our way slowly through small pockets of dim light. The breeze had picked up by then, and I had my hands thrust under my shoulders.

I motioned to Dawn. "Let's stop for now and rest. I'd rather not stumble across an Omegan patrol in the dark. We'll regroup in the morning."

"Alright. I have to admit that's not a bad idea," Dawn replied.

I smirked. "Well, small favors."

Treg cleared the branches and leaves, and made a space between the trees with smooth ground so the three of us had a spot for the night.

"We still going the right way?" I asked Dawn.

The light from Dawn's P-LAD cast the only light around us besides the moon.

"Hmm, yeah, looks that way. We should hit it in another day."

The bushes made a soothing rustle in the wind. I was just about to lean back and get comfortable when I heard a quick shuffle of branches off to the right from us, about ten feet away. It wasn't light enough to see much, and I saw nothing, not even any dim shapes. I jumped up, but the noise stopped and was replaced by the whisper of the wind again.

Dawn tapped her P-LAD and mouthed, "Ambush." My chest tightened, and I did my best to stop the tremor that had started.

I crawled over to Treg.

"What's goin on, Dawn acting stupid?" he asked.

"We heard something."

He looked around the area. "She scan for heat sigs?"

I nodded toward Dawn and twisted my hand in a circle with one finger pointed up. She held her P-LAD up and turned in the direction I showed her. Graphical images of the woods around us cascaded by on the screen. But then, a glowing dot of red and yellow made her stop in place. We looked at each other.

"Looks like one. Might be a vehicle if they're close enough."

"Great, and no guns." My hand slipped to the handle. "What you thinking, Treg?"

He looked around again, his eyes wide, but the thick blackness and dim light from the moon covered everything in a dull dark shroud. "If they're this close, they're watching us too, and we'd have heard from them by now. I think it's a lost patrol."

"Or the Guard snooping around," Dawn said.

"They wouldn't waste time here. It's too easy pickings at the housing units right now." The woods were covered in a blanket of darkness. The branches offered a slight rustle with the little breezes of wind that slipped around us.

The sound happened again, much closer this time. My face flushed from the heat, and I drew my blade. There wasn't time to run anywhere. Whoever or whatever it was moved in quickly. I stood up over Dawn. Treg clutched the muzzle end of his pulse rifle and held it out like a club. I planted my feet and held the knife in a fighting stance.

The rustling stopped once again.

"Who is it?" I whispered into the night air.

Nothing came in response for a few minutes. Then another voice whispered, just above the sound of the breeze, "One…"

I looked at Treg. He replied, "Or none."

The branches rustled again, and the dull outline of a figure stepped out. It was a woman, and I caught sight of her face when a sliver of moonlight passed over her. She had high cheekbones, slender eyes that were fixed and alert like a hungry tigress, and a smirk I would know from anywhere.

Nycole.

"So you survived the crash too." I sheathed my blade. "Where the hell you been?"

"I was thrown free before the landing. Had to get my bearings."

"You could've made contact with us a little sooner."

"Well, how about you? You weren't waving a Valkyrie banner around or anything."

She scoffed and sat. "Anybody got a gun? I'm feeling naked without one."

"Nope, all we got are two dead sticks."

"Well, that sucks."

"Even more when you hear how."

Dawn nodded. "Hello there."

Nycole's brow raised a bit, but she returned the greeting. "Hey yourself."

We figured it was getting too late, and after the food we'd gotten we needed rest. Even Dawn agreed with that one. We made a camp out of a few close tree trunks and some fallen branches. Nycole gave us the scoop on her story. She'd bailed out before we hit ground—she was up top with Jacobs on the nav when she punched out. She came across what sounded like the same Omegan patrol we did. She hadn't made contact but fired a few long range shots their way before her gun got zapped when they activated Darkness.

"He wanted to land that bird. The personnel hold was more secure from a crash but not so much the cockpit. Crazy bastard. Refused the help I offered."

"They have a disruptor," I said with a mouthful of food. "We saw 'em test it. Took our weapons out."

Her eyebrows raised. "Not good. But your P-LAD wasn't affected?"

"No." Dawn flipped the device around. "Guess it was set for weapons only."

Nycole sat with us in a circle, her legs folded beneath her. She held a twig and traced random shapes on the ground with it. "We called them Darkness in the Warrior Product weapons program. Lebabolis was working on that while I was still over there, but they hadn't perfected it. Either the Omegans did it or they stole it. We had some intel on them they'd been working on how to fine tune it, to take out weapons and leave other tech functional."

I said, "Looks like they perfected it."

"So what are you doing out here by yourselves? Jacobs and the rest made it?" Nycole asked.

"Yeah, Jacobs and a good twenty others. He grabbed them and went off to find a Storehouse so they could get back to the fight," Treg said.

"He mutinied? Thought we were set to go for Cataclysm once we got clear of the Omegans," Nycole said.

Dawn sighed. "He had other ideas."

"Crazy jackass. Wouldn't be surprised if he were in custody now." Nycole chuckled.

Dawn snickered. "That's what I tried to tell them."

Nycole asked, "So what's the plan now; you three going for Cataclysm?"

"The plans changed a bit. We lost Nelson too. He was supposed to be with us, but we got separated back in the Crater," Dawn said.

"We're going for the Capital," I said.

Treg eyed me but said nothing. He returned to his meal.

Nycole looked at us. "The Capital is in Lock down. You think they'll just crack the door if you ask nice? They're probably under siege!"

I said, "We're a long way from Cataclysm, on foot with no weapons. What other choice we got?"

"I can come up with a few." Nycole shrugged.

I said, "You don't get it. I made an agreement with Charista."

Nycole said, "No, you don't get it, Worker Product, so let me enlighten you. You don't get into the Capital on a Lockdown. Damn, I've got more access than Ms. Laboratory over there, and I'm not sure I could even do it."

I grabbed a handful of leaves and tossed them to my side. "We have to try."

Nycole eyed the three of us. "Well, good for you. You have any idea how risky that is? You realize they're expecting people trying that? At a minimum the Omegans would be doing whatever to bust in, and you think you'll just be waltzing right in like nothing's wrong and you just want to say hello?"

I said, "I never said it'd be easy. But it's necessary."

"Why the Capital anyway?" Nycole asked.

"It's our deal," Dawn said.

Nycole swiped a hand toward Dawn. "Screw the deal. Charista doesn't have any ships; this Intellectual's just tired of running. What's Kaitlinn or Jacobs gonna say? It's their job to clear a path for you to Cataclysm."

"Jacobs knows; he even tried talking me out of it. And besides, neither of them's here now, are they?" I flung my hands up. "We made a deal for getting Cataclysm, and things got blown to hell. Besides, why are you so interested in not going back?"

Nycole shook her head. "It's the wrong direction, in more ways than one."

I said, "Yeah, or maybe you don't want to go back because it's not in your plans or worse, we aren't expected back there since we were supposed to die when you blew our Hell Hawk up. Is that it, Nycole? Real handy how you bailed out before we landed. Did Jacobs even know about the bomb? I bet he didn't."

Nycole cut her eyes at me. "You're ridiculous. Jacobs wouldn't have let the ship land if he was in on it. Don't be crazy."

I said, "Dawn says Charista's got transport ships at the Capital, so we're headed there. Besides, where can we find better weapons? I'd rather avoid the Easter egg hunt, me."

Nycole sipped her water and wiped her mouth on her sleeve. "Yeah, but getting through security won't be easy. Not even for mister silent entry over here."

Treg snorted a bit. "Told her it was pretty damned impossible, but she ain't changin' her mind."

I debated how much I should tell her or any of them about the voice. I never knew for sure if it was just something through the Link or not, anyway. And she wasn't one to leave with the Action, even when Treg did. I held off.

But Nycole, I just was never sure where I stood with her.

We continued the next morning on our twisting journey through the forest. The roads were nearby, and we used them as a guide but kept off them since the Omegans were always around. I wondered what that test was all about and if anyone knew about it. Charista and Kaitlinn always had good intel on the Omegans, but they never mentioned that little detail. I'd think a weapon that could've shut down every piece of tech we had, even MODOSNet, would've been worth a mention.

(NELSON)

"I DON'T THINK SO." Norg aimed his pulse rifle right at Kaitlinn's chest. Her guards stood by, their rifles fixed on Norg. Kaitlinn's eyes widened, a frown etched into her face. "Just what do you think you're doing?"

Norg smirked. "We're going for Cataclysm; we ain't into your timetable anymore."

"Do you have short term memory loss? How do you expect to make it that far with just the two of you?"

"Make that three," Kado said.

"Oh, now I know you're forgetting things. Kado, we discussed your Link. I'm fully capable of blowing up a blood vessel in your brain, remember?"

"No, I remember pretty well, Kaitlinn."

"Don't try me. You've done a lot of good here and kept the Coalition running, but so help me if you do this, it's going to be the end of you. You'll be dead before you leave the compound."

"We're leaving and you can't stop us."

"You're committing suicide is what you're doing. You go out there and the Omegans find you, you'll be a blob of bloody matter when they're done."

"That's a chance I'm willing to take," I said. "I still don't see why you're so scared to go for it right now."

"It's too risky, Nelson. You have to understand all the moving parts here. You're not responsible for all these soldiers like I am."

The soldiers stepped toward Norg with their guns raised. Kaitlinn activated something on her vest and an alarm buzzed. More soldiers filled the room. "Subdue them! Leave Forrester and Kado alive, and kill Norg!"

Kado grasped one of his guns, flicked the controls on it, and fired it at Kaitlinn. A loud crackling hum filled the room, and a ball of glowing blue light leapt out the muzzle and surrounded Kaitlinn and the troops. They twitched for a few seconds then all of them let out a collection of shrieks and yells before they dropped to the floor. A few more seconds and the ball disappeared.

"What the hell was that?" Norg looked at Kado with wild eyes.

"Stun pulse; they'll be out for a few minutes. We gotta move fast. Grab what you can and let's go!"

We filed out of the building and trucked it over to the nearest Hell Hawk. Norg blasted the soldiers nearby, and we jumped aboard.

A familiar voice sounded from the intercom. "The hell are you guys doing here?"

"Zengus! No time to explain; we're bailing outta here and... how'd you get over here? We heard you were off on other maneuvers."

"Kaitlinn called me back for some kinda emergency at this spot."

"Yeah, that would be us."

"Hah, can't wait to hear this story."

"Tell you on the way. We've got a fix on Cataclysm, and we're beelining for it now."

"Cataclysm? Well, alright, strap in!" The engines revved up and the craft rocked as we launched.

"Set coordinates!" Kado bellowed. "Nelson, get up front on the nav!"

The engine noise went from a deep hum to a shrill whine in seconds, and I braced against the wall when the craft jostled and launched into the air. I made a personal resolution I had to stop flying like this, preferably to stop flying altogether. A pained belch escaped my lips as I wandered to the front.

I grabbed and pulled my way to the cockpit and looked at the navigation. The text on the strange controls didn't appear in English, but my hands flew to controls on the panel like a paperclip to a magnet. In a few seconds, I typed a course onto the nav and heard a beep sound in response.

"Coordinates received," Zengus commented. "That was easy."

"Just don't ask how I did that."

"You got the touch, man; all I need to know."

Kado laid his hands on our shoulders. "Great work."

Zengus asked, "Think Kaitlinn will try to ground us? They aren't too plenty on Hell Hawks these days."

"She's got too much to worry about with the Omegans, and she's already short one Hell Hawk. Now full on to Cataclysm. Nelson, I've got notes from Baudricort on Failsafe. They're scattered but we need to figure out what's going on with it, if there's anything we need to hack or disable. Sooner I know about it the better, OK?"

The text of the P-LAD danced around, but then it focused for me. The notes were from Baudricort, and they talked about controls and listed a diagram of the Cataclysm unit with a reference to an input port. The device was to be inert until the Failsafe was activated. This was how they prevented unauthorized firing of Cataclysm. It wasn't part of the original design, though it was done by the Valkyrie to prevent accidental discharge of Cataclysm.

"Kado, any idea what these controls are?"

He looked at the notes for a few moments, then checked them against his own P-LAD. "This looks familiar. They were developing a new Link around the time the Action split off. People were becoming more resistant to the Audio suggestions, so they developed an internal one that links to the nervous system. It's far more stable and harder to resist. They'd experimented with the Link, and the one used through the headsets, but it was only one method for them. They'd also tried working with the blood, which was more complex, and the earlier version of that. Before the Link was done. There are examples of this happening, and that looks like what they're talking about."

"So the interface is the nervous system?"

"It's in there somewhere. I just don't have all the details. I'll check back through and find whatever she tied it to. If you get any of those inklings you've been getting, please don't be shy."

"Do you think Charista knows about this?"

"I can't be sure. But I say we get this device and figure out a way. Maybe I can circumvent the Failsafe. We won't know until we get there and try. Step on it, Zengus!"

"How long til we get to the Cataclysm spot?"

"From here, at present speed, another three hours. I'm checking the onboard weapons stores, in case we run into trouble. The rate our luck's been going, we're sure to be in for something."

"We got some of Kado's new guns too. Guess we get to see how they work in the real world now." Norg beamed.

Zengus shifted in his seat. "New guns?"

"Yeah, powered by Valentium."

Zengus stared ahead at the landscape that shot past us. "Hmm, that's... even better."

"Hell yeah, it is." Norg slapped Kado's back.

Kado winced and rolled his eyes. "I wasn't looking forward to seeing them in action."

"We can't rightly choose to fight or not all the time. Cheer up. Just maybe we will miss them on the ground."

"First priority is finding and securing Cataclysm. Then contact Llewyn for his status and see where we can help out. If we can activate Cataclysm, we can turn this whole fight right on its side."

THIRTEEN

(ANA)

THE CAPITAL STOOD on a large mountain. Cold gray steel walls lined the squared structure, with sheer sides that made any assault on foot pretty much the dumbest idea ever. Nycole's reaction to my suggestion of going through the air to attempt entry made total sense once I saw the place up close. We'd need a Hell Hawk at least, and then we'd have to hack the security algorithm to let them know this wasn't an enemy stolen craft. And that was all before their defenses engaged. I hadn't any idea what those might be, but as much as Charista had done through MODOSNet and the Link, she must've fortified the hell outta this place.

I was surprised there weren't Omegans around trying to break through. Looked like they were still more about the Valentium, for the time. Kaitlinn also gave the Omegans enough hell to have time for a direct Capital assault, I figured. I hoped she was as good at protecting Nelson as she was at drawing Omegans away from the Range and the Capital.

At least, we didn't need all the hacking I'd figured on. Nycole and

Dawn worked their magic with some access codes and before long, we slipped inside.

It took a little doing to get through security, even with psycho research killer Dawn with us. She and Nycole tried emergency beacons, and Lebabolis security authenticated finally our access. I wondered why they had all that security, but they couldn't find it to spare any tech or resources for their troops in the field. The thought of troops I'd seen and fought along with, some I'd buried, all of whom could've been helped with just some of the weapons and gear that was hoarded around here sent me fuming.

Charista met us at the entrance while we watched the teams seal the entrance up tight.

"What in the world are you doing here?"

Her arms were folded, a stern scowl on her face. That was it, her only greeting to the group and one of the two people with whom she agreed to have Cataclysm delivered to her. It really pissed me off how even now that we were on the same side, she still eyed me like a disapproving parent. After days of walking, eating very little and exhaustion in general, I was surprised at how much resistance I mustered as I kept my hands from clutching her throat right then.

"The Omegans shot us down, and we bailed," I retorted. "Oh, and somebody blew up our Hell Hawk. Don't suppose you know about that?"

Her eyes seethed and she searched for a nasty reply, but her eyes found Nycole and her glance changed quick. It was a brief flicker, and Nycole narrowed hers in some kind of unspoken conversation. I swallowed hard. Nycole gave Charista a knowing smirk in return.

Charista watched me again for a few seconds, then grabbed a small comm from her side. "Of course not. Why would I destroy one of my own officers? Why didn't you check in with Kaitlinn or Jason? They could've helped."

"We might've hit an Omegan patrol before we even got near friendlies."

Charista's eyes darted about us in a visual inventory. "Nelson. He was with you. He didn't—"

"Not so we know. It's tough getting info when your comms are busted."

I thought about the other group we'd seen, the Guard, and why Charista never mentioned 'em. It was like pulling teeth, getting what we even did from Dawn. I kept my mouth shut on that one and hoped Dawn wasn't feeling too generous with the info sharing. *Nice work, Ana. I bet Baudricort would be proud.* The longer I played this game, the easier it got.

"I told them about your ships, ma'am," Dawn said.

Charista said, "Oh? Yes, that's right."

Charista's face twisted as if stung on the heel by an insect. She shrugged the irritation off. "Whatever brought you here, it's time we get on with our primary objective." She spoke a few words into the comm then met my eyes again, this time with a small smirk. "I've notified Harkson. You and Dawn will push on to Cataclysm, and we've got some more... tools for you."

"What about Nelson? Isn't he a crucial part of this too?"

"Nelson, for our purposes, is lost for now. We can't afford to wait anymore, I'm afraid. There's no guarantee he hasn't ended up with the Omegans either."

Dawn stepped up toward my side. "The transports, commander?"

Charista beckoned us over to a MODOSNet terminal, where she tapped controls until diagrams of ships appeared. They were slender and sleek, and nothing like I'd seen. They were longer and skinnier than Hell Hawks. They sure looked fast. Their surface looked seamless, one continual piece of dark shiny metal. Treg stood next to me, his face blank. Wherever these ships were stored and however they came about, the average Warrior Product knew zip about 'em.

"These were in development around the time the Action first broke from Lebabolis. Not even Baudricort knew about them. I'm willing to bet they'll make it."

"You couldn't have brought these around sooner? You realize how many troops are getting killed out there, including your own gray bands?"

"This war got messy fast. Problem is we don't have an unlimited supply of these transport ships. In fact, they're rather short in number. I'm afraid they aren't good for direct assaults. Troops in the field are better off with the Hell Hawks."

"Well, how about letting loose with your garrison?"

"We have to keep enough for the rear guard. This place is our last resort, and we'll defend it to the last."

"Well, now that you're sharing a small piece of your plan, how about letting us in on the rest?"

"It's quite simple, Worker Product. We get Cataclysm and turn it on the Omegans, then that ends them. I can thank Kaitlinn and Jason's regiments for keeping the Omegans occupied until then."

Treg flipped his fingers through the stats on the ships while I took a seat next to Charista. "How's the Pox treatment going?"

"Better than expected." She tapped away on the console, then stopped. "Ana, your brother made it through."

She said the words like she'd read the inventory for a food supply. An excited gasp escaped my lips.

Had I done it?

Was it true?

I choked back a sob at the thought, of Varrick healthy. And now it wasn't just an idea anymore. I felt Treg's arm on my shoulder, and it took me a minute before I answered. "I want to see him."

The terminal sounded with a few beeps, and the symbol of the Valkyrie passed the screen. "In good time. I need to show you part of the gear we'll be supplying you with."

Two soldiers wheeled in a large box that reminded me a lot of the Caches. The cover gleamed a little in the light, black metal with silver trim along the sides. Charista looked at the box as if it were one of her children. "This is the container for Cataclysm. It's very important you place it in here as soon as you get it. Please use extreme care when handling Cataclysm. Any attempts to move or shake it could set it off, so please do not mess this up. I'd rather you had someone like Kado there with you, but there isn't time for a proper outfitting."

"We've handled Valentium runs before; we know about delicate, lady." Treg scoffed.

"I won't debate the safety risks. Just do this as part of our agreement, understand?" Her eyes were fixed on me the whole time, and they narrowed when she mentioned the agreement, as if a verbal slap to my face.

She pulled up several videos on the screen of battles between Lebabolis and the Omegans. At first I thought it was a feed of some of the fighting we'd been into, but faces passed the screen and at one point I recognized Baudricort! The uniforms for Lebabolis looked different, older. Smoke billowed about the soldiers who charged around and fired on each other. In the middle of it was one woman, the Valkyrie. A chill ran through me when I realized why she was familiar. During my Verge, she was the one I had seen who led troops into battle.

The clips showed a force of Omegans in a fight inside the borders of Lebabolis. The Valkyrie stepped about the field, shoulders broad and her head fixed on the scene like a hawk that regarded its prey with serene but laser like focus. She pointed and waved her arms about, directing her troops. They watched her and obeyed with no hesitation. She was calm, cool, even in the sea of destruction around her. I heard the voice who'd spoken to me say, "Across distances I've led you. With valor, strength and victory I've fed you. All evil in this world will dread you."

Charista's face changed. Her scowl softened, and her eyes were stained with a mix of worry and regret. "Years ago the Omegans damaged the borders to Lebabolis and moved pretty far into the Sectors." She eyed me. "We never had time to overhaul them; we were too busy with building back people and infrastructure."

She kept talking, but then I lost all attention to her when another clip played on screen.

"Our army was well trained, but they were overrun. People were in a panic. Worker Products, and Intellectuals especially, aren't accustomed to shows of force and having to defend themselves. They needed something... someone to lead them. The Valkyrie led our troops, but they also stood as a reminder that while we benefit from technology, the old ways are still with us and are always reliable."

I said, "I heard the bedtime stories about her. She and her forces held the Omegans off until Cataclysm finished the job. And you killed her for it."

Charista's eyebrows arched. "Is that what you think of me? You think I'd take our greatest warrior ever and terminate her?"

"See no reason to doubt it."

Charista shook her head. "You haven't heard all of the story. The Valkyrie wanted to break Lebabolis apart, Ana. Harkson, the Coursons and I wanted to retain order."

"You mean slavery."

"I mean progress. Freedom can't exist as anarchy. Without order, the weak fall; they always have. The Valkyrie wouldn't listen to me or the Coursons. She also had the army on her side, so she was too dangerous to be left alone. I had to stand up to her, for the good of the people."

Charista's face clenched. I wasn't sure what happened to her, but she looked like she was in pain telling this story, as if she was being tortured. The usual hard glare I'd known her for was gone, and she looked more like a frightened animal in a trap.

"The Valkyrie was our best and last hope against stopping the Omegans before we had Cataclysm. She had the attention and respect of Lebabolis. But that power went to her head, and she had to be stopped. She tried to shut down our facilities, but it ended up getting more people injured in the process. We just weren't safe anymore with her around. She wanted freedom for all Products, but some of us weren't convinced the Omegans were really gone. And we had no stability without order. If we were left to our own, things would have gone back to people destroying each other. Our system was tough, but in a world close to its end, sometimes order must come before freedom. Now I want to show you where you came from, Ana, because we need you. We need you and the Action, and you need us, even if you don't realize it yet.

"Ana, I'm desperate to stop the Omegans and we need your help. There, I said it." She slid her fingers and moved them briskly about the controls. The screens switched to Product files and histories, and before I knew it, there was mine. My entire existence reduced to a single screen. The only thing that was blank was the parents. Those two fields were cleared out.

"Your records have always been like this. I assume Baudricort wanted secrecy for you, like some of the others who fled to the Action. We eliminated his access for this once we learned what he had done, but not before he damaged a lot of records."

I thought back to his eyes as he lay there dying in my arms. Was he just sorry because he knew he was dying? No, my heart never accepted that. He got people out. That wasn't Baudricort. Was it?

Everything in me figured he wanted me protected by doing this. All of us in the Action knew we were doomed for Realignment if we got caught.

"As I told you, the Action started out as training for our new army. We wanted to resurrect the Valkyrie. Once we learned the Omegans were assembling for another invasion, we knew time was short. Preparing Radomet takes too long, and we needed people who could be made ready much sooner."

The screen switched back to another profile record. I hadn't seen this one before, but a glimpse of the face really resonated with me. It was the face of the woman I had in the Verge, the one on the videos.

"The Valkyrie?" I asked.

"Her name was Petra." Her voice trembled just saying the name. The ember of emotion smoldering in Charista's voice stunned me. It was the first time I heard anything from her other than the cold commanding tone that greeted me on the MODOSNet updates, or Product training speeches or even the dealings we had with her as part of the Action. We'd joked that her heart was just a mechanical device where emotion was as absent as water in a desert. To us she was a Radomet with well-hidden mechanical parts.

But before I could ask about anything else, she continued. "Petra was the Valkyrie. We grew up together, two Warrior Products and friends. She led the army to victory against the Omegans. She was our protectress. I rose up too, but with the regular military. In time I had my own command. But the Valkyrie oversaw the Guard and the true elite of the Lebabolis strength." She strained when she said the word 'elite', as if it bothered her that it hadn't been applied to her or who she commanded."

Charista continued, "When a majority agreed we needed stronger controls, tighter security, Petra resisted. She refused to let Lebabolis go the way they were. She never understood the benefit of order for moving ahead. She insisted on freedom, but we'd seen the Outlands. That's no more than chaos. A lot of people joined her; she had a lot of supporters. Some people can't handle that kind of power. She became rash, reckless. We had a foothold of civilization in this world, and it soon became clear she would only jeopardize that."

"But then why the torture and Realignment?"

"Only for order. People need direction and purpose. You think the Outlands are less harsh than Realignment? I suggest you spend more time out there. All the Outlands offer is blight and a slim chance of survival. You've been out there for a while now; do you really see that place offering anything other than chaos?

"There's more," Charista said and hesitated. She watched me, her brow wrinkled. "Should I continue?"

"I don't know what you're gonna say, so it's up to you."

"Ana, we fought with Petra a lot over what she wanted. Before we stopped her, she went on raids trying to break our system from within. Those raids included attacks on facilities. She was so determined to break up Lebabolis, she lashed out, she and her troops. They stormed facilities, shut down things they could, and in all of this a lot of Lebabolis products were killed. Including, I'm afraid, your mother."

My body went taut at this. The Valkyrie killed Lebabolis products? But there it was: Petra blasted production facilities, and I noticed Sector Five, my home sector. And the woman who had my name laid out to rest.

"I don't understand. She was the Protectress. Why would she?"

"Desperation. She lost her mind, Ana. She started out good. I knew her from little and she was the best we had to offer here, but later in her life she became something else. Intentions, however good, can get blurred with time. I'm sorry to be the one to tell you this, and I don't know why Baudricort never did. I suppose he was too embarrassed about his own transgressions and for not taking better care of you."

"Baudricort started this?"

"He was under strict orders from the Coursons to develop a weapon. He architected Cataclysm to stop the Omegans."

As she talked, Charista's expression softened. I thought of the nomadic life the Action had, and even this location of the Range didn't really offer much other than shelter. We had no structure, at best a haphazard one from Baudricort's half crazed obsession with rescuing people from the mistake he'd created and given to our world.

"I figured in time, once our reach was further, we could consider more freedom. But I care too much about the citizens of Lebabolis, of which you're still one too, to let them flounder in self destruction." Charista breathed a heavy sigh; her eyes were distant.

The vision of Charista as a child seemed as odd to me as a third arm. I wondered how all this time she hadn't managed to pull a coup and kill Harkson to take command of the Coursons and Lebabolis. If there was anything she wanted and liked and desired, it was power. She gravitated to it like no one else I ever knew.

The more she talked about Petra, the more Petra sounded like Baudricort. Quite strong willed; made me wonder how he would've handled her. "So she was brought in for Realignment?"

"That wasn't an option back then. In fact we never had any other chance to convince or stop her. She broke out with the Guard when word was received a group of Omegans massed near our border, and Petra was never heard from again. We always assumed she was lost."

"So she wanted freedom, but instead of that you lay down an even tighter rein on people. How is that any better?" I asked. "The Valkyrie wanted to return the rule and the decisions to the people. Why isn't that better than keeping people living like cattle, producing like pieces of machinery?"

"In time, there could be more freedom, but we can't consider that with the Omegans at our door. You really think we can drop everything with this army hell bent on raiding and ruining everything we've built to date? Dear Ana, you must consider the world Lebabolis developed in. Chaos was the rule, the strong devoured the weak. To leave any society to that kind of rule would be to just invite more problems among those who couldn't defend themselves. Lebabolis has a mission to establish order, and that's our goal."

I wondered if our plans to live free were really considered part of their deal. But I wasn't about to let that thought slip into Charista's cross hairs.

Charista looked at me with sad eyes. "All I can say is when the Valkyrie was gone, I lost a friend and Lebabolis lost a great asset. We've stumbled down the road of progress, but it doesn't mean we haven't made a lot of great advances.

"But now we need something. We're protecting the future of Lebabolis, but we need help guarding its present. Jason and Kaitlinn command our field troops and the Coalition, and are keeping them at bay, but troops need a rally point. If anything, the Valkyrie taught us that having a champion is what spears soldiers on to win. We want you to be that champion for us."

"Me?"

She nodded. "You've got respect of both the military and the people. You were a Worker Product who burst out and thrived. You even outfought Radomet. You showed how the Product system doesn't always serve the best needs. Ana, we want you to be the Valkyrie. Deliver Cataclysm and lead our attack. We'll have Kaitlinn make the troops ready for you so you can lead them into battle. Llewyn's group is near the Range and he needs help. We need it to be you."

"I don't know, what could I do?"

"What you've been doing, what you've been trained to do, what you've always done... what's in your heart. Show the Omegans that they can't control this world and they won't own us."

"But when we have Cataclysm?"

"That's our guarantee. The Valkyrie fought the Omegans to a standstill before Cataclysm finished them last time, and I know you can do it now. The peace will be ensured once we have Cataclysm."

I watched Treg. Leading the attack, the whole attack? How could I be expected to do this? All I had to go on were the words of someone who claimed to be the Valkyrie talking to me in my head.

A few people rounded the corner with a small child. My eyes leapt to them and when I saw Varrick's face, I froze. My throat seized up as if I were about to choke. My eyes brimmed with tears. I felt like I'd been punched in the gut. My breaths came too fast for words. My legs shook, but somehow I stayed on my feet and took an awkward step toward him. I squinted my eyes shut, and the tears dripped over my cheeks unchecked.

"I kept my bargain." Charista stood and watched Varrick as he ran and jumped into my arms.

"Sister!"

I kissed him and rubbed the back of his head, my voice in a full tremble. "Y-you're OK?"

"Uh huh." His voice was bright, like he hadn't recently been sick with a life threatening illness very recently.

My arms snaked around his form and squeezed him tight while my body shook with sobs. I closed my eyelids and let the tears come. I didn't have to be brave, I didn't have to be strong. I felt like I hadn't in many years.

The warmth burst through me like rainfall. My body relaxed, and for a moment I wasn't a leader of troops in the Coalition or even the Action, I wasn't this fearsome soldier, this brutal machine with a Worker Product's heart and a Warrior Product's skill.

And for that moment, I didn't have to be either.

I held my young brother and for just a moment I became a child again too. I let the feeling flow through me. My knees buckled, and I fell to the floor. I opened my eyes and the tears blurred my vision, but I didn't even care.

He was OK.

And with me.

I watched his face, his smile, oh that smile I hadn't seen in forever. I exhaled a sob as the weight of what I'd been through, and not knowing how Varrick was, was lifted in an instant. My heart ached as I wondered what to do so that this moment would last always.

In an instant, what I'd been through, what we had left to do, was all worth it. Doubt melted away like ice in sunlight. A warm energy hit me, and I didn't care where it came from, just that it felt like love returning to me as a river that flooded a dry oasis. I blinked back the tears, and my voice shook with all the agony of not having seen Varrick well, or even at all for so many months.

My voice hitched as I spoke. "Oh, my little man. It's good to see you." I hugged him as tight as I could. "What are they doing with you over here?" I took a gulp of air and exhaled into more happy sobs.

"They let us walk but only inside. They say it's safer."

I laughed. It felt more like home, this cold capital, for the first time ever. Even with Nelson and my other friends still away and under attack, I felt a calmness I'd been missing. I quickly regretted that I had to leave. It was mandatory. We had to get back to the front. There was no way I could let those people be out there.

I had no idea what Charista thought of the Valkyrie or that knife that I had. She never asked for it, but I wondered if someday she'd have aimed it at my back.

The sight of Charista so broken up over what happened to her friend, Petra, made me wonder how much war had messed her up too. War made even the hardest one of us crumble, even just a little.

I smiled at the thought of the light now back in my present, with Varrick at my side. And my future had a glimmer now. If I pressed on and finished my deal with Charista, I had a shot at making a real home with my brother.

FOURTEEN

(ANA)

I WORKED TO PROCESS EVERYTHING Charista had said. It was weird how little I'd known about her before. Even more how sad she was about what she said. Maybe we'd underestimated her all this time. I knew I was ready for this all to be over, and now I knew that maybe she was too. Charista always was the figurehead we saw for updates on the Security of Lebabolis, and to have her not only know the Valkyrie but to have grown up with her was strange.

Charista's story reminded me of how much I never had. A family she knew, choices she wanted, and recognition. It seemed so distant, like one of those stories we heard over and over again about the Valkyrie. It felt like she talked about another race of people or country. I never knew anyone who had it even close like that where I grew up.

I'd never heard anything about her and the Valkyrie. The stories I was told were more about inspiration, not on who was whose best friend.

And now she wanted me to lead the charge. I wanted more than anything to get back at the Omegans, but what to do about Cataclysm worried me. Was Duncan right? Was I crazy, giving it to her? I was too tired at that point for any more strategy plans like Baudricort.

I wished Nelson was here, but I had to think he was safer with Kaitlinn or one of the Guard tribes for then. I'd figure out a way to get him back to his time. Kado had to have something.

The sweeping ceilings and ramps of the Capital's interior led lower below the surface into the mountain. The lighting cast a faded glow everywhere. Charista wanted me to meet with Harkson, and for once I was happier to meet with him after her mood changed so much. I needed a father figure, and as much as I hadn't wanted it to be Harkson, he was the closest thing I had to that here.

While people were locked in at the Capital, they were allowed time for meals and light exercise, as long as shifts were kept. A group always had to be ready for exterior defense and monitoring of the proximity alarms too.

The Capital facility was large over ground and it had a network beneath for quarters. They took their time and built a pretty solid fortress, or at least they had their Products do it for them. The sight of the detailed structures, reinforced walls, quarters, food ration supplies, just got me angrier than I'd ever thought it would make me. I thought about Products I knew, grew up around, and lived with. They suffered and in some cases died so places like this were built. It made that deal I had with Charista as tough to take as the first day we made it.

Some people brushed past me as I walked toward one of the great dining halls. The room was filled with the low roar of people stuffing their faces. I watched the loyal Products, those who either couldn't or wouldn't break and go with the Action, feeding themselves. Their faces filled with contentment of their reward received. I shook my head at the thought that after this was over, they'd just go back to their lives of slavery, doing whatever their master wanted of them. Then I wondered, what if this didn't end for them, if this was where it ended for all of us among the living?

I was about to leave the room when I heard a younger man's voice call out, "Ana!"

A group of products at a nearby table watched me. One man stood, a grin from ear to ear. I stepped toward him. The gentle roar of the crowd eating enveloped us. "Is that really you?"

I searched his face, but nothing in it was familiar. Why hadn't I recognized this guy when he knew me? I'd eaten, but still hadn't gotten any sleep; that must've been it.

He let out a small chuckle. "Haven't seen you since Instruction!"

Then I remembered.

Watson.

Watson was a fellow Worker Product from the same housing unit. He knew me, Treg, Norg and the rest of the Circle well. He'd helped my adopted parents with Varrick on occasion in our housing unit, and if I'd have stayed we would have been fellow facility workers for sure.

"I'll be damned. I wondered what happened to you since I took off." I laughed.

"We heard about that break. Saw you a few times on the MODOSNet updates, until that crash anyway. We thought you died."

"Nah, it was close but we made it."

"You seen Varrick?"

I nodded and brushed a hand quick past one eye. "Yeah, he looks great."

"They've been running people through this contraption since we got here. Say they cured a good thousand people of Pox already."

"Good, that was part of our deal with 'em."

"Treg still with you?"

"Yeah, he's here too. They're sending us on a mission."

"Mission? What's with the outfit?"

"Well, the Action and Lebabolis formed the Coalition—"

"Oh, that's right. How could I forget? You're a big bad Warrior Product now. How'd you even get over on them?"

"Guess they liked how I took care of myself in a fight. So who else is here with you?"

"Oh, a few folks from our Sector, but they kinda mixed us together now. We're grouped by Product."

"What do they have you doing here?"

"Oh, food and exercise mostly. Gets boring a lot these past few months. But some of us are loading up a stash of Valentium. It's slow, and that job has been the same for a while. Don't matter much; I'd rather have something to do."

"Loading Valentium? What for?"

"I suspect it's for resupplying regiments. They gotta be running on empty, much as we see them fighting on MODOSNet."

"I didn't realize they still sent out MODOSNet updates here."

"Oh, hell yeah. Too many of us to jabber to all at once. They give us the latest. We saw that fight in the Crater. They have us hooked in when we aren't on extra duties."

"What kind of extra duties?"

"Oh, like running maintenance, monitoring the perimeter. Kolb over there's the one who caught y'all on your entry beacon in fact. Whatever they got, it's way more boring than facility work. But you don't know about that, now, do you? Kolb heard a few officers talking the other day about some big move that was going down. Something about a Range."

My gut froze up tight at the word, and I thought of our people still out there. They never felt more like mine at that point, and I was terrified they were walking into a place they'd be stuck in.

"Well, just keep your head down, Wats. I may not see you again before they send us."

"Look at you. You know we heard what happened on your Exodus breakout." His eyes beamed. "That was damned brave."

"Aww, well, things get blown up more after they're passed around through a few people."

"Don't sound blown up to me. In fact, Treg told me about it."

My throat clenched at the memory and the sight of myself

through Wats' eyes, and I had to leave at that. "Nice seeing you again, Wats. Just take care of yourself, and I'll pass back any word I can."

"Sounds good. Look, we've been thinking. If you're going to make the Range, we want to come. Can you take a few of us with you?"

"How the hell can we do that? I'm pretty sure you'll be noticed, and they won't take too kindly to something like that."

"Anything, just... I'm getting real bad feelings about this."

"I know. I can tell you, if I have anything to say about it, this war is gonna come to an end pretty damned soon."

"I'm holding you to that."

"Well, good then." I smirked. "Take care of yourself, Wats!"

I needed more time for my thoughts, so I walked further into the halls of the Capital until I ended up in the hangar and watched the sleek transport ships Dawn had gone on about. There they were, five of them. They looked nothing like the Hell Hawks. These were long and slender, and there were very few guns on the outside. They'd better be pretty damned fast, because about all they'd be good for in a fight is a battering ram, or just a target for Omegan gunners. One of the ships was being loaded with Valentium, like Wats had said. Were they supplying troops? Or was it for a run separate from the Cataclysm one?

It had to be. Why the hell would we carry that kinda load with us that far?

I ran my hand over the smooth metal of one of the craft wings when the voice returned to me.

She's lying, you know.

+What do you mean?+

The Valkyrie. She's right about the Valkyrie, but she knows just what happened to her. And she's not dead. Not yet, anyway.

+What makes you so sure?+

Because I'm her.

I exhaled in a gasp. A painful chill arrowed through me, and I clutched my sides in a deep shiver. The techs working on the craft glanced my way, but I just waved them off. The whole time I'd been talking with her, the killer of my mother?

I spun around and plodded back out of the hangar.

+You're Petra?+

Yes.

My whole body jerked upright as if I were a piece of rope pulled taut. I'd been talking with her... her.

+Is she wrong about you killing my mother, then?+

She paused for a long while. *I don't know.*

+Oh, well, you have no idea what I've been through, what I'm going through now, what I'll always go through over this. I don't know who to believe, but I'm thinking I'd be a lot more peaceful without you, so let me know where you are and I'll make sure I end your body wherever it is and whatever state it's in.+

Ana, please, hear me out.

+Why the hell should I even listen to you at all? I need answers; I want to know why this happened!+

What I do know, as dangerous as you think I am, Charista is a thousand times worse.

+I don't care. Why don't you leave me the hell alone?+

I want to help you.

+Help me do what?+

Save your people, your brother, Nelson.

+How?+

Ana, I'm talking about what Charista said, her plan for you to get Cataclysm. Let me help you.

+Why should I?+

Because I once swore to protect Lebabolis and I failed. I want to do what I always set out to do but wasn't strong enough to accomplish because of my pride. I know I don't deserve your attention or help, and I certainly don't deserve your forgiveness. I've tortured myself far longer than you ever could, trust me.

+At least tell me how you're communicating with me all this time. Are you using the Link?+

I am.

+How?+

They set it up so well, they didn't realize someone with enough ability could use it to send their own messages out.

+If you're here at the Capital, or anywhere to know where I'm at, why haven't you just come to me?+

I can't; they took that from me.

+What do you mean, took that from you?+

They took my physical freedom when they made me into a Radomet.

+You're a—how did that happen?+

It was the only way. I was scheduled for Realignment—

+Charista said it wasn't invented at the time.+

Oh, it was. Baudricort was ingenious and quick. We had it around the time we had Cataclysm. They took my troops away and told me they were gassed. They didn't want to take any chances of making them Radomet; they were afraid they would overpower the system and break the coding. They could've busted out of the holding and made a break for it. They wanted them taken care of fast and clean. For me they wanted to experiment and clone me, using their tech to make an army of mindless drones. I was to be the template, kept locked away and duplicated to keep their supply of warriors filled. But I was saved at the last moment by a friend. Instead, I was sent for Radomet conversion. They completed everything except the neural break, which allowed me to communicate like this.

+Why can't you just get out of there; what are you doing around?+

I'm only one person, and I'm trapped. I can't leave the Capital. If my troops were around, I'd have a shot. But instead I've been biding my time. Lebabolis is too powerful. Now with the Omegans at their door it might be easier for me to make a stand.

My head ached with this. Charista was only interested in keeping things to herself. She never stopped her schemes, even toward those who were supposed to be her allies. She wanted control. But the

Valkyrie would've known about the Omegans and how to defeat 'em. Charista wasn't afraid of the Valkyrie destroying the Omegans. She was just afraid she wouldn't be able to control the Valkyrie ever.

You must be very careful and think again about her. She's got no interest in defeating the Omegans. I haven't been able to prove it and the Coursons wouldn't accept it, but I know she's worked out some kind of deal. We fought them to a near standstill and Cataclysm turned them back for years, but I knew just as she did that they'd come back one day. She needed a bargaining chip so they'd agree to give Lebabolis their own land and exist side by side. Two enemies in a truce, however unstable.

+How long have you been like this?+

I stopped counting at around five years, so it's anybody's guess now.

+I've got news for you about the Guard; they aren't gone. At least, not Duncan and his group.+

Wha- how do you know that name?

+Because he's alive, along with your troops. I've seen them.+

What?

+The Guard? I've seen 'em, well some of 'em.+

Really, where?

+When we came through a Sector, they attacked a group of Omegans testing a Disruptor. They were poorly armed, and they turned the Omegans back.+

Where?

+In the wilderness, about a day's walk from the capital. They overpowered an Omegan patrol.+

The voice shuddered. *Unbelievable. They live. So they've joined you.*

+No, not at all.+

Why not?

+I tried, but you wouldn't recognize them. They aren't what you remember. They were more interested in surviving than a fight.+

No, that cannot be. They swore to fight and die with me.

+And now they think you're dead, and their own country turned them away to let them scrap like rodents. Why should they still care about anything?+

They pledged to stand with me and a country, and were cast aside. You can convince them to return.

+I tried but it was a clear no.+

Did you show them the knife?

+Yes, but they think it was stolen.+

What about the beacon?

+What beacon?+

The knife. Built into the handle is a beacon. Only the Valkyrie would know how to activate it.

+Yeah, so what do I do then?+ I pulled out the knife and flipped it around. The raised sigil pressed into my palm.

Rotate the handle to the left until you hear a click. Then push the emblem on the handle. That does it.

I followed her instructions. The handle took a little work but it finally budged, and when I pressed the sigil I heard two high pitch beeps, then nothing."

+So that's it?+

Yes.

+But wouldn't Charista have known about that?+

No, that was never shown to her. Your friend Baudricort—

+You mean my father.+

Yes, of course, your father Baudricort set that beacon up.

+But how do you even know they're monitoring it? They had no real weapons or tech I saw and smelled like they'd been living outdoors for the past ten years.+

When you're short on options your number one has to be hope.

+Now you're sounding like me.+ I clutched the handle in my hand again. I felt it warm up beneath my fingers. +So is this thing sending now?+

Yes, it will continue to unless you shut it off.

+How do I do that, anyway? In case someone we don't like is listening too.+

Repeat the process, but don't do it until you're in their presence. That's your proof that you know me.

+It's a long shot.+

You have to try again, Ana. You can do it.

+I don't even know where to find them.+

Start by looking due west from Sector Two in the Outlands. There once was a settlement there, thirteen miles from the Lebabolis border.

+It's been more than twenty years. What makes you sure they're so intact? That group I saw coulda been all of 'em. The Outlands aren't the best place to rough it on your own.+

You must try, Ana. Remember, I saw you when you made the Verge jump all those centuries back.

+You're the one who called out to me?+

I was. And I saw you do something amazing for someone who was only supposed to be a Worker Product. With no direction, you grabbed control of the situation you were thrust into and made that leap. Even Warrior Products get hesitant at times, but not you. You're a soldier, and whoever trained you did their job well. You completed the mission and helped many people. But now people need you again. Your friends need you. You can't let Charista get her hands on Cataclysm. It's too dangerous for anyone to have. So search, use the beacons, figure it out. It's what you've done, what you've always done.

+What do I say to 'em? They weren't even interested at all; they just wanted to get away.+

Tell them this: Across distances I've led you—with valor, strength and victory I've fed you. All the evil of the world will dread you.

+What is that?+

The Valkyrie pledge. Every member of the Guard knows it. In fact it was so volatile that when Lebabolis disbanded the Guard and sent me for Realignment that code was rendered illegal. If they hear someone speak it, that should give them enough of a push.

+So you worked with Baudricort. My father?+

There was a pause. *Yes, I knew him very well. He can help you.*

+I'm afraid not. He's dead.+

The voice gasped and shuddered. When she spoke again, her voice was stained with emotion. *How did it happen?*

+It's still a mystery. He was killed by a bomb at one of our bases, but we never found who did it.+

Her voice trembled more. *He believed in what I did, what I still do, with every breath I have in my body, in this mechanical shell they've locked me in. Without safety and strength, evil will win. Find the Guard, Ana. Repeat what I said.*

+But their deal to cure Varrick and the rest depends on me finding Cataclysm.+

You made a promise with someone incapable of doing so, I'm afraid.

+But they cured Varrick! I saw him.+

Be careful. I'm an expert on dealing with Charista, and look where it's gotten me. Just remember, things aren't always what they seem.

+I had no choice.+

I know. But now you do. If you don't stop Charista, there won't be much of anything or anyone else left to save, my dear. Be careful. Charista has eyes everywhere, and don't think she's not trying to get into your mind via the Link.

+And the Omegans? Can we stop them at all?+

They want something, plain and simple. Find Cataclysm, and you'll have what they and everyone else who wants power desires.

+Power?+

Control, but power too. And the Guard will give you the edge to find it and defend it if they get the chance, if you show them they can strike back over what was taken from them.

+Even if I do this, and they go along and we somehow manage to turn back the Omegans, what about Charista? She'll still be in power, she'll still have the ability to develop, and she'll come up with something else before long.+

First stop the immediate threat. The Omegans will drain the world for resources before they leave. There'll be no stopping them just yet either. If they do, this planet will no longer be habitable. Ana, your list of enemies is growing, you better add to your collection of friends. If you get to Cataclysm first, Baudricort has something there for you.

+Oh?+

Yes, but you must get to the device to see it. Just don't let other people know about me and our Link at the Capital. They don't like those who are different, and you don't want Charista to get any more plans for you than she already has.

FIFTEEN

(NELSON)

AFTER A BLISTERING FLIGHT across miles and miles of jagged terrain, over and around mountains like some sort of extended rugged machine test, we arrived at the location for Cataclysm. The mountains stared back at us like an angry pack of lions. We glided past a collection of boulders, scattered around like pieces of popcorn spilled on a floor. Our ship weaved slow and steady toward the taller mountains, where my Pull was so strong that I shook.

I clutched the armrests of my seat and took several deep breaths. I hoped getting Cataclysm also meant these feelings would finally stop.

We topped a few more grassy hills and saw a flatland, still with random boulders and rocks, but a level path that slowly arched up to the mountains appeared in front of us. I felt this tug in one direction. It wasn't super strong, but it was enough that if we moved a different way I felt unbelievably nauseous. I noticed a reach of boulders and some reddish soil, and I felt the direction was the right one to go, so I pointed Zengus to where my "feeling" showed me.

Reilly rode next to me in the comm seat. He was pretty brawny, and among Norg and Zengus, that really said something.

He'd been part of the group with Kaitlinn that was supposed to haul us back with her in force. Once Zengus explained things about our situation better though, Reilly went along. His glasses lay across his nose, and he looked on me with a smirk that he held for most people. He was in maintenance, but it was pretty clear if things got physical, Reilly was one of the guys who'd be throwing down early.

We touched down near a cave that jutted out from the side of one mountain like a hungry mouth. The air right inside the entrance was damp. I wiped the moisture that collected on my forehead. Kado ran a scan for signs from any other forces but found nothing. We unloaded, grabbed torches and weapons and headed inside. A dank moist air greeted us on the way in, with a rotting smell of a place that had no ventilation ever. A snake slithered past us into the darkness.

"You never mentioned snakes," Kado muttered.

I shot him a glare. "What am I, a tour guide?"

"Given everything that's happened, I'd expect you know a lot about this place, more than you may even realize."

"You should know by now, it doesn't work like that for me."

The ground was rocky and slippery, and more than a few times one of us slid to the ground in the near darkness. We took slow steps on the soft ground.

"Still got those feelings, Nelson?" asked Norg.

"Stronger than ever. Ready for this to be over. It's weird but I'm walking right where I'm pulled, if that makes any sense."

"As much as anything. I posted Reilly by the entrance of the cave for a sentry. Let's keep an eye out; I don't want us wandering off where we might get stuck."

"Of course."

Zengus lifted his light above and lit up the ceiling, and its jagged slopes of rock pressed into each other in crooked and broken arches.

Zengus pointed at the fractured rocks. "Looks like there's been a few cave-ins here over time. We used to look around in caves like this back at my Sector. Watch your surroundings, case we need to bail fast. Everybody remember your bearings and the way out. It's real easy to get spun around in here if you're not careful."

"Eyes out," Kado murmured as he tapped away on his P-LAD. "I'm scanning the area. Let's go slow here; we got a big prize to haul in. Don't want to waste time looking where we shouldn't."

The cave was filled with silence other than the small sounds we made as we talked on occasion and padded our feet over the unstable ground. I remembered my trip with Ana out of Sector Five in the beginning of all this, when she saved me from having my mind altered and destroyed. I felt another Pull but kept it in check, even though it still shot up to the surface now and then.

The deeper we went, the moister the air got. The Pull got even stronger too, so I knew we were right on target. I walked through a wall of cold air. The chill it sent up the back of my neck stopped me quick. The Pull moved to my throat, and I managed a startled cough.

"You alright?" Zengus asked.

"We're close. Real close. We should even stop and check here; this may be it."

The path widened, and a ledge formed out of the rock off to our right. We fanned out and looked around. The dim light from our torches threw a lot of shadows around, and showed just piles of rock and dirt, with a makeshift path through it all. I scanned my eyes and strained for any more details than my eyes gave me right then. My view settled on one section of rubble and passed over it before I felt myself pulled back there.

I looked off somewhere else again, but my head jerked back as if invisible hands directed it back to the same place. Before long I pointed right at the spot. "There it is."

A smooth ledge jutted out from the floor of the cave up four feet, a wall of rock that flowed up to a platform. Loose boulders were placed all around to make it semi-visible to anyone who wasn't looking right at it.

Norg and Zengus snaked from behind me and stood, their thighs pressed against the ledge. They slid rocks and other rubble away from the spot until they revealed a large crate. I shone my torch on it. The case was covered with black soot and grime, but the light found a few glimmers of metal. It had some markings I didn't recognize; there was too much grime on it. The center of the top part had a larger reflective surface, and I made out the crossed blade and bolt of the Valkyrie.

"Paydirt," Norg muttered.

I grasped the P-LAD in the darkness and activated it. I pulled the notes up on the screen. The letters stared at me in their original state, and after a few minutes they rearranged to form letters and words I understood. Diagrams amid the notes explained how to open the crate, so I directed the others on unlocking it.

I watched and called out details that flowed from my uncomprehending eyes to my brain and out through my mouth. Part of my mind watched the whole scene as if it were some kind of movie. After a few minutes the case was open. For all I'd heard about this device, it looked average to me. I don't know what I'd expected; anything more elaborate than this. Several circuit boards and a swirl of wires with switches. The whole thing emitted a bluish glow. It looked old, even by this time's standards. I wondered if it even worked anymore. It was a lot smaller than I'd thought, for a machine that caused so much destruction.

Norg grunted. "So now what?"

"What do you mean?" asked Kado.

"Let me tell you now what." Zengus' pulse rifle activated and made me jump; it was the only sound we heard in the cave. "I suggest you get to hauling that thing out and hand it over to me good and fast."

"What're you doing, man?" Norg's face was twisted in confusion.

I traded confused glances with Kado. He reached a hand toward Zengus and flinched when Zengus swung his rifle to Kado in response.

"Um, Zengus, what's going on?"

"All that needs to be, Intellectual Product. All you need to know is I made my own deal out of this whole situation. See, you're going at this the wrong way, searching and gunning and fighting for what? Stopping the Omegans? Still think they're out to get us? Why don't you consider just how easy it's been for them, and then let me tell you why. You've got the wrong information on them. We're not their enemies. We're their slaves."

"What?"

"You heard me."

"Zengus, what makes you even think that?"

"I got a good dosage on one of my raids I flew up in Jason's regiment. They've been pulling more of us out to help with the Omegan gathering humans up."

"Gathering humans?" Kado waved his arms about. "Zengus, this is ridiculous. You know Charista's been sending suggestions through the Link for years now. I think your imagination has just gotten away from you."

Zengus sneered. "Wrong again, brain child. You've been fed the same story like most people, even Baudricort. Poor bastard never even realized he'd been helping keep this little scenario going, all those years working on the Link and programming us like the onboard systems of a Hell Hawk."

I asked, "But the way you say it, not just the Omegans were in on this. If they're pulling people to help as you say, someone else in Lebabolis knew."

"Charista." Zengus scoffed as if the effort of saying her name was beneath him, like it was some secret we were all supposed to know.

I felt my knees wobble beneath me, and I steadied myself against the wall of the cave.

Zengus laughed and shook his head in pity toward us. "Y'all still thinking I'm crazy; well, let me just explain it better. We're generations into a gigantic farming experiment."

"Farming for what, Valentium?"

"Us, fool. Us. We're the crop."

"What?"

"You heard me. Centuries ago, the human race were reduced to a stash of embryonic cells in storage. Seems the powers that were back then made arrangements in case the shit royally hit the fan. And when it did, they had their backup plan. Only they didn't realize just how bad shit would get, so thousands of these embryonic hosts sat and stayed. Until another race came along, the Omegans. They weren't even looking for us. They stopped over to drain this planet and thought we'd make good helpers for that before they turned this whole place into dust."

"You're telling me that they reconstituted an entire race? Why?"

"That ain't for me to even begin to determine, brain child. How's about you, Mr. Author? You got any ideas why this all happened?"

The idea of the Omegans and what they did hadn't entered my mind one bit. "No. I'm at a loss. I always figured we'd be wiped out in a nuclear war. But I've no other idea."

"So we'll just have to wait for the book, I suppose. If you live long enough to finish it." Zengus sneered.

Sloshing footsteps grew louder in the corridor behind Zengus until Reilly's face was framed in the dim light, his pulse rifle pointed, the tip glowing and ready. I watched how he regarded Zengus, and it told me whose side he was on.

Zengus nodded, then pointed to the case. "So let's move this thing on out."

"I ain't moving jack nowhere," Norg muttered. "You better shoot me now and save us all the trouble."

"Norg, what would we do without that badass mean you pull off so well?" Zengus nodded to Reilly, who jammed a metallic claw in Norg's arm. The claw came to life with a shrill tone and the sound of metallic gears clinking. "Gotta hand it to those Omegans, they brought all this kind of tech to us for their experiment. We've added tweaks, but I bet it's nothing like theirs."

Norg's body shook in violent convulsions. He took labored breaths as saliva shot from his mouth. This went on for a few minutes, and his eyes shut tight. When he opened them they emitted a pale blue glow.

"And now we have our own drone product." Zengus admired their handiwork for a few moments. There was Norg, in body anyway. But it was pretty clear from his face that he wasn't there. Even the crinkled lines on his brow from his frowns were gone, and his eyes were blank aside from their new hue.

"What the hell did you do to him?" I asked.

"Oh, just a little temporary sedative to make him less interested in being an asshole. Should keep him docile til we can make it permanent back at the Capital. Now, Nelson, Kado, put those puny ass arms to use and help Norg carry this thing out."

I folded my arms. "Why the hell should I listen to you, traitor?"

Zengus laughed as Reilly readied another claw device. "Xander, much as I'd like to kill you, there are plenty of people on the Omegan side as well who'd just love to get a closer look at you. Think I'd deprive them of the pleasure? Hell, no!"

"Save your mind, Nelson. There are other alternatives here. Let's wait it out," Kado whispered.

Norg's body twisted like a piece of machinery and he grasped the handles on the edge of the box and lifted. Once Kado and I grasped and pulled the box came free. My arms got sore in a few minutes.

We slowly walked back down the path way with Zengus and Reilly behind us.

"So the package we'd been talking about and wondering what it was. All this time, it's us. We're not joining up to fight the Omegans; we're being handed over to them."

"How did I let this go this far this long?" Kado's voice was as broken as the expression on his face.

I said, "It's ok, don't beat yourself up. At least Ana wasn't here for this."

Kado eyed me. "She's probably dead, you know."

"No, Kado. I feel it," I said.

"How can you even—wait, you feel it? Like the Pull?"

"Yep." I nodded and smiled at Kado.

Kado asked, "What about the Pull for Cataclysm?"

"That's settled for now," I said.

Kado watched me for a moment then said, "So Zengus, since you have us cornered and will be delivering your package soon, why not tell us more?"

Zengus scoffed. "In case you get free? Hah, not gonna happen. I've contacted an Omegan regiment, and they'll be here within the hour. Your days of running and planning all over this place are over, Xander."

I asked, "Then how about you tell me what I've got in store? Least you can do for me leading you here to begin with."

Zengus said, "As soon as our other inside person is in position, you'll be brought over to the Omegans for processing. They're interested in collecting their experiment and reining it back in. They wanted humans as a worker force, but they also gave them some of their tools and tech, showed them how it worked. And we learned fast, learned how to make a lot of weapons that destroyed things. They kept us going for a long time doing that. But something happened they never expected. Humans developed. We organized and created a society. We were self-aware, and not just these obedient workers anymore. We thought for ourselves and wanted more than they wanted us to have. All the skills left in the species when it was dormant came back to life. The Omegans who were watching over the Colony were way outnumbered."

Kado asked, "So they managed to form Lebabolis the country?"

Zengus said, "Yeah, did plenty. The Valentium they were mining for, they kept on doing that. They made their deliveries to the Omegans. They made a peaceful offer. But things developed and got more involved. Then Lebabolis determined it wasn't ready to keep delivering to their masters. They wanted their own and so they shut the Omegans off and, well, it didn't go so well."

"So all this time, Charista has been part of this experiment too?" I asked.

"Yes," Zengus said.

"And she's never said anything about it?" I asked.

Zengus said, "She had plans to break free; she figured that she could've. The Valkyrie gave her hope, and especially, having Cataclysm, it was a clear option that she could shut them down forever."

Kado asked, "What made her think they'd just let her go like that?"

Zengus said, "Can't say. People have so much power they forget who they are or where they came from. What I know is she's still hell-bent on using Cataclysm and believe me, she'll bring fire down on us all."

I asked, "And what are the Omegans bringing?"

Zengus said, "Don't matter what they're bringing. They're coming to shut all of this down. We've lived on their graces for generations at the cost of giving them everything this planet has. What would you have expected?"

"I don't know, Zengus. Can't see what you could expect from them other than to be their dog," Kado said.

Zengus said, "Better a live dog than a dead duck. You're going into the mill. Least I'm making my plans to get away somehow. Now let's move."

With Zengus and Reilly watching, we formed a detail and hauled the Cataclysm device out of the cave. The box was more bulky than heavy, and I kept an eye on Zengus and Reilly, who both trained their guns on us.

I was next to Kado, and we stood across from Norg. Norg's eyes still had the glazed bluish glow to them, and he said nothing other than a few grunts when the box got stuck against a wall of the tunnel.

Our trip out of the cave was a lot bumpier and quieter than the way in, of course. Reilly walked ahead while Zengus watched us from the rear. I heard Zengus open up his comm. "Cataclysm retrieved transport. Give ETA."

The comm crackled for a few seconds; then came a response. "ETA ten minutes."

Zengus replied, "Good work. How about the others?"

After a few seconds the comm crackled again. "Crucinal and Firebreed? Lost contact with their transport but we saw the blast. No one walking away from that."

My knees weakened.

No, it couldn't have been.

She'd have fought back, right? Wouldn't she have figured out there was a problem? Ana was too smart for that, just to have been locked up and killed.

By the time we made it outside, the transport ships had landed. Their slender black crafts were lined up as if on a showroom floor somewhere. They'd been over our vehicle already, and from the mess of wiring and pieces thrown around, it was a safe bet we were stranded.

Some of the Lebabolis gray bands approached. Zengus motioned them to the Cataclysm device. While others grabbed Kado and me, Norg loaded the device onto one of the transports. They brought us close to our craft.

"On your knees," Zengus commanded.

"Zengus, what's the point now? You've got Cataclysm, Charista has it. Why even waste time on us when you can destroy whoever you want?" I asked.

Zengus said, "Because this was part of the deal. Charista doesn't want anyone around who could get in the way. Which is why she had Ana killed as well."

He watched us as the words sank in. I eyed Kado; he just watched Zengus with eyes so wide and his mouth halfway open. "You unbelievable bastards."

"That's enough from you two." Zengus swung his rifle to my chest. "I think I'll take away the prophet here, since he started all this."

My eyes were blurred with tears and I choked a few sobs out. Was this it for me? Was this how it was going to end? Dying alone here centuries in the future, and what did I have to show for it? Not a whole hell of a lot.

Zengus closed one eye and took aim, but Reilly stopped him. "We got trouble."

Zengus still held his aim. "Who, Omegans?"

"No, something else—you've got to see this." Reilly pointed at something over our shoulders.

Zengus flung his rifle across his back and leaned close. His stale breath had me gag a bit. "Stay right here; I'll be back to finish the job in a second."

I craned my neck for a look at whatever they saw, but the Hell Hawk and the transports blocked my view. But then I heard a noise.

At first it sounded like rolls of thunder. As it got louder, it cleared up—it wasn't thunder but a lot of yelling. A group approached from hills off to the left of the cave across a clearing. None of them looked familiar, and they weren't even Omegans. In fact there were no distinguishing colors or anything. All of them had scraggly manes of hair. In the front of them was a man with a Hell Hawk pilot uniform. I chuckled when I noticed the mane of blonde hair on the man ahead of the group and the crazy look in his eyes.

"I'll be damned," Kado muttered.

"What?" I asked.

"It's Jacobs."

"How can you tell this far away?"

Kado chuckled. "I'd know that mop of hair anywhere."

There he was, his uniform more ragged from when I'd last seen him at the crater, but it was the guy, his eyes wild, but the group he was with I hadn't seen. I scanned the crowd for any hint of Ana, but she wasn't there.

Who were these new friends? Had he lost his mind and hooked up with renegade savages? Whoever they were I just hoped they were on our side. The other soldiers were pretty haggard, but their shoulders were broad and they carried weapons. Some were pulse rifles, some just sticks, but they looked menacing.

Zengus waved the Lebabolis detail, and they loaded up onto the ships. Before long, the night air erupted in pulse fire.

Jacob's group kept their charge up and just broke off into multiple units. They peppered the Transports with pulse fire in random short bursts. The Lebabolis troops hunkered down and laid down fire. The ground shook from the explosions and weapons blasts.

Zengus, rifle held up against his side, dashed back to us.

"On second thought, we may need some help with Cataclysm once it gets going." He clutched Kado by the scruff of his neck. Kado yelled out and fumbled until he was upright. Zengus dragged him off to the ship. I watched him pass Norg, and he swung his rifle into the side of Norg's head. Norg collapsed onto the ground.

Zengus and his group fired up their ships and after return fire from the group with Jacobs, they were up and soared out of sight in a few seconds.

The troops made it to the Hell Hawk, and when they saw me some of them growled in response. But Jacobs waved the others down. He walked close to me, the rest of them close behind. They'd have all been shoo-ins for extras on an episode of *The Walking Dead*.

"The hell are y'all doin here?" Jacobs lifted me to my feet.

"I was thinking the same thing about you," I responded.

He shrugged and laughed. "We got hit after the Crater. Omegan bastards shot my bird up good, had to ditch inside Lebabolis territory.

"You landed?" I asked.

"Hell, yeah, I did. Who the hell you think you're talkin' to?"

"What about Ana?"

"She's fine, least since we landed. We parted ways on our next move. Ana and Dawn took off with Treg for the Capital, rest of us wanted back in the fight."

I felt a lump form in my throat. "They said they killed her."

"Who?"

"Zengus."

"What happened to him?" Jacobs asked.

"Went traitor," I said. "Turned this guy into a drone, at least for a while." I motioned to Norg. He stood up straight, like a machine that waited for its next command.

Jacobs eyed Norg. "Ehh, yeah, well, some of these Guard been working around tech things. I'll have them take a look. Long as Norg ain't trying to take us down for now. So back up a bit. You said Zengus turned?"

"Yep. We'd gotten our hands on Cataclysm and he overpowered us. Took off on those craft you shot at with Kado."

Jacobs rubbed his eyes and took a deep breath. "I just don't know. If Charista gets that thing and can get it to work, I just…" He stared off in thought about what the rest of his comment would've meant, and I had an idea it was something pretty horrific on a global scale. He seemed to also be processing the fact that Cataclysm even existed, as if he'd been an agnostic suddenly shown how wrong they were about the beyond.

His eyes cleared a bit, and then they showed pain as he said, "Ana, gone?" His eyes got misty and he bowed his head for a second. "She was our link; she pulled us together."

His body softened a bit and I felt more tears come down. There had to be a mistake. Zengus just wanted us as broken and defeated as possible. I had to think this was just some mind game of his.

"Who are these people?"

"The Guard."

"Yeah?"

"You bet your ass. They been tearing it up in the Outlands. They're scattered but in groups large enough to cause some serious hell, I'm here to tell ya. We been giving Omegans plenty of crap to deal with."

"That's great but there's more. They struck a deal."

"What?"

"Something about a package exchange. Kado intercepted a transmission," I said.

Jacobs wiped his brow and cast a look around toward the Guard troops. "Package? What, the Valentium?"

I grabbed his arm. "No, you don't understand. The package isn't Valentium at all. It's us."

His face twisted a bit. "Come again?"

"That's right, Jacobs. The Coalition wasn't ever being sent to the Range to fight the Omegans. We're being delivered to them."

"By who?" Jacobs asked.

"Charista."

Jacobs shook his head and took a few uneasy steps around. He looked over the Guard troops. They looked pretty eager for some action, one way or the other.

Sweat glistened his already filthy brow. He swiped at his eyes a bit. "So they get their weapon and they get to turn us loose. For what, I haven't a clue. I- I told Ana she shouldn't have trusted Charista. I tried stopping her, Nelson. I did."

"I know. Tell you the truth, I don't believe that story about her being dead. Just seems too simple for them to try that. They'd do anything to shake us up," I said.

In an instant, Jacobs shook his head and reared up, as if he'd gotten some kind of electric shock. His eyes steeled a bit and his brow uncreased. "Hmm, well, we can't sit here thinking about what might be while there's something pretty big we can do something about."

"The Range," I said.

He nodded. "Something else too, and this lines up with what you said about us being delivered to the Omegans. We've been tracking a large group of Omegans, hitting them when we could, but they ain't stopping for shit, and my best guess on where they're headin' is smack dab where Llewyn is. If we've been sold out, I'm circling back and protecting who I care about that I'm sure's still here. Our people need us; I'm going there. Y'all coming?"

"Hell, yeah. So Llewyn made it to the Range?"

Jacobs nodded. "Yep, well, he best get tucked in quick because there's Omegan patrols all over the place. They're gonna hit the Range hard, and he better be locked in."

"How'd you get in with this group?"

"When I left Ana and the rest at the crash site, I headed for the nearest Storehouse I could think of. It took a while, but then I ran into these guys. It took some convincing but not too much to get them to realize I was no friend of Omegans and definitely not Lebabolis. They brought me to one of their encampments and showed me their setup."

"How many are there out there?"

"This group's five hundred strong right now, but they tell me there's over a thousand, spread around the Outlands. They live apart though; they forage for whatever they can find in the wild and the Outlands."

"Who's their leader?"

"Some guy named Duncan. He ain't interested in getting involved in any combat. They want to keep themselves fed."

"If they got word, if Llewyn called a distress alert, they'd already known about it."

"Maybe but we've got a package out there, Valentium."

"Yeah? That's his big plan? Don't add up at all, man. They're corralling us in. And now we're going to the Range, a dead end. They've got us penned in. What if it wasn't about the Valentium after all?"

"What are you saying?"

"This whole exchange is bullshit. The package they want to trade isn't the Valentium, it's a hostage exchange. They're trading us."

"But for what?"

"We need to get in the open on this. Let's circle around the Range. If the Omegans are gonna hit that, we need to be where they wouldn't expect us. That's what Ana'd want anyway."

SIXTEEN

(ANA)

CHARISTA WALKED ME OVER to Harkson's private quarters where he met me. He was the biggest mystery to me of all the upper echelon of Lebabolis, even more than the Coursons. At least the Coursons were known in the Sectors, and every now and then they showed up in different places, but Harkson was out of sight most of the time. The updates on MODOSNet pretty much all featured Charista with the status of Lebabolis, and Harkson was a ghost in the wind who ran things from some distant place or even another planet.

He sat at his desk slouched as if a king who'd held his reign too long and had gotten fat and bored. His cold eyes examined me inside and out like he was some kind of judge who decreed a verdict on a crime he also determined I committed.

Everything was bathed in dark colors. A wall of monitors filled one side; each screen showed activity from a different Sector. Most of them had Omegan Patrols at one point or another. I couldn't believe how they were so comfortable with this; at least they never said anything about it to me. We were supposed to be in this pact together, but it was clear how much they withheld the longer I stayed over here.

The terminal at Harkson's desk was pushed to the side, and he clutched a glass. His steel grey eyes looked like they'd seen the world and then some. He looked tired but also like he'd just read the book about my life and was ready to quiz me on it.

"I trust Charista told you about the Valkyrie?" He said the word 'Valkyrie' like it was a piece of sour fruit in his mouth or a bacterial infection. His brow drew in a line.

"She showed me the clips."

His eyes still locked on me, he sipped from his glass. "I never liked the Valkyrie. That much power in one person's hands is a recipe for disaster. But these aren't normal times, and people having a focal point drives them more than anything else. People are easy to sway if you've got their emotions. I can't deny the Valkyrie did that quite well. She convinced them freedom was better than security, in fact."

He reached back and tapped the terminal at his desk, and up sprung a holo image of the Valkyrie symbol. He shook his head at the crossed dagger and bolt as if it were an insect he wanted killed.

"Isn't that contraband here?"

Harkson studied the image a little more, then returned my glance with more of his icy gaze. "It was, during peacetime. Symbols are very powerful, Ms. Crucinal, as you may have realized by now. They rally people, give them something to fight for." His lips curved up just a little as he added, "Against unbeatable odds."

I pulled the knife and turned it over and around in my hands. "What does any of this have to do with me?"

His brow raised and he chuckled a little. He looked uneasy about having laughed. I figured there weren't many laughs around here, ever. "So she didn't tell you everything?"

I sighed and slapped the knife on his desk. His eyes jumped to it, then back to me. I leaned closer. "No. How about you do before I raid your supplies and leave with my brother?"

It felt like I was back with Baudricort. There wasn't a word for how done I was with all this mystery and secrets. "I want to know about—"

"Ana, the woman Petra you've seen... the Valkyrie... she's your mother."

I froze in place. My gut was burning, and I heard almost nothing except the ringing in my ears. "What? No, m-my dad was taken as a Deviant and sent for Realignment and my mother was a Worker Product killed in a raid."

Harkson shook his head. "The people you lived with as your parents were in fact taken as part of the Deviant uprising, and yes they were sent for Realignment. We pieced together records in MODOSNet after Baudricort wiped all he did from the system and formed the Action. He covered a lot of tracks; I guess he was worried we'd target any offspring of Deviants and do away with them."

"Wonder how he got that idea."

He ignored my glare. "As I said earlier, the symbol of the Valkyrie was very important at one time. She saved Lebabolis from being over-run, and a lot of people remembered those days. But once it came time to reestablish order and preserve the peace, the Valkyrie was at odds with the plans of the Coursons."

"I've heard this story. She tried to take control back and ended up killing Products, then she disappeared once she went to face a group of Omegans who attacked Lebabolis."

"That's not all of it. The Valkyrie is a wartime leader and we were at peace, but she wouldn't stand down, and she had enough people on her side to be a problem. Ana, that's not all. She killed people. Among them, your mother. Instead of a discussion, she opted for a takeover. It threatened our security. We had to stop her for the safety of it all."

The video showed scenes of Sector Five, a fabrication plant. The one my mom worked at.

"Sector Five produced window tech. This is security footage from when the Valkyrie assaulted the complex. She called it liberation, but this; look, Ana. Look at those people. Terrified, running and being slaughtered."

I watched an army, led by the Valkyrie, proceed through the plants, firing on security and other soldiers. People were laid down in her wake. She regarded the scene with a smug smirk on her face.

He took a sip of his drink. "Ana, you know what's happening out there now. You're closer to it than anyone here. You've seen the bodies and destruction. Not even our best Radomet can hold off this invasion forever."

"Why didn't he just tell me? I was with him for so long, he had every opportunity to, but he never said anything about this." A tear stung my eye when I painfully recalled how slow he even was to reveal he was my father.

"Charista gave you who we want; I'm telling you what we need. We've had to make hard choices. Charista and I don't always agree, but on this we do. We are luring the Omegans into a trap. We've got it set up: fake vehicles, some Hell Hawks, and beacons to simulate enough of a Valentium deposit. They've been after the Valentium more and more; we'll give them their chance to take a huge haul in."

"What makes you think they'll bite? They've been pretty damned strategic so far, from what I've seen."

"It's a risk. We're coordinating with Jason and Kaitlinn. They'll begin maneuvers to draw the Omegans they're in contact with into a path for this location. Once you find Cataclysm, you activate it and hit the distress beacon."

I shuddered at this news. Baudricort had wanted no risk for me or the Action, so he kept that identity a secret. As recorded as it was in MODOSNet, he was able to change those records enough to not be a concern, then put me with the parents who raised me. I felt a lump in my throat at that thought. What did he or they do that they were so ready to take me on. I felt an ache for them, even if they weren't who had me naturally, they were still there for me while I grew up.

"Yeah, I'm out there fighting, and I'll keep on doing it, but what are you suggesting that's any different? Why me, anyway?"

"Who better to become the Valkyrie than her offspring?" The words hung in the air like the echo of a pulse cannon blast. I had no response at first. His eyes pleaded with me. He grasped my arm.

"You were born for this. Take lead of the forces. I know they've used you, but you've got competition. Jason and Kaitlinn are running a lot over there. Llewyn was a ranking member in Lebabolis; you think he'll stay with the Action and accept your freedom? He was with Baudricort, he wanted you dead. Who do you think it was who tried to have you killed? It was him! They are becoming egotistical. Leaders always have a danger of becoming too absorbed in their own glory and forgetting the true mission, the true purpose of why they're there. But you, Ana Crucinal. Not only are you the offspring of the true Valkyrie, you wanted only to save your brother and your fellow people in the Action.

"Some people already say I'm the Valkyrie."

"What do you say? Are you ready to stop listening to what other people think you should be and become what you are? Now is your chance. You thought nothing about running through a Verge centuries in the past because of what Baudricort wanted. You're who we need; who they need. When people see you leading the forces, it will turn the tide. It has to."

"And if it doesn't?"

He watched me for a few moments. He leaned back in his chair and folded his arms in thought. I looked back at the monitors that showed Omegan patrols in contact with a group led by Kaitlinn. The Omegans lit up the screen with fire, and the Action scampered about. The monitors were a collection of chaos. I wondered what else they had in mind if this plan failed. They were so outnumbered, so helpless. What would one person change about that?

"What about when it's over and you've got Cataclysm, and we're still apart from you? We won't join your fold again. We're living free or you might as well kill us, starting with me right now."

"Ana, we want peace, like you. We want things settled. I don't want to house these people forever like livestock. There's no point to keeping that going, as long as there is no more danger, and that's what I and the rest want, no more danger. You do too, right? That's the whole reason you left in the first place. I want things to return to how they were. We'll discuss terms when the time comes. You must understand though, this role you have ends when the war does. And once we give you what we've promised, our agreement terminates into peace unless you decide to challenge us again."

"You cross me, I'll blow Cataclysm sky high and take you all to hell with me."

"I think you're smart enough to know we have as much on the line as you do."

"Yeah, but I've also learned how trusting anyone, even someone who says they're an ally, can be dangerous."

I watched his face. He held my gaze and smiled. "You're wise, like your father."

My thoughts went to Kado, and how I bet even right then he tinkered somewhere on a solution that would change the outcome.

"You'll need to step up your arsenal," I muttered. "They've got disruptors. Any powered devices like guns and vehicles on the ground and in the air are disabled by 'em. It won't be long before they overrun us with that. And even with the Capital sectioned off, you know that won't keep them away from your front door for long."

The comm on Harkson's desk buzzed.

"Chancellor, urgent message from the Coalition. They've made the Range but are engaged with a large force of Omegans. Requesting assistance at once."

Harkson was silent. He pulled a P-LAD out and flipped it around in his hands for a minute or so. He gazed off, his eyes in a daze. Then he looked at me. "Ready to do your part of the deal?"

I shifted up in my seat. "What?"

"The Valkyrie led this nation before when the Omegans attacked, and that was how we kept ourselves safe from them. Now we need that to happen again. And though we don't have the Valkyrie, I think we've got the next best thing... Ana Crucinal, darling of the Action. The girl who outfought Radomets and risked her life to save her brother."

I heard him go on about these stories about me as if they were bedtime tales. It felt weird hearing this again, this time from the leader of Lebabolis himself. I shook my head. Harkson's forehead wrinkled. "I'm not sure you're thinking this all the way through, dear. Varrick was healed, part of the deal you and Charista sealed. We kept our end of the bargain—"

"The only thing we had to face back then was the attack on Sector Five." I gripped the arms of my chair tightly.

"Our deal was to turn back the Omegans."

"Why does it have to be me? Besides, some of my own people haven't taken to the idea of me in command."

Harkson chuckled and stood up. He walked about the desk. "Oh dear Ana, respect for the rank and respect for the person aren't the same. You've passed up a lot of people who are older and have been soldiers longer. How did you expect them to handle you as their leader?"

He grabbed a black rectangular shaped box and set it on the table. After he tapped a few controls the device opened and displayed several bracelets inside. "I can't mind control anyone, at least not anymore. The Link was damaged too much from all of the Valentium disruptions. However, people will remember these. We're spreading the word that the Valkyrie has returned, and it's you. And we're sending another unit to help protect your friends at the mountain range. We need you to be the Valkyrie though. To believe it for yourself. To know that you are the one, the person who will stop these attackers. The warrior who will restore peace."

I eyed the strange bracelets before me. The Valkyrie was always such a legend, I swore she was fifteen feet tall and crushed rocks with her bare hands. The thought of someone else being the Valkyrie was a little much to take.

I also doubted what effect it would have. Sure, the Valkyrie turned back the Omegan invasion in the early years, but from what I had heard that was much smaller than what they faced this time. And what exactly would that do that the Lebabolis military and other products couldn't also do?

"Ana, I need you. Lebabolis needs you. Your friends in the Action need you. We're sending a company of forces with a squadron of Transports. You'll be travelling much faster, so their Darkness shouldn't be a problem. You'll sweep down on the Western Range and catch the Omegans. They'll be off guard. Once you hit, the Action and Lebabolis troops in the field will engage from the sides and catch them off guard. They'll be caught by surprise, and if the weaponry the Action is developing is ready, you'll be able to turn them back."

I gripped the blade in my hands and ran my fingers over the sigil. The crossed blade and lightning bolt that represented freedom. At least, freedom for Lebabolis. I wondered if they included anyone else in that number. They had given Varrick his life back, and the rest of the sick from the Pox, so there was that.

The troops I saw here were pretty big in number. I wasn't sure how many were left for defense, but if I knew anything about Charista, she'd never leave her back door unguarded. She was way too careful about that.

I felt a mixture of good and uneasy about Harkson's suggestion I take the lead here. What was it about me that Llewyn and even Kaitlinn never took seriously when I led that group with the Coalition? Was I just the dumb young girl, even now? The one who never listened, who went off on her own, who dared jump through the Verge even though she was never prepared for it? I wished I knew how to wait at times, how to hold my tongue, to keep silent and let others speak. But silence to me was the worst pain of all. Of all the things I'd become tired of, the worst was having to wonder what people wanted me to be. It was time I drew my own line in the sand and let everyone know about it.

"I do this—" I clutched the blade and eyed Harkson—"we establish our new home in the Western Range, and you show us the shield technology so we set it up for ourselves."

Harkson clasped his hands. His lips protruded and he narrowed his eyes at me. Then, his face softened and he laughed a bit. "See, negotiating your terms. I knew you were a leader. Yes, of course. Contact me when this is over, and we'll set up terms for bringing our shield capability to yours."

I watched the blade on the dagger. The Voice said nothing, and for once it hadn't bothered me. This was my call, just like the others had been, and I knew I had to stick by this. Baudricort wasn't there for help. Neither was Llewyn or Kaitlinn or anyone else in power. It was me, the one they'd chosen. It was my time.

My back was still protected anyway, as long as I had one of my Circle with me. If I had Treg and got near Norg or Zengus, I had a chance. Worst case, I'd lead these troops into the battle and let them duke it out with the Omegans.

I felt a surge burst through me, not because of who Harkson and Charista were, but because of who I was. "OK." I stood up, my hand extended. "It's a deal. Show me to the troops and let's get started."

(ANA)

OUR GROUP OF SEVEN TRANSPORTS left Lebabolis after sunset and soared on a direct course for the Western Range, I hoped in time to make a difference and keep the Action safe. I rode with Treg in the lead ship, because in spite of what they showed and told me, I just knew I was never all the way safe unless I had one of the Circle close by. The deal was tricky, having Treg on board was not.

The Transport shook and yawed about a little as it rocketed to supersonic speed. We'd come in pretty fast when we got there, but that may have been all it took to catch the Omegans off guard. I braced my hands against the walls, but in a few minutes, I realized that wasn't necessary. This ship hadn't vibrated like a Hell Hawk, even as fast as we went. The angry howls of the engines were gone too. Instead, a steady hum was the only thing that let me know we weren't still on the ground.

I wondered about Harkson's reasons for this sudden burst of support. They wanted the Omegans gone, fine. But they had already given us an army. The Action had gear, even at the Range. Harkson stretched Lebabolis protection out a bit thin with these moves; I hadn't figured out his logic on that yet.

I watched the troops at the pilot console. They weren't mine anymore than I was theirs. I looked for some spark or fire in their eyes, but all I saw was a dull coldness. They were under orders from Harkson, not me, and it made me nervous that we may just have to depend on them if shit got serious.

I sat in the rear of the cockpit and watched the pilots as they monitored and adjusted controls without a word. The only response I really got from them was a salute.

Treg waited in the lower hold with the ground troops, in case one of 'em had anything in mind like our little exploding pod from earlier.

One of the pilots spoke, and I just about slipped out of my seat from the surprise at the sound of their voice. "ETA to Western Range, thirty minutes."

His comm buzzed with a reply from the lower hold. "Roger that, ground units on standby."

One pilot glanced my way. One of his eyes was covered with a red lens from the ship navigation tool. "We'll drop ground troops off on a ridge about a click from the Range. That's enough space for them to set up and start their Landcrawlers up. We'll support them from the air after that."

"What kinda guns you got on this bird?"

"Oh, they aren't loaded like Hell Hawks, but they've got pulse cannon. Enough for moderate damage."

I nodded. "OK. So, you got a name or should I call you 'hey you'?"

His face stayed fixed on me, but there was no hint of a smile. He just replied, "Jarin."

"Thanks, Jarin." I leaned forward toward him. "Harkson or Charista tell you about me?"

He shrugged. "Just that you're leading this attack and to take orders from you. I don't know much more than that. I'm told what I need and I guess that's it for now."

"Right." My mind's eye laid out the scene of the fight, as much as I'd known about it. I closed my eyes and took a slow breath. "Once we let the ground troops go we should pull back until they get in position so we can hit the Omegans at the same time as the Landcrawlers, give them more support."

Jarin nodded a little and looked back my way again. "Roger that. We begin deploy procedures in fifteen, better get into seat restraints."

The roar and rumble of the engines built to a loud ear-splitting noise. Our craft dipped down and I saw the others alongside us doing the same, releasing the Landcrawlers and troops so they could get in position.

Jarin studied a few digi maps on his console. An alert beep sounded with a message on the console, but Jarin covered it pretty quick. Not quick enough that I hadn't seen it, though.

I ducked back outside the cockpit to the access way to the below compartments and met up with Treg. Back when we were kids and he was just a Warrior Product trainee and illegally shared information with me, he had told me how it was always important to talk in code if I was ever in a hostage type situation.

"Hey, you OK back here?"

"Mmmhm. They're loading up gear. Should be another two, three minutes before we're out. How are you?"

"I saw some really strange trees at the Capital, forgot to mention it to you. Did you notice?"

Treg paused, and responded slowly. "Like what?"

"It was just these roots. They were really twisted."

"Oh yeah, that's bad. How'd they look up top?"

"Not good. Someone needed to cut 'em down."

Treg paused for a while, then he replied, his voice slow and steady. "Check." His eyes steeled, and he took a few deep breaths.

By the time I made it back to the cockpit, the stars greeted me like a twinkling cloth that covered the outer glass of the ship.

Jarin commented, "A few more minutes, we can swoop in and hit them all at once."

The comm chatter was filled with the other craft giving statuses, weapons checks, everything. If this punch was everything we needed, Kaitlinn's crew should be able to bust in and finish these guys off.

I grabbed my rifle and checked it over. A strange beeping noise came from somewhere. I flipped the rifle around and looked near the power supply. Nothing. I activated the firing mechanism for a test; it looked fine. My comm wasn't being activated either.

What was that noise?

I glanced up and saw something on the console for a second, but Jarin's hand swept over it.

It was an auto destruct sequence.

I kept looking at my rifle and then I held it across my lap.

"Everything OK, Jarin?"

He kept working on the console. "Of course, why?"

My hand grasped the handle of my gun tight. I felt the blood rush to my face.

"I was just wondering why you activated the self-destruct. Something you wanna share with me?"

An electrical zap hit my right shoulder. A thousand tingling daggers stabbed into me, and my arm flung out, sending the rifle tumbling loudly to the floor. Jarin's co-pilot had electro tased me.

"What are you—"

"Shut up!" Jarin left his seat and stood before me. "This is our mission, and I'm afraid it doesn't involve you or your Action."

He grabbed my right arm, still limp from the blast, and placed a restraint on it. I struggled a bit with the left until he shoved me down and jammed his knee into my left shoulder.

"Is that right?" I groaned as he fastened both my hands together and hoisted me back into a seat.

"Completely. You see, other negotiations were made. And Harkson felt it was best he put all his bad eggs in one basket. So we'll turn our troops back to where they'll do some real good, and you and your Action friends can deal with the Omegan horde. I'm sure they'll have a good time turning you into dust."

Jarin and his co-pilot set a few more controls on the console before they turned to leave the cabin, with me still tied down. Jarin paused and clutched my shoulder. He shook his head, a look of pity on his face. "I expected more from a Valkyrie."

I tugged hard against my bindings. My hands ached to go for his throat, but it was no use. The craft wobbled a bit and started to dip downward. Jarin and his co-pilot braced themselves. When they opened the door to the cabin, I heard that battle tested and weary voice who'd never let me down since we were young.

"Yeah, no, this really won't work, you tying my friend up. Your mama didn't raise you better than that?"

I craned my head back to the sight of Treg as he swung at the co-pilot. Jarin ducked aside and grabbed the electro tase again. I writhed in my seat until I flopped to the floor. I crouched as best I could then launched myself toward Jarin. It was all I could do, but if anything I'd take another jolt and give Treg a chance to do away with these guys.

Unfortunately, the co-pilot got his own stun weapon out and knocked Treg downward. Jarin swiped a fist at me and I plummeted back down to the floor. Jarin and the other crew bolted down the hallway.

"You OK?" I yelled. I tried to sit upright but the wobbling ship made it almost impossible.

"Yeah, great," Treg muttered. "So Harkson gave us the raw deal?"

"Whatever gave you that idea? He and Charista are in on this cluster, and I owe them both a world of shit. How bad they zap you?"

"Oh, my ass has felt better."

"Thanks for the update."

"Anytime."

We could both hear the beeping from the console.

"You've got to be kidding me," Treg said, clambering toward the controls.

"No joke. They set the auto destruct and if we can't stop that, we gotta bail."

"What about the crew?"

"Sensor panel indicates they sprung the emergency troop release."

Treg jumped into the pilot seat. I made my way closer to see the console over his left arm. The readout showed the destruct sequence activated with a minute to spare.

"I don't know this ship. It's new tech."

"You gotta do something, Treg." Treg groaned as he tugged the control stick back and forth. The craft slowly pulled back out of its dive.

"OK, so we won't smash into the ground." Treg eyed the console. "They changed these up. The Hell Hawks had an energy discharge relay by the pilot seat. If we can find and yank it that should disable the onboard system. At least it worked like that in the Hell Hawks."

"Give me the downside."

"I'll have to land this metal manually."

"You can swing that?"

"I can drop this bucket. It won't feel too good, but I can handle what she's got," Treg said. He thrust his hands downward. I strained against my restraints. My wrists burned as the couplings around them dug into my flesh.

The timer got to forty seconds. Treg fished his hand about wildly, then he paused, his eyes widened and a smile formed. "That's gotta be it."

Treg moved the handle and the console buzzed with a warning. "Energy discharge selected. Enter code to confirm." A set of number keys appeared.

"Oh, great," I groaned.

"We gotta bail." Treg flung me into the co-pilot seat and attached the restraints as much as he could with my arms still bound. He jumped into the seat and activated the pilot eject sequence. In seconds we rocketed out of the craft straight up into the air.

The canopy flipped away and fell back to the ground. I watched the Hell Hawk careen back toward the ground, and a few seconds later it exploded and sent a blast of hot air and smoke in our direction.

Parachutes on our seats deployed, and we slowly dropped to the ground. I saw the other transports in the distance, along with a few groups of ground troops headed toward the Range.

Treg and I landed fifty yards apart. Once he freed himself he came over and helped unfasten my wrists.

"Shoulda known she'd set us up." I shook my head. "All that talk about coordinates and finding Cataclysm. Guess she figured on another deal. Why did I do this again?"

"Nelson." Treg looked at me.

"If Dawn did a Link pull on me, she'd have gotten the coordinates. But she couldn't have done that while I was asleep." My thoughts drifted to that research lab I was ushered away from by Harkson. "They must've found another way to it. Nelson's useless to them now. He's not in their system or subject to a Pull. Baudricort was lucky he got what he did out of him."

"Once again, Charista missed her target." I clutched my wrists. "Don't suppose you got any weapons outta there before we ditched."

Treg frowned. "Coulda kicked myself, not grabbing one of those morons' rifles on the bridge. Well, sit tight. We just—"

Treg was looking past my shoulder, and his eyes widened. If he was shocked by something, then I knew we were in trouble. I quickly turned around to face our next obstacle.

There was a large group of Lebabolis soldiers approaching us.

Thankfully, their weapons were down. I recognized an officer insignia on one of them in the front. I saw his tag read the name "Clyde". He waved the rest to a halt and came close to us.

"You're Ana, the Valkyrie?"

I smirked a bit. "Some people think so."

Clyde nodded. His face was strewn with sweat and a bit of brownish oily liquid. I pointed toward his face. "You been through a rough ride, huh?"

He wiped a hand at the liquid on his face and checked it. "Yeah, well, Charista never told us one objective of this mission was taking you out."

I clenched my gut. Treg frowned and gave a small chuckle as he shook his head.

"Is that right?" I narrowed my eyes. "What's your wait, then? I'm here, aren't I? Unarmed?"

Clyde watched me. His eyes weren't cold, though. They looked more like that of a fatigued animal. "Don't make sense to. I been fighting and killing people who never fell in line. Deviants couldn't make their lives fit any kind of mold Lebabolis said they should. And now Omegans are destroying all we got and making it disappear. Making us a thing of the past, too. Well, I got to thinking how much Lebabolis took away, much more than they ever gave. It's time I fight for someone who's gonna work for me, not just work me. We have to work together, or we don't work. One or None."

"Yeah? What about your crew there?"

Clyde motioned to the rest near him. "We're all in the same unit. Warrior Products from Lebabolis. Never joined the Action, but that doesn't mean we liked everything they had us do. And now, with the Omegans... we're not fighting against each other anymore. There's too much at stake. We're with you... the Valkyrie."

I looked at Treg. "I'm not sure I'm the one you think I am. But if you wanna help me, our friends are in trouble. We're heading over the next few ridges ahead; that should bring us close to the fight. There's a lot of Omegans trying to get into the Ridge. I have no idea what the others from Lebabolis are gonna do since Jarin and several others tried to have us killed back there."

"We've got weapons. Don't have a Landcrawler; ours was disabled," Clyde said.

"That never stopped the Valkyrie before, did it?" I looked at 'em and suddenly felt very small. I'd held myself up for a while now. Being strong for Varrick, being tough for Treg. But now we were in this fight with people who'd faced down and defeated the Omegans years ago. Was I tough enough to fight alongside them?

Clyde said, "I'm not turning back from this. We need a plan."

I said, "Charista knows where Cataclysm is."

"Cataclysm? What do you mean?" Clyde asked.

"The device."

Clyde shook his head. "The Valkyrie was supposed to destroy it, but she was overrun. So she put in a security measure. Cataclysm cannot be operated without the security measure enacted."

"What measure?" I asked.

"It was on one of her last transmissions," Clyde said.

I thought back to Otto's P-LAD. "I have data from the Valkyrie, but I don't know the code."

I showed the device to the others, but they stared at it with blank eyes. "I'm afraid we can't help you there. But we pledge ourselves and our young to you, the Valkyrie."

"Who are you, and how do you know all of this?" I asked.

Clyde opened the gap in his shirt and showed the mark of the Valkyrie in a brand on his chest. The crossed sword and lightning bolt had been covered by a layer of jagged and whitened hair from over the years, but the mark looked as if it was applied that day. A few of the others followed Clyde's gesture.

"You were with the Guard?" I asked.

Clyde smiled but shook his head. "We supported them and what they stood for. You too."

"Me? What do you mean?"

Clyde chuckled. "Oh, it was years ago, and you were pretty young. But we knew about you, and your parents."

My throat hitched.

"M-My parents?"

"The ones who raised you. They were good people." Clyde approached me and slid his arm around me. "They didn't deserve what happened to them, but they loved you as if you were their own."

I blinked tears from my eyes. The holes in my life hadn't hurt as much as long as I'd filled them with other things, but when I stopped and remembered things I'd never had, they pulled at me painfully.

I coughed so my sobs were stifled. "I know you're on the level now. I need you, and what's left of the Action needs you. The

Omegans are after my friends, and neither of them realize where Cataclysm lies. But we have to watch Charista. She's on the prowl and will stop at nothing until she's got total control."

The soldiers formed a circle. They were disciplined and quiet. Their eyes had flickered with intensity, not the dull blankness that a lot of Products had in Lebabolis. Their arms were well toned, and they looked like an army without an arsenal.

They held their arms up in salute to me.

Suddenly I didn't see a hundred rough troops. I saw a thousand legions of deadly Guard members who I commanded. I felt like the greatest general in the world.

(NELSON)

AFTER A QUICK REPAIR JOB, the craft we had was repaired enough to fly. I turned down a seat though. I'd had way more flying than I wanted for my lifetime. If I ever made it back I was starting a new personal rule: no trips that involve an airport.

Our group loaded up and trekked out toward the Range. After an hour's walk we heard the sounds of a fight. Pulse discharges, the periodic boom from an explosion. We topped a large hill and saw the scene.

There at the Range, the Action was holed up while the Omegans fanned out in an arc that cut them off. Smoke drifted all over the place, and the Omegans moved closer as they pummeled everything in their way.

Jacobs called the group over. "Listen up, that's our people over there taking fire. The ones you swore to protect once. I ain't talkin about Charista's lot. I mean those who were slaves and worked to death for nothing. You wanna get back at Charista, it starts with freein' those people. Remember, One or None!"

"One or None!" the crowd cheered.

The Guard troops formed a solid block formation. At the front they angled the lines and then gave the order to move out. I walked with Jacobs. Norg was nearby too. The blue glow had faded from his eyes, but they showed me nothing. He had to really be bad off to not have complained all this time.

After fifty feet, some of the Omegans noticed us and trained their weapons our way.

"Charge!" Jacobs yelled. The group lurched forward into a fast run, while the Hell Hawk soared above and angled several shots at the Omegans.

The ground rumbled with each blast from the Omegan ships. The Coalition forces returned fire as best they could and shot from every conceivable angle.

Another blast hit close and sent dust raining into my eyes. "We've got to get word to Llewyn! If we link up, we'll have a better chance of surviving this!" I yelled.

"Don't think we got time for that."

I squeezed the handle of my rifle. I'd just learned to shoot this damn thing, and now I was going to be killed. After all I'd been through. I guessed I'd never see dad again and now Ana was gone too. She died for this cause because these people were worth it. That meant to me this was right where I was supposed to be. I looked at Jacobs and Norg and couldn't have been prouder of who I was with.

In spite of how things were right then, a weird calm settled over me. I had a place, a point of existence. I even had a mission. I had to carry this out. My feet planted firmly into the ground.

A heavy rumbling built to our left and we saw Kaitlinn's troops appear from over a rise in that direction. The Hell Hawks glided over the soldiers and traded fire with the Omegans around the Range. Kaitlinn rode in a Landcrawler; she sat up top and directed the troops as they moved.

"She better watch, somebody gonna pop her out in the open like that," Jacobs muttered.

Jacobs Guard troops pressed forward into a melee with the

closest Omegan division. They responded with a heavy barrage of pulse weapon fire. The darts of yellow hot light skewered the crowd, and screams came from all over when soldiers were hit. The group didn't slow down.

Norg stood next to me, silently. He looked to be coming out of that trance, but not all the way yet. I grabbed his arm. It was loud but I had to try.

"You in there, Norg?"

He surveyed the scene around us before his eyes slid to me.

"Norg, you alright?"

He had nothing in response. The best person who could've known what to do here was Kado, and he was long gone, maybe even dead. I thought about Ana again. The realization that I'd lost her, this woman, this character I'd somehow willed into existence. It felt more like I'd lost someone close. A friend or perhaps someone even closer.

I grabbed for a pulse rifle and fired shots back into the Omegan group. They had their own ships come down, and they peppered the area with another shower of fire. From this point, we had a chance to hook up with Kaitlinn's regiment but that meant we had to fight our way through a pretty thick line of Omegans that separated us.

The Action group drove the mobile facilities out into the crowd. They made it fifty yards before they were stopped with fire and turned into flaming roadblocks. The Action soldiers there fanned out on the sides of the flames and fired on the Omegans closest to them.

Jacobs bellowed, "We have to link up with Kaitlinn or Llewyn for any chance of making it out of this!"

I scanned around for the best way and asked Jacobs when I felt some taps on my midsection. I turned to Norg; his eyes were wide, and they gazed over my shoulder the other way.

Jacobs spoke before I turned around. "Son of a bitch."

"What?"

"Ms. Crucinal returns."

There she was.

I'd never seen anything like it—or her.

She was ahead of another group that looked a lot like the one with Jacobs. Some had Coalition uniforms, others looked more like another guard unit. Ana's face was twisted in a shriek, and they were at a full charge.

I watched the group and her and beamed with pride at her ferocity. I forgot where I was for a second. "Look at her. She's something else alright."

Jacobs nudged me. "Easy there, you sweet on her or something?"

I couldn't stop smiling, which made him laugh at me. It was strange to feel so happy in the middle of this fight, but at the same time, it was comforting.

Ana's group headed straight for the line of Omegans that divided us from Kaitlinn. Jacobs and I looked at each other, and he yelled out his command, "Pivot! Up the center!"

The Omegans who had been around earlier with the Valentium returned, and soon we were surrounded. The Omegans and their black and dark grey uniforms and ships closed in on us like an eclipse. With all of us there, there were at least three times as many of them.

The large device I'd seen at the center of them was lifted up in the air, and a low hum rattled and shook the ground. The pulse rifles around me made a weak fading beep sound.

"It's Darkness! They've activated it!"

The Coalition troops banged on and fumbled with their weapons for a few seconds, but it was useless. The Guard troops just flipped their guns around as if they were clubs and charged again. The Coalition troops followed along, and we continued our charge. The Omegans now unleashed more shots into our group, and more yelps and screams came from us in response.

The circle of Omegans around us got closer, but it made our group fight that much harder. This was our chance, and I had hope that Charista had another option, like Jason's regiment for assistance.

Whatever it was, time was running out, and we needed something fast.

NINETEEN

(ANA)

I HEARD THE ROAR of the Guard troops behind me, and they surged with more intensity than I'd ever seen, even more than the attack they made back in Sector Two. We charged right into the center of the Omegan horde, a mess of swung arms and deactivated pulse rifles. Their Darkness only stopped the weapons, not the highly pissed off people who swung 'em.

Out the corner of my eye, I noticed another group apart from the Omegans. They looked like the Guard, and before long I caught some Coalition garb in the mix. After several minutes, we made our way closer to this other group. I thought they were another unit ditched by Charista. But then Treg called out into the crowd.

"Norg! Nelson!"

I strained my eyes and ran toward them. Nelson was hunched over, and I saw his blood covered hand that grabbed his midsection. "What the hell happened to you?"

"Plenty. Let's start with Zengus."

"What?"

"He turned, Ana. He turned on us and took off with Cataclysm and Kado fifteen minutes ago."

The idea of my Circle being shattered again made me stand still. First Otto's death, now Zengus turning on us. Why?

Nelson yanked his rifle up and battered an Omegan who ran toward us in the head until it fell to the ground. Without missing a beat, he looked over at me and said, "He made a deal with Charista."

I stared at Nelson in disbelief. "Had a little training, have you?"

"I couldn't wait around for my bodyguard, now, could I?"

I bit my lip to stop myself from laughing. We were in the middle of a battle without any working weapons. Nelson held up his useless rifle.

"What are we going to do now?"

"The only thing we can. Fight. Don't leave my sight."

"Never again."

The air was filled with fire, energy sparks. This felt unusual; for once we weren't on the run from anyone. We ran toward and were in control.

"One or None! Attack and destroy 'em!" I shouted. My cries took on the sound of an angry predator. My pulse throbbed in my throat. I blinked back the red haze over my vision, but I soon realized it was my adrenaline in overdrive. My face flushed with heat. Suddenly these troops, these whatever they were, represented everything that stood in my way, and not just at this moment or this position. They were also the Lebabolis government that took my parents away. Charista, who dangled my brother and Nelson as her guarantee I'd be on the hook for whatever plan or objective she cooked up. And my mind had one thought in response. "Destroy them all!"

I felt rage course through my veins. My skin bristled, and my ears were filled with the roar of the fight. It made sense to me now, why this felt so right and normal.

I was bred for this.

Like my mother.

These enemies weren't Omegans to me anymore. A feeling took over me like an infection. Memories of seeing Varrick dying on an Action medical bed and how they hid him from me. The anger swelled so much that I hadn't felt the shot that pierced my side. Another fist glanced off my face. When I was close enough, I swung the butt of my rifle into the nearest Omegan. I took a hit to my midsection and doubled over for a second, but jumped back up and was in the middle of a giant fray that spread around me.

I saw their eyes, their inhuman eyes, images of hell and the dogs of Satan about them. They weren't human, and it made the blows that much easier to dish out. I felt the anger and rage as much a part of me as my own blood as what stood in my way, what kept me from the life I wanted, from the safety and security I needed for myself and my brother.

Llewyn came out and stood on top of one of the damaged facilities in the crowd that hadn't burned yet. He watched, and I yelled out to him to take cover, but it was no use. He wasn't concerned about taking a shot. A blind soldier with a rock could've taken him out. What the hell was he doing? Had he lost his mind?

The ships fired a little on us then moved back toward the group that came out of the cave. I saw Norg first; he took shots standing in the crowd. A few Omegans crumbled to the ground in agony when they were hit. Treg and I stood with our backs together and parlayed whoever came within range. I swung my arms until I felt like they couldn't move anymore, then I lunged into a large Omegan and drove them to the ground.

A hot stinging seared my right shoulder, and I saw a bloody blade being pulled out of me by a grinning Omegan. I connected with my good hand and knocked it to the ground. A deep soreness burst through my body. It got hard to breathe; even standing up straight was tough.

The howling around me was intense and kept going for what seemed like hours.

"Ana!"

I heard Nelson's voice but didn't see him. Then, there he was, among a group of soldiers with Norg. They fought their way closer, and we stood near each other, flailing arms, weapons, whatever we could grasp at the horde of Omegans. It felt like we were underground, the way they swarmed about us. Sweat rolled off my forehead and got into my eyes, making them sting.

"You alright?" he bellowed over the roar.

"Think so. Here we go again, huh?"

"Y-yeah, well. Same story, different day."

An Omegan swung a large pole over toward Nelson's head, and I swung my arm up fast to block it. The rod made a loud clang against my armor and glanced off. A tingling shot up my arm until my teeth vibrated. Nelson ducked at the sight of the weapon swung toward him, then looked up at me in amazement. A smile found his face. I felt removed from the fight, like I wasn't there at that moment anymore, that I was somewhere else with Nelson and this wasn't even a thought for us.

His eyes widened and brought me back in an instant. He reached his hand toward me, but then his eyes froze on something behind me. He shouted, but I didn't understand his words.

A searing sensation penetrated my lower back. The stinging scorch was soon replaced by a deep soreness. My arms and legs tingled and went limp. I wobbled on my feet, and there was a strange salty taste on my lips. I brushed a finger over my mouth and drew it back, coated with blood. Nelson shielded me as best he could with his own body.

Dizziness came over me as I shuffled around to a rather large Omegan. He had an insignia like Commander Chun, who we'd seen at Sector Five. I managed a shriek and raised my rifle, but he swung his fist into the side of my head. My feet slipped from under me, and I landed face down. Nelson was by my side, but his shouting soon faded. Everything around me, the screaming and explosions, paled to nothing. All around me was calm.

Then, I entered my own Darkness.

TWENTY

MY HEART FELL when I saw Ana's body go limp. The Omegan who'd shoved a spear into her back stood by and studied her body as it twitched at random.

"Ana!"

I swung my rifle at the Omegan who'd impaled her. The Guard who was nearby leapt around the Omegan and in a swift move snapped its neck.

The fighting continued as I sunk down near Ana and shielded her body from the combat above. The tears streamed down my face, and fear gripped me. What was going on, what were we supposed to do?

Pandemonium enveloped us like a dense fog. The Omegans continued their fight and we stood our ground best we could, but soon we were enclosed in a tight circle by the Omegan horde. I suddenly found myself pulled from the fight, and away from Ana, as much as I'd fought to stay close. I was then back in the scuffle on my feet.

A large horn sounded, and the Omegans stopped their assault.

Our group pressed forward but all the Omegans did was defend at that point. Gradually, our group was subdued and the Omegans wrestled the few who still had strength to the ground. I then noticed I was near Llewyn. He regarded the scene with a grim frown, a trickle of blood oozing from a spot on his head.

"What's the plan?" I asked Llewyn.

He watched me with empty eyes, like his entire country had been destroyed. "Plan? We're a bit beyond that now." His eyes twitched about. The groans of the wounded settled on the battlefield. A group of Omegans on a small floating skiff observed the scene. One of them clasped a device and then spoke to us.

"Pitiful humans, you've lasted much longer than we'd ever expected. You've proven yourselves worthy of lasting for the purposes you've been designed for. My name is Emperor Zakmar of the Omegan empire, and you are henceforth and forever onward our prisoners. You were given the opportunity to serve us, but instead you defied our wishes. All you are, all that you did, all that you made was because we allowed you life. You won't win, you won't live, you won't breathe without us there. You're our crop, and we're reclaiming what is ours. We're taking you to our fortress soon. For now, do listen to what I say carefully and relinquish your weapons to the nearest Omegan at your side. Failure to do so will guarantee your immediate and swift termination. Do not test me; I've been gracious enough allowing you to come to this location freely."

The Coalition surrendered weapons slowly. The Omegans made their way through our group, pulling and reaching for our weapons. The wounded were sorted out. The dead were yanked out of the group, much to the anger of others nearby, but any attempts to stop the removal of bodies was met with brute force from the Omegans.

Before long a pile had developed of bodies. It pained me to look at it, but still I found myself focused on it. One of them reached for Ana.

"You're not taking her."

The soldier glared back at me and raised his hand to strike, but Llewyn grasped his shoulder and spoke a few words in his ear. He nodded and left Ana.

I shrugged and looked at Llewyn. "We've been down before; we can figure this out. I'm sure Charista's got a plan. Another strike, or Cataclysm maybe?"

Llewyn eyed me with a smirk, his eyes narrowed.

"She'd help us, right?"

Still with his eyes on me, he raised his hand. "Emperor Zakmar, I wish to discuss the terms of my surrender with you."

"Yes, we must discuss the terms of delivery as agreed upon by Charista."

I froze at the conversation.

It was him.

The whole time.

The familiarity that Llewyn had, the fact they knew him by name. Well, they'd know him by name because he was a ranking official. But the deal, the very terms that were mentioned in the document Kado uncovered. It wasn't fabricated, it wasn't a mistake. In fact, Llewyn looked to at least be in on it, maybe even the broker of the whole thing.

Llewyn eyed me with pity; a smile found his lips.

I felt rage as it coursed through me. My fists were balled so tight they got sore. "You unbelievable bastard. You sold us out to them. Why, what for? How the hell could you do this?"

"I'm here to survive, Nelson. Look around you. We've fought these people for decades. And you don't even realize we owe them for our very existence."

"What are you talking about?"

"Humans were dormant as a species. After countless wars humans had their biological activity suspended, and it was the Omegans who brought us back to life. They cloned, cultivated and trained us. They gave us some of their tech, which we learned and were even able to augment, like Cataclysm. We were supposed to be their workers, but something happened. While the Omegans were only worried about what they could take from the planet itself, we became aware and developed. Evolution took over and then before long we'd established a nation. With a whole belief system. And they had a harder time controlling us. People like the Valkyrie made it very difficult for us until they were taken by force to get us under control."

"What do you mean, 'us'? Wait, Llewyn—" I reached for him.

He gazed on me with disgust. "Forget it, Nelson. That's how it is here, and if we don't make friends with it, we'll die. Charista is dealing, and I'm doing what I need to survive. I suggest you do the same."

"Dealing? With the same force who wants to kill us?"

"Corral, not kill."

I jabbed a finger toward Ana. "See what you did to her?"

He eyed Ana like someone who observed an entry at a science fair. All he mustered was a head shake. I lunged toward him, but an Omegan clutched me and flung me back to the ground.

I watched Llewyn's dead eyes review everything as he walked off. The whole place and everyone there looked frozen, like a streaming video caught in buffering mode. I felt numb and lost. The weight of this crushed me to where even breaths were difficult. This was my fault.

She couldn't be gone.

No.

Not her.

Not her too.

I couldn't lose her again. She lay there like a discarded mannequin, and I thought back to Mom's helpless and lifeless body on the bed. I clutched her while the rest were pulled and pushed into groups above and around me. I didn't care. It stung like Mom did. I lost her. Who was I, did it matter anymore? I wish it was me, why not me? It's my fault; why can't I just die so other people won't have to anymore?

I stared at Ana and noticed her brow wasn't creased. It was the first time I'd ever seen it relaxed, which made me all the more worried. Her eyes were shut. She lay like a wax figure. The Omegans prodded about the rest of us and divided people into groups. Large orcish looking soldiers stepped about with weapons, moving us into place like frightened cattle. A few who dared push back or resist were bludgeoned intensely.

One of the monitor screens across from us showed teams of Omegans hauling the Valentium store away. Just one of their precious cargoes. From the look of it they were far more gentle with it than with their human payload.

Some of the officers milled about. Zakmar stood fixed, his eyes pouring over us like a bear that is deciding which of us morsels were to be its next meal. "Your government has seen fit to deliver you to us in exchange for a cease fire. I'm not willing to discuss terms of this, and frankly, I could care less about their safety at the moment. We'll handle them in good time. But for now, all you need to know is you'll be transported for processing."

Zakmar strode about us. When he neared me I asked him, "What are we going to be doing there?"

Zakmar responded, "You'll find out soon enough. It's time you humans learn just how much you have was given to you, and since you've proven you can't be productive with your freedom, you'll be returned to the original purpose we developed you for: servants and miners. That is, those who can follow along. The rest, well, we've got ways of handling the non-compliant."

The leader of the Omegans spoke with Charista on a monitor chat, and in the background behind Charista I saw a large box being moved away with that familiar Valkyrie symbol on it. She had won, and the Omegans had no idea. To them, they'd made a deal and an easy grab. I wondered what they had in store for us.

Slavery?

Experimentation?

Worse?

None of it mattered anyway if Charista learned how to break the Cataclysm Failsafe. She had it, us and the Omegans where she wanted us. I thought back to a time that felt so long ago, when I was just a simple man who dreamed of writing this book. I had a crazy pie in the sky dream that I would get published one day, and now it had turned into this.

I held Ana's head on my lap. She was still as a rock, but I refused to believe she was gone. My mind flashed back to Mom on the bed, and my every thought that echoed the words and the sentiment, "Live, you must live! Don't do this."

I knew Mom had to go. But Ana; no, this was wrong. It was too early and just incorrect.

"Don't leave me." As I spoke the words, visions of Mom floated into my head. It wasn't about letting go this time; I couldn't. This wasn't a person who'd suffered a disease where death was imminent. This was someone, an idea, a hope, a picture of strength that I somehow willed into being. How did I do that? Out of despair and the absolute stubborn belief that people dying wasn't the end, that somehow I could make it be about more.

But it wasn't.

Even so, Ana wasn't going. Some way, somehow, she wasn't dying. At least not without a fight.

The Omegans gathered us into small groups and marched us toward giant transport ships where they loaded us like cattle. A few got rambunctious and tried to resist but were quickly silenced with blows to their bodies. They removed our weapons and gear. A fleet of transport ships began to arrive and several people were loaded onto them.

Norg muttered, "Charista's just bought herself time, that's all."

"If the Failsafe is tied to the Valkyrie, she won't have much time at all."

"She'll get hers in time, and hopefully from us," Norg said. "I need me some Grade A payback, and I'm ready to pull the trigger on her."

"First things first. They're loading us and we'll need to size up things." I shuddered as I heard words that Baudricort or even Ana would be saying but they came from me. Treg and Norg looked at me for a moment with awe.

"We're open to suggestions, Nelson; you just keep that going." Treg grinned.

Norg steadied me. "Can't do anything now. Too many of them here. Better wait until it's a one on one thing."

"I'm wondering if they even know about me."

Norg eyed the Omegans. "I can't say for sure, but in any case, you get those Pulls you were talking about, best keep them quiet for now. We got to figure out our new situation and any advantage we got better be secret."

Norg and Treg remained back with the rest of us. Treg came closer and knelt by Ana; his eyes were shrouded in tears, and a deep wince hung on his face as he looked on her. "Anything from her?"

"Nothing."

"They won't take her with us," Norg said.

"Why not?" I asked.

"Heard some talkin'. They ain't no hospital. Anyone going with them's gotta be able to stand on their own. They're looking for slaves, not patients." Norg kicked the ground and grunted in disgust.

I shuddered at what else that meant. I cupped her head in my hand as a sob choked its way out of me. "They better kill me too then; I won't leave her like this."

I shook her body. Tears came loose and wandered down my face, splashing onto her chest. "Come on, you can't do this. You've got to live, Ana. You aren't ready for this; there's more you have to do. Please, just don't leave me. I need you. I've always needed you. Please."

Even the thoughts of returning home escaped me. What? Was that my home anymore? Had I lost everything that made me who I was? Was I still even Nelson? Was this where I belonged now?

For the first time, I heard a strain of emotion in Norg's voice. "We ain't going quietly, Prophet Man, I can assure you. I'm thinking of something."

"Looks to be now." Treg flashed a dagger in his hand. I grabbed for the dagger Ana held and nodded to him. "One or None, right?"

"Fuck-n A."

I watched the Omegans corral the Action and Coalition troops, and then Llewyn appeared. He walked with some of them and made comments.

Llewyn stood with the Omegans in a conference with Charista where it was laid out. The deal, the transfer. Llewyn watched us all, the sweat collected on his brow. My hands clenched into fists and, despite Treg's warning, I launched to my feet. The Omegans didn't grab me until I had a hand on him.

"What did you do? What is this?"

"It's survival; you wouldn't understand."

"Oh, I think I would. Only my version doesn't involve tossing people to the wolves."

"I won't debate the merits of this with you."

"Because there are none."

"Look, it's over, it's done, I made a deal." He turned, but I yanked him back and gazed into his eyes.

"You sold us like a bill of goods."

"We had to stop them; there was no other way."

"What about Cataclysm?"

"It's halfway to Lebabolis by now."

"You let them in on that little tidbit?"

He just eyed me in response.

"Was that even true, what Charista said about the Pox and curing the people?"

"They were able to mask the symptoms, but the disease has too good a stronghold. I must admit, Charista really didn't think that one through. All the while trying to come up with a weapon to attack, she created the greatest one ever. All from an accident."

"How long do they have?"

"Can't say, but you might as well break the news to Varrick's dear sister over there, if she ever comes around."

"Llewyn, what were you even thinking? What the hell did they even offer you to get you to consider anything this stupid?"

"It's not what they offered, it's what Charista offered. A place, status. Baudricort never saw the point of working with people. It was a good thing I killed him when I did."

"You son of a bitch."

"It was either him or all of us under a pile of rubble. Think these people will stop?"

"I think we'll never know now. We had a shot, a good one, and you gave it up for a safe bet and a deal with someone who wants to dismantle this planet. You're a worthless human being, and you're everything that was wrong with the Omegan experiment. They brought back humans, but I see they didn't weed out the assholes this time."

"Be that as it may, I don't expect we'll be speaking much anymore."

"How do you think? Who's to say I won't be able to use my mind about this place? It's served me pretty well so far."

"It has, but tell me, have you noticed anything different lately? That device keeps you stable, but it has also disconnected you. Nelson, I'm afraid you won't be planning or doing much of anything anymore. This world, your world, is no longer. The Omegans will take their control and agree to split the land with Lebabolis. There'll be the peace."

"You made deals with homicidal and ruthless creatures. And you're naive enough to think they'll play nice now that you've divided the sandbox up equally? I think we will be seeing each other again, and I really hope it's with me or someone else pointing a rifle at your chest."

"Save your strength, Nelson, the Omegan work camps are rather rigorous, or so I'm told."

I was about to launch into another tirade, but an Omegan

stopped me short with a jab to my midsection. As Treg collected me from the floor, Llewyn finished and spoke with the Emperor for a while. Charista was on the screen and joined in their conversation. The deals of the terms were simple: we were all to be hauled away to their fortress. The peace was to be established. Omegans took their share of Valentium, Llewyn's fake ruse was just about preparing it and making a signal. The Omegans honed in on the Valentium as a waypoint to get to the Range. Cataclysm remained a mystery. None of the Omegans spoke about it, which worried me all the more. I wondered if they even knew about it. Unless they figured it was a secret that we didn't know about. They must have wondered about that fight back then, and how they were turned back so decisively after being able to get the best of the humans for so long.

And now I understood how the humans came. Like seeds collected from a harvest years back, planted and cultivated for one purpose. But they neglected to think about one key ingredient in the mix. The one thing that sets us apart. The ability to think, to choose. And they couldn't stop that, even after who knows what kind of conditioning and chemical treatments. They'd separated humans into products, and Lebabolis carried that vision over. But they wanted their own piece of the world, apart from the Omegans. And that was the struggle. I knew they wouldn't rest with this deal. Charista had a short time left for herself if she couldn't get her great big gun to work.

Norg neared me. "What's up, Prophet Man?"

"Not much, and all of it bad."

"Yeah, no kidding. We gotta play this cool and let Ana heal."

"What if she doesn't, Norg?"

"Don't even talk like that. We gotta think this through. When we get wherever we're going, we need to figure out our deal. Maybe Kado can help."

"If they don't grab him up and pick his brain first. I'm sure Llewyn gave them the dirty dark about each and every one of us. Surprised they aren't trying some kind of Link on me right now."

"Ana's gone?" Norg's eyes showed more emotion in that one

statement than I'd ever seen. His lip twitched so fast I'd have sworn I was seeing things if I hadn't looked right at it then. He took a few slow breaths and shook his head. "Can't be, man. Just can't be. The Circle can't lose her. I—we can't lose her."

Her hair was strewn across her face, and her cheeks were ashen. It was easy for me to be worried about her, and I thought about Jacobs' remark. Maybe I had gotten attached to her. The sight of her, still as can be, wrecked my soul. Was this it? Was this her end? Why wasn't it more of a deal? Why weren't people around her, doing anything medically to save her? She deserved more than this.

The feelings thrashed around in me, wanting to grab her and shake her, do whatever came to mind in my infinite lack of medical knowledge that was only supplemented by medical TV dramas. There was nothing I could do. Kado was gone, and there wasn't anyone who either could help or was able to right then. I'd seen this all too recently and, while we had no blood connection, this was worse in some bizarre way.

Her high cheekbones were tainted with smudges of dirt and dried blood. She was so full of energy, so full of life. I imagined her about, standing and commanding, rolling her eyes at one of my jokes, anything. But there she lay, like a mannequin that had never been alive.

Then, before I realized it happened, her hand jumped and clasped my wrist, and my heart felt like it had stopped beating. I forgot to breathe and watched Norg. Moisture formed at the corner of his eye; the only other thing he did was grunt and shake. A sharp piercing shock ripped through me, and my heart about burst through my mouth.

Ana took a gasp, and the rest of us fell back. Her brow immediately crinkled again, and a low moan escaped her lips. She blinked her eyes and they opened slowly. She winced.

I watched in amazement and hoped I hadn't imagined this, that this wasn't what had been happening with the Pull and the maps and the strange words. Once I saw Treg's and Norg's faces, I knew what I saw wasn't fake or in my head.

It was real; she was still here.

Treg was the first who found words. "Hey, Ana, you there?"

She squirmed in pain. Her eyes swiveled around. Her voice came in a scratchy whisper. "Mmm, yeah, think so. What happened?"

"Just about everything bad you can imagine," Norg offered.

"Well, that's typical." She wheezed and coughed. A splash of blood hit her lip. "Where are we?"

"The Range. Llewyn sold us out."

"What?"

"The deal, the package. It's us."

Ana heaved. "D-damn prick. Never liked his ass. What'd he get?"

"Not sure, but it sounds like he was pulling for Lebabolis all along. Surprised Baudricort didn't know about it, or let on if he did. Llewyn was the one who killed him all this time later."

"Why?"

"Charista. She made him a deal like she made one with us. Now we know what that's worth."

"They've got Kado. Do we have time?"

"Dunno."

"What about the Guard?"

"They wasted a lot of 'em. Don't know about the others."

"Don't count on 'em." Ana took a labored breath. "It's just us now. They wouldn't even listen to me at the Valkyrie."

"We were in a tough spot; we didn't have a whole lot of choices."

"And now looks like we have none."

"No, but look what we got." Ana raised a shaky hand and pointed at each of us around her. "We'll figure it out." She grimaced but propped herself up after a little effort. A steady trickle of blood oozed from her mouth.

"You sure you're alright?" I asked.

"Ow." She went into a heaving fit but managed to add, "I'll live, I think."

"Doesn't sound too convincing. Stick close to me; I'll keep an eye on you." I clasped her shoulder. She watched me with worried eyes but managed a nod in response.

I breathed the deep sigh I'd held for some time. She was alive, and like the rest of us, she had a chance. And for Ana Crucinal, that's all she ever needed.

VALKYRIE RISING

THE VALKYRIE CHRONICLES

BOOK 3

PAUL HEINGARTEN

"Through this world I've stumbled
So many times betrayed
Trying to find an honest word
To find the truth enslaved"

(MCLACHLAN, SARAH "POSSESSION"
FUMBLING TOWARDS ECSTASY, LEGACY ED.,
NETTWERK, 1993, TRACK 1, AMAZON)

"So needless to say
I'm odds and ends
But that's me, I'm stumbling away
Slowly learning that life is OK
Say after me
It's no better to be safe than sorry"

"A-HA - TAKE ON ME (LIVE FROM MTV UNPLUGGED)", YOUTUBE, UPLOADED BY A-HA, 28 SEPTEMBER 2017, HTTPS://WWW.YOUTUBE.COM/WATCH?V=-XKM3MGT2PE. ACCESSED 29 JANUARY 2020.

T he story so far...

ANA CRUCINAL, Nelson Forrester, and fellow members of the Action have joined up with forces of Lebabolis to create the Coalition in an attempt to fight and repel the Omegans, the alien race responsible for restoring humanity to existence.

Ana meets members of the Guard, the battle-hardened elite warriors of Lebabolis who served under the Valkyrie, but were cast out by Charista once she made her play to assume control of Lebabolis. Despite her best attempts to get the Guard to join the Coalition, their leader Duncan prefers their known existence of living for another day.

While Nelson is originally from the 21st century, he felt strong connections to Earth pulled toward Cataclysm, the sinister weapon humans once used to turn back the Omegans.

But the Omegans know well about Cataclysm, as its technology was developed by them, and they want it back along with the human race, which they refer to as their specimens. Using their military might and other tools in their arsenal, they unleash a barrage of trouble on the fledgling remnants of Earth's native species.

Meeting the Coalition at the Range, the mountainous region once considered for a safe haven by the fleeing Action, Ana, Nelson, members of the Coalition and a portion of Guard troops make a desperate last stand against the Omegans.

But troubles for Ana and company are more than external. Cracks within the Coalition show themselves, and even Ana's childhood friends like Zengus reveal that the fight for victory sometimes pits you against what you love the most.

ONE

(ANA)

I THOUGHT I WAS DEAD.

My last memory was burned into my brain. The Coalition troops I led were in the middle of a swarm of Omegans. The mountains of the Range towered in the close distance, our safe place just out of reach, even as close as we were. The air was stale, full of the scent of smoke from fires, spent weapon rounds, the sweat and foul odor of wounds from so many people, many of whom I'd led to this place.

We had our Coalition, the Action troops who were former rebels of Lebabolis, as well as the Lebabolis loyal "Gray Bands", and some of the Guard, the once elite unit that protected Lebabolis but now a band of renegades, on our side. We even had a group led by Jacobs himself. But even with all of that, the force of the Omegans we faced was too much.

It was the biggest group I'd ever seen of 'em. Their scaly skin oozed with sweat, and their reddish eyes bored into us with a hungry look. We weren't a small group ourselves. The Range was our goal, our shelter from the Omegans. The hope was we'd be too difficult for them to get to, and eventually we'd be forgotten by the Omegans for easier targets. It was Baudricort's and our plan, anyway, until we were surrounded and blocked from getting there.

I remembered the image of Nelson with an Omegan zeroed right in on his head. My body moved before my mind had a chance, and I did what I had to and stopped the Omegan from ending Nelson. But the pain in my chest came a second later. A real fear of dying found me; it was the first time I'd ever felt anything like that. It froze me for a moment. The seconds melted into minutes and longer as my mind skipped gears into lessons and memories from Treg. He hammered it into my head pretty good: do what must be done. Show no mercy. Never accept defeat.

But defeat was too strong this time. After the first darkness hit me, I came to and saw Nelson. He cradled me and said things; I don't remember them. I asked him some questions, but soon I slipped away again. The next darkness I slipped into felt deeper. For a while I thought maybe that was it for me, but then jolts of light burst in. Voices echoed in my head. None were Nelson, though. Some were just babble, but after a while I made out words. Some kinda medical talk that may as well have been gibberish. Whoever they were, this wasn't like Petra's voice when she sent me those messages through the Link. This was different. She'd spoken with me, like a dream I was awake for. She didn't know where she was, but she knew plenty about me and Baudricort.

On a few of the flashes, I saw a room, and some cables and tubes, and I dimly realized I was connected to 'em. Splashes of blood and shouting came, and again I was out.

I wondered if someone, Charista or otherwise, had found my mental connection to Petra and broken it. We'd had conversations, lots of 'em, but they'd stopped recently. I felt a splash of despair dribble over me as I thought maybe Charista had found a way to silence them permanently.

Maybe Charista finally had enough and just had Petra killed. Charista's play confused me. The Omegans were still here and as strong as ever. I guess she knew there was no way we'd have ever stopped them, so she threw us to the Omegans to buy time and space to grab Cataclysm. Our freedom was another of her flags, false fronts.

Thoughts in my head were jumbled, and it took some work to remember. Faces, people, sounds swam around me like a sea of answers, but I was drowning with no luck putting them together. I was desperate to get the picture in focus.

Petra, had I heard more about her? Harkson, he met with me, didn't he? Did he tell me she's my mother?

That piece of me had been missing so long, knowing what it was almost felt wrong. How had I lived that long without knowing it was Petra? But she knew, or did she? She connected with me; how I wasn't sure. But she did. Petra had spoken with me so clearly, but it stopped when I woke up again. It wasn't something I'd heard all the time, but I figured if I was in a fight like we were, there would've been some kind of message break through. She would've helped. She was the Valkyrie. She'd reached me before, anyway. But there was only silence.

I missed having her, even if it was just her voice. I'd never known her but getting that contact and losing it again hurt even worse; I almost wished I'd never known she was out there.

I was more alone than I'd ever been. It was the worst feeling.

So much was left undone and wrecked, and now, maybe that included me too. I couldn't see where my wound was, but the pain alone told me it was bad. I remembered thinking about so much in those few moments. What was going to happen to Varrick, what about Nelson getting home? My worries flooded my head with everything and nothing all at once.

I wondered what the world was gonna be like with Charista or the Omegans running things. If there was a world left at all. Cataclysm was in Charista's hands; my hazy memory served me that piece of our situation. Charista was gonna use it to turn back the Omegans, even if firing it at full power could destroy this planet.

When I finally came to for good and was fully awake again, I was in a room with several others, each in their own state of suffering.

Best I could tell, they looked like our group from the Range. At least, they were in here with me, so we at least had a common enemy. Or so I hoped.

The sting of Charista's betrayal hit me again like a punch and stung as deep as the ache from my chest. I'd fallen for her promise of a truce, of the Coalition. She'd dangled Varrick in front of me, and his cure, because she knew me so well. I wanted to believe it so much. But what did she do, really? She knew what to say that worked for me, alright.

I wondered about Varrick, if he was safe, if he was ever safe with Charista. I felt the lies on top of lies piled around me and wondered if we were ever making our way out of this. For that matter, would any of us be safe again?

Then there was the Pox. Charista claimed she had cured it, and I saw Varrick. That wasn't illness in that body. How could something like that have been faked? It sure looked like Varrick was fine when I saw him at the Capital. No one knew for sure, but I wondered if Charista used that disease on us as just another way to filter more of us out before we infected everyone. Charista promised to cure Varrick and the rest of our people who were sick with Pox in exchange for our help. With that trust in her to come through, we signed ourselves over to be delivered up like some damn freight shipment instead.

Charista seemed to have some of the truth on her side, and things going for her, but I knew there was no way I'd ever trust her again. If she did cure Varrick, it was for some other goal for herself. The idea of him being under her thumb in the city was just about the only thing that kept me from dying.

That, and Nelson.

At least I knew more about the truth, that it wasn't Lebabolis but the Omegans who had us. They dictated what happened to us from there on. I could make sure they had as hard a time getting information from me, that was for sure. Beyond that I didn't know what else I could do. It sure seemed this was the end for us. There was nothing to do and nowhere to go.

For some weird reason I hadn't yet figured, the Omegans still wanted me alive. Whatever they wanted with someone who basically led the rebellion against Lebabolis and fought Omegans, I had no clue. They were so interested in me though, that they even patched me up in the field, as if I knew anything important, like what Charista had been up to. The thought of this mess we were in made me chuckle, but the soreness in my chest stopped me.

The air was a nasty mix of old sweat, blood, and the stench of rotting flesh. Our room was long but narrow. A single door with a big latch was on one side of the wall opposite from me. Next to the door was a bank of windows that were mostly smudged and smeared but clear enough that I made out the dark shapes of the figures who patrolled outside. My eyes and brain worked well enough that I recognized that the bloated ass hulks guarding us were Omegans.

The dank air was also filled with the moans of the wounded. Once I got my eyes to focus a little better, I recognized some of the brave souls of the Action.

Some were Action, some were Guard. No Coalition. The name Coalition stung me like a cruel joke; Charista's promise, empty once again. Should've known that would've always been the case. Once again I fell for her plans, and she led me right where she wanted me, along with the rest of the people she wanted out of her way.

Were these people still with our group? Were they still with me? I wouldn't have blamed any of 'em if they weren't. Their history of being steered, mostly wrong, had to have at least some of 'em ready to bolt from here and me. They'd been led wrong by many, most recently me. How long did they have before their will gave out completely?

I noticed two Guard people were with us in the room. One, a woman with dirty blonde hair, caught my eye. She peered at me with the steely eyes of an animal hunting prey. I wondered if she was the one sent for me, and she just was waiting for the best time to take me out.

I knew we were never gonna have a shot without the Guard. We had some with us, but not the main group that Duncan had. They weren't moving without him being on board. And, well, he said his piece after I'd begged him to join us.

We were tough, but it took more than brawn with a traitor in our group. Llewyn had sat nice and pretty in his number two spot behind Baudricort in the Coalition until Baudricort was killed, and just took over. Since Charista and Llewyn sold us out to the Omegans and we ended up here, I felt myself starting to slide back into how it was during my days of being a product. I should've been used to this. But this was different. This time we weren't issued things like information about our assignment or where we'd be living or what to expect from the government. We were brought here to be kept.

Maybe for good.

I sucked in a breath and tried not to gag on the rank odor. *Time to see what these assholes did to me.* My face was covered with a layer of moisture. Wherever this place we were in was, the ventilation was damn near zero.

As the haze lifted from my brain, I realized the people in this room and across the hall were probably all that was left of our group, the Coalition between Lebabolis and the Action. I hadn't recognized anyone familiar, which worried me even more. I had enough problems trusting the people I did know, and now I was with total strangers, even if they were supposedly on my side. I just knew all of Charista's people were long gone. I hadn't made out a Gray Band in the room so far and hadn't really expected to. They were the smart ones; they knew who to side with. Once again we, the Action, were just a chip worth trading for something. Our human lives once again were reduced to a numeric value. I was a little surprised that some of the Guard were here, considering how much Duncan wasn't for throwing in with us. Even the toughest, most unified and hardcore fighting units disagreed on things now and then, I guessed.

I bet even Dawn wasn't here. I figured her mission was a success and she had been called back to her death chamber.

I hadn't recognized anyone from my Circle either. I wondered what had happened to 'em.

Zengus!

The name smacked me like an insect bite. *I'd heard something about Zengus, but what was it?* My memory was fuzzy, but I swore I'd heard Nelson say Zengus had 'turned'. My childhood buddy, turned and joined Charista? Was that right or had I imagined that too?

Kado... there wasn't anything about Kado.

Wait—was Kado dead too?

Please no, not him too. I can't lose any more people. All this was my fault. I led them to this and they followed me.

Why?

Because of who I was, or who they thought I was. *Look at me now. And I've led others, strangers and people I've known my whole life, people from my Circle, into this. How many of my extended family had I killed too?*

The more I tried to push my fears aside, the worse it got. I tried distracting myself with a mental list of the others. If I didn't know where my Circle was, it felt better to at least imagine what had happened with 'em. Norg wouldn't have kept quiet or behaved too well; I just hoped that hadn't meant he got taken out or anything. Treg too, he wasn't gonna put up with much, but hopefully he could at least hold Norg back. Always better to fight another day, he used to say.

I tried piecing together the rest of what happened since the fight at the Range and how we got here, but it was so blurry. I thought hard, but all that came up was the memory of Nelson next to me while I lay on the ground. Even so, I didn't remember exactly what he'd said. My memories of it were just a puddle of mumbles. I was on and off.

A deep enough breath sent sharp pains down my back and legs. The guards kept a steady pace as they walked back and forth in the hallway outside. Each of their steps made a dull thud that echoed in the hall and into our room.

I wondered what the Omegans were gonna do with us. If they wanted information, they were out of luck. I knew as little as anyone, it seemed. I sure didn't know about whose side was right in all of this. Or even what sides there were anymore. I even let Charista stick Dawn with us, and she was probably one of the bugs that set us all up. Better than a bug, a real person who reported everything we did back to home base probably. *Nice going, Crucinal.*

I finally proved it to myself and hopefully to everyone else. This time, the lesson was gonna stick.

Worker Product; that's what I can do, and that's it.

I wasn't a leader. I hated that the rest of these people hadn't recognized it by now. What was it about me that people still believed in, anyway? I wasn't strong enough for this. And based on the throbbing pang in my chest, I wasn't gonna be around for much longer anyway. I'd led them all down this road, because I was Ana Crucinal. The leader of the Action.

The Valkyrie.

Not quite. If I never heard that word again, it would've been too soon. I sucked in a slow breath until the dank air made me gag and waited as the soreness welled up in my chest in response. I took a long look at the room while I tried ignoring my pain for a little bit. One of 'em glanced my way, and I saw those reptilian Omegan eyes pierce the room in a mental inventory of us. I locked my eyes on theirs until they got bored and returned to guard duty.

I wasn't strong enough to hide it, and I felt fear wrap around me like a snake.

An itchy sounding voice jabbed into the silent darkness. "You awake?"

I knew the voice, but the name that went with it hadn't found its way to the right spot in my brain yet. A dim outline crouched near me, and when I rolled to that side, a face came into view.

Nelson. It's Nelson.

I froze at his eyes.

He was alive.

I hadn't failed him yet.

He was one of the only people I knew I couldn't have let down as long as I was still alive.

I half coughed and let out a cry. Happiness welled up in me, and for the first time since I had come to, I hadn't thought about what we'd lost, at least for a few moments. Joy tugged at my heart, and my eyes burned with glad tears that inched their way down my cheeks. I pawed for him, my throat clenched with relief. My heart raced, and a soreness in my chest deepened, but still I managed a weak sob. The pain was worth it; just seeing him made it worth it. I clutched for his arm until he ran his hands across my shoulder into a half hug.

"Hey, hey, it's fine, you're alright." He slid closer to me. "Be careful about speaking; they did a number on you, including patching a wound in your neck."

I hadn't thought about my throat until he mentioned talking. It felt like someone had rubbed a handful of gravel over my neck and poured acid down my throat. As bad as trying to talk felt, the sight of him here was a blessing to me. Few others, really just Nelson and Varrick, got me feeling like this. I just gazed on him and hoped my look said everything I couldn't right then.

Nelson smiled. Even in the dim light, I saw the gaze of awe in his eyes as he looked over me. "We thought you were dead at first. Even after they worked on you, it was touch and go for a while. Some Action medics treated you, patched you up. You were stabbed, really more impaled by an Omegan spear." He turned a bit and his voice broke as he added, "You'd lost plenty blood."

It was nuts how little I felt my injury during the fight. How had I ever made it? *Easy, Ana, hold it in; don't let Nelson see you like this.* It hurt like hell, but I was able to rasp out a word. "Food?"

Nelson's eyes slid up to the guards outside our room. "Nothing yet, except for water. Think they're trying to figure things out; we've been here for just three days."

I swallowed the lump in my throat, knowing that all this—the battle, our capture, being held with no food—hadn't happened to some other warrior or person, but me and our group. I reached for my legs, and that's when I felt it in my back: a deep soreness. I grimaced and twisted my body so I didn't lean against the wall as much on that spot. Turns out it didn't matter; whichever way I moved felt pretty crappy all the same.

My thoughts drifted to who could get Nelson home for me. If Treg or Norg were around, they could, maybe even Kaitlinn, assuming she hadn't bought it at the Range. I was way past fighting for keeping things going; I had to cover my promises in case this was it for me.

I looked toward the far side of the room where a familiar pair of eyes returned my glance. As much as it hurt, I tightened up my gut at the sight of her while my fists clenched up into balls. The throbbing that started it my chest right then just made me even more pissed she was even considered worthy to be here with us. I choked the words through my throat toward her. It was worth the pain of saying them. "What the hell are you doing here?"

Dawn gazed back and shook her head. "What do you think? She conned me, same as the rest of you. They sent me out here with a detachment and left me for dead."

"You expect me to believe that?" I ignored the fire at my throat. I wished I was strong enough to lay one on her right then.

"Believe what you want, Ana, but think about this: when Charista picks her target, she gets what she wants no matter who she has to sacrifice. Everyone you see here that isn't an Omegan is someone she didn't need any more in one way or another."

Our eyes stayed on each other, and I saw a flicker behind her irritated look. While I looked her over, my mind poured over a dreadful idea on why Dawn was really here. Maybe Charista had left her behind to finish me off? She looked enough to be one of us as far as the Omegans knew. I bet the Omegans would've practically expected us to be at each other's throats after enough time down here with no food. They probably cared about us as much as a worn-out pair of boots; if a few of us killed some others here, we just made life easier for 'em.

"Keep away from me," I muttered.

Dawn scoffed in response. "As if I could hurt you. Your boyfriend over there's right. They worked on you good in the field. It was almost like you being stabbed was an accident. The mere fact you're alive after what they did, I'm beginning to think you're immortal." She slid up and moved to a further corner of the room.

Nelson and I watched her for a moment before he turned back to me. "Dawn's not wrong, you know. I wasn't sure if I'd see you awake ever again. But you are." He smiled as a line of moisture drizzled across his cheek.

I felt a lump in my throat and managed a whisper in reply. "Missed you."

He sat with me for a few minutes like that, his eyes poured over me like a faithful dog... no, a friend. Was he just a friend or more? As bad as I felt, seeing me in his eyes made things seem somehow less horrific.

While I continued my search for an actual comfortable position, Nelson went back over what went down during the fight in the Range. He gave me everything: finding Cataclysm, Zengus turning, and even the experiment. How the Omegans had monitored us after harvesting us over a century ago.

According to Nelson, the Omegans wanted a race of slaves, so they developed us while they also scoured the earth for whatever else was useful to them. When it finally came time for the Omegans to decide what to do with us, we were able and willing to fight back, and we had ideas of our own about what our purpose was.

I hadn't dreamt it could've ever been Zengus against us. The sting from remembering how far back our friendship went to childhood felt like a new wound.

What hadn't made sense to me yet in this was Charista's part. Was she in the dark like the rest of us? She couldn't have known everything. If she knew we were the Omegan's playthings and what they were gonna do, she'd have wanted us on her side, not delivered over like some half assed bargain. Now the Omegans had nothing left to stop 'em except maybe Llewyn's group, a few roving patrols, and Duncan's Guard if they were even stupid enough try engaging the Omegans like we had.

Charista also had Cataclysm, and even though it had a fail safe on it, she had Kado, the one guy on our side and probably hers who could find a way through it. Kado wouldn't have turned on us, but with Charista and all her manipulations there, I was scared about how much Kado was able take before they broke him.

Charista had gotten to Zengus after all, and he was way stronger than Kado. That stung me like a punch to the face. Of all the people with us and all that happened, Baudricort getting bombed in a facility, all the moves and raids by Lebabolis and people who used to live alongside those who joined the Action, now this with Zengus. There had to be some reason why he did it. I had to know.

I took another deep breath and pressed the sides of my head. I'd been awake long enough for it to really bug me how I'd only seen twenty people in this room. I was scared to ask, but I had to know. "What about the others, Nelson?"

Nelson shrugged and eyed the room. His silence at first scared me, but that feeling was just as bad as the pain, so I blurted out, "You seen Norg?"

He shook his head slowly. "Not him specifically, but I saw them move a bunch, I'm guessing down below, but I can't rightly say."

I clung to the idea that we weren't put in here so the rest could be wiped out. I had no way and really no right to think that, but I knew the more I kept my mind on thoughts like that, the better I was gonna be. I felt myself slipping and any positive thought was golden. "So Nelson, any idea at all on where the hell we are?"

I caught the gaze of an Omegan through the clouded window. They watched me and Nelson for a second, and I wished I still had a dagger to throw at them, it would've looked great in their eye socket.

"They call it Ulter. I didn't see a whole lot when we came in there, but there were Lebabolis markings around."

"So then why the hell are we so special?"

"Special? You mean these lavish penthouse amenities only the finest Trivago booking could get?" Nelson patted the floor and winced when his palm landed smack on a pile of darkish colored grime. He made a face as he flung the dark sludge from his hand, then shook his head and sighed. "I think it's more about you being special. They saw you leading troops out there. My guess is they want to talk with you more than most, see what you know."

"Uh huh. And they brought you and these in for convincing me in some way to cooperate."

"Plausible." Nelson's hands fidgeted as he eyed me with a shrug. "Then again, all of this is speculation. Let's just say they haven't been too open to questions."

I rubbed my eyes and strained them in the low light until I noticed some markings on the wall. At first look I figured they were just some kind of gibberish. Maybe something from an earlier group kept in this place, notes on something. Maybe dates if they were captured for a while.

But then the haze in my head cleared a little, and the markings became familiar. The patterns on the wall indicated mining locations. I chuckled at first at the sight from my past; it greeted me like a friend, one that I never even thought I had. It was familiar, something I knew about, a piece of a life I once had that somehow brought me just a sliver of comfort.

I scanned the room again in the low light, but since my eyes focused better, things got clearer and the patterns on the rest of the walls registered in my mind, somewhere. The memory wasn't of these exact walls, but ones a lot like 'em. Memories I'd hoped were gone just jumped back into my head and filled my mind like a ray of sunlight. The walls had this texture to 'em. Even the door handle; once I focused on it, I remembered it from the temporary facilities we used for Valentium processing, exploration, and later, with

Baudricort and the Action as part of the Exodus away from Lebabolis.

I laughed at how something from my old life, which was pretty much a hostage situation in itself, made me forget about the fix I was currently in, even for a minute.

It made sense they'd have taken us to one of Lebabolis' Valentium mine areas; where else could they've fit so many of us? And with Lebabolis so locked down in the Capital, can't imagine it was tough for them to handle whatever pissant unit Charista left to defend it.

"Nelson, I think this place is one of the Valentium processing plants. When I was in Worker Product training, I was part of a group taught to assemble and work in these. It's just a hunch, but it's all I got for now. If I'm right, these places have a good amount of space below. I guess they just funneled us into whatever rooms they found up here." I spoke too much right then, and my lungs rewarded me for it with a bout of heaving coughs.

Nelson patted my back. "Good amount of space below, huh?"

"Yep, I bet they could fit a few thousand, especially if they aren't worried about comfort."

"I saw people being moved but can't tell you how many. I do know there's an elevator close by."

I grinned. "Yeah, that makes sense. Cargo transport, most likely. These plants are pretty well sealed off from the surface too. There's just one main entrance; they learned early they needed to contain the Valentium in case of a rupture, so the outside was covered pretty heavily. Down below there's a heavy cargo lift, but you're not blasting through that. These places are bound up like a shell. There's pretty much one way out from up here, which makes it easy for a small unit to keep us pinned in, another reason it's a good place to stick our group here."

Nelson brushed a lock of hair from my face. "So, escape is impossible?" His eyes scanned the windows before they returned to mine.

"Looks that way." My back ached against the cold stone wall behind me. I pulled my legs up a bit but that just made my tail bone sore that much more. There was no getting comfortable in this place, or maybe that was just me. From the group of us in here, I had no idea when we'd be moving somewhere else or anywhere else at all.

Besides, knowing where you are and knowing what to do about it were two way different things. I was still working on the first part.

TWO

(NELSON)

THE SIGHT OF ANA AWAKE was the best news I'd had since we ended up in this mess. There was so much I wanted to tell her, so much I needed to say, but I knew I had to start with the details of our situation. She did her best to get comfortable while she listened to everything I had to say. Ana's pained expression faded as I made my way through the story, making me feel like a doctor sharing news about a terminal patient with the family.

Even after I told Ana about the Omegans raising human beings, she still hadn't totally grasped the idea. I saw her feverish eyes as they locked on me, as if she hoped I was simply holding the answer back from her. Ever since Baudricort died, she worked more and more to be what he was for the Action. Her eyes said it all to me, but lately that fire had gradually faded from alert action to weary tolerance, and I saw her struggle to get it back. Now that she was so thrown out of commission, she wanted to be in charge, and I guess she felt it was better to look in charge even if she didn't always have all the information.

"So you're telling me," Ana wheezed, "that all this time, we were part of some kinda massive experiment run by the Omegans?"

"That's right."

"Why'd they spend so much time on it and us?"

That was the million-dollar question alright. Also, I had no idea if the Omegans included me in their plan, too. But it was pretty clear whatever they had in store for us, they were probably on the move to round up everyone, even our so-called friend Charista and all those with her back at Lebabolis.

"Ana, I wondered that myself. It's strange that a race of explorers as they call themselves would focus so much on reviving a race. Now we know, I suppose—they were interested in us for something else. They collect and analyze. Somehow, for some reason, they found something useful in us. Enough to spend all this time reactivating our species."

"It doesn't add up. They went all that way to work this and then fight us off; why'd they waste all that time?"

I shrugged. "Well, they wanted to see if we were of any use. They figured we'd be good helpers, as it looked like we were from Earth and at least better suited to the environment. We didn't need any physical assistance with the environment like they did."

"So they got us to minc for Valentium."

"They let you grow and develop. Mining was the Omegan plan."

She coughed a bit. "Yeah, but Lebabolis was a byproduct, one Charista wanted. She must've figured that was her way to rule, make herself Queen of Earth. At some point, she took it on herself and loved the idea of being more than just a flunkie of the Omegans. Of course then she just kept it quiet, so the Omegans never suspected."

"Neither did we. But the leaders, you don't just toss them without some kind of resistance."

"Oh, I bet she did just that, took care of the Coursons and Harkson."

"Unless any of them were in on it too."

"Not only that, but weapons. Cataclysm, our best minds were trained in it. They figured out how to make a tool into a bomb."

"Yeah, they let the world run pretty loose," I said. "What about the Valkyrie, then? Can't imagine why they'd let a leader like that appear."

Ana nodded. "I agree, that couldn't have been in their plans. People need something. Baudricort knew this."

"People need a focal point. It drives them more than anything." I thought of the words I'd just said and how I'd heard them from Harkson. I wondered what had happened to him and the rest of the Coursons once Charista had her great weapon. Was it all in her plan all along to take control once she had it?

Ana stared at me for a while, as if she waited for me to follow up with revealing it was a joke. But the truth hung in the air, worse than the rancid odor that drifted over us without mercy. However it happened, I realized we weren't in control as much as I even thought we were.

Ana rubbed her eyes, but the weariness remained in them. She looked downward, and I felt like it was my turn to carry some of the load, if only mentally. "At least we know why the Omegans are so interested in us, and from the sound of it they won't just do away with us."

"Oh, I'm sure they won't." Ana gazed off into space, her hands writhed together in an odd set of jarring moves. "Charista, the Omegans, Cataclysm..." Her eyes dulled as she muttered the words like names in a police lineup.

I watched her in the hope it would jar my own brain into usefulness, in the hope that between our two heads, we could come up with a plan, a method of dealing with our situation, and in pie in the sky crazy ass fashion, an escape out of this place.

But instead, all I saw in return was the half glazed and totally fatigued set of eyes slightly masked by a tangled mess of hair.

It was obvious she wasn't much for talking at length right then, so I continued. "In case you're wondering if I'm feeling any more Links or Pulls to any of this, I'm not. Something's changed." I'd felt it for a while, but when I said that, I sensed a bit of weight lifted off my chest. I'd held it from everyone. When we found Cataclysm back then in that cave, something happened in me. Before and up to then, I was led like a GPS to that spot, but once we had Cataclysm, the feelings left me. Those pulls I'd felt toward Cataclysm or anything else were gone, and I didn't know what to make of that. At least those pulls gave me some kind of place, or need for being in this place. Without it, I felt once again like an outsider, an infection in this system.

Ana worried me the longer she sat still. She'd never been like this before. When I first saw her back in 2014, this fighter, her spirit, her beautiful strength, no matter what she was against came through in her eyes. Anyone who saw her knew it right away; she had this fire that just explained wordlessly how she got what she wanted, no matter what. But here and now, none of that energy showed. It was almost like she was in some kind of trance, prepared for a long, maybe eternal sleep.

Thick wads of gauze poked over the top of her shirt; some of them were stained red. I remembered the scene around her after we had surrendered to the Omegans. Once the fighting stopped, we were sorted, and some wounded were tended to. Everyone made a pretty big rush of helping her in the field, and the Omegans seemed interested as well. As much as the Omegans had tried to kill us all, with her it seemed they were more interested in retrieval.

She kept silent as I watched her, so I figured I'd better stoke her coals a bit. "You've been down before. Remember how you came back through time for me? You didn't back down, even when you said you were almost killed making that jump across time. And then you had to face me and my stubborn ass. Still, you never backed down, even when I brushed you off again and again. Even when people tried to kill you, you fought with them, and fought off people better trained than you. Ana, I know we're in a tough spot, but we've got to keep pushing. There's got to be a way through this. It seems the longer we go, the further from home I get."

Her eyes drooped a bit when I mentioned 'home'. "You know, there's a good chance you won't make it home. You never know what's ahead."

"Yeah, I don't, but neither do you."

Her face twisted in response. "More suffering? I don't know what's the point anymore. They've got us here. Once again we've been abandoned, and this time I gave us up to our captors. I'm sorry we didn't get you back before."

"It's OK. Besides, my rushing to get back last time was a big disaster." Otto's name hung in the air, as clear as the stench that surrounded us. She said nothing about him. She didn't have to; her gaze filled in his name well enough. He was their brightest mind, but when they tried a run for a Verge to get me back home, Otto paid the price with his life.

Her brow lowered. I stared at this woman, this warrior who I'd been so close to, just about in each other's heads. Her body so damaged and her spirit so low, I really pitied her. I knew what she meant... their fight was now against two groups of people, the Omegans and the loyalists of Lebabolis, both of which could tear us all apart. The Omegans alone damn near destroyed Ana before she went down.

Besides Otto, another name stood with us. As little as I knew to offer, this other name was the one thing Ana had left that would've kept her in this or any other fight. "Don't you think he's still alive?"

"Varrick?" Her body flinched as she spoke the name, as if it was a knife jabbed into her side. "I've wanted and waited so long for him to be OK. I'm beginning to wonder if that moment I had with him at the Capital was our last together." She squinted and bowed her head, her voice trembling as she continued. "Much as I hate to admit it, Dawn's right. Charista's all about pawns. She'll use him and the rest of our sick people, same way she always does. Whenever something happens, and she needs to protect herself, it'll be everyone she can grab in front of her like a shield, a bargaining chip."

Ana trembled as if she realized what that meant. Her body rocked with light sobs. I was speechless. I'd never seen her this distraught. And my mind traveled back thinking of my mom, who was in the throes of her illness and yet refused to give in. I realized that, like Mom, Ana needed my help now.

I clasped her hand in mine. She eyed me with a sad and worried look. "Ana, I know you're hurting. And I feel terrible for what I've done to cause it."

No one was ever able to explain it to me, how this book I'd started writing, this pet project that I thought could at least let me sell a few copies to my friends, had turned out to be some weird kind of transcript of events that came true in this time period.

She smiled and brushed a lock from her face as she gently squeezed my hand. "Don't blame yourself, Nelson. A gun doesn't shoot by itself. People can always destroy themselves, in your time and this one. I trusted too much. That's my problem. I took the word of an insane woman because she dangled one of the most important people to me, and I let her lead me with a lot of other people here, and look where it got us. Duncan was right; he wasn't dumb enough to fall for it and follow me to this, and he's better off for it."

I seethed at the mention of Duncan's name. All I'd heard about him and the Guard, these fierce unstoppable warriors, and so far all I'd seen of it was someone who ran for cover.

"Duncan was afraid. You've done more for these people than he or Charista or anyone else has."

"Or Duncan was just smart enough not to join a fight he wasn't gonna win." Ana's brow creased. "Just what have I done, Nelson? Look at me; my body is fading." Her voice broke again.

At that point, I wanted to cradle her in my arms, but I stopped myself short. She was a warrior and a fighter who took too many hits all at once; she just needed something to bring her back. She'd carried me this far; it was my turn for a bit.

She folded her arms and focused on the others in the room with us. Her eyes looked wounded. She watched the rest of our cell mates with a mixture of fatigue and worry on her face. "I fought hard, Nelson. I fought long. Not as long as some, but long enough. I did my part. Well over my part."

My stomach burned. It could've just been the lack of food, but I thought maybe some of my pangs were desperation. Nervous energy found me as I bolted upright, and I paced about the room. Some of the others looked my way as I wandered around.

"Life is a long shot. Being born is a long shot. Being here and living this long—Ana, there's no guarantees. I know you've lost so much. But we need to find a way because if these people get Cataclysm to work or the Omegans bust in and Charista launches it, there's no telling how worse this'll all get."

"We're not in a bind," she countered. "We're at the bottom of a thousand foot well. There's no climbing out of this, with or without a rope."

"One step, Ana. We take the first and then the next."

Ana stared at me, her cloudy eyes cleared and filled with irritation. She slapped the floor and send a cloud of dust up. "Why, Nelson? What for? Haven't we tried enough already; what else can we possibly do? They've won; don't you get that?"

"There's gotta be a way."

Ana's face wrinkled in despair. "OK, let's be real for a minute. Yeah, you're right, I've been down before, in some bad places. You know how I made it out of tough times in the past? The Circle. I didn't have to be strong all the time. I could walk knowing Treg was watching my back. Treg could fight because he knew Norg was protecting his back. Norg knew he was alright because I'd blast whoever tried something on him when he wasn't looking. But they aren't here. I can't say who all these people are or even if any of 'em are plants to take me out. I didn't even know one of my oldest friends was gonna turn on us. Nelson, how can I even do this?"

"We need to try... for Varrick, Kado, and me. We can run and run again, but at some point we have to fight for people. It's the only thing that makes any of this worthwhile. We still have a chance. Wouldn't Baudr- your father want that?"

The name brought moisture to her eyes. Her lips twitched as her eyes darted off in thought. She took a few deep breaths and looked at me again with a slight nod. "You're right. I said I'd get you back, and I have to do that."

"Now, that sounds like a Valkyrie."

"Sounds like a me." Her brow wrinkled. "I'm a person, and don't you forget it. Besides, I'm not sure what I did getting us here is worthy of being called a Valkyrie."

Ana wrinkled her brow. I'd gotten used to this look from her; she did it right before she came out with something pretty big.

I brushed the locks of hair from her eyes and watched them, red with tears, and I searched for that spark I'd seen that first time I saw her in the bar back in 2014, which, even then, felt like a million years ago. Something was still there, but only barely. Her fire had been reduced to just a few embers.

I laid a finger under her chin and slowly guided her eyes back to mine. "Ana, listen to me. You're the bravest person I've ever known. You've faced down warriors way better trained than you, androids trained to rip you limb from limb, being ripped from your parents and having your brother taken from you, a trip across centuries on your own. Think about it, Ana. You survived, you overcame, and you became something. You didn't wait for something better to happen; you became someone better and made it happen."

She watched me. Her mouth remained turned downward, and her eyes still sagged to the floor. "Became, huh?"

"Yeah, you became someone. And you're still that person; you're just down for a bit. But it doesn't matter how much you are down as long as you return, you get back up, you keep going."

"You're starting to sound like I used to."

"We're kind of in each other's heads."

"Yeah, well, that can be a scary thing."

Her eyes softened as she clasped my hand. "I don't know what I'd have done these past few months without you around, you know."

"I could say the same; who else would pull my ass out of the fixes I've been in here? OK, maybe Norg, but I'd probably get a few pops in the head after all was said and done."

Ana braced herself. "Making me laugh isn't smart right about now."

I felt a little better, like maybe I'd broken through a bit to her. But I had an awful feeling that as bad as Ana was mentally, her physical condition was soon going to be an even bigger problem.

THREE

(ANA)

NELSON LOOKED BACK TOWARD the window as a dim outline of an Omegan passed. "Why don't I see what I can find out from them while they got us here."

I cocked my head. "Whatcha think they'll tell you, Mr. Prophet?"

"Doesn't hurt to ask. Maybe I can get back in touch with some of that Pull magic and find a way to an answer."

"I doubt it, but ya may as well try something while we're stuck here," I said.

Once Nelson was out of earshot, I let out a deep groan. The pain I'd felt and held in around Nelson got worse the longer I was awake. My chest tightened as my eyes teared up. I went from wondering what had happened to me to thinking about just how much time I had left. The fact we were here and not buried somewhere told me they at least wanted us for something. Or maybe they just wanted us out of the way.

But that many people to be handled... that's a lot of work for just getting someone out of your way. Why not just incinerate us?

While I waited for Nelson on his useless errand, my mind flashed back to what had brought us here.

I had to admit Nelson's point. At some point, we had to make a stand. Running forever was a temporary solution. However it happened, we had to stand, and for sure we needed even more help than last time.

Since I'd left Lebabolis and joined the Action, I was never alone, even when I was in trouble. Treg helped me, our Circle, we always looked out for each other. But, they had to think I knew something about us coming to the Range. Why would anyone trust me anymore? We needed to start over somehow. But, I wasn't sure I was even gonna be around for this much longer.

At our last stand at the Range, the Omegans swarmed around us like angry bees. The Omegans were always a threat to Charista, but I bet she'd never faced 'em like we did. And, I held my own with warriors, both from Lebabolis and even the Omegans for a while. People born bred and trained for fighting didn't have an easy time with me.

I leaned to the side, and a sharp sting in my chest radiated through my body and snapped me back rigid. I traced a finger over a line of stitches in that spot. Their jagged edges felt like knotted weeds. I'd seen the quick patching up medics did after the Action was hit by raids and ambushes. They worked so quick on the wounded, sometimes just one medic, other times a team. They swarmed over the injured, and no matter how bad it looked, how much blood I saw or how much of the person's guts were exposed, there was an unspoken belief that they'd be OK, even if they sometimes weren't.

I'd never been stabbed before, and if that's what this was, it felt horrible. My mind went back to that fight, and I wondered again just what it would've been like had Duncan shown up with his people. He wasn't convinced at all that day I tried talking with him in the Sector. I watched the Guard, his group, when they took care of an Omegan unit pretty well. That group was a lot smaller than the one we fought back at the Range, but Duncan's Guard showed zero trouble taking out the Omegans, even though Duncan's group was unarmed then. Hell, the raids we did with weapons on the Lebabolis convoys hadn't gone half that smooth. We stole supplies we needed, but a lot of times it ended up with more scrapes and bruises for us than any kinda haul.

What made a battle-hardened soldier like Duncan and his part of the Guard turn tail? Had Duncan known something all along?

Some mechanical whirs sounded off to my left. A Radomet stood against a wall in low power mode. The sight of it startled me at first; I suppose the old reflexes to those things was still strong in me. Funny how something so sinister and vicious became something I might have actually considered a useful tool. I wasn't gonna count those things as allies simply because of where they came from.

But that said, it was here with us, and from all looks, mostly out of commission. It trembled a bit as if stuck in some kind of continual start up mode, but it just didn't have the juice to do a full online launch. The Omegans had fired Darkness, disabling all our weapons and mechanized tech like the Radomet, and that lasted longer than I thought it would've. The Cybernetic would've been all about and corralled us up quick. But now it looked like it was a dying animal, maimed from a hunt. I watched it with pity, amazed that I'd have ever felt anything like that about a Radomet. Its deep red metal armor caught some reflections in the dim light.

Some people called 'em Clankers because of the noisy way their metallic limbs sounded as they moved. Most of the time when we were on the run from these things or attacking them, I hadn't the chance to look at one so close. But there it was, a mixture of human flesh and red wiring that weaved up its neck to a control access in the back. It would've made sense that this point was one of their weak spots, but I'm glad Treg told me different. Their true mechanics, and core of their processors, was internal. They were wired deep for maximum efficiency.

I watched Nelson as he rapped on the door for a few seconds. The only thing he accomplished was getting the closest Omegan's attention, and they just thrust their finger back toward the back wall of our room in response. Of course, they weren't giving anything up. They probably knew squat anyway; I'm sure they had just sent a bunch of grunts to keep us tied up while they went after the people who really mattered, the people who had what they wanted.

They had us checked off their list. Now it was Charista's turn.

I wondered about Kado and what Charista must be doing to him. He was our brightest, but I wasn't sure how much he could take under the heat of it. Hell, I wasn't too sure about myself either.

I put a lot of hope in Failsafe, but really it was more about believing in what Baudricort had set up with Petra, the Valkyrie. My mother. It was weird that not only was Baudricort my father, but Petra, the one who people looked to, was my mother. It made a little more sense why people looked at me the way they did, but I still hadn't felt like I deserved it. All I ever wanted was to live in peace. Everyone deserved that. I always believed in that, and nothing, not even this injury, changed my mind. I wondered what Petra would've told me to do in this place. Or Baudricort. I came from two smart people, well known for thorough plans, but somehow the ability to piece everything together like they had done was lost on me.

Charista had Cataclysm, and Kado and was gonna fire it; the longer we stayed here or with the Omegans, the higher the chance of that happening. The idea of that sent a chill through me. We had a chance to stop it. Why couldn't we?

Kado had been worried about Cataclysm firing again, even in a normal situation. He said it was too unstable and it could destroy the planet, which is why Petra went through all those steps to hide it and activate the Failsafe. I didn't understand anything that techy, but I trusted Kado's word like my life depended on it.

So, what were we supposed to do? Charista wanted to turn back the Omegans, and she was willing to fire Cataclysm to do it. Back in the day, Cataclysm had shattered an entire legion of Omegan troops and kept Lebabolis safe. But according to Kado, that was a controlled blast, and if it was fired with too much energy, it would be a disaster. As volatile as it was, it may destroy the planet. Charista was so crazy about holding onto her world that she was ready to destroy it in the process.

My thoughts were broken up by a deep throbbing pain in my chest.

The soreness that ran through me fueled my anger, and I let it. It was what I had and what was in my control. The rest of our neighbors looked around, dazed. The realization that we could do nothing about our situation dimly settled on me before long. Ours was to just sit and watch the rest of this happen and let the world go.

The thought struck me, how I'd seen this attitude before, in Duncan's eyes when we first met. Was that really all there was? I wondered if we'd been at this all wrong and it was time we went with the Omegans. We were dead either way. At least the Omegans had spent time getting us back to existing as a race. They weren't in it for a slaughter; that would've been beyond dumb. Maybe they had a plan for us after all. A purpose for us, different than what Charista had in mind with Lebabolis. Different wasn't necessarily better, but it was different, and sometimes that's all you had to hope for.

Maybe it was Charista who was running away. Maybe she knew about what the Omegans did, and Lebabolis was her way of hunkering down to save what was left of us. If that was true, it still wasn't an explanation for why she served up some of her fellow humans like this.

Hope wasn't something that lived on its own. People like Baudricort started it. Others like Marlene kept the fire going. But when it came to me, and the Guard, it wasn't there for us to carry it on. People get used to being in their own way, on their own, surviving. I realized how similar I was to Duncan. I wondered if in a way he was me in the future, a wasted out ragged ass renegade, always on the run and fighting for whatever scraps I was able to get.

FOUR

(NELSON)

AFTER A FEW MINUTES pounding on the door, I managed to get one of the Omegan guards to stand right outside of it. No matter how much I mouthed the words to open the door or pointed to the latch, they only responded with a slow shake of their head and a piercing glare. They jabbed a finger toward the wall behind me, and after a few minutes they raised their rifle to accentuate the point.

I returned to Ana, who had a simper on her face.

"You don't have to gloat, you know."

She coughed. "Sorry. It was a nice try." She bit her lip to conceal a devious grin.

"Get some rest; I'll keep an eye out," I told her.

I slid to the ground and stayed next to Ana. Her breathing eased, and her face relaxed as she drifted off to sleep. I was staying by her side, no matter what. I enjoyed this feeling that watching over her gave me. I felt a little fulfillment at returning the favor, at least one percent of all she'd done for me, and I promised myself, no matter what, I was helping her to the end. I'd looked for things and ways I could assist as my new job. My story was this world and everything in it; at least some part was. But story or no, these people needed my help. And, there was one person in this world I trusted without question, and Ana Crucinal was it. There was no way I'd let her down. She needed me and I needed her; I wasn't letting anything get in her way or mine.

While I watched her face as she slipped into a variation of sleep, I felt the presence of someone else crouched nearby me in the darkness.

"How's she doin?"

The voice was gruff but definitely female. I looked up into intense eyes that burned like the embers at the end of a fire that refused to go out. A mane of dirty blonde hair scattered over her face, some draped over her eyeline. If we'd been in the field, I'd have worried about where the nearest gun, knife, or rock was to defend myself.

I looked at Ana, and with my best shot at optimism, I made my best non-medical diagnosis. "OK I guess, for now," I said warily. "She's just been awake for a little while."

Ember eyes glanced toward Ana and nodded. "She got tagged pretty bad back there. I'm gonna see what these assholes can do to make her more comfortable."

She started to get to her feet, but I grabbed and stopped her. "They aren't too interested in being helpful."

Her glance shot to my hand on her arm, and her face deepened to a scowl for a moment, then came back with a simper. "Well, I think I can be a tad more convincing that you."

"I bet. My name's Nelson."

"Lucyna. I'll be around here, 'till we figure a way to bust out, anyhow."

FIVE

(ANA)

MORE PAIN WOKE ME UP from my nap. I looked to my side where Nelson was before and was surprised to see the Guard who'd watched me earlier there instead. They faced the door, and I couldn't see if they were asleep or not. I tapped their shoulder, and after they flinched a second they turned toward me, and I was looking into the face of a woman a few years older than me. Her blue eyes somehow lit up in the dark room. "Yeah?"

"Hey. Don't think we've met. I'm..."

Her voice was deep, with a slight growl to it. "...Ana. I know. Lucyna, but my friends call me Lucy."

There it was again—I'd never heard my name the way these people said it. She watched me with fierce eyes slightly hidden by a mane of dirty blonde hair. Whoever Lucyna was, she was misguided, and I had to set her straight soon. "So, you're in the Guard too."

Lucyna scoffed. "Damn right; woman's got just as much place in this as a man." She leaned back and rested her back against the wall. A knowing grin found her face with her statement. "And you're the Action."

"Yeah, I guess. What's left of it anyway."

"So ya been screwed over by Charista too?" She chuckled. "The Action had a good idea, but we wondered how y'all were gonna stick it out. You had one thing right—One or None. The only way you make it through isn't alone, but together, working as one. See, with the Guard, we're all equals. Lebabolis only cares about the nation, protecting it at all costs. The Guard cares about each other. We learned way back if you don't care about yourself, no one else is gonna."

"Well, what about Duncan, then? He had to know what was happening at the Range, and at least some of his Guard were involved in the fight."

Her brow wrinkled a bit. "Can't say I know what he was thinking there. We've been through some rough times, and I do know he has a reason for stuff he does."

For a moment, my pain wasn't so bad, and I felt a wave of pride over me at the idea of women serving with the Guard. Why shouldn't they? They were led by one after all. "I gotta introduce you to Nelson. He's... not from around here."

"Yeah, I saw when he tried talking to those guards."

"Heh, yeah, well, can't fault him for trying."

"I gave them a go too... thought I could've gotten some help outta them, but they're as stubborn as they are stupid looking. Figures; I bet they'll only respond to physical threats." She slunk back down to a seated position and pulled her knees in tight.

"Mmmhm. Well, I'm not in much shape for that. Might as well get cozy, since we're stuck here for now."

"Yeah, sucks. Don't see any other way fer now. But I'll tell ya this, if we break out, I'm with you." She gazed upon me, her blue eyes locked onto me and her jaw was set.

I resisted the urge to laugh at her idea of breaking out. "Why?"

"Why what?"

"Why stick with me? I brought everyone to where we got caught and thrown in here."

Lucyna shrugged. "Simple. I seen you out there, leadin' and all. You reminded me of her."

"Her?"

"Petra. I might be loopy from this blow to my head, but I don't rightly think so. Whatever happens from here, wherever we go, let's just say you're stuck with me."

She was impressed by what I had done in the field?

I wondered at first if maybe she needed more medical treatment than me. But that steadfast and loyal look in her eyes silently answered me, and a flutter hit me in the belly. Lucyna's gaze matched the ones I'd seen in Guard troops, and even my Circle when times got rough. Her eyes hadn't flinched since she looked my way. All I saw in her was the smooth and cool look of an honest soul. If we had a few more thousand people like her, our problems would've never gotten this far out of hand, and we'd have never let Charista get so far out of control.

The rush was pretty short, and that familiar quiver soon took its place again. The new voice I was in contact with was called Doubt, and its connection was stronger than any Link I'd had before. "Lucyna, you're thinking of someone else."

Her brow creased. "What do you mean?"

I stared at my palms.

What did I mean?

My brain hadn't sped up much. Thoughts floated in front of me, as my mind stretched for them to make some sense of everything. I ached my brain for a response. "I'm a Worker. I was trained on being a Warrior but that's a lot different than what the Warrior Products went through."

Lucyna's eyes pierced through me, into my very soul, as if her stare was a needle that punctured into my very core for an assessment of a medical condition. She listened to me without making a move at all. When I'd finished, she slowly shook her head. "Worker, Warrior... it ain't about what other people—or even what you—say you are. It's about what you do."

"I've done plenty bad." When I said those words, I chuckled by reflex. There wasn't enough energy in me to give her a full report on all my screw-ups.

My attention drifted off, and again I felt the doubt flare up in me. But I was jolted back when Lucyna stomped her boot against the floor, and again we locked eyes. "Who hasn't done bad things? Look, we all stumble, and we all fall. But you've gotta realize you're meant for something more. We are what we do, but it's a total. You put more good than bad into it. It doesn't excuse the wrong you did, but it makes you someone who does good."

I felt a knot in my throat as she continued. "We heard stories about you. You survived a lot, Ana. Sometimes things are easy; sometimes surviving means you make another poor bastard die before he kills you."

"Well, what about Duncan and the rest of the Guard?" I asked, the shake in my voice pretty clear. "Were they surviving, leaving us in the thick of things without their help?"

Lucyna looked off in thought. "Can't say I've got a good answer on that one. Maybe Duncan saw some things leading up to it and decided better to come back another day, or another way."

She was full of the Guard attitude alright, always living to fight another day. I'd heard that before, but sooner or later, we all ran out of days.

Lucyna let out a grunt and got to her haunches. "Well, I wanted to meet ya. As you can see, we're all a bit cramped, so I'm gonna stretch my limbs a bit, but we'll be chatting more soon."

While Lucyna got up to stretch against the far wall, Nelson made his way back next to me and sat down again.

"Saw you made a friend."

Lucyna bent down in a stretch. Muscles rippled about her arms as she twisted her body with the confidence of a lioness. "Yeah. She took a nasty blow back at the Range, but it hadn't changed her spirit one bit, best I can tell. It's all in her eyes. She'll fight to the last. I'd take her over a platoon of fresh Radomet any day."

I felt Nelson watching me and noticed him out the corner of my eyes. I figured it was his turn again on the attempt to drag my ass up from the gutter of failure I'd sunk to. "What, Nelson?"

"Ana, listen. You've been brave for so long. You came through time to get me, and you led an army to fight the Omegans. Do you remember that? I do; I won't ever forget it, in fact. You not only led them, you endeared them to you. Those people down there, I bet if there's anything on their minds beyond getting the hell out of this place, it's 'what is Ana going to do?' These people are gonna follow you to the ends of the earth; you just have to lead them. It doesn't mean always having the answers, it doesn't even mean always having a plan. But having momentum, just those first few steps, you need that. And I'm with you for it, OK?"

I was about to laugh at Nelson's latest attempt at motivating me when the door to our room swung open with an angry whine. An Omegan filled the entrance, their broad frame blocked out most of the hallway light behind them.

We all tensed a bit, like a group of boxed in animals afraid of being the unlucky one picked for dinner. I felt people's eyes in the room settling on me, and I knew what came next better than I wanted to.

Sure enough, after the Omegan scanned the room for a moment, one of their knobby fingers jabbed toward me. "The Captain wants you." Their gruff voice bounced off the walls like a slap. Together with another Omegan, they marched right up to me.

I pulled my arms in close, it was all I could do. It didn't matter a bit, one fished for my arms and yanked 'til I was on my feet. I yelped from the stabbing pain. Before that, the soreness in my chest had just gotten to the point it hadn't felt any worse but now a few new pains joined the party. I let out a deep moan and swung with my good arm, but I had just enough strength for a moderate tap.

Are people seeing this? Why do they still think I'm some kind of warrior? It doesn't matter who my parents were, I'm next door to dead, when will they all wake up here? I'm no one to follow anywhere.

Nelson hopped to my side quick, he thrust an arm between us. "Easy!" he hollered. "She's still recovering from that stab wound y'all gave her."

My eyes met Nelson's. The pain inside me was too much for words right then. I just shook my head slowly and watched him through my tears. His eyes were wide, and trails of sweat poured off his face.

The other Omegan broke things up when they slammed Nelson in the gut, and sent him doubled over in heaves. "Don't tell us what to do, boy; just watch yourself. We got orders to take you in too—unless you'd rather us stomp your head in here first."

I gasped out a sob. My arms went for him, but the Omegan held me too tight. I wanted more than anything to at least let Nelson know I was alright. But all I got out was some hitched breaths. I did my best to muffle the sobs that started coming out.

What the hell was I gonna do?

They had us.

And I hated each one of 'em for it.

Nelson slowly got back up to his feet. He held his side and eyed me with regret. He started squaring his feet again when the Omegan who'd hit him grabbed a handful of fabric on the back of his shirt. "Alright, I was gonna give you a few more minutes, but since you wanna be smart about it, we'll just take you first."

Nelson flailed against the guard's hold, but he was pinned against the wall. He grunted, twisted, and cocked his head back. "No, you can't do this!"

The one who hit Nelson yanked him out. My throat clenched at the sight of Nelson being led away. I forced some words out.

"Leave him alone, ya bastards! I'm the one you want, not him!"

The other guard clutched my neck until it throbbed. "Don't test me. We been here way longer than we were supposed to be, and keeping you safe was more of a suggestion, as far as I'm concerned. So, shut up and come along."

SIX

(ANA)

THE OMEGAN PULLED ME ALONG; I stumbled trying to keep my balance and ended up careening around as they yanked me forward down the hallway.

"What're you doing with Nelson?"

They tossed an annoyed gaze to me. "None of your business. And if you want to keep living, do me a favor and shut up. Now let's go."

They led me down a lot of twisting corridors. It was too much to take in all at once, especially with my chest throbbing like a Land-crawler had rolled over me, plus I could hardly see because of the tears in my eyes.

Before long they brought me to a room with a set of chairs facing some video screens. The Lebabolis crest flashed on one, and another showed shots of troop movements and map locations. Another Omegan studied the screens as we entered, then they faced me. Their reddish animal eyes narrowed on me and they nodded to a seat, which my escort dropped me in. I let out a gasp when I was jolted into my new resting spot.

My escort left, and the one at the screen spoke. "I'm Ancus,

552

Captain of Security. I understand you're the leader of the faction we captured back at the mountain range."

I blew out an exasperated breath. "Call me whatever you want. What do you even care?"

Ancus' hands clenched. "I care—we care because we're cleaning up a mess Charista started, and we need to be certain that everything is on the up and up. If you help me with information, we may go easier on you."

"Easier meaning a quick kill instead of me bleeding out?"

"That's all you think of us Omegans, isn't it? That we only seek to destroy you?"

"What the hell else should I think? Please, clue me in."

Ancus sucked in a slow breath. He had an air like Baudricort, and it was clear this guy was in charge, definitely here anyway, and probably even higher up. He steeled his gaze at me and took a few measured breaths before he continued.

"I'll get right to it. I'm going to you some questions, and you will respond to them. In case it hasn't been clear already, we're entirely willing to make your stay here even more painful than it has been so far, so I suggest you don't waste my time."

My fists were clenched, but once again, I felt the corner at my back and knew it was time for my mouth instead of something physical. Ancus' face relaxed after I held quiet for a second. He began, "We want to know what Charista has done with your weapon."

"I don't know what you're talking about."

Ancus narrowed his eyes. "You know quite well what I'm talking about. Your weapon; you know it as Cataclysm. It misuses technology of ours, and we want it. How many of you die before we get it is entirely up to you."

I swallowed hard. So, they knew about Cataclysm. "I'm afraid I don't know what to tell ya."

Ancus launched to his feet and quickly came up next to me and close. "Oh, yes you do. We've tracked a group that retrieved it, but all signs point to them flying it back to the Lebabolis Capital."

"Well, there you go; you solved your own mystery."

"We want to know what they've done with Cataclysm."

"So ask 'em, then. In case you hadn't noticed, Charista sorta delivered us to you. What makes you think she'd bother telling me anything important?"

He shook his head, annoyed. "You don't understand. Charista with that kind of power is the last thing anyone wants, including you."

"So what do you need me for? You need Cataclysm; go get it."

Ancus shook his head. "Taking a gun from someone with their finger on the trigger is never advisable. Besides, as your race owes us much for your current existence, you're obliged to help us here."

"Help you?" His words stunned me like a smack to the head. *After all this, our group wrapped up tight, shoved into this hole, starved for days, now we were supposed to help them?*

His mouth curled up at one side.

"I can see you're surprised we'd even entertain your assistance, given how we've come into contact. But yes, we very much would like your help. As you can probably guess, Charista has locked the Lebabolis Capital up in a defensive shield. While blasting through is the approach we'd normally pursue, the Cataclysm weapon makes this quite delicate. We are acting as swiftly as we can, since there's no way of knowing how close she is to being able to fire it yet."

"You want us to break into the Capital?"

"Of course. Your race is cleverly devious. That became clear early on. Surely you can manage to enter a secured site."

I held back a chuckle. At least for a change they wanted the same thing we did: getting Cataclysm away from Charista. But going with 'em, giving them what they wanted; I had to think we removed our last bargain for ourselves.

"So, suppose we break through this impenetrable fortress, and make our way through all the protection and security we both know she'll have in front of her, what in the world are we supposed to do?"

"Secure the weapon and contact us. We'll proceed through and secure the Capital from there."

I strained my head to make sense of the details. Things came into focus a little more. "You're got to realize something. Assuming the few people in our group who might know how to find Charista and Cataclysm in there, she'd never let us within a foot of that thing. She'd kill me and everyone else on sight."

"I would agree. Normally, we'd leave afterward and blow the planet. But you must understand, this world, everyone on it and even several of our nearby ships are in danger if she gets control of this weapon and fires it with enough of a charge."

"But how? All I know is that it neutralizes anything or anyone that's in its target path."

"That's a rather simplistic explanation. A more thorough one is it's a seismic isolator. It pulls in kinetic energy from its surroundings, then releases that energy in a focused area. Depending on the level of burst, any number of effects like breaking rocks, busting metal, even shattering bone. Initially, the technology used by Cataclysm was employed in locating Brescar deposits, even jarring them loose when necessary. But, with some clever modifications and a lack of concern for the consequences, Charista has created this weapon. It uses our technology; therefore, it is rightfully ours."

Something in the way he said her name made me wonder. My brain had gotten less fuzzy at that point, and I started getting more of those old gut feelings back.

"You had Charista running things for you."

"Indeed, this experiment needed a liaison. She provided us a way to let humans develop and give us time to focus on other exploration elsewhere. For a time, it went well..." Ancus' brow wrinkled, and he folded his arms. "However, years ago we became concerned that Charista had become more interested in this project than her initial assignment warranted. We sent a force to take her out, but we were too late; she'd already assembled the weapon, and she stopped our initial group. Sadly, we recognized the signal a little too late as a

Brescar powered weapon. And, based on our analysis, Cataclysm can be fired at a controlled level, which is likely what was done earlier to neutralize the Omegan contingent we sent initially. But Charista knows we're back in greater numbers, and the kind of energy that Cataclysm harnesses shouldn't be released at a level necessary to destroy us."

The level of Charista's deceit was a little much to get a hold of. "So, she'd destroy the earth to keep you away. Isn't that what you're trying to do anyway: blow all of this up?"

He took a deep breath and shook his head. "Hardly. We're explorers and catalogers first and foremost. Earth is just a stopping point for us. However, we saw potential in your kind to help us on worlds with similar atmospheres to this planet. Trust me, our leader is in no way interested in abandoning a project that took so long to come to fruition. One way or another, we're leaving this world with Cataclysm and our specimens. Not all of us were interested in your kind, but now that we've invested all this, we're collecting on our investment. And most important, we're removing Cataclysm even if we have to sacrifice a few more of you to get it."

The way he talked about humans as specimens just made my mind numb. Everyone I knew, loved, cared about, even hated—just specimens. The Lebabolis system was just one layer in the situation. We were an experiment within an experiment. My rage crept up; my face tingled with stinging heat. But I remembered once again my father's advice: keep your head or you'll end up dead.

Ancus went on. "You're looking at us, someone you're on the assault against, as a ruthless enemy. But the truth is, your kind initiated this. Earth was dormant when we arrived, and we reinitiated your race by our own choice—"

"To become your slaves."

Ancus chuckled a bit and nodded. "That's a rather narrow view, again, not a surprise from your kind. The bigger reality is your planet's climate is shared by a number of worlds. We're explorers, not destroyers. But over time, your race began to exude the worst qualities we could've expected. Jealousy, anger, lust for power. In time you became more and more difficult to control. And you'd formed your own civilization. Lebabolis."

"Still, you never gave us much choice, the way you chased us around."

"You think that was chasing? We were collecting. But your kind is so quick to fight, to be scared. Your fear is your greatest weakness, and mark my words, it will one day destroy you again."

"Thought that was your job."

"Hardly. Truth be told, I was never for your usage in this manner. I've studied your kind; how do you think your population was already reduced to the state it was when we found you?"

I'd never thought much on it, but his point was hard to brush off. I don't think even Nelson could've explained what caused this entire planet's population to disappear. And, as hard as it was to admit, we owed the Omegans for our existence, after all. "Alright, your point is coming in clear. Suppose I agree, and I get the others to go along too. Just what do we get in return for helping you?"

Ancus said nothing for a bit; he just eyed me up and down, and I felt the superior tone of his look as he watched me like a vegetable he was waiting to sprout and become useful. "A chance to live, to repopulate, to grow. And for some of you, a place with us away from here."

Away from here?

I hadn't thought of that possibility, but given everything that we were into here, and just how much we ended up prisoners after pretty much our best effort, maybe a chance to start over and away was the best bet.

"You'd just let us live after that?"

Ancus' eyes narrowed. "Some of you perhaps."

"And what would you do with the rest?"

"Your options would be to stay on this planet, which is floundering, or to join our exploration efforts."

"If you want to leave and take us, why don't you just do that and vaporize Cataclysm from space?"

"It isn't that simple." Ancus sighed. "The effects of an energy release from Cataclysm can extend off planet. As close as we'd need to be, we'd end up in the residual explosion. Even in dormancy, Brescar still holds a tremendous amount of energy. Not even our Darkness system can touch it because of the self-sustaining force. No, the device itself must be deactivated properly or it could be just as dangerous as if it were fired. It isn't safe otherwise. If you have any attachment for this barren rock of a planet, you'll take me seriously. We want this Cataclysm for ourselves and won't be leaving this place until we have it."

I folded my arms. "You're pretty quick to say we're useless destructive creatures. Well, you brought us back, so you're a little responsible too. You can't just leave because you don't like how things are going."

Ancus' face twisted in a deep scowl. "Listen, child, you're about to have much bigger problems that you realize. Our leader is tired of the delays and is coming here, expecting us to deliver Cataclysm to him. To make things easier, we had your group captured, and now we're sending transports for you all. We'd hoped you'd convince your people to help us first. Trust in this, we'll get what we want, even if it leaves you all bone dry. We'll get what we want out of your people whether it means a few of you die or all of you die."

"Well, why don't we skip all the bullshit and-"

The pain in my chest went from a mild throb to a heavy deep soreness. The room around me began to fade. Ancus continued talking, but his voice and words faded too. I watched his angry face, jowl twisting and gnashing his words out, bits of spittle flung off his lips.

The pain roared inside of me, much deeper than before. I took some strained breaths, but that only made it worse. Nothing I did made me feel better. I braced my hands on the sides of the chair.

His words were blank to me; I heard none of 'em. I clutched my chest; and I saw his expression change. He reached for a comm, and my legs turned to rubber. I slid off the chair to the floor in a heavy thud.

SEVEN

(NELSON)

THE GUARD WHO LED ME AWAY looked like a football lineman. The back of my neck and shoulders burned under the grip of their knobby hand that kneaded my flesh until it felt like it was on fire. I quickly got dizzy with all the twists and turns we took through the hallways. I watched the trail of fluorescent bulbs snake past marking our winding trip. I heard the sounds of muffled voices behind the walls as we walked. The Omegan jerked and grunted, as if that drowned them out.

I attempted to crane my head for a better look around the area, but with them dragging me around it was pretty much impossible.

"Where the hell are you taking me?" I asked.

"Shut up and keep moving, earthling."

The dank odor of a sweaty gym locker room flooded my nostrils. I felt like a prisoner being interrogated in a war movie.

After a half hour of twisting and turning through hallways, my forced march ended in an open room. A single light hung from the ceiling, and a rotten odor hung in the air, the same rancid smell as in our cell. I hoped what I smelled wasn't rotting human flesh.

Cabinets lined the walls, reminding me of that first room I was in with Havens when I first came to this world. I did my best to hold in a chuckle at that thought. It was kinda weird, how the temptation to laugh struck me then, but the idea of just how much I'd gone through in what was just a bit less than two months was too wild not to find a little hysterical. Or maybe I had finally found my reason to check out of reality for good.

In the middle of the room was a single chair, and it was quickly obvious the seat was mine. Lineman pointed me to it, but I was in no mood for moving a step further. My moment of humor passed quickly into indignation. The ache in my neck, the dizziness, and being yanked from Ana just ratcheted my bad mood to the worst level it had been in a good while. There's only so many times a guy can be shot at, beaten, chased, imprisoned, starved, and so on before he just has enough. Even I had my limits.

So, we began an impromptu standoff, a Mexican standoff, or Omegan standoff in this case. I was belligerent enough to figure whatever I was in for with these jerks wasn't gonna be made easy for them. It was tough to keep the facade going though, as the hunger pangs that had racked my stomach for the past several days started to go into overdrive.

"What's this all about?" I asked with as much indignation I was able to muster.

Lineman's eyes narrowed, and I was a little tickled at the realization I'd pissed him off. Their biceps flexed as they reached for my arm. It surprised me how some of the Omegan physique was very human like. The lizard skin, not so much, but their faces and even expressions gave me an eerie feeling that there was more to these things than Ana's group or even the Omegans let on.

Lineman snorted and spat. "You'll find out soon enough. Now sit before I hit you again." He growled. He thrust me into the seat and attached restraints to my arms, then checked a few terminal screens before he stomped out of the room.

Beads of sweat formed on my brow. My back gave me about nine thousand complaints and promises of pain to come. My thoughts of what I was in for got clouded with worry about Ana. I felt more and more tied to her, and the sight of her like that in the cell, injured so badly, made me even more angry I wasn't there for her. I wished I had more strength or at least fought harder to stop them from taking her away. Norg and Treg could've done something more, I bet. *What were they doing with her? She was barely able to stand. There's no way she was gonna make it through any heavy interrogation.*

Ana had been there time and again to protect me, and when it was my turn, what did I do? Not near enough. Ana hadn't deserved this.

All I thought of in that moment was to try centering myself to what I knew so far, so I repeated to myself. *Nelson, you wrote a novel back in 2014, and somehow it came to life. You've got this tie to this world. You're gonna figure out a way to get out of this. After all, you're what got you into this mess in the first place.*

My mind raced for ideas, options, anything. In the past, at times like this, things rearranged themselves before me, like when I learned the location of Cataclysm or when I learned to fly one of their Hell Hawk aircraft just from watching the controls. But this was different; something had changed, and I wasn't sure what.

It slowly sank in that I was without those mysterious powers that Ana, Baudricort, and Kaitlinn found useful, and the lack of any bargaining chips worried me. In a few seconds, I had to talk with the Omegans and give them something, but I didn't want to give them so much they had no reason to keep me anymore.

I attempted a stretch, as best I could with my hands locked down. When I flexed my arms, I felt that familiar pressure against one of them and looked down at my one definite tie to this place.

The bracelet on my wrist was my tether, according to Kado, and something that couldn't be removed without risk to my very life. I thanked heaven that so far, the Omegans seemed to have gotten the memo how dangerous it was to remove that bracelet from my arm, or they just hadn't needed that to threaten me with just yet. The armlet was my only link to home and what that meant: people, places that at the present were all long gone and dead, just like me. But this little device was my hook back to where I was supposed to be.

Home seemed as far away as another galaxy though. I was part of a transaction, and from all appearances they were ready to close out accounts and leave me and the rest like trash from yesterday's party.

My hopes went to Kado and that he was still alive. It was a hope we all shared, Ana and me in particular. Aside from being one of my best shots at going home, Kado was the best of the Intellectual minds now.

Kado had to be alright in some way. Charista needed him to activate Cataclysm. Whatever the solution was, it lay with Kado, but he was being tortured, I was sure. Poor guy. At least Ana was sort of ready for a fight, and people like Treg and Norg pretty much lived for it.

I sat there for ten minutes. The only noise around was a periodic grinding sound that sounded like gears turning. Finally, another Omegan entered the room. This one had a different uniform on and they looked a little more kept up than my last escort. A thick cover of reddish hair on their head swirled down in a series of braids. Either I was really lonely for physical contact, or this new Omegan had a distinctive feminine curve to their build.

I watched her and wondered what this was all about. Was she just trying to scare me? Her eyes met mine with a scowl so intense I had to look away. If she was here for torture, I wished she'd get on with it.

Red Hair took her time and paced around me in silence. She eyed me from head to toe like a lioness that surveyed a wounded gazelle. The dull staccato thump of her boots filled the room with a slow cadence, a march of measuring me up. Our eyes met several times as she looked me over. She cocked her head at one point, then shook her head slowly. My pulse raced in my throat as I braced for whatever was to come next.

She paced again around me; a slow hiss escaped her lips. I felt my body draw tight. What was this? Her slow measured footsteps were the only noise in the room as she walked slowly behind me. My heart paused a second when I thought I heard the sound of a blade. But no; she kept her gradual pace around until she faced me again. She bared her teeth, and I took a long swallow. I had to hold it together. Whatever was gonna happen, I had to. For Ana. She wasn't in shape for much; it was high time I did something myself and carried a bit of the load she'd dealt with for a long time now.

If this was what I was up against, I had no idea what they were putting her through right then. Somehow, I found my nine millionth tank of reserve. I let the sweat beads roll off my face, and I took my best calm breath while my gut was ready to burst out of my body and become a red splatter on the nearest wall.

I eyed her with my best possible stink eye. Whatever she had planned for me, I wanted it as difficult as possible for her.

What was I in for? They must've known about Ana and the rest, but had they known about me and Xander too? Was that why they singled me out? Were they about to execute me? That couldn't be, could it? They sure were aggressive against us in the fight though, and it was hard to imagine they weren't out to kill us all back then. We were their spoils, handed up to them like pieces of silver.

What bothered me most of all was, if they were so eager to kill us back then, why hadn't they just taken us out? Why the move here, to this place? And, if the relocation here and now was for me, why go through all this to kill me quietly? They could've just gassed us in that room and made it easy on themselves.

Then a reason settled on me like dew, and I realized why they hadn't gotten rid of me yet.

Information.

The Omegans, by their own admission, had studied earth for at least a few centuries, and I realized if Ana and her group found my book, there's no telling what a sophisticated race like the Omegans unearthed with more advanced technology. If anyone was a prime target for them, it was me and my link to this place. I had a fountain of information in the past, but it seemed the spigot was clogged as of late. I prayed whatever methods of extraction were coming happened quick and painless.

A lump formed when I considered another alternative: interrogation-slash-torture. I wondered if I was in for more Link connections like the one Baudricort had treated me to. He was determined to see what was in my brain, and he hooked me up to that contraption that almost drove me insane. I'd hoped it was soon behind me, but again, how could it ever be? After a few minutes of parading around me like an interested scientist checking on her favorite lab specimen, Red Hair stopped in front of me and leaned in close. "So, you're the one they call Xander."

I cringed at the mention of that name. "Yeah, I suppose."

Red Hair nodded and crossed her arms in thought. "Allow me to introduce myself; my name is Dera."

Dera studied me and waited for my response. I scoffed. "First of all, call me Nelson. Second, I'd be happy to shake your hand, but I'm a little constricted here."

Dera chuckled. "Yes, well we can't be sure you wouldn't try to escape."

I shook my head. "Can't imagine why. Tell me this, Dera. I noticed none of you messed with this thing on my wrist yet; I assume you know what it's for."

She nodded. "It's a transit beacon. One of the tools we made available to humans over time."

Dera said 'tools' in a way that made me wonder how many of them were thrown into the experiment, where humans were allowed to think of themselves as the creators but in reality were just the recipients. The Hell Hawks, the Landcrawlers, the P-LAD. They were so fascinated with us they gave us all kind of toys to see what we were able to make with them.

"So, have you ever sent your own people back in time before?"

"When the need calls for it. Time for us is just a storage method of sorts. Temporal transport has plenty of helpful uses, but once we found out Charista was sending people back and for what, we knew she'd reach well beyond any reasonable limits we were willing to tolerate."

"What was she sending people back for?"

Dera shrugged. "A number of crimes, abducting figures from the past, bringing them forward. Why, you yourself, Xander, your whole purpose of being here was one of her trips over the centuries to pilfer."

And now the very entities in my book world were telling me what my place was. I couldn't have held in the laugh if I tried.

"You know, I just have to say I'm stunned I came up with this."

Dera's face went taut, and she blinked for a few seconds. "What do you mean, came up with this?"

"Oh, you know, this book that I wrote centuries ago." I continued on in my book description. If I did ever make it out of here, I knew my book pitch was gonna be rock solid after this many re-tellings of it.

Dera shook her head, and I suddenly felt like the kid who mouthed off in class to the wrong teacher.

"Don't start telling me about that falsehood of a book! Allow me to show you just how insignificant you and all humans are. And by the way, you should stop talking about anything in that book as your idea. You didn't create this world. You received the idea for it because of us."

While my brain did somersaults in an attempt to determine if I'd been fed a huge pile of dung by Dera or my entire worldview of this insane experience qualified as such. Dera watched me, her arms folded like a suspicious parent. She opened one of the cabinets on the wall and pulled out a greenish translucent bracelet and put it on her right arm. The device settled on her wrist, and after several clicks, it filled the room with a low hum before it went quiet again. Dera tapped on its surface for a moment until a green glow filled the room with holographic images of space. Dera glanced around the three-dimensional spread, then moved her hands once she saw what she wanted. In response, the display rotated and zoomed in on a planet.

After a few enlargements, I saw it was Earth. But not the Earth I remembered, and not the Earth I'd come to here. This one was in ruins, the view flipped through cities, reduced to charred remains. Buildings, sadly leaning to one side in disrepair. Roads and highways, broken and spent.

"This is how your planet was when we found it," Dera said. She still moved her arms about so the display moved in response.

"We naturally take our time in a world in this condition, since we had no way of knowing what it was that caused such a mass extinction. But in our research of your world, we were able to locate a collection of your life forms in embryonic state. Since we were in part looking for useful entities from this place, the decision was made to invest time in your race."

She eyed me and continued. "Flash forward a century or two of monitoring your kind, and we've been brought to some interesting conclusions. Your species is truly, enjoyably predictable. Always thinking of yourselves as the center of everything." She patted my arm as she stood and paced about me.

"Be that as it may, to answer your question about the transit portals, we well know about them and made sure as soon as it looked like our issues with the human population were getting beyond a reasonable resolution we had to shut them down, and we did so quickly and in force."

Shut down? Trapped here forever? "So, I can't go back home?"

"Not without our assistance. So, you see my dear boy, you are somewhat indebted to us before the fact anyway."

I felt the indignation swell up in me.

"Point is, you started us on the path to existence again, but you also gave us enough tools that we made an earth ending weapon. That's kinda how we roll." Fear gripped me at the idea of the life sentence she gave me with no thought or concern.

"I want to know about who took the weapon, Nelson." My name rolled off her tongue like a conciliatory gesture, and for once I saw her hard gaze soften a bit.

"His name is Zengus." Once I said his name, a chill shot through me, as if I'd conjured him up by some voodoo incantation. I wondered how much more I should've said. Just saying the name of the guy who betrayed us like that pissed me off. I knew I had a few cards left here, and I hoped I hadn't played them all just yet.

Dera stepped around toward the door she had come through and stopped. She bowed her head in thought. "Your people were taught the principles of the device but to be used for other technological means. Cataclysm harnesses Brescar particles as an energy source. That was only meant to be set up as a power supply. But your brighter minds learned its destructive potential."

"Like I said, give us a torch, we'll start a fire eventually. I'm sorry, but my mind has been wiped for a while since we found it."

Dera sneered; she looked like she was about to laugh at something I'd just said. "Be that as it may, when we realized what had happened; we tried to break through and retrieve it. We sent a team in under guise to pull this out, but it was missing."

"Taken by the Valkyrie," I said.

Dera nodded. "Not even Charista knew its whereabouts. And that was dangerous enough. But now she does have it."

My mind was flung back to the cave, with Kado, Norg, and Zengus. Finding Cataclysm made me feel like a kid on Christmas morning, for at least a few seconds. We all wanted it and looked for so long. Still, I was in shock over how Zengus had been in on it, and I still wondered just what and how Charista was able to get through to him and what he was offered to make that kind of switch on us.

She then launched into a deeper discussion of her plan. I was simultaneously amused and terrified of how much information she revealed to me, like a master villain who made that one crucial error in a film that let the hero have just enough information to save the day. But again, what if this wasn't any ploy and it was just a post-script before I met my end?

"Look, I've gotta get home; my dad needs me. I miss him, I have a life and a place back there. It isn't much, but it is home." Even as I said that thought, what had been my mantra ever since I was pulled to this time, the idea of Earth itself being gone made me think more about things. I mean, for me, I could still go back centuries ago and live a life. The routine had a sense of comfort for me at that point. Life isn't always about climbing Mount Everest or something. The moments between were something I missed more than I realized. I knew I could have still had some kind of life that maybe was mired in mediocrity but also in completion. There was a decent shot I'd have met a girl and settled down. What was there to care about what happened with these people? Aside from this device on my arm, I had no physical tie to this place.

At least, that's what my head knew. My heart reminded me of something more. It reminded me that my home in 2014 wasn't the whole picture anymore. New Orleans was still home, but I also knew since my little trip here that being with Ana felt more like home than I'd ever thought it could.

Dera smiled a bit. "I'm sensing your inner debate. Nelson, I'm sure you're a dutiful son in your time. But here you are part of so much more, and you could really make a difference."

"Why? I'm just someone who got a really long-distance call."

Dera shook her head. "The fact you were contacted or reached like that isn't something to take lightly."

I laughed. "You really are forthcoming with a lot of information."

"Things happen," Dera said. "People become what they always were meant to be. It's in your wiring. As much as your kind can and often does take its own destruction out on anything including itself, the truth remains that our original path is set from birth. The Product system proved that. This Experiment showed your race has enough potential without the violent tendencies if they can be controlled. You might think us willing to destroy. I'm telling you we are charting other worlds close by, and we need sentient races that can help us. It's too much work for us to do without some assistance. Your world here is near its end, and we offer you a chance to extend your life elsewhere."

EIGHT

(NELSON)

"MY DEAR NELSON, the fact is that we are traveling through your world. Our Brescar—you know it as Valentium—was spread to your world by us. It is our energy source, and in our exploration of various systems, we typically provide ample supply for us to use. Once on a planetary body, it replicates itself, so we have a sustaining energy source."

Dera leaned against the wall directly opposite from me. For the first time since she entered, she relaxed her frame a bit and crossed her arms in thought for a few moments before she continued.

"We use these deposits as a home base to examine planets with no worry for lack of energy for our machines and processes. Brescar provides us with several advantages. We've been able to harness its energy potential as a very efficient fuel source. And its volatility, when controlled, can be a quite useful aspect. It has increased our space travel speed exponentially. And we're enjoying the time displacement of being in your galaxy, which seems to move at a rate much slower than ours."

I felt my mind slip a bit at the idea of time displacement; it was enough that I was yanked this far ahead, but the idea of time across galaxies – I wasn't quite the physics student even on my best day.

Dera continued, "We've estimated that one of our years equals about 500 here, so we've been looking around for everything here that might be useful. Also, Brescar has given us the ability to mark our path. Its signatures are easily tracked by our systems, which made it so easy to zero in on your Valentium locations. Normally, we'd have ditched your useless rock of a planet by now. But, having Brescar in your hands isn't acceptable for us, especially our leader. Cataclysm, however, was well shrouded, and I must admit Charista has gone well beyond anything I'd ever assumed her capable of."

"Wait, what? How?"

"Nelson, your face still informs the naive interpretation that you and your kind are the controlling force of all in this world, and I'm telling you that isn't even remotely close to the truth. Delusions are as much a part of your race as are oxygen and water."

"But, I was pulled in directions. I knew where Cataclysm was before anyone else did, including people using scanners."

Dera studied me for a minute before she gave me a shrug in response. "Brescar has a lot of potential, a lot of power. Its ability to lance the fabric of space time is probably as good an explanation as any."

"Lancing space time? You'll have to be more specific."

Dera chewed over her response for a minute or two. She paced around, her arms folded in thought before she continued.

"In all purposes we shouldn't have ever been here. But Brescar has a certain concentration of dark energy that opened up these windows. If I recall properly, your kind referred to them as Verges. That's how Ana was able to travel back to you, centuries in the past, and then bring you forward, correct?"

I swallowed hard. It was like she was a lawyer cross examining me on trial. "Yeah, that's right."

Dera gave me a condescending gaze as she spoke. "The substance your people know as Valentium is the culprit, I'm afraid. It's quite useful here as a means of power generation, but there's much more to it than that. Our race has been able to pass through dimensions in our exploration. We have traversed several universes already and are merely stopping through here. We collect things we think are useful and discard the rest."

She said it with the ease of someone giving directions to their house. Travel, not just between worlds, but universes and dimensions?

"Look, you still haven't explained how I knew all those centuries ago to write this book about a conflict. You've monitored humans long enough to know things that have happened aren't too far from what I wrote."

"Your kind has likely never experienced this, or you wouldn't be as surprised by my explanation. Physical bodies aren't the only things that can travel through these windows. Essences can move back and forth; memories, thoughts."

"But how would that work?"

"Thoughts travel for our kind beyond space and time even. And with this portal, it seems some of that information has traveled back to you in yours."

She eyed the holograph for a moment before she returned my look. "We have found that certain bleed overs can happen when making trips like we've done here and there."

"Bleed overs; what are those?"

"When affecting space time, there's never an even or neat transition. Undoing the fabric of time always leaves threads. Things slip through."

"Things?"

"Thoughts, ideas, people, events even. What I can say in your case is you're the lucky or dubious recipient of a reasonable portion of our current history."

There it was. I felt a mix of relief and amazement pour over me. My ideas came from here. From these people and what they did. Was I mad at them or was I grateful? I thought more about it. We held onto memories of people. Maybe there was a way they lasted through time as well.

"Earthling, we've no part of your story. We've seen copies of your work, and they say nothing at all about our invading race. Your story, while an entertaining one, stops with the nation being turned back by your heroine."

Her gaze was like a cheetah that savored every bite of the gazelle it had just subdued. Her words were anything but reassuring. Dera folded her arms and studied me some more before she continued. "All right, enough small talk. Your species has the Cataclysm weapon they never should've created, and we want it back."

Cataclysm again. That pile of used electronic looking junk was more valuable to these people than anything. The fact I was Pulled to it the way I was felt like some sick insult. I made a note if I ever got back, I wasn't gonna look so bad on thrift store items again.

"Need it back? Why'd you even let humans build one if we're part of your experiment?"

Dera's eyes flickered. I'd gotten a lot better at reading emotions from these things, but I wouldn't say I was ready to be an Omegan shrink by any means. My best non-trained guess is that they were sincere though.

"Nelson, I know we haven't given your kind much reason to trust us, but believe me, there's much more at stake here if that Cataclysm weapon is activated. I need to stop it, and I can't do it without your help. We're not marauders, much as you might believe. If Charista decides to detonate this device, it could cause a major disruption and could even have temporal effects if the Valentium is affected."

I swallowed hard. Dera's sympathetic glance melded quickly into one of intimidation. "I'm a patient person but not without limits. I'll give you fair warning here, I don't recommend you test me here."

"Continue."

"You have access to the leader of Lebabolis, Charista. We need to establish a communication with her."

"Can't you do that yourself?"

"We tried, but her systems have scrambled all attempts we've made to connect. It's important that we reach her." She cleared her throat, and for the first time since I met her, Dera's gaze softened a bit. Something about Charista had her worried.

I sucked in a deep breath and thought for a moment. "If anything Ana's told me about Charista is true, she's hunkered down right now and is never gonna let any of you get to her." I wondered what was going on over at Lebabolis Capital right then. Charista was hard at work on Cataclysm with Kado, and I worried just how long we all had before she cracked through the Failsafe to launch it.

"Well why don't you go get it yourselves? You know Charista has it. You've got the firepower. What're you waiting for?"

"Surely, you can reach a channel she has left open." Dera said.

"What makes you think we could do anything like that? From all appearances, she abandoned us at the Range. But let's say we can get to her and she miraculously throws out the red carpet. What do you expect us to do with Cataclysm that you can't by yourselves?"

"Since Cataclysm is Omegan technology in essence, there is a hope here. A Spike could bring it down and make it inoperative."

"A Spike?"

Dera nodded. "It's a device that must be attached to Cataclysm. Years ago our team attempted an insertion, but Cataclysm had been removed before it could be done. It only works if it's attached to the device; being in close proximity won't do it. We've been tracking Charista's signal and also the signature of Cataclysm for some time now. We figured the best course was to eliminate it and her. She shut us down though and acquired a tight shield. We had no choice but to summon our military, which is what you've been facing. And they will only escalate until they achieve their objective, no matter what."

"Why do you need us to do this?" I asked. "Shouldn't you be asking Ana right now?"

"We are, believe me. But we need more than her in on this. We need as many of you as possible to know about this and make it happen. Cataclysm is still very dangerous."

"Are you sure about that? It looked pretty beaten up when I saw it. Whatever it's been through, it looks kind of ragged."

"Trust me, it's still very functional. And if Charista manages to fire it, it won't go well for anyone here, including you and your friends."

Dera sighed and checked a device on her wrist. She tapped a few controls onto a display, and it responded with a series of beeps. A deep amber light reflected on her face, and she squinted for a few seconds before she smiled again and returned to our conversation. Dera glared, then took a seat in the chair across from me and clasped her arms. A deep sigh escaped her. She suddenly looked exhausted, and I thought, as much as we'd been on the run, so were they. They must've been getting tired, maybe more than they let on.

"We want to send a group into Lebabolis to retrieve the device under a guise."

"And you want us to help you?"

Dera nodded. "Forcing entry is never an issue for us, but to keep Charista from activating it, we'll need to be very covert."

"You'd better keep Ana on the hook too. Anyway, how do you expect us to just walk in?"

"I admit it won't be easy, but we've identified several in your group who might have special access to the Capital."

The way Dera said it, one name popped into my head. And Ana was gonna love it if that's who Dera meant. I wondered what the bigger challenge was: getting into the Capital or keeping Ana from tearing Dawn's head off.

So, that was it. I wasn't this big conduit, this channel of the future. I was just a guy who won some really bizarre intergalactic temporal lottery ticket, and I had no clue how to even begin comprehending the prize, if this could've ever been considered a prize.

I should've felt relief, and I did, but that was soon replaced with the dread of a kid left behind by the school bus. Was I really stuck here for good? Was Ana my only shot back, and was she gonna be OK herself?

I turned to Dera, who seemed to be enjoying my mental shuffling. "So, if we're not in control, what is it about us you're so damned concerned with? Why all this bother of having us kept here as your prisoners?"

"We needed to make sure Charista didn't have anyone among you with any other weapons. Your race has an impressive ability to destroy itself. Decades of training hasn't removed that by one degree, but we'll get use out of you yet. We'll keep you in check, but we're not having any part of your self-destruction. Charista knew this all too well, more that you can imagine. And she will be dealt with in kind too." Dera sneered. "If you help us, we can make your time here— What's the earthling word?—agreeable."

"Agreeable, like not putting me back in that rotting morgue smelling place of a room?"

Dera nodded her head a bit. "Perhaps."

"You know I'd be a whole lot more willing to help you guys out if you'd start with telling me how I can get home."

"The windows have been shut, thanks to our Darkness system. We won't allow anyone the chance for a trick maneuver on this until we have our prize secured." Dera jerked her head in response.

Dera activated the green projection on her gear again. "There's more to the story, Nelson. We're not just looking for your help. Truth be told, you need our help, and as a sign of good faith, I'm going to show you exactly why. First of all, you need to know that this world of yours is spent. Your race and our Brescar are the only two remaining assets of use to us or any civilized beings, I assure you."

She explained some basic details about the condition of the core and Earth that had been impacted over so many years. How all the radiation, some from just normal existence but a lot from nuclear weapons, ravaged the core and makeup of the planet until it was almost too brittle. "At this rate, the Earth will disintegrate in a matter of years."

"Is that so?"

"Yes, quite. The planet will quite literally pull itself apart in its own rotation. We wanted this experiment to have time, but I'm afraid that time is almost up, so you see you're out of options when it comes to habitation here anyway."

The thought of the world ending shook me. Of all the ideas that went with that, topping the list was that I needed to stop this. I had to do something; if there was anything my life was going to be worth, let it be stopping that. What good was going home just to let it happen unchecked? I couldn't let her—and the rest—have their lives end like that. "So, if we do this, what will you do for us?" I asked.

"What if I told you we could set up a portal for you to get home?"

I laughed. "Well, I've tried trips home, and the last time I did that some of your people snuck up and blew us all to hell, killed someone I knew." I thought of Otto and the guilt of that trip that I'd attempted that brought that down on us.

"You can see what I mean. Our military is hell bent; the loss of your life is but a move in the right direction to them. Help me help you and the others, Nelson."

"Look, there's one person here I trust fully; her name is Ana Crucinal. She swore to me she'd get me home. It hasn't been easy for her, and you guys damn near killed her. So, excuse me if I'm less than hopeful about you saying you're now gonna put me on an express train back to 2014."

Dera folded her arms and bowed her head in thought, like a judge pondering a sentence to give a convicted defendant. After a minute or two, she took a slow breath and continued.

"Nelson, I've told you the truth. Much as I can accept you being hesitant to believe me, you must realize that we have it within our power to vaporize you and your little band three times over, yet you're still here. Don't misinterpret that gesture from us as anything other than a gift, and believe me further when I say we're not above considering the alternative that leaves you and this world in waste. I implore you to return to Ana Crucinal with this offer and strongly encourage her to consider it. For the safety of you, your people, and this world."

As blunt as she was, I wasn't in any place to argue with that. We were a bunch of cockroaches to them down here, the rest of our group even further below. They could've just sealed off ventilation and choked us out, but they were keeping us, not well, but alive. I thought about what Ana would've said, suggested, or offered in this case. I figured the best plan right then was to keep Dera talking.

"So, your plan is to have Ana lead a team into the Capital."

Dera shrugged. "Of course, that is assuming she survives."

I jolted up. Until right then, any thoughts about Ana not still being OK were just in my head. But this was someone else saying it, and someone who had up to date info on it. My breaths quickened until they burst out of me. My arms ached under the tension of the restraints. "What?"

"Her injuries, I'm afraid, were more severe than we initially believed."

My mind played a thousand games with me. *Of course she's telling you this, Nelson. She wants you scared enough that you'll play along and since you're not cooperating yet, she'll dangle what's important to you. Don't listen.*

Oh, do you think so? Are you ready to chance that it's fake? What if Ana's on a bed somewhere, screaming for some kind of medical fix or something and the only thing that will keep her going is for Dera to send a notice on her device to the team working on Ana right then.

Are you willing to bet that?

Are you willing to bet her?

Are you?

I thought back to her in pain in the cell. She wasn't in tip top shape, but she was alive. A chuckle burst through my throat. "You've gotta do better than that. I saw her not that long ago. She'd looked better, sure, but you can't expect me to believe that."

Dera just gazed at me for a moment. "Tricky thing with medical treatments. When someone is expected to have the worst outcome, oftentimes the best option is to mask the symptoms as long as possible."

My gut was sore with the realization and I groaned. "You've sedated her, and it's wearing off." My pulse pounded in my throat, and a huge pain slammed me in the belly. It was a lie; it had to be.

Dera reached for my arm, but I pulled it back. She eyed me with a tinge of pity. "We'll try to save her, but we also need assurance from your group you'll cooperate regardless."

When I spoke again, my voice trembled. "You find a way; I don't care how, you save her. If she dies, you'll get nothing out of me."

Dera's eyes narrowed, but she managed a slight nod. "She's valuable to us; we're having someone work on her now. That's all I can say at the moment."

"You better say more later," I said. "You better be telling me she's gonna recover." The sting from this news hurt, but it wasn't new. This time though, it was about her. And, I hadn't even thought about how I was gonna live without her. Even if I left this place as planned, that thought was too unpleasant to spend any energy processing.

The ideas were stewing in my head, and I'd felt a headache building for a while. It had probably started back in the Range, but I knew if I didn't let some steam out, I was gonna be in a world of hurt.

"Would you just do me a solid? No fancy demonstrations with holograms, no tales of adventure where you and your people cherry pick burned out civilizations. Just tell me what's so damned important to you here that's keeping you from pulling out and blasting us all from space?"

Dera glared at me for a while. She let out a guttural moan and then snatched a comm device from their chest and growled some commands into it.

"I can't figure it out; why are you so keen on speaking with Charista? You had your way with us; why aren't you moving on to take her out next?"

Dera eyed me and sighed. She looked away as if she debated if she should reveal something to me. Then our eyes met again.

"Because she's one of us. Charista is an Omegan."

NINE

(ANA)

WHEN I CAME TO, I WAS STANDING, staring at my feet. My vision cleared slowly, and I made out three pairs of boots: mine, another human's and the thick blunt ones of an Omegan. An awful ringing noise filled my ears, another lovely new discovery. Hands clutched and held me up on both sides. My face felt like it was on fire. The floor wobbled, and soon I realized I was in an elevator, and the ringing in my ears was the lift mechanism. I caught Lucyna out the corner of my eyes, and the heavy build of an Omegan guard who worked the controls of the lift while they braced me with their free arm.

"Easy," Lucyna cooed. "You're fine."

Fine was a word I'd heard too often around the Encampments and on the relocations. When raids happened and people got shot, 'fine' was thrown around by the medics like another one of their bandages. They used it for calming someone down, sometimes to ease the pain of someone they couldn't save. Meds weren't always available, so hope had to do now and then, even if it was to keep someone positive about dying. I shuddered at the idea I was now in that place, and just what kind of 'fine' I was.

"Lucyna, what the hell happened? Last thing I remember I was talking with Ancus about what I knew, then I come to and you're holding me in an elevator."

"They said you fainted. After they couldn't revive you, they came back to our cell and said they needed help with you. I volunteered. You were unconscious and had some fresh blood from your chest wound. I guess whatever they did hadn't taken, so they tried getting help from the rest."

My brain grappled the pieces Lucyna gave me and slowly worked them around. I remembered the room and speaking with Ancus. He said something about their leader coming here. The floor of this elevator and my cell were about the most stable thing my feet had been on for some time.

Next to the Omegan's boots I noticed a silver-gray staff resting like it was a third leg. *I guess that's so we behave,* I mused. My legs gave a little and I felt myself drooping towards the floor when Lucyna caught me.

The angry whine of the elevator machinery as it lowered us got louder. We clanged to a quick stop, the doors opened and we stepped into a dimly lit warehouse area. A blast of warm air threaded my nose with a strong sour smell familiar to me.

Valentium.

So, I was right about those marks on the wall. We were damn close to the mineral if the odor was that strong. Fear lashed me. With energy processing, we were always trained that we had to wear protective gear, but here we were pretty much naked around a big enough deposit to have a strong odor, and we'd been here for quite some time.

My pulse quickened, but I then figured there must've been containment. The Omegans had to have known about its volatility. As we stepped through the cavernous room, I noticed some familiar Lebabolis markings on crates we passed. They greeted me like long lost enemies, a reminder of my old life, one I'd sworn I'd have forgotten by then.

They processed the Valentium in places like these so it was more stable and produced the power they needed. These places hadn't been used since new processing methods were discovered, and I'd always heard the Valentium was cleared out of these facilities.

Or was it?

Was that why we were here, to harvest what was left of it before this place became our common grave? We had plenty of room. In fact, some of the caverns in a place like this could be big enough to put a unit ten times the size of the one we had at the Range. But still, there was no sign of the others, not even down here. Was Nelson mistaken? If he wasn't, then where were they? Or worse yet, were they already gone? Were we the last, kept alive for whatever use we still served? The worry about them settled on me like dust. Beyond our thirty in the cells and the Omegans I saw, this place was either deserted or the rest had been hidden better than I could've ever imagined. I was again afraid we were alone.

I motioned to Lucy to hang back a bit as our Omegan escort trudged ahead. The pain in my chest got worse with every step, and I knew I had to do something, not for me, but for the ones I cared about.

"Lucy, we don't have much time. Promise, if anything happens to me, you'll take care of Nelson and Varrick."

She avoided my gaze. I guess she wasn't denying how 'fine' I was anymore either. Just when my panic was about to hit overdrive, her gaze lasered back on me so sharp I forgot to breathe for a few seconds.

"You're gonna make it, alright? Stop talking like that."

A sob escaped me. "Yeah, well, we can sit here and say that, but I need your word. Nelson, the guy who was near me in the cell, remember him?"

"Of course, the Xander guy."

"Right. The other is Varrick; he's held somewhere in the Lebabolis Capital. If I don't make it out of this, you've got to help them, you've..."

My voice trailed off as I broke down into trembles. The pain got stronger; even crying hurt. I was glad Nelson hadn't seen me like this. Lucyna snaked her arm over me and leaned close. "Don't worry."

Brakus' voice echoed ahead of us. "Hey, let's go."

Lucyna barked back in response, "We're coming, dammit; just wait."

Lucyna snaked her arm under my shoulder in a half hug and held me up as we continued through the large warehouse.

Lucyna's strong hand held my shoulder in a firm grip. I straightened up a bit; it felt good just knowing someone was still here on my side. At least I wasn't gonna die alone. The fear around and in me made me tremble, and she responded by gripping me tighter and closer.

Lucyna asked, "Brakus, where you taking her?"

"She needs fixing. Ancus don't want her dying before he's through with her."

Before he's through with me? So, I was in for more interrogation. They must've heard enough about me, probably from Llewyn. After Llewyn handed us all over, I bet he gave 'em everything, and I bet they made it all peaceful like, as if getting some of their experiment was all they wanted. What deal could Llewyn have expected to make?

Besides, didn't Llewyn have an idea about the Omegans and what they were up to? If he knew enough to sacrifice us like he did, he must've had some plan of his own going on. But what could that've been?

Charista at least had Cataclysm for a bargaining chip. She'd have cast Llewyn aside too though, first chance that she needed another edge. No wonder Llewyn never lead anything.

What about Nelson though? I remember they roughed him up in the cell as they grabbed me. I'd made a promise to Nelson, and I'd let him down too. My track record in this got worse with each passing thought. How much worse could things possibly get?

I glanced toward Lucyna, and her eyes told me she wondered

what Brakus' words meant as much as I did. I took a sigh of relief, but it sent another wave of agony through me, and I doubled over with a wince. Fear grabbed me when I realized the hurt came from my wound.

The Omegan growled. "Hey, this isn't rest time; get up."

His face was plump, just like his frame. His red glowing eyes glared at us from the two slits in his face. When I just stared back, he lunged toward me, but Lucyna put out a hand to stop him. Her nostrils flared as her lips drew into a line.

"Easy! She's wounded. You want your special friend to live, go light on her."

The Omegan braced and squared his shoulders as he leaned toward Lucyna. At first, he looked like he was set for a punch to Lucyna's face. I bet he was one of their field troops, probably more used to getting their way by bashing whoever was in their way around. And, I bet he never heard a woman give him lip either. He eyed us, probably remembered some earlier order to not let me die or something, and instead a guttural growl was his initial reply.

"Come on, let's go." He sneered at Lucyna in response.

Lucyna inched her arm further again under my shoulder for more support. "Meet Brakus, asshole of the moment."

"Mmhmm. What's his deal?"

"He's in charge of getting you down here, and not much else. They pulled someone else to help carry you at first, but I wanted a chance to spend more time with the legend."

A tinge of awe hung in her gaze over me. *Me, a legend?* What had she heard about me? What was I to her? She'd trained with the best and toughest force Lebabolis had ever seen, and I was taught to assemble machinery. And, I hadn't even gotten to do that; I ran off before that life started for me. My main skill so far was running. Had she missed the part where I led our people into capture?

"Legend? You're thinking of somebody else."

"No, I'm not. We heard about you in the Outlands. You took out a group of Lebabolis sentries armed only with a pulse rifle and one helluva disregard for authority. That ain't easy, even for a Warrior Product. Trust me, word got out on you quick."

"The stories you heard on me aren't much more than that."

"That's not what Baudricort told Duncan."

I froze. "Duncan knew Baudricort?"

"Sure did. We came from Lebabolis, didn't we? Duncan got help from Baudricort and likewise. How else you think an Intellectual would've started up the Action, with all those stolen vehicles and tech?"

"The Guard was with the Action?"

"At first, anyway. We both knew Lebabolis had it wrong. The Guard was in the best place to make a break first, but Charista knew that too well, so she dealt with us quick. But yeah, all that business on the Breeding Assignments, Products, punishing the Deviants instead of thinking maybe they had a problem and needed some help. We always helped those who needed it. Baudricort gave us help when he could, clued us into shipments, and even set up a crude commo system for us. I figure he must've been caught at some point, because the contacts with him dropped off to nothing. We knew though that Baudricort always wanted to break free and we supported him."

So, he was more into breaking out earlier than I realized. I remember him with the Action, so in charge, so sure of things, but with this tinge in his eye, of something. Sadness, doubt, or maybe something else.

Lucyna continued. "The Guard fended for themselves, but sometimes even the best need a little help. He let us know of some cargo shipments with less secure routes. He talked about you to him, we knew about you for a while. Had to think a lot of it was his imagination but when I saw it, well, that locked it in for me."

"I dunno, I've seen enough to want to stick around you."

I shook my head. "What the hell was Duncan's plan then? I thought the Guard was all about full out attack, no mercy whatsoever. Was there a chance, had we had a chance there at all?"

Lucyna shrugged. "You gotta realize something else about the Guard. We learned to survive all this time, with just what we grabbed from someone else. You don't live that long if you're always jumping right into the fight every time. A warrior's gotta be smart about things sometimes too."

I wondered just how close the Guard was if they heard as much about the Valkyrie as she seemed to. And they knew about our troop moves. I guess those runs into the Sectors like the one we'd seen earlier weren't the only time they broke into the city, and supplies weren't the only thing they were out for either.

I looked up in time to catch Brakus' glare toward us. "One more word out of either of you, and you'll both have an unfortunate accident. Now move."

We lurched forward behind him, my arm wrapped around Lucyna's waist, and tossed a look toward Brakus. He held his frame up like the fate of the Omegan nation counted on us going wherever the hell we were headed. He cast a glare our way now and then.

I returned his gaze for a moment then turned back to Lucyna "Oh, he's a charmer. Ya know, for a minute I thought they might go easy on me."

Lucyna brushed the hair from my eyes. "So help me, whenever we get loose, first thing I'm doing is popping his sorry ass."

We passed by a bank of lights, and I got a better look at Lucyna's face. It was smeared with sweat and some grime. A bloody bruise lined one side of her head; from the looks of it, she had taken a nasty blow. The rest of the story on her though, at least all I needed to know, was in her eyes.

"Ya know, Ana, this world would be a lot better if we could just pop a few assholes now and then."

Lucyna didn't look much older than me. She sort of reminded me of Marlene, this girl I'd seen trying to escape Lebabolis back before I joined the Action. Lucyna and I could've been fast friends if we'd met in the past. I felt a little like I was back with some of the Circle. I squeezed her shoulder, and she leaned in to me. "Easy, don't make me laugh; it hurts that way."

We shared a grin. These Guard people looked better to me all the time.

Lucyna's face said volumes about how tired she was. As bad as she looked, I didn't want to even think about me, more than I had to anyway. My body shuddered with soreness as I laughed at her comment about slugging Brakus, but I welcomed the pain. It felt good, her being here, someone who shared this mess of a situation with me. I'd have also liked Nelson, Treg, or one of the others from the Circle, but Lucy turned out to be pretty close to that. She felt like a lifetime friend in very little time. I had no idea why I felt that way so quick. And honestly, I wasn't in much shape to care, just as long as she was here and on my side. So many people weren't these days. As much as I knew I should've been more careful with trusting someone new, I just didn't feel any doubt with Lucy.

It's strange how some of the people who crossed your path made this instant connection with you, like somehow they were always meant to be there. And in some way maybe they always were; you just hadn't known it yet. It could've just been the fact she hadn't yelled at me like the Omegans did or the fact she actually worried if I was OK. Not even Dawn had been that worried about me, unless it meant her ass was on the line.

For a second, I felt like I'd known Lucy for way more than two days, and I was even a little angry it took yet another shitty situation like this before she and I met. How many others in the Guard, maybe even Lebabolis, were caught in this system, made to be something they weren't at all, but were good people, who might've had good ideas on a better way to live?

We had wasted so much time in this fight already. All our moves, scrounging food and fights over these pathetic pieces of land and their structures along with the barren Outlands... We could've done a whole lot better working together on figuring out a long-term solution. If we'd done that, no telling where we might have been by then.

Lucy's lips trembled as she stroked my head. "Easy. It's gonna be fine." Her eyes disagreed with her words though, as she shot a piercing gaze towards Brakus.

I nudged her arm. "Lucy, am I gonna die?"

She pulled up a hand tightened into a fist and brushed the side of her cheek with it. Her lips drew into a line, and a weary glint filled her eyes. I'd seen that look before. It wasn't fatigue, though she had plenty of that. No, this light from her gaze was more of a cold animal stare, like a wild creature who'd seen too much and knew just how to survive it all. I closed in on her and hoped like hell some of that energy she had passed over to me again. I needed something to get me going. It bolstered me. I flexed my arms, even though my chest still ached. I waited for her to give me the 'fine' response, like a condemned prisoner waiting for their execution order.

I imagined Lucy'd taken care of more than a few people over the years. I figured at least some of those were wounded, and I bet she'd given bad news more than once. That strength, that confidence; I wondered where it came from? My tank was near empty, but hers sure wasn't.

Lucy leaned in close, her voice dropped to a whisper. "Ana, listen. Strength isn't about being the strongest, the toughest, the least afraid, or never getting hurt. It's pressing on in spite of. No matter how much it hurts, no matter how much you're scared, no matter how much things seem like they'll just never work out. There ain't a one of us in the Guard who hasn't been scared at one point, not even Duncan. Being afraid's what keeps you alive. It's the overconfident assholes that get themselves wasted. So, rest up. You're in a bad way, but you're not out of this fight. Understand?"

Seeing this strength looking back at me, and knowing she was one of them, the Guard, I knew whatever she said to me was gonna be real. Maybe not what I wanted to hear, but what I needed to hear. She took a slow breath before she continued. Her mouth formed a line. "The reason I don't say more about your condition is I don't know. I've seen bad wounds, and yours isn't great. I'm playing along and hoping Brakus and these morons really want to help you like they say. Tell you this much, good or bad, I won't leave your side until I know you're better."

There it was in her eyes, her word. The promise of someone from the Guard, and I felt in my gut, as wrong as I'd been about other people, I just had a feeling here these people weren't steering me anywhere I didn't want to be. Sooner or later, if I trusted enough, someone was gonna come through.

Her words flowed through my ears better than any medicine could've right then. I clutched her arm tight and gasped. The fear of dying hung over me like a heavy blanket. I'd never felt this kind of pain, and the fear it put into me was nothing I'd felt before either. Being on the run was one thing, but I always felt OK when I did those hops and flights and runs all around the Outlands. I had felt tired, beat up, angry as hell before, yes. But my body had always felt OK during all of that, and now it didn't.

Running had been my number one for a while now. But, I thought about Lucy and the Guard. They'd been running too, way longer than I had, and what had it gotten them? Maybe sometimes, it wasn't about where you ran, but where you stood. As long as we stood here, though, we were just a part in someone else's plan. And, if I got notice and respect from someone like Lucy, well, maybe I hadn't lost anything after all.

Brakus brought us to a med station, such as it was. A bare metal table that had seen its share of dents, scratches and scorches in its time. To the side were two monitors with a collection of wires draped over them. A bank of lights cast a faded glow over the room.

Brakus nodded toward the table. "Lie here; I'll get the medic."

The air was cool in there, and it smelled of chemicals and disinfectants. With Lucy's help, I pulled myself up onto the dented metal surface. The cold steel against my back sent a shiver through me. The warmth I'd felt in the elevator was gone, and in its place was deep cool murky air. I jammed my hands under my armpits and worked on slowing my breaths and hoped the soreness went away. The table steel on my back was my latest wall, and maybe the last one I was up against. So much had been left undone.

TEN

(ANA)

A FEW MINUTES LATER, Brakus returned with another guy. His tousled brown hair draped over a youngish face and an earnest smile. He cocked an eyebrow as he gave me a once over from the doorway. The calming blue in his eyes warmed me enough that I hoisted myself up through a series of groans. I felt a little better about Brown Hair until I saw the gray band on his arm. My chest tightened, and the pain came on ever stronger until my breaths turned to huffing. I felt my body stiffen as new aches rocked it, and I felt like I was gonna throw up.

This was it; their first attempt at me had failed, so they sent me here for this ass from Lebabolis to do me in. But why the production? They could've wasted me with a big enough rock in the field once I went down—oh whatever; I had no idea what was happening anymore. I only cared about survival, and this jackhole was the latest thing in my way.

My eyes darted to Lucy. "Uh uh, no, not him."

Lucy glanced at me; a deep scowl formed into her face in response. Her eyes darted back to Brakus and the medic. She regarded both as if she were a wild predator. My eyes swept the room for anything that could've been used as a weapon. If this was it, I had to be ready. I was gonna make 'em, or at least this guy, pay for this. For all of it. I knew Lucy had my back too; whatever I couldn't finish she was gonna handle just fine.

The needles to my right, attached to one of the medical consoles, were a good first bet. OK, they were a crappy choice, but they were the closest, and if I got him in the eyes that would work nice. Gray Band and Brakus still had the advantage, but at least Lucy wasn't gonna go down easy, I bet. Very least this "medic" was gonna get a broken arm and not get to do whatever he was about to.

Brakus snorted. "Whatdya mean, 'not him'? He's who we got." He thrust his arms to his side in disgust, but it also felt like a challenge. Brakus stepped towards us until he and Lucy were about an insect bite away from a brawl, and I only wished I felt strong enough to jump in on her side.

Gray Band's brow wrinkled, but he just dipped his head. He looked back down the hallway he had come from as if he was waiting to be dragged back there like the useless drone he was, at least to me.

Brakus let out a deep growl and jabbed a finger toward Gray Band. He then eyed Lucy and me, so I said, "He's one of theirs, don't you—oh, forget it. He's not touching me. I don't care how, don't care who; find somebody else." I averted my eyes and watched Lucy. We spoke only through our shared glance, and I knew no matter what I tried right then, she was with me right until the end.

"There isn't somebody else." Brakus' voice melded into a growl. I mused to myself I may have clogged his simple mind with too many complex instructions. As long as they had us here, I intended on making this as difficult as I could. I added one more to my list of goals included: wreak havoc with these people. Any way possible.

I shook my head and scoffed at Brakus. "Bullshit. We had plenty of medics. We had about a thousand troops at the Range when you took us in, and I bet there's plenty of people in that group I'd trust enough for working on me, not some goddamned Gray Band. Brakus, there's gotta be at least one of our medics here."

"There ain't any more; no one well enough anyway. Now look, I got orders to get you stable. Otherwise, I'd just as soon shove another spear in, this time through your heart, and finish the job they were supposed to back there. But I'm under orders, so lucky you. This guy here, you wanna live, he's your best bet." He studied us as we chewed his latest offer that was more like the scraps from last week's dinner than anything useful.

I shrugged. "What about one of your people, then. Don't you have medics too?"

Brakus chortled. "Do I look like a medic? All we got here is soldiers. This place isn't high priority, so you get minimum treatment, shelter and whatever food we can scavenge. All we're supposed to do is keep you alive. Nobody ever said how comfy ya had to be." He eyed me up and down. "Besides, you aren't in a position for giving orders."

I asked, "What about whoever patched me up? Can't they take a look; they got me here alive, didn't they?"

Brakus chuckled. He shook his head and eyed Lucy as well. My throat seized up as I realized something. *I wasn't alive because of the Omegans. I bet whoever had saved me paid with their own life.*

"Yeah, they did. And if they hadn't gotten smart and tried overtaking some guards, they wouldn't have been blown away and coulda helped you out. Afraid you're outta luck."

They all stared at me for a few seconds. Brakus broke the silence with another grunt. "I don't know who you think you are or what you think you are, but you'll listen to me and follow along. Don't you worry, we can hook you up nice and good, keep you alive, only you won't like it any."

Gray Band's eyes darted back and forth between Brackus and me. When he neared the table, he walked right into Lucy's outstretched palm. "The lady doesn't want it." Lucy steadied herself. Her shirt moved over her bulging arm muscles. She cut her eyes toward Gray Band and locked in on him.

I wondered what Lucy did when she was in Lebabolis. With her kind of strength, they must've had her running security details all over the place. I bet she never needed a gun; she was scary enough without one, and she liked me. I imagined her on foot chasing down Deviants and arresting them barehanded. So far, meeting her was the only good thing about being here.

Gray Band pointed toward my chest, his eyes narrowed. "The lady may not want it, but without medical help she's going to die. No human's tough enough to survive that kind of wound alone. I saw what happened to her back there at the Range, you know. I was with the Coalition there. I also watched what they did just to keep her alive. Brakus said she'd just collapsed onto the floor before you came down here. It's fine, really."

Gray Band stepped toward me, but Lucy blocked his way. Their eyes met, and he added, "I'm unarmed. You really think they yanked you down here for me to do her in? That wound's bad enough; a swift enough kick right there, and she'd be a goner. Besides, you really think Brakus here'd let me try something after all this?"

I had to admit this was probably the dumbest way to do someone in. He could've killed me about eight times since he got here. I figured I was safe, but I still wasn't ready to let him know it. "You're a good talker, but so far you're not making me feel good about this." I heaved.

Brakus shook his head. "I'm gettin bored here. You can croak for all I care, but I got orders to keep you alive. Stall all you want, whatever. It's on you now." He turned and stabbed a finger in Lucy's face. "And you, tough girl, you best not get any ideas."

Lucy's jawbone twitched, and she gave Brakus a fiery glare in reply. She glanced at me, as if waiting for a silent command to go after Brakus.

"Alright, I really should get started." Gray Band's brow creased, his eyes coated in concern. His glance flicked to Brakus and then Lucy. "Look, can I just speak with her?"

Lucy eyed him and me then nodded. She stepped back but held a look on me that said a thousand words that she was staying close by.

"So help me, Gray Band, none of these guards will save you if you hurt her one bit, got me?"

Gray Band cocked his head and cleared his throat. A few beads formed on his forehead, but he managed a slight nod. Lucy eyed him another few seconds and then backed up, her eyes fixed on me, her expression like a protective mother bear.

Gray Band sat on the edge of the table. His eyes pleaded with me. He looked like he was about to tell me I had hours to live.

"Why are you even helping me?" It was my common response, for so long now. I missed back when people looked out for each other. It was better when I was young, if only a little. These days, even people who seemed to want to help me did anything but that.

Gray Band's face relaxed. "Would you believe I'm bored? I've spent several days with this crowd wide awake fixing people up best I can. It's not easy being the only medic around that's 80 percent well or better. Talk with me when you can say the same."

He explained how he was with the rest of our group down below. He talked about the near thousand ragged and Action troops in that fight that were now crammed up tight in this place. They were hidden even further below, in one of the spent shafts for Valentium, another hundred feet down. I felt better hearing about the rest of our people. Knowing for sure was nice; at least what I did hadn't gotten 'em all killed... yet, anyway. They were never gonna listen to me if we all got out of here though.

Gray Band had the air of a medic, alright. Medics, even in the Action, were well trained, and a lot of 'em knew it too; he wasn't an exception.

"I thought all you Gray Bands were Charista's favorites. Did you miss your ride or something?"

"Favorites of Charista? Is that any way to talk with someone who's fought with Jason's regiment?"

Charista didn't compete with many people for control, but Jason was one of 'em. If anyone had a chance of taking the lead of the Lebabolis military and making a play for total control, Jason was the guy. But, he chose country and order instead of the Action, even when Baudricort risked almost everything reaching out to him to break loose and leave. Baudricort considered it a big failing when he didn't get him with the Action.

My eyebrows raised. "Oh yeah? You're telling me you were with him?"

"I was. And during the fight against the Omegans while Kaitlinn handled the central Outlands and your group took the south, Jason headed them off at the north. They put up a big fight and had turned back a lot of the Omegans, but they just kept coming. They had one thing we didn't—plenty of fresh bodies."

Gray Band sighed. "We heard about Kaitlinn and the move to secure the Range with your group. We wanted to help. I know what you must think of us, the loyalists to Lebabolis, but we serve Lebabolis, not Charista. Harkson and Charista only wanted to serve their own interests. So, we tried to make our own move, and we were cast out from the regiment instead."

"How about Jason?" I asked.

"He's in Lebabolis, under the garrison order. Jason's not loyal to Charista either, don't misunderstand. But he also doesn't trust the Action. He and Baudricort never quite saw eye to eye, and, with the Omegans around, well, I guess he'd rather stick with the most fortified group for now. I wouldn't rule him out though; he's got a lot of troops who follow him. They figured it was better to group up against the Omegans."

"Funny, I thought that's what we were doing when we joined Charista."

"Charista wants control, and my guess is after a while we were more useful as a bargaining chip. She needs Cataclysm activated, and now that she's got it, she'll hole herself up until she gets it working, or they pry it from her cold dead hands."

"I heard they want to grab it back."

Gray Band stuck a needle in my arm, and I groaned as I felt heat flush through into my veins.

He tapped my cheek to get my attention. "You alright?"

"Yeah, keep going. So, the Omegans want Cataclysm. Isn't it their tech; can't they just reproduce it?"

"They could, but they don't want something like that in anyone else's hands. Trust me, I was brought up in the Intellectual Product system, and even though they trained me in medical, they covered a bit of the tech stuff, including Cataclysm. It's beyond lethal. If they even accidentally misfire it, it might bend the fabric of time itself. Charista is ready to use it, and she's got no clue what it will do."

Fear gripped me. For the longest, the enemies I faced were all external. This was different, and I froze with every new wave of pain that racked my body.

Lucy watched Gray Band for a while, their eyes locked. She held that stare, that Guard stare I'd seen in the eyes of Duncan's crew back at the Sector and on the field. Lucy's eyes looked like they weren't human for a few seconds. The battle had never ended for any of us. We'd been caught, and even though we weren't fighting right then, it was still on. I hated that I was like this, that they had done this to me. I was so weak; how much could I keep on going? At least I had one ally here. I hoped I had more, like Norg and the rest. If I got outta here at all in one piece and alive, it wasn't gonna happen alone.

Lucy held fast by the wall with her eyes locked on us, especially Gray Band. Her expression faded from protection to concern, and I realized that, of these people, this guy was the best at that time for helping me. The biceps on Lucy's arms bulged with her sharp breaths. Without a word I leaned back onto my elbows and nodded.

"Alright, now we're getting somewhere. By the way, the name's Ethan."

"Tell me straight, Ethan. Am I gonna die?"

Ethan's eyebrows arched. "If you are, I'm sure wasting my time then, aren't I?"

My throat hitched as I replied, "No jokes. No lies. Tell me."

The light mood from his eyes faded, and in its place was the cool collected gaze of a field surgeon about to jam their hands into a chest wound gushing blood. "I'll work on you like you were my own daughter."

I felt some tension release from my body. I lowered myself back down to the table. "That's better. Daughter, huh? What's her name?"

He kept his eyes on his work, but he whispered, "Clara."

That name, that single word and the way it trembled out of his mouth, had a helluva story with it, I bet. I also felt like I'd heard it before somewhere. There were probably a lot of families broken up in the Exodus. Joining the Action wasn't an easy choice for anyone, especially when not everyone in your family felt the same way. People wanted the best for their loved ones, and sometimes that meant letting them slip out while the ones left behind could stall and cover as best they could.

Even as Ethan started to prepare me for the procedure, my hazy mind managed to pull up a familiar memory, and the name he said registered something. Of course—the little girl we found after one of the raids. That was her name too.

"Was Clara, with the..."

"...Action? Yeah, she and her mother left in the Exodus. We didn't know how much time we had, and I figured I could give them more time to escape and delay them being caught in a search if I reported myself in, and them as deceased. I hoped Lebabolis found me useful as a medic, which thankfully they did. They were tracking Deserters on MODOSNet, and I did what I could to stall that without being noticed. Handy thing about Intellectual train- ing, they showed us enough of the system to cause a little damage. Plus, others who stayed to let their families get away like me had the inside track on some of the systems. Anyway, all that was over a month ago. I like to think Clara and Jean are still alive, but I heard what Lebabolis did to some of those Encampments. Can't say most days that I hadn't regretted staying and letting them go without me."

"Well," I said, "I ran into a little girl named Clara. She survived a raid. Hadn't seen anyone else, but I know people tended to scatter."

A tear jagged its way down his cheek. "Dirty blonde hair, bluish eyes?"

"Mmmhm."

Sad joy found his face just like that, and I lost any fear I had of him. He wasn't some hired assassin or a rogue interceptor serving Charista. He was a father who missed his family.

He stayed in that moment for only a few seconds more, then coughed himself back to fixing me, his eyes steeled over once again, but not before another stray drop leapt from one of his eyes. "They don't have the best equipment here, but I'll do what I can. I'll have to knock you out for a few, OK?"

As I watched Lucy and Ethan, a strange calm came over me. Thoughts of Baudricort filled my head. Maybe Ethan was legit, or I was just too tired and broken to care anymore. Wherever this feeling came from, lying down suddenly felt like a good idea. I said to Lucy, "I'm as sure as I can be about all this right now. I just know I've never felt so bad before, so getting that to stop is my number one right now. If there's more for me, it only happens after Ethan here works his magic."

ELEVEN

(NELSON)

LINEMAN RETURNED AND LED me back to the cell. Walking back was easier than my trip there at least. Dera had given me enough to think about for a good while.

Not only did the Omegans know about my work, but nothing that had happened had had anything to do with it; at least it wasn't my creation. I felt free in a sense. My connection to this world was either gone or a hell of a lot looser than before. Of course, that also meant whatever control I had or thought I had was also gone.

Whatever the case was, I still meant something to them. They hadn't escorted me around and treated me to this if that wasn't true. I'd have been lumped in with the rest a hundred feet below me if I wasn't special at all.

I just hoped I still had a way back. But, I'd found myself wondering, could "back" mean more than one thing? At that point though, there were several "ways" back I wanted. One of them was by Ana's side again.

What I meant to the Omegans, I wasn't sure. But whatever it was, I still had time. I needed Ana to be better.

I wondered about Dera's comments on Charista. All this time she was running things? As an Omegan? How could that have been? She looked human enough, on the outside anyway. Whether or not that was true, I knew the only one I'd trust with sharing that information was Ana.

I wondered what had made Charista switch sides. She must've had some of kind power play in mind. She wanted to destroy them and anyone who was against her like the Action. Whose side was she on other than her own?

I felt more and more like I had slipped into a large pool of quicksand, and each question only pulled me down further. I knew I was tired of trying to feel the Pull, and I hadn't been able to anyway. I wanted to focus on what I knew from now on.

I had no good feelings about what was in store for us. At least I knew part of their plans meant a trip off planet for us—and for good. That explained why they spent so much time with humans, and why they weren't interested in wiping us all out, at least not yet. They just wanted the ones they couldn't control to be eliminated. I wondered what visiting another world was gonna be like, but then again, I wasn't sure I'd ever see the outside of this place again. Charista was hot and heavy to get Cataclysm working, and if she wasn't careful, we were all gone.

Dawn eased her way back over to me after I'd been sitting for a few minutes. She eyed me but kept quiet as I got as comfortable as I could.

I was only gonna feel better when we were back calling our own shots. I laughed to myself when I realized I was sounding more and more like Ana.

I looked at Dawn. "I appreciate the sympathetic eye, but are you gonna tell me what you're thinking? You look like you're about to say you took the last cookie or something."

Dawn scoffed. "You still don't get it, do you? I get what you, Ana and probably the others are thinking, about the Omegans, if they're going to be taking us off world and all. But, I'm telling you, you shouldn't count Charista out just yet. Charista had lots going on, and not just at the Capital. She had projects all around Lebabolis, spread out. Sometimes it was because there were closer things available where she went. Others, it was a matter of keeping things split up in case she was hit by anything at any time. She must've known about the Omegans and what they'd do at any point, so she made a play to protect herself. Sector 5 was a major research arm for her. She was working on a lot of tech, things like masking tech that scrambled radars. The scramblers like Hell Hawk 91's got? That came from Charista's Sector 5 research."

I thought back to that place, I was taken there and almost got to see the inside before Ana busted me out. Later on, we made a stand against the Omegans there. Maybe they found out about it then. I guessed that explained why the Omegans wanted to hit it the way they did.

"They got wise, but Charista had been a few steps ahead as usual. She's got her plant reconfigured, only this time she's got one of her people watching over it."

"Llewyn."

"I see you've been paying attention. My suggestion to Ana, as long as she comes back in one piece, is we go after this place. She may even have hidden Cataclysm there all along, in plain view of the Omegans."

Anxiety ripped through me. The longer I stayed in that room, the worse it got. Aside from my worry about Ana and getting back to her as soon as possible, another thought popped into my head. If controlling Ana is what Dera and the Omegans wanted, they failed. All they just did was piss her off.

TWELVE

(ANA)

I CAME TO ON A BED with Lucy and Ethan nearby. My breathing was very slow, and I focused on my body for a few moments while I lay still. What was different? I still felt the pain in my chest, but now a lot of stiffness went along with it. I tried a deep breath and winced from a new pain. So, I still wasn't dead. But, I sure the hell wasn't living too well, either. Wherever I was, it wasn't the place that I was when Ethan started working on me. This room was lit just a little and the set of doors on the walls told me it had to be some kind of utility closet. Instead of a steel table, they had me on a bed, which felt much better.

"She's awake," Ethan murmured, a warm smile on his face. "How're you feeling?"

"Flattened, even more than before. Were you here the whole time, Ethan?"

"No, but this one was." He grinned and nodded toward Lucy, who smiled.

Every time I moved, I was rewarded with a patch of heat on the mattress from where my body had been lying. I also noticed a layer of sweat covered me all over.

"Hmm, yeah, feels a little better, soreness is less."

"Anesthesia'll do that." Ethan snickered as he tapped and adjusted several monitors.

"Alright, you've had your look. Am I gonna make it or not?"

"We'll see."

"What? I thought you were gonna fix me."

Ethan rolled his eyes. "Look, I did what I could with these supplies. I bought you more time."

Lucy and I shared a look, and my eyes met Ethan's again in a silent threat.

Ethan glanced at Lucy and back to me. "Look, without what I just did, you'd have probably bled to death in a few days, OK? Those chest pains you're feeling aren't a head cold, you know. You were pretty lucky; that stab missed several vital organs by inches. By the way, your lung was clipped, but I was able to patch that. You must be special to the Omegans for them to drag me up here like this, but be that as it may, you're still a human and you need to heal, so listen to me and take it easy for a few days."

"I'm not going anywhere soon."

"No, and that's a good thing, at least in your case." Ethan turned to Lucy. "When you're settled back in your cell, keep her legs up for a while. If she starts feeling more of that soreness or worse pain after a day or two, have them get me."

With that, Brakus came back with another Omegan who escorted Ethan away.

Lucyna walked me back. Without Brakus nearby, it seemed easier even though I was stiffer than before. I leaned on Lucy for our trip to our cell.

"Lucy, you're someone I need around me."

"I can deal with that."

"Norg really needs to meet you."

She flashed a worried look. "Norg... big guy? Scowls a lot?"

"Yeah; you met him? Didn't see him in either cell up there."

She shrugged and averted her eyes as we got out the elevator and trudged toward our cell.

"Saw him with the medics working on you in the field. He was pretty forceful, even gave the Omegans a time. He's got that Guard spirit alright. They took him away around the last time I saw the medics."

Something in Lucy made me stop and watch her. Seeing her and knowing she was with me, actually with me, sent a wave of calm over me, much more than any of the meds that Ethan had pumped into me.

She had this air, and I knew when she talked about how bad my wound was that she wasn't going to steer me wrong. I'd been wrong about Charista for sure. But here was someone I knew had always been on the outs. Charista had way more to lose by being honest than anyone in the Guard.

Our chances in this place were still pretty crappy, no doubt. But no one moved forward alone. I realized that more and more each passing hour.

(NELSON)

WHEN ANA AND LUCYNA came through the door to our cell, I could see she was as weak as I'd ever seen her. I jumped up to help Lucyna, and together we carefully brought Ana to her place by the wall, and we eased her down to a sitting position.

Ana was so pale and had this dazed look on her face. She was so far away from that woman who came across time for me, and who tried so hard and so many different times to convince me to jump through for her.

The sight of her like this broke my heart. I kept the concern out of my voice the best I could.

"How're you feeling?"

Her hair was stuck down to her forehead from sweat. She took a few slow breaths; her glance toward me was slightly dulled.

"Nelson, gotta tell ya, I've been a whole lot better."

"Guess so. Can't imagine you get impaled all the time."

"Heh yeah no." She whimpered as she shifted to her side for a better look at me. A few of the others in the room watched her as she moved herself gingerly.

She let loose with a deep, weighted sigh. "How about you? I would've pounded that bastard who popped you under other circumstances."

"I'll be OK. I had a nice chat with Dera. I've got news for you when you're ready."

Her eyes were heavy, but there was still an edge there, a glint that I'd seen before. It was faint but still there, thank God. Fires don't last forever though, not without some help. Leaving wasn't even on my mind. I saw a thousand cries for help in her eyes, way more than she was physically able to say on her own.

I nudged closer to her. I used to think this feeling I had toward Ana was a part of my Link to this place and time, but no, this was more. The feeling I had when I was near her was almost like the Pull I'd felt in the past to Cataclysm, only more of an emotional tie than just the physical one. And seeing her in this shape worried me like I'd never felt before, ever.

She lowered herself to the floor and laid her head on the makeshift pillow of rolled up clothes. With every attempt she made at a more comfortable position, she moaned and grimaced. After a few minutes of this, she pounded her fist on the floor. While she tried to get into some semblance of a comfortable position, I spelled it out to her, everything I'd learned. About the whole cover-up, the Omegan experiment on humans.

"Ana, it's worse about Charista than we thought. There's more to her than we could've imagined ever."

Ana nodded. "Charista needs to pay for this. The Omegans want to get her and Cataclysm. That's the play. But we're stuck here for now. We want the same thing."

"But if we do with the Omegans, we'll just be their prisoners, right?"

"Probably."

I asked, "So what is our option then?"

Ana pressed her lips together firmly. "We take it back."

"Take what back?"

"Control." Her eyes darted about the room. When they came back to me, I figured it was time for a bomb to be dropped. I didn't think she'd be ready for any of this, but not knowing how much time we had here, I figured it was best we get on with things.

"Ana, there's more Omegans around us than we realized."

"Huh?"

"Charista is an Omegan."

Ana blinked, as if something was caught in her eyes. She did nothing else at first, as if stunned from a blow to the face.

"What?"

"I was interrogated by one of the Omegans here named Dera. She gave me a lot of details about Charista and what they want from her. But it's true. Evidently, many years ago when this experiment was started, they wanted to monitor things, so they left some of their own, namely Charista. I'm not sure what happened to the others, but she was there. It was her the whole time."

Ana squinted. "But she looks human."

"I know. I guess with all their brilliance they've figured out making a doppelganger of humans as well."

Ana shook her head. I knew where she was at mentally because I was in the same neighborhood.

Ana wheezed. "How the hell could—oh, I can't be surprised anymore. Nothing that happens now is in our control; we've been dangled at the end of a string over a pit of fire. And at any point they're gonna cut our cord and we'll be gone."

"Dawn's got some ideas on how we can maybe get inside, if we ever get out of here."

"You trust her, Nelson?"

"As much as I can trust any of these people. Even more than her, I trust Kado, and he said that if Charista gets control of Cataclysm and manages to fire it, there's no way of knowing what might happen. She wants to stop the Omegans, but she isn't sane enough to think what she's risking in the process. Kado researched it and told me in the cave when we found it. It's unstable. The Quantum energy it has harnessed could rip the fabric of reality apart if it malfunctions."

"And she's crazy enough to try it."

"Of course. She's got her own world, and she won't let it go no matter what."

I thought about what that meant, having a world and not letting go. There was so much I'd held to, even in this place and that connection I'd had. Now that it was gone, I wished it was back. Without it, I felt incomplete.

"There might be a way out of it," I replied. "Dera talked about Cataclysm and something she calls a Spike that can shut it down. But to do that, they've got to get this device implanted in Cataclysm. It won't work otherwise. They tried to do this years back, but Petra stopped them when she stole Cataclysm and hid it."

"Was Petra hiding it for the Omegans or for Charista?" Nelson asked.

"I'm sure neither. Petra knew it was too powerful for anyone. And since destroying it was too risky with the link to the Valentium, she did the next best thing: hid it so it would be out of everyone's reach for years."

"We have to get to Charista." Ana glanced off as if she'd listened to someone else make that statement, and she nodded her head in agreement.

"But isn't she hunkered and bunkered in, locked up tighter than a drum?" I asked. I saw a spark behind Ana's eyes begin to take shape.

"Yep. It's impossible or at best not even remotely easy. But whatever has been? The Omegans are rounding up Valentium, and they need more, but if they're getting it as fast as they say, soon the places to look for it will run out, so they'll be focusing on the Lebabolis Capital before long. Then they'll have to face her. How will we handle Charista and the Omegans at the same time when we couldn't stop either before?"

I said, "We've got some decisions to make. First of all, how much we want to cooperate with these people."

"These people, the ones who corralled us in here, took away everything, gave us little to no food, these people?" Ana coughed.

"Everyone wants something," I said. "We know what they're after. Maybe we should give it to them. We'll get further for now if we play along. They're sending transports for us all. We aren't staying here. Anyway, they didn't waste their time on us just to bury us here, so the human race was given another shot, only this time we've been tagged for our usefulness. It's the damned product system again, but this time there's only one classification."

"Slaves."

"How long do we have?" Ana asked.

"Dunno. A week? Days? Less?"

FOURTEEN

(ANA)

T HE NEXT DAY, I WAS ABLE to sit up more. The pain was still there, but it had gotten better. Nelson never left my side during the night, and I was glad for that. I felt better just knowing he was close. The sight of him calmed me and made my pain, and our situation, easier to take.

Lucy kept watch too, from the corner of the room. My faithful sentry and new friend.

According to Nelson, we had a few days, if that, to try something before the Omegans took us away for good. Once again, things were out of our hands, and we were about to leave this place for more of the unknown. I hated that more of the Circle weren't close by, but it was what it was. I was alive, and that meant there was a chance.

They started bringing us food. Nelson claimed it was his doing, but I think they wanted to save their collective asses with their leader until our transports arrived. I figured the Omegans were busy enough out on the prowl, hitting Charista. Since they had us locked up, they had more time to scour for the rest of the Valentium. All we had to do was sit and wait for something to happen, whenever and whatever it was.

610

I had to think Duncan was long gone. A good warrior always knew to avoid a fight they couldn't win. But, no one avoided this fight, if what I'd heard about Cataclysm was true. Simply running from a weapon like that while still staying on this planet was suicide.

What was the point anymore? Maybe that was just it. Maybe Duncan was tired of the fight. All those years, it never came to anything good for him, only survival in whatever existence the Guard had in the Outlands. Maybe they just had no one else left to fight for? I still had Varrick and Nelson. It would've been a lot harder for me to keep going without them around.

Aside from Nelson and my new watchdog Lucy, I was grateful my mind had cleared more each hour since I woke up from Ethan's procedure. I felt more like a part of the group in the cell instead of just another casualty needing attention.

Every bit of strength that came back to me focused one thought into my mind stronger each passing moment. *I wasn't meant to die in here, neither were the rest of our people. We've just gotta wait for our time, our opportunity. We'll get free from this, no matter what. That's what Baudricort would've wanted.*

A warrior always needed all the facts they could get on their situation. The rest was just belief and determination for the outcome you wanted. That's what Treg told me once. None of his lessons over the years had ever left me.

I thought back to the procedure and Lucy. She was ready to fight Brakus and Ethan; I bet all I had to do was just tell her to and she'd have gone off on 'em. Even though she was wounded, still a prisoner, overpowered, she hadn't backed down, hadn't given up. That Guard spirit was amazing. She was ferocious. And she believed in me. Maybe that voice I'd lost contact with changed form, and it was now her.

Soon my thoughts went to our escape, and if that happened, what came next. A list formed in my head, one that had been building for a time. I knew there were two people I'd be damn sure saw me with their own eyes once I was free. Most important was

Charista. Once and for all, her ass went down. I didn't care if she took me with her. Of course, that was only after I had a little talk with Llewyn.

As bad as Charista was, I at least respected the fact she never changed. She always looked out for herself, always would. Llewyn, on the other hand, sold us out. The thought of having a go at him fueled me and got me distracted from thoughts about what our escape might look like and my frequent pain.

I knew I was better when my mind went to planning again, Baudricort's mind working through me. It warmed me and turned my urge to cry about him into missing him. It wasn't as good as him being there, but thoughts of him were all I had, and that had to be enough.

Since I'd woken up, Nelson started wandering around the room, stretching his limbs. Once he had enough of that, he plopped back down beside me.

"You doing OK?"

"Pain's a little better, so I guess I'll live. How bout you?" I asked.

"Eh, guess about the same. I've been trying to find out what I can about the Omegan guards but so far nothing."

"Nelson, just forget it. We're not getting anything out of them."

He nodded for a moment, then grinned and arched an eyebrow. "Well, good thing they're not the only ones I tried getting information from."

"Oh?"

Nelson's eyes got this twinkle that I'd gotten used to during my time with him. It came over his eyes when he had something clever in mind. I was glad the days were gone when that cleverness involved him running off on his own and leading me on some crazy chase.

"I know Dawn's the person you trust least in here, maybe even less than the Omegans, but she and I chatted while you were getting the what have you, and Dawn drops the tidbit that Charista had other sites for research and weapons."

"So what? If they're all holed up in Lebabolis on a Lockdown, all the other sites are shut off. There's no point in being around any of 'em; they're just a bunch of structures with no power and no defenses at all."

"Actually, no," Nelson said as he held a finger up toward me. "Turns out they're not all dormant, and Dawn's pretty sure he went to one."

I squinted hard at Nelson and hoped my improving mind hadn't taken a step back. He gave me a half smile in return, and continued. "Dawn told me she overhead him mentioning coordinates for a destination. They tie into one of the old facilities in a Sector."

So, Llewyn's little move was more strategic than we'd realized. "Really now."

"Yep. He's holed up with reinforcements, waiting for Charista to meet him there."

"I don't get it. Why'd she split her numbers when she's in the Lebabolis Capital, the obvious target?"

Nelson crossed his arms in thought. "Maybe she thought she had more time for a getaway?"

"I guess. Charista's so crazy, who can tell what she's thinking anymore."

"What do we do?" Nelson asked.

Names, places, people, thoughts fell more into line in my mind. Through that recipe of memory, plans were the next ingredient that came together, and one idea bubbled its way to the top of the rest. Even I had to admit this thought was a bit crazy, but sometimes, when so much is against you, a little crazy is what you need.

"Nelson, it's really simple. We steal Cataclysm. Just grab it back. The Omegans want it. Charista's got it. Let's grab it; then we'll definitely be calling the shots."

Nelson sighed. "Stealing a weapon from the middle of a combat zone in the most heavily fortified place known from an insane woman who'd probably cut her own head off first to stop us. Am... I missing any details here?"

"We can stay here, wait for our ride, and let whatever happen to us. But, if we go with the Omegans, we'll lose the chance to claim this world as our home; we'd only be transplants in a foreign place, way below zero. Or, for maybe the first time, we take control. If we can get Cataclysm, then they all have to deal with us."

Nelson nodded. "Won't be easy."

"We've gotta try. Maybe it won't work, and Charista fires Cataclysm and ends all of this. Maybe the Omegans won't be stopped and they'll take us away to be their specimens for the rest of our probably short lives. Life's got plenty of bad outcomes. But we won't have a chance at a decent life if we don't try something other than lining up like pieces of freight."

"You have a point. Well, we know they've gotta get us up top first, so what, we make a move then?" Nelson asked.

"They're only transporting us, so maybe they'll have a smaller group of soldiers. I mean, we're all in here, weaponless and half starved. They wouldn't waste the number of troops they fought us with at the Range if we're just being loaded onto ships."

Nelson nodded. "Good chance of that. Let's say we do it, bum rush these bastards and get one over on them. Then what? We've gotta deal with the Omegans storming the Lebabolis Capital, then get through to Charista and grab Cataclysm, right?"

I stroked my temples, working my brain into deeper thoughts. "Yeah, but breaking into the Capital's probably gonna be tougher than making our way through the fight that's gonna be happening outside. See, there's one thing Charista was always good at—security. Locking her precious Capital up tight was never a problem. Kado and Otto used to tell me all about the security systems. It pretty much went over my head, but I figured that if they were that impressed it had to be pretty severe a system."

"Can the Lebabolis garrison even hold off the Omegans with their firepower and Darkness?"

Once again, my painful history as a Lebabolis Worker Product gave me a handy bit of inside information. "Nelson, you don't understand. Intellectual Products in Lebabolis studied Valentium for a long time and found a lot of uses for it. Beyond the energy production from Valentium, Intellectuals developed newer uses for the substance; some involved using it to strengthen metals and things."

"Yeah, like walls?" Nelson asked.

"Yep. Those outer walls of the Capital are laden with Valentium reinforcements. Baudricort told me so himself. I bet the Omegans know it too, or they'd have blasted it to kingdom come long ago."

"Oh right; I remember how bad that Verge site blew up when you shot at all the concentrated Valentium there," Nelson said.

"Yeah. They're gonna have to work their way in without blowing the place apart, and so would we." I pulled my legs into a crossed position, grimacing from the effort.

Nelson glanced about the room. "We're in a spot, aren't we?"

"When are we not?" I chuckled weakly.

I'd started trying my regular routine of getting comfortable when a shrill alarm in the hallway stopped me, and I edged upright again. Cascading red lights filled the rooms with swarms of beams. They bounced off the walls and lit up people in our cell as they swirled about.

"What the hell's that?" Lucy asked.

I wondered if Kado had gotten Cataclysm working and Charista had activated it. If that was the case, we were all in for something.

But it wasn't that. Omegan soldiers ran past us down the hall. Some bellowed, "Enemy force approaching!" Maybe Jason's regiment in Lebabolis had busted loose and come looking for us? Maybe they figured out that not only Charista wasn't on the up and up, but she was actually an Omegan.

I looked at the door and was surprised when my vision snapped to as if something in me reset. My pulse picked up a bit. The others in the room crept near the window at the mad scene that unfolded. I turned to Lucy.

"Seeing as how we're all locked up, whatever's going on has gotta be bad for 'em." A wicked smile found my face. Lucy and I shared a glance, and she grinned as well as she edged toward the door.

Several loud blasts rumbled outside, and the jolt knocked

everyone off their feet. I braced against the wall and gasped from the impact. Shouts and yells rang out and got louder.

I felt my midsection tighten. The wounds, the fear, got pushed down. The switch flipped, and I was ready. Adrenaline saturated my body like water on a desert plain. I was ready to fight, with whomever it was and make them pay for every drop of blood they took from us.

The lights dimmed. I whispered, "Lucy, back up from that door."

We crouched low in the darkness. The sound of our breathing was drowned out by the growing sound of pattering feet. I felt the incision in my chest throb, and I coughed a bit. Whomever it was, they were gonna deal with us for sure.

The first one came into the hallway. The dim light showed a mane of hair, and the glow of a pulse rifle shot a beam of light around the room. They got close to the door and flung the rifle up. "Lucy, that you?"

She looked toward me then shook her head. "Yeah! Berg?"

"Yep."

"Well, damn; I wouldn't be happier to see your ugly ass if you had food."

Berg grinned, his eyes fixed on Lucy for a moment. He yelled back up the hallway, "Sir, in here; they're in here!"

"And below," I added. "Lots more below."

WHILE THREE OTHER GUARD TROOPS headed down the elevator to see about the rest of our group, Berg herded us together and we began our climb up the stairways to the outside. Berg took the lead; his large frame almost filled the entire stairway ahead of us. I was close behind, with Lucy and Nelson helping me.

"So Lucy, this guy's a friend of yours?" Nelson asked.

Lucy chewed her lip for a few steps and kept silent. Her eyes said plenty though.

"Hey, you sweet on him or what?" I asked.

Lucy tried holding back a smile, but she failed miserably. "Let's just say we know each other pretty well."

"Uh huh."

When we got topside, Berg directed us behind a destroyed vehicle, then he took off to join the fight. I happily sucked in the fresh air and eased myself next to the huge burned out hulk of charred metal while everyone followed suit. It felt good to be outside again and breathing air without the stench of rot.

The Omegans had left a small detail, as I'd suspected. Most were hunkered in a circle, firing on whatever Guard troops came close, but at that point it was pretty useless for the Omegans, even those who ran about, firing every way they could.

There was plenty to see elsewhere, especially overhead. Hell Hawks swooped about and fired on the Omegans at will. The Omegans fired back at the attacking Guard troops and managed to hit some of the aircraft, but the Guard's onslaught continued. The roar of another ground unit got really loud and clear in the near distance as more Guard troops, hundreds of men and women, charged the Omegans. I marveled at the skill they showed.

Lucy howled with delight at the scene around us.

"How'd they find us? I hadn't turned the beacon back on." I said.

The sight of Dawn to my right made me clench again, but there was too much else to see for me to have focused on her long.

I turned back to the fight and soon was fixated. It was unreal. The Guard swept forward, a lot like they did that time I saw 'em back in the Sector when they attacked a group of Omegans with sticks, rocks and spent rifles. But this time, they were armed and so much more fearsome.

These Guard troops weren't just scavengers like the others I'd seen before. This was a pack of hungry predators, their prey our soon to be former captors.

Several loud explosions slammed into the ground, and we ducked for cover. I winced in pain as my chest was enveloped with a deep throbbing. I clutched it as Nelson and Lucy help me to my feet.

Once I was standing again, I spotted the Omegan transport in the distance about 100 yards from us. The Guard had blasted away all of its escorts, and there it stood, waiting for its cargo like a faithful animal.

The air crackled with pulse weapon fire, and the clang of weapons that found their mark. Off to my side, I heard a familiar voice shouting orders and caught a glimpse of Duncan as he surged past. He looked a lot different than the last time I'd seen him. He was full on in the thick of it and slugged through the fray with the intensity of a battle tested warrior. He fired his weapon over and over, sighting and taking out Omegans on all sides.

A Hell Hawk swooshed by overhead—it looked like a Hell Hawk, but in much more disrepair than I'd ever seen. Guess these guys just made the most of what they had and got by. However they survived, they made it with no help from anyone else, just scraps of food and gear they managed to steal. And I thought the Action was tough for making it on their own like they did. The Guard had even less, and they lasted way longer than the Action could've ever claimed.

After several minutes, the Guard wiped out the remaining group of Omegans on the scene. The Hell Hawks swarmed about and blasted the rest of the Omegan vehicles nearby until they were smoldering wrecks except for the nearby transport.

Berg jogged close by again and waved us all back down to the ground. "Better stand down for now; once the Guard gets into a fight it's not always easy for them to disengage. Good idea y'all lay low for now until we get things settled."

Lucy rolled her eyes and grabbed his shoulder, a definite smirk on her lips. "OK, cowboy, just tell the Old Man we're over here so they don't zap us too."

The collection of wrecked vehicles oozed fire and smoke into the air. I felt a wave of strength shoot through me like a well-aimed sniper shot and beamed at the Guard troops. I wanted to know 'em all and figure out what I had to do different this time to get 'em to join us for real. I knew we needed 'em if we'd ever have any shot at all of winning this mess.

The Guard troops closest to us turned and braced their weapons for a second before they saw Berg and gave shouts and raised their hands up in joy. Duncan headed over to Lucy, and after a few seconds of greeting, she pointed towards us.

Duncan smiled as he approached. "I figured they'd mount a big offensive with their force to capture you. We pulled back and circled around, so we could hit 'em when they least expected. Omegans are tough, but they've got their weak spots too. We've fought them long enough to know how to get over on them."

He watched his troops like a proud parent. These warriors who'd lost so much: their country, their purpose, in some cases their families. I realized then, Duncan probably wasn't just a leader to his people, but a reminder of their time with Petra when answers were easier, doubts were smaller, and the enemy clearer.

Duncan checked back with his group on the roundup of any gear from the Omegans. I caught a few glimpses of Guard troops that passed nearby, eyeing me and my fellow former prisoners with awe.

The looks the Guard troops gave me made me uncomfortable. These people went through ten times what I'd seen. I should've bowed to 'em for what they'd survived. I wondered if I was ever gonna feel like I belonged with 'em.

After Duncan checked with the Guard troops that ran around picking up all the gear they could, Duncan returned to my side. "Thanks for the beacon, by the way."

I shook my head. "Huh? I hadn't turned it on."

"I did," Lucy said from behind us. As she walked closer toward Duncan and me, she shrugged and ran a hand through her hair. When she caught my open-mouthed gaze, she added, "If you didn't think each and every one of us in the Guard knows all about the Valkyrie, you weren't paying attention." She laughed. "When you went down in the Range, I saw it on your waist. You still don't get it, do ya? You think that knife you had all this time is just some piece of gear? You never wondered what the hell that was gonna do against a pulse weapon? I activated it. Whatever happened to that blade since, it was sending and gave the Guard our exact location."

I grabbed for the blade out of instinct, but of course it wasn't there. Duncan smirked. "Oh I'm sure we'll uncover it and a bunch more once we get the rest of your people free."

Suddenly, thoughts of other names came into my head, like Dera, Brackus, and Ancus, and fear gripped me thinking they may have circled around for their own surprise attack. "Duncan, there were some officers in that group watching us, Ancus... Dera... Brakus?"

Duncan squinted at me. "No clue; you can sift through that pile we made of the rest of them, but I'm thinkin' those were your run of the mill grunts. Anyone who was a leader or of any important most likely bailed before we came callin."

As I watched the Guard troops, I felt a lump form in my throat. I was more than grateful for the reinforcements, but what lay ahead of us was still pretty scary. I knew I needed help, but the words to ask for it still weren't easy for me. "Duncan, I can't do this without you. I'm pretty sure Charista's hell bent on firing Cataclysm to stop the Omegans."

"Wouldn't put it past her." Duncan wiped his brow.

I looked at the rest of the Guard troops as they mopped up the scene. "So how many more are there of you?"

Duncan gazed about him in a mental inventory. After a few seconds, he replied. "This is about it. Any other stragglers ain't gonna be worth what these are here."

Duncan turned in time to catch Berg as he trotted up close.

"Sir, we've located the loading mechanism for this facility. Confirming approximately two thousand troops down below. We're working on getting the system to run again; it's been out of service for a while, but it's our best chance at getting all those people out quick."

Duncan nodded. "Let's get them outta there, then."

As Duncan waved a few of his troops over, we walked toward the rear of the Valentium Facility. "You did pretty well against these Omegans," I said. "Ever think about picking on a group your size?"

Duncan laughed. "What you got in mind?"

I chuckled at his question, since I knew damn well he knew exactly what I meant. As much as I'd bombed last time I asked him, I figured if I didn't try again, our shot at Charista and surviving any of this was zero. So, I went into the story, what we'd learned so far. "The Omegans want to collect Cataclysm and release us, which to me is another way of saying they'll wipe us all out."

Duncan sighed. "Lot stacked up against you, ain't there?"

"Yeah. Look, we really need your help. You can't know how hard it is for me to say that. As long as Charista stays in power and the Omegans are at our door, none of this fighting ever ends. And it needs to. I need to stop 'em, and I need your help."

As I heard myself say what I'd denied for so long, I felt the weight I'd carried with it lift off me. A sob forced its way out before I caught it. I hated feeling helpless, but I was equally tired of denying I was. I slumped to the ground. My chest stung bad. I had a feeling that pain was gonna be around, maybe for good. My annoying little friend. I'd never felt more scared and angry at the same time. I knew what I had to do, but how was I gonna get there? I needed help, plain and simple. But, I'd said my piece. The rest was up to Duncan.

My voice quavered more, but by then I didn't really care anymore. "Duncan, I don't understand. You say you recognized me by my eyes. So why didn't you join up with us; why not? Is this it; are you leaving again? We need you... I need..."

He crouched beside me, his eyes full of compassion. He grasped my shoulder and a glint of moisture hit his eye. "I tell ya, these old eyes have seen plenty. Fights, scratching for food to survive, even some of my own people turnin' on each other when times got a little too rough. I still remember how it was, though. The days when Petra was with us, leading us. And when I first saw you back in the Sector, I felt like it was true, that you were somehow her or her daughter. But, my head was so stuck in survival mode so long, I ended up ignoring it. I wanted to think it wasn't real, that you weren't real, and us meeting didn't happen, anything at all. But then I saw you in that fight. You were outnumbered by the Omegans in every way, but you didn't back down. That's when I knew, sure as anything, who you were, and that I needed to help you. You've changed this old fool, and you reminded me of a time when things were better. I want to make that time come again, and I figure best chance is together, and with you. I ain't going nowhere that isn't by your side. All of us."

My throat seized up hearing about Petra. I felt in my heart that she wasn't gone; I'd never believed that she was. I'd heard her voice on the Link, and that was good enough for me, because it had to be. But now, the sight in Duncan's eyes, this strong man who let a few tears loose just talking about her, made her all the more real and what she meant to these people. She got them to stand and hold the line. I realized too, that was who I came from. And it was time I took my spot in that line.

He motioned several Guard troops over, and as one they formed an arc facing me. It was like when I saw that group of them in the Sector, but now it was only honor and respect for me in their gaze.

Duncan bowed to me. "I'll never doubt you again. You've got the Guard behind you, Ana Crucinal. All the way with you to the very end."

I felt a catch in my throat, and a few more teardrops eased their way down my face. All I ever wanted was to find a place of my own. I thought by running I'd have found it at some point. I always figured if you searched long enough, the sheer odds of finding what and who you were supposed to be was greater.

But all this time chasing it, I had flown past people ready to give that to me. Right then, I saw it in Duncan's eyes. It was also in the eyes of the others here, reflected back to me. Stories behind each glimpse, each person... regret, relief, and a rally to stand. These people wanted more, needed more, and deserved more. I wanted to find a place to be safe, but I'd never thought until then that I had that place all this time since I left Lebabolis. These people were the home I'd looked for. They were the safety I wanted and needed. My family was way bigger than I could've ever realized.

ONCE THE GUARD had picked the Omegan corpses clean of gear, they formed up and lined all their vehicles around the area outside the Ulter Facility. The sight of the five Hell Hawks, three transports, and hundreds of soldiers gave me even more hope than getting out of our cell did.

The Guard troops had some different markings on their uniforms; I figured they were some kind of grouping, maybe for where they lived. They had survived for so long out here, it made sense they had some kind of system going. They probably formed a society, with someone like Duncan running things. I wondered how different they were from what Lebabolis had. At least their deal wasn't about anyone living as slaves like the sweet Lebabolis Products did.

We had our biggest challenge ahead of us, but I knew with the Guard around it was at least in reach. The Guard troops milled about, some checked their newly taken Omegan gear while others took a look at our group for any familiar faces. I smiled when I found Lucy in the crowd. She'd gotten with her old group, her face lit up as they crowded around her, sharing stories about the fights and our recent capture, I'm sure. She waved me over.

"Ana, meet my clan; we're a scrappy bunch." She pointed to me, her eyes sparkling with wonder. "This here's the Valkyrie."

When they saw me, their expressions faded into ones of reverence. One of 'em remarked, "She looks just like her."

A knot formed in my stomach. Hearing the word 'Valkyrie' and the way they said it still felt like it was meant for someone besides me.

SIXTEEN

THE LARGE ELEVATOR IN THE REAR of the facility, once used for transporting Valentium out of the caverns for shipments, was shut down, but Berg, Duncan, and a few Guard people got it running again, and we started moving our group from the cavern up slowly.

After about twenty minutes, they began coming out. All of 'em looked dazed, whether they were Guard troops, Action soldiers, or the Gray Bands.

The Guard already assembled outside gave cheers when people appeared, and the shouts got louder whenever one of their own showed up in the freed groups.

I wondered what food the ones kept below ate, if they had anything at all. We were given next to nothing, so I had no clue what they'd have tossed down into that hole. When those coming out of the cavern saw me, their expressions picked up, like I was a pool of water in a desert or something. A few smiles even came my way too. I hoped I was still the person they thought I was.

Treg was in the first group. His face was covered in dirt and grime, but he managed a huge smile, and wrapped his arms around me. He released when I grimaced.

"You OK?"

"Yeah; they patched me up, and it's still taking a little getting used to."

"We thought you were a goner."

"Think again," I said. "I was too stubborn to die. So, how was it down there?"

He smirked and cut his eyes at me as if I'd expected a story about a secret underground paradise instead of the grimy hole it was. "Mostly dark, except for a few lights."

"A little ironic, huh? I was the one trained for places like that, but you went there instead."

Treg bent back in a stretch. "Woulda gladly traded. The smell of Valentium residue was bad, but after a day or two the other odors took over."

"No need for a detailed brief." I giggled.

"How about you?" he asked, his eyes steeled with concern.

"I'll live."

"You better. So, they actually helped you out? That's wild."

"More like they got one of ours to do it. Well, a Gray Band named Ethan."

"Oh, yeah, I saw him a few times. We kept him busy down there. The Omegans yanked him after a few days. We figured he was the daily meal or something."

I grinned. "Glad you and the rest are back. We need everybody we can get at this point."

Norg found me soon after. All that time down in the hole did nothing good for his personality; no big surprise. He managed a grin when he saw me, though.

"Hey you."

"Hey yourself. Ready to get back in the fight?"

"Beyond ready. What's the plan?"

"It's developing. But, if I've got any say, and I do, it includes a trip to whoop Charista's ass once and for all."

"Hell yeah." Norg nodded with a devious grin.

Along with Treg and Norg, we drew close, and the Circle came together, our smaller version of it, for at least a moment. We watched each other with a mix of happiness that we'd managed to keep together and wonder over what could've happened to Zengus, our childhood friend turned traitor.

Jacobs joined us after a while of the troops clearing the elevator. His hair was as dirty as I'd ever seen it. He took a drink of water and was already set to go. "So, what're we doing?"

"We're figuring it out, but it's gonna revolve around shutting Charista down for the last time."

Jacobs wiped his mouth, his lips formed into a tight line and he nodded. "Works for me. Just get me in the air. I'll do a helluva lot more damage topside."

His eyes were red, but that fire was still there. I swelled up under the gaze of a true Action soldier. If he and I made it outta this, I promised myself to ask him just how he got so in with a group of Guard troops to lead them into our fight at the Range.

"There's your ride." I pointed the Hell Hawks out to Jacobs.

Duncan had walked near the aircraft and was talking with the crew when I whistled for his attention.

"Duncan, got room for another flyer?"

Duncan looked at the Hell Hawks around him and then back to Jacobs. "I suspect they can arrange something."

Jacobs nodded. "Great." He sauntered off and soon joined the group of pilots, like a long-lost relative being welcomed back at a family reunion.

As more people came up, the crowd filled further around us. I soon noticed Nelson standing next to me. "Looks like you got your army."

"Sure does." I turned from the scene of people checking weapons and equipment and gazed into Nelson's eyes. I would've loved if he had one of his epiphanies right then, like when he physically found Cataclysm. But, I had a gut feeling those were gone forever. "The Guard, with the rest of Kaitlinn's forces, are our fist. But, we need some kinda finesse to slip inside. Maybe there's a back door in, something the Omegans don't even know about."

Dawn's voice popped off to the right of us. "How about the displacement portal?"

"Do what now?" I asked.

Dawn narrowed her eyes and smiled. "Over the years, Charista became obsessed with Valentium and other possible uses for it. The time jumps were a nice extra, but jumping through space has an advantage of its own. It started as a way to get access inside the Capital from a Station close by outside. We created a prototype around the time the Baudricort and the Action made their break, and after that it was abandoned until things settled back down. I know where the prototype is outside the Capital. Trust me, if there's any kind of siege going on there, it's the only way in."

"But is this it even operational anymore?" I asked.

Dawn shrugged. "It's a risk, but I say it's worth it considering what we're trying to do."

"And you know how to activate it?" I asked.

Dawn nodded. "I've got some access, but I'll need a higher-level credential if we're gonna do this. I didn't have the upper tier access for that project."

"Well, that's just great. You've taken this time to tell us this why?"

Dawn's face twisted in a sneer. "Look, Ms. Lookin-For-Ideas, don't shoot something down just because you don't like it. I was about to tell you there's someone who just might have a way into that portal... Llewyn."

Just when Dawn had me ready to slug her, she laid a golden egg at my feet. "Continue."

Dawn's face beamed. "Before Llewyn pretended to be all cozy with the Action, he was leading the Intellectual Design team. They did plenty around Lebabolis, not the least of which included security.

He had access to a lot, and I'll bet if he made the deal he did with Charista, he's still got all that access and maybe more we couldn't even think of yet."

I watched her, and too many times of the switches and double crosses crept up in my brain. "Dawn, just tell me this. After all we've been through, why in the ever-loving hell should I give this information of yours serious consideration?"

Dawn nodded, and her head sank for a moment. Then her eyes met mine again. "You don't get to own betrayal. Charista left me here, same as you. You might call me a Gray Band like those others, but I'm done with what Charista's been doing."

"That goes for me too." Ethan had walked up close with a few other Gray Bands during our talk. He grasped the Gray Band on his arm and ripped it loose. The other Gray Bands did the same. I looked at them on the ground, tossed out like garbage, and watched their faces as they looked at me with grim determination.

"Well, alright. We need all the help we can get. And let's get something straight. We called this the Coalition since it was Lebabolis, but I think we can all agree that Lebabolis stands for something none of us want. We want to be free, and that's what the Action always was about. Baudricort died making sure that lived on. He must have known about what was going on or at least had some idea to want to move us so far away from the Lebabolis lands. You are now and will always be members of the Action."

That name floated in the air and felt as comfortable to me as anything I'd known. It was so much more than the escape it meant to me at first. It was the family I never knew I needed, a cause that I wanted, and a future that had the most promise of any I'd had yet.

Still, my gut hadn't been the best guide for me so far, so I gazed deep into Dawn's eyes for some flicker, any hint of doubt behind her glance. I wanted to believe what she told me, but I knew too painfully well how much my gut had steered me places I shouldn't have been, so my head took the reins for a bit.

"Alright, Dawn. You've got an interesting idea here. But first off, we've gotta find out more if Llewyn even has this thing you're talking about. We've spent too much time chasing promises of deals that fell through."

I looked at Nelson, and he nodded. "How about we ask some people who could've been closer to Llewyn?"

Kaitlinn's name sat right in front of me. She may have had an idea. I hadn't seen her with the groups coming out of the cavern, though. I walked through the growing crowd with Dawn and Nelson following a few feet behind. After a few minutes, I found Kaitlinn chatting with Nycole. Nycole gave me a once over glance and nodded. Kaitlinn's lips curved slightly in a smile, but her eyes had another message.

"So you're alive," Kaitlinn said.

"Looks that way," I answered.

"What are you looking to do?"

"For one, get some payback. Two, get rid of the big problem called Charista. I think you'd at least agree with me on that one. Three, knock her house down and start over the right way."

Kaitlinn nodded her head as she eyed the troops. "I can go along with that. Much better than being ditched down a hole again. So, what's the play, Valkyrie?"

I caught a look at Dawn watching us from the corner of my eye and chuckled a bit to myself. "So, Dawn over there says Llewyn might have some kind of super-secret access that we can use to break into the Capital while all hell's breaking loose outside. Are you familiar with anything like that, or are you, Nycole?"

Kaitlinn's brow creased, and she shook her head slowly, but Nycole cocked her head back. "I know what she's talking about."

I eased closer to Nycole. "Do tell."

She ran her hands around her weapon, caressing it like it was an infant. Her eyes looked off in thought. "Kind of makes sense, after all. Llewyn was running research programs for Charista, so him having that type of access wouldn't be the biggest shocker. Besides, during our fight with the Omegans at the Range, I saw something he was carrying."

I waved Dawn over as Nycole continued. "He had it on his hand; looks like a Verge tether bracelet but not so much. The upper tier has them. They grant privileged access. I bet you anything, you get one of those, you can slip past security, even if they're being overrun."

Kaitlinn clasped her chin in thought. "But you still need to bust in there during a fight that will probably be going on and tearing the place outside apart."

Dawn breathed a confident sigh. Kaitlinn's face was pretty static, though. Out of any of these people, I trusted her the most. Any leader worth anything had to be on the straight and narrow, since any mistakes they made usually cost lives.

"OK," I said. I eyed Kaitlinn and swallowed hard. Duncan had thrown in with me, but without her this whole idea was just as hopeless if Duncan wasn't on our side.

"Kaitlinn, I think you'll agree there isn't any other way out of this that doesn't involve a move against the Capital. You've got the bulk of the troops at your command here. I know I steered us wrong before, but I'm just asking that you—"

Kaitlinn thrust her hand up. At first I thought, *Yeah she's done. She's heard this all too much, just like Duncan did when I approached him the first time.*

But instead, she said, "I've sworn an oath, years ago, before a lot of you were old enough, to fight for and protect Lebabolis. I did that because I believed in the city, but not Charista. This twisted joke that Charista has put upon us has to be stopped. We're ready. And the daughter of Petra is as good a person I can think of to throw in with. We'll come between the Omegans and do everything we can to fight them so you can bust in and take back our world. We'll start over. I promise myself to you, Ana Crucinal. I pledge my loyalty and my troops to your watch."

Kaitlinn's mouth curved into a smile. I swallowed hard again and cleared my throat.

"OK, well, the outside fight is key to this idea. You've got to give the Omegans and Lebabolis garrison enough to handle until we can nab Cataclysm."

"We'll rain hell on them to the last. How long do you need?"

"We'll need a day or two to hit Llewyn."

Kaitlinn's eyes looked at the assembled troops. "Do your best; we'll hold them off as long as we can."

DUNCAN RETURNED from the Hell Hawk team. "OK, our assault is lining up. We'll give those bastards a what for they've never seen in their lives. How's the other part of our plan coming, getting inside to Cataclysm?"

I sighed. "Whatever we do, it's gotta be fast. I dunno what Charista is doing or how far ahead she's gotten with Cataclysm. If Kado hasn't figured it out, I'm sure she's pressing him every which way she can, and I don't even wanna know what that means. We've got to make our play before we lose our chance to do anything.

"We gotta get a hold of Cataclysm or at least stop her from using it. We've got a way in, but I'm throwing in a lot with Dawn, who I don't fully trust, but it's the best option we have. So, while you and Kaitlinn take the fight to 'em outside, we'll be ducking and weaving through the back door."

Duncan grinned. "Now you're thinking like the Guard. Doesn't always have to be a full-on assault. Dash and move, keep them off balance; you'll get more done that way. But the Omegans still want Cataclysm too."

"Absolutely; they're after Charista as well, so the Omegans and Lebabolis will be focused on each other. We need to give them something else to think about while we snatch and grab the prize from under both of them, and that's where you come in. Think you can provide enough of a distraction?"

"I suspect we can give them enough to worry about."

"Duncan, you know chances are not everyone's gonna make it."

His face got somber. "Been awhile since anyone told me that, but we're ready to do our part. This is what we have always been about. Protecting and serving the Valkyrie."

It all felt right, but I knew, and the fear rose in me when I realized just what this was for. We weren't only fighting for the right to exist freely anymore or even the right to have consideration as human beings. This was to save this world. Charista was crazy enough to take it all with her if she didn't win. What was I willing to give up for the same?

I knew the risks too; nobody with a clear mind could've ignored 'em, either. Not even the world-weary ones of the Guard. We'd already faced a small detachment of the Omegans, and it had almost landed us in our graves. This move was still gonna take a lot of effort, and a big move from the Omegans. Could I lead them from afar? I wasn't gonna be in the front for this assault.

"Battles have to be fought on multiple sides," Baudricort would say. I'd heard it when they talked about the big move to the Range. He knew that Lebabolis was after us, and in the Outlands we were open and vulnerable. Same way here; by moving on Lebabolis and fighting the Omegans again, we were putting ourselves out there. There were gonna be casualties. I felt odd about that. Were any of these people's lives worth less than Varrick's? Hadn't they all fought to survive; didn't they deserve that right?

(ANA)

B Y THEN, MOST OF THE GUARD troops had finished digging through the rubble of Omegan ships and had gathered nearby. Duncan and I walked over to them. As we got close, their cheers got louder. Some threw the crossed arm salute; others just waved their weapons high.

We had six hell hawks and a dozen ground vehicles, along with a force of two thousand. They all still looked ragged, even the Action people, and was that really a surprise? Food and hygiene were pretty much always low on the list of what we had going for us. But outward appearances only mean so much. I wouldn't have traded the heart of one of these for ten thousand Lebabolis regular troops.

We were as mixed up a group as we ever were. Shreds of the Action, pieces of the Guard, wrapped up into one big ol mess. On top of our numbers, we had a plan that was part desperate, part crazy, and totally necessary. As Baudricort said, you fought the battle you needed to with the weapons you had.

Duncan and Kaitlinn stood on either side of me. I watched the troops. I'd been here before, like back in Sector 5 when we first faced off a group of the Omegans as the Lebabolis and Action combined.

But this time it wasn't for a facility or just a sector. So much rode on this. And, even Nelson; his trip home still hung in the air, a promise I knew that whatever happened, I was gonna keep.

I felt Baudricort's presence again, like I always did when I addressed the troops. I wondered what he'd have thought of me, how I turned out. I also thought about his plans, and maybe this was part of it all along, having me here, leading them just like he did. As I spoke, I heard echoes of him when he addressed the Action.

"Our lives haven't been our own," I began. "We've been made to be something, a part of Lebabolis, but you also as the renegades, the Deviants, who wouldn't or couldn't belong to the laws of Lebabolis. We've all been controlled. Up until now we went along with it. At first, because we didn't know any better. But now, we're awoke. Now we know just what is going on and how they've tricked us."

Shouts came from the crowd. My chest was still tight, but the feeling I got when I saw their eyes, locked on me, hungry and with a gaze that wasn't angry, wasn't threatening, but more like the cold stare of an animal ready and obedient for any order. They'd have died for me, they'd have killed for me. I loved each of 'em for it.

"We're gonna get the people responsible. You know who... Charista and the Omegans. We'll make them pay. Like most of you, I was born into a world of fear. I was afraid of not being able to produce, afraid of being labeled a Deviant, afraid of the Realignment, and right now I am just done. It's time we stop running and start fighting. It's time we take a stand and tell them all that this is our planet and we aren't going anywhere. The only time you are who you truly want to be is when you stand for something."

Murmurs rose in the crowd. I saw the Guard's faces with snarls and nodding. Nelson beamed.

"We've been living in a system created by the Omegans and Charista, and I'm tired of it. Tired of being an experiment. Tired of living in a world where I'm a piece of machinery. Aren't you? I say it ends and we take our world back."

Lucy gave out a shrill whoop in response, and many other Guard members followed along.

"I dunno about you, but I'm tired of being told how I need to live. We need to stand firm, to tell the world this is who and what we are. It starts with taking control back. We have to get to Cataclysm. Charista's trying to turn it on to stop the Omegan advance, and with the help she's got she has a pretty good chance of it. Well, I'm here to tell you we're about to be all the trouble that Charista and the Omegans can stand."

I went from being speechless to knowing just what needed said. Again, I felt the touch of Baudricort on me. I gasped, and a tear formed at the corner of my eye as I swelled with the vision, with their vision, not because I was chosen, but because I was ready. Most of all, I hadn't missed it. I'd run, and my path led me here, to this point. Charista was doomed. The Omegans were the least of her worries. I felt the strength of ten brigades of warriors coursing through me right then.

"We can't live in a world where there's something like Cataclysm. We have the chance to do something, to become something more and most of all, to earn something. What are we earning? Our future. Yours, mine, the future we won't see except for those who come after us. People generations before did it; they lived, they suffered, they made mistakes and they overcame to get to a point where a new generation took over. And now it's our turn."

The solders cheered again, and several thrust their rifles high. I watched the scene and smiled a bit before I turned back to Duncan.

"We're sending a small group including myself into the Lebabolis Capital using access Dawn here knows about. We've all seen the Omegans, and most of us have gone up against them before. I don't have to tell you, there's no guarantee that all of us are making it out of this alive. This whole plan is risky, and it could all fail. But the worst risk is sitting, waiting, and hoping this all blows over. Because that's what we've been doing, and this time, there's no definite idea it will."

The more I talked, the better I felt. The pain from my wound hurt less. It helped seeing the look in their eyes. They watched me, and I knew they understood what we had to do. After centuries of a lie, they were ready for the truth like a thirsty man wanted water. The cheers from the crowd fed me. I started seeing myself more in their eyes. Their faces felt like hands on my shoulders, holding me, supporting me. They pressed me on.

"It won't be easy. Nothing worthwhile ever is. But we need a plan. Duncan and Kaitlinn are our wedge. Drive a spike into the battle. The Omegans will be attacking the Lebabolis Capital, trying to bust through. You have to disrupt, to distract and to take as many of them out as you can."

Duncan stepped forward. "We'll give them plenty to think about, won't we?"

The Guard troops erupted in shouts in response.

"This is for everything we are, everything we love, everything we want to be. This is for tomorrow. This is for your future. The world doesn't happen like you want; you need to earn your future. Are you with me?"

I was sure of it, even though the voice I'd heard was stopped, that this was my time, and my mission was gonna work.

"Every Guard member dead equals five of theirs. You got me? Be fierce, be relentless. Fight for your Valkyrie. Fight for tomorrow, and earn your future!"

***

THIS GROUP WAS MORE than just the Action or the Coalition, where both had their own hidden spies who planted explosives or flipped on us just when things seemed normal. This was everyone who was considered unworthy by Charista and everyone left for dead or being collected by the Omegans. We finally had a common ground, each of us. Even with the odds stacked against us, I felt better about who I was going into this with.

Nelson looked different too. His normal worried glance wasn't there as much. Instead, he had a glimmer behind those eyes of his. If I didn't know any better, I'd say it was hopeful. That was the best word I had to describe it, anyway.

The air was dry with a mild wind. I glanced up at the sun overhead and worked on a reading on one of the P-LADs for Llewyn's location when Nelson stood next to me.

"Maybe you shouldn't go in with us on this, Nelson. There's plenty of places you can hang back until this blows over. We have to yank Cataclysm, and I don't trust any of these other people for that."

"Well, that's fine, but remember I don't trust anyone here like I trust you. Further to the point, I don't need anyone else here like I need you. You go, I follow; I'm not leaving your side."

He said it firm and quick, with no wavering in his voice. His eyes backed up his words too.

As people scattered to various transports and ships getting ready, I watched the scene with Nelson. The air was filled with energy again. It was different than the Action days even, when our main goal was getting to where we could hide. For the first time, it felt like we were in charge.

Lucy's voice to my left jarred my thoughts.

"I don't recall giving you permission to go somewhere without me."

She was all geared up. As vicious as she looked even when we were in that cell, with the pulse rifle and gear she looked like her own little ball of Cataclysm.

"You make that stuff look good."

She stepped close, a small smirk on her lips. "Mmhmm, well again, I don't recall you giving permission to go anywhere I won't be with you."

I clasped her shoulders. Her eyes said everything her mouth didn't, and it was nothing I didn't already know. "You're absolutely right. Believe me, having your kinda muscle at my back is something I'll sure miss, but we need the most punch we can get outside. Those Omegans have to be held at bay long enough."

Lucy nodded and glanced away. "We'll give 'em every bit of hell they deserve and more." Her eyes finished the thought, with more of that Guard gaze. Resolute, crystalline determination. That kind of attitude wasn't trained; it was bred.

I leaned in until our foreheads touched. "You take care of yourself."

Her eyes looked into mine. "You too."

We pulled back, and she glanced at Nelson. "Take care of our girl."

"You know it." He nodded.

EIGHTEEN

(ANA)

NELSON AND I WATCHED AS LUCY darted off to join Berg and the rest of the Guard. After a few moments, Nelson leaned in close. "Didn't want to tell them about Charista being an Omegan?"

"Too many moving parts right now. They'll know when the time's right. We've gotta get this done first. Won't matter much if she blows us all up, now, will it?"

Nelson nodded. "True. So, between us, what do you think our chances are? We didn't do so well against just the Omegans. Now what do we expect to do against them all?"

"Whatever it is, whatever happens, at least we can say we stood together and fought."

He glanced my way, then back to the crowd about us and gave a shrug. "You know, something feels different about it this time. We're on the outs and all, but we've got something different here."

"A bigger group to get mowed down by the Omegans and Lebabolis?" I chuckled.

"No, a chance. I feel it."

"What do you think we should do?"

I watched the whole scene, our assembled group, and felt Baudricort's presence. "Nelson, we've got a shot if we keep working together. Stay close to me when we go for Llewyn."

Nelson watched me. "So, you think we can grab his access."

"I do. I've been wrong before, but something in my gut tells me a turn's coming."

Nelson stood by me, and together we watched our army. For the first time, it really felt like that to me... our army. The Action was close and was sure welcoming enough, but it was the baby of people like Baudricort, and for a while, Llewyn.

Nelson glanced at me. "We've got more muscle now, I'll give you that. But that still is gonna take a lot for us to bust through Lebabolis."

"This is what it looked like when I first got with the Action, Nelson." He watched me with curiosity, that little boy sense of wonder. I lightly punched his shoulder. "When Baudricort started the Action, it was pretty slipshod. That's why they called us 'rag tags', among other things like Deviants. We were a mixed bag, all different Products from different Sectors. We just had enough guts and knew how to steal some vehicles and get enough of our people away to start. From there it was just more of the same. But that little rag tag group was enough of a problem that Lebabolis was constantly coming after us. They sent raids and everything they could, but it wasn't until Charista herself stepped in that they were able to get us in any kind of position to bargain."

"We were on the run, and they couldn't stop us. The smaller fish gets eaten up by the bigger fish, but only when it can be caught."

"Well, alright." I grasped Nelson's shoulders. "Listen, there's no way to make this easy. This'll get pretty rough."

Nelson's brow arched. "As opposed to the playland we've been through until now?"

"Hey, I mean it." My voice hitched as I went on. "This could go very wrong for a lot of us, maybe even me."

He squinted, and he blinked as if I'd just punched him in the face. The look he had was probably like the one I'd had when Baudricort said the same to me. There always was a chance things weren't gonna end well during Exodus, and knowing now he was my dad, it made sense, the fear in his eyes. Now as I said the same thing to Nelson, it made it all fit into place different. If it was my time, I knew I'd had plenty of chances. And I'd made a few things good. Varrick still had a chance, and so did Nelson. If I had any small part in that, all the better. Things didn't happen because of one person, but because many acted as one. One thought, one goal, one idea.

"I'm not trying to scare you, Nelson. I just wanted you to be ready for what I think is ahead of us."

"OK," he said.

"If something happens to me, I want you to get to Duncan. Or if he isn't around either, find the next highest-ranking member of the Guard, and tell them to get you to Kado. If he's still around, he's gonna be your best bet to get out of this place."

"I can do that. But I won't have to, right?"

It hurt my heart, knowing that I wasn't able to give him an honest answer that he'd have wanted to hear. "Here's hoping. Just know I'm seeing you through this one way or another. You still don't have my permission to die."

I thought about our approach to this. Duncan had the experience and I knew I could trust him, but I still wondered if this was gonna work. How much could they have done against both the Omegans and Lebabolis? And were we gonna be able to get into the Capital? We had to work quick. Charista wasn't slowing down at all, and my one hope wasn't a huge one, but it was what I had.

I knew a huge battle was ahead of all of us. Everyone did, even Baudricort probably.

What would he have advised? What would he have done?

I wished I'd had some kind of message from him that told me what to do, but there was nothing. I was on my own, except for those with me in the flesh. However unsure I felt, I knew it was right that I should lead it. It was dangerous and maybe deadly doing that, but who leads from behind? It had to be from the front. The Guard wasn't about waiting back to see how things went; neither was I. But then again, sometimes being a leader meant you put people in the places they needed to be to ensure victory.

Nelson watched the vehicles as the Hell Hawks powered up and the troops started getting on board the land vehicles.

"We've got to keep our eyes open. We both know we aren't getting to the Capital or Llewyn without running into the Omegans again. They're scouring the Outlands and the odds aren't in our favor for a quick trip over there. I can pretty much guarantee the heat's gonna pick up not long after we book outta this."

"Well, I'm staying close to you," Nelson said.

I grasped his shoulder. "You better."

"But these Spikes, they've gotten it; I've seen these before. If we can get a way to disrupt their power, we can control the fight. We can slip over, and we can get to this token and get it all done before it's time for Charista to fire her weapon."

"Wait, you telling me that you, Ana Crucinal, scourge of the Action, is entertaining something other than a full-frontal assault?"

"When you put it like that—"

"—I'm right?"

I shoved Nelson. "—or you make me want to smack you. Listen, it makes sense, don't it? We get forged access and find our way into some Lebabolis units running defense. Then, we slip inside the Capital."

I hadn't seen the Capital, but everything in my mind told me it had to be sealed up pretty tight.

Nelson asked, "So how the hell are we getting in there? Won't it be fortified?"

"Yeah; won't be easy. Dawn's got an idea, but it involves our next stop."

"Llewyn?"

"Mmmhm."

Nycole walked by, a large pulse rifle cradled in her arms. It was bigger than a Lebabolis issue, and after a few seconds I realized that it was Omegan in fact. Two large barrels were housed in a twisted collection of tubes and wiring with a large sighting computer that let off a bluish glow from the console readout.

"Oh, that's very you," I commented and nodded.

"I agree. So, heard you say my name."

"Yeah, we need someone who knows the ins and outs of Charista's restricted areas. We're not gonna have much time once Dawn gets us in there."

Nycole slung the rifle over her shoulders. Did they teach all these Warrior Products that move? "Once we're inside, we can't be sure what we'll run into, but with the fight going on outside, they'll have every gun and person available to the exterior defenses. There's as good of a chance of sneaking in there ever will be."

"Problem," Dawn commented.

"Oh?"

Dawn sighed and paused, glancing at all of us for a moment. "First of all, the access is limited to a small number. Remember, this is a prototype. We can safely move five people across. Once we go through, that's it. Without another token, no one else is getting through. Also, the token is biometric. I was never granted access; I was only on the research and development team. There's a slim chance I can get my testing access enabled; better shot is if we get access on a Lebabolis priority level."

"How the hell do we do that?" Nycole asked.

Dawn shot Nycole an irritated look. "I don't have the tools to forge one here. But if we can get to someone who had that access at one point, we might be able to use theirs."

"Alright, say we get this credential we can't get and slip into this transport that we don't even know if it's been deactivated, what do we do inside?" Nelson asked.

I shrugged. "We locate the lab. Dawn, you know more about the labs and locations, that'll be your job once we're in there.

Dawn shrugged. "I'll do my best."

I cast a side glance to Dawn. "We'll need 'spot on'. We have to get to where she's got Cataclysm. We get there, we find Kado too, I bet."

Jacobs walked up. He looked ready to make trouble, all decked out in his flight gear.

Nelson asked, "So just how do we stop her? I thought the whole point of this incursion was to not startle Dawn into firing Cataclysm but to sneak it?"

"We can go as sneaky as possible, but in the end it's gonna take someone yanking it out of her hand." I said.

Dawn asked, "So we grab it and take out Charista?"

"I take out Charista. She and I have plenty unfinished business."

Jacobs asked, "But then what? We'll still have the Omegan and even Lebabolis armies to deal with."

I looked at Jacobs and the rest nearby. "The Omegans only want Lebabolis and whatever humans they can use for their slave trade. The Lebabolis soldiers who remained loyal are under Charista. If they realize she's gone, they won't be able to put up a fight. Duncan can keep them all at bay long enough that we can get this thing shut down and fast."

Jacobs laughed. "It's a wild plan, but I gotta say, as good as any I've heard since I joined this outfit. I'll take the four Hell Hawks and be ready in the air. These Omegans aren't as good with flying in our environment, so we should be able to give them enough problems for a while up there. On the ground, I leave it up to Duncan and the Guard."

"They'll remember us for sure."

"OK then, we go do this thing."

"There's another thing," Dawn said.

"Of course there is. What?"

"If you're not familiar with the layout in the Capital, it can be tricky. We better have someone who knows their way around, since we don't want to waste any time finding Charista's laboratory."

I scoffed. "Why do I get the feeling you're the prime person for that part of the job?"

"Seeing as how I'm one who set this tech up, yeah, seems like a no brainer." Dawn's eyes narrowed.

"Mmmhm."

Duncan shook his head. I looked at him and saw his eyes, his warrior eyes, and we had a moment. His look said plenty to me, about being in the field and the guilt I already felt about even thinking about ditching the front-line assault went up even more.

Duncan sighed and pointed to my chest. "We're all warriors in this, and a fight isn't always done with the weapons and bloodshed. Sometimes we need people in on the backside, slitting the throat of the enemy and whatnot before they can know what hit them."

"If we get to this weapon and stop her, we take away her big threat."

"And you save the whole thing. We'll give them plenty to think about on the outside."

"Gonna be tough; they had their way with us back at the Range, and I'm not even talking about Lebabolis proper at this point."

Duncan said, "We're ready. We've been wanting and needing a country and a cause. Looks like at least for now the country is gonna come one day. The cause is already here." He winked at me. There it was; they threw in for me this time. I felt twenty feet tall and like I could've heaved a Hell Hawk into the air with my bare hands. This was happening. I had a place, a mission, and most of all, a calling.

"Besides, he and I have unfinished business to attend to." Duncan's brow creased. "Well, what about all the brainy types in your group, maybe someone can figure out a way in there?"

I saw Dawn's face in my mind, and my gut clenched at first, but I sighed and returned Duncan's gaze. "There's one. Not sure just how much we can trust her, but she may have a way."

"Yeah, who?"

"Her name's Dawn, but I gotta tell ya, Duncan, I'm pretty wary on this one. Can't say I trust her a full 100 yet."

As much as we'd been through, it always seemed that she was in the places with us when things went bad. It just never sat with me that she'd be someone we could trust all the way. She wanted to report back to Charista. But now that wasn't anything she had a part of anymore, and she was bound to be the person that could be into some of this.

"You think you can do all this?" Duncan asked.

"We have to try. There's no telling how close Charista's getting to have her weapon operational, so we can't waste time. If Dawn here gets us in, we'll slip in the back door and isolate Cataclysm."

"But then what? You'll be surrounded by her best troops in minutes."

"Tell ya the truth, I haven't thought that far ahead. I just know if she fires that thing it could be the end of us, and that's something I'm not waiting on. We have to act now. We silence Cataclysm, and then we silence Charista. Agreed?"

"It ain't gonna be easy, standing up to a legion of Omegans and Lebabolis. But we're ready for a fight, long as we can make it count."

I swallowed hard and looked into his eyes. "We'll get our part done."

Duncan smiled. "I bet you will. And, we'll give 'em plenty to deal with out there."

NINETEEN

(ANA)

IT BOTHERED ME A LOT THAT I wasn't gonna be on the ground with the rest of the boots, but Duncan made a great point that without me making my way into the rear, it wasn't going to be possible. They knew the odds against them; the idea of them wading into this fight, against two enemies, was pretty suicidal at best. But we had an advantage that we didn't have to beat them into submission just then.

From there, we would lay out our demands. The only concern was whether or not the Omegans were gonna go along with it. There were more troops that would be lost from this. The hope was that we could get in there before too long and the damages were too severe.

Duncan gazed over the horizon toward Lebabolis. "Can't say what's gonna happen once we get there, ya know."

"Yeah, I know that. You think this'll work?"

"Good a shot as anything of working." He looked toward me, with a compassion in his eyes. "Your parents would be damn proud, you know."

I swallowed a lump in my throat. "That's good enough for me, I suppose."

"You needed to hear it plain and clear. I don't mince words or give out compliments I don't need to be messing with. I've seen people with three times your strength and not one tenth your heart. If we've got a future at all in this world, it's because of you. You brought us back, and I wanted you to know that in case I don't get a chance to tell you again."

I nodded. "Thanks, Duncan. I'll see you when this is over."

"Here's hoping, Fiery Girl."

(ANA)

T REG AND NORG TOOK THE CONTROLS of our Hell Hawk, and we started toward Settlement 2216. I felt good about us finally having a path, one we controlled, not some deal with another group. But, I wondered what waited for us at the Settlement. For Llewyn to have agreed or even wanted this place as his own, he must've either thought he was gonna be hidden enough and not a strategic property, or just holed up so well armed that no one was gonna have any kind of luck busting in.

We had a small group, but I had to think the more important part was keeping the Omegans and Lebabolis armies from destroying each other and giving Charista a chance to fire her weapon.

Nelson sat in the back of the cockpit with me. He scanned the scenery without a word.

"Hey." I nudged him. What's going on in there?"

He gave me a weak smile in return and sighed. "I dunno; was thinking about what Dera said about my book."

"Oh, about it being a hole in the time that sent it back to you?"

"Yeah. I guess I thought I was really onto something and had this wild ability to make it come true."

I patted his arm. "Isn't it better knowing you're not some kind of deity or something that could cause all this kind of trouble too?"

"Hah. Well, I guess when you say it that way. Still, would've been nice to be able to pick out a Powerball number or something."

We shared a laugh.

"Still think I can make it back home, Ana?"

I hoped one day that question from him wasn't gonna make me knot up inside. What was it about not knowing an answer to a question that drove me nuts? "You know I'll do everything I can on that."

NORG CALLED US OVER. "Ana, you gotta see this."

They pointed me to one of the scans on the Settlement showing population. A thousand troops but then another grouping of people that included some children.

"Those sigs aren't showing up as Lebabolis; why?"

"Because they're ours."

My throat clenched shut. "What?"

"Yeah, Charista sent them there for some reason."

"Guess she didn't want them to be in the way. Varrick, is he there?"

"Yeah, he is; all our people."

MY HANDS BALLED INTO FISTS. Llewyn's insurance policy. He wanted something there so we couldn't blast him, even if we got enough firepower together to do something. That bastard!

"Pull back on the assault."

"Come again?"

"I say, all troops, do not engage. Form a barrier around the Settlement. Anything tries to leave, turn it back or turn it to ash."

We were hurting for troops. I wondered if any of these soldiers down there would've thought about joining up with us. Maybe some of 'em weren't here because they wanted to be, maybe some wanted out. They were holed up in there; it was worth a shot. But if we were captured, it was over. I preferred to take charge first and negotiate later.

I strained for ideas. Llewyn could also have Valentium in there, and he could just as easily blow it if he saw us coming. An explosion from that wouldn't be as bad as Cataclysm, but it would be enough to knock us out. Plus, we needed to get more fuel ourselves. Our stores weren't endless, and if we were making a trip up Capital way, we better get some for the trip.

Nycole pointed to the console where the energy store readout displayed. "Look, we've got limited fuel here. If we're gonna make it to the Capital, we've gotta be smart, plus, gotta think they aren't expecting a group at all, and with the way things are around here, I'd rather come in quiet on the ground, make like we're a roving troop looking for sanctuary first."

I clenched my hands together, hoping for a nugget of an idea to appear. "Maybe we can pull some troops from Duncan; reinforcements?"

Nycole shook her head. "No, we'll only draw more attention on ourselves. Once we get inside, move quick. Shoot anything that moves that isn't one of us. You run out of ammo, make 'em pay for every shot they take at us. Copy?"

Everyone came back with a "Roger".

Our convoy careened toward Llewyn at Settlement 2216. He'd set himself up nicely; they carved a natural boundary out of rock and he had a nice living arrangement set up. Even a garrison of troops. They made him provincial over a new territory sanctioned by Lebabolis. Too bad nobody told him that I was coming to collect due on some old debts.

Llewyn was one guy in charge I knew the least about. Charista was a public figure. It was impossible to not at least see her daily on those situation video updates from Lebabolis on MODOSNet. Baudricort was even more familiar, even before I found out about my link to him. Llewyn, on the other hand, was always associated with someone else. The leaders of Lebabolis had no kids I or anyone knew about, or maybe they were just kept hidden pretty well, like I was.

I thought how it was strange that I never saw Llewyn's family. He was one of the adults I knew back in Lebabolis, but aside from seeing him at some gatherings or reviews, I had no contact with him at all. But in the Action, things were so scattered, people left home like I did in the middle of the night. Families were separated all the time. I sure had no one I knew of other than Varrick at the time. I wondered if the reason Llewyn didn't have any family was that he was another plant like Charista, another Omegan hiding in plain sight running their experiment.

"Set down on the ridge near the back of the Settlement."

TWENTY-ONE

(ANA)

THE SETTLEMENT WAS A LITTLE MORE than a refined Sector. They had sectioned off the key production facilities and some housing units as well as an admin building. Llewyn had enough to give himself and his crew of tag-alongs energy and space to forage for themselves outside of their electro barrier.

Nelson swung his P-LAD over the area. "How are we gonna find him?"

I eyed Nelson. "Llewyn's a pampered wuss. Look for the biggest or nicest looking unit. Bet ya a crate of Valentium he'll be there. That's where I'm going."

"Not alone you're not," Nelson said.

"Never thought otherwise. Get troops to cut off escape routes out the Settlement and surround Llewyn's quarters."

Nelson and Treg came with me. As soon as we landed, alarms buzzed and some troops swarmed toward us. I tensed at the sight of their gray bands. Loyal to the end. So be it.

There were around fifty of them. Llewyn had a nice little piece of the world set up. I wondered if he knew all along about Charista too.

A spray of scorching pulse rounds heated the air around us and slammed into the walls behind us.

Me and our group slunked down against a barrier as the pulse fire beat a steady pattern into the wall above me. I activated my comm. "Llewyn, this is your only warning. Give up or we end you."

"You're in no position to make demands, Ana Crucinal."

The familiar whine of the Lebabolis klaxon alarm blared out, along with an announcement by Llewyn: "Raiders spotted inside compound; activate defensive protocols and neutralize them."

A barrage of pulse fire rang out around me. The barrage kicked up a cloud of dust and rocks that rained down on us as we hit the dirt. Once the few Lebabolis crafts they had swung up and opened fire I got back up and dashed down the ledge.

"Attack! No quarter!"

Our group cascaded down into a group of Gray Bands. They fired at us at random. Our group returned the volleys and also added some good old muscle. The air was filled with the crackle of pulse fire and the blunt pounding of fist on armor or bare skin.

"I see you, Ana."

"Yeah, well come on out; are ya scared of me or something?"

Over the comm came a response. Llewyn sounded pretty confused. "How in the world did you ever get free from the Omegans? They told me you'd be shipped out."

"Yeah, guess again. You realize what Charista's trying with Cataclysm, don't you?"

"Of course; she's trying to destroy the Omegans once and for all."

"Don't you realize what could happen to us all if she uses too much energy? Did Baudricort have to read those maps to the Range to you slow? There won't be a place to hide if Charista blows this all up with Cataclysm. Not even the Omegans want her to fire it. Look, we don't want this fight. Come out and let's talk. We can stop the Omegans once and for all—why don't you want that? Isn't that what you want? You and Charista, in your happy little kingdoms? You know where she's really from, right?"

"Yes, I know she's an Omegan, Ana. You aren't the only one with access to deep information. Only difference is I use mine when beneficial to me. You see, I want them to blow each other up. I've got my piece here, and we're staying. This is your chance to start over; I suggest you take it."

"I trusted an insane woman enough for a lifetime, Llewyn. You're not looking too good to me yourself right now either."

"Everyone's a villain or a hero, depending on perspective. You can join us, leave or die."

"I need your access; you'll either help me or I'm taking it from you."

"Good luck. It's an embedded chip. You won't get it unless you cut it out of me."

"That can be arranged, Llewyn."

"So, that's your wild scheme, Ana? Breaking into the Capital, using my credential?"

"You're not quite as dumb as you look."

He responded with a laugh that broke into a coughing fit. "You can forget that. I'd rather stay here and live. You can wander into the lion's den all you want for all I care; leave me out of it."

"Ya know, Llewyn, I always wondered just what was it about you I never liked."

"That's interesting. I never had to wonder about you. I never liked you from the start. You and your 'anointed one' airs. The way Baudricort went on about you and why we had to save some measly runt Deviant over so many others. It sickened me, thinking of the lives he wasted trying to save yours. Setting those charges did the trick."

That stopped me in my tracks. The charges in the room that killed Baudricort, my father.

It was him. "You bastard!"

"Oh come on now, don't be so sad. You know I'd hoped you'd be in there with him, but I suppose I'll have to finish you the hard way."

"Hard way, Llewyn? We've got boots on the ground here; think your people can last long against some Guard troops? You better reconsider that while they rearrange their limbs."

"Ah, I see. The direct frontal assault. Yes, that was your first, best and only move, now, wasn't it always? Risking your life, little as it's worth. Shame your dear departed father never had the decency to give you other ideas in mind, such as watching the rear guard so you can always make a hasty retreat."

Our way to Llewyn's quarters was almost clear when I heard over the comm, "Ana! He's escaping! Hell Hawk to the far east wall!"

There he was. Running like a coward. He always was in the rear, even when we were on the same side, and now he was ready to leave these people, his protectors, once again. I froze for a second, and my gaze locked in on him so tight that the sides of my vision got dark. However true or false it was, I focused on him, Llewyn right then, as the source and cause of everything that had happened.

Rage gripped me tight, and I took off running. I heard shouts behind me to duck and stop, but I ignored them. My vision was like a laser, dead sighted on Llewyn as he scrambled toward the Hell Hawk. The pain in my chest got a little worse as I huffed. My lungs sucked in waves of air. I came upon a Gray Band woman who blocked my way by firing on me. I danced and juked around until I was right on her and punched her in the face. I kept my pace after that.

My sight was never clearer. I beaded in on Llewyn better than if I'd looked through a scope from a thousand yards at a dead center target.

I passed another group of Action soldiers, and they waved me on.

"Give her some cover fire!" Treg yelled.

The heat from a nearby pulse shot singed my face, but I couldn't have cared less. Llewyn was still a good hundred yards ahead of me, but I just ran all the faster. My lungs burned and my wound sent a deep pain into my chest, but I didn't care. Whatever I did, I wasn't letting him get away. If he didn't want to work with us, if he was too stupid to see the bad play he had made, he really was as useless as I thought he was.

By the time I got to his pad, he'd gotten the ship revved and ready to launch. The craft lifted off several feet in the air when I leaped for a landing skid and grabbed it.

You're gonna pay for what you did.

To them.

To him.

And to me.

My shoulders burned fire as I hoisted myself up. I was driven, and nothing was gonna stop me. They might as well have cut my arms off if even that would've worked.

I remembered how Baudricort's body looked on the floor. The pained look in his face, his eyes filled with regret over everything he'd tried to make right that was left undone. It was my turn to set it right, and it started here.

The Hell Hawk wobbled a little from the uneven load I put on it. I grabbed for the door release and saw him with a pistol in his right hand aimed for me.

I thought about everyone who'd stood in my way. Llewyn was just the latest in this long line.

It's over.

You're over.

You're done.

We grabbed the door at the same time, him pushing, me pulling, and then I was flung loose. My right hand held on to the craft while I dangled. I looked down for something else I could grab and then heard him over the whine of the engine.

"You just don't know when to quit, do you?"

His pulse pistol was pointed right between my eyes. I sucked in a deep breath and held it. What now?

The craft shook a little and he stumbled, and I got another idea. I swung and kicked my legs more, and the craft shook further. He swayed his arm to steady himself, and that was my cue.

I hauled myself up and grasped his right wrist.

I yelled over the roar of the whining turbines. "So long, asshole!" I yanked him out of the craft, and he plunged to the ground, his screams drowned by the engines. The craft dipped further, and I yanked myself in to steady it. I thought about the controls, what I'd seen them do. This was nothing I was used to, but I did my best. The comm crackled to life. "Ana, you OK?"

"I'll be great if one of you fly folks tell me how to land this damned thing!"

TWENTY-TWO

(ANA)

AFTER LLEWYN WAS KILLED, the mop-up went a lot different. Seems that even Llewyn had his own collection of forced troops.

Our group formed up behind me, and we faced a company of Llewyn's Gray Bands. They eyed us, weapons drawn. The air was quiet; the only noises were the almost silent hum of pulse weapons engaged.

I raised a hand up. "We're not your enemy any more than you are ours. You've got to believe me here."

"Why should we?" a girl called out, further back in the crowd. She stepped forward, her rifle swung downward but still in her hands, her finger very much on the trigger. Our eyes met.

"I can't know what you're all thinking right now, but I can imagine you're figuring you're safe here. I'm telling you you're not. Have you heard about Cataclysm? Well, Charista has that, and whatever Llewyn told you about her, don't believe it. She's as ruthless as anything, and while you may think she'll protect you from the Omegans, you better start thinking about who'll protect you from her."

A man spoke. "Easy for you to say. We heard you and yours were captured by the Omegans."

"Yes, that's right. And I've got news for you there. They're coming to get us. All of us. We're not a civilization being built up. We're a bunch of specimens being prepared for a life of labor in service of someone else. Who do you want to serve? Charista? She's kept you all quiet by feeding you promises of a good life. One of security and a feeling like you're accomplishing something. The Omegans? We're a find to them. They saw something in us I'm sure I'll never fully understand, but they felt it was worth it enough to start this project and have us as an experiment for centuries, growing us like a crop. Well, the harvest is here, and unless we stop them both, we're gonna end up as slaves or vapor when Cataclysm fires."

"How do you know we'll be vaporized?"

"I've got it good from my friend Kado. He was one of our top Intellectuals, and he's studied this device almost as much as Baudricort, the man who developed it. It is unstable and the force it uses isn't one that's ever been able to be contained."

Another man spoke. "But what's our alternative then? Serving you?"

Grumbling arose in the crowd. I realized how I looked to them right there, and it made sense. They'd been under someone's rule, and what was I? Another person who was a conqueror?

"The difference with me is I don't want you to kneel before me. I want you to stand with me. I want you to fight with me. I want you to join me, so we can come up with a better world. We've been given another chance here. But chances don't last long without action. I did as much as I could, and I'll continue until I'm gone, but I can't do this alone. All of you, think about what you've done, think about your lives. If there's just one shred of hope in you, one bit of happiness over a life that you started to feel might be yours, I'm just asking you to dwell on it and not let that go. The future can be yours if you work for it."

I saw another little girl in the crowd and after a second I remembered her face; it was Ethan's daughter Clara. I stooped down to her. "Hey, Clara, how are you feeling?"

"OK, better now." Clara smiled.

"I saw your dad, you know."

Her eyes widened.

"Yeah, he helped fix me up. He's with us."

Ethan walked up, but when he caught sight of Clara he stopped in his tracks. His eyes widened and brimmed with tears, and his legs jerked until he was on his knees in a soft whimper, his arms extended. Clara shrieked and tearfully bolted into his arms, and they shared a warm embrace. Their sobs were muffled by their hug.

Faces in the crowd softened more at the sight of Ethan and Clara's reunion. I pointed to them. "This is why we're doing this. This is what we want. This world can destroy itself or build itself. Building takes more time and effort, but is so much more worth it. We are better off together than alone."

As it turned out, the idea about Cataclysm being the problem wasn't new to these people. Ideas and plans had simmered among them for a while, and Llewyn hadn't much more loyalty from these than Charista had from most of her people. It was more cooperation from fear once again.

Once we made our case and explained what the Guard had set out to do, it hadn't taken long for even the strongest Gray Band loyalist to flip over. Now we had the credential, some extra bodies for the fray, and maybe just a little bit more momentum.

"I'm one of you, or I was," I told the crowd. "I want more, but freedom. I want people to be free again. I'm not your enemy; I want to be your friend."

Their eyes looked all too familiar to me. That look, that tired, confused, frustrated look we had in the Action was all over these people's faces.

"We're all supposed to be dead, you realize that? I'm not trying to scare you or anything, but if you think about it, we were supposed to be dead many times. I was almost killed more times than I can count.

Makes me wonder what the hell I even did joining up with the Action. They killed my own father. And, my mother... I don't know, she's probably dead too." My throat tightened when I added, "I know a lot of you have similar stories, or worse. But regardless, we're alive. Today, and now. That means for us, all of us, we've got a choice. We can run and hide, take care of ourselves, and hope that this fight ends without any trouble. If it does, we can go on, letting other people tell us how we should be, even if it's from a distance, and we're there just hiding and hoping we are never found while we scavenge for enough to survive on.

"Or we take control and earn our future. That's right. We can draw a line, and say, 'This stops now, and you will hear me.' We take the fight back to them. There's no Darkness or Cataclysm that will keep us down if we stick together, believe, and become what we were always meant to be. I can't do it alone, and I really don't want to. Not anymore. The Omegans have bigger numbers than us. But numbers start with anything more than one. And we keep it going, free our people in the Capital, and we take back what is ours.

"We have a plan. Duncan is leading a group of Guard troops, and they'll engage the Omegans trying to bust in at the Lebabolis Capital. If he were here now, I bet he wouldn't turn down help from you. I won't lie; besides, you know damn well that fight will not be easy. I can't promise any of you will even make it back. I also have no right to ask you, but I am anyway. Why? I'm asking you because I believe in what is to come. I believe this world will be better, but only when people like you and me make a stand and say we aren't standing for this anymore.

"What we fight for is tomorrow. We fight for the future. The only way in this life you survive is when you make that happen.

"You were all loyal to Lebabolis, and that's fine. They gave you plenty over the years, and you served them with the expectation of protection and purpose. Many of you know the Action; some of you may even know me. But let me tell you just what you don't know. You've been serving a country lead by an Omegan. Yes, that's correct.

The world of Lebabolis is one that was set up for us to believe in. We've been serving a false idea. I say this because like you, we were also tricked.

"The Action stands for something, and it's not about fighting Lebabolis. It's about restoring order. We were sold an idea that Lebabolis was the way, but it isn't.

"Think about all we've been through. And now Charista, the leader, who has been proven to be an Omegan, is about to fire a weapon that, if it works, could destroy this place. I have to think that inside each of you is this spirit, this will, this want. You all want something: to live and be free.

"That's what we want to. But sometimes, those in power get greedy and twist things for their own. I'm asking you to step out and believe. I don't care if you like me or us, don't even want you to be in service to us. But I do want you to believe. In what? Tomorrow. Believe that you can be free. Believe that you can be more than just a worker serving a nation. This world is rich, but only if we share the resources with each other. We're attacking Lebabolis now and are going to put a stop to this, but we need your help. I'm asking you to think about it and join us."

They brought the sick from the Action out, and in the crowd I saw Varrick. When our eyes met, he bolted to me into my waiting arms. I hoisted him and hugged him close as I let a sob out. I turned from the crowd, but then I heard something. It sounded like someone clapping. The sound grew quick until it was all around me, and I looked back. Faces that were weary were happy again, and I realized that maybe I had something with these people, and maybe they were just the ones we needed.

A man stepped toward Varrick and me. The compassion in his deep blue eyes was warming.

"Ana, we've been here because we were told we had no choice. We'd believed that for so long, but we're ready to throw in. If you're out to end this fight, and bring peace back to us, we're with you. We all are."

With that, he thrust his hands up in the Valkyrie salute. Others in the crowd quickly joined in until they all were. I stood up, my shoulders back, and felt the pride surge through me.

I felt more strength and hope, that maybe we had as good a shot as we ever had at getting what we wanted. But when I looked at Varrick at my side, still weak, I knew we had to take care of our own first, and that meant the sick like Varrick kept out of harm's way.

I knelt beside Varrick and savored that smile of his for a moment before I cleared my throat. "Little man, we have to fight Charista and the rest before this is over."

He nodded. I looked up at the others who milled around, and a few Gray Bands came closer.

"I want you to stay here, hunkered down. It's better for you." My voice cracked as I said it. As much as I promised myself I wouldn't, the fear over what we had ahead of us wasn't something I could've ignored.

"You can't take us all." The voice came from above me, and I looked up into the blue eyes of the man who'd came forward.

I only nodded at first. "Will you –"

"-watch over him? Of course. We'd been keeping your sick long enough anyway. Come on, little one, let's get hunkered down."

I clutched Varrick's arm and pulled him into a tight embrace. "Next time I see you, this'll be over."

"Promise?" Varrick asked.

"Yep."

I got back to my feet and eyed the blue-eyed man. "What's your name?"

"Wes."

"Wes, take care of my brother."

His mouth formed in a line. "They want him, they'll have to come through me first." I imagined he'd seen things like this before, as a lot of us had – families separated, some for good. This fight had done far more than take people's lives.

I steeled myself as best I could. I hoped it wasn't the last time I would see Varrick, but no one knew for sure. "We'll contact you when we're safe, Wes."

Wes gave a quick salute with a hopeful smile before he led a group with our sick to find shelter in the Settlement. After a few moments, I turned and saw our forming group. They gave me that look they were ready for the fight we faced. "All available ships, everyone who can hold a gun, anyone who wants to be free, follow me."

Once we raided Llewyn's supplies and armed up with more gear, we formed up into our attack formation. This unit was even more colluded now; we had some Lebabolis issue craft and weapons at our side.

I smiled at the idea my goal was in sight, Varrick and Nelson free at last.

I held the bag with Llewyn's hand in it. Nelson looked sick as he watched it with weak eyes. "Well, that's awfully disgusting."

"We're a little short on options now, best we could do."

"Just don't put it next to me on the ride to the Capital, please."

"With Llewyn's credentials, we should be able to break through their access portals so we can get inside."

"Just how you think that's gonna work? They'll be trying to get in every which way they can. Don't you think they'll see you?"

"Yeah, well. I never said this was gonna be easy. Hell, I never even said we'd make it out of here. But it's not about us; it's about what we're stopping."

"You really think you'll be able to do that?"

"Hey, who're you talking to? I believe and I—"

"—become, yeah, yeah, I know. But Ana, this isn't some speech. You're gonna wade into the deep of a fight, with people way more trained than you. Don't you think that's a little suicidal?"

"It is, but I don't have the luxury to debate the alternatives. Frankly, I don't see any others that don't involve us blowing the whole damn thing up, and I'm sorry but there's plenty of our people who will get vaporized from that, and that's just not good enough for me."

As we left the encampment, I called Duncan on the comm.

"How's the war going, Duncan?"

Explosions rang out in the background. "Busy as hell, but we're hanging in. You get that piece you wanted?"

"Yeah. Making a beeline there, and we're bringing you some friends to help out."

"Tell 'em to come in blasting and we'll have plenty of fight to share with 'em. Out."

TWENTY-THREE

(ANA)

TREG PILOTED OUR HELL HAWK away from Settlement 2216 toward the Lebabolis Capital. He kept us low and gunned the engines. Dawn was next to him on the Co-pilot, working some navigation out for us to get to the portal outside the Capital. Time was never on our side, but at that point there was the unspoken fear we were on the verge of being too late.

Nelson sat with me in the seats behind the pilot, and he pointed at the landscape that zoomed by. "Lots of greenery."

"Huh? Oh, the trees?"

"Yeah. Reminds me of this place back home, City Park."

"What's a 'park'?"

"Oh, there just these open spaces with trees, sometimes ponds, benches, really just a big place for people to go and relax with their friends or family, or just be alone."

As he talked about this other place, his eyes gave me a little more. There was this remembering, maybe a little longing for something he'd forgotten but suddenly was reminded about. The idea of relaxing sounded great, and assuming we made it through what we were about to, I hoped I had the chance for Nelson to explain me just how you relax like the way his eyes seemed to remember it.

An alert indicator buzzed from the console. So much for thoughts on relaxing. I wondered if that meant we were spotted and about to come under fire.

I figured it was either that or... "Treg, how's our fuel reserve?"

He tapped the controls. A greenish hologram of the dials and meters jutted up from the console. You didn't need to be an Intellectual Product or Hell Hawk maintenance tech to know what the red dials meant. Treg gave me a worried look.

"How long?"

Treg sighed and looked back at the controls. "We could maybe get half way there before we have to ditch. With this Spike on board though, that's not gonna count for much."

"It won't count for anything." A deep ache bloomed in my gut at the thought of what we may have given up in doing this. Duncan was ready to do his part, but here we were, the secret piece of the puzzle, but it wasn't gonna count one damned bit if we were still miles away.

Thoughts swarmed in my head. Nelson hunched over, his hands steepled near his mouth. "What about a Valentium station?"

"Maybe the Omegans hadn't made it to all the Valentium depots yet." I grabbed the comm. "Hell Hawk 91 calling available Action units; any fueling depots available? Scrambled frequency respond with scrambled code."

The comm crackled with static, and a voice burst in. "Action Unit 106. Hell Hawk 91, receiving you spotty. Repeat last transmission, over?"

Nelson and I looked at each other. I tapped the Comm. "Hell Hawk 91 here."

Dawn scratched her head. "Action 106. I heard about them. They were part of Jason's regiment but were cut off by an Omegan assault, shut off from the Capital."

Nelson and Dawn's eyes widened. Treg muttered over his shoulder, "We ain't got time for being picky; see if they can help our situation out, already."

I tapped the comm again. "Action 106, we are flying in-bound to Lebabolis Capital, but we're low on fuel. Can you assist or advise on any available refuel points?"

"Capital? I thought that was under siege by the Omegans."

"Yeah, that's the rumor. But we're trying something else."

"You're in luck, 91. Got ourselves at a Valentium plant. We're holding for now, turned back a few Omegan groups since. Guard troops helping out here."

"Well, bless my stars! You're a little piece of luck we've been looking for."

"Goes both ways. If you can give us a ride over to the Capital, we'll hook you up with all the fuel you can hold."

"Done deal."

"Great; we'll send you coordinates. Head over here."

Once the comm shut off, I looked at the others with me. Nelson nodded with a smile. "Things have to go right now and then, don't they?"

Lucy wasn't as convinced. "Not like the Guard to be so open on the comm channels. I think we'd better go in easy on this one."

I nodded. "It's a risk, but then again, so is trying for the Capital on vapor."

TWENTY-FOUR

(ANA)

W E ARRIVED AT VALENTIUM PLANT X8G6S just in time. The place was deserted but not yet on complete shutdown. Nelson, Treg, Ethan, Dawn, Lucy, and I headed inside while the rest stayed with the ship in case we had to book out fast.

The air inside was thick with the smell of freshly harvested Valentium. The Omegans had just been here and maybe were still around a bit.

Where were the troops? I wondered. The Action 106 unit was so definite. *Could I have read the signal wrong?* No, I'd never seen someone fake a location beacon.

The others knew just like I did what that smell meant. "Keep your eyes peeled. Guns drawn, anything that doesn't identify itself, blow it away."

We canvassed the area. I wasn't sure what I was looking for but somehow knew I'd get what it was when I found it. Treg and Nelson kept close by me too.

Treg kicked a pile of debris with his boot, and it scattered onto the floor in a crumble with a low sounding crash.

"They sure didn't worry about cleaning up, did they?"

"No, not really. Think we need to split up a bit here. Anything we need isn't gonna be too obvious. The Omegans would've taken that long ago when they hit this place."

The lights flickered, just like the rest of the city and sectors had. The power grid was definitely compromised.

"They'll have their own circuit at the Capital. Charista never let anything like this happen there. I bet she had all the power she could use and then some."

"She kept the power for herself literally and figuratively." Nelson shook his head. "Any thoughts, Ana?"

"How about you? Don't suppose those Pulls of yours kicked back in any?"

"I wish. Would've made a lot of things easier here, but no, I got nothing."

"Why don't we hit some of the databanks here? Maybe we can locate something there."

The systems room lined the southern wall of the room. Huge walls that jutted up twenty feet from the floor, a self-contained box in the room kept the data for this plant secure. It was important for the monitoring systems to be sealed off from the Valentium in the event of a meltdown. Data had to be preserved. The lives running this place weren't as important as the information about its processing to Charista.

The systems were in offline mode, but Dawn had an easy time getting things back on track. She activated a hologram interface and whizzed through the screens and commands. It got to be so much of a blur of slipping and flying objects in the imaginary space that I looked away for a bit. Otherwise, I was gonna be sick.

Dawn smirked and pointed to the screen. "Here it is, the data we need. The Valkyrie was careful, but even Charista and her people didn't think of all the weak spots. They trusted someone pretty high up, at least for the time."

Treg pointed to a display of containers that appeared. "Those look like fuel pods. Come on, Ethan, let's start loading these up. You guys see what else you can dig while we're here."

While Treg and Ethan headed off to grab Valentium, Dawn tapped a control, and I was stunned when a huge holograph image of Baudricort's head swiveled in the air in front of us. He had a slight smirk on his face; I remembered the look pretty well. It wasn't a big surprise that was the expression they captured of him since it was pretty much his damned resting face. It was a mixture of boredom with a slight curiosity, as if he'd planned everything out, so why would anything be such a surprise to him? Damn, I wished I could've just said two words to him right then.

"Don't suppose you can tell us anything else about that Failsafe, in case Kado can't help us once we get there, huh, Dawn?" I asked.

Her eyes danced between the holograph and me. "It's bloodborne tech. Something they'd experimented with but decided against when the Link was developed. The project was largely scrapped, so I guess that's why they went that direction. They wanted something that wasn't obvious and easy to get to."

"So, the bloodborne tech activates Cataclysm?" I asked.

Dawn nodded. "Activates it, shuts it down, whoever has the proper controls implanted in their bloodstream has total control of the weapon."

"Is it something that can be hacked?"

Dawn said, "There isn't a system that can't be broken into, as long as you've got the patience and time. Charista doesn't have a whole lot of either, but she's got a damn lot of nerve, so I suspect she's gonna squeeze Kado until he either gives out or she's got her great big gun in her hands."

A gruff and familiar voice shut us up quick.

"Sounds like a helluva plan to me."

Zengus stood with a platoon of troops next to him. He wore some kind of modified tech. It was a battle armor, but it had a look like it was something for a Radomet maybe.

"Couldn't keep yourself away, could you?" I sneered at him.

"It was just too easy. And this Omegan tech is pretty damned handy for tracking. Can't be blocked by even the best stuff on Lebabolis; kinda convenient that way."

Zengus trained a pulse rifle on us; its purplish beam came to a point on my chest. Lucy stepped toward Zengus. "You're fighting the wrong people, Zengus. Why dontcha put that gun down and we'll talk?"

"Talk? Is that what your offer is, Lucyna? Talk? You forget what I've been through, what we've been through? Talk's all I've ever got outta anyone from the Action. When we were in the Sector, good little Warrior Products who were ready to do their part for country, Mother Lebabolis, and serve, it was just talk then. When Baudricort decided he could make his own world and gave us a chance to not just serve but to be part of something and be free, that was talk too. But all it ever got us, all either of those ever got us, was a lot of moving, fighting, and dying. I lost a lot of friends in the Action and even before we left. I'm sick of it, man. I'm ready to leave this all behind."

Nelson asked, "And you think joining up with Charista is leaving it all behind?"

"She's been trying to protect us, way more than the Valkyrie ever did. She ain't perfect, but she's got enough behind her to make it a smart move in my book. Charista isn't with the Omegans; she'll keep us here."

"She *is* an Omegan," Dawn said.

"Yeah, but she ain't with them." Zengus walked around and pointed to the building we were in, part of Lebabolis, and in that way, part of the Omegans too. I couldn't have just brushed that off if I'd wanted to, except the part about throwing in with a person who'd sold me out way more than I cared to count.

Zengus thrust his arms out. "What's there left here anymore? What's worth anything?"

"The world you live in is what you make it," I said. "You can bitch and moan about why something isn't the way you want it, but unless you knuckle down and do something about it, nothing ever changes. Charista did plenty making this world something for her. Only problem is that it was only for her, with her collection of pets. If you go with Charista, you'll always be another piece, a part of some other machine. She likes you now, 'cause you're her lapdog and you're running her errands. But one day, when she's done with you or you get a little too hard to control, she'll end you. Are you too stupid to realize that?"

"I've fended for my own this far. And besides, I take you all in to Charista, it helps my position out more."

As much as Zengus and I had the exact same destination in mind, I knew same as going with the Omegans going there in chains under Zengus' watch was the wrong way too. The troops with Zengus fanned out in a large circle. Each soldier held a staff with an electrified end. The glow at the staff showed me that they were Valentium alright.

"Nelson, I can't be sure, but those tips look like Valentium. Whatever you do, don't get hit by one or that's it for ya."

His eyes widened. "Oh? Yeah, um sure. Piece of cake."

"Zengus, you mean to tell me you'd take a chance of killing us before you bring us to Charista?"

"I'm just being careful, seeing as how you busted out from the Omegans and all. Gotta say, Ana, someone who wasn't ever supposed to be a fighter, you held your own pretty well."

Lucy and I traded glances. She nodded toward Zengus, and we started our unspoken dialogue. Her eyes went to the soldiers nearest him before she looked back at me. Lucy pointed toward the troops then clenched her fists.

Zengus arched an eyebrow and went over to one of the solders to tell them something. While he talked with them, I leaned closer to Dawn, my voice in a whisper.

"Dawn, what would it take to fire up the furnaces in this place?"

She looked at the controls for a second.

"Need an answer now, Dawn."

"OK, well I can probably do it pretty fast."

"Then do it, now."

"You sure about that? It's gonna get pretty hot in this place."

A drop of sweat fell into my eye, and I squinted to clear the burning sensation. "Dawn, I'm pretty sure they're about to take us in or kill us quick. So, fire the furnaces up and we make a break for the exit. Whichever of these morons don't get vaped will be one less that we have to deal with out there. Send a silent comm to our group outside to have the Hell Hawk ready for a quick launch to knock this place out if things get bad."

Zengus returned to us and approached me. "Gonna be so nice getting you back where you belong as somebody's pet or something. You weren't anything special, and you never will be."

His sour breath made me wince. "Just remember, you got a place in this world, but it isn't leading anything other than yourself, and by all looks you're not too great at that either."

He grabbed me by the scruff and marched me out. My pulse sped up to a rattle in my throat, and I focused on breaths. Treg had shown me how to keep your body in control so you could be more effective when you had to be. As we walked, I already felt my midsection tighten. It was gonna be much easier to do what I wanted next. I just hoped my chest wasn't gonna punish me too much for it.

I sucked in a quick gulp of air and ducked and rolled away, sprung up in a fighting stance.

Zengus eyed me with curiosity. "Oh, you want to play, do you?" The other guards surrounded us, but Zengus waved them back. "No, no, I'll handle this one; we're old friends."

We circled each other. I felt a mixture at that moment. Sadness at the betrayal of my friend of so many years. I knew Zengus as long as anyone in the Circle except for Treg. That kind of history made this move of his pretty exceptionally ridiculous, and it was the only thing that kept me from trying to kill him outright. I had to know. Some part of me still had to know just what made him do it. I clung to the idea it was a Link that did it. That would've been a simple explanation, one I would've gladly accepted. But there was never anything about a Link. Zengus just was turned. And it was gonna eat at me for the rest of my life. I'd never understand it in a hundred lifetimes.

A snarl escaped his lips as he lunged for me. Several quick jabs to my midsection, and I was sprawled out. As I gasped and coughed for air, I heard his laughs over me.

"You never were anything." He spat his words out like a piece of rancid meat.

His arms wrapped around me and squeezed. I grunted against his hold and jerked around, but he held me fast. My hands raced around for something, anything. But what? His arms squeezed on me tighter, and it got really tough to breathe.

Hold steady, Ana. Don't let the bastard win, you've got to...
BLAM!

My ears rang at the noise. Zengus' body jerked and suddenly went loose. I felt warm liquid spurt on my arm and realized then he'd been shot. Before I was able to stand up, several more pops sounded. I saw Nelson and Lucy crouched down, and Zengus with his group of soldiers were piles of bloody messes. There by the entrance was Treg and Ethan, pulse rifles in check. "You guys OK?"

"Yeah." I smiled. "Glad you peeked in on us."

"Well, you should've told me you felt social. Come on, there'll be time enough for that later. We've gotta book it to the Capital!"

I followed the rest out of the building but stopped a moment to look back at what had become of my friend there on the ground. I'd never know what happened with him, I guessed. The look of him there really burned into my head with questions. *Just what has this been worth? Can you keep going like this; are these lives less worth it than those you're trying to save?*

TWENTY-FIVE

(ANA)

W E FLEW LOW ON A trajectory toward the Capital. A few trails of smoke slinked from below up into the skies around us. My vision started to really narrow toward the Capital where she was. I held onto hope that our plan was going to work. It felt good to think that everything was going to end up right, but just as fast as I had myself convinced, the doubt, fear, and worry started again.

Once we get there, we'd need to break off into groups. The first group would engage the fight. Omegans and Lebabolis would be at each other's throats, so our best shot was looking like one of them. Lebabolis had the fortress so we'd go with that. That would also give me the best shot at getting through the line to them. It was a risk, but this whole damn thing had been pretty risky.

The fight was as bad as I could've imagined. The Omegans had reinforcements, and their ships hovered in a solid arc a hundred yards from the Capital entrance. They looked like they had enough firepower to level the place, and the only reason I imagined they hadn't was for fear Charista might activate Cataclysm and wipe everyone out.

The landscape we crossed toward the Capital got worse the further we went. Housing units and facilities were blasted and belched black smoke into the air. The ground around the Sectors was charred with explosions and fires that burned out of control. I wondered just who of our people would be left at the Capital once we got there. Their defenses were tight, but I couldn't imagine they'd hold off the Omegans for that long.

The alert sounded in the cockpit. Treg turned back. "Brace yourselves; we got contact. Patrol of Omegans."

The Hell Hawk bobbed and weaved into an attack pattern. I grit my teeth at the tightness in my chest. Others in our group spoke on the comm. "Roger that. Taking fire now."

The blare of pulse cannon shook the ship, and explosions rang out around us.

"We're not gonna get them to stop; let's see if they'll give a chase. Ground units checking in; how you guys doing?"

"Hanging in tough but not sure about the rest."

I glanced downward at our group of troops; they were engaged in their own fight with the Omegans. At least with Duncan down there, I felt better about them running things and fighting them off. At least they'd be kept at bay.

I looked at Nycole in the cockpit. "So, think this'll work?"

"The credential? Best chance we got of any."

"Yeah, well, was hoping for something more definitive from you."

Nelson leaned from behind me. "We'll find a way or make one, right?"

I tapped his hand on my shoulder. "Hell yeah we will."

We neared the northeast quadrant, and Dawn nodded to us. "The portal's on that side; hit it!"

Nelson, Dawn, and I headed down the rear exit of the ship. We connected our suits to the drop mechanism.

"Ever jump out of these before, Nelson?" I asked.

The look in his eyes when he spotted the ground answered my question, but still he said, "No, not at all."

I clasped his chin and gently turned his head and eyes back to me. "Gonna be OK. Just stay close to me, and you'll make it."

A sparkle of doubt filled his eyes. He knew as much as I did that nothing we did here was a sure thing except giving up. But that wasn't in my plan.

"Always," he said.

Dawn insisted on going first; she wasn't too sure herself, but I just knew she wanted to be down there and get into the Capital to find out herself just why she wasn't included. *Well, Dawn, seems to me you weren't in on Charista's little rule the world plan after all. Guess you missed a meeting or two along the way.*

Once we left the Hell Hawk, I heard a lot of explosions from the front of the Capital. The Omegans were blasting the Lebabolis garrison who'd been out in the field already. They were dug in, two lines that blasted each other. In the distance, I saw the Omegans had some of their bigger ships. They hovered in place like large black vultures. The only thing keeping them from blasting anymore was the Valentium.

"They've gotta take it by hand," I said over the comm. "But they're careful too because they don't know what Charista has planned. She's got a lot in store for them, but they can't be sure where or when the big bang's gonna happen."

TWENTY-SIX

(NELSON)

A SMASH LANDING AND WE WERE on the ground. Ana groaned a bit and clutched her chest.

"You alright?" Nycole asked. Ana only nodded and coughed in response.

The roar of troops were about us. The air was perforated with electronic punches of pulse blasts from above and on the ground.

"Let's move!" Nycole shouted. We pulled up and saw our group headed toward the southeast wall. Nycole grabbed the credential from Ana's hand. She still hadn't said anything.

"Hey, you OK?" I asked as we jogged.

She replied back, "Fine," but the trickle of blood from her lip made me doubt that assessment. She ran at half speed but never said a thing about hurting or anything else for that matter.

The portal was off to the side in some woods.

"Let's hope this one isn't shut down, or we'll be in a bad way for sure," said Dawn.

Nycole slipped the credential in—the unit powered off. We froze and stared at it as if none of us had just seen it do that. Nycole screamed and pounded it. "Come on, damnit! Work, you piece of shit!"

She pulled back on the unit and re-entered the card. Still nothing. I looked up and noticed a Valkyrie flag billowing in their crowd, but off to the left, heading in our general direction, I saw another group. This one was not-so-friendlies. I pointed them out to Ana.

"We got company," Ana said. "Omegan ground troops; they're gonna give our people on the ground hell. We'll be an appetizer for 'em if they catch us in the open. What's doing with that thing?"

"Jack is what's doing. You wanna try?" Nycole waved Ana over.

Ana studied the credential. "Damn, wish Kado were here right now." She tapped the portal console, and a prompt appeared. Ana spoke several things into it, but none did any good.

She then swiped the crimson liquid from her lips and grasped the credential. Her blood smeared a spot on the card, and she slammed the card home. The console went black again for a few seconds, then it flashed a couple of times and came to life, indicating a successful authentication.

"Yes! You got the touch, girl. Gotta teach me that trick one day. Activate entry portal now!" she shouted at the console. "Request R&D lab."

A purple light enveloped us just as I saw the front of an Omegan tank come into sight, and then we were gone.

Dawn spun towards us. The last thing I saw was a wave of purplish light, and then I was unconscious.

"EASY NOW, you're not going anywhere."

Nycole had us restrained against a wall in a room in the Lebabolis Capital. Ana was to my left, Treg and Dawn to my right.

"What in the hell is this, Nycole?" Treg asked.

"Insurance, dear." She folded her arms, a P-LAD between them.

"I had to get you in here because we need your services. Well, more to the point, hers." She pointed at Ana.

Ana's brow creased. "Yeah? What the hell you think I'd do for Charista?"

"You'll activate Cataclysm, of course."

Ana seethed. "You're missing something. Kado's the brainiac of the group, and you've already got him."

"And he's done fantastic work, but there's one piece that is still missing. At least he was able to find out."

"What's that?"

"Cataclysm's Failsafe, the system implemented by the Valkyrie to prevent it from being fired, has a catch. It can only be activated by the Valkyrie. There is a bloodborne system of nanotransmitters that will engage the system and allow Cataclysm to fire again."

"Well then, you're really in bad shape then, aren't you?" Ana sighed through a laugh.

"No, you don't understand. The Valkyrie saw to it that one person had those transmitters in their blood. It's you, Ana."

What?

All this time?

Ana's eyes widened, and she glanced off for a moment in thought. Then, I thought back to something I'd seen. Baudricort's message to Ana. It's in your blood. So it was that. He had held his cards with the person who he wanted to protect and did protect until he was blown to bits.

TWENTY-SEVEN

(ANA)

"WONDERFUL!" CHARISTA CLASPED her hands together and surveyed us, lined up like a selection of choice meat for her next meal. I searched her eyes for some clue of what she was thinking. Someone who had gone as far as she had and given up as much for the idea of herself ruling the whole planet seemed to be way past any kind of reasoning, but I kept watching.

Flanking Charista were three Radomet, with a fourth one slumped over. It looked like a Radomet, but its metallic body was golden more than reddish.

Also alongside Charista stood Nycole, and that was the more difficult thing to figure. Had I really done it again, pulled in this far by another? Nycole averted her eyes from us and spoke only to Charista. "I've got them where you want them. What's the next move?"

Charista said, "Well, I gave Kado enough time to work through Cataclysm to launch it and that hasn't gotten us anywhere. Now I think it's time for Ms. Ana Crucinal and company to see just what they know."

"We've learned it's a blood-based key," Nycole offered. "The question is where it would've been kept."

Charista nodded and walked toward a wall that had several spears mounted on it. She studied the weapons for a moment before she took one and turned back toward me.

"So, after all this time, the one missing piece happens to be the one person I'd tried to have killed." Charista angled the spear toward me. "Tell me, Ana, just what do you know about your blood?"

A smirk crawled over my face, and I mustered what strength I had left in me. I made myself a promise right there—no way they got blood from me while I was still alive. I was gonna fight her on this until the very end.

My face burned, and I felt my anger flow through my eyes as my glare bored into her. "My blood is better than yours will ever be. Just how many people have you double-crossed to get to where you are? See that fighting going on right outside? That's your people, the Omegans, trying to bust in here. Good on you, making yourself a fortress so tight that it might not happen. But it's gonna come for you, one day or another. You might kill us, but it won't stop what's happening here. And, by the way, it clearly hasn't sunk into your head yet that what you're trying could destroy the planet."

Charista sneered. "Ana, I think you underestimate the strength of the outer walls I've lined with Valentium. But the chance you happen to be correct is a chance I'm willing to take. The Omegans want the universe; I'd rather have my own spot here. Ah Ana, I'll miss these chats of ours. You see, child, you never did have a chance. You were made to think you did, all of you. The problem is without something to hope for, your race doesn't prosper. The Omegan experiment of raising and nurturing your race for several centuries showed us that in spades."

"You treated us like your equipment, but now you're going to have to find something else."

"Oh, I think I know just what to do." Charista chuckled. "Thanks to all these years of humans producing food and tech, we should have enough resources to last us long after you and your kind are gone."

Charista's arms twitched, and the next thing I knew a blade was about an inch away from my right eye. Nelson shouted, "Don't, Charista, no! Damnit, stop!"

Charista's response to Nelson was only an eager glint in her eyes. "I'm completing this experiment, starting with Ana. Don't worry, Ana, your blood won't go to waste. It will be put to use starting up Cataclysm. Your dear old parents thought they could hide their secret with you. Well, they were wrong."

As she clenched the spear tightly, she began to ease it closer to my neck. Focused on her work, she muttered, "Congratulations to you, Ana. You finally have a use in this world."

As she got closer and closer, I took a slow shaky breath in. *Was this finally it?*

I decided to close my eyes so she wouldn't get the satisfaction of seeing the fear in them.

But then, Nycole spoke up. "Wait, Charista, I've got an idea. There are better ways to handle this."

My eyes crept open again. Charista's gaze was still locked on me, but her eyes quickly darted toward Nycole. "Other ways?"

"Well, yes. There's one, anyway."

"One?"

"That's right. One... or none."

If someone had described to me secondhand what I saw right then, I'd have sworn it was a lie. But it was real. I watched in awe as Nycole spun low, her leg out, and connected with a nearby Radomet. Her boot clanged its leg and shifted it just a little. The Radomet behind her swung a fist down on her head, but my reflexes kicked in and I flung my arm up to stop the blow. My forearm throbbed, and a deep ache burst from where I was hit.

The look on Charista's face told me I wasn't the only shocked one in the room. "Foolish girls. And you, Nycole, I thought better of you than siding with Ana."

Nycole flung herself at a Radomet. Sparks flew as she writhed, her arms and legs colliding in sprays of sparks. Charista stepped back but stumbled a bit, dropping the spear. The Radomet swung its fist and connected with her face, sending her sprawling to the floor in a loud yelp.

Two Radomet surged toward me. I leapt through one of their legs and slid behind them. A throb built in my chest.

I scrambled for Charista's spear, grabbed it and thrust it toward the Radomet.

"You're crazy, Charista. There's a legion at your door; don't you realize that?"

"They can come all they want; the sequence has been activated."

"The what?"

"The sequence, my dear, for Cataclysm."

The Radomet swiped at my head, but I managed to duck and roll away several feet until I ended up alongside Nycole. "You mind telling me what the hell's going on?"

A Radomet connected with Nycole's back, sending her forward a bit. I thrust the spear back, blocking them.

Nycole shrugged. "I just figured we'd never last if we didn't have some kind of cover. So, I improvised. Charista had me looking for you, so I figured I'd be the one she'd least suspect of doing something like this."

"Yeah, well, a little prior notice woulda gone better with the rest of us." I smirked.

I had to admit, her little act got us to Charista. But time was running out. Nycole grabbed a pulse baton and launched herself in the middle of the pack of Radomet. They were all a blur of sparks, her yells, the flinging of her weapon and the loud crashes when her staff, foot, leg or even head made contact.

"Nycole! The neck!"

She twisted the baton at the neck of one of the Radomet, and it made contact. The Radomet jerked its body straight and shook in place while swarms of electrical sparks flew from it. I ran toward the other Radomets while they took aim at me. I leapt into the air, my feet aimed at one of the Radomets as it swung at Nycole's head. I connected with the Radomet and knocked it so it collided with the other Radomet.

Before either android had a chance to get back upright, I thrust Charista's spear deep into the neck of the one on the top, shoving it through to the bottom one. After a few seconds of wild jerky moves, both Radomets shook and then after a few sputters, fell silent. The lights on their faces dimmed.

"Impressive," Charista muttered with a frown. "But there's more you need to worry about, Ana."

Loud whirs sounded behind her as another of Charista's creations made an entrance. The pair of green glowing eyes wasn't the only thing unusual about this one, but it was sure the first thing I noticed about it. It was another Radomet—well, it looked like one but a little different. This one had lighter colored armor, almost golden, two staves on its back, and a collection of jagged spikes on its arms.

The worst part was the face, though. It wasn't gruesome, just painfully familiar. I hadn't seen it before, but not even Charista needed to introduce 'em. My feet were fixed to the floor, and my pulse rattled in my throat.

The gold Radomet stood beside Charista. She walked around it, her arm snaked over the smooth gold armor, and with a chuckle she looked back at me. "What's the matter, Ana? Don't you recognize her? This is the true Valkyrie. Petra. I've made some enhancements. You think you can take the Radomet down and kill me? Well, you've got something else to worry about first. Why don't you see how you can do against her?"

Nycole was braced near me; her stance told me all I needed to know about her being ready for this fight too. But I knew we had to take care of other things first.

"Nycole, you've gotta find Kado. I can't leave here; Charista would shoot me down the second my back is turned. Find Kado. See what he can do, he's our last shot. Here, take Llewyn's credential."

"You sure about this?"

"I am."

"That Radomet's not just some warrior product you know."

"I know." My eyes never left Petra's for a second.

Nycole's hand found mine and squeezed before she ran off.

I noticed an attachment on Petra's arm I hadn't seen on a Radomet before. A needle was at the tip of it. Charista caught my glance and chuckled. "I see you're noticing this isn't a typical Radomet, and you're quite right."

Petra made a pass, and I rolled to the floor to avoid her. I was rewarded for that move with a deep throb in my chest.

Petra stood directly in front of me, her eyes wild like an animal that honed in on its prey. Her face, other than the fact it was like I looked in a mirror at myself twenty years into the future, showed not even a hint of recognition.

I tried the Link.

+Hey, you're in there, right? We've been talking all this time, so I know you're in there. Please, answer me. Anything.+

Her response was a sharp jab to the right side of my face. I sank to my knees quick, and needle-like pain blurred my vision.

Charista clapped. "Come now, that's no way for a Valkyrie to fight. Did you just think you could inherit that title without having to do anything about it? You think you're special? Try earning something for once in your life."

I ignored the bitch against the wall and flung myself toward Petra. I slammed my fists into her midsection, but aside from some groans it did nothing. "What the hell'd you do to her, Charista?"

"I activated her, dear child. You're looking at the pinnacle of our existence. Warriors for protection that don't know the word retreat or panic or anything except obedience. You've seen regular Radomet up until now. Well, Petra here is the first of a new line. They'll save us from everything—the Omegans, any of the Guard—these new Radomet are the ones that will last to serve me."

"I don't think so." I whipped out the dagger and swiped toward

Petra. She watched me with an animal stare. I waved a hand in front of her face, but nothing I did made her lose that blank stare. "Come on, Charista's right there; let's get her."

"Nice try, Ana, but you can scream into her ear all day and she won't hear a thing. I've adjusted her hearing with some tweaks to the system. Now, I'm the only one she can hear and respond to."

+Petra, please. Anything!+

Instead of showing any recognition toward me, Petra shoved me into the rack of spears, it sent me and the rack tumbling to the floor in a loud crash. I needed something, a way to get through her. But she had no hearing, and seeing me did no good either. I needed another way to signal.

After I avoided another swing of her blade, an idea came to me. While Petra assumed an attack pose and lurched forward fast, I spun away from her to the far end of the room. I grabbed the handle of the dagger and twisted. The beacon activated, but Petra kept coming. Her lips drew back over her teeth in a crazed sneer, and she lunged for me.

+Mom, wake up!+

I thought of anything; nothing came to mind. She drove her blade into my shoulder. The pain in my chest deepened, and it sent a spurt of blood onto my hand, and I dropped my dagger.

Petra reached for the dagger and held it with her free hand. She eyed it with curiosity, then smashed the handle of the dagger, crushing it into a collection of sparks, and she dropped what was left of the weapon to the floor.

The fear rose up in me. *What can I do? There has to be a way I can get to her. To touch her.* My mind raced back at the thought of 'touch', something Duncan had said.

Sometimes, even the best beacons need the right touch.

I saw the dagger's busted handle on the floor. I ducked a blow from Petra and flung myself across the floor. By the time the blade and handle shards were in my hand and I turned, she was already on top of me. Her metal hand dug into the flesh of my neck and she had me raised up in the air.

Charista beamed. "And now Ana, finally you see what all your efforts, all your plans, all your beliefs have become. Petra, kill Ana Crucinal now."

Petra pulled me in closer. The room began to dim; I was fading fast. Had to focus more. My eyes locked in on hers, and as I felt her grip tighten, I jammed the broken beacon into her neck. An electric jolt hit me, and her hand released me to the floor.

Petra's body lurched and jerked. Her arms flung around at random, and she finally collided with the floor. I raced over to her and saw her face; the light was off but her eyes were wild. Trails of sweat ran down her face. I watched her eyes as they blinked for a second. Then she spoke in a raspy voice. "Who am I?"

Charista had approached us and stood nearby. "What's this? What's this going on?"

I pulled myself up and faced Charista. My vision had narrowed to her. She was my one target, my one focal point.

"As I said before, you're done. Oh, I think that peak you were talking about just passed you by."

Her eyes narrowed. "You're not human. What are you? You should've died long ago. I tried killing you too many times; why are you still alive?"

"I'm alive. I'm more human that you'll ever be. Because I'm a woman who became what you never could be."

"And what's that?"

"A Valkyrie."

Nycole's blade thrust deep into Charista from behind. Charista's eyes widened, and her hands clutched my throat. We fell to the floor like that. I panted and felt the pain in my chest as well as my shoulder.

TWENTY-EIGHT

(ANA)

NYCOLE YANKED HER BLADE FREE from Charista, sending Charista's lifeless body tumbling to the floor. I felt myself sinking to the floor when Nycole caught me and eased me down until I was next to Petra. I pulled her into my arms.

Kado raced into the room as Nycole caught me. He carried Cataclysm and laid it gently on a table near the wall. He went back and forth between the device and me. While Nycole checked my wounds, Nelson stayed close by. The room was a jumble of their voices, but my ears had tuned them out.

All I really was interested in was Petra. Her body twitched, and she gasped. Her eyes flung open. "What am I?"

I coughed so the sob wouldn't take over my voice.

"You're Petra, you're the Valkyrie. You've been captured and reprogrammed as a Radomet, but you're going to be OK."

"Charista?"

"She's dead."

"And you?"

I fought with myself over telling her or not. She was in bad shape; maybe I should wait until later. But what if there wasn't a later?

"I'm—I'm your daughter. Ana."

Her eyes focused on me, and her breaths slowed a little, and then she shook with weeping. "Is it true?"

"It is. I never knew about you."

"And that's my fault. I'm sorry, dear. I wanted to protect you. Your father and I both did, but we were in too far. The only thing we could do was to get you away from us. If Charista knew who you were, she'd never stop trying to find you, and I didn't want this for you. You deserved a chance."

"I got one. Dad got me out."

"Where is he... Baudricort?"

"He's gone. We had a spy; they took him out." My voice always shook when I talked about Baudricort, no matter how long it had been.

Petra's eyes widened at the news about him. She pulled a hand up and rested it on her chest. Her eyes dimmed with sadness, and she shook her head. "All of it was useless... the fighting. Why couldn't Charista realize that? This fighting went on too long. We were faced with annihilation from the Omegans, and we had to do something. But to Charista, that became a weapon, and I knew if I didn't hide it from her at all costs, it meant the end of us."

Blood oozed from her mouth as she shook. "It's done. I can go. It's OK."

I pulled her closer into my arms. "No, it isn't."

She eyed me with a mix of sadness and utter fatigue. "You still have work to do."

My eyes stung with sweat and tears. I nodded toward Charista's lifeless body. "Killing Charista was my work."

Petra shook her head. "No, it was mine. Yours is the future. You told them to earn theirs, and they have. Now it's time to build their future." She shook with a coughing spell.

Fear latched every pore of my being. I thought the fight against Charista was the biggest challenge, but I'd forgotten all about the road that came after.

"How do we do this, without repeating all the bad?"

"It won't be easy. There'll always be the chance of this happening again. But the fight to hold onto the good's worth it. You and the others are worth it."

"If I survive this wound." I looked down at the new blood that had formed on my chest.

Petra saw it too, but shook her head. Then, she smiled at me. "You will, because you're my daughter. Take care of Varrick and yourself. Find your happiness."

"Stay with me, Mom; you'll be OK." I shook her, and my voice quavered. "I just got you; I can't lose you like this."

"What about the Omegans?"

"They're done here," I said. "I guess they realized after all this time it wasn't worth it. Not even to blow us up. They want to take Cataclysm with them and leave."

Petra nodded and watched me with wide eyes. "You can't let them take it."

"I know. But they'll be here soon, and there's no place left to hide. I think about all the times I wanted to be away from here. Even if it meant leaving the planet. But I realize now, your home and your life are what you make 'em. And if you run over everything and ruin and fight and hate and let that swirl around, nothing good ever comes from it. But if you build, care, love, things will get better. Maybe not today, tomorrow or next month, but if you work at it long enough you can accomplish anything."

Her eyes studied me with wonder. "I wish I could see you live, my love. But I'm not so sure."

"Mom, what is it?"

A new trail of blood that oozed from her chest answered my question. The gaping holes from the console attached told me what she meant. This was it. It wasn't fair. There were so many questions, so little time. I wanted to know; I needed to know why this had to happen, why it had to be like this.

But a realization crept into my thoughts. Through all the doubt and questions and hope, I had at some point heard a reason for all of this. I knew the truth: It's not important that we have everything that happens to us explained, but instead that we make the most of the time and situations we're given. Death came for us all, but the most important thing was how we lived, not how we died.

"Mom, I'm scared." I heard the words from me, calling this woman "mother", and not just knowing, but feeling its truth. All this time I had wondered what she was like. Had she known me, had she regretted how it went with me? Her face answered most of my questions, and my heart filled in the rest.

Life gave us half a picture, and left us to fill in the rest the best we could. My eyes stung, and the lump in my throat stayed there. I needed her to stay, but my gut told me that just wasn't happening. I needed her to know how much I loved her, that I didn't care about how things went, that I knew she did what she could. Baudricort and she did everything they could with what they were given.

She smiled weakly. Tears streamed down her face. "I know you're scared. There's still bad out there, and it will always be a scary place. Just find something for yourself, OK? Find people, friends, a family, a purpose. Build something. It's much harder to build than destroy, but it's worth it. It's what humans can do when they don't let darkness cloud things. Your father and I tried to correct this. We failed but not in everything."

I took in her features. I needed to anchor her face in my mind forever. I swallowed the lump in my throat and gazed through blurred vision at this woman. There wasn't even a chance she wasn't my mother; the resemblance was dead on. It was like I looked into a time altered mirror that showed me thirty years into the future.

"How'd you do it, Mom? The Link, talking with me like that?"

She sniffled and shrugged. "Not even Charista could keep me from my daughter. And your father helped a little with the Link."

I chuckled through more cries at her talking about me as family. The family I never had, and never would. I knew the future wasn't set but wished like anything that my past had been different. I had to admit I had a safe childhood. Emily and Jordan took care of me with everything they could, as much as two Products in the Lebabolis system could do, and did their best to share love with me. I realized the truth that, as much as I hated the word, I was a Product after all. But I wasn't a Product of Lebabolis; I was one of Baudricort and Petra. Equal parts strength, knowledge, determination, and compassion. Their best parts, combined and hopefully all part of who I am.

Their story was ending, but mine wasn't. Forever now, they were my parents. I finally knew at last. It wasn't for me to just know, though. I had to pass it on. Carry over what they started.

Charista twitched in the corner. "She was one of them, Mom."

"I know. That's why I hid Cataclysm from her. I wanted to destroy it, but there wasn't enough time. I had to do something. The Failsafe was the best option to keep her from using it. I locked it with the one person I knew more than anything I could trust."

She shook in my arms. "You did it, Mom, you know? You saved us all."

"It wasn't just me." I shook my head. It wasn't at all just me. There was no way I'd have made it this far without everyone. Even Dawn and her tricks got me further than I'd been before. I knew I owed them a lot when this was all over.

Her wheezing deepened. She slunk further back against the wall. "Ana."

I leaned in closer.

"You're the best thing I've ever done. Keep me close, and I'll watch over you, OK? Death isn't the end, just a short time away."

"Mom, no!" I bawled. But it was too late. Her eyes slid shut, and she collapsed against the wall. I fell on top of her, and it seemed like an eternity.

She was gone.

It was over.

The pain I'd felt, of all we'd been through. Baudricort, me, Treg, Nelson... Nelson! The suffering that Charista had released on us because of her own grasp for power. Even the Omegans. It was over. I trembled at the thought of sweet relief, mixed with the pain of losing my mom.

Nelson, Nycole, and Kado stood by in silence. I sobbed without a thought for them or anything else at that moment. What else really mattered?

After a few moments, Nelson slid down to my side and wrapped his arm around me. I watched him through my tears.

"Where does it end, Nelson? Charista kills people, we kill Charista, my mom dies, the Omegans take us... it just goes on and on."

"What do you mean?" he asked.

"Petra led people, Baudricort led people, but they always ended up dead. I'm no better than the warriors; I've led people to their deaths. I couldn't save Otto."

Nelson took a slow breath. "You gave them something he didn't have, maybe what he never had: Hope. You showed him and everyone who saw you what they could do if they tried, if they just believed. You showed them what they could become."

There it was. My own words came back to me, like a long lost loved one. I eyed Nelson. He watched me with warmth in his gaze. His smile made me relax and remember more about the good I'd come from and the journey I still had ahead.

Nycole joined us on the floor. "I know this is a bad time, but we still have the Omegans to worry about. Last I saw, they were making their way through the Guard."

A quick sniffle and I nodded. Nycole's eyes said plenty about the pain she felt for me, but there was also that reminder about the job. It wasn't done, and it was up to us to finish it.

"OK. Let's do this. Kado, get me into the address system; I wanna get a message to the outside."

Nelson helped me to the console, and Kado worked with the controls a bit until he handed me a mic.

"Here, this will broadcast to the entire Capital and on the speakers to outside."

I grabbed the mic and sucked in a deep breath. I watched the monitors, showing where the Action and Guard troops still brawled with the Omegans.

"Commander Patrach of the Omegans, my name is Ana Crucinal. Charista Mantisword is dead. I have what you want: the Cataclysm Weapon. Enter the Capital building and go to the third level. I'm in here with the device. I suggest you don't try anything smart, or I'll activate Cataclysm and level you and your entire force. You have five minutes to comply."

We watched the scene on the external monitors as the Guard stood back. They kept at the ready though; nobody, not even me was gonna tell Duncan to back off at that point. Patrach strode into the entrance with a group of soldiers.

While we waited, Kado ran through the sequencer for Cataclysm with me.

"It's pretty simple, actually. Your blood has the key to activating this device; you just place your finger here, and it arms in seconds.

I stared at Cataclysm, the source of a lot of our trouble so far, and shook my head at the fact this was now in my hands. I realized then how Mom must've felt with this device, and I knew I wanted it as far away from me as possible, just like she probably did.

After a few minutes, Patrach and his crew entered, and we were face to face with him and his aides. The lines in Patrach's skin were deeper than the average Omegan I'd seen, and his eyes looked a bit more ragged. I held myself up every bit as much as I could.

"You can examine Charista's body, but I'm sure you'll find she's as dead as someone can be."

Patrach nodded to one of his troops. "See to it."

Patrach watched his soldier walk toward Charista for a moment before he turned back to me. "Is that the Cataclysm device over there?"

"It is, but before we go any further on that, we need to discuss terms."

His brow raised. "And you're the humans we've been trying to retrieve? I must tell you, you've given some of my better troops a time, so my compliments."

"Commander, I appreciate your words, but the truth is your race and ours need a new agreement. We've worked for you for centuries and built many things. We've shown our use, but we won't live like slaves anymore. If that's all you thought of us, I may as well flick this switch now because we weren't born to be equipment."

"Strong words from a foolish mind. What do you suppose I say to my people though, the ones who'd spent time cultivating and developing your race, the years we've spent here, and the lives we've lost? Are we supposed to just abandon this? Simple creature, charity isn't a word familiar to Omegans."

I nodded. "I thought you might say something like that. Allow me to offer a truce. Your Brescar, you've been pulling it out of all the deposits on the planet. You say it's yours, OK. Leave us and take it with you. We only want to live free and will not press the issue, as long as you let us be."

Patrach's face twisted in disbelief. "Living free, on this decrepit world, with no viable source of energy? Are you mad?"

"No, just tired. And, ready for no chains. We need a world that doesn't depend on things like Brescar."

"The world will always depend on things like Brescar."

"I can't say you're wrong there. But we need time to remember what is more important, and that doesn't include killing each other just to get more power."

"Until that happens, you'll be setting your people up for an ancient existence they've never known. How long before they're rioting and at your throat?" Patrach's chuckle was as deep as it was sarcastic.

"We have a long road, no doubt. But we need time to find a better way so we don't lose control again. Some won't follow, but we'll deal with that in time. It won't be easy; nothing worthwhile ever is. But it's necessary. Our race has been through plenty, and though we know how to tear down, to destroy, to break apart, we're also good at building. We've done it before; I know we can again."

Patrach gazed at me for a long while. "Your species is rather troublesome, and I think if anything we've learned yours isn't a kind worth a bother. I'd rather see Omegan lives be spent looking at more viable worlds anyway. That said, I don't spend Omegan lives lightly. Your race wants these terms, then you must offer suitable compensation for what our kind has given yours. I entertained this meeting because I wanted to see up close just who it was that would've dared resist me for so long. It troubles me why anyone would risk anything for this forsaken rock."

"This forsaken rock happens to be our home."

"And this is the way your species treats a home? Decimating it until near oblivion? We found your kind dormant, like seeds scattered to the wind. We've scoured this planet for over a century, girl. And the little we've found of use has no bearing on what we think of this place in general. Why would you be concerned with us destroying it?"

"Besides the obvious part of us living on it, it's our home. It's not much, with a dubious history. Plenty of wars, suffering, destruction and death. But it hasn't been all bad. People haven't been all bad. And we're willing to start again. To try again."

He narrowed his eyes and scoffed. "Why?"

"Because someone needs to. Because someone else did in the past. Thousands, millions of someones got up and did their part and kept things going. Others tried destruction and conquest, but enough did plenty to build. The better, calmer minds took control of what they could and made something out of it. I have to think through all that, what we've done and what has happened to us, even you bringing us back, had to have been for a reason. I'm willing to look for it here."

"It doesn't seem worthwhile. Your species was on the verge of extinction when we found you."

"However that happened, I'm willing to bet we can correct that."

Patrach's brow creased, and he took a deep breath before his eyes narrowed again. "I do admire your will, but let me give you another item to consider. Several ships from my fleet surround this planet and at any moment, I can have them open fire, reducing this world to mere clouds of cosmic dust drifting into dark space. Does this bring you to any easier decision?"

I swallowed a lump in my throat. Faces came at me, and the thumping of my pulse in my throat ratcheted up. My thoughts raced; did we really have a choice. Was there nothing left as an option?

Then as clear as I'd once looked on Baudricort, it came to me.

I jammed my finger into the Cataclysm sequencer. Patrach bolted forward, but Nycole held him back. "What are you doing?"

"I have an item of my own. You can destroy this planet, and you're a far superior force to anything on it. You've got us, except for this. I've got the Cataclysm device set for global destruction. You might destroy us, but I bet even your fleet won't be able to escape before I blow you up too."

"You're insane! You've proven everything about your race, how evil you can be and destructive."

"Nothing you didn't already know, but I'm actually proving something else. I'm prepared to do away with all of this," I muttered. Our eyes locked for what felt like ten minutes. He grunted and eyed the rest of the Cataclysm device. The hum was the only sound in the room. Treg braced himself near one of the guards.

"You'd destroy the planet?"

I realized finally in that moment, it's not about what you're willing to die for.

We all die. Some for a cause, like Baudricort and Petra. Others for much less than. The people killed in Lebabolis, had they died for anything? Weren't their lives worth as much as mine?

No, it wasn't about dying for something.

It was about what you just aren't willing to give up.

For me what I wasn't giving up was simple. The life that I'd been given—the child of two people who fought so hard for what they believed, they gave up their own daughter to live in safety so they could make their play to stop the world from disintegrating into Chaos.

It was also Varrick. My brother from the moment I felt him in Emily's belly. My brother in spirit and in heart. The one I'd seen go through ridiculous pain and suffering, and wasn't out of the woods yet. He was still around and there was a future for him, I'd be damned if that wasn't the case.

And then Nelson. I went from being curious to being interested, to now, the thought of his not being in the same place as me wasn't even thinkable. While I knew it had to happen, it was gonna happen on our terms. Not Patrach and the Omegans, Charista, nobody.

My line wasn't in the sand. It wasn't a huge banner. It wasn't some fancy battle armor. It was people that I could not for anything do without. If the Omegans wanted us off world to waste away in slavery, we'd all join each other in death.

Patrach heaved, and beads formed on his forehead.

"Leave us, take the Brescar, and leave us be. We let you go, and you let us live."

"It's an ongoing fight, you know. Your kind is rife with discontent. In time they'll be gunning for you if you're not careful."

"Maybe. I'll take the chance."

Patrach shook his head slowly. "I've heard enough from the sentimental aspect of your reason. You'll need to make this worth my while if you expect me to leave all of you alone."

"We can't give you Cataclysm. Even in good faith. It's too dangerous. It must be dismantled, but only after you've left this planet and us alone."

"That's not a call for you, girl. That device was around well before you were even born."

"It is a call, it's my call, and I'm making it. Leader, you may command the Omegan Empire, but on this planet people take a stand now and then, and that's what I'm doing."

His eyes lanced into me with red fury. He let out a guttural growl and gnashed his teeth a bit. I felt that familiar ache in my gut again, but I also knew I had to do this.

"I must admit, I admire your nerve. Given different circumstances, I may have even considered offering you a rank in my legion."

"Thanks, Leader, but my place is here with these people."

"So be it. We'll settle with our Brescar. The sooner we're done with this wretched planet, the better."

TWENTY-NINE

(ANA)

I'D BECOME A DIPLOMAT WITHOUT even knowing it. The deal we ended up with on the Omegans was involved, but it was pretty simple. In exchange for them vacating this planet and leaving us to it, we returned their Brescar. A lot of our people were against it, and it took some doing, but once the Intellectuals started researching, they began developing newer methods for synthesizing the residue of what we had left and restoring our regular power.

So, we slipped back into a darker period, but after a while I noticed a change. People became closer. Without technology to help us, hold us, train us, strain us, people relied more on each other. It almost felt like the Circle, but on a much bigger size. Hope was a trip that never ended, Baudricort used to say.

We held a funeral for Petra, finally burying her with the honors she deserved. The wound of seeing her die in my arms was still fresh, but I knew there was nothing anyone could do about that. It helped having Nelson nearby and seeing the faces of so many people, grateful for the woman who held up faith in a time when it seemed like nothing would ever be right. I was happy to know that finally and for always, my parents had a resting place next to each other.

The harder part of our existence after the Omegans was getting everything dismantled and deciding on a new system. People left unchecked are a dangerous thing. Freedom can be a difficult system, especially when some of the choices people had available to 'em involved destroying themselves or worse, an encore of the world Charista had set up. But that's why the Valkyrie remained important and always would.

In time after beginning to rebuild, a system came about. Freedom, representation, and a fair say for more people. It wasn't perfect, but it was better than before. And sometimes better is all you can hope for.

Still and all, the Valkyrie remained a thing. It bothered me less, in later years. People like to know, or needed to know someone was out there, standing guard, watching the lines, ready to step in when someone else got out of hand. Sooner or later, someone always did. Humans are many things; one of them is stupid forgetful idiots. Eventually, someone wants more than they had, and they had enough strength to try something about it.

Even with a new government in its stages, people still clung to traditions of old, and I found myself right in the middle of one of 'em.

I FIDDLED with the handle of my dagger. The newly formed blade and handle gleamed even in the evening light. I stopped twirling it around my hand long enough to catch Duncan looking at me. "We really need to do this?"

"It's what we do, Ana."

Duncan lit a fire outside in the common gathering area just outside the Lebabolis Capital ruins. The deep orange and amber flames danced around like excited worshippers. He pointed me to a spot on the ground and motioned for me to kneel, then he began.

"Our crest, the blade and bolt, has a rich history. When we were formed, when the Valkyrie was first known to us, she gave us this symbol and told us what it means. The blade represents all that we know, all that we control. Weapons like the blade were made for protection, defense, and sometimes for attack. But they were made by humans. They are controlled by humans, and we must always remember to respect that which we control and also master that which we can control, so it never controls us.

"The bolt represents all that we cannot control. Nature, the weather, life, death, disease. This world has been shaken time and time again, by forces beyond our control. It isn't ours to control these energies, but to respect them and learn to use them, to work with them. This planet is our home, and we must always remember that while we live here, we are only part of this entire system."

"So, we have the two, the known and the unknown, the controlled and the uncontrollable. They intersect because our world is never without each of these forces. We use what we can control and deal with what we cannot. To guide us is the Valkyrie. Lebabolis gave us the Valkyrie but as our watcher. The Valkyrie is over and above Lebabolis, because she isn't a ruler. She isn't a governmental official. She is strength, honor, and discipline. She is what is best in us, and that only when we are at our best will we ever matter in this world. Petra was our leader, and she's gone. She defended us until she couldn't anymore. And through our struggles to claim our lives back from the Omegans, one has risen and proven herself. Ana Crucinal, daughter of Baudricort and Petra, we salute you, your heart, your strength, your honor, and your iron clad will to never lay down even when the odds are overwhelmingly against you. You are in my mind, heart and soul what the Valkyrie was, is and will be. I pledge all that I have, muscle, skin, bone, blood, and the heart that pumps it, to your service as long as I shall live. Hail Valkyrie!"

The rest of the Guard joined in a chorus of shouts, "Hail Valkyrie!" Their voices continued, cheers and hollers, praises. Even with the flames close by, a chill swept through me. I looked at their faces, eyes lit up the same as when I was surrounded by them back in

Lebabolis. But unlike then, they weren't sneers. It was respect, honor. I saw myself through their eyes and felt a surge of pride at their vision, knowing it wasn't for someone else but for me.

Once the ceremony finished, people wanted to see me, meet me, touch me. It still felt bizarre, but through all this I'd managed to accept a few things. I knew I'd been given something, and it was up to me as well as whoever came after me to never let it become me. I was always Ana Crucinal, and the Valkyrie was something I was, but not all that I was. As much as my parents had given me an example, I knew I'd always have the lesson of Charista in my mind too, because someone with a lot of power didn't always have a clear path.

Nelson met up with me several hours later near one of the building areas for new housing units. His smile warmed me as much as it ever did.

"How does it feel?"

"Being the Valkyrie? Eh, not bad, I suppose."

His brow arched. "Not bad? You still having trouble with this title after all this time?"

I laughed a bit. "No, no, not at all. It's something I'll probably still have to get used to, but I'm learning."

"Well, good for that. Listen, Kado sent me a comm a little while ago. I think... it's time."

My gut tensed, since I knew what that meant. "OK, let's see how this is gonna go."

KADO'S new laboratory was way different than anything I'd seen him work in before, the residual Valentium powered some of the monitors and terminals, but I knew that was a short-term deal. The tech we had left in here was our price for a ticket, a one-way trip for Nelson.

Nelson and I joined Kado in his lab around a table with a monitor on it. It was so nice seeing him back in his element. He had been so ragged and exhausted when we saw him with Charista. This time, he was all cleaned up, and that inquisitive spark I knew and loved was back in his eyes, brighter than ever before.

"So, I've been able to deconstruct Cataclysm and have released its energy. I've been able to open up a small Verge for a single passage. It's going to implode once used and then that will be it."

Nelson watched him, his eyes wide. "Alright then."

"Indeed. Nelson, your way home is here, it looks like."

He strode about the room, his eyes taking things in. He folded his arms about. His eyes were filled with a lot of things, mostly joy, but when our eyes met a tinge of something else was there."

"Kado, can you give us a moment?"

"Of course." He handed Nelson a piece of paper with scribbled notes. "Coordinates for the return. We'll set them up for the Verge before you leave." Kado smiled at us then left.

"Tell me what's on that mind, Nelson."

A tear snaked down his cheek. "After all this time and all this searching and fighting, to finally get it here, just seems surreal."

"We've fought for this so long, and I knew you wanted this. I wasn't giving up on this ever. I also knew I wasn't doing it alone. I'm glad that Kado got something to happen for you after everything we've been through."

"Yeah." Nelson's reply lingered in the air with a lot of hesitation. His mouth hung open, and fear slipped over his gaze.

"What; tell me."

After a deep breath, he shook his head. "I wanted to get back for so long, I hadn't thought about what I was leaving."

"You mean like getting shot at and killed more times than I could count? Getting hooked up to one contraption after another? Being worshiped as a prophet and the assorted pressure that goes with that?"

That got a laugh outta him. I knew what he meant, and truthfully, I'd denied it probably as much as he did.

"I really want to stay, but my head won't let me. My heart, on the other hand, wants to remain here more than I can say." He clasped my arms and gazed into my eyes, and I knew it wasn't anything I'd said but something I'd felt. All this time we'd been together, it grew between us and was there, no denying it. My face flushed, and he pulled me closer.

"How can it be," he whispered. "You can be this close with someone ever?"

Without another word, we embraced. I gasped out in a loud cry and held him with all that I had. Was he the one who had given me this? A million images and feelings rushed through me. A lifetime of memories forbidden, of love withheld, of want, need for this man. My body shook, and he held me close. I'd lost so much already, was I ready for this loss too?

THIRTY

(NELSON)

ANA WALKED WITH ME ALONE to the Verge. Seemed the best way to do this. It had started with just me and her, and now it was gonna end that way.

Or would it?

Do things really end? I mean, yeah, our lives do, but the people in them, the feelings we have, do they end? I still loved and missed my mom. It was so real, and there was nobody on Earth, or even God, who could've changed how I felt. The feelings were as much a part of me as my very soul, and I was damned glad for it.

Ana and I stood by the Verge. The familiar swirl of purple waves greeted me like an old friend, and my throat clenched up, knowing the moment I'd dreaded was finally here.

I had to say goodbye to her.

I watched the swirling sea of colorful patterns in silence. I felt my chest move with my slow, deep breaths. Ana's fingers tickled mine, and our hands clasped.

"I thought I'd know what to say right here." Ana's voice was low.

A lock of hair slipped over her face, and a tear glistened in her eye.

710

"Yeah, I'm not much better, and I'm supposed to be the one with the gift for words here."

"You've got plenty of gifts, Nelson. Don't you ever doubt that."

"No, and you either. You're a leader now. In charge."

"World better watch out."

We shared a nervous laugh. Her face beamed with a smile. The light in her face and being drew me to her, and before I knew it she was in my arms. We embraced, two bodies meshed together as if they'd always been that way. Our lips met in an invitation neither offered nor refused. Visions flashed through my mind, me and her, her and me. Walking, laughing, living a life together. One that would never be. Marriage, kids, old age, happiness, heartache; they poured through me like a river of memories. All this time I'd convinced myself she wasn't real, but somehow she was. I hadn't created this world; I was just lucky enough to have been linked to it. A world I never belonged to. A world I was just the storyteller for.

She trembled a bit in my arms as she spoke. "I think I figured it out, about you. At least how I've felt. I didn't think it was this way before. I wanted to meet you because it solved a mystery. It filled a piece in for me, and that was enough. But all this time together, and what we've been through. I with you, I'm who I am, not what I need to be."

"What do you mean?"

"I'm scared a lot of the time, Nelson. I don't let them see it, don't let the soldiers or those who call me Valkyrie see it, because I can't. This isn't a world for the timid. Leading it isn't anyway."

I clasped her head gently. She smiled with her eyes shut in my embrace. But then she eased her eyes open again and stared at me, eyes, mind and soul completely open to me.

"Listen to me, dear one. Being afraid makes you human. I bet anything those soldiers out there all have some kind of fear. Fear isn't a bad thing. Fear of dying makes you fight that much harder to stay alive, right? It's gotten you and the rest this far. The trick is not to let it control you. And definitely not to make decisions that affect people out of fear. That's the wrong way."

Tears streamed out of her eyes, and her lip trembled. "Promise me something," she said.

"Anything."

Her amazing eyes were wide with so many emotions. I took her face in; I had to remember it somehow and always. The way her hair was strewn about her face. Another tear sneaked down her cheek.

"Find your joy. Live your life. Think of me from time to time."

"Always. And you, take care of that kid. You're all he's got left."

"Yeah well, been this far for him, you know me..."

"...never backing down."

We laughed again. Her lips were soft and for that moment, I didn't have to go anywhere. I was home. With her. But that wasn't the way of things.

"You gonna lead now? Figure out where all this is going? Seems you're the one to do it."

She laughed again and swiped her hand over her face. "I'm not one for delegating. I'd never last in that position. These people would drive me nuts. Look how crazy you made me, chasing your ass every which way."

"Good point there."

"It needs to be Kaitlinn. I think she'd do it. I'm happy to advise. I just need... to make something for myself."

I nodded. "Treg?"

"He's who I know. And one of the people whose known me long-est." Her lips formed a tight line as more tears fell unchecked down her face.

"He's a good man."

She nodded, her lips slipped down to a pout and she sniffled. "Dammit, you tell anyone about this, so help me I'll come back through that Verge somehow and beat your sorry ass."

"Your secret's safe with me, Valkyrie."

"OK. Remember, never forget. Our lives are linked always, by more than just days."

We wrapped arms around each other once more for the last time. "I love you, Ana Crucinal."

"I love you too, Nelson Forrester."

THIRTY-ONE

(NELSON)

THINGS WERE A LOT DIFFERENT since I came back. I mean, yeah the same, like it was still my city and all the people there in it were around, but what I knew since my— I've come to call it my detour—I look at things different.

People especially.

The story about Tina's murder got handled. The DNA at the scene was tracked back to a corpse found by the wharves. I never bothered to dig, once they informed me I was in the clear. I still think about her and what might have been from time to time.

Would there ever be another who matched me so well, who knew me so fully, who felt so much like an extension of myself? I thought of Ana's words to me a lot, about finding my happiness. I learned while finding it is important, it's equally crucial to accept it. Things and life don't typically happen as designed. We sometimes need to find happiness in things, even if they are the mundane day to day variety.

In my dreams, I still went to her sometimes, and I knew that wasn't changing for any length of time. I took comfort in writing the novel and looking in on Dad. I came back into 2014 at the moment I left, and Dad hadn't suspected anything and was still there as much as ever. I happily jumped in and resumed my watch over him.

Talking with Mom at her graveside on Mother's Day and other times of the year helped me through it too.

The thoughts still came to me from time to time, about the distant time to when I was part of one of Earth's greatest battles.

Was I ever gonna talk about what happened to me? Tell Harvey or anyone else? There's no way they'd have believed it anyway. I had the fortune of the book and the ability to pass it off as the wily imagination of a writer. If people only knew the truth.

I can still remember the feel of her against me, her taut arms that held me tight. Even the way she smelled. What was that? It wasn't the scent of flowers, but it was calming. Warm. I knew for sure if I had one thing left on this earth it was finishing my novel. At least by that time I had no problem figuring it out. My only concern was remembering.

And doing them justice. Doing her justice.

I smiled every time I thought of her at that ceremony, when she officially became the Valkyrie. She pushed it aside for so long, but finally realized it was who she was and accepted it. But she chose it and made damn sure we all knew it, even me.

There was no telling Ana Crucinal anything otherwise. I watched her, her face once again clean, hair kept perfect, those beautiful eyes, I watched her, pride for her overflowing in me like a brook in spring, like she was the loved one at a graduation or something.

She had the benefit of a long history of people and groups who did ridiculous amounts of things to screw up the world. But like a cat with nine lives, the human race had once again survived another day. In part due to outside help, but also due to no small amount of tenacity from people like Ana.

I couldn't have been prouder or more torn about leaving. I do sleep better knowing that she will exist. Knowing that in spite of how much the Darkness or Cataclysms of the world can threaten it, there are still those willing and able to stand up, hold a weapon and lead others to victory.

I MET Harvey at a new place he wanted to try out in the suburbs called "Ales".

"You'll like it, man, really! They've got this really hot bartender, been trying to get her number and all."

"Oh yeah, now I know why you made me go all this way out of the city for a damned drink, passing up all those watering holes along the way." I shook my head.

The line of taps faced us like cars backed up on the interstate. Harvey nodded at a girl who poured a dark stout into a glass. She had short hair with a color I wasn't sure existed anywhere else in this world, even the one I'd just visited. She slammed the tap back closed and spun on her heel with the grace of a dancer. Her form fitting black shirt and jeans resembled a catsuit. She eyed us, a lock of hair drooped low over her eyes.

"Yeah?"

"Need a beer, babe."

She narrowed her eyes toward Harvey. "It's Sarah, not babe. Gimme a sec, k?"

She made her way down the bar and busied herself picking up some empty glasses and tip money. I heard Harvey next to me grunting some kind of approval at the particular view. I had to admit she wasn't bad, but only if I removed comparison with a certain other.

"Nelson, you're telling me this whole thing was just some kinda scam?"

"Yeah, I don't get it either. Apparently, they'd been doing this with other people. I looked into it at the police office, and one of their detectives clued me in."

"What the hell they pull that on you for? I mean, no offense, but

I'd have thought they'd go for someone with more means, money, fame, whatever."

"Yeah, thanks for that. I dunno, guess some people just want to have something they can control. Gives them a feeling other than being completely helpless all the time."

I heard myself say it, and the symbol jutted into my mind like a ninety-foot billboard right in front of me. The whole line to Harvey; I figured that while a lie wasn't great, if I went on and on in depth about what really happened, somewhere, somehow that would get out, and then I'd be looking at way more than just people wanting to know about my trip. Saying you've traveled centuries to the future and back even now and even in this town is a pretty easy way to get yourself locked up. New Orleans loves its crazy and doesn't hide it, but I suspect even people in this town would draw a line in a second if they heard my story. I figure I'd let everyone just see the book and let the talking go there.

We proceeded to down a few drinks as I pondered my upcoming employment search with Harvey's feedback. Harvey was nowhere even close to getting even the name of Sarah's subdivision, but I noticed her flash me a wink at one point after serving up one of our rounds.

After Harvey finished his latest drink, he turned to me. "So, you wanna do something next weekend? I'm gonna be starting vacation and feel like hitting the road, maybe cruising up the coast."

"Long as you can keep it simple or foot the bill; remember I'm between jobs."

Harvey patted my shoulder. "No worries, man."

"Alright. Just let me check in on my dad first."

"How's he doing?"

"Eh, alright, I suppose. He's slowed down a bit and isn't driving anymore. I've been taking him around, and our neighbor's been helping out too."

"That's good."

"So, yeah, give me until Saturday, and I think I can slip away for a little trip."

The end of the day found me back at my laptop. The lucent glow of the screen greeted me in a familiar sight like it was some kind of therapist. I looked at the words on screen like they were dear friends, since now, they really were.

Seeing pictures of them, real people now, in front of me. I feel like I've been welcomed to a relative's home on Christmas Eve and I'm surrounded by them. I'm comforted they'll always be with me. How could they not? They are as much a part of me as I am of them. And maybe, this can serve some purpose after all. Maybe after all the trying, the jobs, the searches, the battles, the struggle, this can stand up for someone and remind them that as bad as life can get, as much as illnesses like pox and cancer and everything else can rip our most beloved from us with no rhyme or reason whatsoever, there's plenty that makes this place worth it. Plenty that makes us still worth it. But the key is like that phrase "One or None". It's not to say that only one person gets their way. It's that we come together as one.

We can't control people, but we can love them. When we did that, things got better from there.

THIRTY-TWO

(ANA)

T HE SUN STILL BURNED MY FACE when I looked at
it, but now the feelings were different. Before, I had
thoughts of the war, of the Exodus, of Baudricort and the
whole fucking mess that started us on this journey. Now, it's almost
like a dim, even pleasant reminder of all we've been through.

Our best minds got together, and with a network of trees, they
carved out living quarters for many. It was a small start, but in time it
grew fast. The new civilization Renovare consisted of the former
Lebabolis Products, surviving members of the Guard, and of course
the Action. A group no longer divided by Product assignment but one
that worked toward a goal. The word 'united' was still a stretch for us,
but we sure operated more as a group in the Rebuilding instead of a
series of separate factions.

The Lebabolis facilities remained in place, all steadily broke
down into piles of rubble with each passing year. Their sight was a
reminder to us of where we'd been, and a place we needed to never
be again.

As if a reminder was all we needed.

I knew better.

People still looked to me, but the stories about me and everything that happened got told less and less as time went by. The less people looked at me like some superhero, the more relieved I felt. I just wanted to be what I once was, find that girl I used to be before the fighting, killing, and dying started. I hoped that one day I would find her.

At least, I had help in that search from Treg, who became my partner in recent years. It wasn't something that happened right away, as during the rebuilding process we had our own work to handle. But in time, that childhood connection grew stronger.

He always knew about my heart and Nelson, but Treg was a lot of what was right about my past and present. I figured he was my best shot at a brighter future too. And we did that, each day one step at a time.

Renovare rebuilt as a place of ideas and growth, and Kaitlinn was a natural for its first leader. I listened to speeches by Kaitlinn since she took office. She was the elected leader of the new government we formed. I wanted no part of it but agreed I stayed around, ready like the Valkyrie always was, in the ongoing fight of keeping everyone safe. Even after all we'd been through, a peaceful world still needed help now and then.

I didn't have the stomach for Kaitlinn's kind of diplomacy, and I knew she was the one to take it over. In our new world, people governed instead of being formed, directed, and assigned to a place someone else determined for 'em. Things weren't perfect, but we made strides toward that.

Jacobs fought until the end, but the fight outside of Lebabolis took its share of casualties, and he was one of 'em. We buried him along with all the brave who gave their lives for our future with honor. Freedom always came with a price, and I hoped we never ran short of people like Jacobs who paid that final price without question.

Lucy survived the fight with the Omegans, and I was the least surprised about that. After a little while, she even forgave me for not having her along on our mission to Llewyn and Charista, and in the months and years since we became as close as any sisters could've ever been.

Dawn joined up with Kado, and while she and I still weren't any closer at all in recent times, her with Kado was a lot better than the days when I wondered what she was up to during the days of Charista.

I still thought of Nelson so much at times; I probably always would. My other half. The one who reminded me, more than many, after his impossible journey, that I hadn't known everything there was to know about the Valkyrie.

I've learned it meant being a protector and all, but also someone who was loving, who held on to those they cared about. And sometimes, there were ways beyond the physical ones where we kept people close. Our time with people in life was always limited, but also the emotional connection went way beyond the physical presence. Thankfully, the emotional link continued long after a person's death, but only if we spoke of 'em and told the world about them, and lived for them, because that's what they wanted for us, right up to the end.

Even with this new life I had, a piece of me always stayed back in 2014 with Nelson, just like a bit of him remained with me in a way. Two souls, connected yet apart. Forever. Some nights I dreamt about him and what he ended up as. A famous author who created worlds people enjoyed. I wondered if anyone from his time even had an idea how real his stories became.

Varrick got healthier. He walked with a limp and always would, they told me. It was a trade-off I gladly accepted for him to be alive and with me. I just wished I could've saved Petra.

I still cried for her sometimes. How long we'd been apart, how I never knew her at all. My mother. My real mother. She was still a part of me, even though I never had her in my life. That thought was one of the things that kept me going now. Even though she wasn't with me for very long, she was with me in my mind and heart always.

After all, she was part of me, and that was something no one ever took away.

Not even Charista and all her plans and schemes.

Kado was as much a part of the technical side as in Lebabolis, if not more so. The creations he, Dawn and their new crop of mentees made kept us running, and I grew prouder of him each and every day. We've begun the slow climb back with technology, with the hope that just maybe this time we remembered our past and avoided the mistakes there.

We've worked on our strength and made sure we maintained a defensive force with members of the Guard as well as the new blood as they grew into their new roles in Renovare. Duncan has been everything I could've hoped for in a friend, mentor, and someone who kicked people's asses into shape, even mine sometimes.

Norg began again too; he started a new family. He still grumbled at times, but that was just Norg. The day he stopped that was the day I worried about him.

My Circle. Those who I'd never made it without. We saw each other still, much less than I liked, but I know like any true friends, they're around whenever I need them.

So we stood, once again, out of the pile the world was sinking into very steadily. The Omegans were good for little other than their promise of leaving, and that was only after I threatened 'em with the one thing worth more to 'em than any of us – their lives.

Once Nelson was safely away, we deactivated Cataclysm once and for all, then turned the device into a series of unrecognizable scraps. The Omegans left with their Brescar. I figured that was the last time we saw 'em, but then again, who'd have thought they'd have been here to begin with?

Whatever the case, we had our own work to do. Lebabolis wasn't built in a day, and I bet nothing actually worthwhile ever was, either. Of all things humans had potential for, our race had a strong attraction to stupidity, and no amount of knowledge got around that completely. We always wanted more, fought for more, needed more, took more, and did all of that way more than we gave. And that had always been our problem. It wasn't until people or a group of people stood up and said 'No, that's enough' that things ever changed.

The Valkyrie did that – stopped people from going too far, and still did – but it was never a job for one person. It was always a group effort. So that was my mission, as the Valkyrie, I trained our growing army. It was what I've known, and thanks to people like Treg, I've passed on things I've learned. That included the most important lesson: that even with strength and power, there still has to be thought.

The Action and my Circle taught me it was possible that a Warrior, a Worker, and an Intellectual worked together, and along the way became some of the best friends in the world. That's what we needed through this. "One or None" soon became only a distant memory of our rally, our time when we pulled together, but the best part was that the call to unity still lived. It wasn't spoken anymore, but it was around more than it ever had been. It was on the faces of people who worked together on the rebuilding, those who were segregated into different Products in the past, but instead were all together, free citizens who worked for the common goal and were allowed to, free from the strict rule of Lebabolis.

As much as I learned about people in the Rebuilding, I learned about myself too. It wasn't easy, but over time I got better. Treg said my attitude was grown in my first 23 years of life and it took at least that many centuries before I changed again. I just smacked him.

Whatever became of me in the end, the Valkyrie remained a symbol. But now it meant more than what it represented in the beginning.

It meant hope for tomorrow.

Some people in our new society set stones in the ground as a symbolic marker for our time with the Omegans. As much as they'd done to us, they gave us a chance again. As bad as it was in our second start, we owed the Omegans for that option. I looked at the rocky markers now and then, large smooth discs that sat in the center of our new Capital. Gifts weren't given often, and the careless always risked running out of favors before they knew what happened.

We stayed on the watch though. Because people always forgot their way sooner or later. The Omegans gave us another chance. Making it count was up to us. For now, and for always.

As much as we made sure that, like our motto One or None, that Every...One was taken care of. Especially those who weren't able to fend for themselves. The Rebuilding hasn't been perfect by any stretch. There was still disease, and challenges like getting enough food for everyone, but no one could've argued we were headed to a better place.

My mission now was to chase good. I found people who needed help and got it for them, either myself or through someone else. Until no one was left out or alone, we still had work ahead for us.

Our potential covered so many things, like blowing up all we know and love, and spreading misery until everything on this planet was destroyed and we were all in our own self-made hell, or the alternative: chase good. For any who asked what that looked like, I told 'em it meant caring for people, looking out for those who can't do it for themselves.

Whenever times got tough in the years of Rebuilding and after, I thought back to the ceremony, when they made me the Valkyrie, and Duncan's words about the bolt and blade emblem, the intersection of things under our control and those that weren't. And while the Charistas, the Darkness, and the Llewyns and all those who wanted the way of burrowing deep into everything about greed and destruction, I and everyone who valued the good rose up and did something. It was truly up to us.

After all, we had no way of knowing when our time in this life was up. But we knew this moment existed and we were in it, and for that moment and for however long after that, we had a choice. Either we sank into the muck of the power hungry and destructive or we rose into the growth toward that destination of who we were always meant to be.

"We are not now that strength which in old days
Moved earth and heaven, that which we are, we are,
One equal temper of heroic hearts,
Made weak by time and fate, but strong in will
To strive, to seek, to find, and not to yield."

TENNYSON, ALFRED LORD. "ULYSSES."
POETS.ORG, HTTPS://POETS.ORG/POEM/
ULYSSES. ACCESSED 26 JANUARY 2020

"Now this is not the end.
*   It is not even the beginning of the end.*
*   But it is, perhaps, the end of the beginning."*

WINSTON CHURCHILL ADDRESS TO THE
HOUSE OF COMMONS, PALACE OF
WESTMINSTER, NOVEMBER 10, 1942

THE VALKYRIE CHRONICLES SERIES

All of these titles are available individually on Amazon.com

ALSO BY PAUL HEINGARTEN

The Harvest (short story)

Leave from Absence (novel)

The Monitor (short story)

Natural Election (short story)

WANT SOME FREE BOOKS AND STORIES?

How would you like to receive future novels from me for FREE? Go to my website at www.paulheingarten.com and click on the "Krewe of Paul (VIP)" link for more information.